AF322880

THE COMPLETE
HAMMER'S SLAMMERS
VOLUME 3

Other books by David Drake:

Hammer's Slammers
The Dragon Lord
Time Safari
From the Heart of Darkness
Skyripper
Cross the Stars
Birds of Prey
The Forlorn Hope
At Any Price
Killer (With Karl Edward Wagner)
Active Measures
Bridgehead
Ranks of Bronze
Lacey and His Friends
Counting the Cost
Kill Ratio (With Janet Morris)
Fortress
Dagger
The Sea Hag
Target (With Janet Morris)
Explorers in Hell (With Janet Morris)
Vettius and His Friends
Rolling Hot
Northworld
Surface Action
The Hunter Returns (With Jim Kjelgaard)
Vengeance
The Military Dimension
The Warrior

Old Nathan
The Jungle
Justice
Starliner
The Square Deal
The Sharp End
Igniting the Reaches
The Voyage
Arc Riders (With Janet Morris)
Through the Breach
The Fourth Rome (With Janet Morris)
All the Way to the Gallows
Fireships
Redliners
Patriots
Lord of the Isles
With the Lightnings
Queen of Demons
Servant of the Dragon
Lt. Leary, Commanding
Mistress of the Catacombs
Paying the Piper
Grimmer Than Hell
Goddess of the Ice Realm
The Far Side of the Stars
Master of the Cauldron
The Way to Glory
The Fortress of Glass
Some Golden Harbor

THE COMPLETE
HAMMER'S SLAMMERS
VOLUME 3

DAVID DRAKE

NIGHT SHADE BOOKS
San Francisco

CONTENTS

INEXTRICABLE DISENGAGEMENT: THE WAR GAMES OF DAVID DRAKE

AN INTRODUCTION BY BARRY N. MALZBERG

"Hammers Slammers" no misnomer, that is what war accomplishes, combat demands, training forces: it *hammers*, it slams, it breaks you down, reduces to nullity. They'll tell you that training first breaks you down "only to rebuild you" but that is snare and delusion, brochure hype, a sell because what training breaks it never replaces, cannot replenish, you become something else if you are restored at all, some foggy mountain breakdown self. War guts, eviscerates, makes all of us the same living and dead, in so doing blurs—as is training's purpose—the line between living and dead to indistinguishability. The only difference in these extreme conditions is that the living perceive themselves as dead while the dead perceive nothing at all.

Believe this: it is not only the outcome of assessment, it is taken from the pulp of experience. I settled for Basic Training at Fort Dix in the last months of Eisenhower's sleepy post-Korean Army; Drake was in the flames of Johnson's Vietnam. We appear to have reached the same conclusions however and our work is much closer than one might think. The shuffling, burnt-away assassins of my FINAL WAR are Slammer dropouts, not rejects.

Extreme conditions flatten, make us all the same, combat is among the most extreme conditions and Drake's Slammers, dead-gone mercenaries fighting in squalor for their own squalor inherit Remarque, Mailer, Heller. Only sentimentalists believe that there is a difference between mercenaries and "ideological" warriors and there are no sentimentalists in foxholes, no foxholes in sentimentalists. They grieve and gravitate these warriors and they leave ideology to the landlocked, protected homefront. Their ideology is their etiology: survival.

To live through Hammer's Slammers is to pay the piper, to understand that these blown-out functionaries are our own idealized selves no longer idealized. David Drake has through furious refusal to compromise, from refusal to special plead, taken us into the bowels and apparatus of wartime as has no science fiction writer; he is the inheritor of the cold flare of military fiction's history and his rifle sight, his shot pattern is exact. Exact and exacting; a freezing, burning, incontestable body of work.

Barry N. Malzberg
New Jersey: 2005

DEDICATION
To our architect and builder Derwood Schrotberger
Writing a novel and moving to a new house are both stressful occupations. The fact that I was able to combine them is a comment on Derwood's consummate skill, which reminds me that architect originally meant Master Builder.

ACKNOWLEDGEMENTS
Those of you who notice the echoes of *The Glass Key* and *Red Harvest* by Dashiell Hammett in this book are correct. Those of you who don't should go off and read Hammett's splendid novels at your earliest convenience.

When I'm at the crux of my plotting, I tend to talk at those around me. When I did this time on the way to the state fair with friends, my wife, Jo, and Mark Van Name made suggestions which were precisely on point. I adopted both.

THE SHARP END

The room housing the Officers Assignment Bureau was spacious enough to have three service cages and seats for twenty around the walls of colored marble. Nobody was waiting when Major Matthew Coke entered, though a single officer discussed alternative assignments with a specialist.

Coke stepped into an empty cage. A clerk rose from her desk in the administrative area across the divider and switched on the electronics.

"Yes sir?" the clerk said pleasantly. "Is there a problem with your assignment?"

The Frisian Defense Forces reassigned scores of officers every week. Normally the operation was impersonal, a data transfer to the officer's present station directing him or her to report to a new posting, along with details of timing, transport, and interim leave.

This office handled problems. President Hammer, in common with other leaders whose elevation owed more to bullets than ballots, felt most comfortable with a large standing army under his direct control. Professional soldiers are expensive, and unless they are used, they either rust, or find ways to employ themselves—generally to the detriment of the established government.

Hammer's answer to the problem was to hire out elements of the Frisian Defense Forces as mercenaries. This provided training for the troops, as well as defraying the cost of their pay and equipment.

Sometimes the troops engaged were merely a few advisers or specialists. When somebody, a planetary government or the rebels opposed to it, hired a large force, however, the OAB would be standing room only.

Officers on Nieuw Friesland knew that the only sure route to promotion was through combat experience. The Frisian Defense Forces had sprung from Hammer's Slammers, a mercenary regiment with the reputation for doing whatever it took to win… and a reputation for winning.

So long as Alois Hammer was President and the commanders of the Frisian

Defense Forces were the officers who'd bought him that position in decades of bloody war, bureaucratic "warriors" weren't on the fast track to high rank. You paid for your rank sometimes in blood, and sometimes with your life; but all that was as nothing without demonstrated success at the sharp end, where they buried the guys in second place.

Not everybody was comfortable with Hammer's terms of employment, but the Forces were volunteer only and the volunteers came from all across the human universe; just as they had to Hammer's Slammers before. A certain number of men, and a lower percentage of women, would rather fight than not. Alois Hammer's troops had always been the best there was at what they did: killing the other fellow, whoever he was.

A draft going out to a hot theater was a ticket to promotion. Officers would crowd the Assignment Bureau, begging and threatening, offering bribes and trying to pull rank to get a slot. Mostly it didn't work.

The Table of Organization for a combat deployment was developed by the central data base itself. Changes had to be approved by President Hammer, who was immune to any practical form of persuasion. The Assignments Bureaus were open because people prefer to argue with human beings instead of electronic displays, but that was normally a cosmetic rather than significant touch.

You could also appeal to Hammer personally. In that case, you were cashiered if you didn't convince him. Old-timers in the Assignment Bureau said that the success rate was slightly under three percent, but every month or so somebody else tried it.

There were no large-scale deployments under way at the moment, but there were always glitches, clerical or personal, which had to be ironed out. The clerk smiled at Coke, expecting to learn that he'd been assigned to a slot calling for a *sergeant*-major, or that he was wanted for murder on the planet to which he was being posted.

Coke's problem was rather different.

"I'm here to receive sealed orders," Coke said, offering the clerk his identification card with the embedded chip. He smiled wryly.

The clerk blinked in surprise. There were various reasons why an officer's orders would be sealed within the data base, requiring him or her to apply in person to the bureau to receive them. Coke didn't look like the sort to whom any of the special reasons would apply. He looked—normal.

Matthew Coke was thirty-four standard years old—twenty-nine dated on Ash, where he was born, fifty-one according to the shorter year of Nieuw Friesland. He had brown hair, eyes that were green, blue, or gray depending on how much sunlight had been bleaching them, and stood a meter seventy-eight in his stocking feet. He was thin but not frail, like a blade of good steel.

Coke was in dress khakis with rank tabs and the blue edging to the epaulets that indicated his specialty was infantry. He wore no medal or campaign ribbons whatsoever, but over his left breast pocket was a tiny lion rampant on a field of red enamel.

The lion marked the men who'd served with Hammer's Slammers before the regiment was subsumed into the Frisian Defense Forces. Its lonely splendor against the khaki meant that, like most of the other Slammers veterans, Coke figured that when you'd said you were in the Slammers, you'd said everything that mattered.

Considering that, the clerk realized that Major Coke might not be quite as normal as he looked.

"Face the lens, please, sir," the clerk said as she inserted the ID card into a slot on her side of the cage. Electronics chittered, validating the card and comparing Coke's retinal patterns with those contained in the embedded chip.

A soft chime indicated approval. Coke eased from the stiff posture with which he had faced the comparator lens. He continued to smile faintly, but the emotions the clerk read on his face were sadness and resignation.

"Just a moment," the clerk said. "The printer has to warm up, but—"

As she spoke, a sheet of hardcopy purred from the dispenser on Coke's side of the cage. Coke read the rigid film upside down as it appeared instead of waiting for the print cycle to finish so that he could clip the document.

His face blanked; then he began to laugh. The captain at the next cage glanced at him, then away. The clerk waited, hoping Coke would explain the situation but unwilling to press him.

Coke tapped the cutter, then tossed the sheet across the counter to the clerk. "It says my new assignment is Category Ten Forty-seven," he said as the clerk scanned the document. "That's survey team, isn't it?"

The clerk nodded. "Yessir," she said. "You'll be assessing potential customers for field force deployments."

She didn't understand Major Coke's laughter. "Isn't this what you were expecting, sir?" she asked as she slid back the hardcopy.

"What I was expecting…" Coke explained, "… after the way I screwed up my last assignment on Auerstadt…"

He was smiling like a skull, as broadly and with as little humor.

"… was that they'd fire my ass. But I guess the Assessment Board decided I couldn't get into much trouble on a survey team."

He began to laugh again. Despite the obvious relief in Coke's voice, the sound of his laughter chilled the clerk.

EARLIER: AUERSTADT

There was a party going on in the extensive quarters of General the Marquis Bradkopf, National Army commander of Fortress Auerstadt. Next door in the Tactical Operations Center, Major Matthew Coke of the Frisian Defense Forces was trying to do his job—and General Bradkopf's job—through a real-time link to the pair of combat cars in ambush position thirty kilometers away.

The combat cars were named *Mother Love* and *The Facts of Life*. They and their crews were Frisians; and the sergeants commanding them were, like Coke, former members of Hammer's Slammers, the mercenary regiment whose ruthless skill had transformed Colonel Hammer into Alois Hammer, President of Nieuw Friesland.

"We're getting major movement into Hamlet 3, sir," said Four-four—Sergeant-Commander Dubose in *Mother Love*, stationed for the moment on a dike south of the three hamlets called Parcotch for administrative purposes. *"Nearly a hundred just from the direction of Auerstadt. Most of them are carrying weapons, too."*

The three clerks in the TOC with Coke were National Army enlisted personnel, two women and a male who looked fifteen years old. They were chattering in a corner of the open bullpen. One of the women had brought in a series of holovision cubes of Deiting, the planetary capital, where she'd gone on leave with her boyfriend, a transport driver.

There was a National Army officer listed as Commander of the Watch, but whoever it was hadn't put in an appearance this evening. In all likelihood, the fellow was at General Bradkopf's party.

That was fine with Coke. The best a National officer could do was to keep out of the way of the advisor hired from the Frisian Defense Forces.

Though all the raw data was provided by the combat cars, processing by the base unit in the TOC added several layers of enhancement to what the troops on the ground could see. Coke checked the statistical analysis in a sidebar of his holographic display and said, "There's a hundred and seventeen up the Auerstadt Road. They're *all* armed, and ninety percent of them are in spatter-camouflage uniforms."

"Bloody hell," said Sergeant-Commander Lennox from *The Facts of Life*. *"We've got regulars from the Association of Barons? Then it's really going to blow!"*

"And Four-Two has spotted another eighty-four coming down from Hamlet 1 and points north," Coke continued, watching his split-screen display. "The only thing I can imagine from an assembly this large is that they're planning to attack the fortress itself in a night or two."

Two companies, even of fully equipped regulars, weren't a threat to a base the size of Fortress Auerstadt; but Parcotch was only one village of the ninety or a hundred within comparable distance of the base.

The direct views from sensors in the combat cars filled the lower right and left quadrants of Coke's display. The top half of the screen looked down at an apparent thirty degrees on a panorama extrapolated from the separate inputs and combined with map data.

Mother Love was a klick to the south and east of Hamlet 3. *The Facts of Life* was within 500 meters of the hamlet's west edge, and that was the problem. Lennox's vehicle was only 500 meters east of Hamlet 2 as well, where the incoming troops had parked a launching trailer full of short-range guided weapons.

The combat cars were in perfect position to do a number on the enemy concentration in Hamlet 3, but Coke wasn't willing to put Lennox between two fires.

"Any chance the Nationals might send us some support?" Sergeant Dubose said wistfully.

"Any chance the tooth fairy is making a run by your car tonight?" Sergeant Lennox retorted tartly. She was a lanky woman who shaved her head and was just as tough as she looked. *"Sir,"* she continued, *"let's do it. If we rip this one, the locals'll*

get their heads out of the sand."

"Not in your present location, Four-Two," Coke said. "If they salvo the full load of missiles, there's no way you're going to survive. Particularly with whatever's happening in Three."

"*Sir, look,*" Lennox said. "*The personnel are going to be in Three with the others, getting a pep talk or whatever the hell they're doing. The launcher's no threat!*"

"We don't—" Coke started to say.

A mortar fired just outside the TOC.

"Hold one!" Coke shouted, spinning from the console and grabbing the sub-machine gun he'd slung over the back of his chair. The National Army clerks jumped up also. They'd been frightened by Coke's reaction rather than the mortar's flash and hollow *CHUG!* through the TOC's doorway. The vacationer's glittering holoviews spilled onto the floor.

Cheers and laughter from outside the TOC told Coke there was no danger. The shell popped thousands of meters in the air, casting harsh magnesium light across Fortress Auerstadt. General the Marquis Bradkopf was using parachute flares to provide fireworks for his party.

Which suggested a way out of Coke's immediate problem.

In theory, Coke's console was linked to the National Army net. Rather than go through the complicated handshake procedures, however, Coke turned to the rack system at the adjacent bay.

He switched the unit from standby to operations and waited a moment for it to warm up. When the light went from amber to green, Coke keyed the address of the heavy battery of the artillery battalion attached to the fortress defenses. The clerk responsible for the communications bay watched Coke in concern from across the room, but she didn't attempt to interfere.

Marquis Bradkopf began hectoring a subordinate outside the door of the TOC. Drink and anger slurred his words so that Coke couldn't make them out. A woman's voice wove a descant around Bradkopf's.

"Battery Seven," a man said. "Yeah?"

"This is Fortress Command," Coke said crisply. "I have an immediate fire mission for you." As he spoke, his left hand addressed a target information packet on the Frisian console. "This will require seeker shells, so I'm authorizing you to release them from locked storage."

"What!" said the soldier on the other end of the line. "What? Look, I'll get Chief Edson."

Theoretically, the Frisians were in advisory capacity without direct control of National Army forces. As with other large organizations, somebody who was willing to claim authority was more than likely to be granted it.

The mortar fired again, lofting a second flare into the night sky. There was static on the land line, masking a half-audible conversation at the battery end.

National Army heavy equipment was generally of off-planet manufacture, ranging from good to very good in design. The local personnel were of low quality, however, and virtually untrained. Coke didn't dare call an ordinary fire mission to support units within half a klick of the intended impact area. Battery 7's 200-mm guns were capable of nail-driving accuracy at thirty kilometers, but the crews were as apt as not to drop their heavy shells directly on *The Facts of Life*.

Technology could eliminate the problem. The battery was issued four Frisian-manufactured seeker rounds, one per tube. These self-steering warheads were designed for use against ill-defined or moving targets, and combined with satellite photos of Parcotch Hamlet 2 they would obviate the friendly-fire risk.

"Chief Edson," a businesslike voice said. "Who is this?"

"Major Matthew Coke," Coke said, "acting Fortress Command. Where's your battery commander?"

"Who the fuck knows?" said the chief, the battery's ranking enlisted man. "Look, Major, I don't care about your authorization—I flat don't have the codes to open the special locker. Maybe Captain Wilcken does, maybe the Marquis does—maybe nobody. Forget the seeker warheads, they're just for show."

"Prepare the battery," Coke snapped. "I'm on my way."

He dropped the handset onto its cradle and rose. More figures drifted through the shadows of the split screen. Lennox and Dubose held their silence, as Coke had directed them at last transmission.

Coke settled his commo helmet, slung the sub-machine gun over his shoulder, and started for the door. General Bradkopf and his entourage burst through from outside.

"Coke!" the Marquis roared. "Where's—there you are!" He pointed an index finger at Coke's face. "What's happened to my tanks?"

Bradkopf was in his mid-fifties. His body was fleshy but powerful, since swimming and exercise machines controlled the grosser results of the dissipation nonetheless evident on his face.

"Sir, you and I discussed using the combat cars for an ambush patrol," Coke half-lied. His mouth was dry, and his palm was sweating on the grip of his sub-machine gun.

This could get him reprimanded. If Bradkopf was angry enough, he could even have Coke recalled to Friesland.

The group oozing into the TOC behind the Marquis included most of the higher male officers of Fortress Auerstadt's complement. Among them was Captain Wilcken, a twenty-year-old of excellent family and the titular commander of Battery 7.

Each of the men had a woman in train. The redhead on the Marquis' arm was approximately a third of his age.

"*You* said you wanted to send out one of the tanks with a patrol," Bradkopf said, his memory unfortunately quite accurate. "For communications."

For stiffening, actually, but the lie was a harmless one. When he'd gotten down to serious planning, he realized that he didn't dare saddle Frisians—*his* troops—with any of the National Army units in the fortress. The locals lacked noise discipline, fire discipline, and target identification skills. A Frisian combat car was the largest thing around and therefore the most likely target for the National troops who did manage to shoot.

Furthermore, the locals lacked guts.

"*I* said I'd think about it," Bradkopf said, "and now I find you've stripped me of all my protection! Are you a traitor?"

"No sir," Coke said, "I'm not a traitor. I—"

I screwed up badly, but Bradkopf wasn't the man to admit that to. Coke had taken the chance that the Marquis wouldn't notice the two combat cars—not tanks—normally parked near his quarters were missing. If Bradkopf hadn't decided to shoot off flares for his party, Coke would have gotten away with it.

If.

Coke couldn't quarrel with Bradkopf's assumption that the commander of an 8,000-troop base was unprotected if two foreign combat vehicles left his presence. It was just that protecting *this* commander was in no sense a military priority for Coke.

"*Six, this is Four-four,*" Sergeant Dubose reported tensely through Coke's commo helmet. "*The troops are moving out of Three in civilian trucks and wagons. Over.*"

"General Bradkopf!" Coke said. "Association forces are maneuvering to attack this base tonight."

Not in a few days: in a few *hours.*

Fear of a bad rating in his personnel file had turned Coke's skin hot and prickly. The prospect of imminent combat washed him cool again. Major Matthew Coke was a professional and an employee; but first of all he was a soldier.

"What?" blurted the Marquis, sounding amazingly like the gunner on phone watch at Battery 7. "An attack *where?* Have you gone mad?"

"*Six, this is Four-Two,*" Sergeant Lennox reported. There was a lilt, almost a caress in her voice despite the flattening of spread-band radio communication. "*The rocket pod's moved out of Two. It's being pulled by a tractor, now. I'd say it was time, boss. Over.*"

The partygoers gaped without understanding at the multidirectional byplay. Most of them were drunk or nearly drunk. Captain Wilcken was white-faced but sober. The glance he exchanged with Colonel Jaffe, equally well-born and head of the garrison's supply department, held more terror than confusion.

Coke keyed his helmet. "*Six to Four elements,*" he said. "*Take th—*"

He didn't get the last word, "*them,*" out of his mouth before the split display behind him ignited with gunfire and explosions.

"I'm sounding the general alarm," Coke said calmly as he turned his back on the Marquis. He uncaged and pressed one of the special-use switches at the side of his console's keyboard. The artificial intelligence sent an alert signal to every node on Fortress Auerstadt's communications network. The siren on the roof of the TOC began to wind.

The holographic display shimmered with the cyan hell engulfing Parcotch.

A Frisian combat car mounted three tribarrels in its open fighting compartment.

Each weapon fired 2-cm powergun ammunition at a cyclic rate of about 500 rounds per minute. Because the barrels rotated through the firing position and had time to cool between shots, a tribarrel could fire sustainably for several minutes before burning out. In that time, the powerful bolts of ionized copper atoms could peck halfway through the side of a mountain.

Nothing *Mother Love* and *The Facts of Life* faced at Parcotch had armor protection. The targets, unprepared Association soldiers and the civilian helpers driving the vehicles, wilted like wax in a blowtorch.

The Facts of Life's two wing guns hit the trailer of anti-tank rockets and the tractor towing it. That was overkill—a single tribarrel should have been sufficient—but the rocket pod was the only real danger to the Frisian vehicles, and Lennox hadn't survived to become a veteran by taking needless risks.

Cyan bolts licked the pod. The solid rocket fuel burned in a huge yellow ball, technically not an explosion but wholly destructive of everything within its ten-meter diameter.

At least one of the missile warheads *did* detonate. The white flash of forty kilos of HE punctuated the saffron fireball. The tractor-trailer combination blew apart. Blazing debris rained across the landscape, igniting the houses of Hamlet 2 and the heads of the ripe grain in the paddies.

On the other side of the display, *Mother Love*'s three tribarrels clawed the infantry packed into the civilian vehicles. Ammunition and grenades went off in secondary explosions, but the stabbing cyan plasma itself did most of the damage. The Association troops were too crowded to fight or flee in the first instants of the ambush, and those instants were all that remained to scores of them.

A stray bolt ruptured the fuel tank under a truck cab. Kerosine, superheated and atomized by the plasma, expanded into an explosive mixture with the surrounding atmosphere—

And flash ignited, just as it would normally have done when injected into the cylinders of the truck's diesel engine. Bodies and body parts flew up in the mushrooming flame, but most of the Association troops had already been killed by gunfire.

"You wanted to know what?" Coke shouted over the wail of the siren. He gestured to the screen which glowed with the light of the scenes it displayed. "*That's* what, General, and there's a lot more Association units out there tonight than those."

An automatic cannon opened fire from a bunker on the perimeter of Fortress Auerstadt. The gunners probably didn't have a real target. They were shooting at shadows or livestock.

That was the right response to the present circumstances. With the base fully alerted, any attack Association troops made would be fragmentary instead of coordinated and overwhelming. In all likelihood there would be *no* attack. At daybreak the National Army would be able to concentrate on scattered companies of their opponents.

"Why that's…" the Marquis said, staring at the console display. "That's a massacre!"

Coke was surprised that his nominal superior had enough military knowledge to make that perfectly accurate assessment of what was happening in Parcotch.

As soon as the shooting started, the combat cars' drivers fed full power to the lift fans. Howling like banshees as the fans sucked in vast quantities of air to pressurize the plenum chambers, spraying water and soupy mud in all directions from beneath their skirts, the fifty-tonne behemoths accelerated toward Parcotch Hamlet 3 from two directions.

While her wing gunners destroyed the rocket launcher, Sergeant Lennox had opened fire on the community itself. Lennox didn't have a line of sight to the vehicles leaving the hamlet eastward from *The Facts of Life*'s starting position half a klick distant. Instead she shot up the buildings.

The structures had thatch walls and roofs of corrugated plastic sheeting, supported by wood or plastic frames. All the construction materials were flammable at the temperature of copper plasma. Houses, the school building, and the community center all burst into flame, spreading panic and confusing the enemy.

Everything moving this night was a foe and a target. The Frisians' only chance was to hit hard and keep on hitting before the enemy forces could organize their superior numbers. In the morning, every corpse in Hamlet 3 would be tagged as an Association soldier or an Association supporter. Like other forms of history, after-action reports are written by the survivors.

Mother Love bounced onto the Auerstadt Road from the dike which had concealed the vehicle in the darkness. The gunners depressed their tribarrels, raking the troops who'd jumped into the fields to either side of the causeway. A gout of steam flew up at each bolt, whether it hit a flooded paddy or superheated the fluids within a soldier's body.

The flames enveloping the hamlet rolled in redoubled fury, whipped by *The Facts of Life*'s powerful drive fans. The combat car bellied through the blaze at a walking pace, firing continuously from all three weapons. Cyan bolts cut down the soldiers who had jumped from wagons and truck beds to run toward the fancied safety of the buildings.

Lennox made a point of destroying each of the stalled vehicles. Blazing fuel geysered over the paddies, igniting rice and troops alike.

"Good *Lord!*" the Marquis said. He turned from the display to Coke and continued, "Get those tanks back here *now*, you fool! How dare you leave me at risk at a time of such danger?"

"Yessir," Coke said. "They're on their way back now."

The Facts of Life bulldozed burning wreckage off the causeway, clearing the route by which to return to Fortress Auerstadt. The driver was buttoned up within his compartment, using the curved bow slope to butt aside a truck festooned with corpses.

The tribarrels continued to fire. The visors of Frisian commo helmets could be switched to either light enhancement or thermal imaging modes. The latter could pick up bodies even through the shallow water of the paddies.

Captain Wilcken blurted something, clawed his personal sidearm out of a white patent leather holster, and pointed the small-bore projectile pistol at General the Marquis Bradkopf. Colonel Jaffe was drawing his pistol also.

Part of Coke's mind reasoned:

Wilcken and Jaffe were supporters of the Association of Barons. They intended to assassinate Bradkopf in conjunction with the attack, leaving Fortress Auerstadt leaderless at the moment of crisis. In panic, Wilcken has gone ahead with the plan even though circumstances have obviously changed....

That was with the conscious part of his mind. Reflex thumbed off the safety of Coke's sub-machine gun as his left hand slapped the foregrip and his finger took up the slack in the trigger.

The first bolt blew plaster from the wall above the TOC's doorway. The next four hit Wilcken in the chest and neck at point-blank range, virtually decapitating him.

Officers and their gorgeously clad mistresses screamed and threw themselves down. Coke body-checked the Marquis, knocking him to the side and clearing a shot at Colonel Jaffe. Jaffe's pistol was only half out of its holster. To Coke's adrenaline-speeded reactions, the colonel didn't seem to be moving at all.

The air stank of burned flesh and vaporized blood. Wilcken toppled backward, his head dangling onto his chest by a tag of skin. The pupils of the dead man's eyes had tilted up into the skull.

Coke's second burst winked cyan on Jaffe's corneas. The colonel's chest burst like a blood-filled sponge. The pistol in his hand fired a single shot into the floor. The bullet moaned away in sparks and a spurt of powdered concrete.

"Traitors!" gasped the Marquis, half-sprawled where Coke had knocked him, supporting his torso on the spread fingers of his right hand. They were—*uh!*"

Coke was poised for a further threat, sweeping the bullpen over his sub-machine gun's holographic sights. The iridium barrel glowed white from the nearly instantaneous bursts. Heat waves trembled through the haze of powergun matrix and smoldering fabric.

Officers and their women hugged the littered floor, some of them with their hands crossed over their heads. The trio of enlisted personnel huddled behind the overturned table at which they had been sitting.

No one else was touching a gun. Jaffe's disemboweled body thrashed, but he was as dead as the headless Captain Wilcken. Everything was safe—

Except that General the Marquis Bradkopf vomited blood onto the concrete floor, then pitched facedown into the bright pool.

The hilt of a narrow-bladed dagger projected from his back. Bradkopf's youthful mistress stared fixedly at the weapon. There was blood on her little finger and the heel of her right hand. Her tongue dabbed at it.

"Bloody hell," Coke whispered. He didn't shoot the girl, the third of the assassins. At this point, it wouldn't do any good.

"*Four-Two to Six,*" Sergeant Lennox reported gleefully. "*We've done all there is to do here, boss, so we're heading back to the barn. Out!*"

Bradkopf's sightless eyes stared toward the split display of the carnage achieved by the troops who, by his orders, should have been guarding his own person. In that professionally significant aspect, Coke's gamble hadn't paid off after all.

TANNAHILL

Limping slightly, Lieutenant Mary Margulies entered the orderly room for the first time in seven months.

"Hey, El-Tee," called Kerry, the 305th Military Police Detachment's first sergeant. "*Good* to see you. You look like you're getting around okay."

Margulies grimaced. "Twinges, that's all," she said, "but the bastard medics put me on a profile anyhow. I'm being transferred out, Top. Stuck behind a desk, I suppose."

She was a stocky woman whose black hair was her only affectation. She'd removed padding from her commo helmet so that she could coil a longer braid when she was on duty. As a platoon leader in a war zone, she had been on duty virtually all the time, awake or sleeping, until a routine convoy escort went sour.

"Ah…" said Kerry. "You suppose? You got a copy of the actual orders, didn't you?"

"Oh, I got them all right," Margulies said with a wan smile. "Long enough to see I was being transferred back to Camp Able. Then I threw the chip and reader right through the window. *I* don't belong on Nieuw Friesland. Curst if I don't think I'll put in my resignation if that's what they want from me."

She nodded toward the detachment commander's door. "The Old Man in?"

"Ah…" Sergeant Kerry said. "No, Major Yates had an Orders Group at Tannahill Command this morning. Ah…"

Margulies smiled harshly. "Go on, Top, say it if that's what you're thinking. A crip like me shouldn't be in the field where she could get good people killed because she's hobbling around."

"No *sir*," Sergeant Kerry said. "*Hell* no, sir. What I meant—and I know that nobody but the recipient reads assignment orders until the recipient's signed off on them—"

Margulies laughed, this time with genuine good humor. "Top, you've got seventeen years in the FDF and the Slammers before them. Let's take it as read that you knew my orders before I did, all right?"

Kerry grinned. "For the sake of argument…" he said.

His fingers touched keys on his desk; the integral printer hummed. "I guess there's no harm in me giving you a hardcopy replacement of the assignment orders you lost, is there?" he said.

A flimsy spooled out of the printer slot. Kerry tore off the document and handed it to the lieutenant without looking at the contents. "I think you'll find," he continued, "that Camp Able on Nieuw Friesland is just a transit stop, where you'll join your new unit. You've been assigned as security to a survey team, El-Tee. You're not supposed to be in combat; but if things were peaceful, a survey team wouldn't be there trolling for business."

"Well I'll be hanged," Margulies said, reading the data through for the first time. "I was so scared they were going to stick me at a desk that I…"

Kerry affectionately scratched the corner molding of his desk as though the piece of furniture were a living creature. "Different strokes, El-Tee," he murmured. "Personally, I don't find I miss getting shot at in the least."

"Well, I'll *be* hanged," Margulies repeated with changed emphasis. "Do you know where this survey team—"

She blinked. "Oh," she said. "Oh, sure you know where we're going."

"Cantilucca," Kerry said, returning the smile. "I looked it up. West Bumfuck is more like."

His lips pursed in sudden concern. His fingers started to summon Margulies' personnel data, then realized doing so now couldn't help the situation. "Ah—don't tell me you come from Cantilucca, El-Tee?" he added.

"Not me," said Margulies with a broad grin. "But I know somebody who does…."

EARLIER: TANNAHILL

"Sarge…" Lieutenant Mary Margulies said as Angel Tijuca slid their two-seat air-cushion jeep between a pair of road trains. The huge vehicles had accelerated slowly, but they were maintaining 50 kph now and there was just enough clearance to spare the jeep's paint. "If you don't take it easy, you're not going to survive the last three days of your enlistment."

Margulies didn't sound concerned. Her eyes continued to search the roadsides instead of glaring at her driver.

Angel laughed infectiously. "Now, Missie Mary," he said. "Don't get your bowels in an uproar. And anyway, it's not three days, it's two and a wake-up."

In public Sergeant Tijuca was never less than deferential to his superior officer, but he and Margulies had gone through a lot in the year he'd been driving her. Angel was ending his enlistment in the Frisian Defense Forces, and Margulies was curst sorry to see him go.

"Only if you survive," Margulies remarked, but she wasn't serious. Angel's willingness to take chances was just as important a reason for her keeping him as her permanent driver as his skill at the joystick was.

Angel accelerated to 60 kph. The jeep passed along the right side of the road trains at an increment that was slightly faster than a man could walk.

The convoy consisted of ten articulated road trains, each of which had three track-laying segments with a driver in the lead cab. There was a gun tub crewed by Brigantian troops on the center segment of each individual train, but the convoy's real security was provided by the four combat cars manned by Frisian military police under Lieutenant Margulies' command.

The war was over, but the fighting might not stop for years. Brigantian regiments, spearheaded by armored companies of Frisian mercenaries, had swept across

Tannahill's Beta Continent. The armies of the continent's local population, mostly Muslims of South Indian descent, had been smashed if they stood and run down if they retreated.

The guerrillas, supported by the local communities even when they weren't actually members of those communities, were a more difficult problem. They were controllable, at least for as long as the Brigantians of Alpha Continent could afford to pay their Frisian mercenaries, but Margulies suspected it would be decades if not generations before the locals accepted Brigantian domination.

That was somebody else's worry. Margulies had a convoy to take through eighty klicks of—literally—Indian Country.

"Yes *sir*," Angel said. "Inside a week and a half, I figure, I'll be back on Cantilucca with a forty-hectare gage farm of my own. Three more days here. Three days objective to Delos, that's the cluster's port of entry. Maybe a day to get transport from there to Cantilucca, another day's transit, and bam! I'm home, with a discharge bonus in my pocket. How long can it take then to buy some land, hey?"

Tijuca began to whistle a flamenco tune. Margulies smiled at his enthusiasm. She noticed that despite the sergeant's air of heedless relaxation, every time they overhauled a road train his eyes flicked left. He was checking through the gaps between vehicles to see what was happening along the far treeline.

Combat engineers had defoliated, then burned off, strips a hundred meters wide along either edge of the road. Ash flew out from beneath the jeep's skirts. It merged with the yellow dust which the trains' cleats raised from the gravel road surface. The breeze was slightly from the right, so for the moment the jeep was clear. Tijuca kept them ten meters out in the burned zone—comfortable, but by that amount the closest vehicle to the enemy if the guerrillas decided to start something.

"Take us back across between the second and first trucks," Margulies said. "I don't believe in giving anybody long enough to compute the lead on a full-deflection shot."

"Your wish is my command," Angel said. He goosed the fans, let the jeep settle into its new, higher speed, and angled the vehicle sideways across the line of heavy trucks. It was an expert job, as difficult as threading a needle blindfolded.

"My command is your command," Margulies grumbled. Her commo helmet slapped nose filters in place automatically, but she tasted the chalky dust on her tongue.

She wished that a battery of Frisian howitzers rather than Brigantian artillery was providing call fire for the run. Brigantian artillery was reasonably accurate, but Margulies didn't trust the indigs to react as fast as Frisian hogs would if anything blew.

The chance of an ambush was less than one in ten, but Margulies' platoon had provided security on this run fourteen times already.

"You ought to come to Cantilucca, Missie," Angel said, throttling back to 60 kph. "You'd love it. With a tract of top gage land—"

"Sarge," Margulies said, "I'm a city girl, born right smack in the center of Batavia. I wouldn't know which end of a hoe to use, and I don't even *like* gage. Alcohol works just fine for me."

When they crossed the road, Margulies hunched higher in the seat to view the left treeline over her driver's head. Angel watched the potential danger area also, navigating with his peripheral vision. A sub-machine gun was clamped beside his seat. Though it was ready for use, it didn't interfere with his driving the way a slung weapon would have done.

"Huh!" Angel said. "The only thing you can get from booze that you can't from gage is a hangover. The good stuff—the pure stuff, we're not talking about refinery tailings, sure—there's no side effects at all. You just go to sleep when you come down. Why would anybody want booze over gage?"

"Because if something pops, I can deal with it if I'm hung over and I can't if I'm in a gage coma," Margulies said tartly. That was true enough, but it wasn't the reason she relaxed with alcohol instead of stim cones of gage. It was all a matter of what you got used to—

Like everything else across the board. There was no question that a city was the most dangerous combat environment you could find: stone and concrete ate troops. Nonetheless, Margulies was always more comfortable patrolling or even fighting in a city than she was in the open air like this.

Not that it mattered. She was here to do a job.

This portion of the route was through lowlands. The soil was mucky, and there were frequent potholes where the treads of road trains had chewed through the gravel. The trees outside the cleared strip were five to ten meters tall. Their foliage was vaguely blue.

Margulies' four combat cars flanked the convoy front and rear, fifty meters out from the road. Because of the size of the road trains, the convoy was more than half a kilometer long even when closed up properly. The tribarrels of the combat cars could still sweep the full length of it on straight stretches.

They were coming to one of the route's few major curves, nicknamed Ambush Junction until the guerrillas hit what turned out to be a platoon of Frisian tanks instead of the Brigantian armor they'd expected. The route had been quiet as a grave since then.

Margulies keyed her commo helmet. "White Six to Rose One," she said, calling the driver of the leading road train. She glanced up at the cab looming beside her. Because of the angle, she couldn't see the Brigantian to whom she was speaking. "Can you crank up the speed a little? This isn't a place I want to hang around. Over."

A wash of hollow noise flooded Margulies' helmet, racket echoing from within the driver's compartment. The cab was lightly armored but not sound-proofed. A moment later the Brigantian said, *"All right, we'll see, but I don't want to put this sucker in the bog either."*

The background noise shut off. It was as effective a close-transmission signal as more standard commo procedures would have been. Presumably the Brigantian notched his hand throttle forward, though change came very slowly for mechanical dinosaurs the size of the road trains.

The leading combat cars pulled farther ahead and swung a little closer to their respective sides of the cleared strip. Margulies hadn't bothered to give her own people orders. They knew what the situation was and had been dealing with it for the better part of a month now.

There was new growth where Frisian tanks had blasted hundred-meter notches through the vegetation with their main guns. The flushes of new leaves were red and violet.

There wasn't enough silica in the soil to glaze when struck by powerguns, but steam from the high water content exploded main-gun impacts into craters that could swallow the jeep. During file ambush, one of the panzers had swept out into the forest, deliberately scraping its steel skirts across the dirt to uncover the guerrillas' spider holes. The arcing scar was still barren save for speckles of low growth.

Angel hung off the left front fender of the leading road train as the convoy squealed and rumbled into the long right-hand curve. He glanced at Margulies to remind her that this wasn't the position *he* would choose for a plastic-bodied jeep, though whatever the lieutenant wanted…

"Yeah, ease back, let them pass us, and we'll cross to the right side between the second and third trucks," Margulies agreed. She was holding her 2-cm shoulder weapon at high port. Now her index finger pushed the lever at the front of the trigger guard forward, off safe.

She had a bad feeling about this spot. That was nothing new. She'd had a bad feeling about it every bloody time she crossed it.

Angel eased the fan nacelles closer to vertical, raising clearance beneath the skirt to slow the jeep as ordered. He kept the power up. The wasted charge was a cheap price to pay for greater agility in a crisis. Margulies rose in her seat to get a better view back along the convoy.

The lead road train's quad automatic cannon was swung to starboard, aiming at the inside of the curve. That was fine, but the crew of the second vehicle was doing the same cursed thing instead of covering the left side of the route as each alternate crew should do.

Margulies swore and took her left hand from the powergun's forestock to key her helmet—as a command-detonated mine went off under the third segment of the leading road train.

The charge buried beneath the gravel was huge, at least fifty kilos of high explosive. It lifted the segment, blew the track plates and several road wheels from the suspension, and dropped the 30-tonne mass on its right side.

The blast stunned the gun crew atop the middle segment and flung several of them out of the tub. The jeep flipped like a tiddlywink.

Margulies didn't hear the explosion. The shockwave gripped like a fevered giant's hand, crushing her in conditions of intense heat. She couldn't see anything but white light. Both her shins broke against the dashboard as she and the jeep spun in different trajectories. There was no present pain, but she heard the bones go with tiny clicks like those of fingers on a data-entry keyboard.

Margulies' world reformed as she lay prone on soggy ground. She wasn't sure whether or not she'd been unconscious. Her skin crawled, and all her senses were preternaturally sharp.

Twenty meters away the leading road train was skewed across the gravel. The rear segment lay on its side, but the coupling still held. The segment had acted as an anchor, bringing the huge vehicle to a dead halt. The cab door was open. A splotch of blue uniform marked the driver huddling in the ditch beside his abandoned charge.

The combat cars maneuvered violently, engaging the weapons shooting at them. Explosive shells raked the road train, igniting the two upright segments. Margulies thought part of the cargo was ammunition. Tracers or rocket exhaust trails fanned from a position at the treeline.

The second road train had tried to pass on the right side of its disabled fellow, but the ground to that side was apparently even softer than that on which Margulies lay. The vehicle had sunk in over its running gear, hopelessly mired. The gun crew jumped from the tub and hid between the bogies.

The driver fired a pistol from his cab doorway. Machine gun bullets sparkled on the armor, starred the windscreen opaque, and punched the driver's lungs out through the back of his rib cage.

Margulies had lost her 2-cm powergun and her commo helmet. She didn't wear a pistol because it got in the way in a jeep's tight seating. Anyhow, she couldn't hit anything with a handgun. She wished she had one now. Her legs ached so fiercely that she had to look down to be sure that they hadn't been blown off at the knees.

Angel Tijuca ran toward her. A guerrilla machine gun combed for him, aiming low and making the black soil spurt upward. Angel tumbled, slapping at his pelvis.

Powerguns and automatic cannon fired at the rear of the convoy, out of sight around the curve. Small arms were probably involved also, but the sound was lost in the blasts of the heavier weapons.

Margulies tried to crawl toward the center of the convoy. Ash on the ground made her sneeze violently. The machine gunner shifted his aim toward her. The guerrilla wasn't very good, but it could be only a matter of time before he found the range.

Angel jumped to his feet, scooped Margulies up, and staggered toward the road with her in a packstrap carry. "Fucking ricochet," he said. "Knocked me—*down!*"

Margulies' toes dragged the ground. The pain in her shins was indescribable. Angel's normally olive complexion had paled to a jaundiced yellow, and his skin gleamed with perspiration.

"Not there!" Margulies cried. She wasn't sure if she was speaking audibly. "That truck'll blow any minute now!"

"That's—" her driver gasped "—the next—thing, M-Missie."

He tumbled into the mine crater with his burden and released her. The pulverized soil was pillow-soft, but the reek of explosive residues clung to the pit chokingly. The machine gun sent a last spiteful burst of white tracer over the jeep's crew before casting off for other targets.

Angel had lost his helmet and sub-machine gun, but the butt of a pistol projected from the left cargo pocket of his trousers. He drew the weapon as he lurched out of the crater.

Margulies tried to follow her sergeant, using her knees and elbows for purchase on the loose soil. It was like swimming through molasses. Every pulse tightened a red-hot vise on her lower legs.

Angel ran to the coupling which linked the overturned third segment to the pair whose running gear was undamaged. The machine gun and the guerrillas' light cannon traversed toward the motion, but the Frisian was fairly well covered by the bogies of the second segment. Cannon shells fanned the flames already snorting through holes in the cargo box.

The coupling was torqued and immobile. Angel aimed his pistol at it point-blank, covered his eyes with his right forearm, and fired. The 1-cm powergun bolt sprayed blazing steel in all directions.

Angel's battle dress smoldered in a score of places. He squinted, fired again, and again, and again.

At the fourth bolt, the coupling parted with the sound of a shattered bell. The overturned segment slid a meter from the remainder of the burning vehicle.

Margulies knelt at the top of the mine crater and waved her arms. She knew what Angel intended to do, knew also that she couldn't stop him as she wished she could. But if the guerrilla gunners concentrated on *her*, then there was at least a chance Angel would succeed.

The light cannon shifted aim toward Margulies. It had a three-round charger, so the tracers snapped out in trios. They left tight gray helices in the air, like the tailings of a metal drill.

Angel ran toward the road train's open cab. The machine gun pursued him, bullets flickering against the chassis and treads a half-step behind. The cargo boxes breathed blowtorch flames from every shell hole.

An explosive bullet buried itself in the rim of loose dirt beneath Margulies and detonated. The shock threw her back as though she'd been hit by a medicine ball. She lay at the bottom of the crater, wheezing and blinking at the sky for a moment before she resumed crawling upward.

When Margulies regained the crater lip, the only combat car she could see had been hit in the skirts by a shoulder-launched rocket. Air gushing through the jagged hole in the plenum chamber slowed the vehicle's motions to those of a half-crushed cockroach, but the tribarrels were still in action.

The two-segment road train staggered across the cleared ground like a drunken streetwalker. When one bogie or another found a soft spot the gigantic vehicle lurched, but each time inertia dragged it from the potential bog.

Angel was steering toward the guerrillas' automatic cannon.

Three buzzbombs like the one that had disabled the combat car burst on the road train's bow. The shaped-charge warheads went off with hollow *thocks*, like the sound of boards being slapped together. The cannon, the machine gun, and at least a dozen guerrilla riflemen were firing at the vehicle.

Ricochets and explosive shells danced across the cab like a fireworks display. The protective windows were starred white, the armor was holed in a hundred places, and gray smoke or coolant trailed back from the power plant to mix with the flames shooting from the cargo boxes.

The cab door opened fifty meters from the treeline. Angel somersaulted from the vehicle. He splashed into a muddy trench gouged by a main-gun bolt in the earlier ambush. He didn't move. A machine gun had hosed the side of the cab as the Frisian left it.

A guerrilla stood up in plain view to aim her buzzbomb at the road train. Smoke spurted from the back of the launcher as a rocket motor lobbed the missile into a near-side bogie. The warhead's pearly flash enveloped the running gear for an instant. The track broke, shedding links behind it and pulling the vehicle slightly to the left as it continued to trundle onward.

A single cyan bolt winked past the guerrilla's face. She dropped her useless rocket launcher and unslung the automatic rifle from her back. Angel's second pistol shot hit her in the chest. She spun as she fell to the ground.

The road train kept up a walking pace as its battered bow crunched through the stunted trees. A guerrilla leaped desperately for the cab, caught his sandal in metal torn by gunfire, and toppled screaming beneath the second set of bogies. It wouldn't have made much difference if he'd set his feet properly, because an instant later the munitions in the second segment exploded.

The first charge bulged the sides of the cargo box. Margulies ducked in time, before the shock wave compressed the mass of burning propellants and detonated them. A blast hugely greater than that of the guerrilla mine flattened vegetation in a hundred-meter radius and sent tonnes of excavated soil skyward on an orange fireball.

The surface waggled, flipping Margulies like a pancake. She hit the ground again and bounced onto her back, stunned but no more severely injured than the mine had left her. Dirt rained down for tens of seconds.

All the shooting from the left side of the roadway ceased. A guerrilla, stark naked and bleeding from nose and ears, ran out of the trees. A tribarrel on the combat car roaring forward from the rear of the convoy cut the man in half.

The Frisian vehicle swung around the bogged second road train, ripping the right treeline with its full firepower. The guerrillas on that side were already disengaging. Hoses of cyan plasma devoured the few snipers trying to provide a rear guard for the main body.

Artillery shells began to land on both treelines. They were late as Margulies had feared, but at least they were accurate.

She saw a Brigantian carbine, dropped or flung on the ash ten meters from the crater. She crawled toward the weapon, ignoring the pain in her legs.

Halfway between her and the smoking gap in the treeline, a man in Frisian khaki rose on one arm and waved his muddy pistol at Margulies. Her eyes filled with tears of joy, but she continued to crawl.

NIEUW FRIESLAND

The door opened and a full colonel stepped unexpectedly into the anteroom. Sten Moden rose to his feet and saluted crisply.

"Captain Moden?" the colonel said. "Could I speak with you for a moment?"

Which, when asked down a gradient of three steps in rank, was a rhetorical question if Moden had ever heard one.

"Yes *sir*," Moden said, sounding as alert and ready as he knew how. His tailored dress uniform was brand new; he'd had his hair cut that morning—he'd showered afterward to wash away the clippings; and for the first time in his military career he was wearing all—all but one—of the medal ribbons to which he was entitled.

Not even for this purpose would Sten Moden wear the most recent citation for bravery. That would be too much like drinking the blood of his own troops.

Moden followed the colonel, Dascenzo according to his name tape but not somebody Moden knew or knew of, into a comfortable office. One wall was a holographic seascape. Waves surged from horizon to horizon without a hint of land.

The view could have been from Dascenzo's home-world. Moden's suspicion was that the view was intended as a soothing backdrop for interviews by an officer with a medical rather than personnel specialty.

Moden wasn't worried about his physical profile. If that was the only determining factor, the Frisian Defense Forces would give him a new assignment with no difficulty. The fact that he was talking to a colonel instead of an enlisted clerk proved what Moden was afraid of: there was a problem with his psychiatric evaluation.

"Please, sit down," Colonel Dascenzo said. He gestured toward a contour-adapting chair. "This isn't anything formal, Captain. I'd just like to chat with you."

The chair into which Moden lowered himself was the only piece of furniture in the office, save for Dascenzo's own console with integral seat. Moden wondered how many sensors were built into the chair or focused on its user from the surrounding walls.

Captain Sten Moden had given the Frisian Defense Forces valued, even heroic, service, so no invasive methods would be used on him. Apart from that, however—

The FDF would recompense its veterans for past service, but the organization had to look to the future as well.

"I've gone over your file, of course, Captain," Dascenzo said. "I must say I'm impressed by it."

Moden decided a slight smile was appropriate. "Thank you, sir," he said. "All I'm looking for now is a chance to continue serving Col-C-President Hammer for the foreseeable future."

"Well, that's what I wanted to check with you about," Dascenzo said. He looked serious, though he wasn't scowling. His expression was probably as calculated as Moden's own. "You do realize that you qualify for a pension at one hundred percent pay?"

"Yes sir," Moden agreed with a measured nod, "and I very much appreciate the honor implicit in that offer. But I'm still able to provide the FDF with useful service, and I'd like to stay on the active list for as long as that's true."

"The extent of your injuries…" Dascenzo said, letting his expression darken into a frown. His voice trailed off, forcing the captain to decide what the question really was.

Moden decided to take a chance. He rose slowly to his full enormous height. "Sir," he said as he gripped the arm of the heavy chair with his right hand, "my injuries were extensive. What remains of me, however—"

Moden's biceps muscles flexed, threatening the weave of his uniform jacket. He pulled with the inexorable strength of a chain hoist.

"—is more than you'll find filling most of the slots in the FDF!"

The chair jerked upward with the sound of ripping metal. Only then did Moden realize that he'd been tugging against the conduits serving hard-wired sensors rather than merely gravity.

"Sorry, sir," he said ruefully, looking at the wreckage of a piece of very expensive equipment in his hand. He'd made the point he was trying to make. If he'd blown his psych profile off the map, then he may as well hung for a sheep as a lamb. "But strong and stupid has a place in an army too."

"Bloody *hell*, man," Colonel Dascenzo murmured. "Look, put that thing down before you drop it on your foot and do yourself some real damage."

His expression softened as Moden obeyed him. The chair balanced awkwardly on the ends of tubes which had stretched and twisted before they broke. "You really do want to stay in the service, don't you?" Dascenzo said softly.

"Yes sir," Moden said, standing formally at ease. "I really do."

"There's a team being formed to survey a planet called Cantilucca," Dascenzo said. "They'll need an officer with a logistics background. Do you want the slot?"

"Yes sir," Moden said. "I'd like that very much." He heard his voice tremble with the relief he felt.

"You've got it," Dascenzo said matter-of-factly. He touched the keyboard of his console. "Assignment orders will be waiting for you in your quarters."

The colonel threw another switch, then looked up at Moden again. "Captain," he said, "you don't have to believe me, but I just turned off all the recording devices. Would you answer me a question, just for my personal interest?"

"Yes sir," Moden said. He flexed his right hand behind his back. Now that it was over, he too was surprised at the amount of force his body had been able to deliver to the task he had set it.

"*Why* do you want to stay in uniform so badly?" Dascenzo asked.

Moden smiled, amused at himself. "Because I screwed up," he said. "I therefore owe a debt. For a while I thought I should kill myself—I suppose you know that?"

Dascenzo nodded, tapping the data-gorged console without taking his eyes off Moden's.

Moden nodded also. "I decided that wouldn't pay anybody back," he continued. "I don't know *who* I owe, you see, but that wouldn't help anybody. I—I *believe* that if I'm given duties to perform, then someday I'll be able to… balance the account." He barked a humorless laugh. "Does that make me crazy, Colonel?" he asked.

"Captain Moden," Dascenzo said, "'crazy' isn't a term I like to use when discussing professional soldiers. What I do know, however, is that if all you want is a chance to do your duty—I'd be a traitor to Nieuw Friesland if I took you out of her service. You're dismissed, Captain."

Dascenzo rose and extended his right hand across the desk to shake Moden's hand. The psychiatrist was smiling sadly.

EARLIER: TRINITY

The sound dived into the night of his mind, twisting deeper like a toothed whale hunting squid in the darkness a thousand fathoms down. It found him, gripped him, and tore him back to surface consciousness from the black gage coma in which he slept.

He didn't know his name. He didn't know where he was. But the whine of the base unit to which he'd plugged his commo helmet was the call of duty, and not even the half-dozen stim cones of the past evening could deny his duty.

He stabbed the speaker button, cueing the unit to continuous operation. "Go ahead," he croaked.

He couldn't see anything. Existence was a white throb shattered by jagged bands of darkness.

"Cap'n, it's Filkerson," a man said, his voice pitched high and staccato. "That load of local-manufacture pyrotechnics that arrived today, I can *hear* the crates, they're *chirping*, and I don't like it a bit!"

Shards of light spun. They reformed suddenly into present surroundings and the past life leading up to them:

He was Captain Sten Moden, Base Supply Officer serving the regimental field force of Frisian troops on Trinity. He was in semi-detached quarters, three rooms and a bath connected by a dogtrot to the Base Intelligence Officer's suite.

The earthen berm surrounding Trinity Base's ammo dump was 400 meters to the west of the officers' lines. Filkerson was sergeant of the dump's guard detachment tonight, which meant this was a *real* problem.

"Right," Moden said. "Alert the emergency team. Start dousing the crates *now*, don't take any chances. Are they in a bunker?"

Spasms wracked his muscles, but the aftereffects of the gage would pass shortly. It was like being dropped into ice water while soundly asleep. Why in *hell* did a crisis have to blow up the one night out of a hundred that he overdid it on stim cones?

"Blow up" wasn't the most fortunate thought just now.

"No sir, there wasn't time!" Filkerson said with an accusatory tone in his voice. "This is the batch that came in after hours, and you told us to accept it anyway!"

"I know what I did," Moden said flatly. He'd donned his trousers and tunic while talking. Now he pulled on his boots and sealed their seams. He didn't bother with the strap-and-buckle failsafe closure. "Handle your end, Sergeant. I'll be with you as soon as I make a call. Out."

He broke the contact by lifting his commo helmet from the base unit. He settled the helmet on his head with one hand as he switched the base to local and keyed a pre-set.

As he waited for the connection, Moden shook himself to rid his muscles of the last of the gage tremors. He was coldly furious, with Loie Leonard and more particularly with himself because of what he'd let Loie talk him into doing.

"Yes, what is it?" a woman said. She sounded irritated—as anybody would be, awakened two hours before dawn—but also guarded, because very few people had this number.

"Loie," Moden said, "it's Sten. I need you here at the base soonest with manufacturing records for everything in that load of flares and marking grenades you just sent us. There's a problem, and part of it's your problem."

He squeezed the desk support hard so that the rage wouldn't come out in his voice. Tendons rippled over the bones of his hands. Moden was a big man, so tall that almost anybody else would have claimed the finger's breadth he lacked of two meters. He had difficulty finding boots to fit him, though now that he was in logistics, it was a lot easier than it had been with a line command.

"Sten, I'm at home in bed," Loie said in irritation. "I don't have any records here, and I don't see what there is that couldn't wait for dayli—"

"Soonest, Loie!" Moden said. "Soonest, and I mean it!"

He switched off the base unit so violently that the stand overset. He ignored the mess and started for the door.

Sten Moden had held his present position for thirteen standard months. Most of the field force's munitions were shipped from Nieuw Friesland. The expense was considerable, but powergun ammunition and self-guided shells for the regiment's rocket howitzers had to be manufactured to the closest tolerances if they were to function properly.

Supplies of other material were available cheaper and at satisfactory quality on Trinity. Because the local government had hired the Frisians at a monthly flat rate, cost cutting had a direct, one-to-one effect on President Hammer's profit margin. Sten Moden was responsible for procuring food, bedding, soft-skinned vehicles, and hundreds of other items on the local economy.

Trip flares and smoke grenades were high usage items for the field force. Forges de Milhaud had underbid other suppliers on the past three contracts. In the course of his duties, Moden had gotten to know Loie Leonard, the woman who owned the company.

Know her very well.

Moden didn't have a vehicle at his quarters, and he didn't want to waste time summoning one from the motor pool. He began to jog toward the munitions dump, letting his long arms flap instead of pumping them as he ran. The floodlights illuminating the four-meter-high berm emphasized the yellow-green cast of the local soil.

This afternoon Forges de Milhaud had delivered a load of pyrotechnics after working hours. Indig labor crews had to be off-post at sundown, so deliveries couldn't be properly sorted and inspected for quality.

According to standard operating procedure, Moden should have refused to accept the load until the next working day when it could be processed properly. This was an 8th Night, so delivery would take place after the weekend.

In normal circumstances, Moden might or might not have followed SOP. He didn't like red tape, but it was a fact of life in any complex organization. The field force had a twelve-day supply of flares and grenades on hand, so there was no duty-related reason for the supply officer to cut corners.

But Loie called him, explaining that she needed acceptance *now* in order to meet her payroll. Moden had called Filkerson, telling him to let the drivers dump their cargo where it could be sorted in the morning of 1st Night.

And Moden had visited Loie at a hotel near the Forges offices. Later she went home to her family, and Captain Sten Moden, exalted by gage, returned to Trinity Base.

"Sir! Sir!" Filkerson screeched over the helmet earphones. *"We've got a fire, a real fire, in the center of the pile. We can't get to it with the hoses!"*

Moden broke into a full run. He switched his helmet to override the carriers of all his subordinates. "Supply Six to all personnel in the dump area. Get outside the berm now! Run for it! There's nothing inside the berm that's worth your life!"

He wasn't sure whether the emergency team was on the same channel or not. He hoped so, or at least that they'd have sense enough to follow the dump staff when the latter started running for the entrance.

Still running, Moden keyed his helmet to a general Trinity Base push. "Supply Six to Base Operations!" he said. He was gasping with fear and exertion. "General alarm! We have an emergency situation at the ammo dump. If it blows, debris may injure personnel anywhere in the compound and start fires! Over!"

Moden was twenty meters from the separate outwork shielding the entrance to the dump. A burp of orange flame flashed momentarily above the berm. The ground shuddered, and Filkerson screamed over the unit channel.

A firetruck on a hovercraft chassis howled through the dump entrance, slid up on the outwork as it made the necessary ninety-degree turn, and accelerated down the branch through which Moden was entering the dump.

Moden leaped sideways to save himself. The panicked driver hadn't noticed him. Four firefighters with airpacks and flame-resistant garments, and three of Moden's khaki-clad guard detachment, clung to side-rails of the speeding vehicle.

The siren on the headquarters building began to wail. The floodlights around the dump flickered.

There was another explosion, much brighter and louder than the first. Shells and rocket motors emerged in sparkling parabolas from the fireball, screaming like banshees. The ground shock staggered Moden, though the berm protected him from whizzing fragments like those that sprayed overhead.

The entrance gate, cyclone fencing on a tubular framework, was torn askew. Two khaki figures ran out as Moden entered. The troopers clung to one another, though neither man appeared to be injured.

Moden grabbed them both in his huge arms. "Where's Sergeant Filkerson?" he demanded.

"Via, he's back there!" one of the troopers screamed. "The shack came down on him and we couldn't get him out!"

Moden flung the pair out toward safety. He'd thought of ordering them to help him, but they didn't look to be in shape to do that or anything else just now.

The guard shack had been to the immediate right of the dump entrance. It was constructed of dirt, stabilized with a plasticizer and compacted.

The locally made pyrotechnics had been off-loaded adjacent to the shack, as good a place as any since they couldn't be processed at the moment. When the pile exploded, the shock wave shattered the near wall of the building and collapsed the rest onto Filkerson, inside using the radio. It was hard to believe that anybody beneath the heavy slabs could be alive, but Filkerson's voice still moaned through the commo helmet. The sergeant had been—in a manner of speaking—lucky.

The floodlights went out. The dump glowed red in a dozen locations, bunkers where further material had been ignited by the previous blasts. Moden thumbed his helmet visor to light-amplification mode and began shifting the ruin of the guard shack, chunk by chunk.

The choice was speed or caution, and under the present conditions speed won going away. Moving the mass of shattered walls was much like playing pick-up sticks. There was always a chance that when Moden's huge muscles bunched to hurl a block clear, the remaining slabs would shift and crush Filkerson like a caterpillar on the highway; but if Moden waited for specialized rescue equipment, blast shocks were going to make the pile settle anyway.

Besides, there was nothing else Sten Moden could do except watch helplessly the destruction caused by his failure to do his duty.

The edges of the crumbled guard shack were jagged rather than sharp. Moden should have been wearing gloves for the job. The pain didn't bother him, but the film of blood was slippery until it dried to tackiness.

Moden grasped a shard, found it set firmly, and stepped to the side to take instead the 80-kilo block that held the previous one in place. He lifted and threw the block aside. Filkerson's head and torso were beneath. The man moaned softly.

A bunker on the other side of the dump erupted in orange flame. The initial open-air blast had shifted the armored doors of some bunkers. With the volume of sparks and larger chunks of burning debris, it was inevitable that the fire would spread.

The Lord only knew how it had started. Perhaps a fuze had been defective, perhaps a ruptured membrane had brought two reactive compounds in contact. Perhaps there'd been no manufacturing flaw whatever, but one of the crates had been crushed with disastrous results when the load was dumped unceremoniously.

If lightning had struck the pyrotechnics, it would still have been Sten Moden's fault. The only reason the load was in the dump this night was that he had accepted it improperly.

Moden gripped the slab lying on Filkerson's legs, so that the whole weight wouldn't shear down on flesh like the blade of a roller mill. "It's okay, Sergeant," he murmured.

Only when Moden spoke did he realize how loud the background rumble was. The ground trembled at a low frequency that tried to loosen his bowels.

Filkerson's eyes opened. "Via, Cap'n," he said. "Get me out of here, right?"

He was still speaking on the unit push. Despite the radio augmentation, Moden understood the words only because he watched Filkerson's lips form them.

Another bunker blew up, belching the roof of steel planks and tonnes of dirt overburden. Moden staggered forward. He turned and lifted Filkerson onto his back. His left hand cushioned the man's buttocks while his right gripped Filkerson's arms, flopped over Moden's shoulders and across his chest.

Moden stepped carefully through the tumble of slabs and started for the nearby gate at a trot.

A bunker in the center of the dump detonated. The shock wave set off three more bunkers simultaneously. The cataclysmic blast hurled the two men over the four-meter-high outwork protecting the entrance.

The sleet of debris riding the wave front chewed off Sten Moden's left arm, but Filkerson's body saved the captain's torso.

NIEUW FRIESLAND

Tech II Niko Daun was one of the tough jobs for the Enlisted Assignments Bureau. He'd rejected his automatic assignment, and the first live clerk he'd seen hadn't been able to help either.

That put Daun across the desk from Warrant Leader Avenial, the section head. Daun's quick gaze danced out through the clear wall at the open bullpen where most of the section's requests were processed, then back to Avenial. The technician looked nervous and very, very determined.

Avenial smiled. "Don't worry, Daun," he said. "If you get as far as me, the problem gets fixed. That's as true as if the Lord carved it on stone."

And it was. Not every disgruntled trooper got to the section head, but it was Avenial's truthful boast that he *never*, in seven years in the post, had needed to pass an applicant up the line to the Brigadier in charge of the bureau.

Personnel files carried two kinds of carets marking a trooper for special treatment by Assignments. A white caret meant the trooper either had a valuable specialty or that the trooper had been noted as particularly valuable because of his or her behavior as a member of the Frisian Defense Forces.

A red caret indicated a trooper who'd had a service-incurred rough time, so Assignments was to cut an appropriate amount of slack. Treating veterans well is a matter of good business for a military force and the state which employs the force, though Avenial wouldn't have cared to be the person who stated publicly that Colonel—President—Hammer had no interest in the subject beyond good business.

Daun's personnel file bore both white and red carets.

The technician's complexion was dark—darker than Avenial's, though Mediterranean rather than African stock seemed to have predominated in his ancestry. He was short and slight, but the psych profile didn't indicate a dose of the Little Guy Syndrome that had made many of Avenial's assignment tasks harder than they needed to be. Most of that sort of fellow migrated to combat arms anyway, where they either learned to control the chip on their shoulder—

Or lost chip, shoulder, and life. Hopefully before they had time to screw things up too bad.

"I told the lady out front," Daun said, nodding toward the bullpen. "I won't serve with, with indigs. If that means changing my specialty, then all right. I don't care about rank, you can *have* that."

Avenial nodded. His eyes were on the screen canted slightly toward him from an open surface of the otherwise cluttered top of his desk. He wasn't reading the data displayed there, just using it as an excuse to be noncommittal for a moment.

The clerk who'd dealt with Daun—hadn't dealt with Daun—was new to the section. She might work out, but Avenial hadn't been impressed so far. This particular problem would have been a stretch for any of his underlings, however.

"Well, I don't think we want you to change your specialty, Daun," Avenial said mildly. "We need sensor techs, and it looks like you're about as good as they come. In line for a third stripe, I see."

He crooked a grin at the applicant. As an attempt to build rapport through flattery, it was a bust.

"I told you, I don't *care* about rank!" Daun said. "I'll resign before I serve with indigs. I'll resign!"

"Well, we don't want you to resign," Avenial said. "So we're going to fix things, like I said."

He gave Daun another kind of look—hard, professional, appraising. "You say you won't serve with indigs," Avenial said. "What other assignment requirements do you have?"

"None," Daun said, meeting the section head's eyes. "None at all."

Avenial smiled again. "Fine," he said. "That tells me what I've got to work with. Plenty for the purpose, plenty."

He touched his keypad, changing screens in sequence after only a second or two of scanning the contents of each.

"The lady said she could *assign* me to a Frisian unit," Daun explained, "but once I was out in the field, the needs of the service prevail. If the—the unit commander decided I was the only one who could do a job, it didn't matter what I thought about it. And in my specialty, they might well put me in a sector staffed by indigs who couldn't handle the hardware themselves."

"She told you the truth," Avenial agreed approvingly.

Enlisted people expected to be crapped on and lied to. It seemed to Avenial that some of them almost begged for it. It went with the image. He'd had troopers make false statements about a pending assignment, statements they *must* have known were false, in the obvious hope that by saying nothing Avenial would give their lie validity.

Avenial didn't do that, and nobody in Avenial's section did it more than once that Avenial heard about. He was funny that way; but then, he slept at night without knocking himself into a coma on booze or gage. Life has a lot of trade-offs.

Avenial's finger paused on the next screen key. "Umm," he said. He looked up at Daun. "What do you know about survey teams, kid?" he asked.

"I can learn," Daun said crisply. His expression changed slightly. "So it'll be out of sensors after all?"

"Hell, no, they need sensor techs," Avenial replied. "Now, mind, everybody on a survey team better be able to do more than their base specialty. How's your marksmanship?"

Daun shrugged, smiled—a little wryly. "I've been practicing since my last assignment on Maedchen. Not great, but I'm getting better."

The lines of Daun's face flowed naturally into smiles, but this was the first time his nervousness had permitted one. He hadn't believed Avenial when he said that it was going to be all right. Well, they'd been lied to and lied to, why should they expect this warrant leader to be different?

"You see, kid," Avenial explained, "your specialty's too valuable for me to, say, reclassify you as a cook. Besides, if you're that good at running sensors—"

Daun smiled again. He'd loosened up, sure enough.

"—then it's what you like to do, so why should we fuck with it? Right?"

"No argument, mister," Daun said.

"So the trick's to put you somewhere that you're under Frisian command at all times," Avenial continued. "That's a survey team. Until the survey team makes its assessment, there's no indig employers *to* report to. Even if your unit commander's an asshole, he can't out-place you. You see?"

Daun nodded enthusiastic agreement.

"Now, the catch is," Avenial said, "you're out with—"

His eyes scanned for a figure on the screen.

"—five other guys, FDF troops. That's not like being in the middle of an armored battalion. There's not supposed to be any shooting going on, shooting at you, I mean. But I can't tell you it's safe."

He raised an eyebrow at the technician.

Daun shook his head and smiled. "Mister Avenial," he said, "I'm not…"

His hands flipped palms-up, then down again, in a *Macht nichts* gesture.

"I could have gotten a job with a communications firm, I could have found something safe," he said. "I wanted the, you know, the travel."

Daun meant *danger*, but he was ashamed to say it. Smart enough to be ashamed that he was a young man who wanted to be able to say he'd been *there*, the place civilians hadn't been. Ashamed to be proud of being what he was, a member of the finest military force in the human universe.

But proud nonetheless, as surely as Jumbo Avenial was.

Daun swallowed. "I'm not afraid," he concluded. "But I won't be any place that I have to depend on indigs."

Avenial nodded. "Just wanted to be clear about the situation," he said.

His lips pursed, then grinned like those of a frog swallowing the biggest fly of its life. "There's one problem remaining," he said. "The slot in a six-man survey team is for a Tech Four. You're only a Two."

Daun looked stricken. "What does that—" he began.

His mind paused in mid-thought, then resumed smoothly like a transmission shifted from the lay-shaft to a front gear with only the least clicking of teeth. "If there were a way you could arrange for me to get the assignment on a provisional basis, mister, I would be personally grateful to you. I've got more saved up than you might think because there was no way to spend it—"

Avenial, still grinning, waved Daun to silence. There were times he'd been insulted by an attempt to bribe him, but this wasn't one of them.

"What I thought," Avenial said, "was that we'd just get you the extra stripes. Stripe, really. Like I said before, you're due for your third already."

"I—" Daun said. "I…"

He sat up very straight in his seat. "Mister Avenial," he said, "you don't need my money, I understand that. But some day you may need something from me. Let me know."

"Just doing my job, kid," Avenial said.

But someday it *might* be good to know a guy who could make walls talk and knew what anybody he pleased was saying, right up to the President… Yeah, that just might be.

Daun rose to his feet. "I'll wait for my assignment, mister," he said. "Ah—do you have any notion when it might come through?"

Avenial touched another button. "It just did, kid," he said. "You're bound for a place named Cantilucca."

EARLIER: MAEDCHEN

As Technician Niko Daun dealt the last cards, Bondo, one of the two Central States soldiers in the game, grumbled, "If I get a decent hand this time, it'll be the first tonight."

A dripping soldier entered the twenty-man tent that served as living quarters for the battalion's Technical Detachment. His boots slipped in purple mud as he tried to seal the tent flap. He thumped the ground, cursing in a monotonous voice.

"You're only a rubber down," objected Sergeant Anya Wisloski, Daun's Frisian Defense Forces superior, partner, and—for the three months they'd been on outpost duty—lover.

"Yeah, but that's on Hendries' cards, not me," Bondo said. "I want some cards of my own."

Daun picked up his own bridge hand. Based on what the dealer had, everybody else in the game was looking at great cards.

"What *I* want," said Anya, "is some decent weather. I haven't seen the sun since we've been up here."

Anya was short, dark-haired, and white-skinned. Her waist nipped in and her chest was broad, but the breasts themselves were flat. She was several years older than Daun's twenty-one standard—how much older she'd avoided saying—and had gone straight into the Frisian Defense Forces while Daun had four years of technical school.

Daun trusted his own judgment inside a piece of electronics farther than he did Anya's (or most anybody else's, if it came to that). There was never any question about who was in charge of a group when Anya decided to *take* charge, however.

Another gust pelted the tent as a colophon to Anya's statement. For the most part, today's rain had been a drizzle, but occasionally big drops splattered to remind the battalion outpost that there were various forms of misery.

Support Base Bulwark was almost as isolated as a space station would have been. Weekly convoys brought food, replacements, and very occasionally a team of journalists from one of the major cities.

The journalists never stayed long. Sometimes the replacements didn't either. Troops who shot themselves in the foot or, less frequently, in the head, during their first week at Bulwark were a significant cause of attrition.

The base was sited on a low plateau, chosen for its accessibility by road rather than for purposes of defense. Higher peaks surrounded it within a five-klick radius.

The sensors themselves were expected to alert friendly forces if the Democrats massed in numbers sufficient to threaten the outpost. Daun had his doubts, but he realized the Democrats might be just as sloppy as their Central States opponents.

Heavy construction equipment had encircled the perimeter of the base with an earthen wall. The same construction crews then dug bunkers into the sides of that berm. During the months of constant rain, the bunkers filled as much as a meter deep with water.

The infantry protecting the base lived in tents on the bunker roofs. They had no protection except—for the ambitious ones—a wall of sandbags. The tents weren't dry either, but at least the troops didn't have to swim to their bunks.

Conditions for support personnel within the base weren't a great deal better. Walkways constructed from wooden shell crates led between locations, but for the most part the makeshift duckboards had sunk into the greasy, purplish mire. The Tactical Operations Center was an assemblage of the high officers' four living trailers placed around a large tent.

The whole complex was encircled by a triple row of sandbags and dirt-filled shell boxes. The construction engineers had trenched around the protective wall to draw off water. Because of the lack of slope the would-be channel was a moat, but at least it prevented the TOC from flooding.

The 150-mm howitzers of the four-tube battery were on steel planking to keep them from sinking to the trunnions. The guns slid during firing, so it was impossible to place accurate concentrations when the sensors located movement. Because rain and the slick ground made it so difficult to manhandle the 45-kg shells, most firing was done at random when battalion command decided it needed more ammo crates for construction.

The remainder of the support personnel lived in tents and slept on cots. Most of the tents were sandbagged to knee-height, three layers. Higher than that, the single-row walls fell down when the slippery filling bled through the fabric.

The two Frisians' assignment was for six standard months. The indigs were here for a local year—twenty-one months standard, and at least three times longer than Daun could imagine lasting under such conditions.

"Oh, sure, it'll dry out in spring," Bondo said as he scowled at his cards. "Dry out, bake to dust, and blow into every curst thing from your food to the sealed electronics. You think equipment life's bad in this rain, wait until spring."

The purpose of this Central States Army outpost in Maedchen's western tablelands was to service a belt of sensors brought at great expense from Nieuw Friesland. In theory, the sensors and the reaction forces they triggered would prevent infiltration from the Democrat-controlled vestries on the other side of the divide.

Bondo was quite right about the sensor failure rate. The Belt no doubt looked impressive during briefings in the capital, but the reality was as porous as cheesecloth. Infiltrators had an excellent chance of penetrating the eastern vestries unnoticed, and an even better chance of evading the Central States Army's half-hearted reaction patrols.

"One club," Bondo offered.

Daun didn't blame the rain or the quality of the hardware for the rate of sensor failure. Quite simply, personnel assigned by the Central States government weren't up to the job of servicing electronics this sophisticated.

Central States field teams wouldn't follow procedures. For example, they regularly used knives or bayonets to split the sensor frames to exchange data cartridges. The special tools that would perform the task without damage were lost or ignored. They didn't understand their duties. At least a third of the cartridges were inserted upside down, despite the neon arrows on both casing and cartridge, and despite anything Daun could say to the troops he was trying to train.

And they didn't *care*. As often as not, a field team huddled in a sheltered spot within a klick of the base instead of humping through the rain to service the sensors for which they were responsible. In the morning, they returned with the circuit marked complete—and there wasn't a curst thing Daun or Anya could do about it.

"Three no trump," Anya bid. She grinned coldly around the table.

Daun had already drafted an assessment for the Frisian Defense Forces Maedchen Command, back in the capital Jungfrau. In it he stated flatly that the system wasn't working and could never work as presently constituted.

Nieuw Friesland should either withdraw support from the Central States, or the

FDF should insist that the Central States hire a detachment of Frisians sufficient to perform all field as well as base servicing tasks. Otherwise, the inevitable failure would be blamed on Frisian technology rather than the ineptness of the Central States Army at using that technology.

Anya wouldn't let Daun transmit the assessment. It wasn't that she disagreed with him—quite the contrary. But she didn't believe anything a Tech II said could change the policy of bureaucrats on Nieuw Friesland… and there was a good chance Daun's opinions, once released, were going to become known to the Central States personnel she and Daun shared a tent with.

There are a lot of ways to get hurt in a war zone. Pissing off the heavily armed people closest to you wasn't a good way to survive to a pension.

But the situation grated on Daun's sense of rightness, as well as making him feel he was a bubble in a very hostile ocean.

"Too rich for my blood," Hendries said. "I pass."

Daun stared at his cards again. They hadn't changed for the better. He had four clubs, three of each other suit, and his high card was the jack of hearts.

He knew his partner was asking where his support was greatest; and he knew also that the proper answer was: nowhere.

"I pass," he said aloud.

Anya grimaced.

"Pass," said Bondo.

Daun laid out his wretched hand. His partner's expression softened as she saw just what Daun had dealt himself. Hendries glared at his cards to determine a lead, a nearly hopeless task under the circumstances.

The tent flap tore open. "Hey!" called the Central States soldier who stuck his head in. "Smart guys! Your fucking pickup's gone down again. The screen in the TOC's nothing but hash!"

"Bloody hell," Anya muttered. She laid her cards down. "My turn, I guess," she said to Daun. "You were out all morning with the satellite dish."

Daun stood up, waving his partner back. "Look, you were up the mast last night. Besides, I'm dummy. I'll catch this one."

"Hey!" the messenger from the Tactical Operations Center repeated. "Colonel Jeffords isn't real thrilled about this, you know."

That was probably true. The amount paid to Nieuw Friesland by the Central States government for Anya's services was comparable to what the colonel himself earned. Daun's pay was at the scale of a senior captain. The money didn't go into the two technicians' pockets, much of it, and if it had there was still no place to spend money out here on the tableland. It still provided a reason for some of the locals—Jeffords certainly, and apparently this messenger—to get shirty about off-planet smart-asses whose equipment didn't work.

"I'm on the way," Daun said. "Just let me get my gear."

He buckled his equipment belt around his narrow waist, pulled on his poncho, and tried to punch the larger working canopy down into its carrying sheath. He could only get it partway into the container, but that would hold it while he climbed the mast.

The slick fabric still shone with water from when Daun had had to use it that morning. It didn't matter—to the job—if he got soaked, but rain dripping into an open box could only make a bad situation worse.

The messenger disappeared. Daun sighed and followed him. "I'll catch the next one, Niko," Anya called as Daun stepped out into the rain.

The flashlight strapped for the moment to Daun's left wrist threw a fan of white light ahead of him. He could switch the beam to deep yellow which wouldn't affect his night vision, but it didn't matter if he became night-blind. He'd need normal light to do his work anyway: many of the components were color-coded. The markings would change hue or vanish if viewed under colored light.

Rain sparkled in the beam. Reflections made it difficult to tell what was mud and what was wet duckboard. The crates were likely to shift queasily underfoot anyway.

Three months more. How the locals stood it was beyond him.

Daun couldn't blame the soldiers he tried to train for being apathetic. It was all very well to tell the troops that their safety depended on them servicing the sensors properly, but a threat to lives so wretched had little incentive value.

Daun and Anya complained, but professionalism and a sense of duty would carry the pair of them through no matter how bad things got. The vast majority of the Central States personnel were conscripts, and the conscripts with the least political influence in Jungfrau besides. Daun was sure that at least eighty percent of the outpost would have deserted by now, if there was any place to which they *could* desert.

Light through the walls of the tent turned the TOC into a vast russet mushroom, though the fabric looked dull brown by daylight. Daun could hear voices, some of them compressed by radio transmission.

It was conceivable that the problem was inside the TOC, either in the console or the connecting cables. Daun was tempted to check out those possibilities first, but he decided not to waste his time. The console was of Frisian manufacture and sealed against meddling by the locals.

The cables had been laid by the previous pair of FDF advisers. They'd done a first-class job; Daun had checked and approved every millimeter of the route the day he and Anya arrived. Unless somebody'd driven a piece of tracked construction equipment through the TOC, the conduits should be fine. The indigs were capable of doing something that bone-headed, but Daun would have heard it happening.

The thirty-meter mast was a triangular construct set in concrete and anchored to the toiler housing the battery commander. The unit telescoped in three sections. Daun could lower the mast to save most of the climb, but re-erecting it would require help to keep the guy wires from fouling. He didn't trust the indigs to do that properly even during daylight.

He squelched to the base of the mast, hooked his safety belts, and began to climb the runglike braces which bound the three verticals together. The mast was formed from plastic extrusions, not metal, but the rungs still felt icy to Daun's bare hands. They were also slick as glass.

The sensor wands' removable recording cartridges provided extremely precise information on all movements within the coverage area. If a human passed within two or three meters of the wand, the retrieved cartridge could determine the state of health based on body temperature and pulse rate. Such data were remarkable but useful only as the raw material for a historical overview.

Base Bulwark collected coarse sensor readings in real-time, via coded frequency-hopping radio signals. As the messenger had implied, this was the second miserable night in a row that the ultra-high gain antenna atop the mast had failed.

Last night a matchhead-sized integrated circuit had blown: the sort of thing that happened only occasionally with Frisian hardware, but always at a bad time. Anya had unplugged the blown chip and replaced it with a good one.

Anya, simply glad to have the antenna working again, had pitched the bad chip out into mud and darkness. If she'd instead saved the fried unit, Daun would have examined it to determine the cause of failure. Long odds the problem was due to manufacturing error, but there was always a possibility that a short within the box was causing a hot spot.

The chance to diagnose the underlying problem instead of merely fixing the symptom was much of the reason Daun had volunteered to climb the mast. Besides, he liked the hardware part of his work well enough that he preferred to be doing it instead of playing cards with strangers he couldn't respect and didn't much like.

There were guy wires on each of the three sections of the telescoping mast. When he reached each set of guys, Daun unhooked one of his two safety loops, rehooked it above the wires, and repeated the process with the second loop. At no time did he trust merely his boots and grip to keep him on the mast. Daun wasn't so much cautious as perfectly methodical. The notion of cutting corners to lessen his exposure to the chill drizzle didn't cross his mind.

Viewed from the top of the thirty-meter mast, the lights of Bulwark Base had a surreal innocence, like the gleam of will-o'-the-wisps in a nighted meadow. Rain softened the patterns and dusted glare into sparkle. The scene wasn't beautiful but it had a dignified tranquility, far removed from the muddy truth. The glowing canvas of the TOC could be the entrance to the Venusberg, and Daun could imagine that flashlights in the tents on the perimeter were cupids twinkling around the goddess of love.

The receiving antenna at the mast peak was enclosed in a weatherproof capsule about the size of a soccer ball. The covering was dull gray plastic which was reasonably sturdy but remained transparent over most of the electromagnetic spectrum. Wherever possible, the sensor wands transmitted over microwave frequencies, but those without a line of sight to the receiver used VHF or UHF as circumstances required.

Daun arranged the working canopy over the capsule. When he had it stiffened into position, the monomolecular sheeting blocked the rain completely. Before then, however, he managed to pour what felt like a liter of cold water down the back of his neck from the canopy's folds.

He sighed, clipped his light to a strut so that it shone down on the work, and opened the antenna capsule. Two of the micro-miniaturized circuits were black instead of the healthy gold color. That was neither surprising nor a problem. When one chip blew, it could easily have overloaded its neighbor. Daun's repair kit contained at least three replacements for every chip on the chassis.

He opened the cover wider as he prepared to pull the failed chips. An irregularity on the inner face of the cover caught his eye. The plastic had blistered and turned silvery on the side facing the chips that had failed.

The antenna didn't draw enough juice to heat the cover even slightly. A short circuit which blistered the plastic that way would have vaporized the circuitry, chassis and all, instead of popping a chip or two.

The energy that had caused the antenna to fail had come from outside. The most likely outside source was a precisely aimed X-ray laser on one of the enemy-held hilltops overlooking Bulwark Base.

Feeling colder than rain could make him, Daun reached up to key his commo helmet and alert the camp. The shock wave proved he was too late.

The warhead went off with a hollow *Klock!* that blew one of the TOC trailers inside out in a sleet of aluminum. The weapon, a laser-guided anti-tank missile, was configured to defeat heavy armor with a shaped charge. A straight fragmentation or HE warhead would have been better suited for the present task. This was along the lines of killing mosquitoes with an elephant gun.

On the other hand, an elephant gun *will* kill a mosquito. Little survived of the trailer, and nothing of anyone who happened to be in it.

The canopy flapped skyward in the blast. The antennas whipped violently and a guy wire parted, either overstressed or cut by flying shrapnel. Daun hugged the mast with both arms as his feet slipped from the rungs.

Buzzbombs and crew-served automatic weapons raked the bunkers on the north and west perimeter of the base. Tents collapsed or exploded, flinging out the corpses of troops huddled beneath canvas for shelter.

While the antenna was deadlined the previous night, the Democrats had moved an assault force into position in the gullies close to Bulwark Base. Tonight they had taken the antenna out of commission again in order to make their final approach through the rain. The Democrats knew they had nothing to fear from the garrison's patrols or the watchfulness of the troops on duty on the perimeter of the base.

Another terminally guided missile impacted, this time on furniture near the center of the TOC. The tent shredded in a reddish appliqué over the white flash at the core. Bits of missile casing, and fragments of equipment converted into secondary projectiles, riddled the three remaining trailers.

The mast swayed even more violently. Daun lost his grip. He was hanging by his safety belts. The broken guy wire whacked across his helmet and bound his outflung arm to the antenna mast.

Half a second later, a third missile detonated in the Technical Detachments tent.

For an instant, the flash threw the silhouettes of the dozen startled occupants against the canvas. Then the tent was gone, the flash was a blinding purple afterimage on Daun's retinas, and Sergeant Anya Wisloski shrieked into her commo helmet like a hog being gelded.

Daun's legs flailed as he tried to find the rungs again with his feet. The mast had torqued and bent over so that he hung out in the air. Most of his weight was on his left forearm, bound to the mast. He thought the bones might have broken. The pain was inconceivable.

He didn't scream. His ears still rang with the sound of Anya's cry.

Figures, some of them waving weapons, lurched from tents. The TOC's instrumentation ran off a portable fusion power plant adapted from the drive unit of a Frisian armored vehicle. There was plenty of excess capacity. Most of the living quarters within the berm had electric lights run through a variety of jury-rigged conductors, with telephone line predominating.

The Central States personnel were backlit by their own illumination. Democrat troops had quickly crossed the skimpy wire entanglements by throwing quilted padding over the barbs. They opened fire from the berm, knocking startled defenders down like bowling pins.

Daun managed to grip a rung with his right hand and take some of the weight off his tangled arm. The mast swayed, dipping slightly with each movement. Sooner or later one of the twisted poles would snap and collapse the whole tower. Daun *had* to get free before then.

A ricochet moaned past his face. The bullet sounded lonely, like a dog unjustly kicked. Daun thrashed his lower body and finally hooked his right leg around the tilting mast.

In one of the gun pits nearby, the crew was trying to depress their 150-mm howitzer to fire directly on the attackers. A buzzbomb described a flat arc that climaxed on the gun's recoil compensator. The projectile burst with a white flash and a blast of shrapnel that was invisible except for its effect on the crew.

The gunners spun away and fell. Open powder charges sprayed across the gun pit and ignited in a fierce red flare. The gun captain crawled back toward her position through the flame, dragging loops of intestine. She pulled herself onto the trail and died, reaching vainly for the firing lanyard.

Trip flares attached to the wire on the south side of Bulwark Base began to go off. The sappers leading the Democrat assault had disconnected the flares on their approach routes. Members of the garrison stumbled over their own mines while fleeing into the night.

A truck, one of the few vehicles assigned to the base, drove south out of the engineer compound. Scores of troops clung to the cab and body. Some of them shot wildly.

Democrat riflemen and machine gunners opened fire. Bullets sparked on the frame and slapped troops from the vehicle. The truck continued to accelerate, skidding on the slick surface. Its eight driven wheels cast up a rooster-tail of mud, water, and duckboards.

Two buzzbombs sputtered toward the moving target. One missed high, sailing over the berm to vanish. The other went off close alongside. Would-be escapees tumbled from the bed, but the run-while-flat tires permitted the truck to keep going.

The gate to the road south from Bulwark Base was three X-frames connected by a horizontal pole and strung with barbed wire. A flangelike extension of the berm was intended to force vehicles to slow for a right-angle turn when entering or leaving the base.

The truck hit the gate, crushed it down, and roared over the berm's sloped extension in low gear. A Central States soldier ran along behind the vehicle, trying to climb aboard. He lost his footing on the berm and sprawled.

As the truck disappeared, the soldier rose to one knee and tried to shoot at the vehicle. Mud clogged his rifle. He flung the useless weapon after the truck. A moment later, a Democrat machine gun nailed him into the berm with a burst of golden tracers.

The leg Daun had flung around the mast cramped because of the awkward angle. That pain was lost in the red throb of blood returning to his left arm now that he didn't dangle by it.

With no tools and one good hand, Daun couldn't unwrap the guy wire that held him. It was spliced into his safety belts and apparently pinched by a fold of the slowly collapsing mast. He'd lost the wrist light when the first missile went off.

He supposed that was a good thing, because otherwise he'd have been a lighted target. He giggled hysterically.

Daun heard a thump over the shooting. He looked down. A dark parcel lay on an expanse of softly reflectant aluminum. Someone had tossed a satchel charge onto the roof of the battery commander's trailer.

Daun clutched the mast with his free arm and tried to find footing for his other leg. He closed his eyes instinctively. Blood vessels in his eyelids reddened the yellow flash that streamed through them.

The blast flattened the trailer and flung Daun upward like a yo-yo shooting the moon. The guy wire broke again, but the safety belts held.

The mast toppled with the grace of a falling tree, slowly at first but accelerating as it neared the ground. Daun was underneath. Remaining guy wires zinged as they parted.

A Democrat parachute flare drifted down through the overcast to illuminate the encampment. The mast rotated as light bloomed. Daun stared down through the latticework at the ruin of Bulwark Base instead of up into the clouds that would otherwise have been the last thing he saw.

A pole in the base section had broken, causing the mast to twist on the remaining verticals before it hit the ground. Daun slammed into the mud, beside rather than beneath the structure to which he was bound.

The impact knocked all the breath out of his body. The antenna capsule snapped off and bounced twice before coming to rest beside the technician. He didn't quite lose consciousness, but the shots and screams around him faded into a thirty-cycle hum for a few seconds.

The rain had almost ceased. The flare sank lower. Vertical objects cast jagged shadows that cut like saw-teeth across the surface of Bulwark Base.

Daun lay with the mast on one side of him and on the other the low sandbag wall that had once protected the Technical Detachment's tent. The missile had destroyed the wall it hit and the structure beyond, but it spared the sandbags on the opposite side.

Someone just across the wall was moaning.

Daun tried to free himself from the tangle in which he lay. His left leg was pinned and his left arm was still tethered to the mast. He could move his head as far as his neck flexed, but he couldn't crane it high enough to see what was holding his limbs.

The bunched jacket held his right arm almost as tightly as his left. There was no possibility of tearing the tough, weatherproof fabric.

Daun heard voices nearby. He opened his mouth to call for help. One of the voices said, "Watch it! This one's alive!"

A machine pistol within the area the Tech Detachment tent had covered fired a short burst downward. The muzzle flashes were red and bright.

Daun wore a pistol as part of his required equipment. It was in a cross-draw holster on his left side, where it was least in the way when he was working. He could no more reach the weapon now than he could fly back to Nieuw Friesland under his own power.

"They were playing cards," said one of the Democrats.

"Hey!" said his partner. "We're just supposed to be taking guns and ammunition."

"So I'm searching their wallets for items of intelligence value," the first Democrat snarled. "If you're smart, you'll keep your fucking mouth shut about it, too."

The sky blazed orange as the light of an explosion reflected from the low clouds. The ground shock lifted Daun, the mast, and the sandbag wall an instant before the airborne shock wave punched across them. The ammo dump had exploded.

Daun hit the ground again. He was still tied to the mast. Sandbags collapsed over him.

Individual shells detonated during the next fifteen seconds, some of them at a considerable distance where the initial explosion hurled them. The first Democrat was cursing. The blast had knocked him skidding in the mud.

"There's one!" cried his partner. Two machine pistols fired together. Daun felt the whack of little bullets against the sandbags over him, but he wasn't the target. The moans of the soldier on the other side of the wall ended in a liquid gurgle.

"Hey, lookit!" shouted the second member of the Democrat clean-up team. He was standing beside Daun, but the Frisian could see only a triangle of cloud through the jumble of collapsed wall. "Look at *this!*"

"Bloody hell!" said the first man. "That's a bloody powergun. The Cents don't have bloody powerguns!"

"*I* do," said his jubilant partner. A bolt of cyan plasma lanced skyward.

"You cursed fool!" the first Democrat said. "Don't do that! Somebody'll shoot us! Besides"—his voice changed slightly into that of a hustler calculating his chances—"it's not worth anything much 'cause we can't get ammo for it. Look, though—just for the hell of it, I'll give you two hundred lira for it. For the curiosity."

"Fuck you," said his partner. "This is *mine.*"

The two Democrats stepped onto the bags covering Daun. They hopped from him over the fallen antenna mast.

"Look," the first man was saying, "half of it is mine anyway…."

Daun's lungs burned, but he was afraid to breathe. The detached part of his mind noted that the second Democrat should be very careful about standing with his back to his partner this night. Otherwise he might die for the trophy, as surely as Sergeant Anya Wisloski had died.

LAWLER

The platoon leader's door was open. Trooper Johann Vierziger paused in the day room and raised his knuckles to knock on the jamb.

"Come on in, Vierziger," called Lieutenant Hartlepool in false jollity. "You haven't been with us long enough to know, but we're not much on ceremony in this outfit."

Vierziger had been transferred to the 105th Military Police Detachment on Lawler as soon as he'd completed basic training with the Frisian Defense Forces. He'd arrived a week ago, and had seen action—with the FDF—only once according to his records. That action had occurred the night before.

"Thank you, sir," Vierziger said. He was a short man, dainty except for telltale signs like the thickness of his wrists. Pretty, Hartlepool thought when the fellow was assigned to his platoon, and a nance.

Hartlepool had nothing against queers, not so it got in the way of his duties, but this was ridiculous. The One-Oh-Fifth wasn't some parade-ground unit for show. They, and particularly 1st Platoon, A Company, were in firefights at least once a week.

Hartlepool couldn't imagine who'd thought his platoon was the place to stick an effeminate newbie. He'd liked to have met the bureaucrat in an alley.

"Sit down, sit down," Hartlepool said, gesturing to the seat in front of his desk. Malaveda, who now commanded First Squad, was in the room's third chair, backed against the wall to one side.

Platoon leaders didn't rate a lot of space at the best of times. Hartlepool had a glorified broom closet, but he knew there were lieutenants in the 105th who *shared* comparable quarters. Accommodations in Belair were tight. Expectation of war brought people to the capital, either for its fancied safely or because they believed there was money to be made.

"Thank you, sir," Vierziger said. His face bore a slight smile, but he obviously didn't intend to volunteer anything unasked. He sat down gracefully without touching the chair with his hands.

Vierziger reminded Hartlepool of somebody, but the lieutenant couldn't place *who.*

"Well, we've got some good news for you, Vierziger," Hartlepool said. The cheerful tone was wearing thin, but he didn't know what other persona to adopt. "To begin with, *Sergeant* Vierziger. On the basis of Sergeant Malaveda's report—"

He nodded to the non-com. Malaveda's forehead glistened with sweat. He stared at the wall across the desk without acknowledging the remark.

Hartlepool cleared his throat. "Based on that," he resumed, "and my analysis of both yours and Malaveda's helmet recorders from last night's incident, I requested that Lawler Command grant you an immediate field promotion. I'm pleased to say that they've agreed."

"Thank you, sir," Vierziger said. He reached across the desk to take Hartlepool's proffered hand. His grip was firm and dry, almost without character.

"And thank you, Sergeant Malaveda," Vierziger added, glancing at the non-com. "I trust your promotion will come through quickly also. You deserve it."

He was perfectly appropriate in words, tone, and expression, but Hartlepool got the feeling that Vierziger was laughing at them. It was like watching a master artist accept the congratulations of a six-year-old on the quality of his painting.

Vierziger's faint smile made memories click into place: another man, dark rather than blond, but small and *pretty* and queer…

"Ah, Vierziger?" the lieutenant asked. "Do you—did you happen to have a relative in the FDF? In Hammer's Slammers, actually?"

Vierziger shook his head easily. "Not me," he said. "No relatives at all, I suspect, though it's been a very long time since I was home."

Hartlepool thought of asking where Vierziger called home. He decided not to.

"I, ah…" he said. "I met Major Joachim Steuben once. He was an interesting man."

He raised an eyebrow, an obvious demand that Vierziger reply to the non-question.

Vierziger smiled wider. The expression was as unpleasant as a shark's gape. *The lieutenant had been playing games with him. The lieutenant would never do that again.* "So I gather," Vierziger said. "Hammer's hatchetman, wasn't he? Until someone shot him in the back."

"Bodyguard, as I heard it," Hartlepool said. He chewed on his tongue for a moment to stimulate the flow of saliva in his dry mouth. "Well, he's been gone for some while now. Almost since Colonel Hammer's accession to the Presidency."

"Seven years," Vierziger said. "Seven years to the day I joined the Frisian Defense Forces. Or so they told me."

Vierziger's battle dress uniform was perfectly tailored. That wasn't surprising, since Frisian MP units were traditionally strac, even on field duty. On Vierziger, however, the garb hung so perfectly that he might have modeled for the tailor.

Hartlepool cleared his throat again and tried on a brisk, businesslike expression. "Along with the promotion, Vierziger," he said, "you've been reassigned. You're, ah, quite remarkable. Of course you know that. Somebody seems to have decided you're too valuable for a line unit here on Lawler."

He was betting that Vierziger was too new to the FDF to know that the statement was utter nonsense. Nobody got transferred so quickly unless his commanding officer made a *"This or I resign!"* point of it with echelon.

From Vierziger's icy smile, he knew exactly why he was being transferred. Hartlepool had been shocked speechless by the images recorded by the new recruit's helmet cameras the night before.

Granted that Johann Vierziger was a valuable member of the FDF, the fellow was still too dangerous for Hartlepool to risk having him around. It was just that simple.

"Very well, sir," Vierziger said. "My service with you has been interesting. I wish you the best of luck in the future."

As if he were a commanding general speaking to his staff as he stepped down.

Vierziger stood up. "Am I dismissed, then, sir?" he added calmly.

"What?" said Hartlepool. "I, ah—I'd tell you your new assignment if I knew what it was, of course."

Hartlepool didn't know how he'd expected Vierziger to react to the notice of transfer, but he'd expected *some* reaction. The lieutenant felt as if he'd tried to climb one more step than the staircase had.

"It doesn't really concern me, sir," Vierziger said. "I'll serve in any capacity to which my superiors choose to assign me."

Vierziger's voice was without expression, and his face was a skull..

If the man was what he appeared to be, he was a tool like the pistol in his belt holster or the knife whose hilt projected from his boot top.… But guns and knives will not act of their own accord. Nobody could watch images of the previous night without wondering whether Vierziger was at heart as uncontrolled as he was unstoppable when he went into action.

"Yes, well," Hartlepool said. "Good luck in your assignment, wherever it is, Sergeant."

Vierziger threw him a crisp salute. He looked like a boy in uniform—or a girl—as he turned on his heel and left the office.

"He isn't human," Sergeant Malaveda said. He could have been remarking on the quality of the local beer. His eyes swung toward the doorway now that Vierziger was gone, though he hadn't looked at the man while they were together in the small room.

"He's a hell of a gunman, though," Hartlepool said, as if he were disagreeing. "Well, we'll see what they make of him on a survey team. He'll be going to Cantilucca as part of the security element."

Malaveda raised an eyebrow.

"Via, yes, I know what his assignment is!" the lieutenant snapped.

He looked toward the empty doorway himself. "Major Steuben was like that. From the stories, at least. And the same kind of eyes. But Joachim Steuben's been dead for a long time."

Sergeant Malaveda stared at him. There seemed to be a chill in the room.

EARLIER: LAWLER

Though Vierziger, the trooper driving Sergeant Malaveda's air-cushion jeep, was a newbie to the Frisian Defense Forces, he obviously had a lot of time in other armies on his clock. Malaveda guessed he was on the wrong side of thirty standard, but it was hard to be sure. Vierziger had the sort of baby-faced cuteness that some men keep from early teens to sixty.

It was one more reason for Malaveda, who shaved his scalp to hide the fact his hair was receding at age twenty-six, to dislike Vierziger.

"Pull up here," Malaveda ordered as they eased toward the mouth of the alley by which they'd approached the rear of the target building. "And *don't* get out where the street light'll show us up."

The newbie obeyed with the same delicate skill he'd shown while navigating the alley in the dark. In light-amplification mode, the visors of Frisian commo helmets increased visibility to daytime norms, but they robbed terrain of the shadings, which the human brain processed into relative distances. Vierziger was a good driver, Malaveda had to admit—

To himself. There was no way he was going to praise the little turd out loud.

Vierziger switched off the fans. The hollow echo that filled the alley even on whisper mode drained away.

"Who the hell told you to shut down?" Malaveda snarled.

The newbie turned and looked at him. Vierziger's expression was blank but not tranquil. Malaveda felt ice at the back of his neck.

"Nobody did, Sergeant," Vierziger said. His voice was low-pitched, melodious, and just enough off-key to reinforce the chill Malaveda felt in his glance. "Would you like me to light the fans again?"

Malaveda scowled. "That's not what I said. Just remember, you may *think* you're something, but you're serving with the best, now!"

Vierziger faced the alley mouth again. He drew his 2-cm shoulder weapon from the butt clamp that held it vertical beside his seat and checked the magazine. "I'll keep that in mind," he said.

Malaveda scowled, but he didn't restart the discussion for the time being.

Lawler was a highly developed world with a population of nearly forty million. Even so there should have been enough room and resources for everybody.

The ostensible cause of—not-quite-war, but soon—was that the central provinces of the occupied continent wanted to retain links with Earth, while the coastal provinces wanted a Lawler that was independent and, coincidentally, ruled by coastal-province oligarchies.

The Junta of Central Province Governors had faced a planet-wide vote which would have been dominated by their opponents' political machines. They forestalled it by raising their own army—and hiring two armored brigades from the

Frisian Defense Forces.

The Junta couldn't afford to pay the mercenaries forever just to stand around and look tough. Malaveda figured there'd be a riot pretty soon in one of the border cities. The Planetary Front—the thugs from the coasts—would kill people putting the riot down, or anyway the Junta would say they had.

And the Junta would respond, with FDF panzers the cutting edge of the blow.

For the time being, Malaveda and the rest of 3d Squad, 1st Platoon, A Company, 105th Military Police Detachment (Lawler), had a problem which didn't in the least involve local politics. A trooper named Soisson had been guarding a warehouse in Belair, the Junta's capital. Soisson shot the fellow on duty with him, then ran off with a truckload of powergun ammunition.

The ammo was probably an afterthought—the most valuable thing the bastard could grab after he'd nutted. It had to be recovered, though, and Soisson had to be brought back dead or alive. The tradition of the White Mice, the field police of Hammer's Slammers, was that dead was preferable.

Soisson was supposed to be hiding in a front apartment of the three-story building across the street. Malaveda waited in a backstop position thirty meters from the rear door. Lieutenant Hartlepool would take the main part of the squad in by the front and catch Soisson in bed—if everything went as planned. The lieutenant had stationed Malaveda there just in case.

Malaveda waited with a newbie who obviously thought he was hot stuff, even though he didn't actually *say* so. Malaveda lifted his sub-machine gun to his shoulder, aimed it at the apartment building's back door, and *clocked* his tongue against the roof of his mouth.

He lowered the weapon and looked again at his driver. "I guess you think you've seen action, don't you?" he said.

Vierziger turned, raised an eyebrow, and turned back. "I've seen action, yes," he said softly.

"Well let me tell you how it is, buddy," Malaveda said. "You haven't seen anything till you've seen it with the FDF. Lieutenant Hartlepool, the Old Man? He was in the White Mice when Major Steuben commanded them. He was a friend of Major Steuben's."

Vierziger looked at him. "Joachim Steuben didn't have any friends," he said. His tone was as bleak as the space between stars.

Malaveda waited for the newbie to take his glacial eyes away before saying, "You know a lot—for a guy who enlisted three months ago!"

"I know too much," Vierziger said, almost too quietly to be heard. "I know way too much. Now, let's just watch and wait, like we're supposed to. All right, Sergeant?"

As if a fucking newbie could tell a sergeant what to do! But Malaveda didn't feel like saying anything more. He'd had a creepy feeling about Vierziger from when the bastard was assigned to the squad. Vierziger made everybody's skin crawl. Being alone with him in a jeep was like, was like—

There was a sound in the alley behind them. Malaveda, keyed up, started to swing his sub-machine gun toward the noise. Vierziger—

Malaveda didn't see the newbie move. There was the sound, and Vierziger was—

standing in the jeep—

facing backward—

his 2-cm weapon in his left hand, held at the balance, a hand's breadth from his hip—

where it counter-weighted the pistol pointing in his right hand, a gleam of polished metals, the iridium barrel and gold and purple scrollwork on the receiver.

Malaveda hadn't seen the fucker move!

Vierziger slipped the pistol back into a cut-away holster that rode high on his right hip. It wasn't an issue rig, and it looked like it ought to be uncomfortable for driving; though he'd driven all right too.

He sat down again and smiled faintly at Malaveda. "Just a rat," he said. "Jumping onto the manhole cover back there. Where you have humans, you have rats."

Malaveda nodded in the direction of the pistol, now out of sight again. "Where the hell did you learn to do that?" he asked.

Vierziger shrugged. "Practice," he said. His face was unlined. He looked like a choirboy in this soft illumination, street lights shimmering from the damp brick walls of the alley. "And I had a—talent for it, I suppose you'd say."

"Bloody hell," Malaveda said.

A slow-moving car went by, the first traffic since the MP jeep took its pre-dawn station in the alley. The vehicle's windows were polarized opaque. They reflected the knife-edged whiteness of the hood-center headlight.

Malaveda didn't want to speak, but he heard himself say, "Could you teach some-body to do that? To— draw that way?"

"It's just practice, Sergeant," Vierziger said.

He looked at his companion again. Malaveda couldn't have explained what was different about the newbie's expression, but this time it didn't make him shiver to see it.

"It isn't hard to shoot people, you know," Vierziger said. "The hard part is knowing which ones. They don't always come with labels."

He smiled. Malaveda wasn't sure if the statement was meant for a joke. He smiled back.

The artificial intelligence in Malaveda's commo helmet projected a sudden emptiness through the earphones. The non-sound was the absence of the static which would otherwise have crackled when somebody opened the push but didn't speak.

"We're going in," a radioed voice whispered; Lieutenant Hartlepool or the squad leader, Sergeant-Commander Brankins. You couldn't tell in a brief spread-band transmission.

Malaveda threw the sub-machine gun to his shoulder again. Vierziger flicked him a side-glance and smiled faintly, but he didn't otherwise move.

Malaveda hadn't heard how they'd located Soisson. Chances were the tech boys had swept the low-rent district till they picked up the signature of the electronics in the powergun Soisson ran with. The deserter might have sold the weapon or traded it for something more concealable, but even so it was a link in the chain that would lead back to him.

Whoever had the sub-machine gun would be bent outta shape when a squad of armed men rousted him at this hour. Watching the back door wasn't necessarily going to be a tea party, but Malaveda was just as glad not to be in the snatch team.

All hell broke loose.

The initial gunfire was from the front of the apartment building. Malaveda couldn't see who was shooting, but the hiss*crack!* of powerguns and reflected cyan light quivered over and around the structure.

It didn't sound like a raid, it sounded like war.

The back door opened halfway. A man peered through the crack.

Malaveda aimed his sub-machine gun. The holographic sight picture stuttered around the man. "Come out with your hands up!" he shouted.

The man started to duck back inside. Vierziger blew his head off in a flash of saturated blue.

The quality of light reflected from a third-floor window above the doorway changed. Malaveda noted the event subliminally, but his brain hadn't processed it into *somebody just slid opaque blinds open behind the polarized pane in order to see me/shoot me* when Vierziger fired again. The window shattered. The 2-cm round smacked a belt of powergun ammo slung around the man aiming a sub-machine gun. Hundreds of charged disks gang-fired, touched off by the 2-cm bolt. The blast must have cleared the room.

Soisson had made contact either with fifth columnists set up by the Front, or with a criminal gang that might as well be a government for the weapons in its arsenal. Either way, the snatch squad had walked right into a hornet's nest.

Malaveda ripped out half his magazine with no better target than the whole rear of the building. He hadn't expected things to blow up this way. It had spooked him.

Vierziger fired at another of the top range of windows. He must have seen something or he had the devil's own luck, because there was a man behind the disintegrated pane. The fellow had been pointing a shoulder weapon.

He'd been wearing body armor too, but that didn't help him against the energy a 2-cm bolt packed. The body hurtled backward, propelled by the shock of its colloid structure suddenly vaporizing. The victim's sleeves were burning.

The sub-machine gun recoiled against Malaveda's shoulder. That and the quivering gaps across his field of view, his visor blacking out the cyan dazzle to save his eyesight, combined to focus him on the job at hand. *It's not like this is my first firefight.*

The back door was still ajar. The first victim's feet stuck out of it. Malaveda sensed motion within the building. He aimed, squeezed. His three-round burst lighted the torso of a gunman. Vierziger center-punched the fellow with a bolt at the same instant, then fired again.

The second round was apparently to clear the magazine. The delicate-featured killer turned his weapon up with his left hand and stripped a fresh five-round clip through the loading gate. The gun's iridium muzzle glowed from the amount of plasma energy it had been channeling downrange.

Malaveda's commo helmet spluttered with clicks and hisses, sign of a lot of panicked activity that wasn't addressed to him. The people at the front of the apartment building—the survivors of the snatch team—were calling for serious backup.

The hostiles inside must know that, and know besides that when a platoon of combat cars—or even tanks—arrived, it was all over for them. They had to break out fast, before the FDF came down with both boots.

When Malaveda was sure his partner had reloaded, he emptied the sub-machine gun into two windows chosen at random on the top floor. He thumbed the release button and reached down to his belt pouch for a fresh magazine.

Sirens and screams clawed what had been the night's stillness, punctuated with the slapping discharges of powerguns. A blast too loud for a grenade shook the opposite side of the apartment. Windows facing the alley shattered. Shards of the panes snowed onto the sidewalk.

Vierziger—

Malaveda's mind flashed with a montage of his partner in various stages of what had happened next.

First Vierziger's left hand lifted his 2-cm weapon up toward his shoulder, the girlishly perfect fingers of his right hand curving to the grip. *Then* Vierziger faced the back of the alley, the shoulder weapon out to his side and the pistol, again the pistol, pointing.

Three shots, strobe-light quick, winking on the face of the man lifting the manhole cover from beneath. Cratering the flesh, rupturing the skull itself with the pressure of gasified nerve tissue. The eyes blanking, the sub-machine gun dropping back into the utility passage converted to an underground escape route; the cover clanking down, catching the dead man's fingers for a moment before gravity tugged them loose.

Vierziger holstered the pistol. He bent, switched on the jeep's drive fans, and hopped out beside the vehicle. "Come on!" he ordered. "Watch our back."

"What?" Malaveda said. He jumped clear of the jeep. He felt as though he was partnered with a ticking bomb. He didn't understand what was happening, but he was afraid not to obey the newbie absolutely.

Vierziger revved the fans to full lift and reached for the steering yoke. The bottom half-meter of a second-floor window across the street blew outward, shattered by the muzzle blast of a machine gun firing explosive bullets.

Distortion through the window pane caused the gunner to aim his initial burst high. Chunks blew off the facades of the buildings to either side, hiding the alley mouth for an instant in a cloak of brick dust. Other projectiles burst in vivid red florets on the walls and among the garbage well behind the jeep.

The gunner didn't get a chance to correct his aim.

Surrounded by the *blam!blam!blam!* of projectiles and whizzing bits of casings mixed with brick chips, Malaveda spun and aimed. He walked a line of cyan flashes across ten centimeters of wall, up the transom, and into the window—

As Vierziger reholstered his glowing pistol. He'd drawn and fired twice in an eye-blink. His bolts had punched the gunner in the face, one to either side of the nose. The barrel of the machine gun tilted up and vanished as the gunner slumped.

"Watch our back!" Vierziger repeated. He slammed the jeep's control yoke forward. The little vehicle skittered ahead. It held its alignment but slid slightly to the right when it emerged from the alley and met a breeze down the main boulevard.

The manhole cover hadn't budged since Vierziger shot the man who'd lifted it. Malaveda kept the steel disk at the corner of his eyes as his conscious mind followed what his partner was doing.

Vierziger's holster was metal or a temperature-stable plastic, because it didn't melt or burn from contact with the pistol's glowing iridium muzzle. Judging from the way he'd drawn it both times that speed was an absolute essential, the richly decorated handgun was Vierziger's weapon of choice.

He nonetheless handled the heavy 2-cm powergun with an ease that belied his slight frame, as well as with flawless accuracy; and it was with the shoulder weapon presented that he waited now.

The jeep was too light to be stable without a man aboard. Its flexible skirts hopped on irregularities in the pavement, spilling air from the plenum chamber.

Vierziger fired twice as the vehicle bobbled its way toward the building. His first bolt ignited the interior of a room whose window had shivered away in the bomb blast. Malaveda hadn't seen a human target, but Vierziger probably had, and the baby-faced killer had hit everything he'd aimed at this night.

The flare of cyan plasma filled the enclosed space momentarily. An instant later everything flammable, including the paint, was a mass of orange flame. The transom belched a great fireball when something, munitions or an accelerant, added its energy to the inferno.

Vierziger's second shot was into the window from which the machine gun had fired. Malaveda hadn't noticed additional movement there until the bolt hit the muzzle of the automatic weapon just lifting back over the transom to fire. Plasma converted fifteen centimeters of the gun's steel barrel to gas. The superheated metal erupted in a red secondary flame as it mixed with air.

How had Vierziger hit a target so small at thirty meters, with an off-hand shot?

The jeep crashed into the half-open doorway at 50 kph. That was fast enough to crunch the front of the vehicle pretty thoroughly, though without doing serious damage to the building. The jeep's plastic frame fractured in a series of angry clicks.

Vierziger fired the remaining three 2-cm rounds into the wreckage. He picked his spots, blowing open a pair of fuel cells with each squeeze of the trigger.

The hydrocarbon fuel normally realized its energy in a cold process using an ion-exchange membrane. Now it blazed outward, enveloping the jeep in fire hot enough to involve the body panels and upholstery as well. The mushroom of flame rose roof high. It barred the building's rear street door as effectively as the presence of a tank could have done.

And that freed Vierziger and his partner for other activities.

Malaveda thought he saw the manhole cover move. He fired, rattling the disk in its coaming as the powergun bolts blew divots off the top of the steel.

Vierziger stripped in a fresh clip, then tossed Malaveda his bandolier of 2-cm ammo. "Follow me, swap guns and *load* when I tell you!" he ordered. "Now!"

The newbie had no business giving a non-com orders, but the present situation ignored what the Table of Organization might say. "Yes*sir!*" Malaveda shouted.

Vierziger wasn't wearing body armor; he'd claimed it would interfere with his driving. Now he reached left-handed into one of his tunic's front bellows pockets and drew out a red-banded grenade that he had *no* business carrying.

He struck the safety cap off against the side of the building with casual ease. Malaveda had seen troopers trying to arm a grenade that way, proving how macho they were. He'd never seen anybody succeed so perfectly, and with such little concern, as Vierziger did now.

Vierziger's right hand was on the 2-cm weapon's pistol grip, holding it like a massive handgun. He fired point-blank into the edge of the manhole cover. Sub-machine gun bolts made the steel disk stutter. The heavier charge flipped it like a tiddlywink. Vierziger tossed the grenade into the opening, put his back against the alley wall, and fired another bolt down the hole to disconcert anybody who might have the notion of throwing the grenade back up.

The lid hit the pavement a meter from the hole, spinning on edge with a nervous *clang-g-g-g* until the grenade went off beneath. It was a bunker buster. It atomized a mist of fuel through the air ten cubic meters of tunnel, then detonated the mixture in a blast that ruptured the pavement all the way to the mouth of the alley. Vierziger, poised with his knees flexed, rode out the ripple of concrete, but the unexpected jolt knocked Malaveda down.

Vierziger jumped into the pillar of gray smoke gushing from the manhole. "Follow me!" he shouted as be disappeared underground.

Malaveda followed. It didn't occur to him not to.

There was a ladder. Malaveda climbed down it, facing outward; clumsy because of the sub-machine gun in his right hand and the bandolier of 2-cm ammo swinging from his left. The helmet slapped filters over Malaveda's nose as he stepped into the noxious efflux from the grenade explosion. Four rungs down, he switched his visor to thermal imaging.

In thermal mode, the helmet converted temperature gradients to shapes. Malaveda hopped forward to keep from stepping on the pair of bodies scrunched at the base of the ladder. Another corpse lay on its back a few meters down the tunnel.

Vierziger moved ahead of Malaveda. The atmosphere swirled with blast residues which showed as pastels on the helmet visor.

The tunnel was purpose-built as an escape route, not a converted sewer main. It was round with a two-meter cross-section. The walls were monocrystal filament wound on a resin core. The matrix shattered when the fuel-air explosion flexed it beyond its resilient capacity. Swathes of monocrystal hung down like ancient cobwebs, but the structure hadn't collapsed as yet.

Vierziger fired his heavy shoulder weapon. Shock waves down the tunnel made Malaveda stagger, even though he was behind the shooter. Hot vortices spun off to both sides of the ionized track, expanding until they filled the cylindrical space.

The tunnel dead-ended at the ladder up into the alley. The lid on the alley end had locking dogs to avoid the risk of discovery by a utility crew. Either would-be escapees had undogged the lid, or the heavy jolt of plasma had flexed the disk enough to spring the bolts.

Vierziger broke into a run. The 2-cm weapon was butted against his shoulder. He fired twice more. Each jet of plasma heated the air like a mulling iron thrust into a beaker of wine.

"Feed me!" he screamed, still running, thrusting the shoulder weapon out behind him. Malaveda grabbed the gun by the forestock, too close to the glowing iridium muzzle, but he didn't drop it.

He slapped the receiver of the sub-machine gun into Vierziger's hand. Vierziger holstered the pistol that was pointing again as if by magic and presented the automatic weapon. He hadn't slowed.

Malaveda stumped along behind the killer. Sweat broke out all over his body. The filters kept his lungs free of ozone and the poisons streaming from empty cases which spun from the powergun's ejection port. His eyes burned and patches of bare skin prickled.

A corpse sprawled as a mass of indigo and purple in the midst of the tunnel's cool gray. The man had been partly dismembered by a bolt that struck at collarbone level. His right arm, tangled with a gun sling, hung by a few fleshless tendons; the spine was all that connected the head and torso.

Steep concrete steps led up from the other end of the tunnel. There was a handrail. Two bodies were tangled in it as they sprawled down the steps.

The armored door at the upper landing was open into the tunnel. Light flooded the passage. The panel started to swing shut. Vierziger triggered a burst at the doorway, perhaps hoping to ricochet a bolt into whoever was operating the powered mechanism.

Malaveda stopped and switched his visor to straight optics. He braced himself against the wall to aim the reloaded shoulder weapon past his partner. He was panting, drawing gasps of poisoned air through his mouth. Ozone burned the back of his throat.

He fired. Vierziger hunched at the base of the stairs, the sub-machine gun's muzzle questing back for the unexpected shooter. The door's upper hinge blew away in a cyan flash. The plating glowed white/yellow/red in circles concentric with the point of impact.

Malaveda ignored his partner's gun. The door sagged, kinking the lower hinge and freezing the panel half-open. Tears blurred Malaveda's eyes, and the sight picture danced wildly. He fired anyway and hit the lower hinge squarely. The door toppled onto the concrete landing like a dropped safe.

Vierziger was already up the stairs. Malaveda followed. He could no more have made that pair of shots during a training exercise than he could have ripped the door loose with his bare hands.

In the newbie's company, Malaveda was operating at well above what he would have guessed his best day could be. He didn't know whether the cause was emulation or a justifiable concern for what Vierziger might do to him if he screwed up.

The steps were slippery with body fluids. Malaveda grabbed the left rail; the 2-cm bandolier clanged against the tubing.

Vierziger tossed a grenade left-handed ahead of him. It was an assault bomb with a contact fuze . The blast was instantaneous, but the glass shrapnel was safe beyond a two-meter radius. Vierziger was through the haze-veiled doorway while the echoes still sounded.

The sub-machine gun snarled out four separate bursts with only a heartbeat between them. Malaveda caromed off the transom as he followed his partner. He wasn't in shape for this. His body armor felt as though he were wearing a well-stoked oven.

Nobody was in shape for *this* except Johann Vierziger, who wasn't human.

"Feed—" Vierziger said.

Malaveda snatched the sub-machine gun away and replaced it with the 2-cm weapon. He tried to say, "Only three in the magazine!" but his voice was a croak, and he didn't imagine the devil who led him didn't have the information already.

The room was an unfinished basement, open except for concrete support pillars. It held stacks of cased weapons and ammunition, as well as crates Malaveda couldn't identify at first glance.

Three bodies, two of them women in nightclothes, lay between the tunnel door and an elevator at the opposite end of the basement. Single-person lift and drop-shafts couldn't have serviced the heavy goods stored here. A woman's legs wedged the cage doors.

The grenade had pretty well devoured a man holding a bell-muzzled mob gun near the doorway. Vierziger's powergun bolts had lifted off the back of his head anyway.

Malaveda didn't see a fourth corpse, but he knew there must be one. Vierziger had fired four times, after all.

Vierziger ran to the elevator. Malaveda reloaded the sub-machine gun as he followed. The barrel was badly burned by use. He'd have changed it for a new one if he'd been sure there was time. He wasn't sure of anything at all.

He saw something to his left, down a cross-aisle among the goods stored on pallets. He pointed the sub-machine gun but it was a corpse lying on its back, the face blasted away by a tight quartet of powergun bolts.

Vierziger drew his pistol and fired twice to his right, down another aisle. Cyan bolts chewed the ceiling above him as he shot, blasting gravel and a spray of calcium burned from the cast concrete.

The man in ambush had clamped his sub-machine gun's trigger as he arched backward in death. Vierziger had seen, drawn, and killed before the victim could react to the appearance of the target he'd heard running toward him.

Beside the elevator was a firedoor of mesh-reinforced vitril, displaying a concrete staircase which led to the upper floors. No one was on the stairs. Vierziger tested the door to be sure that it opened from outside the smoke tower. It did. He tugged another grenade from his pocket, armed it, and tossed it up the stairs. He slammed the door shut.

Malaveda hunched aside. Vierziger grinned horribly at him. "Don't worry," he said. "It's gas."

The grenade bubbled open in waves of black haze that quickly filled the volume beyond the vitril. The doorseal, intended to prevent smoke from entering the stair tower, acted equally well to keep the contents of the grenade inside.

It was gas all right—KD nerve gas, which would oxidize harmless within two hours of use in an Earth-type atmosphere… and would paralyze the diaphragm muscles of anyone who breathed it or had skin contact before that time. Malaveda would have suffocated slowly and inexorably if a bullet had hit his partner's grenade during the firefight.

Vierziger ejected the nearly empty magazine from his pistol. To reload, he had to pluck a fresh clip from a belt pouch with the thumb and index finger of the left hand which still gripped the 2-cm weapon.

The woman jamming the doors had been very beautiful. Her filmy pajamas were of a natural fabric that had flashed like guncotton when the bolts struck her, leaving only a net of ash on the body.

Malaveda faced about to guard their backtrail. He felt as if he were in a bubble, he and Vierziger together; cut off from everything he'd for twenty-six years thought was the real world.

The 2-cm gun firing spun him around again. Vierziger had blasted the lock from the emergency hatch in the elevator's ceiling.

"Feed me!" he ordered crisply. Then, as Malaveda traded sub-machine gun for 2-cm weapon, Vierziger added, "Give me a leg up."

Malaveda made a stirrup of his hands. The dangling bandolier and sub-machine gun clattered on the cage floor. *Bloody hell it could have gone off!* But that was only a vagrant thought as he straightened his legs and boosted Vierziger through the narrow opening.

"Come on!" Vierziger said, thrusting a hand—his left hand—down toward Malaveda. "I need you to open the doors *now!*"

Instead of obeying instantly, Malaveda yanked open the latches of his ceramic body armor and shrugged the clamshell away. He probably wouldn't fit through the emergency access with it on, and he was already dizzy from the heat and confinement of exercise while wearing the armor.

He didn't try to explain what he was doing to Vierziger. Malaveda had to concentrate on *what* he was doing if he was going to achieve a fraction of what his partner expected....

Re-slinging the gun and ammunition, Malaveda rose and took Vierziger's offered hand. He jumped and the little man pulled—like a derrick. Vierziger's physical strength was as shocking as everything else about the deadly man with the features of a child. Malaveda's right elbow scraped the edge of the opening and the sub-machine gun's muzzle rapped on metal, but Vierziger's tug was precise as well as effortless.

The sergeant knelt in the litter and lubricant sludge on top of the cage, then rose to his feet. A sagging cable brushed his shoulder. He had his second wind since he'd dropped the back-and-breast armor. A moment before, he hadn't been sure he could go on.

"Switch," said Vierziger, offering the 2-cm weapon. The elevator shaft was vaguely illuminated from above, but most of the light streamed up through the access port.

The little man was using Malaveda as a pack train; which was perfectly appropriate under the circumstances. Now that he was sure of the sergeant's obedience, the edge that had earlier promised, *Do this thing, or I will kill you without hesitation,* was gone from Vierziger's voice.

Vierziger nodded to the knife he'd already thrust into the juncture of the doors closing the elevator shaft from the first floor. He placed his boot along the edge, ready to thrust the door fully open as soon as Malaveda broke the seal. The top of the cage was eighty centimeters beneath floor level, not a serious problem.

The knife was a sturdy tool with a single edge on a thick, density-enhanced blade about twenty centimeters long. It could serve for a weapon, but it was obviously intended for more general purposes than killing. Here it made a functional prybar.

Malaveda gripped the knife with his left hand, crossed his left leg over the hilt to push the other door, and aimed his 2-cm weapon at the crack. Vierziger nodded approvingly.

The sergeant levered the knife with all his strength, using the thrust of his left boot as both anchor and supplement. The doors banged open to their stops. Vierziger was through the doorway like a lethal wraith, the sub-machine gun snarling. Malaveda heaved himself over the floor ledge, feeling like a hippo in comparison to his partner's grace.

But he got there without stumbling. The torso of a startled man in a business suit vanished in the huge flash of a 2-cm bolt, though Malaveda wasn't really conscious of pulling the trigger.

According to the plans and 3-D holograms with which the squad prepared for the raid, the apartment building's foyer faced the street through a wall of clear vitril. No longer. Armored shutters with firing slits had slammed down moments after the shooting started.

Vitril now covered the floor like a field of diamonds. Powergun bolts had shattered the former expanse into bits ranging from pebbles to dust. It was rough, but it didn't have dangerous edges.

A trooper in light-scattering Frisian battle dress lay under the crystalline debris.

Malaveda couldn't tell which of the squad it had been, because an explosive bullet had decapitated him/her.

Three men and a woman crouched by the slits, shooting outward or preparing to when the pair of Frisians appeared behind them. All four of them were dead by the time Malaveda stepped into the foyer. Vierziger had shot them in the back of the head. The purple-haired man on the left of the position was on the floor. His three companions were slumping in various stages of the same motion, like a slow-motion image of a single event.

The armored shield glowed in several places where it had absorbed plasma energy, but all those strikes had been on the outer face. Vierziger hadn't wasted a bolt.

A dozen more people of both sexes tumbled out the stairwell door. Despite being in various stages of undress, they were slicker-looking types than the shooters had been. Malaveda had killed the first of them. The woman behind that victim was shrieking, "The basement's full of gas!" when the 2-cm bolt sprayed her with the remains of her companion.

A tremendous blast shook the building. The shock wave down the stair tower projected the last would-be escapee into the foyer like the cork from a champagne bottle.

Nothing the snatch squad had on hand would have packed that wallop, and there hadn't been time enough for support to arrive. The residents themselves had planned to blow the place from the top down to cover their tunnel escape route.

The foyer lights flicked off, then on again but with a yellowish hue. The system had shifted to emergency power. The building was a *fortress*. It could have held out for hours against almost anything but what had arrived—the devil in the shape of a new recruit.

A woman knocked to the floor drew a pistol from the sleeve of a garment apparently too diaphanous to hide anything. Vierziger shot her hand off. Chips of vitril, now pulverized, erupted in the cyan jolts as the flimsy target vaporized at the first round of the burst.

Malaveda noticed movement and swung. A man threw down a carbine as though it were as hot as the white, glowing muzzle of Vierziger's sub-machine gun. "No!" he screamed. His eyes were closed.

"No," agreed Vierziger, touching Malaveda's hand on the forestock. He lifted the 2-cm weapon to a safe angle.

The armored shutters rang under multiple powergun bolts. A thirty-centimeter splotch went from gray to red to bright orange. The survivors of the squad were concentrating their fire, but the armor remained proof against small arms.

"That's the, the s-s-switch," said a small man whose beige suit would have paid Malaveda's salary for a year. He pointed to a short baton. The man the sergeant shot had flung it onto the vitril in his dying convulsions. "To set off the bombs."

Vierziger nodded to Malaveda. Malaveda scooped up the device, careful not to touch the red contact points.

A grenade went off outside. The concussion lifted dust from the foyer floor without affecting the armor.

"Now," said Vierziger. "We'll need the controls to raise those doors. And we'll need a white flag, because our colleagues don't seem ready to accept my radioed assurance that we've captured the position."

He gestured to a man wearing a tunic that glittered as if diamond studded. "Your shirt will do, I think."

"The controls are here, right here, mister!" a woman whispered, tugging Malaveda's sleeve to get his attention. "Right here!"

She pointed to what looked like a trash chute in the wall between elevator and stairs. The cover plate was lifted to display a keyboard.

"Besides," Vierziger continued, smiling at the captive stripping before him, "I'd like a better look at your pecs, handsome."

He laughed. It was the most terrifying sound Malaveda had ever heard in his life.

MAHGREB

"I'm looking for a piss-ant named Barbour!" roared the stocky man who slammed open the double doors of the officers' canteen. "Lieutenant Robert Barbour? He thinks he's lifting out of here today!"

The man's gray hair was shaved into a skullcap. He wore his rank tabs field-fashion—on the underside of his collar, where they wouldn't target him for a sniper. His aura of command obviated the need of formal indicia anyway.

Barbour set down the chip projector he was reading and got to his feet. The projector was loaded with an off-planet news feed, nothing Barbour cared about one way or the other. It was just a means of killing time while waiting for the boarding signal of the ship that would return him to Nieuw Friesland. Killing time and taking his mind off other things.

"I'm Barbour," he said. His voice squeaked.

The dozen or so other officers in the canteen stared at Barbour when he stood up, then quickly looked in any direction except that of the two principals to the encounter. Conversations stopped, and the four poker players at a corner table huddled their cards between their cupped palms. The lights twinkling in enticement from the autobar looked *loud.*

"Do you know who I am, Lieutenant Barbour?" the stocky man demanded. When the canteen doors flapped, Barbour saw two nervous-looking aides waiting in the starport concourse. Unlike their principal, the aides wore scarlet command-staff fourragères.

Via! Barbour *did* know the fellow. Know of him, at any rate. Tedeschi didn't spend a lot of time in the headquarters in Al Jain, where Barbour had worked until six days previous.

"Yes sir," Barbour said. He restrained himself from saluting. Field regulations again. In order to encourage his command into a war zone mentality, General Tedeschi, commanding the FDF contingent on Mahgreb, had forbidden salutes.

"You're General Tedeschi. Sir."

"You're bloody well told I am!" Tedeschi snapped.

He looked around the canteen. From his expression, he'd just as soon have swept it with a machine gun. "You lot," he said. "Take a walk. Now!"

The trio nearest the doors were out before the order had been fully articulated. The cardplayers left their stakes on the table, and there was hand luggage beside several of the previously occupied chairs.

Hellfire Hank Tedeschi had no manners and no patience. He successfully completed campaigns in minimal time and with minimal casualties among his own troops, because there was absolutely nothing else in the universe that mattered to him. He would cashier an officer in a heartbeat, and he was rumored to have knocked down underlings who didn't jump fast enough to suit him.

Tedeschi believed in leading from the front. He'd killed people with his pistol, his knife, and his bare hands.

"What's this about you deserting your post, Barbour?" Tedeschi demanded. "The job here's not done, you know."

The anger previously in the general's voice had been replaced by menace. Barbour knew this was an act Tedeschi had practiced, but it wasn't *merely* an act. Tedeschi was a clever man as well as a violent one. As a means of intimidation, he let people see the raw emotions bubbling from his psyche.

"I'm not deserting, sir," Robert Barbour said. "I've requested a transfer to another branch of the service."

He didn't add, "As is my right." That would be pouring gasoline on hot coals.

"Like hell you are," Tedeschi said. He gestured Barbour back into the chair from which the lieutenant had risen. "Sit."

Barbour obeyed. Instead of sitting down across from Barbour, Tedeschi put one of his boots on the circular table and leaned his forearms against the back of his knee. "The job here needs you, Barbour," the general said. "*I* need you. Are you hearing me?"

"Sir…" said Barbour. He didn't know how to continue.

Tedeschi wouldn't have given him the opportunity to go on anyway. "Look, what's the problem?" he demanded. "Is it me? Do you have a problem with the way I run things here?"

"Lord, *no* sir," Barbour blurted. Tedeschi could have been back at Camp Able for all the effect he'd had on Barbour up till this moment. Lieutenants in the headquarters bureaucracy didn't expect to have anything to do with commanding generals.

"Then your section CO, Wayney," Tedeschi pressed. "Trouble with her? Tell me, boy, tell me *now*."

"Sir," Barbour said. Tedeschi was leaning forward, compressing his cocked leg and bringing his brutal, swarthy features threateningly closer to Barbour's face. "Captain Wayney's—she's no problem, sir. She's fine."

Captain Wayney wasn't a brilliant intelligence technician. To tell the truth, she wasn't even a good one. But she was far too good an administrator to get in the way of an underling who *was* brilliant. Wayney not only handed Barbour the tough ones, she let him run with his whims. The result had been a series of striking triumphs for the section which Wayney headed.

"Look, I'll make you a proposition," Tedeschi said, leaning back a few centimeters. "You get an appointment on my personal staff. You report to nobody else, and I leave you the fuck alone. *And* you jump two pay grades to major. When this operation's over, which I expect to take another six to nine months standard, you have the choice of accompanying me to my next posting—as a light colonel. Fair, Barbour?"

Barbour stared up at Tedeschi. He didn't know how to respond. The whole thing was beyond belief.

Instead of reacting directly to the proposition, Barbour said, "Sir? Why are you doing this? There's eighteen people in Technical Intelligence. You don't need me."

Half of Tedeschi's face smiled. "Right, eighteen," he said flatly. "All of them can do thirty percent of what you do. Two of them can do about seventy percent. That a fair assessment, Lieutenant?"

Barbour swallowed. If he'd thought about the question—which he hadn't—he'd have figured that Hellfire Hank knew nothing about the operations of Tech Int. He was too busy running around in a combat car and biting the heads off Kairene guerrillas.

Dead wrong.

"Yes sir," Barbour said. "Wellborn's maybe better than that, but okay, that's about right."

"And not a cursed one of them can do the rest of what you do, the magic part," Tedeschi said, his voice like a cat's tongue, rough but caressing nonetheless. "I said six to nine months standard to finish the job."

He slammed the heel of his right fist into his left hand, a sudden stroke and *whop!* that made Barbour flinch back. "I don't need shooters, Lieutenant," the general continued. "I got shooters up the ass, I got shooters better than me, and that's *plenty* fucking good! The difference between six and nine is knowing where the bastards are to shoot. Do you see?"

"Sir," said Barbour miserably. "I can't do that anymore. Target people to be shot. I can't."

"Do you want people to die, is that it?" Tedeschi shouted, his face ramming closer to Barbour's again. "If the operation goes the long way, it'll boost our casualties by fifty percent. You know that, don't you?"

Barbour nodded. Again, there was nothing wrong with the general's analysis. There was a pretty direct correlation between losses and the length of time people were running around, firing live ammunition.

"Also about double the number of local wogs get greased," Tedeschi added, "not that I give a flying fuck about that, but maybe you do?"

"I don't…." Barbour said. "Sir, if I don't do it, it's not my responsibility. Sir."

"That last operation," the general said, "blitzing the headquarters of the Seventy-Three Bee regiment—that was fucking brilliant. That's the sort of thing I need to get this operation over, quick and clean. Right?"

Barbour's face formed itself into something between a smile and a rictus. He was afraid to speak.

"Come on, Barbour," Tedeschi said. He took the junior man's chin between a thumb and finger that could crush nutshells. He tilted Barbour's face to meet his hard blue eyes. "Tell me that you're going to stay with me till the job's done. Not for the promotion. For the *job*."

Barbour stood up carefully, lifting his chin out of the general's grip. "Sir," he said, staring at the wall beyond Tedeschi's left shoulder, "I'm sorry, but I can't do that job anymore."

Tedeschi slammed his boot back onto the floor. He wasn't quite as tall as Barbour, but he had the physical presence of a tank.

"I'd spit on you, Lieutenant," the general said, "but you'd foul my saliva. Go to fucking Cantilucca, fuck around on a survey team. You're not fit to associate with the people doing *real* work."

Tedeschi slammed out of the canteen.

A few moments later, other officers returned to their drinks and belongings. They looked curiously at Lieutenant Robert Barbour, who remained where the general left him.

Barbour was crying.

EARLIER: MAHGREB

The incoming shells screamed down on Lieutenant Robert Barbour like steam whistles pointed at his ears.

They're landing short!

Barbour ducked in the fighting compartment of *High Hat*, the combat car in which he rode as a passenger. The regular crew, Captain Mamie Currant and her two wing gunners, didn't react to the howls overhead. Barbour raised himself sheepishly as the first salvo hit beyond the grove 500 meters distant.

Black smoke spurted. A sheet-metal roof fluttered briefly above the treetops. The blasts of the four shells with contact fuzes were greatly louder than the remaining pair which burst underground.

"Party time!" cried the gunner at the left wing tribarrel. He waggled his weapon, but he obeyed Currant's orders not to fire.

Currant's driver and the drivers of the other thirteen operational cars in her company—three were deadlined for repairs—gunned their vehicles out of the temporary hides where they waited for the artillery prep. The combiner screen beside Currant at the forward tribarrel showed the separated platoons closing in on the village of Tagrifah from four directions, but the crew—including the captain herself—was too busy with its immediate surroundings to worry about the rest of the unit.

The six tubes of the battery of Frisian rocket howitzers firing in support of the operation could each put a shell in the air every four-plus seconds during the first minute and a half. Reloading a hog's ammunition cassettes was a five-minute process for a trained crew, but that wouldn't matter today. The hundred and twenty ready rounds were sufficient to absolutely pulverize the target.

The second, third, and fourth salvos mixed contact-fuzed high explosive with cluster munitions, firecracker rounds. The outer casing of the latter shells opened a hundred meters in the air with a puff of gray smoke, raining down submunitions. Bomblets burst like grenades when they hit, carpeting a wide area with dazzling white flashes and shrapnel that drank flesh like acid.

Because the glass-fiber shrapnel had little penetrating power, the firecracker rounds were mixed with HE to blow off roofs and other light top cover. From a distance, the exploding submunitions sounded like fat frying. The effect on people caught in a firecracker round's footprint was also similar to being bathed in bubbling lard.

"C'mon, c'mon, c'mon!" the left gunner called, hammering the heel of one hand on the fighting compartment's coaming.

The two cars of 3d Platoon—understrength, so Currant was accompanying them—were to the immediate right, fifty and a hundred meters distant, approaching Tagrifah from the south. *High Hat* lurched repeatedly, throwing Barbour against the coaming. His clamshell armor spread the impact, but he still felt it.

Currant's driver kept the skirts close to the ground so as not to spill air from the plenum chamber as he accelerated the heavy vehicle. The meadow wasn't as smooth as the barley fields to the west and north of the village. Sometimes what looked like simply a flowering shrub turned out to be a rocky hillock against which the steel skirts banged violently.

Incoming shells drew red streaks across the pale dawn, plunging down at the targets Barbour had pinpointed in and around the village. The grove of deciduous trees swayed and toppled over. Rounds going off in the soil beneath the trees rippled the surface violently enough to tear their roots loose.

The whole mass heaved again in a gush of dirt and black smoke. Foliage and shattered branches flew skyward. A shell had detonated explosives stored in tunnels beneath the grove.

When the trees fell, Barbour should have gotten a glimpse of the village. All he could see were a few poles lifting above a roil of dust and smoke. In the far distance, the combat cars of 1st Platoon tore across the green barley, spewing plumes of chopped grain from beneath their skirts.

The fields and meadows serving the village weren't fenced. Three boys chatted on a knoll, watching the goats for which they were responsible.

The boys jumped to their feet to watch the first salvo scream in. When the combat cars appeared, two of the boys ran back toward the village, while the third threw himself face down and covered his head with both hands.

The local goats had long black-and-white hair. They circled in blind panic as the armored vehicles charged through them. The animals' mouths were open to bleat, but the sounds were lost in the shrieks and explosions of the artillery prep.

A goat sprang to the right, then tried to turn back to the left when it realized it had underestimated the combat car's speed. It tumbled directly in front *of High Hat's* bow skirts. The 50-tonne vehicle rode over the beast without a noticeable impact.

The shellfire stopped abruptly. The enormous howl *of High Hat's* fans, driving the vehicle and supporting it on the bubble of air in the plenum chamber, was quiet by contrast.

As the pall of smoke and dust drifted lower across Tagrifah, *High Hat* roared past the running goatherds. One of the boys knelt, flinging his arms out and pressing his face in the dirt as a gesture of supplication. His companion simply stared at the huge vehicles. Tears ran down his cheeks.

Barbour looked back at the boys. He had to turn his whole body, because the back-and-breast armor held his torso rigid.

The combat cars braked as they neared the remains of the grove which had sheltered the south side of the village. Thirty-centimeter treeboles were scattered like jackstraws. They lay across one another, heaved up on the support of unbroken branches.

Barbour thought the tangle was impenetrable; the cars would have to go around. Captain Currant had a brief exchange over the intercom with her driver.

High Hat slowed to a crawl. The driver's head vanished within his separate compartment in the forward hull. The hatch cover clanged over him.

The car butted into a treetrunk, skewing it forward and sideways. The roots, dripping clods of yellow clay, locked with those of another fallen tree and jammed firm.

The fans howled louder. Dirt rippled up around *High Hat's* skirts. Air pressure was excavating the ground under the plenum chamber. The combat car shuddered, then leaped ahead, tossing fallen trees to left and right.

Munitions in the tunnel beneath the grove had shouldered the surface aside when they exploded. *High Hat* dipped into the long crater, blasting the loosened soil into the air. The car continued up the far side at a fast walking pace.

Tendrils of foul black smoke, the residue of stored explosives, rose where the combat car passed. Barbour thought he saw a human arm, but it could have been a twisted root instead.

The village Barbour had targeted was a ruin almost as complete as that of the grove.

A few minutes earlier, a casual observer would have taken Tagrifah for a harmless place, typical of this region of Kairouan. Even a patrol of the Frisian mercenaries in the pay of the Boumedienne government would probably have passed on, accepting the black looks and turned backs of the inhabitants as the normal due of an occupying army.

Robert Barbour had identified the village as a Kairene regimental headquarters without, until this moment, coming within fifty klicks of the place.

A few figures moved within the settling dust; women, an old man. A goat nosed a ripped grain sack with apparent unconcern for the raw wound on its left thigh.

With the fans at low speed, Barbour could hear scores of voices wailing. It was hard to believe so many people remained alive.

The houses of Tagrifah were wooden, raised a meter off the ground by stone foundations. Each crawl space served as a fold for the family's goats. Most of the foundations had collapsed from a combination of airbursts and the ground's rocking motion when delay-fuzed rounds went off beneath the surface.

"Via, Bob!" Captain Currant said, clapping her passenger across the shoulders. "It's a walkover! You're a fucking genius!"

Barbour had spent five years with the FDF, specializing in technical intelligence. He'd often surveyed the results line units obtained from his targeting information, but this was the first time he'd been in at the kill.

Literally at the kill.

"Didn't leave us much to do," the left gunner remarked. He turned and flashed Barbour a broad grin. "Which suits me just fine."

"It wasn't me," Barbour muttered. "It was the artillery."

He was holding the grenade launcher which Mamie Currant had handed him when he climbed aboard her car. He hadn't fired such a weapon since he'd gone through training so many years before.

As the wing gunner had said, there was nothing in Tagrifah left to fire *at*.

"Don't sell yourself short, Bob," Currant said. "Popping shells off into the brown doesn't do a curst bit of good. You told them where the targets were, and by the Lord! You did a great job."

She gestured over the combat car's bow. The driver had unbuttoned his hatch. "Like that," she said. "*That* was the big one."

That had been a circular pit a meter deep, surrounded by a fence of tightly bound palings and covered by a thatch roof. A shell from the first salvo had plunged through the roof and exploded on the target hidden within—an 8-barreled powergun, a calliope.

Calliopes could be used against ground targets, but they were designed to sweep shells and rockets from the sky. If this weapon and the three similar ones at the other cardinal points surrounding Tagrifah had been given time to get into action, they would have detonated all the incoming shells a klick or more short of the target. Company D would have had to fight its way into the village while flashes and dirty clouds quivered in the distant sky.

From the outside, the structure around the gun pit looked like a small shed, suitable for drying vegetables or holding community-owned tools. There was nothing about the shelter to arouse hostile interest.

The bodies of four Kairenes lay mangled among the calliope's wreckage. The victims were a boy, two young women, and a man in starched green fatigues. The Kairene regular had been in the gunner's seat, responding to an alarm from the calliope's search lidar. When the shell went off, the civilians had been trying to drop the poles that supported the roof of the shelter. The calliope would have been in operation in another five seconds.

Flight time for the 200-mm shells was less than seven seconds from the point at which they came over the calliope's search horizon.

Swatches of smoldering thatch lay around the shallow crater. The blast lifted the roof straight into the air, so fragments fell back over the same area in a burning coverlet.

One of the Kairene women had been stunningly beautiful. Her unbound hair was a meter long. The blast had stripped all the clothing from her upper torso. Her legs and body from the waist down had vanished.

The calliopes' laser direction and ranging apparatus was a low-emissions unit which worked in the near ultraviolet. It had been difficult to detect, even when Barbour knew from other indications that something of the sort must be operating.

Barbour had arranged for a utility aircraft fitted with broad-band detection instruments to overfly Tagrifah on an apparently normal hop between a Frisian firebase and a Boumedienne government post a hundred klicks to the west. The calliopes didn't fire, but two of them switched from search to their higher-powered targeting mode to follow the aircraft. That gave Barbour their precise location.

With those two in hand, he'd sent a van with a concealed high-gain antenna past Tagrifah at a kilometer's distance. The remaining calliopes gave themselves away by the electromagnetic noise of their loading-chute motors, one per gun tube, which ran at idle when the weapons were on stand-by. Barbour triangulated by plotting the signals—any electromagnetic radiation was a signal for his purposes—on a time axis calibrated against the van's route.

It was a slick piece of work, not something just any tech spec could have managed. Barbour stared at the lovely, naked half-woman as *High Hat* passed.

He'd accompanied the attack on a whim. Because Barbour was the only person familiar with the target, Command sent him to Firebase Desmond to brief the troops told off for the operation—Company D, 3d of the 17th Brigade.

Barbour had met Mamie Currant during one of her visits to Frisian HQ in the capital, Al Jain. They'd gotten on well then, so it was natural for Mamie to suggest Barbour join the operation he'd set up in person, and natural for him to accept.

Tagrifah was nothing new for Robert Barbour. This was exactly what he'd done for a living during most of the past five years. What was new was seeing it as it happened.

A tribarrel fired on the other side of the village. Currant immediately keyed her commo helmet. Barbour wasn't in the company net, but the firing wasn't sustained. It couldn't have been a serious problem.

Barbour's nostrils were filtered against the dust, but the smell got through regardless. Smoke, earth ruptured upward by shells, explosive residues. And death, mostly human, from fire and disemboweling and flaying alive.

Tagrifah had a common well. The women congregated around it in the first dawn, drawing household water and exchanging gossip while adult males were still abed. Barbour hadn't targeted the well, of course, but one of the firecracker rounds strewed its trail of bomblets across the women and spilled them in a bloody windrow. Some of the corpses looked like bundles of rags rather than something once human; rags of predominantly red color.

One old woman, apparently unharmed, sat wailing in the middle of the carnage. Her blank eyes didn't react to the combat car, though the vehicle moved past close enough to stir her garments with the air vented beneath the skirts.

Mamie followed Barbour's eyes. She leaned close to him and said, "It's not us that did this, Bob. It's the sons of bitches who deliberately used civilians as a shield. We can't let them make up the rules for their own benefit."

"I know that," Barbour said. He didn't really know anything at all. He was pretending that he saw Tagrifah in a recorded image, with the camera lens between him and reality.

He pointed. "That was the headquarters," he said.

More accurately, the Kairene HQ had been concealed in a bunker beneath *that*, the mosque and the attached madrassah in which village boys were schooled in reading, writing, and the Koran. Girls as well as boys here in Tagrifah, and apparently a mixed class besides.

Kairouan had been settled three centuries ago from North Africa, where both Islam and Christianity had developed unique strains. Even so, Kairene society had departed to a surprising degree from its roots. Tagrifah could have been an interesting subject for study, before the shells hit.

The stone-built religious buildings had collapsed to rubble which barely filled the large bunker beneath. Gray smoke rose through the interstices of the jumbled stones. Mixed with the ashlars and broken roof beams were the bodies of the pupils, seated on the madrassah's floor at dawn to begin their lessons.

Some of the children were still moving. Captain Currant touched her helmet key again. Barbour heard the word "medics" in the request.

A preplanned operation like this probably had second echelon medical support laid on at the firebase already. The troops wouldn't need help, but the medics and their equipment would get a workout nonetheless.

The radio antenna serving the Kairene headquarters had run up the minaret. The vertical mast was still standing, pure and gleaming in the sunlight, though the building had crumbled around it.

The mast made a fitting monument for Tagrifah. Barbour had initially identified the village as a hostile center because of the signals emanating from that antenna.

The Kairenes had limited themselves to burst transmissions: data collapsed into the smallest possible packets and spit out in a second or two instead of over minutes. They might as well have flown battle flags and set off fireworks for all the good their attempts at concealing their signals had done. They hadn't understood that they weren't dealing with hicks like themselves, they were facing the *Frisians.*

More particularly, the Kairenes faced Lieutenant Robert Barbour. Barbour's tuned instruments not only pinpointed the source of the transmissions, they ran the packets through decryption programs which spat the information out in clear faster than the Kairene units in the field would be able to process it.

"It wasn't a mistake!" Barbour said. "Tagrifah *was* a regimental headquarters!"

"Curst right it was!" Mamie Currant agreed. "Look at there."

She gestured this time by waggling the muzzles of her tribarrel. A hand and arm clutching a 2-cm powergun extended from beneath a collapsed house.

The weapon wasn't of Frisian pattern, though it might well take the same ammunition. The Kairenes had been well equipped with small arms. They lacked artillery and armor, but they would have put up at least a good fight if the Boumedienne government had attempted to reduce them with its own forces.

Guerrilla bands with powerguns, familiar with the terrain and dedicated to victory, could wreak holy havoc with an invader's lines of communications. Boumedienne's troops would have flailed blindly, destroying random villages but taking disastrous casualties whenever they tried to move in less than battalion strength.

The money cost to Boumedienne of a Frisian brigade was considerable, but it was the difference between victory and the sort of bloody stalemate that is perhaps the only thing worse than losing a war. Tagrifah was proof the money had been well spent.

Four more combat cars approached from the east. The armored vehicles spun on their axes to extend the line on which 3d Platoon crawled through the village. The cars closed up. Another platoon was in sight to Barbour's left.

"Bunkers under every one of them?" Captain Currant asked/observed as she scanned the wreckage.

"Yes, that's right," Barbour agreed. The part of his mind that spoke retained its professional detachment.

In every instance, the foundations of the houses they passed had collapsed into a crater instead of mounding above ground level. Delay-fuzed rounds—there was no need for true penetrators, designed to punch through the plating and reinforced concrete of fortresses—had sucked the fieldstone foundations into the bunkers the houses had concealed.

Barbour had pinpointed the individual bunkers by having patrols set off small explosions in the ground, never closer than a kilometer from the village. Analyzing the hash of echo returns was more a matter of magic than science, despite the help Barbour's computers provided.

The results showed how perfectly he had succeeded. He wondered whether the villagers had built additional houses to conceal bunkers, or whether the Kairene military had limited their bunker locations to the existing buildings. Either way, there was a perfect equivalence.

The operation's planners had laid firecracker rounds down to follow the HE in order to catch soldiers stumbling from their shattered bunkers. It didn't appear that any Kairene regulars had made it that far.

Civilians lay individually and in groups near the doorways of their collapsed houses. An infant cried on the ground, between the bodies of its father and brother.

The car beside *High Hat* slowed. A gunner hopped from the fighting compartment, picked up the orphan, and remounted the vehicle.

Most of the dust had settled, but many of the house roofs burned sluggishly. Black smoke bubbled from the damp thatch. Occasionally the fans of a passing combat car would whip fires to bright flame, but mostly they remained glimmerings beneath an oily sludge.

The four-car platoon from the north of the village joined, bringing the company to full strength. Captain Currant spoke, switching her helmet from one sendee to another.

As a company commander, Mamie rated an enclosed command car with better communications gear and a specialist to run it. Like many other FDF officers, she preferred an ordinary combat vehicle.

Military doctrine for millennia had been that a commander's job was to command, not to fight; Aggressive officers had never accepted that formulation; and when the dust settled, the victorious side was normally the one whose officers were aggressive.

High Hat rotated twenty degrees, then backed a few meters and settled onto its skirts. The remaining combat cars were shifting also, forming a tight defensive laager in what had been Tagrifah's open marketplace. The vehicles' bows faced outward, and their massed tribarrels were ready to claw.

They would have no target. Occasionally civilians blind with smoke and tears stumbled toward the laager. They ran as soon as the gleaming iridium shapes registered on their consciousness.

"There's a battalion of Boumedienne's boys coming on trucks," Currant explained to Barbour. "We'll wait for them, then head back to Desmond. There's nothing here the locals can't handle, now that we've done the real work."

She clapped Barbour on the shoulder again. "Now that *you've* done the real work, Bob. This one was all yours."

The dikes protecting Robert Barbour's mind crumbled, letting unalloyed reality wash over him. *The smoke and screams and the stench of fresh entrails…*

It hadn't been an atrocity. It was a necessary military operation.

And it was all his.

CANTILUCCA: DAY ONE

The sailor at the *Norbert IV*'s boarding hatch pointed to a row of low prefab buildings 300 meters in from where the vessel had landed. The freighter's leave party—the whole crew except for a two-man anchor watch—had already stumped most of the distance over the blasted ground. The crewmen carried only AWOL bags, while the disembarking passengers had much more substantial luggage.

"There's the terminal," the sailor said. "The left one's Marvelan entry requirements. If there's nobody home, go to passenger operations beside it. Pilar'll be there, no fear."

"Not," said Mary Margulies, surveying the lighted buildings, "the fanciest-looking place I've ever been sent."

"At the moment," Matthew Coke said, "they aren't shooting at us. That's something."

It was late evening. The sky was purple. Cantilucca was supposed to have two moons, but either they weren't up or they were so small that Coke lost them in the unfamiliar stars.

The sailor snorted. "You want shooting?" he said. "Go on into Potosi. I guarantee you'll find somebody there who'll oblige you."

Johann Vierziger looked at him. "A tough town?" he asked.

His voice was delicate, effeminate. Coke didn't know what to make of Vierziger overall, but he'd watched the sergeant run the combat course at Camp Able. Whatever else Vierziger might be, he was surely a gunman.

"Tough enough, boyo," the sailor replied, eyeing Vierziger speculatively. "But it's a place a fellow can have a good time if he wants one, too."

"It appears that we're our own baggage handlers," Sten Moden said. He lifted his twin-width suitcase in his only hand. "Shall we?"

The big logistics specialist started down the ramp, drawing the others after him. Vierziger moved immediately to the front. Each member of the survey team carried a concealed pistol, but they were under Coke's strict orders not to draw their weapons unless he ordered them to.

Coke was uncomfortable. This wasn't either a combat operation or a routine change of station. He didn't know how he was supposed to feel.

Cantilucca's starport was a square kilometer bulldozed from the forest and roughly leveled. The earth had been compressed and stabilized.

There hadn't been a great deal of maintenance in the century or so since the port was cleared. Slabs of surface had tilted in a number of places, exposing untreated soil on which vegetation could sprout. The jets of starships landing and taking off limited the size of the shrubbery, at least in the portion nearer the terminal buildings.

There were twenty-three ships in port at the moment. Most of them were freighters of around 20 KT displacement, like the *Norbert IV*. Gage was big business, and Cantilucca grew the best gage in the universe.

Niko Daun chuckled. He was toward the rear of the straggling line—Lieutenant Margulies alone walked behind him, looking frequently over one shoulder, then the other.

"Here we all are in civilian clothes and everything," the young sensor tech said. "We look like a bunch of businessmen."

Coke glanced back at Daun. "That's right," he said wryly. "We *are* businessmen. Or ambulance-chasing lawyers, that might be closer."

The survey team's luggage, two pieces for every member except the one-armed Moden, had static suspension systems. When the systems were switched on, they generated opposing static charges in the bottom of each case and the surface beneath it. The cases floated just above the ground and could be pulled along without friction.

On terrain as broken as that of the untended starport, that was only half the problem. Because of their contents and their armored sidewalls, the cases were extremely heavy. They wobbled on their narrow bases of support, threatening to fall over unless the person guiding them was relentlessly vigilant. The poor illumination didn't help either.

"Not bad training for life," Coke muttered.

"Sir?" Sten Moden said, turning his head back.

"Just talking to myself," Coke explained. "Sorry."

A bus pulled away from the terminal area. Its wheels were driven by four separate electric motors. One of the drives shrieked jaggedly as the bus headed toward the gate of the port compound.

"It's a lot easier," Sten Moden said without emphasis as he watched the bus go, "to replace a bearing than it is to replace a driveshaft *and* a bearing."

The bus didn't have headlights. A spotlight jury-rigged to the driver's side window swept the road and a stretch of the fence surrounding the compound. The forest beyond was a black mass. The sky had some color still in the west, but it no longer illuminated the land beneath it.

"Let's hope the soldiers aren't any better than the mechanics," said Robert Barbour.

Coke didn't have any more of a handle on the intelligence specialist than he did on Vierziger. Based on Barbour's personnel file, he was an easy-going man who was brilliant in his field. He had a bright career ahead of him, despite a lack of ambition outside his professional specialty.

There was no question about Barbour's qualifications. Coke had thought he himself knew his way around a sensor console, until he saw what Barbour could do casually with one.

In the flesh, though, the young lieutenant was withdrawn and apparently miserable. The file would have indicated if Barbour had survived a close one, as had happened to Daun. Maybe he'd had trouble with a woman. The Lord knew, there was plenty of that going around.

"They don't have soldiers here, Lieutenant," Johann Vierziger said. "On Cantilucca they have thugs, gangsters."

"We're not going to prejudge the situation," Coke said sharply. "Our report on the quality of potential allies and opposition is just as important as whether we recommend Nieuw Friesland accept an offer of employment here in the first place."

"Sorry, sir," Vierziger said. He didn't sound ironic, but neither was he making any effort to appear contrite.

The sergeant had made a statement which he knew, and which *Coke* knew, was correct on the basis of the score or more similar planets they'd both seen. Coke didn't know what Vierziger's background was—his file began at the point he enlisted in the FDF; but he knew the little gunman *had* a background. Nobody got as good as Vierziger was by spending his time at the target range.

Coke laughed. "Hold up," he called to Moden and Vierziger. He stopped where he was, set down the cases he was pulling, and motioned his team closer.

Lights from the terminal brightened that side of the faces watching Coke, but even there the flesh was colorless. Opposite the terminal, the team's features lacked detail.

"Look," Coke said, "we're here now, we're on our own. From this point on, we're on first-name basis."

Nobody reacted openly. Shutters clicked across the eyes of the more experienced trio, Moden, Margulies, and Vierziger.

"I don't mean," Coke explained hastily, "that we've suddenly become a democracy. Fuck *that* notion. You *will* take my orders, or I'll have you court-martialed on return to Camp Able."

A starship across the compound tested its landing motors. Plasma flared in an iridescent shimmer above the vessels, lighting the team members and the shattered ground about them. Vierziger grinned in broad approval.

"We're all good at our jobs," Coke resumed as the jet's rumble faded away. "And we'll be living in each other's pockets while the operation goes on. I trust that we can maintain real discipline without pretending we're back in base somewhere. Okay?"

The other members of the team nodded—Margulies with obvious relief. The last thing any sensible officer wanted was to serve under a commander whose first priority was that his troops *like* him.

Coke smiled and nodded. "Saddle up, troopers," he said. He switched on the repulsion units of his cases and resumed the last stage of his trudge to the terminal buildings.

Vierziger fell in beside him. "I'm not used to thinking of myself as 'Johann,'" the little man said with an unreadable substrate to the comment.

"Better get used to it, Johann," Coke said.

Vierziger's eyes were always on the far distance, the shadows which might be hiding an ambush. His cases tracked as nearly straight as the ground permitted, never tilting far enough to be in danger of toppling over. The little man's peripheral vision chose the best line possible across the field.

"People generally don't trust me," Vierziger said, as if he were commenting on the magenta glow of the western horizon. "That's understandable, of course. But I want you to know that you could trust me, can if you want to."

A speck of light now at zenith had been fifteen degrees further east when Coke left the freighter. A moon, then, rather than a star; but merely a speck.

"I'll keep that in mind," he said aloud.

Vierziger laughed without malice. "The only difference between me and the pistol in your holster," he said, "is that you're more likely to hit the target if you aim me than if you aim it."

Coke looked at the little man. Neither of them spoke for a moment.

"Watch out for this," Vierziger said, gesturing toward a raw pit with the index finger of the hand gripping one of his cases.

The pit separated the two men by its width as they avoided it. "Why?" Coke asked.

"Because I think that's what I'm here to do, Matthew," Vierziger said.

He took two longer strides, then released his cases. They stood as sentinels to either side of the door as the gunman entered the terminal with his delicate hands free.

Coke walked through the doors a step behind Vierziger. Coke had been a combat soldier all his career, so he was irritated to be treated as an object for protection. Another part of him, though—

It was the job of the security element, Margulies and Vierziger, to protect the survey team's staff personnel. Coke, as team commander, couldn't object with even a frown at his people doing their jobs.

A hissing static broom shut off as the door opened. A woman, hidden until then behind the counter, stood up. Her lustrous auburn hair was caught in a braid and coiled on top of her head.

As Coke judged the mass, the hair would dangle to the floor if she removed the ornate silver combs pinning it up. Unlikely that she let it down often, though; the arrangement would take an hour to rebuild.

The woman wore black, relieved only by the massive silver crucifix hanging across her breast on a chain of the same metal. She was full-featured rather than fat and could have modeled for Rubens.

"Yes, gentlemen?" she said. Her voice held a touch of sharpness, a sign of uncertainty otherwise hidden. She appeared to be alone in the office. Two men had entered, well dressed but men and strangers, and there were further shapes looming outside the door.

"We're passengers from the *Norbert*, ma'am," Coke explained. "We're looking for the entry control office."

He hadn't forgotten the sailor had said that would be in the left-hand structure. The center building was the only one that was lighted, however.

"Oh, they should have told me!" the woman said with a stricken look.

Her eyes focused on the door. The panels had once been clear, but years of grit blown by nearby landings had blasted them to a pebbled surface. "How many of you are there?"

"Six," said Coke. "Is there a problem?"

"Not for six," the woman said. "I was going to take the operations van home anyway. My husband has our—"

She caught herself, flushed, and continued. "You see, the port bus just left with your ship's crew. They didn't say anything about passengers. I suppose they wanted to get into Potosi before dark."

Her skin was white, though from her dark lips Coke suspected she would tan to an umber color. She wore neither make-up nor, apart from the combs and crucifix, any jewelry.

"I'm Pilar Ortega," she said. "I'm the, well, I'm the passenger services officer, but for the past few months I've been sort of running Terminal Operations—to the extent they're being run."

"What sort of entry formalities are there?" Coke asked. "Cantilucca is part of the

Marvelan Confederacy, isn't it?"

The building was none too clean. From the sound of the static broom which the team's entry had interrupted, Pilar was doing not only the terminal director's work but also that of the janitor.

"Here, I'll log you in as well," Pilar said with a grimace. She turned to a console and brought it live. "Call your friends inside, will you please?"

Coke nodded to Vierziger, who moved to the door.

"The clerks in the Commission office next door have all gone home," the woman explained as she sorted through electronic files. Her fingers were tapering. They moved a light pen with short, positive strokes to control the holographic data. "High Commissioner Merian is… isn't as diligent as he might be. To tell the truth, so long as the port duties are paid, the Confederacy doesn't bother much about Cantilucca."

The team entered the terminal building in a smooth movement, forming a chain to slide all the luggage inside ahead of the personnel. Pilar looked up from her console to eye the cases. "It'll be tight," she murmured, "but we'll fit."

"Is the city far?" Johann Vierziger asked. His voice was calm and melodious, but his eyes never rested more than a second in one place. Watching him was like following a tiny, ravenous insectivore as it snuffled through the leaf mold.

"Two kilometers is all," Pilar said. "The usual separation in case of a landing accident. But sometimes the road—"

She looked up again. "There are people here who inject tailings from the gage refineries. It can make them dangerous. It's better not to be on foot when you're out of town. Potosi isn't anything more than a town."

Without changing her inflection she added, "May I see your identity chips, please?"

"Gage tailings are poison," Margulies said as she gave Pilar her ID chip left-handed. She and Vierziger were both nervous, though that wouldn't have been obvious to many outsiders. "Why use them when the whole planet's full of the pure stuff?"

"Poor people, of course," Pilar said primly as she fed the chips into a slot on her console. "Gage on Cantilucca is controlled for export. If you expected"—she glanced up sidelong, then back to the console—"to find it running free for the taking in the gutters here, I'm afraid you'll be disappointed."

"That won't really affect us one way or the other, Mistress Ortega," Coke said. "Ah—are there dangerous life forms on Cantilucca?"

"Only the human beings," Pilar said. "Some of them. Many of them."

The console popped the ID chips forth one at a time at half-second intervals. Pilar scooped them into her hand and distributed them to the members of the survey team. Though she scarcely glanced at the imprinted legends, she returned each to its owner on the first try.

"There," she said as she closed down the console again. "In theory, you should come in tomorrow when the clerks are on duty and go through this again. But I can't imagine anybody will mind. Half the time nobody shows up next door at all."

She took a deep breath and shook herself. "Are you ready to go?" she added.

"You bet we are," Margulies muttered, eyeing the translucent door behind her. A starship coughed plasma again, brightening the panels into feathery iridescence.

Pilar stepped into the office on the other side of the counter and returned a moment later with a dark wrap. She opened the gate in the counter and said, "This way, then, please. The van is right outside."

Vierziger led again. He moved with serpentine grace, that one. He didn't appear to have hastened to get from one end of the room to the other ahead of his companions, but there he was.

Coke was impressed with Vierziger. Lieutenant Margulies' face was unreadable, but there was more to her expression than mere professional appreciation.

The night was as Coke remembered it, warm and muggy. He couldn't understand why the woman had bothered with an overgarment, until he noticed that it turned her into a shapeless blob without sex or individuality. He wondered whether that was more of a comment on Potosi or on Pilar's personality.

Beside the building was a four-wheeled van whose windows were broken out. Pilar got in while the team members wrestled their luggage into the back through the doors in both sides. The only seats were the pair of buckets in front.

Sten Moden opened the passenger door and swept his arm down in a courtly gesture toward Coke. "Rank hath its privileges," he said in a booming baritone.

"Bob, give me a leg up on top," Margulies called. "It's crowded inside, and I like the view from up there."

"I think perhaps I should ride there instead," Johann Vierziger said.

"*I* don't think so," Margulies snapped. Niko Daun chuckled.

Barbour made a stirrup of his hands. He grunted as he took the weight of the close-coupled woman, but she got a boot on the window frame and flipped herself neatly onto the vantage point.

Coke allowed himself a grin as he took his seat beside Pilar. The six of them had a lot of sorting out to do, with each other and with a job they were all new at. So far, so good.

The van was diesel powered. Pilar coaxed the engine to life with difficulty, and it ran rough after it caught.

"Are there aircars on Cantilucca?" Coke asked over the engine noise. From the amount of racket, there was no insulation in the firewall or body of the van to deaden sound.

"A few," the woman said. "It's hard to get maintenance on them. It's hard to get anyone to do *anything* in Potosi."

She engaged the torque converter. The van surged forward instead of picking up speed in a rising curve as Coke had expected.

"Except," Pilar added, "to swagger around with guns looking tough."

The van had a bar headlight across the upper hood. It worked, though its icteric cast suggested low voltage. The yellow light swept the gate of the starport compound, open and unguarded. Something hung from a pole just beyond the woven-wire fencing.

"Sir!" Margulies shouted.

"It's all right!" Coke called back. He'd seen the object as soon as Margulies did. "*He* isn't any danger, at any rate."

A corpse with its hands tied behind its back dangled by one ankle from a cross-pole. Either by chance or intention, the scene duplicated one of the Arcana of a Tarot deck, *The Hanged Man*.

"Yes," Pilar Ortega said grimly. "That's also very popular in Potosi. Dying, I mean."

Either the breeze through the windowless van was unexpectedly cool, or the hormones flooding Coke's system were playing hell with his temperature regulation. He slid open the front seam of his dress jacket and let his index finger rest on the trigger guard of his pistol.

He began to smile. Survey work might not be as different from what he was used to as he'd feared.

Coke had decided to enter Potosi quietly and not to arouse the locals' attention until he'd been able to view the situation on the ground. Frisian commo helmets with their array of vision-enhancing capacities would have marked the team even more clearly than would entering armed to the teeth.

Being able to see into the nighted forest would have been more calming to Coke than the weight of a 2-cm weapon in his hands. He supposed he'd made the right decision at leisure aboard the *Norbert IV*, but it didn't feel that way just now.

The van drove past a lean-to of brushwood and scrap sheeting. An open flame glimmered through the doorway. The shadow of an occupant ducked across the light.

"We're booked into a place called the Hathaway House," Coke said. "Is that near your house, mistress?"

"My *husband* and I have a suite on the other side of town," Pilar snapped. "Terence is in charge of cargo operations."

"I see," Coke said in a neutral voice. He saw, or thought he did, quite a lot. "I was only concerned that we were taking you out of your way, mistress. We're perfectly capable of making our way on foot. The cases are awkward, but the suspension takes all the weight."

The van rattled along at 45 or 50 kph, about all the pavement would allow. The vehicle steered with a pair of thumbwheels set on the arms of a control yoke. Pilar looked down at her hands for a moment, then raised her eyes to the road again.

"I have to go right past the Hathaway House to get home," she said. "Potosi has only the one street fit for a full-sized vehicle. There are alleys, but they're generally blocked."

"You're going out of your way to help us," Coke said, watching the woman with his peripheral vision. "I don't want to put you to needless trouble."

"Many of the people, the men, who come to Cantilucca are a rough sort," Pilar said. She still didn't look toward Coke. "I shouldn't have reacted like that to you.

I'm sorry."

"No problem," Coke said. "Were you born on Cantilucca?"

He knew what he was doing, and a part of his mind didn't like him much for it, but he was tense. This sort of game, this *hunt*, was a way to take his mind off wondering whether the next shadow was going to erupt in gunfire.

"Marvela," Pilar said. She wasn't a good driver; she had a tendency to overcorrect. At least she kept her eyes on the road while she talked. "We met when Terence was working in the port there. When he returned home to Cantilucca to run cargo operations, I—we married and I came with him."

From the glow in the sky ahead, the van was nearing the town proper. They passed a straggle of hovels like the first one. The dwellings weren't so much clustered as squatting in sight of one another, like a pack of vicious dogs penned together.

There was hinted motion, but no figure appeared in the open. There'd have been trouble had the team walked this way from the port. Nothing they couldn't have handled, but it would have gotten in the way of Coke's intention to start out with a low profile.

"Do you miss Marvela?" Coke asked. His eyes swept broad arcs though his head moved only slightly.

"No," Pilar said. "No."

She paused. "But I wish we hadn't come *here*. Cantilucca is a…"

She grimaced. Coke wasn't sure whether she was unable to find words to describe the planet, or if she was simply unwilling to voice them.

"There's too much nastiness here," Pilar said finally. "A man can go wrong anywhere. But on Cantilucca, it's very difficult to live decently."

Nothing wrong with my instincts, thought a part of Matthew Coke's mind; and another part scowled at the smug realization.

The van came up the far side of a dip and rounded a slight curve. Potosi lay directly ahead.

The town had no streetlights, but the ground floors and occasionally one or two of the higher stories were dazzles of direct and reflected enticement. Instead of having common walls, the buildings were set separately, sometimes behind a walled courtyard. Barkers doubling as armed guards stood outside business entrances, shouting to the traffic through bullhorns.

Pilar slowed the van to a crawl. The theoretical right-of-way was fifteen meters wide, but hawkers and shills narrowed the street, grabbing at pedestrians. Coke saw a trio of crewmen from the *Norbert IV.* The sailors stayed together as they crossed from one set of premises to the next. Though the men wore pistols openly, they looked more apprehensive than dangerous.

There were no other vehicles on the street. A pink-haired woman with wild eyes stuck her head into the van on Coke's side. Her breath stank. She shouted something about the tray of electronic gadgets in her hand. The casings of gadgets, at any rate. Coke wouldn't have bet they had the proper contents.

He ignored the woman. She shouted a curse and spat at him. The roof post caught most of the gobbet instead.

The members of the survey team were in civilian clothing, but Margulies still wore her field boots. Her right leg described a quick arc, across the open window and up out of sight again. The hawker spun backward, tray flying as her eyes rolled up in their sockets.

It didn't seem to Coke that an action of that sort should arouse comment in Potosi; nor did it.

The ground floor of each building was walled like a pillbox, generally as a form of appliqué to the original structure. In some cases the strengthening took the form of sandbags behind a frame of timber and wire, but fancier techniques included cast concrete and plates of metal or ceramic armor.

In general, two or three upper stories were as-built. Many of the structures now had several additional stories added with flimsy materials.

Banners, lighted signs, and occasionally nude women or boys were displayed in second- and third-floor windows. There was always a screen of heavy wire mesh to prevent objects from being thrown in—or perhaps out. Music pumped from street-level doorways, different in style at every one; always distorted, always shatteringly loud.

Every major starport had a district like Potosi. The difference here was that Potosi appeared to have nothing else.

As Pilar had said, no proper streets crossed the road from the port, but the setbacks between adjacent buildings created de facto alleys. One or more gunmen stood at each intersection, strutting arms akimbo or profiling on one leg with the other boot against the wall.

The gunmen weren't in uniform, but they wore swatches of either red or blue—a cap, an armband, a jacket—and never both colors. Most of them ran to crossed bandoliers, with knives and holstered pistols in addition to a shoulder weapon.

They eyed the van as it passed. A heavy-set, balding fellow with bits of red lightstripping twisted into his beard stepped after the vehicle, then changed his mind and took his former station. Coke relaxed slightly. He heard Vierziger sigh behind him, perhaps with disappointment.

"Are those your police?" Coke asked their driver.

Pilar sniffed. "There are no police in Potosi," she said. "None that count, at any rate. Those are toughs from the gage syndicates, Astra and L'Escorial. The Astras wear blue."

A leavening of ordinary citizens shared the streets with the thugs, shills, and roisterers. Laborers; farmers in a small way, in town on business necessity but without money to spend as a few of their wealthier fellows had for the moment; clerks and office workers going home, hunched over and covered by capes like the one which concealed Pilar.

Somebody clanged a stone against the back of the van. Coke didn't react physically. He wondered if he should have put two of his people on the roof, so that Margulies wouldn't be clocked from behind. Too late to change plans now without precipitating the trouble he wanted to avoid.

"It isn't always this bad," Pilar said apologetically. Her hands were stiff on the control yoke. "Both the gangs have been hiring recently and bringing men in from the fields. It's, it's worse than any time in the six years we've lived here."

Coke didn't bother to ask whether "years" meant standard or the shorter Cantiluccan rotation.

"These are farmers?" he said, frowning at two bands of a dozen each, kitty-corner from one another at an intersection and only ten meters apart. The gangs glowered at one another as they postured.

A short man with a blue beret hopped up to the side of the van. He braced himself on the window ledge and shouted, "Dog vomit!" at the red-clad gang on the opposite corner.

Niko Daun clutched beneath his tunic. Sergeant Vierziger raised his left index finger to prevent his fellows in the back of the van from moving. His eyes were on the opposite side of the vehicle, however, ready to react if a L'Escorial thug decided to shoot through the vehicle at the challenger.

None of them did. The van rumbled on.

Pilar swallowed, showing that she too recognized how dangerous the past instant had been.

"I meant guards from the fields," she said, watching the roadway. "Some of them were farmers. Some of them were sailors who jumped ship or were discharged on Cantilucca for bad behavior. Many of them are just, just *badmen*. They've come to Cantilucca because word's out that the syndicates are willing to hire anybody who'll carry a gun and swagger."

"But there's no formed units of mercenaries on Cantilucca?" Coke asked.

"No," said Pilar. "No, we've at least been spared that."

So far, Coke thought. *But only so far.*

The van passed a three-story building on the right, set back in a walled courtyard. The structure was painted entirely blue, although several different shades had been mixed promiscuously. The whole facade was sheathed in concrete, and there were firing slits on each level in place of normal windows.

"Astra headquarters?" Coke asked. He thumbed toward the building, but he kept his hand below the level of the van's window so that only Pilar could see it.

"Yes," she said curtly—without looking toward the garish structure.

There were half a dozen guards at the courtyard gate, staring at everything which passed in the street. Their scrutiny drove pedestrians crowding to the left, the way a plume of cloud forms downstream of a hilltop.

Nobody looked at the guards. Nobody. Just for the hell of it, Coke turned deliberately to the right. His face wore a blank smile. The Astras glowered, but they were doing that anyway.

The guards were in full blue uniforms instead of wearing tags and scraps of the color. An elite force, then; and if those slope-browed slovens were the syndicate's elite, the Astras at least should be willing to pay for professional support.

"I'd think," Coke said in a neutral tone, "that there might be advantages to a dwelling closer to your place of work."

"Yes, I've thought of that too," Pilar said, giving Coke a brief smile. She was obviously glad of human contact. "But the part of Potosi past the two headquarter buildings is much quieter. The side toward the port is, well, you've seen it."

"Seen enough to imagine the rest," Coke agreed.

Somebody had sprayed scarlet paint on the pavement four hundred meters beyond Astra HQ. On the left side of the road, a group of twenty or so thugs sauntered from a heavily fortified building, also red, and surged across the street to form a cordon. They called to one another and jeered the civilians they blocked.

Pilar touched her crucifix with the tip of her right index finger and whispered a prayer. She stopped the van and cramped her wheels for a tight turn back the way they'd come.

"What is this?" Coke said. He opened his door and stepped out onto the running board. His eyes scanned front and to both sides, looking for the glint of a pointed weapon or the flash of a shot. His being was centered in his body, ready to send it in any direction.

The van's rear doors slid back as the rest of the team readied for action. Margulies' boots thumped on the roof.

"It's nothing, it's just a game they play every once in a while," Pilar said. She tried to ease the van into a turn, but the crowd recoiling from the cordon held the vehicle fast. "We'll have to go back and try to circle off the road—oh!"

"The idea seems to have caught on with our friends in blue," Margulies called from the roof of the van. "They've got the road blocked behind us now."

"Do you have any orders, Matthew?" Johann Vierziger asked in a voice as sharp and lethal as a cat's white eyetooth.

"No!" Coke said. *Not the guns, not yet.* "Mistress Ortega! What's the best way through?"

A three-wheeled jitney stopped at the cordon. The driver might have turned as more distant traffic did, but a thug pointed his sub-machine gun at the little vehicle.

L'Escorial gunmen poked and prodded the passengers, a pair of sailors and their local whores. A gunman took the liquor bottle from a sailor, drank from it, and handed it back. The business wasn't a formal search, just harassment and almost good-natured—until the end.

A gunman lifted up the bandeau of one of the prostitutes to uncover her breasts. The woman's nipples were tattooed blue.

The gunman's quick feel turned into a vicious yank. The woman screamed. Another L'Escorial thug bashed her behind the ear with a pistol butt.

Half a dozen of the red-clad gunmen converged like soldier ants to the sound of an intruder. They kicked and punched, stripping the prostitute as she tried to crawl away from them. One of the men thrust the muzzle of his 2-cm powergun between the woman's legs.

Coke's vision focused into a narrow tunnel. His mouth was half open and his skin was cold.

He didn't know her. She was nothing but a whore and a stupid whore besides, a whore who took an indelible stand in favor of one gang of thugs over another.

But he was going to do it anyway, violate his own orders and he'd have had the *balls* of any team member who did the same—

The L'Escorial lifted his powergun, laughing, and kicked the woman instead. His nailed boots tore a double row of gashes in her buttocks; but that came with the turf. She continued to crawl, ignored now by the gunman and other citizens alike.

The two sailors and the remaining woman slipped through the cordon during the incident. The driver left the jitney where it was. He ducked into a doorway marked DRINKS & ENTERTAINMENT.

Pilar shut off the van's engine. "There's no way through or around," she said. "No safe way. They—"

She closed her eyes and whispered something with her finger on the crucifix again.

"This doesn't happen very often," she continued in a resigned tone. "I suggest you take beds in one of these—" she grimaced "—places. That's what I'm going to do. It will be quite horrible, but… you can't tell what they'll take it into their heads to do. Many of them mix tailings and alcohol together. It makes them crazy. Crazier."

"This doesn't look like a great neighborhood a-tall," Niko Daun said, looking around at the dingy buildings.

He was right. The add-on levels above the original constructions were reached by rickety outside staircases. The signs reading BEDS or SLEEP or (in one case, and perhaps little more of a lie than the others) SAFE LODGINGS were always on these outside stairs.

"How far away is the Hathaway House?" Coke asked Pilar as he continued to scan.

"It's right across the street from the L'Escorial building," Pilar said, "but that's the problem. It wouldn't do you any good to walk around the, the armed *children*, because they're exactly where you want to go."

"Hathaway House may not be any better than these flops anyway," Sten Moden suggested. He didn't sound concerned.

"There's six of us," said Robert Barbour. "We ought to be safe enough for the night."

"The Hathaway is a decent place," said Pilar. "I mean really *decent*, the only one in Potosi. But you can't get there. It doesn't have any back door. That'd just be another point to guard."

"I would say," Vierziger said coolly, "that it's not too far to carry our luggage if the lady doesn't want to drive us."

"It's not *want*," Pilar burst out angrily. "It's not *safe* to cross that gauntlet, safe for you!"

People with great need or great confidence were getting past the cordon. A gunman in red cordovan boots cut a citizen's belt and sent him scampering away with his trousers around his ankles.

Women were fondled, generally roughly. A few people were relieved of small objects—a gun, a chip recorder; perhaps some money. For the most part the cordon was an irritation, not an atrocity.

But it could become an atrocity at any moment, Coke knew. The only apparent check on the gunmen's activities was their own desires. There was no sign of external control.

Coke glanced up at Margulies on the roof of the van. He'd order her into a firefight without hesitation, but this was something else again. At the start, anyway.

"Mary, it's your call," he said.

She shrugged. "I'm not thrilled either way," she said. "But we came here to get information. I guess we may as well go do that."

She hopped down, bracing her left hand on the van roof. Her toes took her weight, so that she landed as lightly as if she'd stepped from the side door.

"All right, that's what we're going to do," Coke said. "Whatever comes, we're going to take it. When we're in the hotel, we'll take stock—but not before then. Understood?"

Sten Moden shrugged. Daun said, "Yessir," very quietly, and Robert Barbour nodded. The intel lieutenant looked nervous, which was actually good: that meant he understood what was likely to happen. Coke thought he'd be okay.

"You mustn't do this!" Pilar said. "Please, just come with me."

She started toward stairs marked CLEAN LOCKED BEDS, rising from the unpaved alley beside where the van was parked. A man—or perhaps a woman within the ragged garments—lay supine just below the first landing.

"Nothing without orders, Matthew," said Johann Vierziger. "Nothing. I understand."

Coke nodded. "Let's do it," he said, hefting his own pair of cases from the van and starting toward the cordon.

"Please!" called Pilar Ortega. "Please, Master Coke! You don't know what you're doing."

She was wrong there… but that didn't necessarily mean that the business was survivable.

A few additional gunmen wandered out of L'Escorial headquarters to join the cordon. One of them brought a carton from which he tossed thimble-sized stim cones to his fellows.

Other L'Escorials left, bored by the lack of activity. Three of them headed for a ground-floor establishment whose doorjamb and transom were outlined in red glow-strip.

Many of the dives in the immediate neighborhood were marked red. None of them had blue anywhere on their signs or facades.

"S'pose they'd all go home if we waited a bit?" Daun asked.

"No," said Barbour beside him. There was tension in the voices of both technical specialists, but many things need to be tight to function. Neither of the men sounded as if he was about to break.

The 400-plus meter stretch of road between the rival headquarters had largely emptied since the cordons were established. The only traffic was of pedestrians crossing from one bar to another or climbing stairs to a flophouse.

A few drivers returned to their vehicles and ran them into the alleys. The jitneys had large-diameter wheels and often studded tires (though not all of them *had* tires). They could probably get along well enough off the pavement, though a serious pothole would overbalance them sideways. The little vehicles had narrow tracks and a high center of gravity.

The survey team, pulling its luggage toward the L'Escorial cordon, stood out like six sore thumbs.

The gunmen quieted speculatively. They didn't break their rough spacing across the width of the street, but there was a slight edgewise movement to concentrate in Coke's line toward the doorway of Hathaway House.

The door was metal-faced. It opened a crack. An orange-haired woman in her late middle age looked out. She closed the door after surveying the situation, but a triangular viewport opened immediately toward the top of the panel.

A blond man in his mid-twenties walked from the center of the line toward the end which the team approached. The fellow wore a crimson vest and cutoff trousers, high boots with rows of spikes around the calves, and a waist belt heavy with pouches of spare magazines for his sub-machine gun. His right arm and left leg were tattooed in patterns too stretched and faded to be identified in the bad light.

Coke paused a meter short of the blond man. Vierziger was a pace behind him; the rest of the team slanted back in precise echelon. Under the present circumstances, Moden instead of Margulies brought up the rear.

"Good evening, sir," Coke said to the presumed L'Escorial leader. He let go of the hand-grips of his luggage.

The blond man pointed his sub-machine gun into the air and shot off half the magazine in a single ripping burst. A cone of cyan bolts flicked toward the stars.

As their leader fired, most of the other L'Escorials in the cordon followed suit in a ragged volley. They carried a wide variety of weapons, though high-quality powerguns predominated. The night was a bedlam of *whack*s, hiss*cracks*, and propellant flashes of red, orange, and yellow supplementing the powerguns' saturated blue.

Not all the gunmen aimed skyward. A burly, bare-chested man wearing garnet-studded nipple rings with a chain slung between them pointed his chemically powered fléchette gun at the front of Hathaway House. He fired twice.

The crashing reports of the hypervelocity weapon rattled shutters and screens against the windows they protected. The building's facade was concrete containing very coarse aggregate. The tungsten fléchettes blew out craters in sprays of yellow-green sparks. A piece of gravel the size of Coke's clenched fist flew back across the street. It smacked the wall fronting L'Escorial headquarters.

The gunman rocked with each round from his high-recoil weapon. He was lowering the muzzle for a third shot when the L'Escorial leader batted him across the temple with the sub-machine gun's barrel.

"Fuckhead!" the leader shouted as his henchman sprawled facedown on the pavement. The victim's hair, scorched by the white-hot iridium, stank obscenely. "You want to kill us all?"

He'd knocked the fellow unconscious. From the eyes of the man with the fléchette gun, he'd been flying so high on gage and other drugs that he probably wouldn't remember the lesson in the morning anyway, though he'd feel it.

The L'Escorial leader turned. He waggled the glowing muzzle of his powergun in Coke's face. "Where do you come from, dickhead?" he demanded.

"We're businessfolk from Nieuw Friesland," Coke said quietly. "Though the last stage of our voyage was through Delos."

"Everybody comes through Delos if they're coming here, dickhead," the leader snarled. He pointed his weapon one-handed at one of Coke's suitcases. "Open that. *Now!*"

"I'm sorry," Coke lied, "but they were hold baggage on shipboard, so they're time-locked. They can't be opened for another day and a half."

"Want to bet?" the gunman said. He fired.

The survey team's luggage was plated with 40-laminae ceramic armor beneath a normal-looking sheathing. The thin laminae shattered individually without transmitting much of the shock to deeper layers. A few rounds from a 2-cm weapon would have blown any of the cases apart, but the burst of 1-cm pistol charges from the sub-machine gun only pecked halfway through the plating.

Furthermore, the ceramic reflected a proportion of the plasma. The spray of sun-hot ions glazed Coke's trouser legs—the business suit was much more utilitarian than its stylish cut implied.

The L'Escorial gunman's bare knees blistered instantly, and the fringe of his shorts caught fire. He screamed, dropped his weapon, and began batting with his bare hands at the flames.

The case started to fall over. The burst of gunfire had smashed the forward static generator in a shower of sparks.

Coke grabbed the handle of the case. "Please, sirs!" he cried in a voice intended to sound terrified. "We're businessmen! Please!"

"Fuck you!" a tall man with a pair of pistols cried. "You're dancers, that's what you are!"

He fired twice into the pavement at Coke's feet. Glass and pebbles from the compressed-earth roadway spattered Coke's legs above his shoe tops. Coke staggered forward, lifting the front of the damaged case in his left hand. He squeaked in simulated terror.

The fear was real, but not terror, not anything that prevented Matthew Coke from acting in whatever fashion was necessary.

He didn't *know* whether or not the actions he'd set in motion were survivable. It was like a free-fall jump. Once you'd committed, you could only hope the support mechanism—static repulsion, parachute, or whatever—would work as intended. The team couldn't change its collective mind now.

A 2-cm bolt blew off the lower back corner of the damaged case and the rest of the static suspension. With the plating and the hardware inside, the case weighed nearly a hundred kilos. Coke lurched onward with it, bleating. He was through the cordon, but a bullet could flick through the back of his head and take his face off at any gunman's whim.

Mary Margulies touched the latch of her tight-band case with a finger so swift that the luggage appeared to have flown open by accident. Frilly underwear and lounging garments flew out onto the roadway.

"Hey lookee-lookee-lookee!" shouted a gunman. He grabbed a teddy and modeled it against his scarred chest.

The cordon collapsed into a rush for loot. The clothing had no value except as a matter of amusement, but that's all the cordon was to begin with: a way for men with a childish mindset to amuse themselves.

"Hey, sweetie!" a gunman cried. He grabbed, not very seriously, for Margulies' crotch. The lieutenant weaseled past with her remaining suitcase. "Stay with me! I'll give you more dick than all five of them pussies together!"

The door of Hathaway House opened in front of Coke. His left arm felt as though the shoulder tendons would snap with the weight of the case they supported. He stepped aside to check on his team.

"Get *in*, curse your eyes!" Johann Vierziger shouted. "I'll handle—"

Vierziger slid one of his cases into the doorway with a sweep of his left arm.

"—this!" and he sent the second case after the first, skidding like driverless cars.

Though the static suspension balanced the weight of the luggage, its inertia was unchanged. Vierziger's movements, as smooth and practiced as those of an expert lawn-bowler, required strength that one wouldn't assume in someone as pretty as the little man.

A voice yelped from inside the hotel. The door started to close, but Barbour was there, using the mass of his cases to slam the panel fully open. He twisted aside. Niko Daun followed him in.

A pair of L'Escorial gunmen were dancing. One wore a pair of delicate panties as a crown; his partner had thrust his arms into leggings whose multiple shimmering colors shifted as they caught varied light-sources. Other L'Escorials cheered and clapped, or pawed through the open case for their own trophies.

Coke pointed Margulies *in*. She obeyed at a hasty rush, aware that her presence as a woman made the risk to every member of the team greater. The expression on her face was set and terrible.

Sten Moden tossed his huge case after her, picked up both of Coke's cases in his one hand and tossed them; and wrapped his arm around Coke's waist. Moden swept the major with him into the lobby of Hathaway House. Coke could as well have wrestled an oak tree for the good his protests did.

Somebody had to be last in; and yeah, that was probably a job for the security detail, for Sergeant Vierziger, but it didn't seem right…

The sixtyish woman with orange hair started to push the door closed. Daun and Barbour were already doing that. Vierziger danced backward through the opening.

The panel clanged against its jamb. It rang again an instant later: a L'Escorial had fired a powergun into the armor as a farewell. The door's refractory core, lime or ceramic, absorbed the discharge without damage.

The woman swept her hair out of her eyes. She was healthy looking though on the plump side. A man of similar age with a luxuriant, obviously implanted, mane of hair stood to the side, wringing his hands.

Several tables stood in a saloon alcove off the foyer. A few men were seated in the shadows there. They stared pointedly at their drinks rather than at the newcomers. The silence within the hotel was a balm after the noisy violence of the street.

The woman planted her arms akimbo, fists on her hips. "Welcome to Cantilucca, mistress and sirs," she said. "Now, if you're smart, you'll head right back to the port and take the next ship *out* of this pigsty!"

"Oh, Evie, it's not so bad as that," the man said. "It's just with the, you know, with the syndicates on edge like they are, there's more, ah…"

"More murderous bandits in town than usual?" the woman snapped. "Yes, there are, and it's an open question whether they kill everybody else off before they kill each other or after!"

"I'm Georg Hathaway," the man said, bowing to Moden—probably because the logistics officer was the most imposing presence of this or most other groups. "This is my wife Evie, and I'm sorry for this trouble, usually things are better, it's just there are so many of the patrolmen in Potosi these last few months, and you know, the boys will let off steam."

"Usually things are *almost* bearable," Evie Hathaway said sharply. "That hasn't been the case since the bandits began gearing up to fight—and they *don't* fight, they just squeeze decent citizens harder yet. When will it stop, I'd like to know?"

"Evie, now, don't upset the gentlemen and lady," Georg Hathaway said. "They've had a difficult time already, we mustn't make it worse. Are you the Coke party, then, booking from Nieuw Friesland?"

Moden gestured, palm up. "This is Master Coke," he said. "You have rooms for us?"

"Oh, we have rooms, all right," Evie said. "What we don't have is patrons who can pay us for them. Since this trouble started three months ago, nobody with money and sense comes anywhere near Potosi."

She stared fiercely at Coke. "And we have *our* standards. Are you here on behalf of the gage cartel on Delos, Master Coke?"

"No," Coke said, "we don't have anything to do with gage."

Hathaway House was a two-story building. The lobby, saloon, and service quarters were on the ground floor, while the guest rooms were up a flight of stairs. Judged from outside, the protective concrete wall was of equal thickness all the way up, so Coke didn't see any need for special arrangements.

"Speaking of gage," said Niko Daun hopefully, "I don't suppose this would be a good time to have a cone or two?"

Moden looked at the younger man with an icy fury that shocked Coke. "No," the big man said in a voice as still as death, "it would not. Not so long as the operation is going on."

Daun blushed. "I'm sorry, sir," he said, looking toward the lower wall molding, gray against the lobby's general peach decor. "I just thought that since we had a break after, well, after…"

"There's no breaks until we lift out of here, T-tech, Niko," Sten Moden said more gently. "But I'm sorry, it wasn't mine to speak—"

He nodded formally toward Coke.

"—and I'm sorry for my tone. I—wouldn't care for others to make such a mistake as I made in the past, thinking I could let down."

Margulies and Vierziger had conferred briefly. The lieutenant trotted upstairs to check protection and fields of fire there, while Vierziger prowled the ground floor. The Hathaways watched him askance but neither of them spoke—even when he disappeared into their own quarters.

"Bloody hell," Coke muttered. He peeked out of the door's triangular viewport.

The cordons were still in place. The L'Escorials had rolled an armored truck into the street to face the Astra line. It looked like a four-wheeled van covered with so many metal and concrete panels that it could barely move. The vehicle mounted tribarrels in a cupola and in a sponson to either side. There were firing slits as well, though Coke judged that they did little but weaken the already-doubtful protection.

Robert Barbour opened one of his cases. The interior was packed with electronics. He began to extend the case into a full-featured communications module.

"Come on, Daun," he said. "We need to get some information if we're going to do our job."

Niko Daun gave the room a bright smile. "We're going to need information if we're going to survive the tour, *I'd* say," he remarked cheerfully.

The sensor tech unlatched a case of his own. It too was full of gear. He took out a series of sensors, broad-band optical and radio frequency, whistling under his breath.

Clothing hadn't been a high priority for a team operating out of range of support—save for the suitcase Margulies had insisted on bringing as a decoy, and *that* thought had earned her a commendation if Coke lived to write it.

"Ah, would you gentlefolk not like some refreshment?" Georg Hathaway suggested. "We have what we like to think is a very good beer, I brew it on the premises myself, and there's local cacao as well, good enough to export, if it weren't that no one cares for anything but gage on Cantilucca."

"Gage and killing," his wife said bitterly. "And mostly killing. I don't think it'll stop before there's only one of the bandits left."

"About how many men do the gage syndicates employ, mistress?" Coke asked as he continued to look out the viewport. Barbour and Daun would give him much more precise data in a moment, but in some ways there was nothing to equal the naked eye.

"Too many," Evie said. "And they're hiring more every day."

Georg—eyeing the array of devices the tech specialists were assembling—said cautiously, "Sirs, I'd judge that Astra and L'Escorial have at least a thousand, ah, employees each. They aren't all in, ah, the patrol branch, but most of them are."

"Usually most of them are out in the fields, bullying the growers," Evie Hathaway said. "But they've been bringing them into Potosi since the trouble started."

She raised her arms and combed her fingers through her artificially bright hair. She looked tired and frustrated, a woman near the end of her tether. "I hope the growers are getting some benefit. Because it's *hell* here for decent folk."

The makeshift armored truck revved its air-cooled diesel engine. The separately bolted body panels vibrated at different frequencies, creating a grinding rattle. For the crew, it must have been like riding in a cement mixer—but maybe they were so stoned that they wouldn't feel the effects of their silliness until the next morning.

Niko darted up the stairs to arrange his equipment from high vantage points. Margulies came down, wearing a satisfied expression, and gave Coke a thumbs-up. The upper floor and roof were secure in her—expert—estimation.

"And there's no police force, I understand?" Coke said.

The tribarrel in the armored truck's cupola pointed up at twenty degrees, probably its maximum elevation, and fired a two-round burst. The rich cyan of the high-powered 2-cm charges flashed in reflection from the facades.

"Police?" Mistress Hathaway crowed. She pointed into the saloon. "Police? Look at them there, afraid to go out without covering up so they won't be seen! Oh, we've *got fine* police here in Potosi!"

The two men drinking morosely at a corner table did, now that Evie called attention to the fact, wear white uniforms. Dingy white uniforms. They hunched their shoulders under the lash of her tongue. Drab capes like the one with which Pilar covered herself hung over the backs of their chairs.

"Evie, now, don't get yourself into a state," Georg murmured, wringing his hands again.

The gunman in the armored truck rotated his barrels manually, then fired another two rounds. The ill-maintained tribarrel jammed again at the third loading sequence.

One of the policemen turned and glared from deep-sunk eyes. "Look, what do you want us to do?" he demanded. He waved a shock baton, the only weapon he carried. "Go out and arrest them all, and for what?"

He made a face as if to spit, then thought better of it. Sinking back over his mug of beer he added, "Better I should shoot myself. At least I could be sure it was quick if I did it myself."

"Find someone worth a bullet!" Evie Hathaway snapped, but she'd lost the edge of anger. Exhaustion reasserted itself.

A ripple—three pairs—of hypervelocity rockets cracked down the street in the opposite direction, well over the heads of the L'Escorial cordon. The Astras must have brought one of their own armored vehicles out, though Coke couldn't see it from his present vantage point.

The projectiles were aimed deliberately high, just as the L'Escorial tribarrel had been; but that sort of game could get out of hand as quickly as Russian roulette could. A red-clad gunman spread his fringed leather kilt and urinated in the direction of the Astra line.

"You gentlemen—and lady, of course," Georg Hathaway said cautiously, "are in the instrument business, then? You plan to sell instruments to the gage syndicates?"

"Not exactly," Coke said curtly.

"I've got a hook-up, sir," Barbour said. "Ah, Matthew. You can have a panorama here on the console or fed to your helmet."

Coke glanced briefly at the data console. A holographic globe a meter in diameter hung above the base. The image was a schematic of the center of Potosi. Buildings appeared as simplified versions of themselves, while vehicles and armed personnel were icons—red and blue, as indicated.

The L'Escorial armored car revved and backed slowly away, its tribarrels pointing toward the Astras. While turning to the courtyard, the vehicle's right rear fender bashed a gatepost. The engine stalled. The car rolled forward a meter.

Gunmen in the cordon hooted and catcalled at the vehicle's crew. The driver started his engine again with a cloud of black smoke. He advanced into the middle of the street and cramped his wheels to get a running start at the entrance. There was plenty of room, but the single side mirror wasn't adequate for backing so clumsy a vehicle.

The armored car lurched into reverse. It roared backward in a shower of sparks and concrete powdered from both the vehicle and the gatepost it scraped. The gunmen clapped and cheered ironically.

Johann Vierziger sat on a stuffed chair with his hands crossed in his lap, watching the scene in the holographic display. His face wore a grim smile.

The sensor tech had returned from upstairs. He shook his head and said, "I told them I'd never work with wogs again. Lord knows *that* was the right decision."

He grinned. Coke had read the kid's file. Daun was obviously as resilient as he was skilled in his specialty; but then, he was young too.

"Master Hathaway?" Coke said. "I under—"

"Georg," the host said, nodding. "Please, call me Georg."

"Georg, then," Coke said. "I understand that there are no professional military units on Cantilucca—no mercenaries, that is. Is that your understanding as well?"

"Well," Hathaway said, "both syndicates have Presidential Guards. They're mostly soldiers from off-planet."

"But not off-planet *units?*" Coke pressed. The guard forces in full uniform might be individually more skillful than the ruck of ex-farmers and ex-sailors carrying guns, but they obviously lacked the discipline necessary to carry out complex maneuvers.

"No, not that I've heard of," Hathaway said. "That would be much more expensive, surely?"

"That depends on what you're assigning values to," said Mary Margulies.

Coke had thought the cordons might disperse when the armored vehicles left, but a score of red-clad gunmen remained. Traffic was picking up slightly. The citizenry had decided that the gunmen didn't mean serious trouble.

"They can't bring mercenaries onto Cantilucca," Evie Hathaway said unexpectedly. "Because of the Confederacy."

"We'd heard the Marvelans left Cantilucca pretty well alone," Sten Moden said quietly.

"The Confederacy doesn't care anything about law and order here, so long as they're paid their money," Evie said. "*Blood* money, I call it. But they won't let a proper army onto Cantilucca. For fear they'd take over and the Confederacy wouldn't be able to drive them out."

Georg Hathaway looked at his wife in surprise. "What's that, Evie?" he said. "I hadn't heard that."

She turned slightly away. In a less forceful voice she said, "When the Marvelan delegation was on Cantilucca a year and a half ago, the overflow from the High Commissioner's residence stayed here. One of the aides explained that to me when, when I was complaining to him."

"Aides…" Georg repeated in a flat tone. "That would be young Garcia-Medina, I suppose you mean?"

"It might have been!" said Evie. "I was complaining about the horrible situation, that was all!"

"We have," Johann Vierziger said, "a war of sorts outside. I don't think adding one inside is necessary at the moment."

"No, no," Georg said. The innkeeper's forced smile quickly asserted its own reality over his personality. "That's old business and nothing to it, not really, not even then. Pardon me, mistress and masters, for letting the stress of the moment get the better of me."

The whole team was assembled in the lobby of the hotel. Coke grinned wryly at his people. With the corner of his eye still tracking developments in the street peripherally, he said, "Well, what do the rest of you think? Niko?"

The sensor tech grinned and flipped his hands palms-up in a noncommittal gesture. "I can set you up to count the change in the pocket of anybody in town, sir. Just tell me what you want."

Coke nodded. "Bob?"

Barbour looked through the space occupied by his holographic display. His hands hovered over the console keyboard, not quite touching it.

"There's something over six hundred powerguns live in the three-klick radius," he said. "Given the ratio of powerguns to other weapons outside, that roughs in well with a total of a thousand shooters in town at present."

He looked at Coke; his eyes focused again. "What else would you like to know, Matthew?"

"That'll do," Coke said. He'd deliberately kept the parameters of his question vague. The team members were answering each to his own specialty, just as they should. "Sten?"

The logistics officer nodded twice before he spoke, as though his mind were a pump and he was priming it. "Yes," he said. "What Mistress Hathaway says rings true. If so, we'll either have to infiltrate the personnel or arrange a combat landing. I doubt we'll be able to get the Bonding Authority to cover either option."

"Is that a deal-breaker, then?" Coke asked. "Shall we just pack up and go home?"

Moden shook his head. "There've been precedents," he said. "They aren't talked about officially, but you hear about them in the bars around Camp Able. It affects the price and the size of the force to be risked, however."

"I don't like the idea of going in on a non-bonded operation," Margulies said with a frown.

"*We* won't be going in anywhere," Coke said. "And the decision isn't ours. We're just here to assess possibilities."

The Bonding Authority on Terra guaranteed that both parties to a hiring of mercenaries would perform according to the terms of the contract. That is, the troops would obey the orders of the contracting local party—whether the latter was a recognized government, a rebel movement, or an interstellar business conglomerate extending its holdings by force. And the troops would be paid even if that meant the contracting local parties starved or starved every civilian on the planet, in order to meet their obligations to the mercenaries.

The Bonding Authority didn't take a moral stand: money has no smell. Though one could argue that forcing adults to keep their word was itself a way of instilling morality on human weakness.

Margulies grimaced and nodded.

"Johann?" Coke said.

Vierziger sniffed. "A company of infantry, backed up by a company of combat cars," he said. He snapped the fingers of his left hand dismissively. "It could be done with less. These people are hopeless, quite hopeless."

"How about panzers instead of cars?" Margulies suggested. "This is a city of bunkers."

Vierziger shook his head. "There's too many hiding places for buzzbomb teams," he said. "Tribarrels can break up the facades almost as fast as a twenty-centimeter main gun could, and a car has twice as many eyes as a tank to watch for launchers.

Even that's risky, but the infantry needs the firepower support."

Margulies pursed her lips. "We could use the local allies, whichever side, to unmask ambushes?" she said, the question implicit in her tone.

"Dream on," Vierziger said scornfully. Margulies shrugged and nodded agreement with her nominal underling's judgment.

"May I ask just what business you goodfolk deal in, please?" Georg Hathaway said in a cautiously distant voice.

Vierziger raised an eyebrow at Coke. Coke scratched the side of his neck. No point in trying to conceal matters. Theirs was, after all, a legitimate commercial operation.

"We're representatives of the Frisian Defense Forces," he said, nodding toward Mistress Hathaway to include her in the explanation. "Our superiors had been told that one or both gage syndicates here on Cantilucca might be interested in hiring high-quality mercenaries. The FDF are the best, period. We're here to assess prospects for doing business and to report back to our superiors."

Evie Hathaway's face hardened by increments as Coke spoke. When he finished, she said harshly, "I don't think you made a very positive impression when you arrived, *gentle*folk. I doubt either the Widow Guzman or the Lurias will be interested in paying for the services of more like yourselves."

"Evie, now, don't be that way," her husband begged. "I'm sure these—"

"No, no," Coke said. "Mistress Hathaway is right. I suppose we need to do something to correct the situation immediately."

"People are drifting away from the roadblocks, sir," Barbour commented.

Coke had seen as much through the viewport, but there were still twelve or fourteen L'Escorials in position. About right for the purpose.

Margulies raised an eyebrow. Coke nodded. Margulies and Vierziger unlatched another pair of cases.

"How thick are the walls?" Coke asked.

"You *won't* start a fight in here!" Evie Hathaway shouted. "You have to kill me first! This is a place of peace!"

"Ma'am, I wouldn't think of it," Coke said truthfully. "Anything that happens will be out on the street. I just want to be sure that none of the—side effects—will be dangerous to your structure."

Barbour adjusted a set of controls. A ghost of Hathaway House glowed as a sidebar to the schematic of the immediate streetscape.

He looked up at Coke. "The front wall is nearly a meter thick," he said. "Glass-reinforced concrete, and well shaken down. There's a slight batter, but nothing that should matter."

"Well, that's right," Georg said in surprise. "I thought, Evie thought, really, that we shouldn't spare expense on protection if we were going to get the kind of guests we wanted."

The innkeeper looked at the cases the security detail had opened. Like those of Barbour and Daun, they were filled with equipment. This time, all the equipment was lethal.

Margulies and Vierziger began handing out weapons to the rest of the team.

Vierziger handed each member of the survey team a vest woven from beryllium monocrystal. Moden and Daun had carefully lifted the segments of ceramic plate from the exterior walls of the luggage. The plates fitted into pockets in the vests, forming body armor almost as resistant as the clamshell hard-suits which the FDF issued for normal field operations.

Coke took off his loose outer jacket and paused. "I don't think I want armor for this," he said. He was—

Well, of course he was frightened, a *turtle* would be frightened if it was about to walk into this one. It was his job, and anyway it'd be all right.

"I think you ought to wear it, sir," Margulies said.

She'd completely emptied the suitcase on which she'd been working. Weapons and ammunition lay in neat stacks on the tile floor around her. She stood up and latched the case, then twisted the hand-grip 180 degrees. She slid the luggage over to him.

"I think he ought to wear armor also," said Johann Vierziger, "though I'll admit I wouldn't myself if it were me."

He smiled. His face was that of an ivory angel. "I prefer the freedom. But what I really think is that I should be the one to go outside, Matthew."

Coke shook his head forcefully. "It's my job," he said. "And anyway, it'll be all right."

He thrust his arms through the holes of the vest he'd prepared, then mated the front closures. His outer jacket was cut to hang the same whether or not there was armor beneath it. He pulled it on.

"Helmet?" said Barbour without looking up from his console display.

Coke shook his head brusquely. "The implant will do in a pinch," he said, tapping his jaw. The right mastoid contained a miniature bone-conduction radio transceiver. "They'd react to the helmet the same as they would if I went out in full uniform."

Barbour nodded without concern. It was his job to offer information to the action personnel. He didn't—couldn't—control what they did with the information.

Vierziger slid Coke a second case, emptied and prepared as Margulies had done with hers.

Coke looked down at the luggage, then at his security detail. "One's enough," he said.

"Two, Matthew," said Vierziger.

"Two," echoed Margulies. "What do you intend to save them for, sir?"

Coke laughed harshly at himself. There was a tendency in any combat unit, particularly with those which operated beyond resupply, to fear using up munitions which they might need later. At its worst, that attitude could mean a position being overrun because the defenders were unwilling to cut loose with everything they had, lest they be out of ammo when the next attack came.

Margulies and Vierziger were right. Unless Coke made the next few minutes *re-*

ally memorable for the L'Escorials, ten times the hardware the team had brought to Cantilucca wouldn't be enough.

"Right," he said. "Two." He took the suitcases.

Niko Daun put his hand on the door latch. Moden's strength would have been a better match for the mass of the armored panel, but the powerful officer's one arm carried a three-tube missile launcher. The unit was intended for vehicle mounting, but Moden held it as easily as a lesser man might have done a 2-cm powergun.

Margulies and Vierziger were in position to either side of the door, she with a sub-machine gun, he with his hands empty, though he'd slung a sub-machine gun for patrol carry along his left side. The embellishments of the pistol in the high-ride holster on Vierziger's right hip winked in the foyer lights.

Robert Barbour sat at his console, calm or comatose. Coke supposed the former but it didn't matter, not now, as he nodded to Daun and started toward the door, sliding the cases beside him.

Coke stepped through the doorway and shivered in the warm, muggy air. L'Escorial gunmen turned in surprise to face him.

Coke set his luggage against the front wall of Hathaway House. Each of the big cases was a meter long and sixty centimeters high. They were thirty centimeters deep as well, but the volume wasn't important anymore. Coke left the pair in a very flat V, end to end, almost parallel to the reinforced concrete facade.

He stepped quickly toward the cordon's leader, the blond man in vest and cutoffs. The fellow's legs were an angry color; he'd have blisters across the whole front of them by morning, if he survived that long.

A gunman with a bayonetted grenade launcher stuck his weapon toward Coke's face. The bayonet was a spike rather than knife-style. Coke swept it aside with his left hand.

"Excuse me, sir!" Coke called to the leader. "I believe you're in charge here?"

"Who the *fuck* do you think you are, you little prick?" the L'Escorial demanded in obvious amazement. He pointed his sub-machine gun like a huge pistol. The muzzle wavered, but not so much that the 1-cm bore ever drifted away from Coke's face.

"I'm Matthew Coke, my good fellow," Coke said. "I'm afraid I have to complain about the behavior of yourself and your friends."

The need to hold a persona protected Coke against his own fears. This wasn't *him* facing a gang of bored, drugged-out thugs, this was a prissy off-world businessman who couldn't imagine violence as raw as the norm of this hellhole.

A gunman whacked Coke in the back with the butt of a 2-cm powergun. Coke staggered forward, almost into the muzzle of the leader's automatic weapon. The armored vest saved his kidneys, but it did nothing to lessen the inertia of the solid blow.

Coke flailed his arms to get his balance. "Now that's *just* what I mean!" he cried. "What sort of impression do you think that behavior makes on visitors? If you don't apologize immediately, I'll have to take action to bring this to your superiors' attention as clearly as possible."

"What the hell is he talking about, Blanco?" asked a gunman. He still wore a pair of lacy undergarments from Margulies' case over his scarlet beret.

What he's talking about, you moron, is the warning required by FDF regulations before FDF personnel use deadly force in a non-contractual context.

Blanco, the L'Escorial straw boss, stepped forward, poking his sub-machine gun toward Coke's eyes. The iridium bore was pitted from the long burst of a few minutes before.

Coke hopped backward. Another gunman tripped him. Coke twisted like a cat as he fell, catching himself on his left hand instead of sprawling on his back. Blanco kicked him in the side with cleated boots.

Coke scuttled toward the doorway of Hathaway House, doubled over. He dabbed his left hand down like a deer running with a broken foreleg.

L'Escorials shouted and kicked. One of them swung his 2-cm weapon as a club. Because Coke was moving, the massive iridium barrel smacked him in the small of the back instead of across the shoulders. Again the vest saved him from crippling, perhaps fatal, injury, but the shock made Coke's mind go white nonetheless. He plowed facedown on the pavement.

The plated door flew open. Johann Vierziger stepped out, grabbed Coke left-handed by the back of the collar, and half-pulled, half-flung, the major into the foyer.

Sten Moden swung the door closed. A L'Escorial stuck his foot in the crack. Margulies kicked the gunman's knee, then shoved him clear of the opening with the sole of her boot. Several L'Escorials pushed from the other side of the panel, but Moden's strength overmastered them.

Someone emptied the 30-round magazine of a projectile weapon against the front of the door. A L'Escorial screamed, wounded by a ricochet or at least by spatters of the bullets after they disintegrated on the armor.

The door locked on three wrist-thick bolts worked by a single handle. When the panel slammed against its jamb, Niko Daun slid the bolts home into metal tubes set deep in the concrete.

"Open this—" Blanco shouted, his voice attenuated by the massive door and wall.

Margulies touched a thumb switch, detonating the pair of directional mines in the suitcases outside.

The lobby lights went out. Emergency lighting, glow-strips powered piezoelectrically by the structure's own flexing, drew pale yellow-green arrows down the staircase and from each doorway. Barbour's holographic display remained a ball of sharp-edged pastels. Dust, shaken from all the surfaces of the room, filled the air chokingly.

Georg Hathaway opened his mouth as if to scream, but no sound came out. Evie put an arm around her husband's shoulders and another on his nearer elbow.

Coke staggered to his feet. Margulies tossed him a commo helmet. The other team members were already wearing theirs. Vierziger offered Coke a 2-cm powergun, muzzle up.

The double crash of the mines had been terrible despite the wall's protection. Coke heard his own voice with ringing overtones as he said, "Right, open it."

Daun tried to obey. The blasts had warped the door and jamb together. The sensor tech braced a bootsole on the wall for a fulcrum. Despite his straining, it wasn't until Moden slung his missile launcher and tugged the handle that the panel swung open.

The huge doughnuts of dust and smoke from the blasts had spread and dissipated by the time Coke came through the doorway—third, after Margulies and Vierziger, their guns pointing. Coke switched his visor to thermal imaging because the longer infrared waves penetrated the haze better than the normal optical range that light-amplification mode would have used.

A directional mine was built into one face of each suitcase, beneath the 40 ceramic laminae which the team had removed to use in its body armor. The outside of each mine was thousands of faceted steel barrels the size of the last joint of a man's little finger. The inside was a layer of cast explosive.

The mines went off like shotguns whose bore was the full plane of the cases containing them: six-tenths of a square meter. The pair, set to cross the edge of the L'Escorial cordon at a shallow angle, had swept the street like a gigantic buzzsaw.

All that was visible of Blanco was a left foot and left boot—from the ankle down. The mines' steel sleet hadn't had time to spread when it hit the L'Escorial officer. Blanco's torso must have been above the plane of the projectiles, but the shock wave had flung it indistinguishably into the bloody ruck.

Someone's right arm lay a few meters farther on. The radius and ulna were fleshless, but the hand and upper arm remained unmarked as a freak of the explosion.

Another gunman, still clutching a sub-machine gun, gasped on his belly in the middle of the street. He'd been at the edge of the area the projectiles cleared. Blood from a dozen pellet wounds pooled the pavement around him. The blast had stripped his clothes off. There was a ragged wound where his penis and scrotum should have been.

Vierziger glanced at Coke. Coke nodded. Vierziger shot the L'Escorial behind the ear, then reholstered his pistol. Coke blinked at the speed and smoothness of the motion.

Most of the gunmen's bodies lay against the wall fronting the L'Escorial compound. A L'Escorial wearing oil-stained coveralls and a short helmet—one of the armored truck's crew—ran out the open gateway. He gaped at the carnage.

Coke pointed his powergun at the L'Escorial and shouted, "Hold it!"

The L'Escorial carried a pistol in a shoulder holster where it would be out of the way aboard his vehicle, but he seemed to have forgotten he was armed. He didn't look so much frightened as dumbfounded, like a man who'd met a talking dog.

Holding his weapon with the muzzle pointed but the stock in the crook of his arm, Coke walked over to the L'Escorial. More gunmen scampered into and out of sight through the gateway. Nobody else left the courtyard. The armored vehicle's engine roared to life, then stalled with a clang as an inexperienced driver tried to operate it.

Coke lifted the muzzle of his 2-cm weapon. He reached into his purse with his left hand and removed a business card, which he stuck between the L'Escorial's pistol and its holster.

The card read:

MAJOR MATTHEW COKE

Frisian Defense Forces

Representative

The chip embedded within the card would project his image and description through a hologram reader.

"Go on back inside," Coke ordered. "Tell your leaders that we didn't come here to have a problem. We're here to do business on behalf of our principals, and that'll be *very* good business for the side that strikes the deal. Do you understand?"

The L'Escorial stared at the shoulder weapon, not at the man holding it. His eyes were wild, and he gave no indication of having heard a thing Coke had said.

Coke sighed. There was such a thing as making a demonstration *too* effective.

He put his left hand on the gunman's shoulder and rotated the fellow to face L'Escorial headquarters. "Go on," he said. "Tell your bosses that this just involved a few individuals—it wasn't important."

Coke pushed the man gently. The L'Escorial stumbled, then broke into a shambling run around the gatepost and out of sight.

Coke turned, though it made his skin crawl to do so. Backing away from the red-painted structure would have sent a signal of weakness to the gunmen certainly watching through firing slits in the upper floor of the building.

The street was a smear of blood and pulped organs. It reflected the light of advertising signs. Coke's bootheels shimmied as he stepped. He felt dizzy, and the stench of disemboweled corpses made him want to vomit.

A few of the bodies which the mines slammed against the courtyard wall were still alive, at least technically. Coke didn't want to think about that. There was nothing he could do now if he wanted to. He wasn't a medic.

He was a killer, no more and surely no less.

May the Lord give them rest; and may there be rest for the slayer, in his time.

The team, all but Barbour—visible through the open door at his console—waited outside Hathaway House for Coke's return. Daun blinked in amazement and a certain distaste. Moden and Margulies, the combat veterans, were grimly silent.

Johann Vierziger smiled.

"I gave a card to a citizen to deliver up the street, Matthew," Vierziger said in his liquid voice. He gestured with an open hand toward where the Astra cordon had been. The mine blasts brought the blue-clad gunmen running a few steps toward the scene, then scurrying back into their compound to take stock. "Now what?"

"Now," said Matthew Coke, "you await developments here, and I take care of some personal business."

Coke stepped into the lobby of Hathaway House. He was shaking. He hadn't done anything to burn off the adrenaline with which his body had pumped itself in preparation for fight or flight.

The Hathaways stood with arms entwined about one another's shoulders and their other hands linked at waist level. Georg was blank-faced. Evie's expression was one of slowly dawning joy.

The three men from the saloon now stood in the broad archway where the alcove joined the lobby. One of the policemen opened and closed his mouth like a fish gasping silently on the dock. The third man, a civilian whose ragged clothing had once been of good quality, still carried his drink. He didn't look particularly interested, in the carnage or in anything else.

Coke tossed the 2-cm weapon to Margulies. She caught it at the balance. He still had a pistol in a belt holster beneath his jacket.

He thought of taking off the armored vest, but after a moment he decided not to waste the time. "You," he said to a policeman. "Does that shock baton work? Give it to me."

"Huh?"

Vierziger stepped behind the man and slid the fifty-centimeter rod from its sheath.

"Hey!" the policeman cried. He and his partner jumped in opposite directions sideways, as though the little killer's presence were a bomb going off between them. "Look, what are you—"

Vierziger switched the baton's power on. He touched the tip of the slim rod to the inside of his own left forearm. The powerful fluctuating current crossed nerve pathways and flung his arm violently out to the side.

He smiled again, turned off the power, and tossed the baton to Coke. "Fully charged," he said.

Coke slid the baton beneath his waistband. "You'll get it back," he said to the policeman. Half his face grinned. "Or somebody will pay you for it."

He looked at Moden. "Sten, you're in charge till I return," Coke said. "I don't expect potential employers to react that quickly, but if they do, set up a meeting for tomorrow."

He touched his brow with one finger in a wry salute. "See you soon," he said, and started for the door.

Margulies fell into step with him. "I'm coming," she said.

Johann Vierziger shook his head. "Three can be a crowd, Mary," he said in his cultured, mocking voice. "Matthew will probably be all right. . . and besides, as he says, it's a personal matter."

"Three?" said Niko Daun. Margulies nodded, turned, and leaned the extra shoulder weapon against the wall beside the door.

Barbour looked up from his console. "I'll be tracking," he said. If there had been any more emotion in the statement, it would have been a challenge.

Coke laughed out loud. The whole team thought he was behaving like an idiot—but he'd earned the right a few minutes before to do that. The *whole* team, himself included.

"See you soon," he repeated, and he stepped out into night fetid with death.

Scores, perhaps as many as two hundred, L'Escorial gunmen clustered around the windrow of bodies in front of their compound. An armored truck—not the one that had appeared before, but a similar design—illuminated the scene with its quartet of bumper-mounted headlights. One man sat cross-legged on the top of the wall, holding a liquid-fueled lamp, and other gunmen waved a variety of electrical handlights.

There wasn't much effort spent on caring for the wounded, assuming some of the victims were still alive. For the most part the L'Escorials stared, sometimes calling in wonderment. The sight appeared to touch them no more than a particularly vivid traffic accident would have done.

Coke expected the L'Escorials to react to him, perhaps to try to stop him. None of them seemed to notice that he'd left Hathaway House. The pool of light over the bodies acted as a curtain shrouding everything beyond the direct illumination.

A crowd of spectators aggregated quickly now that civilians realized the syndicate gunmen would pay them little attention. Coke noticed that a number of the onlookers covered blue garb with cloaks of neutral gray: Astras who wanted to see what was going on without themselves becoming causes of war.

Coke walked quickly up the street to where Pilar Ortega had abandoned the port operations van. Three filthy locals were in the vehicle now. One of them was trying to shoot something into his thigh with a homemade hypodermic. The injector's barrel was a hundred-centimeter length of hose.

The staircase to the flophouse Pilar entered was helical and of engineering-grade plastic extrusion. It had been salvaged from a starship. Despite hard use and lack of maintenance, the structure itself was solid and safe.

The stair's only attachment to the building was looped wire between it and external tubing—water pipes, electrical conduits, and a downspout from the gutter. The wire was of no particular type or strength. Baling wire alternated with insulated power cable and what looked like glass-core data transmission line.

The helix wobbled at Coke's every step and from any breeze or tremor. He didn't suppose it was going to collapse under him—and he could probably ride it down if it *did* break away; the staircase itself was plenty sturdy enough.

But it put the butterflies back in the pit of Coke's stomach.

The bum who'd been sprawled on the stairs when Pilar climbed them had vanished. Another man now lay halfway up, weeping uncontrollably and holding an almost-full bottle of clear fluid.

Coke entered clean locked beds, the building's fifth level. The salvaged staircase rose another two meters, but there was no doorway opening onto it from the level above.

The end of a counter protected by a hundred-millimeter mesh of barbed wire narrowed the doorway to half its designed width. A bar with a barbed wire apron closed the other half to prevent anyone from bursting into or out of the flophouse, though Coke wasn't sure why either should have been a problem.

No one was behind the counter; the gate into the flophouse proper stood open. The sign on the back wall read:

SPACE 5
BUNK 10
SOLO BUNK 25
LOCK 25

A board from which hung a dozen cheap keyed padlocks indicated the protection you got for the extra twenty-five pesos. Sten Moden could probably have twisted the barrels off their hasps… but men as fit and strong as Sten Moden didn't spend the night in a flop like this.

Coke raised the bar carefully and walked into the establishment. He'd had full immunization treatments before he left Nieuw Friesland, but there was no point in testing Frisian medical science against the filth that lurked on those rusty barbs.

The flophouse filled the entire level, an area of about ten meters by twenty. It was lighted by glow-strips, scraped and speckled but still able to provide a reasonable amount of yellow-green illumination. The good lighting was probably a safety feature—for the building's owners as much as for the staff and clientele.

A narrow aisle separated two banks of cubicles. Each contained a filthy mattress. Instead of solid panels, the cubicles had walls of coarse barbed wire netting.

The remainder of the flophouse was bare floor on which the lower grade of derelict sprawled and shivered and moaned. Twenty-odd were present tonight; varied in age and sex, but uniform in their utter degradation.

Something was going on toward the back of the big room. Men clustered around one of the cages, shouting and laughing in cracked voices.

Coke's face became still. He slid the shock rod from his waistband with his left hand and strode quietly down the aisle.

About half the cubicles he passed were occupied. Some of the men—few were women—in them were lost in their own worlds. Empty stim cones or cruder injectors lay on the mattresses with them.

One man was bent in a tetanic arch. His eyes bulged and his face was purple. Coke was pretty sure the fellow was dead, broken in convulsions by the wrong dose of gage tailings, but the fact impressed him as little as it did the flop's ordinary denizens.

Other caged occupants called or even tried to grab Coke as he strode by. None of them was coordinated enough to actually touch the Frisian. They didn't necessarily see him. The drugs and drug impurities with which they'd injected themselves were capable of turning any movement into a wild hallucination.

Pilar Ortega was in an end stall. She stood erect with her arms clamping her over-wrap to her, as if by squeezing hard enough she could make herself vanish. Her eyes were wide open, but she didn't see Coke coming down the aisle toward her.

Seven or eight men gripped the mesh of the cubicle. One of them was the clerk who should have been behind the counter. They had all dropped their pants. They waved their penises at the woman as they jeered.

The clerk was a fat man, completely hairless. He wore a sleeveless black pullover, his overalls pooled around his ankles. As Coke approached, unnoticed in the drug-fueled hilarity, the clerk reached down into his trousers and came up with a key.

"Lookie what I got, Miz Fancypants!" he cried in a voice pitched higher than the size of his gross body suggested. "You think you rented the only key to your lock, did you?"

"Yeah, I wanna *see* them pants!" the man beside him cried. "I'll bite them—"

Coke whipped his shock rod across the bare buttocks of the four men directly before him.

The men screamed as they leaped convulsively into the wire. The cubicle swayed, but its steel-tube frame was strong enough to withstand the impacts. The men at either end of the cage, untouched by Coke's quick sweep, looked around in surprise, all but one fellow crooning and drooling in his own private dreamworld.

The clerk turned. He bled from a score of fresh punctures and gashes scattered from forehead to mid-thigh. "You—" he shouted.

Coke flicked the clerk with the baton, this time on the lower belly just above his genitals. Flailing limbs hurled the clerk against Pilar's cage a second time. The structure's resilience threw him facedown on the floor. Coke stepped aside to let him fall.

A derelict raised the jagged top of a bottle. Coke held his right arm crooked to the side. His hand hovered over the butt of his holstered pistol. To draw, he would shift his hips left while his hand swept aside the tail of his jacket. He wasn't Johann Vierziger, but it was a maneuver he'd made many times before....

"Try me," he offered in a trembling voice.

The derelict dropped the bottle. He backed into the wall and pushed himself flat against it.

"All of you," Coke said. "Out ahead of me." He eased into an empty cubicle, permitting the men to pass without touching him. "Pilar, open your door and come out. It's all right now."

The clerk was whimpering. He paused on hands and knees to draw up his overalls.

"Did I tell you to do that?" Coke screamed. He lashed the clerk's buttocks again, reaching from the cage to take a full swing with the shock baton. The *whack!* and blue spark flashed terror across the derelicts' countenances.

"Go on! *Move!*"

The group shuffled and stumbled out, fettered as Coke intended by their dragging trousers; all but the wide-eyed fellow mumbling in his reverie about Maureen. Coke let him be.

Pilar came out of the cubicle. Her face was as still as that of a woman in shock, but her eyes moved febrilely.

"It's all right," Coke repeated. He touched Pilar's shoulder to guide her down the aisle. "Ahead of me," he said.

He walked in lock-step behind the woman, reaching past her with the shock baton. Someone groped from a cage despite the warning. The baton's charge snapped him like the popper on a bullwhip into his cubicle's walls.

The clerk and the gang behind him had shuffled to the counter at the front of the room. "Stop!" Coke ordered.

The men cringed as they obeyed. The features of most of them would have looked leprous even under better lighting than that of the glow-strips.

"Now," Coke said. "Return the lady's money." In a gentler voice he added, "You paid fifty pesos?"

"Please *God* the money doesn't matter!" Pilar said, clutching the crucifix beneath her cape.

"That's not the point," Coke said. "You bastards! Make it a hundred pesos. Now!"

"But I can't," the clerk wheezed. His tears diluted the line of blood trickling down his cheek from the gouge in his forehead. "I *can't* get into the cashbox, only Master Delzine can open it!"

The box was a massive canister—too massive for a support structure as flimsy as the upper floors of this building—strapped beneath the counter. The inlet was a doubly-kinked tube with one-way gates, proof against any but the most sophisticated methods of drawing coins back along it. The clerk could hold out the clientele's fees, if he wanted to risk the owner's spot checks; but he couldn't retrieve money once dropped into the box.

"All right," Coke said. "Make it up yourselves. A hundred pesos."

"The money doesn't—" Pilar repeated.

"Shut up!" Coke snarled. "They're paying for what they did. Or else they'll do it again!"

The men squatted to rummage in their fallen trousers. Coke drew a figure-8 with his shock baton, touching the tip to cage supports on both sides of the motion. The sparks snapped loudly in the nervous silence.

Two of the men took off their shoes. The clerk, who'd found only ten pesos thus far, came up with an additional fifty-peso coin.

The money lay in a ragged pile between Pilar and the men. Coke couldn't tell exactly how much there was; and anyway, the amount didn't really matter, Pilar was right there, though the principle mattered.

"All right," Coke ordered. "Head down to the street, all of you. Get going!"

He wasn't going to leave any of this lot ten meters above him. Maybe none of them could throw straight, but all they needed to do was get lucky with one brick or bottle. They shambled and crab-walked out the doorway.

Pilar relaxed so completely that Coke was afraid she'd fainted. He caught her. Her body was warm and trembling.

"I'm all right," she murmured, but it was a moment before she stepped forward. She bent, scooped the money into a pocket of her cape, and edged past the counter.

The men were partway down the staircase. The clerk had hiked up his overalls. When he saw Coke appear at the doorway above him, he dropped the garment again and hopped downward, holding the railing with both hands. The structure jounced violently. Several of the derelicts lost their footing. Half sliding, half stumbling, they made their way to the street.

Five steps up, Coke shut off the baton and slid it beneath his waistband again. When he moved, the men watching could see his holster, not that any of them had doubted it.

"I didn't bring you here to shoot you," Coke said in harsh, ringing tones. "But if I can see any of you thirty seconds from now, I *will* shoot him. Go!"

The clerk and derelicts stumbled into the traffic, pedestrians, and jitneys that had resumed when the syndicate cordons terminated at the mine blast. Coke took a deep breath. His knees wobbled. He held the rail firmly in his left hand as he followed Pilar down the remaining steps.

"You wouldn't really shoot them, would you?" she asked.

"They're gone," Coke said, avoiding the question. "It doesn't matter now."

He massaged his left forearm with the fingers of his right hand. He'd been gripping the shock baton hard, harder than he'd realized until just now when he suddenly felt the ache.

"Look," he said, "is your husband at home? I can take you there. Or we can get you a room in the Hathaway House; it seems to be a nice place. Like you said, a decent place."

Pilar shook her head. "I'll go home," she said. "I'll be all right, now."

She looked toward her van. She noticed the heads of bums silhouetted against the unglazed windows. Coke offered his left arm to her right hand.

"No problem," he said, whisking his tongue across the syllables like a blade over a whetstone. He walked beside Pilar toward the vehicle, flexing his left hand to be sure that it would obey his needs.

"Terry won't be home," the woman said stiffly. Her fingers lay in the crook of his elbow, light contact but warm nonetheless. "He's found quite a number of friends here since he learned to shake the money tree."

"He's smuggling, you mean?" Coke said. His tone counterfeited the sort of polite interest that he thought was appropriate to the statement. Below the surface, his mind considered alternatives with the icy logic of a bridge player assessing his hand.

Pilar stopped. A sailor walking behind them cursed as she blocked his path. Coke drew his pistol and pointed it without a word. The sailor started back and jogged across the street.

Coke reholstered the weapon. "Sorry," he murmured to Pilar.

"You work for the Confederacy?" she said tightly. She stood as though her feet had grown through the cracked pavement. "You're investigating port duties?"

"Not us," Coke said easily. "From what I've heard thus far, we're out of business if the Marvelan Confederacy learns that we're here."

By taking Pilar's hand in his, he made her meet his eyes. In a more sober tone than before he added, "We're with the Frisian Defense Forces."

"Oh," the woman said. The datum fell into place. "Oh!"

"We're not maybe the best thing that could happen to Cantilucca," Coke said, still looking directly at her though her eyes had lifted away. "But we're better than what I've seen here so far."

Pilar gave him a bitter smile. "Sometimes I think the best thing that could happen to Potosi, at least, would be a fusion bomb," she said.

Coke squeezed her hand. He stepped to the van, reached in through the window, and dragged one of the occupants out by the throat. The local squawked after Coke flung him on the pavement. He didn't say anything before he hit the ground, because the Frisian's fingers gripped too tightly to pass the sound.

The remaining two bums bleated. They slid to the other side of the open compartment. Instead of reaching for them, Coke pointed his pistol at the left member of the pair.

"You have five seconds," Coke said. "One. Two."

The local jumped up and stuck his head and torso out of the far window. Coke shifted his weapon's centimeter bore toward the other derelict. "Three. Four."

The local tried unsuccessfully to rise. His limbs were spastic with fear. He seemed afraid to turn and face the opening.

Coke pointed the gun muzzle sideways and said, "Go on, you're all right, I'll give you the time."

The local thumped out into the street and began crawling after his fellow. He was moaning about his bottle, but the only bottle the trio had left in the van was empty.

Pilar stood close beside Coke. "You're very direct," she said in a voice too neutral to be disinterested.

"Yeah," Coke said. He looked at her again. "What you see is what you get."

Pilar smiled wistfully. "No," she said, "I'm afraid that what *I* get is something else again. Perhaps I should have seen it, but I was younger then."

She opened the door of the van. The ignition card clinked against the handle. "Thank you very much, Master Coke. I—I appreciate what you've done. I'd invite you home for a drink, but people might get the wrong impression."

Her face hardened. "And it would *be* the wrong impression."

Coke bowed formally. He wore a half smile.

Pilar suddenly leaned close and kissed him on the cheek. Then she was in the van, shutting the door needlessly hard.

Coke watched her drive away. He was smiling more broadly now. Someone watching him might have noticed the similarity of the expression to that which Johann Vierziger wore after killing.

The remaining five members of the survey team waited for a moment after Major

Matthew Coke walked out of Hathaway House with a pistol and a commandeered shock baton. Georg Hathaway started to close the heavy front door. Margulies touched the innkeeper's arm to stop him.

Hathaway glanced around. The four Frisians besides Barbour stood in a concave arc, facing out the doorway so that among them they watched a hundred meters of the streetscape. All of them held weapons.

"Oh," Hathaway said. "Oh. I wasn't thinking of that."

Margulies nodded without replying, and without ever taking her eyes off the amazed clot of L'Escorials across the street. Her left hand returned to rest lightly on the foregrip of her sub-machine gun.

"There," Vierziger said with a slight relaxation of the drumhead tautness beneath his insouciant exterior. "He's clear of anything we can do—unless we want to follow him."

"Which we do not," Moden said. He set down the missile launcher with care. The weapon he carried comfortably was so heavy that if it dropped, the shock would seriously damage it.

"There's no organization," Barbour offered. He had directional audio from the spectators across the street, as well as a holographic view sharper than that of the others' naked eyes. "People run inside saying they're going to report to Raul or to the Old Man, but they don't come back with any orders."

"Raul Luria is head of L'Escorial," said Georg Hathaway. "With his son Ramon, and Ramon's son Pepe."

"Pepe is a weasel," Evie said in clipped tones. She looked at the Frisians and added, "We have rooms prepared for you. You'll share baths; I hope that's all right. But surely you'd like something to eat or drink?"

It was hard to read her expression. The sudden destruction of a dozen gunmen had opened a window on the woman's mind, but its interior was still thick with the dust of long depression.

"I wouldn't mind something to drink," Niko Daun said clearly. "You say you've got local cacao?"

"And I think I'll have a beer or two," Sten Moden added, quirking the younger man a smile. "It's been a long day. Not that it's over yet."

"Here, I'll serve you gentlemen," Georg said. "And lady of course. Evie, I wish you wouldn't say things like that, you know, in public. Though Pepe's off Cantilucca now, I believe."

The local patrons had returned to the alcove in which they'd been drinking. Vierziger walked to the table of the third man, the civilian, and said, "Good day, sir. My name is Johann Vierziger, and I'm a sergeant with the Frisian Defense Forces. May I ask who you are?"

The fellow looked up. His face was handsome in a hollow-cheeked fashion, but there was a gray glaze over him that was more an aura than skin tone.

"My name's Larrinaga," he said. He was younger than he looked; thirty years standard at the most. "And I'm nothing, that's who I am."

"Pedro's had a difficult time this past year," Georg said; half-confiding, half in an attempt to forestall the wrath of the little stranger who made him *very* uncomfortable to watch. "His wife died. She was an artist in psychic ambiances, a very fine one, known all across the galaxy."

"Really?" said Niko Daun. "I've worked in PAs myself. Who was she? The wife."

His tone wasn't precisely dismissive, but there was a challenge in it. Daun didn't regard himself as a top PA artist, but he didn't expect to find a better one on this wretched planet.

Hathaway drew drinks. Larrinaga looked up and said, "My wife was Suzette. That was her working name. She was a saint. And there'll never be an artist like her. Never in all time!"

"Suzette was from here?" Daun blurted. "Blood and martyrs!"

Margulies raised an eyebrow in the direction of the sensor tech.

Daun turned his palms up. "She's—" he said. "Well there's taste. But the best PA artist in the galaxy, yeah, you can make a case for it. I'm amazed…. Well, I didn't think she'd have come from a place so…"

He looked at Larrinaga, who was staring morosely into his beer mug. "Suzette's work is so tranquil, you see," Daun said. "It's not what I'd expect coming from Cantilucca. From Potosi, anyhow."

Georg handed out beverages in rough-glazed ceramic mugs of local manufacture. The beer, for all his praises of it, had an oily undertaste that Moden found unpleasant. He'd drunk worse in the field, wine that had rotted rather than fermenting properly… and there were worse things in life than bad booze.

Daun sipped his mug of frothy, bitter, cacao drink with approval. His lips pursed as he considered Larrinaga and the situation. A Tech 4's pay didn't run to art the like of Suzette's, but there was always the chance…

"I wonder," he said, "if there's any of your wife's work still on Cantilucca? Some minor pieces, perhaps, that—"

The local man clutched his empty mug with both hands. He began to cry. He made a convulsive gesture that would have swept the mug against the wall to shatter.

Vierziger, who was standing arm's length away and didn't seem to be watching, caught the mug in the air. He set it on the serving counter.

Larrinaga lurched up from his seat. "I'm going to go piss," he said. He angrily wiped his eyes with his forearm. "That's fair, isn't it? I've pissed my life away!"

"Pedro?" Hathaway said. "Can I show them the draft? It's not the same, but they'll get the idea."

"Do what you please," Larrinaga called as he left the alcove.

"He leaves it here," the innkeeper explained as he opened a cabinet beneath the serving counter. "He doesn't have a place of his own anymore."

Margulies returned to the saloon alcove. She'd taken a beer to Barbour at his console. "Trouble with the gangs?" she guessed aloud. "They robbed him?"

"Well, not quite that," Georg said. "You see, when Suzette died, Pedro sold his house to the factor of Trans-Star Trading on Cantilucca. His name's Suterbilt."

"Suterbilt is a criminal," Evie said from the lobby. She sat in an upholstered chair, knitting as her eyes stared into time. "He's no better than the thugs he bankrolls."

"Now, Evie, you know we shouldn't say things like that," Georg said. "But Suterbilt has, well, a financial stake in L'Escorial. That's personal, not TST."

The innkeeper was setting up a table-model hologram projector. Niko moved to help him. The unit had a lot of flash and glitter, but it looked clumsy compared to the trim projectors in use on Nieuw Friesland.

"So a shotgun sale?" Margulies pressed. The story would probably come out, from Mistress Hathaway if not from her husband, but Margulies didn't want to wait.

"Not that either," Georg said. He obviously felt uncomfortable speaking about the gunmen and their masters, though the chance to gossip with *these* folk had attraction as well.

"Not really, at least," he continued. "Pedro had been taking a lot of gage, mostly gage, because he'd loved Suzette so much. He wouldn't have sold at all if he hadn't been, well, if he'd been in better condition. Because Suzette's greatest masterpiece is a part of the home where they'd lived, you see."

"And then he lost the money," Evie added harshly. "He was drugged *silly*, and he gambled, and he lost every peso of the price."

"The price had been a good one, though," her husband said quickly. "Master Suterbilt didn't cheat him, not really, since the art can't be moved and its value's only what it's worth on Cantilucca."

"Suterbilt didn't cheat him in the notary's office, you mean," Evie said. "He left that job for his friends at the roulette table."

Her fingers clicked the needles with mechanical precision. Moden thought of the old women watching the guillotine; and realized for the first time how much, and how rightly, they had hated the aristocrats being beheaded.

"Why can't the PA be moved?" Daun asked in surprise.

"What?" said Georg. "Because it's built into the fabric of the room, sir. You'd destroy the whole thing to try to move it."

The technician frowned. He didn't argue, but it was obvious that he couldn't understand the problem.

"There," said Hathaway. "Watch this. It's the holographic draft Suzette did before she created the ambiance itself."

He dimmed the alcove lights. The policemen were watching from their table. Larrinaga reappeared from the rest room. He stood in the archway instead of reentering the saloon.

A psychic ambiance was just that, a recorded vision—a waking dream—capable of being transferred to recipients in the focal area. It couldn't be copied, because it depended on inputs too subtle to survive the duplication process. Though the PA was immaterial, the artist normally started with a visual or auditory sketch, just as medieval fresco artists drew cartoons on the wall before applying a coat of fresh plaster on which to fix the paint.

Suzette worked visually. The holographic sketch was of a verdant paradise, a mythic place in which fountains played and the geologic features seemed themselves alive though immobile.

No animals could be glimpsed, though the movement of plants hinted their presence. Above all, the shifting holographic image was suffused by light and a warmth for which the objects described could not themselves account.

The sketch began to repeat itself. The second time through, individual facets merged into a whole greater and quite different from its parts.

Daun frowned. He could *almost* grasp the unity to which the intersections of light beams were building in this holographic shorthand.

"It's her, you know," Larrinaga said abruptly. "It's Suzette. She did a self-portrait, she built it into our house so that I'd never have had to be without her. And I threw it away!"

He began to weep openly. Georg Hathaway shut off the chip projector; Margulies brought the lights back up. Though Hathaway House was a fortress, the bright internal illumination prevented the weight of the protective walls from crushing the souls of those within it.

"There, there, Pedro," Georg said awkwardly. "Maybe I shouldn't have done that. I know it bothers you."

"Everything bothers him," Evie said, knitting with tiny clicks unaffected by her words. "It's Pedro's life now, being bothered."

"It's still possible to see the PA, isn't it?" Niko asked, looking from Georg to Larrinaga and quickly away again.

Hathaway pursed his lips. He started to say something, then glanced toward the archway.

"Can I have another beer, Georg?" Larrinaga asked. "It'll have to be on credit, of course."

"Why of course, Pedro," Hathaway said enthusiastically. "You're not a patron here, you're our friend."

He gestured Larrinaga toward the serving counter instead of drawing the mug himself. A transaction had taken place, and everyone within earshot knew it.

As Larrinaga stepped past him, head bowed, Hathaway said, "The ambiance can only be viewed with Master Suterbilt's permission, and that's hard to come by. He's aware of its value, you see. He keeps—well, there are six L'Escorial, ah, security personnel in the house at all times. Suterbilt doesn't live there, but he visits frequently."

"The last time I went there and asked to see Suzette," Larrinaga said with his back to the others in the saloon, "they beat me unconscious and left me in the street."

He drank in order to create a pause for effect. "I think," he resumed, "I'll go back there tonight."

"Yes, I suspect you *will* do that," Johann Vierziger said in a voice like the purr of a well-fed leopard. He set down the mug of cacao from which he'd been sipping with evident approval. "It's the sort of thing a worthless bastard would do, after all."

The little man's enunciation was so precise that it was a moment before the words themselves registered on the others. Daun stifled a snort of laughter. Margulies raised an eyebrow; Sten Moden pointedly failed to react.

"Sure I am," Larrinaga said loudly. "You bet, that's just what I am."

"Oh, you mustn't say that, sir!" Georg Hathaway blurted. "Pedro isn't that at all. You don't know what he's like inside!"

"Nor do you, Master Hathaway," Vierziger said with sneering intonation. "All we know is the side he shows the world. That side is a sniveling, self-pitying bastard."

The words wouldn't have cut as deep if there'd been emotion behind them instead of cold disdain. Larrinaga winced as though he'd been stroked with a barbed whip. The mug trembled. He set it down and walked to the outer door.

Barbour looked at the local man, calculating the door's opening against the movements of figures in his holographic display. There was no need to keep the armored door closed; but there might have been, and Barbour would have said so if there were.

The door closed behind Larrinaga. "Oh, I wish you hadn't said that, good sir," Hathaway murmured miserably, though he didn't look directly at Vierziger as he spoke.

"Why, Georg?" Evie Hathaway demanded. "Does the truth bother you so much? Has saying, 'Oh, Pedro just needs a little time to get straightened out,' made things better? For anybody?"

"Well, he blames himself for having sold the house," Georg said. "And it was Pedro's fault, I know, partying with Master Suterbilt who'd been trying for years to buy the ambiance and Suzette wouldn't hear of selling to him. But it's a shame that one mistake should ruin his life."

"The major's coming back," Barbour called from the foyer. He looked toward the policemen and grinned. It was the first smile any of his teammates had seen on his face. "He's returning your shock baton, gentlemen."

"One mistake can ruin more than a man's life, Master Hathaway," Vierziger said to the innkeeper. "It can ruin all eternity."

He smiled tightly, terribly. "Of course, I've made many more mistakes than one."

Coke entered the lobby. He closed the door behind him, then rested his back against the cool metal surface.

"Any excitement, sir?" Margulies asked.

"Matthew, please, Mary," Coke said with his eyes closed. "And no, nothing to speak of. The usual run of port-city foolishness, nothing serious."

"What's the next order of business, Matthew?" Moden asked. "We continue to wait?"

"I could use one of those beers," Coke said, snapping alert again. He strode into the saloon alcove. From there he continued, "Yeah, we wait. I figure it'll be days before either side makes an approach. Two gangs may make this a tough place, but it sure isn't an organized one."

"Is organized better, Master Soldier?" Evie Hathaway demanded from her chair.

"Evie, *please*," said Georg.

"Yes, ma'am," Coke said, taking the mug the innkeeper had drawn him. "It is. Highly developed parasites see to it that the host body stays healthy. Less developed ones, roundworms and the like, are often fatal. Cantilucca has a bad case of round-worms, I'm afraid."

"And your prescription?" the woman said. She'd stopped knitting so that she could turn to look directly at the Frisian leader.

Coke drank, then shrugged. "Arsenic or the equivalent, Mistress Hathaway," he said. "The trick is to titrate the dose, of course, so that you only get the worms."

"In the short term, Matthew," Mary Margulies said, "would you have any objection to me doing a little sight-seeing in the countryside? Tomorrow, maybe?"

Coke shook his head "No, we need to learn as much about the place as we can," he said. "Potosi may be the head of the planet, but it's not the whole place. Ah—I'd rather you didn't go any distance alone."

"I'll go along, sir," Robert Barbour said. "That is, if you'll permit me. I'll have the AI in this console dialed in to take care of ordinary business in an hour or two, now that you're back."

"No, that's fine," Coke said "Just remember, we're in a fluid situation. Things might happen pretty fast. And I'm *Matthew*."

"My old driver came back here when he got out of service," Margulies explained. "He came from a place called Silva Blanca. It's supposed to be fifteen klicks away."

"Good," said Coke. He handed his mug to Hathaway for a refill. "It'll be good to get a professional's viewpoint about the situation here."

"I'm not sure there's enough arsenic, Master Soldier," Evie Hathaway said. She had resumed knitting. "Certainly there can't be too much."

CANTILUCCA: DAY TWO

The messenger at the door of Hathaway House flashed his gray cloak open toward the viewslit, displaying a blue uniform jacket with chromed buttons and frogs. By trying to look simultaneously self-important and inconspicuous, the man gave the impression of a rat tricked out in pheasant plumage.

"A lady wants to see Major Coke!" he hissed meaningfully, casting a wary glance over his shoulder toward L'Escorial headquarters.

Coke nodded toward Mistress Hathaway at the door. He was shrugging into his body armor. The location of Hathaway House wasn't ideally neutral, but the team hadn't been sent to Cantilucca to be fair. Just to strike a deal, and that seemed to be a practical proposition.

"A bit earlier than I'd figured," Coke said to his three fellows. "Niko, you're ready on your end?"

The sensor tech grinned brightly. He patted a magazine pouch on the right side of his waist belt, opposite the holster clipped for cross-draw.

"The bugs're here," he said, "not in my case." He waggled the attaché case in his left hand.

"Sten, you're comfortable with the hardware?" Coke went on, shifting his attention to the man who would remain behind in the hotel lobby.

"Quite comfortable," the logistics officer said. His arm swept across the terminal, changing the display from streetscape to a close-up of the Astra messenger's face, then back. "This isn't my specialty, but I've probably spent as much time at consoles as you or Bob have."

"Come *on*," the messenger whined. "Do you think I like standing out here?"

"Do you think we care?" Niko Daun snapped. The suddenness with which the young technician's smile broke and reformed indicated that he was jumpy, reasonably enough.

Johann Vierziger grinned at Coke. Neither man bothered to speak the obvious truths.

Coke settled a gray cape over his armor, his attaché case, and a slung sub-machine gun. "All right," he said. "Then let's do it."

The messenger scampered ahead. He was probably afraid to be seen with the trio of Frisians. It was late morning and the sun was hot. L'Escorials had removed the wrack of bodies from against their wall, but the stench of rotting blood was fierce even against the reek of garbage and human excrement.

The gates to the L'Escorial courtyard, vertical steel bars in a wall-height framework, were closed. Half a dozen gunmen sat beneath an awning inside, playing cards. The concrete around the titular guards was littered with gage injectors and empty bottles. None of the men paid any attention to traffic from Hathaway House.

The messenger was ten strides ahead of the Frisians. He turned around and waggled his hands toward them in a pulling motion. "Come on, come along," he urged.

"We'll get there, little man," Johann Vierziger said calmly. "And the more surely if we watch what we're about, not so?"

Though the messenger wasn't a prepossessing physical specimen, he was bigger than Vierziger. Nobody hearing the comment smiled at it, however.

A combat vehicle converted from a bulldozer was now parked in the entrance to the courtyard in front of Astra headquarters. Metal plates were welded to a framework around the bulldozer's sides.

The add-on armor didn't look to Coke as if it'd stop much. The earthmoving blade which protected the front would originally have been tempered soft so that it wouldn't shatter if it hit a rock. The alloy steel *could* have been surface hardened during the conversion process, but he doubted that it had been.

The vehicle mounted a twelve-tube launcher for hypervelocity rockets. These could be extremely effective weapons, capable of penetrating more than a meter of ferroconcrete; but the mounting was fixed in azimuth, so that aiming a salvo required the vehicle itself be turned toward the target.

The messenger led the Frisians past the 'dozer's worn tracks. Astras on the vehicle and around it had their guns out. None of them spoke to the Frisians, but Coke heard several deliberately loud sneers about the pansies come to call. At least the blue-clad guards seemed to be more alert than their rivals down the street.

"The Widow's waiting for you, gentlemen," the messenger called, several strides ahead again. "*Do* come along."

Niko Daun stumbled twice while easing past the converted bulldozer. The first time he slapped his hand against the armor covering the commander's station on the right side of the vehicle; the next time he caught himself on the gatepost. He'd touched his belt pouch before either slip, but there was nothing noteworthy in that.

The sensor tech patted the jamb of the doorway into the headquarters building as well. Each time his hand touched, he left behind an irregular disk of self-adhering material, as unremarkable as a splash of clear lacquer. Each palm-sized swatch contained an audio pick-up and transmitter, powered by micro-flexions in the crystalline structure of its matrix material.

Though not precisely invisible, the bugs appeared to be merely areas of random gloss to anyone but an expert looking for them. Cantilucca wasn't a place where the survey team expected to find expert sensor technicians.

The front half of the ground floor was a single room, thronged now by fifty or sixty blue-clad gunmen. Men in full uniform formed a corridor, not quite a gauntlet, between the outer door and the inner one in the partition wall at the back. Astras in less formal attire were relegated to stand behind the elite.

Vierziger led. Daun, with another bug palmed and waiting, walked behind him, and Coke brought up the rear. The air stank of nervous sweat.

"These are the tough guys?" sneered a man as big as Sten Moden. A scar twisted up his cheek and forehead, filling one eyesocket with a mass of pink tissue. "Don't look much to me!"

"Now, boys, the Widow wants to see them," the messenger pleaded.

"This one looks like a fairy!" cried a man carrying a sub-machine gun and a slung grenade launcher. He reached out to pinch Vierziger's cheek.

Coke lifted his hand into the air, visible to everyone in the big room. Simultaneously, Vierziger's light cape ballooned as his arm moved.

The muzzle of Vierziger's chased and carven pistol bloodied the Astra's lips. The fellow yelped in surprise and would have lurched backward. The men behind hemmed him in too straitly to move.

"Does he indeed, my friend?" Vierziger said in a lilting whisper. "That's not surprising, is it? Since he is a fairy. Do you have a problem with that?"

The little killer punctuated each sentence by tapping his pistol forward, hard enough to chip the Astra's teeth. Blood smeared the iridium barrel.

Coke said nothing. His hand held the fat tube of a bunker buster. The grenade's red safety tab was lifted, and only the Frisian's index finger held down the arming spoon.

"Do you?" Vierziger's pistol lifted so that the muzzle centered on the Astra's right eye.

"No sir. *No sir!*"

"Just as well, isn't it?" Vierziger said conversationally. He tugged out the Astra's shirt with his left hand and wiped the pistol clean with it. The weapon vanished as suddenly as it had been drawn.

Coke put the live grenade back under his cape. Vierziger walked to the inner door. The corridor between the Astra lines was half again as wide as it had been before.

Nobody spoke for a moment, but pandemonium broke out in the anteroom when Coke closed the door behind him. Most of the noise seemed to be laughter, directed at Vierziger's battered victim.

Dark wood paneled and furnished the inner room. There were no windows, and the several lights were point sources which accentuated the darkness beyond the surfaces from which they glared.

An old man, a lushly attractive young man, and a woman in late middle age sat on the other side of a heavy table. The woman rose to meet the Frisian delegation. She had strong, handsome features, but she was trussed into clothing a size or more too tight for her soft weight.

"I am Stella Guzman," she said, extending her hand to Coke's touch. "The Widow, you may call me. I've been president of Astra since my husband passed on three years ago."

The woman's male companions stood up as she identified herself. The younger one put his hand on Widow Guzman's shoulder in a gesture of ownership. He smiled: appraisingly at Coke, disdainfully at Daun, and at Johann Vierziger with a spark of different interest

Coke found the young man's warm glance at Vierziger to be utterly disorienting. Presumably wolverines can be considered sex objects also… but this Cantiluccan gigolo wasn't by any stretch of the imagination of the same species as Johann Vierziger.

"This is my friend and advisor Adolpho Peres," the Widow said, covering with her own hand that of the man's on her shoulder. She patted it affectionately. Either she didn't see the look Peres gave Vierziger, or she was very complaisant.

"And on this side," she went on, extending a hand toward the other man, "is Simon Roberson, who has been of great help in Astra's business transactions. Master Roberson is a goods supplier with outlets all over Cantilucca."

Roberson wasn't, in fact, nearly as old as Coke had initially judged. Rather, he was sick with worry. The cause of the merchant's stress could have been any number of things; but given that Roberson was the man Evie Hathaway said bankrolled the Astra syndicate, Coke would have been interested in hearing the fellow's assessment of the relative strength of the sides.

The weaker party was usually willing to pay more for support….

"Mistress, gentlemen," Coke said, bowing over the hand. "These are my associates Master Daun"—he nodded—"and Master Vierziger. As I'm sure you're aware, we're part of a survey team for the Frisian Defense Forces."

"This is a lovely table," said Niko Daun, stroking first the underside, then the top, of the piece. In fact, the wood was dented and ringed from long use. He beamed a smile toward the Cantiluccans.

Peres sneered at the sensor tech. "Sit down, gentlemen," he said to Coke. "I doubt we'll need help from mercenaries, but we're willing to listen to your offer. Will you try some of my private-stock gage? Or perhaps liquor?"

Roberson glared at the gigolo with impotent hatred. Widow Guzman winced, patted Peres' hand again, and reseated herself.

"Water for us, I think," Coke said. He unfastened his cape and hung it over the back of the heavy, leather-upholstered chair. The fuel-air grenade was clipped to his belt again, with the safety tab latched down.

"I wouldn't mind trying your gage, Master Peres," Vierziger said in his usual soft, cultured voice. Coke wondered where the little man came from originally. "A demi for a start, if you please."

"We don't have an offer for you, mistress," Coke said. "We're a survey team, as I said. We're here to observe conditions on Cantilucca and report on them. I'll be sending message capsules to Nieuw Friesland on a regular basis, probably daily, while we're here."

Vierziger took a pale green stim cone from the tray Peres offered him. "If you have proposals, we would of course forward them to Camp Able," Vierziger said as he set the injector against the inside of his left wrist and triggered it. "If not, well. We'd have to look for other interested parties."

It was useful to have two FDF negotiators present, though the team hadn't been deliberately structured that way. Vierziger was along simply as muscle, as a bodyguard.

Whatever the little man had been in the past, it wasn't merely a sergeant in the field police.

"Stop this nonsense!" the Widow Guzman snapped. "At any moment, it all could—burn, explode. What is it you're offering, Major Coke, and what price do you put on your… merchandise?"

"That depends somewhat on the circumstances," Coke said, nodding at the woman's candor. Peres hadn't brought the water Coke requested. He'd have liked something to do with his hands besides spreading them on the tabletop. "How many troops of your own are there?"

Peres frowned, then shrugged. "Eight hundred," he said. "Nine hundred, perhaps. And we have six tanks."

"And L'Escorial?" Coke said.

Peres and Roberson exchanged glances behind the Widow's head. If it wasn't an ulcer that grayed and twisted the merchant's features, he was sure on the way to giving himself one.

The Widow Guzman stared toward the far wall. Her eyes were empty and her plump fingers tented before her. Coke thought of Pilar Ortega touching her crucifix as she contemplated bleak horror.

"The same," Peres said at last. "About the same."

"Neither of your syndicates have tanks," Vierziger said with a lazy smile. "For the sake of discussion, let's assume L'Escorial employs, say, two hundred men more than Astra."

His smile broadened, sharpened. "Of course, that's twelve fewer than they employed at this time yesterday."

The merchant giggled nervously, then choked.

"Details like that make a difference, you see," Coke said mildly. "Not an insuperable difficulty, but a difference."

He paused. When he continued, his mind broke the stream of words into thought segments, each as precise as if Coke were taking aim instead of speaking.

"Based on my provisional assessment," he said. "I doubt my superiors at Camp Able would be willing to hire out any force smaller. Than a company of infantry and a company of combat cars. Fighting vehicles. To either of the parties on Cantilucca. And that will be expensive."

Roberson leaned across the table. "*How* expensive?" he rasped.

Johann Vierziger was examining his manicure. "As a matter of comparison…" he commented toward his almond-shaped fingernails, "… less expensive than being burned alive in your house, let us say."

"Approximately three thousand Frisian thalers per day," Coke said crisply. This was money, not lives. He was out of the mood of stark calculation which had gripped him moments before. "With add-ons, perhaps ten percent over. I estimate that the operation will take forty days, and as much longer as you dally about on your own end getting started."

"That's ridiculous!" Roberson blurted. The quoted figure had shaken him from his shell of despair. "That would make the cost of hiring your soldiers equal to the value of the gage the syndicate ships in a half-*year!* Not the profit, the *value!*"

"In other words, a quarter's value of the gage shipped from Cantilucca as a whole," Vierziger said with a gentle smile. "Since control of the total would be in the victor's hands. Perhaps your hands."

"And you could reduce your in-house security force," Coke noted. His tone was flat, factual; not in the least cajoling. *This is the deal, people. If you aren't smart enough to take it, be assured somebody else will be.* "I know, man for man the cost is much lower; but what the FDF offers is victory, and what you're buying from those buffoons outside—"

His thumb hooked dismissively toward the door behind him.

"—is a stalemate that's about to collapse on you."

"It won't work anyway," said the Widow Guzman. She groped blindly to the side to grip Peres' wrist. *Hell of a thing to have to depend on that one for human warmth.* "You can't bring your armored cars to Cantilucca without the Confederacy learning, and for *that* they would react."

Peres bobbed his head at the beauty of the thought emerging from it. "How much for just the infantry, Master Coke?" he asked. "That shouldn't be very much, should it? We can slip men into the port in twos and threes, that won't be a problem. Marvela doesn't watch very closely."

"The cost *of three* companies of infantry," Coke said, "which would be the minimum I'd recommend—to my superiors—without armored support, is approximately the same. A Frisian infantry company isn't simply a hundred troopers,

Master Peres; but I take your point about the need to infiltrate the units rather than bringing them in formed, on a single hull."

"That's too much money," Roberson moaned. He sat bent over, clutching his lower rib cage with both hands. "I can't possibly manage that. We're running at a loss as it is, with the force doubled and gage production down because we've squeezed the farmers so hard already."

The Widow looked at the merchant with a face as blank as ice ready to shiver off a warming window.

"Now I'm not sure the difficulty's as great as you suggest, Simon," the gigolo put in unctuously. "Perhaps if the three of us go over the books…"

He pressed the Widow's hand, then returned it firmly to her lap. This was Peres the Businessman, Peres the Wheeler-Dealer, not to be distracted by a woman's needs.

"I've *gone* over the books," Roberson retorted. "I've *been* going over the books. That's why I'm concerned, *Master* Peres."

Coke stood up, flanked by his companions in a motion so coordinated that it must have appeared pre-arranged. "We'll leave you to your considerations, mistress, gentlemen," he said. "Perhaps you'll have occasion to see us again before we leave Cantilucca."

Vierziger opened the door and stepped through it in the lead, as before. The anteroom had emptied except for ten or a dozen Astra gunmen. One of them threw the Frisians a mocking salute. The tension of the party's entrance was gone.

The door to the private office was thick. It thumped shut behind Coke, amputating all but the first syllables of the voices raised within.

Coke smiled. Lieutenant Barbour's software would polish and enhance the conversation into a form more clearly audible than it was for the three principals inside the office.

The jitney driver, looking both puzzled and pleased at having reached Silva Blanca safely, went off in search of a bar. The two Frisians were paying him as much for a day trip as he'd normally have earned in a week.

Of course, they hadn't gotten back to Potosi yet; and it had taken the cold stare of Johann Vierziger (who'd wandered over "aimlessly" during the negotiations) to put the driver into a mood to deal. Margulies figured she owed her sergeant one for the help, not that he'd exactly *done* anything.

The Lord knew, though, she understood how the jitney driver felt. She didn't suppose she could have a better man to back her in a firefight… but she wasn't quite convinced Vierziger was human.

The village consisted of twenty-five or thirty buildings, constructed for the most part of local timber with shake roofs. Each house had its own chest-high fence of palings. A few chickens ran in the courtyards, though there weren't as many as there should have been. Most households had small kitchen gardens as well.

The driver had stopped his three-wheeled vehicle as directed, in front of a largish red-painted house. It was the only structure in town that wasn't naturally weathered wood, so Barbour had suggested the village headman likely lived there.

The intelligence officer was probably right. They couldn't be sure until somebody acknowledged the Frisians' presence.

"Hello?" Margulies shouted again. Nobody responded. Again.

She shifted the strap of her sub-machine gun. Probably not the best way to reassure the locals who were keeping indoors, but the gun was heavy, the sun was hot, and it had been a kidney-pounding ride in the curst jitney.

"The next time," she muttered to Barbour, "I check to see if a planet's got aircars before I agree to take a mission on it."

"There's aircars in Potosi," Barbour said. "One at least, from the signature. It probably belongs to one of the syndicates, though. Like everything else bigger than these cyclos."

Barbour viewed the village with interest and less apparent irritation than Margulies felt. From what Barbour said during the ride to Silva Blanca, he'd been purely a staff officer before transferring to the survey service. Probably hadn't seen as many mud/stick/straw hovels as she had in the field police.

At least the intelligence officer was loosening up a little. Margulies had been a bit worried about him during training. Couldn't complain about his competence, but a six-man team was too small for somebody whose eyes always seemed focused on his memories inside.

Margulies pulled out a handkerchief and lifted her helmet to wipe her brow. She wasn't going to turn straight around and return to Potosi. She was too stubborn for that, and anyway she didn't relish an immediate fifteen klicks in the jitney.

But she *was* getting ready to kick a gate open, and kick down the door of the house beyond if it came to that.

An argument erupted from the house in the next courtyard over. At least three people shouted simultaneously. Each voice seesawed higher, building on the volume of its competitors. It was obvious that none of the speakers was listening to the other two.

The door opened fiercely enough to slam against the front wall of the house. A young man surged out, twisting his arm free of the older woman and man who had tried to hold him back.

"Sure, I'll stay here!" the young man shouted. "Stay here and starve, that's *a fine* idea! Why should I go to Potosi and live like a human being, hey?"

"Live like a filthy killer!" the woman shrieked. "My son, a killer like the killers who take everything we grow! Will you come back and rob us yourself, Emilio?"

She tore the front of her dress open. Her breasts sagged like banana skins. "Why don't you just shoot me now? Wouldn't that be easier than breaking my heart?"

Margulies motioned Barbour with her toward the gate into the adjacent courtyard. The low fence permitted them a full view of the events.

"Look, I'll be able to send money back to you, Mother," the boy said. He glanced at the woman, then jerked his eyes away in horror at her histrionic self-degradation. "Look, we're all starving here!"

"Blood money!" the woman shrieked. "Blood money! I'd rather die!"

She flung herself on the ground. It wasn't an effective ploy, because it freed the boy's arm from her gripping hands. He half-ran, half-skipped toward the gate. His father followed, bawling, "Emilio!"

The door of the headman's house opened a crack. When those within realized the strangers were going next door, a little man scurried out. He wore red pantaloons, a loose shirt of unbleached cotton, and a red headband.

"You there!" the headman shrilled. "Strangers! You don't belong here! I've called for help, you know. You can't just come in here with your guns and order us around!"

The only thing Margulies had said since arrival was "Hello?" Barbour hadn't said that much. The whole business was informative about the social structure of Cantilucca, all right.

As Emilio reached for the gate-latch, he noticed the Frisians for the first time. He recoiled abruptly. The boy's father grabbed his arm from reflex, but both of them stared over the fence at the strangers instead of carrying on their quarrel.

"You there!" the headman called. "Strangers! Come away from there at once!"

Margulies made a quick decision and turned toward the headman's compound. "We're here to see a friend of mine," she said. "Angel Tijuca. Can you tell me where he lives?"

Emilio snatched the gate convulsively open and darted into the street. His father gestured toward him, but the near presence of the Frisians kept him from following the boy. Emilio carried a short staff and slung his possessions from it. The bindle was so slight that its presence was better proof of poverty than nothing at all would have been.

"Blood money!" his mother cried. The boy bent forward, as though he were hiking toward Potosi against a sleet storm.

"We don't have any Tijucas here," the headman said. "You should go away now, before the guards arrive."

The fellow was short to begin with. He splayed his legs deliberately so that his eyes barely glinted over the fence. Margulies had the impression of a turtle peeping from a shell of palings.

"There's a vehicle with four driven wheels on the way, Mary," Barbour said. He looked doubtfully at the sub-machine gun she'd insisted he carry. His expression wasn't so much frightened as confused, that of a bachelor confronted with a squalling baby.

Margulies wasn't sure how Barbour had gathered the data—so far as she knew, the intelligence officer wore a commo helmet just like hers, with only the standard sensors. She'd have been willing to take Barbour's word for the situation, even without the headman's confirmation.

"That's no problem," she said, her voice reassuring. Though the implication was that there wouldn't be any trouble—and probably there wouldn't—Margulies' mind was considering the quantity of troops and weaponry carried by a patrol vehicle, and the degree to which she could count on Barbour for backup in a firefight.

Not far, she was afraid. Of course, he might draw attention away from her by shooting himself in the foot.

"Angel was from Silva Blanca before he joined the Slammers," Margulies continued calmly to the headman. The local shifted his weight from one leg to the other, at a rate which increased with the intensity of Margulies' gaze. "And I got the impression he intended to return here after he retired. I just—"

An open car roared up from the other end of the town's only street. It had four oversized tires mounted on outriggers to keep the vehicle from tipping during off-road travel; a 2-cm tribarrel was mounted on a central pintle. There were four men aboard, one of them at the grips of the big gun. The muzzles swung as the vehicle swayed on its long-travel suspension.

The patrolmen wore red; red gloves, in the case of the driver.

Emilio's parents disappeared within their house The boy was out of sight also, though Margulies thought he might have ducked behind a hedge. She didn't think there'd been enough time for him to have walked around the sweeping curve of the road to Potosi.

The vehicle shimmied to a halt. "Drop those guns!" shouted the man at the tribarrel. "Drop them right now or s'help me, I'll kill you!"

The driver was extending the collapsed shoulder stock of his sub-machine gun. The other two L'Escorials pointed weapons as well. The fat bore of the grenade launcher wavered between Margulies and Barbour without ever quite aiming *at* either one of them.

Margulies set her fists deliberately on her hips and faced the car, arms akimbo. "I'm Lieutenant Mary Margulies of the Frisian Defense Forces," she said in a harsh, hectoring voice. "An ally of L'Escorial *if* your Masters Luria can come to terms with President Hammer. Who in the hell told you to point a gun at me, *boy?*"

The driver's foot slipped off the brake. The car had a hub-center electric motor in each wheel. Their torque jerked the vehicle forward. The gunner fell back, lifting the tribarrel's muzzles. It was pure luck that he didn't manage to trigger a burst while he was at it.

The back of the vehicle was full of food and personal gear in wicker baskets. The tribarrel's gunner untangled himself from the clutter, awkwardly helped by one of his fellows. "Shut it off, Plait!" he shouted. "Shut it off, you dickhead! D'ye want to kill us all?"

The driver, a rabbity-looking fellow, cut the power. The motors' singing wound down against friction, leaving the village quieter than it would have been without that contrast.

The gunner slapped the grenadier on the shoulder to point him out of the crowded car, necessary so that the gunner too could step down behind him. The driver and the remaining gunman got out also. They stood on the other side of the vehicle; perhaps for the sake of cover.

The headman scurried out his courtyard gate to join the group in the street. "I told them they had no business here," he said. "And I called you right away, just like

I was supposed to, sir."

"We do indeed have business here," Margulies said, frowning at the gunner, the apparent team leader. "I came to visit an old friend of mine from the FDF—Angel Tijuca. He was my driver for a year and a half."

The grenadier stared at the gunner. The gunner frowned in turn. "You know Angel, then?" he said.

"Yes, he was my driver," Margulies repeated. The L'Escorial didn't sound hostile for a change, so she didn't add a gibe to the statement. "He got me out of a tight spot. A really tight spot."

"Why's she here, then?" the driver asked plaintively. "Why this dungheap?"

Jalousies covered the windows of the houses. Corners of the slats tilted up as eyes peered from within. The Lord knew what the tableau would seem to people who couldn't hear the discussion.

A naked child opened the door of a house halfway down the street. An adult arm shot from the shadows and dragged him back inside.

"Look, if you're friends of Angel, then there's no problem you being here," the L'Escorial gunner said. He scratched his beard stubble in puzzlement. "But he's not here, lady, he's in Potosi."

"*Where* in Potosi is he?" Margulies demanded. She massaged the palm of her left hand with her right thumb.

"Well, he's in headquarters, I suppose, lady," the gunner said. He was unsure of himself and nervous of giving offense—under circumstances where, moments ago, he'd thought he and his tribarrel were the Lord God Almighty.

"He's our training officer, lady," the driver blurted. "He's training officer of the L'Escorial syndicate."

"Well, you missed the live show," Sten Moden said as Coke opened the door of Hathaway House, "but you're in time for the first rerun."

The logistics officer had been sitting at the console the whole time Coke's party was gone. He stretched, reaching up to the lobby's high ceiling. His lopsided figure looked like an archaeological treasure, an oversized monument dragged from the midst of ruins.

Evie Hathaway stuck her head out from the kitchen. She ducked back, though she could still overhear the Frisians' conversation.

The team had effectively commandeered the lobby, the only volume in Hathaway House big enough to serve them as an operations room. They had to treat the Hathaways as allies. Georg might be ambivalent, but Evie's support was willing. Coke and his team had proved they were willing to stand up to the syndicates—if only to get a better price for the FDF's services.

"Getting good signals?" Niko Daun asked as he stripped off his cloak.

"Clear as a bell," Moden agreed. "The guards on the tin can at the gate think Dobrynyev, who quit the poker game a winner, was cheating. Though they're not sure how."

"Dang!" Niko Daun joked. He was brilliantly cheerful from success, from the end of immediate danger, and from having been part of a dangerous and successful *team* operation. "Now I gotta go back and stick a personal shadow on Dobrynyev so we can be sure. Knew I should've done that!"

"Let's see how the leaders' conference went after we were gone," Coke said. His tone was a little sharper than he'd intended. The men had a right to be pleased; it was just that the job wasn't finished yet

"Ready to roll," Moden said mildly. He touched a control.

"*We can't pay that!*" Roberson's recorded voice said in impotent fury.

"*I'd pay anything if I thought it would work,*" the Widow said. Despair made her empty, while it drove the merchant to frustrated anger. "*But if we hire them, then the Lurias will simply bring in more foreigners of their own. Thanks to Suterbilt, they have first look at possibles coming through the port.*"

"*You don't understand, Little Star,*" Peres interjected. His tone was disdainful, only lightly screened by a pretense of affection. "*In a fingersnap, these mercenaries will go through anything L'Escorial can put up. Spaceport toughs and petty criminals, that's all their best is.*"

"Good assessment," Coke murmured.

Vierziger gave the other men a lazy smile, like that of a cat awakening. "I don't like them with brains," he said. "But I'm not convinced that Master Peres has disqualified himself as yet."

"*A gun is a gun,*" Roberson muttered. "*And just how did you expect to fund these wonderful troops, Peres? Out of your purse?*"

"*I didn't expect to fund them at all, old man,*" the gigolo sneered. "*After all, the transaction can't go through the Bonding Authority.*"

"*Will they agree to that?*" the Widow asked.

"Smart lady," Niko said to show that he'd picked up something from the discussion among the officers earlier.

"Not smart enough just to hire us and be done," Johann Vierziger said. "Wait and see."

"*They'll have to agree to it,*" Peres insisted. "*They know as well as we do that the Marvelans would have to take action if they heard we were bringing in a mercenary regiment. If the Bonding Authority's informed, the Marvelans will hear about it. The Frisians are here to deal, so that means they're willing to go outside the normal channels.*"

"Maybe," Coke said. "*Maybe* we're willing."

"*I don't see how that follows,*" Roberson said, but his voice had lost its vehemence.

"*So our Frisian visitors arrive,*" Peres caroled, "*they clean up our problem. They board the ship we provide, though they don't know the ship's ours. And the ship never gets home. The credit chips are aboard the same vessel, so they're never presented for payment. End of story, yes?*"

"You see?" Vierziger said. "My type after all."

"But can we be certain they'll agree to act outside the Bonding Authority?" the Widow said. *"Surely they'll recognize the danger."*

"It's not our doing, you see," Peres insisted. *"The Marvelans really would quash the operation if they heard about it. We'll offer Master Coke a lagniappe of his own, five percent say. Enough to retire on happily, if he sees matters the right way and explains them to his superiors."*

"I wonder," Sten Moden observed, "how carefully Mistress Guzman has gone over the contracts her friend lets on her behalf?"

Vierziger tittered. "Definitely my type," he said as he stretched his delicate, deadly fingers before him. "Dumber than dog squat."

Daun glanced at the gunman uneasily.

"I'm not sure. . ." muttered Roberson, but he wasn't sure enough even of his objections to proceed. Generalized fear hung over the merchant, darkening his vision and blurring details into a miasma of formless danger.

"We don't have any choice," the Widow said abruptly. *"Every day our situation gets worse. I should have sold my interests to the Lurias when Pablo died, but it's too late for that now. I'll call Major Coke."*

"Not yet, Little Star," Peres said. *"We don't want to look too eager and make them suspicious. Wait for this evening and we'll say we've been able to raise the money after all."*

"In a way," Sten Moden said, "it *would* be surprising if clients understood just what they're buying from soldiers, and how much it's really worth to them."

As he spoke, he unconsciously kneaded his left shoulder with his remaining hand.

"All right," the Widow said. *"If you say so, Little Heart. That's what I'll do."*

Moden switched off the recording. Mistress Hathaway looked out of the kitchen again.

"And our move, Matthew?" Vierziger asked. He had his pistol out. He was rubbing the metalwork with a synthetic chamois which he carried folded in a pocket.

"L'Escorial doesn't seem to think they need us," Coke said, pursing his lips as he considered. "We should do something about that."

"Pepe Luria is off Cantilucca," Evie Hathaway volunteered from the doorway. "He's the active one, though he's the grandson. Raul and Ramon are probably waiting for him to get back before they start the killing. In earnest."

Coke nodded. "Do we know where the syndicates' installations are?" he asked Moden.

The logistics officer grimaced. "I can make some guesses," he said. "For fine tuning, we're going to need Barbour. Though if"—he turned toward the kitchen doorway—"Mistress Hathaway is willing to provide some local knowledge, I think we can do a pretty good job right now."

"What are you planning to do?" Evie said crisply.

"Something very costly to the syndicates," Coke said. "Are you in?"

"Yes," the woman replied. Her voice was just as flat as Coke's had been.

"Get on with it, Sten," Coke said. He looked at Johann Vierziger. "Come along, Johann," he said. "You and I are going back to Astra headquarters to give helpful advice."

"Yes, I thought that might be the case," Vierziger said, rising easily from his chair.

His fingers twitched the pistol in and out of his holster twice, to be sure that it didn't bind. He was smiling.

"Patrol One to Base," announced the console. The voice was recognizably that of Margulies, despite the stitching and compression of spread-band radio. "We're coming in. So don't get nervous when the door opens, Johann."

Coke paused with his hand halfway to the latch of the front door. It swung in, pushed by Barbour while the security lieutenant watched the street in a would-be negligent fashion.

"When did you become Patrol One?" Moden asked.

"Well, it didn't seem right to identify ourselves in clear," Margulies said in mild embarrassment. "If you like, sir, I can be Three from here on out. We don't know who's listening in."

"On this benighted planet, nobody is," Barbour said as he seated himself at his console.

He obviously didn't want to look like a mother desperate to check her child after the first day of school. Equally obviously, that *was* how he felt about having handed his equipment over to somebody else, however apparently trustworthy.

"Johann and I are going out," Coke said. "I'd like to hear about your trip when we get back, though."

He reached for the door again.

"Just a moment, sir," Barbour said. "Let me find Peres for you. He's left Astra headquarters."

Coke blinked at the intelligence officer. "You were listening in on all this while you were gone?" he asked.

"Yes sir," Barbour said. "Through the console. Ah—perhaps I should have asked your permission?"

He looked up in sudden concern. Barbour's sandy hair and unlined face gave him the appearance of being a boy at least a decade younger than he really was.

"I won't tell you how to do your job," Coke said. "I just—well, I didn't know you could do that from a remote location. Without special equipment."

"Yes sir," Barbour said. He grinned suddenly, unexpectedly. "Commo helmets are more special than most people realize. If you know how to program them, which isn't any great trick."

Right, thought Coke. He'd heard exceptional cooks talk the same way, in absolute honesty. *Oh, there was nothing to it.* Nor was there, for them. As opposed to 99.7 percent of the people who might have attempted the same dish, with results ranging from mediocre to disastrous.

The console display shifted fluidly as Barbour spoke. It locked into a section of streetscape five hundred meters west of Astra HQ. "Here's where he's gone, sir," Barbour explained. "I think he's on the third floor."

Coke hooked a finger to Evie Hathaway to join the group about the display. "How in blazes did you determine that?" he asked. "How did you even know Peres had left the building?"

"Voice print," Niko Daun said/guessed.

"Right in one," Barbour agreed. "I told the software to analyze audio inputs and track Peres through it. He'd gone out past the bug at the courtyard gate a few minutes after you'd left, telling the guards he was going to the Bucket."

"The Bucket of Blood," Mistress Hathaway said. "Yes, it's in that building all right. It's an Astra bar. No worse than most places, not really."

"I tracked him through the external sensors here on Hathaway House," Barbour said in obvious—and justifiable—pride. "He was traveling with three companions, talking frequently enough that I could follow the audio after I lost video… though even with enhancement, I'll admit that there was a lot of guesswork at the end, sir."

"Your guesswork is what laymen call genius," Coke said. "You don't need to be modest with me, Bob. And Via! Call me Matthew, all right?"

"We need to place more sensors up and down the road," Daun said. "Visual, too. I'll get on that right now."

"Would you prefer to find Roberson, ah, Matthew?" Barbour asked. "Mistress Guzman hasn't left the building."

"No, no," Coke said. "Master Peres is the choice for this approach." He smiled tightly. "He's a gambler. That's what we need."

Niko Daun opened his case. He sorted through it with practiced fingers, pulling out items from several different pockets.

"Let me get something to drink," Margulies said, "and I'll give you some backup, kid. No rest for the wicked, hey?"

She walked toward the saloon, rubbing the shoulder where the strap of her submachine gun had hung during the jitney ride. At the archway she turned and said, "When we all get back, Matthew, I'd like to talk to you about L'Escorial. I don't know how important it is."

Coke nodded. "Sure," he said.

"Shall we visit the Bucket of Blood, Matthew?" Vierziger said. "I wonder if the ambiance is as high-toned as the name."

He giggled as he opened the door.

The shill for the Bucket of Blood was a woman in pirate costume on whose shoulder perched either an aviform or a bird-featured robot (the thing/creature certainly wasn't a Terran parrot). She was bare-breasted, overweight, and seemed desperately tired.

From the way she kept trying to wipe invisible cobwebs from her face, Coke suspected that the woman had already overloaded on gage. Additional cones could no longer stave off the crash into near-coma that was due in an hour at the latest; they could only prolong its duration.

The outside stairs serving the third-floor tavern were wide enough for two to pass if they were careful. The burly Astra who came out while the pair of Frisians were midway above the second landing was deliberately clumsy. He lurched toward Vierziger, in the lead, in an obvious attempt to crush the smaller man against the railing for a joke.

Vierziger shifted stance and dodged past the Astra, right shoulder to right. Vierziger's hand moved too, probably with something in it, though even Coke couldn't be sure. Hand or object made the Astra's head *tunk* like a hammered melon. The man slid bonelessly down the stairs to the landing, where he sprawled.

The woman who'd accompanied the Astra out of the bar stared at the Frisians without speaking. Coke politely lifted his commo helmet as he passed her on the stairs.

The Bucket's waiters were husky, and the man in a protective cage by the door carried a beanbag gun. The big-bore weapon fired bagged shot at low velocity, giving the projectile an impact like the fist of the most powerful boxer who ever lived.

The beanbag gun could break bones, but it wasn't generally fatal. Coke presumed the intention was to avoid dangerous penetrations rather than to spare troublemakers' lives, however.

All the bar's staff and most of the clientele wore blue, though some of the patrons were obvious sailors who'd simply tied on a neckerchief of the correct color as a temporary measure. The music was loud and there was a life-sized holographic sex show going on in one corner, but the place wasn't exceptionally bad for its type.

Exceptionally tough was another matter. Most of the people, staff and patrons alike, carried guns. One wrong word and the bar would sound like Settlers' Day celebrations on a frontier planet.

Peres wore black, not blue. He and the three men with whom he'd left Astra HQ were in a corner booth with three women and a boy. Stim cones stood to attention on the table, with empties littering the stained floor beneath. Peres groped the crotch of one of the women beneath her dress, but his heart didn't seem to be in the activity.

Coke approached, Vierziger a pace behind to his leader's off side. An Astra with Peres looked up and grabbed for the machine pistol he carried in a shoulder holster.

There wasn't enough elbow room on the banquette seats for the fellow to draw. Peres saw the attempt, glanced blank-faced toward the oncoming Frisians, and broke into an oily smile.

"My friend Master Coke!" Peres called over the glass-edged music. The gigolo reached across the girl he'd been fondling to lay a finger of restraint on the wrist of the henchman with the machine pistol. "And Master Vierziger as well! Can I hope that you're here for pleasure?"

"Business first, Master Peres," Coke said. "But if it goes well, then in a couple months we'll all have both time and a reason to celebrate. Is there a place you and we could. . .?"

"Here," Peres said without hesitation. He chucked the girl under the chin. "You lot, get out of here. We need the space."

"Hey!" said the girl. "You told us that—"

Peres' three henchmen stood up. The boy and the other two women were leaving the booth without objection. Peres hit the protesting woman with the same hand that had been between her legs a moment before. Her head snapped back and she sprawled across the banquette.

The guard with the beanbag gun turned at the commotion. When he saw Peres was involved—and that Peres didn't need further help—he looked away.

One of the Astras with Peres carried gloves thrust through the epaulette loops of his sleeveless blue shirt. He took the pair out and pulled one of them on. It had fishhooks sewn into the back, points forward.

The other two women shrieked and grabbed their fellow. They dragged her out of the booth before the Astra was ready to punch her. He aimed a kick, but she was too groggy to react.

No bones broken, just a bruise or two.

Coke smiled at Peres. The escorts sat down again.

Coke thought of the ruck of blood and offal the mines had left of the L'Escorial cordon. This time he fantasized that the uniforms were blue, and that some of the pellet-torn faces were those of the men before him.

He sat on one end of the semi-circular banquette; Vierziger took the other end, across from his leader, so that they both had a way out of the booth. In a room full of guns and blue garb, that wasn't a free ticket home, but it was better than having to ask permission of Peres and his thugs before getting to your feet.

"What I was thinking, Master Peres. . ." Coke said.

"Adolpho, please," the gigolo said. "And Matthew and—"

He cocked an eyebrow toward Vierziger and smirked.

Vierziger smirked back, for the *Lord's* sake! "Johann, and of course you may," the little killer said.

"We realize that you're doubtful about committing so much money without certainty of the result, Adolpho," Coke resumed. "I'd like to show you that quite apart from armed force, we can help you through planning and—data collection."

He'd almost said "intelligence," meaning it in the military sense. Peres might have misunderstood by taking the word at its general meaning. That would have been correct also; but the wrong thing for Coke to have said aloud.

"What do you have in mind, then?" the gigolo said. Peres wasn't as stupid as Vierziger claimed while listening to the bugged conversation. Rather, he had no experience of the world outside Cantilucca, and he was too young to realize that Cantilucca was a *very* small pond.

"Your competitors warehouse their gage," Coke said. "With the information my colleagues and I provide, you can snatch the whole amount without any alarm being given. That's pure profit, a good quarter of the cost of the FDF's services."

"We could never do that!" said the Astra holding the hooked gloves. He looked as though Coke had told him to walk on water.

"Besides which," Vierziger said with a smile, "that will leave your L'Escorial friends with severe liquidity problems. They won't be able to bid for comparable services for several months."

Peres looked from one Frisian to the other. His right index finger sorted out one of the unused stim cones in the pile before him. He flicked it across the table to Vierziger. "Try this," he directed.

Vierziger rotated the thumbnail-sized gray cone. The casing didn't have the usual markings, lines, or spots to indicate the contents. "Gage?" he asked.

"Gage *and*," the gigolo said. "Go on, try it."

Vierziger shrugged and set the injector to his left wrist.

Peres wheeled and looked at Coke again. "*Why* are you offering me suggestions that'll handicap you in getting the Lurias to jack up your price?" he demanded

Coke smiled. "I'm not on Cantilucca to raise the price," he said. "I'm here to deal on the terms my superiors set me."

The smile broadened and grew as terrible as the one that played over Vierziger's lips in the aftermath of the mine blasts. "It may be that your L'Escorial friends think the way they greeted me cost them only a dozen dead. They would be wrong. It's cost them everything they have—so long as the Widow is willing to meet our minimum demands."

"The Widow is willing to do whatever I tell her," Peres sneered. "But how can I be sure you're not playing a double game? Let's you and him fight, hey? Astra and L'Escorial… and your troops land to loot the ruins."

A shudder rolled through Vierziger's frame. Coke looked at his companion with unexpressed concern. The little gunman waved a negligent hand when the spasm passed.

"What is it?" he asked Peres.

"Gage," the gigolo said. He smiled. "But cut with first-distillation tailings. Are you afraid now?"

Vierziger laughed. "Afraid of what? Dying? No, Master Peres, not me."

Vierziger flexed his hands above the table, showing that the nerves and muscles all responded normally. He laughed again. His voice sounded like snake scales scraping on rock. The nearest gunman groped toward his hip holster, then caught himself.

"There won't be a fight," Coke said to Peres. The pulse of the music overrode the discussion anywhere beyond the booth itself. The gigolo's decision to negotiate here had been a reasonable one. "There's only a few watchmen in the warehouse. I can show you how to get through the walls, and how to disconnect all the alarms before you start the operation."

"Are you afraid of a fight, Master Peres?" Vierziger asked in a voice too soft to be a gibe… and with a grin that could have sharpened knives.

"No," the Astra leader snapped. He looked at Coke. "Money in my purse so that there can be money in yours, hey? Very reasonable. So we'll do it—but you'll come along, Matthew, so that we can be *sure* the deal is that reasonable."

"All right," Coke agreed. "We'll go to your headquarters now and I'll brief you. I'll need a hologram projector—or I can get one from the hotel."

Peres' lips tightened. "We have projectors. We're civilized here, not some backwater, you know!"

Coke didn't laugh in the gigolo's face. Again, it wouldn't have been politic.

"Then let's go," he said, rising. "After I brief you, I'll send a message capsule to my superiors to update them. The operation itself will take place tonight, if you can get your end together that quickly."

"Yes, of course we can!" Peres snapped. He looked at Vierziger, rising also. "Are you going?"

"I wouldn't miss this for the world," said Johann Vierziger, stroking the inside of his left wrist with his right index finger, his trigger finger.

Coke viewed his surroundings from a cool vantage point above his flesh and prickling nerves. He would see Pilar when he routed the message capsule toward Nieuw Friesland. There would be time for dinner afterward, and other things.

And it might be the last time Matthew Coke had.

Sten Moden emerged from the alley between a pair of six-story structures. Washed clothes hung by an arm or leg from poles thrust out of windows on the upper floors. The washing was the first sign of domesticity the Frisian had seen on Cantilucca.

The area behind the buildings along Potosi's single street was given over to garbage, storage, and living quarters. In a few places the forest had been cleared. Generally the trees had died when human activities stripped their bark or poisoned their roots. Derelicts used dead limbs for firewood and sheltered beneath the fallen boles.

This ten-by-twenty-meter space equidistant from the two syndicate headquarters was one of the formal exceptions. Four large trees had been left at the corners to support a roof of structural plastic. A metal post peaked the center of one end; the sheeting was rectangular, while the area it covered was a rough trapezoid. One of the corner trees was dead, but for the moment it seemed steady enough.

The fenced area under the rigid marquee garaged vehicles ranging from jitneys to the elaborate aircar beneath which projected the legs of a man in multi-pocket overalls. The four lift fans whined in different keys. They were spinning out of synchrony, obvious even to ears less trained than Moden's.

A boy of twelve or so was in the driver's seat, adjusting controls in obedience to orders which the man under the chassis shouted. The boy saw Moden and chopped the car's throttles. "Father!" he called. "A man is here. A big man!"

Moden waved to show that he was friendly. The fence around the garage was a combination of woven wire, barbed wire, and the body panels of wrecked vehicles welded to metal posts.

The chained and locked gate was metal plating on a tubular frame. Judging from the power cables, it could be electrified. Moden didn't feel a prickle when he passed the back of his hand close, but he didn't actually touch the panel to be sure that the power was off either.

The man who pushed himself into sight from beneath the aircar was dark-skinned and solid-looking; in his late thirties or maybe forty standard years, though Moden didn't consider himself any judge of age.

"Yes sir?" the mechanic called.

"I want to rent a vehicle," Moden replied. "Maybe several, there's six of us. We landed from Nieuw Friesland yesterday on business."

The man relaxed slightly. He wiped his hands carefully on a rag, giving himself time to consider both the request and the stranger making it.

"My name's Moden," the logistics officer went on, adding reassurance. "Besides, I've worked maintenance myself and I wanted to see what your operation was like. Who decided to bring a Stellarflow to Cantilucca?"

He gestured toward the aircar, its fans now at idle.

The mechanic's face changed again, this time to an expression of interest and even hope. "I am Esteban Rojo," he said. "I am the owner here, though not of the aircar."

He glanced over his shoulder and called to the boy, "Pito? Go on back to the house now. It's time for your lessons."

He unlocked the chain. Moden stepped aside so that Esteban could swing the gate outward. The boy darted through, following the one-armed stranger with his eyes until disappearing into the alley.

Esteban gestured Moden into the enclosure before chaining and relocking the gate. "You're familiar with the Stellarflow, then?" he asked.

"There's people who swear by them," Moden said, looking critically at the ornate aircar. "Not the people responsible for maintenance, though. And I wouldn't have thought you could get parts for one closer than Earth. Are there many aircars on Cantilucca?"

"This one," the mechanic said glumly. "Adolpho Peres, a friend of the Widow Guzman, bought it on Delos and shipped it here. He's given me a tennight to get it running properly."

"No spares, I gather?" Moden said. He didn't ask when the tennight was up, nor whether the Widow's gigolo had bothered to state the obvious "or else" at the conclusion of his orders to Esteban.

"Stellarflows are of the finest Terran engineering," the mechanic quoted in flat irony. "They never break down. This one must have been damaged in shipping. But it's up to me to fix it!"

He shook his head. "I can't get the fans to synchronize," he said. "Peres says the car was fine on Delos, but I don't believe him. I think the problem's electronic, not mechanical, but I couldn't have gotten control boards from Earth in time even if I'd ordered them five days ago."

Moden walked around the aircar, lifting and closing access plates. "You couldn't get parts on Earth either," he said. "From the serial number, this unit's older than either of us are."

"Stellarflows are of the finest Terran engineering," Esteban chirped. "They never wear out."

"Right," said Moden. He opened the side door and lay down on his back in the driver's compartment so that he could look under the dashboard. "Their engineers' stools don't stink, either. Just ask them."

The logistics officer carried a multitool. He used it now to loosen fittings behind the wood-veneer interior panels. His size and single hand made it difficult to work in the strait confines, but he proceeded without asking for help.

"I thought it might be the fans themselves," Esteban said, peering through the opposite window in an attempt to follow what was going on. "They'd been replaced in the past with standard units, Gurneys, instead of Stellarflow parts. I thought that might be the problem, but the fans synch fine when I jury-rigged a chassis from a ground car."

"You do a lot of work for the Astras, then?" Moden asked. His face was hidden, but his casual tone fooled no one.

"I work for whoever pays me!" the mechanic snapped. "Or doesn't pay, half the time. The cyclo drivers, it's their livelihood. They haven't got any money when they break down, and sometimes they forget to pay when I get them running again. Do you have a problem with that?"

"Quite the contrary," Sten Moden said. He folded the powered multitool into its belt pouch, then straightened with a flat plug-in module in his hand.

"This car has an autopilot," Moden said.

"Yes, of course," the mechanic agreed. "But we don't have guidance beacons on Cantilucca. You can't engage it."

"Right," said Moden. "And the board driving it is identical to the board driving the manual duct controls. Except with luck this one isn't shot."

He handed the module to Esteban, who took it with dawning comprehension.

"May the Lord bless you and keep you, Master Moden," the mechanic whispered. Relief flooded through the dikes of insouciance with which the man had tried to protect himself against the coming deadline.

"Well, we're not out of the woods yet," Moden said. "If this board's packed it in too, then we cobble together something from scratch. Refrigerator controls from big trucks—four of them in parallel, that might work. Do you have reefer trucks here?"

"I could never manage that in five days!" Esteban said.

Moden got out of the car. "We can do it in twelve hours," he said flatly. "I'm not looking forward to dialing in four separate units though, I'll tell you that. But chances are this one's going to work."

Esteban, holding the module as if it were his first grandchild, started to crawl under the aircar again. He stopped. "You want to rent vehicles, Master Moden? What sort of vehicles? Anything you please."

"We'll talk about that later," Moden said. "Right now, I want to get my hands dirty."

His face set, then smiled again. He took out his multitool. "I've been in admin too long."

The big Frisian sat down, lay back, and slid himself under the blocked aircar with the certitude of the tide coming in.

The man guarding the garage beneath the building holding the Ortegas' apartment wore brown trousers, a green shirt, and a carbine which fired fléchettes. He slid the gate closed as Pilar squeezed the port van into a space that was only wide enough by the thickness of the paint. Ten other vehicles, one of them a scarlet armored truck, had virtually filled the parking area.

"We'll have to get out through the back of the van," Pilar apologized to Matthew Coke.

Coke slipped between the seats ahead of the woman. "I've made low-level drops under worse conditions," he said, forcing a chuckle. He was keyed up and working very hard to conceal the fact.

You couldn't let your men know that you were as nervous as they were. Besides, the process of *acting* calm brought a degree of real relaxation.

"I appreciate you escorting me back, Matthew," Pilar said. "It's been... Until last night I could pretend it wasn't as bad as it seemed, but now I'm frightened to be out alone after dark."

"My pleasure," Coke said. "Besides, I could use the drink you offered."

The interior of the garage was painted half red, half blue. Both sides had staircases. Pilar walked toward the red one.

"Only a drink, you understand," she said. She didn't look at her companion as she spoke, and her left hand clutched her crucifix.

"I understand," Coke said in a neutral voice.

The guard smirked at the couple. He turned away when Coke gave him a flat glance from the base of the stairs.

"L'Escorial?" Coke said mildly. There was room to walk beside Pilar. He followed two steps back in order to keep his right hand clear of her if he had to draw.

"Not exactly," Pilar said. She paused just below the ground-floor landing to let a party of sailors exit noisily onto the street. They sounded happy, even the man who was reciting the Lord's Prayer in a singsong.

Pilar started up again when the way was clear. "The top floors, the fifth and sixth, are a, a brothel," she said. "They have the same—staff, I understand. But the entrances to the two floors are off different stairs so that there won't be fights. Our suite is on this side of the building, that's all."

The cape she wore for concealment draped her full hips and swayed as she moved. Coke smiled at the thought of Salome and the seven veils. Far more effective than just flaunting your bare tits over a railing... though that worked too; anything at all worked when a man was going into the red zone and needed to reassure himself.

Pilar had kept her explanation flat, purely informative. She cleared her throat and added with a touch of embarrassment, "It's actually a *good* location in Potosi, you realize. The security is so much better than at other buildings."

The door at the second landing had three separate lock plates, though they seemed to work from a single electronic key. As Pilar began to open them, a L'Escorial gunman turned at the floor above and continued down the stairs.

The man was drooling and wild-eyed from gage tailings. He held a 2-cm powergun. The loading gate was open, indicating that there wasn't a magazine in place, but Coke couldn't be sure whether or not there was a round in the chamber.

Coke walked up two steps and stood so that he blocked the stairwell. His hands were under his cape, the left one holding a needle stunner. Unlike powergun bolts, the little charged projectiles would penetrate the light film of the gray cape. "Good evening, sir!" he called. "L'Escorial forever!"

"Fuck you," the gunman mumbled. He braced himself against the wall and pointed his weapon at the Frisian's face.

"Inside quickly!" Pilar screamed as she flung the door inward.

Coke shot the L'Escorial in both knees. The gunman's legs splayed outward like those of a dancing marionette. His tailbone slammed violently down on the step behind him.

The powergun was pointing at the ceiling when it went off. Cyan light and the *wham!* of enclosed air superheated filled the stairwell.

The 2-cm bolt shattered the lower half of the cast-in-place concrete. It left a cloud of powder and the rusty squares of reinforcing wire across a meter-wide crater.

Coke lunged into Pilar's suite and slammed the metal door behind him. He held the panel shut while the woman reset the triple locks.

"Well!" Coke said, expelling a deep breath. He stripped off his cape and threw it down. He felt hot and trembly.

The floor was carpeted. Coke put the needle stunner on safe and dropped it onto the cape. His grip had been so fierce that his hand hurt. He'd trained himself to shoot ambidextrously, but using his left added a level of stress—

Necessary here so that he could have drawn the powergun with his master hand.

Pilar removed her own cape. Her face was calm until the composure crumbled like ice in a spring freshet. She threw herself sobbing into Coke's arms.

"I hate this place!" she cried. "This house and this town and this planet! Oh Lord, I wish I were dead!"

Coke stroked the back of her neck with his left hand. With his right he tilted her face and kissed her. Her lips were wet with tears.

"Don't wish that," he whispered. "It's not as bad as that."

"This place is Hell and I'm in Hell," Pilar moaned. "Oh, if only we had never left Marvela…."

Coke kissed her again. He lifted her breast against his broad chest with his left hand.

"Please," she said. She put her hand to his and twisted her torso away. "Please."

The room was lighted by three globes, weaving a simple pattern as they hung unsupported in the air. The furnishings were of handmade wood rather than the plastic extrusions that Coke had seen everywhere else in Potosi. The syndicates preferred to import goods and even food rather than to turn the labor force into production of anything except gage.

Coke held Pilar by waist and shoulder. He kissed her again. "Your husband isn't here," he said. "You know he isn't going to be back tonight."

He thought of adding that Terence Ortega had gone to an apartment at the other end of town at midday. Barbour would warn them if Ortega left.

Coke decided not to explain that. Telling Pilar there was an electronic tag on her husband would have indicated the degree of preparation that Coke had made for this moment.

Coke was romantic—you didn't stay a soldier because of the pay and benefits. But you didn't survive as a soldier if you didn't plan each possible step, and that carried over to the rest of Coke's life as well. Women tended not to see things the same way.

Pilar snatched herself out of his grip again. "Terry's behavior doesn't affect *my* vows!" she said angrily to the far wall.

"Pilar," Coke said softly, "I'm—not real settled just now. Forgive me if I misspoke."

He put his hands on her shoulders and guided her around to kiss him again.

"Oh, Matthew," she said, "you could have been killed, I know. Because of me. But…"

Her fingers brushed his cheek, dusted by tiny fragments of the concrete ceiling. He kissed her, pulling her toward him without resistance.

"Matthew," she said desperately. She caught his hands as they rose again toward her breasts. "Matthew, I'm so sorry, please."

She stepped away, still holding his hands. "Let me get you that drink, but then I'm afraid you'd better go."

He lifted his chin and dipped it again. His face was as placid as that of a saint's statue. He lowered his hands to his sides. "That's all right," he said. "But I don't think I'll have the drink."

Pilar began crying again. She swallowed the sobs, but the tears pulsed down her glistening cheeks. She held her crucifix with both hands. "I'm sorry, I just can't," she whispered. "I want to, but I can't."

An internally lighted button controlled each lock-plate from the inner face of the door. Coke thumbed the buttons in turn, switching them from green to red.

"No problem," he said without emphasis. He donned the cape again. His hands and the needle stunner vanished beneath the gray shimmer.

"Matthew?" Pilar said. "Please? Call me when you've gotten back to Hathaway House safely."

Coke looked over his shoulder at her. "I've got various business tonight," he said.

"If it goes well, I'll probably see you tomorrow when I send another message capsule off from the port."

Pilar caught the door behind him and kept it from swinging to. She watched through the crack.

Instead of going down to the street, Coke started up the stairs toward the brothel.

Moden and Esteban Rojo could have finished the job in an hour and a half, if they'd had good luck and the right tools. They had neither.

Removing the Stellarflow's lower electronics module required either special equipment or great care. Moden was careful, but years of vibration had crystallized a plastic bearing. The joint snapped, and then they had to cut the other three straps as well because the clamps had frozen.

Four hours after they'd started—straps replaced with pieces cut from sheet stock, bearing freed in a sonic bath from the multitool, and journals cannibalized from one of the pair of redundant trunk-lid cantilevers—Esteban ran the fans up and down in perfect unison before shutting off the power.

"As good as new!" he announced.

Moden stretched mightily. "Which means," he said, "it's almost as good as a Frisian aircar that would have cost half as much free-on-board… but Via, some people have to have their Terran technology."

He'd acted in place of a hydraulic jack when the bow of the car had to come up twenty centimeters. Judging from the weight, Stellarflow had used iridium for the frame. Moden ached, but it felt good to have been doing physical labor again.

"Will you eat with us, Sten?" Esteban asked. He tossed a rag to Moden so that the big man could wipe his—hand. Esteban's mouth opened in embarrassment

Moden pinned the rag between his knees and dragged his hand through it determinedly. "Got the big chunks off," he said.

He looked at the mechanic. "At your apartment, you mean, Esteban? I don't want to be in the way."

"We have a cafe," Esteban said with dignity. The Frisian had skirted as delicately as possible the question of whether Esteban could afford to feed guests, but the well-meant concern still rankled. "My wife and children run it, Pito and our daughter Annunciata; and I help when there's time. But I ask you there as a guest, not a customer, please?"

"Then I'd be honored," Moden said. He flicked the rag through the air, caught it in a fold; and folded it a second time, into a square, against his thigh.

Rojo's cafe was on the building's second floor, with the entrance and sign—The Sacred Heart—near the mouth of the alley down which Moden had walked to reach the garage behind. A dozen locals were present in the single small room, two families with children as well as individual adults. The food odors were piquant and wonderful.

The girl who shuttled plates from the serving window was in her early teens and strikingly beautiful. "My daughter, Annunciata," Esteban said proudly. "Nunci, I want you to meet Master Sten Moden!"

The girl dropped into a curtsy, though she carried a serving plate in either hand and there wasn't, Moden would have thought, space enough for her knees to dip as they did.

The patrons of The Sacred Heart sat at a single table supported on six pillarlike legs. The table was of native wood with a subtle grain, polished by use into an attractive brazen patina. Seating was on the pair of full-length benches. There was barely enough room between the cafe's walls and the ends of the table for patrons to edge by to the side away from the door—the side from which Nunci served.

"Rosaria!" Esteban called. A woman, older and much fatter than Annunciata, stuck her head out of the serving window.

The mechanic gestured to the cafe's patrons, all of whom were staring at him and his huge companion already. "Everyone! This is our great good friend, who repaired the aircar which had me tearing out my few remaining hairs. Rosa, your special chicken and rice for our guest—and plenty, he has the strength of ten men and no doubt he eats like ten!"

"Well, I'll be able to do justice to the meal," Moden said. The undoubted virtues of Hathaway House didn't include the cooking of Master Hathaway, who attempted that task.

Esteban led the Frisian to the open seat in the center of the table, facing the door. Moden's knees straddled the table's central leg. There was a general shifting and good-humored discussion to create a second place into which Esteban squeezed himself.

Pito popped out of the door to the kitchen and presumed living quarters, carrying a basket into which he dropped dirty dishes. They were plastic and crude, locally pressed from exterior sheeting.

Esteban whispered in his daughter's ear. She passed the message to her mother at the window and received two small glasses with a bottle of ruby liqueur, three-quarters full.

"From my father-in-law's farm," Esteban said as he poured. "That's where we get the food as well."

Annunciata reached past to put a serving platter, not a normal dish, of chicken with rice and a variety of heavily processed vegetables on the table before Moden. "Grandpa Mordechai won't grow gage," she said. "He says people must eat, mustn't they?"

"To your health!" Esteban said, raising his glass.

"And yours," the Frisian responded. He jostled the neighbor on his right in grabbing his glass. The liqueur was thick, almost a syrup, with a fruity flavor. Not unpleasant, and there was enough alcohol to bite the back of Moden's tongue.

"Both syndicates have been after Mordechai," Esteban said with a frown. "L'Escorial pushed him off his old farm, so he terraced a hillside that nobody claimed. I helped, the whole family helped, and his neighbors too. He's stubborn.

I agree with him, but I worry."

The food was delicious. "Have things gotten worse recently with the sides arming?" Moden asked through a bite.

"No, no," Esteban said. "Since so many of the gunmen came here to Potosi, there's fewer left to bother the farmers. Most of the farms grow food for themselves, but they grow gage too for one syndicate or the other. So that they'll be protected."

A family got up to leave. The wife paid Rosaria with three separate credit chips. From the prices chalked beside the serving window, the five dinners totaled less than ten pesos—one and a half Frisian dialers. The citizens of Potosi didn't have easy access to credit terminals which could have combined the small amounts into a single chip for convenience.

The outer door opened. The chatter stilled. Three men wearing blue shouldered in. All carried powerguns: a pair of sub-machine guns and the third man festooned with four separate holstered pistols as well as a selection of knives.

Esteban stood up, awkwardly since he had to step over the bench to do so. Citizens—his neighbors—slid to either side, half-crouching toward the ends of the room.

"Gentlemen," Esteban said, "this is not a bar. I'm sure you'll find better entertainment elsewhere."

The leader of the Astra gunmen appeared to be the man with the pistols. "You got a red sign downstairs," he said. "We thought we'd check the place out."

"The sign is the sacred heart of our lord Jesus Christ!" Rosaria blurted from the serving window. "We have nothing to do with L'Escorial here!"

"Nunci," Esteban said in a low voice. "Go help your mother in the kitchen."

"She stays," ordered an Astra. He wagged the muzzle of his sub-machine gun to emphasize the point.

"They used to have a red sign," the gunman to the leader's other side tittered. "It had a little accident when we come by it."

The trio moved further into the cafe. The local patrons flowed behind them on both sides and out the door, like damping fluid when a shock absorber compresses.

Moden wore a pistol in a belt holster. He wasn't a particularly good shot. He certainly wasn't good enough to drop three men in the fraction of a second he'd have before the sub-machine gun aimed at him blew his head off.

"Please," Esteban said. "This is just a cafe. We have no sides, we are poor people."

The leader took the bottle of liqueur and drank directly from it, eyeing Moden past the plane of sluggish red fluid. He handed the bottle to the man aiming at Moden. "Who's the crip?" he asked.

"My name's Sten Moden," the Frisian answered calmly. His hand lay on his lap. The closed flap of his holster was in sight of the gunmen. "I'm from Nieuw Friesland, a businessman."

"He's a leftie!" said the Astra who'd warned Nunci not to leave. "Get it? A leftie!"

Without warning he triggered a single shot. The cyan bolt struck near the top of the kitchen door. Wood blew outward in blazing splinters, leaving a hole the size of a soup plate in the thin panel.

Rosaria screamed. Nunci stood transfixed, and Esteban's fists balled.

Sten Moden gripped the table's central leg. He lifted and hurled forward the massive piece of furniture with all his strength. Both sub-machine guns fired, into the tabletop and ceiling as the huge club pistoned toward the three Astras. Moden felt the shock of the bolts through his hand, but the table was too solid for the light charges of a pistol or sub-machine gun to tear it apart.

The tabletop hit the far wall, or almost, with a soggy thump. Moden pulled back, then slammed his weapon toward the wall again with his shoulder behind it.

There was a gurgling cry. When Moden withdrew the table the second time, sub-machine guns and other accoutrements clattered to the floor behind it.

Annunciata screamed. She threw herself into her father's arms.

Moden gave a convulsive gesture that slammed the table back down on its six legs. He was trembling all over. He had to brace his hand on the scarred top in order to continue standing. Powergun bolts had blown smoldering craters in the wood.

Moden didn't try to look over the table to see what had become of his victims, though he knew he ought to. One of the Astras might still have enough strength to pull a trigger....

But probably not.

The Rojo family spoke or cried in four vocal ranges, all of them incoherently. The Frisian closed his eyes and opened them, drawing deep breaths.

The cafe's outer door flew open.

Mary Margulies lunged in behind a sub-machine gun. Niko Daun followed her with a set expression and another sub-machine gun.

The would-be rescuers looked at Moden, then looked at their feet. "Blood and martyrs," Niko said.

Margulies straightened from her crouch. She put her weapon on safe and cleared her throat. "Ah," she said. "Barbour, you know he monitors the audio from the helmets. He thought you might need a hand."

Sten Moden looked at his palm. His adrenaline-charged grip had left white valleys where it held the corners of the table leg.

"No," Moden said. "One was enough."

CANTILUCCA: DAY THREE

The outer fence surrounding L'Escorial's gage warehouse was woven wire, five meters high and topped with a Y of razor ribbon. The forest had grown to and entwined with the wire despite evidence of desultory attempts to burn it back. The diamond teeth of Coke's powered cutting bar opened a man-sized hole with one sweep of his arm.

The vegetation in the four meters between the fencelines was cut to knee-height scrub. There was a single row of buried toe-poppers, located so that the mower could straddle them. Daun marked a safe pathway with white tape.

The sensor-controlled directional mines placed every ten meters along the inner fence were even less of a danger. Daun turned them all off with a deactivation signal, just as the watchmen would have done while mowing or carrying out other maintenance operations.

"Who do these bozos think they're dealing with?" the sensor tech muttered disdainfully to Coke.

"Bozos like the Astras behind us," Coke replied.

Well behind them. Coke had decided he and Daun would breach the defenses alone. Vierziger wasn't happy to be a kilometer back in the forest along the road, but that was the only way Coke could be *sure* the Astras would stay where they belonged.

The last thing Coke wanted was a line of trucks to come driving up while he and Niko were in the middle of the wire. He'd seen relief in the sensor tech's eyes when they went over the plan the first time. Daun had more reason than most to doubt the competence of indig forces.

"Wait here, sir," Daun said crisply.

The sensor tech darted across the cleared area to the nearest directional mine, a lump against the inner fence. After a moment's manipulation there, he moved ten meters down the line to another lump. He tossed something to the ground.

"All right, sir," Daun said, this time using helmet intercom. "I've pulled the fuzes. I didn't want somebody turning them on again at a bad time. It can happen by accident, even, lightning or a plasma discharge."

"No, we wouldn't want that," Coke agreed under his breath.

He was smiling. He remembered he'd had doubts about how the kid would perform after the experience which got him transferred to a survey team. Just fine, so long as Daun could be confident of his backup… and for that, so far, so good.

The warehouse was a huge hangar constructed primarily of structural plastic, but strengthened at the corners by pillars of reinforced concrete. A bank of lights on the roof was intended to flood the interval between the fencelines. Many of the bulbs had failed without being replaced.

It didn't really matter. The guards didn't patrol the exterior, and there were no windows in the building proper from which to observe their surroundings.

The gage syndicates had achieved parity of incompetence. That was fine until somebody arrived who knew his ass from a hole in the ground.

Daun set a small transducer close to the nearest of the inner fencepoles. He stepped swiftly toward the next support, holding a similar transducer and unreeling the thin cable which tied it to the box he'd set on the ground.

"Don't touch the fence yet, sir," the tech ordered; needlessly, because they'd gone over the plan in the lobby of Hathaway House, and Matthew Coke knew better than to jump the gun in an uncleared detector field anyway.

"Right," Coke murmured. He preferred a subordinate who might irritate him with unnecessary warnings to one who let him walk into disaster because, *I thought you knew!*

Daun turned a switch on the control box. "There we go!" he said. "All right, sir. It'll think the circuit's complete even if you blow everything down between these two posts."

"No need for that," Coke said. He thumbed the cutting bar live and swept it up and down with his left hand in a nearly perfect catenary arc through the fencing. The blade whined and sparkled happily.

If L'Escorial's builders had used beryllium monocrystal or some other refractory material for their defenses instead of steel wire, the Frisians' task would have been more difficult. But if a frog didn't jump, it wouldn't hit its ass on the ceiling....

Coke crouched in the opening as Daun sprinted for the building forty meters away. If Coke had to supply covering fire—he carried a sub-machine gun, with holstered pistol and a 2-cm weapon slung just in case—he didn't want to be so close to the warehouse that he couldn't cover both ends of the building with his peripheral vision.

Daun wrenched up a lid on the ground outside the building. It wasn't locked shut. The tech stretched on the concrete pad, holding a light down in the cavity with one hand and reaching in with the other. Bob Barbour claimed this fusion bottle was the sole power source for the warehouse.

Fusion bottles didn't fail, and the output of one was more than sufficient to power the building's lights, sensors, and motor-driven trackways. Coke still found it hard to believe that there wasn't at least a battery-operated emergency radio, despite Barbour's assurances. If Bob was wrong, well, he was also ready to jam the transmission within a microsecond.

Niko Daun ran back, bent halfway over and flushing with excitement. "Okay, sir!" he said quickly. "Okay, whenever you want it."

Coke keyed his helmet to channel one. "Go," he said. "Out."

"Roger," said Johann Vierziger's voice, a whisper like tendons rustling on dry bones. "Out."

Coke checked all his weapons. "Niko," he said, "why don't you wait here. I'm going to wait by the door in case they open it when they hear the trucks."

"No *sir*," said the sensor tech. "I'm part of this team." He closed the case holding his equipment and unslung his sub-machine gun.

"Glad to have you along," Coke said with a quirked smile. He started around to the front of the warehouse, walking just inside the inner fenceline.

It wasn't really true. Daun's combat skills were coming along, but firefights wouldn't ever be the boy's strong suit. On the other hand, he was probably better than most of the guards they'd be facing in a moment. And anyway, Coke wasn't about to tell the kid who'd performed splendidly that he'd be a fifth wheel in what came next.

Coke expected the first of the vehicles coming up the road to be a flatbed truck configured as a ram with a sloped steel bow and extra weight in back to add momentum. Instead he heard the hum of a jitney, one of those Sten Moden's mechanic friend had supplied to the Frisians.

Coke frowned, but then he thought about it for a moment. Vierziger had kept the Astras on their leash. If the gunman wanted to arrive before the locals now, there was no real reason he shouldn't.

Instead of coming to the first of the two gates on the approach road, the jitney bounced off the pavement and whined to the hole Coke had cut in the outer fence. Though the Astra convoy was running without lights, the twenty big flatbeds were audible by now.

Vierziger left the jitney at the gap in the fence. He jogged the rest of the way to Coke and Daun. He wore two bandoliers and a garrison belt hung with various munitions, but none of the equipment jingled or clattered as he moved.

"We were going to let the Astras take it from here," Coke commented mildly.

"No, Matthew," Vierziger said. "We were going to do it right."

"We still have to wait for the ram," Coke said.

"I can open the warehouse doors if you'd like, sir," Niko Daun said. "So long as the power's still on, like it is now."

Coke blinked. "You can?" he said.

Johann Vierziger smiled at him. The harsh illumination from the roof floodlights made the little man look like a gnome, an incredibly vicious gnome.

"Sure," Daun said.

He reslung his sub-machine gun and fumbled in the small tool pouch on his belt as he walked to the latch plate beside the sliding doors. The kit Daun had left back at the fence contained the special equipment he needed for the outer defenses, but he wore what he considered basic tools whenever he had his trousers on.

"I hope he remembered to put the curst gun on safe," Coke grumbled.

"He did, Matthew," Johann Vierziger said. He faced the door, but his eyes were far away. He flexed his empty hands twice, then readied his sub-machine gun. "He's a very careful lad. A credit to you as his commander."

"I'm ready," the tech said. He'd pressed a flat disk held by a magnet or suction cup to the latch plate. A coil of thin flex ran from the disk to the squeezer in Daun's hand.

"Just before the truck rams the first gate," Vierziger said softly. "Then cut the power when the door's half a meter open."

Vierziger hadn't said anything during the planning session when Coke proposed a battering ram to enter the warehouse after they'd shut off the building's power supply. If the sergeant had made this suggestion, Coke would have vetoed it as needlessly dangerous to members of the survey team. Now, with adrenaline surging through his blood, Coke couldn't imagine another way to have done it.

But Vierziger had *known* that all along.

The trucks were in sight, snorting and rumbling up the approach road. The ram plate on the lead vehicle was a V-shaped blade intended for a ground-clearing bulldozer.

"Don't the guards hear them coming?" Niko asked in a combination of wonder and nervousness. He had nothing to do but wait until Coke gave him the order.

"They're not guards," Coke murmured. He switched his visor to thermal imaging, then through light amplification and straight visual mode back to thermal again.

Just to be sure. "They're employees who don't really believe there's need to guard anything. Drunken, stoned employees."

"Are we really going to put all this gage in the Astras' hands, Matthew?" Vierziger whispered.

The bastard had known all along!

"No," said Matthew Coke. "We're going to burn it here."

Daun squeezed, then dropped his clacker and grabbed the separate control clipped to his breast pocket. The double doors rumbled back. The lead truck slammed into the gate with sparks and a tortured squeal—

The lights on the warehouse roof dimmed and vanished, the doors froze the width of a man's shoulders apart—

And cyan hell broke loose as Johann dived into the building behind his blazing weapon.

Expanding echoes of Vierziger's bolts glowed in Coke's thermal optics. A man writhed on the floor, his face gone. Coke leaped the body, firing twice between his legs while he was in the air.

The warehouse offices were in three partitioned cubicles to the left of the doors. The remainder of the building's volume was a single room, ten meters high and stacked with drums of gage on pallets.

The car of the overhead rail and hoist system jogged forward on the inertia of the laden pallet slung beneath it. Because the building's power was off, circuitry hadn't shorted when Vierziger hit the control cage with a long burst. The operator lay slumped in his saddle, his clothing afire.

There was motion from the middle cubicle. A man stepped out. He lurched backward, shot simultaneously by Coke and Vierziger.

Coke dropped his sub-machine gun and aimed the 2-cm shoulder weapon instead. Vierziger ran down the center aisle. He would take any L'Escorials at the back of the building before they realized what was happening in front.

Coke fired twice through the open doorway of the center office, then twice into the door to its left. The bolts of sun-hot copper ions ignited the desk and furnishings of the first, and blew the extruded plastic door of the second into the cubicle's interior.

Coke loaded a fresh magazine. He was shifting his aim to the third office when a figure ran out of the burning center cubicle. He swung the heavy muzzle back as his finger took up slack on the powergun's trigger.

A woman, stark naked and screaming. She held a bandeau top in her left hand. No threat, no danger.

Coke aimed past her at the remaining office. He stroked his trigger twice to flush out anyone hiding there.

Niko Daun stepped alongside his commander. He fired at least half his sub-machine gun's magazine into the screaming woman. Gobbets of flesh and bone spewed away like wood chipped by the teeth of a router. She spun back into the flames of the office from which she'd fled.

"I got him!" Niko shouted. "I got him!"

The lead truck hit the opening hard enough to jounce the double doors nearly open. The driver managed not to stall his motor. He backed a few meters and accelerated again, cutting his wheels to slide the left door back against its stops.

Nobody else came out of the offices. A body lay in the corner away from the cubicles. As Vierziger entered the building, he'd dropped the fellow. Coke hadn't noticed him before.

Sprinklers opened above the burning offices. They were fed by standpipes in the roof, even though the pumped water system went off when the power did. Coke surveyed the ceiling, then put a bolt into the end of each standpipe where it joined the front wall of the warehouse. He fired until he'd emptied the 2-cm weapon's magazine, then reloaded again. Water gushed down the inner wall and splashed across the concrete floor. There it could do nothing to affect the flames.

"All clear in back!" Vierziger reported over channel three. Several quick bursts of sub-machine gun fire snarled from the rear of the warehouse. "All clear in back!" Vierziger repeated, simultaneous with another burst.

Steam and smoke billowed from the burning office cubicles. Another Astra truck drove into the warehouse. Its headlights brightened the gray mist but did little to illuminate the building's interior. The Astra gunmen didn't have night vision equipment. They shouted to one another in anger and confusion.

The gage was in double-walled 150-liter plastic drums. For shipment, the drug was dissolved in a matrix of ethyl alcohol. Because Coke knew what to look for, he could already see the fires started at the back of the warehouse where Vierziger had raked pallets with his sub-machine gun.

"I'm coming out!" Vierziger called over the unit push. "Do not shoot, I'm coming out!"

Coke grabbed the foregrip of Niko Daun's sub-machine gun and lifted the muzzle high. The sensor tech might not have heard the warning, might not have understood it—might have dropped his gun on the concrete and triggered a shot wholly by accident. Firefights weren't Daun's proper job, so it was the commander's duty to see that no accidents occurred.

Adolpho Peres swung down from the cab of the second truck. He wore body armor and a helmet that must have weighed nearly ten kilos. "Start loading the gage!" he bellowed. "We can't wait around here long!"

The gigolo waved his machine pistol. He turned his head as he spoke. Coke stepped toward him, releasing Daun.

Peres saw the motion past the edge of the helmet's cheek plate. He must have thought he was being attacked, because he tried to swing the gun onto the Frisian.

"I'm a friend!" Coke shouted as he lunged forward. Instead of directing the weapon upward as he'd done with his own trooper, he jerked the machine pistol out of Peres' hand. "We've killed them all for you!"

The office cubicles were fully involved by now, hammering the men in the front of the warehouse. The right side of the ram-equipped truck was only a few meters from the fire. The plastic body panels started to soften; bubbles appeared on the front fender.

"Who?" Peres shouted. "Coke, is that you? Manuel!"

The last call was for the gigolo's bodyguard, a man nearly as tall as Sten Moden and broad in proportion. Coke saw Manuel's vast, weapon-festooned bulk several meters away, groping in what was for him a gray fog. Vierziger's assessment of the big man was that a gun-jeep had more brain cells and could carry even more weapons—but that choice was for Peres to worry about.

Johann Vierziger stepped up on the Astra leader's other side. "I'm here, Matthew," he said. "Now let's get out of these gentlemen's way, shall we?"

"Peres, we'll leave you to load the gage," Coke shouted in the gigolo's ear. "We'll meet you tomorrow morning to arrange contract terms!"

The warehouse had become a steambath because the heat boiled water off the concrete. The flow from the sprinklers had decayed to irregular dribbles, noticeable only if a drop happened to splash you from above.

"Yes, of course," Peres replied. He snatched his helmet off in frustration at its weight and the degree to which it limited his range of vision—not that he was going to be able to see much more without it. "Manuel! Sanjulio!"

The three Frisians broke for the door. Coke's finger on Daun's wrist gave the sensor tech guidance he might or might not have needed.

A third truck drove into the warehouse and collided with the second. The drivers shouted at one another, and the rest of the convoy stopped in confusion on the approach road.

Coke led his men toward the gap he'd cut in the fence. "I think we'd best stay in the woods and hump our way back," he explained. "I'm not thrilled about walking the six klicks into Potosi, but L'Escorial is going to see the flames before too long and come out with guns blazing."

"Does Peres realize that?" Niko Daun asked. The point had obviously escaped the tech himself.

"Here, wait by the jitney," Vierziger said.

"We can't drive it back through the forest," Coke objected. "It's not a skimmer. We'll just have to abandon it."

"Sten's going to pick us up in a moment," the gunman explained. He looked at the sensor tech. "Niko," he went on, "the Astras don't know the gage is burning yet. Whether they'll realize that a fire here will call the owners' attention is an open question."

An unlighted aircar slid low over the treetops. Sten Moden was at the controls. He dropped vertically to hover on fan thrust directly behind the jitney.

Coke half-climbed, half-tripped his way into the vehicle's other front seat. Vierziger and Daun got into the back.

"Is there anything else you ought to have told me?" Coke demanded in a loud, generally directed voice.

"Well, you didn't want to walk either, did you, Major?" Sten Moden said as he pulled the joystick toward him to add power. "Esteban was still doing tests on the Stellarflow, so I asked if he'd mind me putting it through its paces tonight. Does pretty well, don't you think?"

The Stellarflow was too massive to accelerate quickly, especially with a load that included the logistics officer, but it had a good deal of power. Starlit glimpses of the treetops close beneath suggested their speed was 200 kph and rising. Moden swept them in a broad arc that would approach Potosi from the north, opposite to where all the commotion was occurring.

"Look, I'm not going to argue with success," Coke said after a moment "But the next time, don't pull this sort of thing behind my back, all right? You guys act like a team, and I'll promise not to act like a little tin god."

He realized as he spoke that something very basic had changed in the structure of this survey team; and that he was pretty sure it had changed for the better.

They were out of sight of the warehouse at this altitude, but the whole sky behind them glowed red from the swelling inferno.

Matthew Coke's bedroom had a window which opened out onto the alley beside Hathaway House. When he leaned his elbows on the ledge, he could watch the building across the street. As a result, he wasn't surprised to hear his commo helmet click, then warn in the voice of Lieutenant Barbour, "Matthew, two men are walking toward us from L'Escorial headquarters. There isn't any other exceptional behavior from that direction."

The breeze blew from the south. Even at this distance it carried with it a whiff of burned vegetation, burned plastic, and—present only if you knew it was there—burned flesh.

Coke lifted himself back from the ledge. One of the approaching visitors was garbed in an ensemble of scarlet and vermilion, a well-tailored outfit and clearly expensive. The two close hues made his plumpish figure seem to shimmer.

The other man wore a red beret, but the remainder of his clothing was khaki. The garments looked a great deal like Frisian battle dress.

"Right," Coke said as he snatched the gray cape from the hook by his bed. "Action stations, though I doubt there'll be trouble. I'm coming down."

The shooting had gone on south of town until nearly dawn. The fact that it hadn't spread to Potosi proper meant the syndicates really didn't want the lid to blow, despite all their deadly posturing. That might change when the L'Escorials realized just how badly they'd been hurt by the fire.

Margulies slammed down the stairs ahead of Coke. She slid her left hand along the balustrade against the possibility of her heel catching on a tread as she jumped the steps three at a time. Vierziger was already with Barbour in the lobby, his proper location.

Georg Hathaway stood by the door and wrung his hands. "I'm sure there won't be any trouble," he murmured. His voice sounded like that of a dying sinner claiming confidence in his salvation.

"Johann, take the upstairs today," Margulies ordered as her boots hit the tile floor.

Vierziger raised an eyebrow. He looked spruce and trim. Somehow he'd managed to scrub away all the soot and matrix residue which had settled on him during the firefight.

"This is—"he began.

"Not today, Sergeant!" Mary Margulies snapped. "We're trading today."

She flashed a near-smile of apology to her subordinate, then to Coke.

"I think I know this guy," she explained in an undertone. She pointed toward the streetscape in Barbour's display. "I think he used to drive for me."

Barbour didn't comment, but his right hand moved. Half the hologram screen became a facial close-up of the man in khaki.

"Via, that's Angel, all right," Margulies said. "Via, he looks bloody awful!"

Margulies' friend carried a sub-machine gun, but it was slung muzzle-down over his back. His cheeks were hollow and his skin looked flaky, almost mildewed.

His well-dressed companion raised his knuckles to rap on the door.

Hathaway shivered and smiled falsely. "Ramon Luria," he murmured with a nod toward the holographic display. "Raul's son, that is."

The knock was crisp and imperative—three short strokes.

"Let your guests in, Master Hathaway," Coke directed. "There won't be any trouble."

If one of L'Escorial's leaders had come personally, that was certainly true. For so long as he was here.

The door sighed open. Ramon Luria waved a hand expansively. "Hathaway!" he said. "It's been too long since I sampled your beer. And you, sir, you'd be Major Coke, I assume? The very person I've come to see."

If you watched Ramon carefully, you could tell that he was nervous. His movements had a birdlike suddenness, and there was a tic at the corner of his left eye. At a casual glance, though, the syndicate boss was utterly relaxed.

"Hello, Angel," Mary Margulies said from a corner of the lobby. She stood with the sole of her right boot against the wall behind her. "I made a trip out to Silva Blanca just to see you the other day."

"El-Tee!" the man in khaki said. "Blood and martyrs, Lieutenant! What are *you* doing here?"

"Same as you, Angel," Margulies said, answering a more limited question than the one Angel asked. "I'm pulling security while my boss does business."

Coke suddenly realized why Margulies leaned back against the wall. That way she had an excuse for not offering her hand or her arms to her former comrade.

Angel's skin puckered and shook because muscles were twitching randomly in response to the commands of damaged nerves. He appeared to have been pulled from his grave to come here—and from the look in his eyes, his worst problems weren't the physical ones.

"Major Coke doesn't need security, El-Tee," Angel said. "We're all friends here.

I was, I was—"

His eyes darted toward Ramon. The syndicate boss pretended not to notice him, instead eyeing the lobby with an avuncular smile.

"I'd been partying a little, I mean, when you guys landed," Angel rattled out, "or I'd have been over before. I've been telling Ramon here and the Old Man, if the FDF wants in, hire them. There's no better!"

"Angel's our training officer," Ramon said, deigning to glance at his companion. "And he assists my son Pepe, our… shall we say 'war chief'?"

He laughed, a throaty sound and as threatening as jovial. "Angel Tijuca," he added. "Since I gather not all of you are familiar with our boy?"

"Rather than stand in a doorway," Coke said, "why don't we adjourn to the bar."

He nodded. "I'll buy the first round."

Ramon waved the idea aside. He wore rings on all four fingers and his thumb. The bands were set with rubies, diamonds, and what Coke judged was a large amethyst.

"I'm just the messenger, really," Ramon said. "I came to invite you back to our house to discuss future affairs with my father, Raul. I aid him, and Pepe even more so when he's home. But the Old Man still makes the final decisions."

"Your son Pepe isn't here, then?" Coke said with a bland smile.

"That's correct," Ramon answered with no smile at all. "But he'll be back soon, Major. And you will want to have come to a decision with my father before that time, do you see?"

He bent his lips up at the corners. The warning couldn't have been more explicit if he'd drawn and charged a pistol.

"I don't mind discussing my employer's business at any good location, Master Luria—" Coke said.

"Ramon, please, just Ramon," Luria said with another glittering arc of his hand.

"—but when we arrived, there was some difficulty with your men," Coke continued. "And since from the sound of matters last night, people are pretty worked up still, I don't know that your home would be the best place to talk business. For me, that is."

"Don't think anything of it!" Ramon ordered. "Those imbeciles you killed, you did me a favor. With so many in Potosi all together, the men need disciplining or they'll get completely out of hand."

"I'm not sure *they* feel that way," Margulies remarked from where she stood against the wall.

The veneer of bonhomie slipped from Ramon's face. "They feel whatever way the Lurias tell them to feel!" he said. "If I, Ramon Luria, tell you that you can visit my home without concern, that is so. Will you doubt my honor?"

"The Old Man doesn't think it's a good idea for him to show himself with things like they are, Major," Angel Tijuca explained with desperate sincerity. "Out in the street, I mean. Like you said, things got pretty excited last night. You'll be all right, truly."

Coke shrugged. There wasn't really a choice about going. He just hadn't wanted to appear too eager. "All right," he said. "Mary, you want to tag along?"

"You bet," Margulies said as she shifted herself onto both feet. "Maybe Angel and I can catch up on things while you talk business with the important gentlemen."

Niko Daun stepped into the doorway from the kitchen. His action station was first floor, rear; Vierziger and Moden guarded the upper story for now.

"I wonder if I could go, sir?" the sensor tech asked. He already wore the ammo pouch filled with bugging devices. "I'd sort of like to see the place."

"No, stick around," Coke ordered. He didn't want to try planting hardware in L'Escorial HQ while Tijuca was there. Margulies' friend might recognize Frisian equipment, which could be embarrassing—or worse. "I won't need a gofer, since we're just across the street."

He grinned at the syndicate boss to draw attention away from the exchange which had just taken place. "You know," he said, "you could have just phoned yourself."

Ramon waved his hand. "Would you have accepted the invitation had I not shown myself willing to visit you?" he said.

"You've got a point," Coke said. He deliberately checked that his sub-machine gun was on safe. Slinging the weapon muzzle-down across his back, he added, "Let's go talk to the Old Man, sir."

Ramon Luria ushered Coke ahead of him through the door marked BOARD ROOM. An old man in red and a middle-aged one wearing a business suit of Delian cut were already seated within.

Instead of wood paneling, the walls of the sanctum in the basement of L'Escorial headquarters were covered with holographic screens. If the equipment had been perfectly tuned, an observer would almost think he was standing at ground level and the building didn't exist.

In fact, the hardware had all been installed at stock brightness and coverage settings, which varied from unit to unit. One of the thirty-odd screens was dead and three others operated at less than half their proper resolution. The set-up made Coke think of a diorama viewed through distorting mirrors.

Ramon waved proudly at the walls and said, "My son Pepe brought these back with him from Delos on his last trip. Pepe is very up-to-date, very civilized."

There was no sign on the streets of the gunmen who had been omnipresent throughout Potosi since the survey team arrived. Civilians moved in nervous spurts, like birds on the verge of a violent storm.

The table in the center of the room was a black synthetic oval. There were thumb controls at eight points around its circumference. Each was a shallow dome paired with a shallow depression.

Coke casually fingered the bump nearest him. Nothing happened. If the system had been operating, his touch would have brought live a workstation linked to the data bank within the table.

"I am Raul Luria," the old man at the head of the table said without rising or preamble. "Potosi is mine, *Cantilucca* is mine. For too long I have allowed the Guzman syndicate to exist—out of affection for the late Pablo, so close a friend of mine. But after last night—"

Raul Luria rose with the staggering difficulty of a ship's mast being stepped by amateurs. The man seated to Raul's left looked alternately bored and disquieted by the rhetoric.

"—after last night, I have no more compassion. They must be crushed!"

The old man—the Old Man—pointed a crooked index finger at Coke. "Where do you stand in that, foreigner? Shall we crush you too?"

"I represent a business firm, sir," Coke said mildly. "We can supply personnel and equipment that will permit you to achieve your stated goal faster and more cheaply than you could in any other manner. I don't see why we can't strike a deal that will benefit both parties."

"One of the possible problems, Major," Ramon Luria said with his back to the door behind Coke, "is the sort of arrangement Friesland has already made with the Astras."

"And what you had to do with the raid last night," Raul Luria grunted as he bent, joint by joint, back into his chair. "If you're working with those pigs, I'll see to it that you're slaughtered with them. I swear it!"

"Father, we agreed there's no profit in discussing the past," Ramon said, his voice quivering between fear and contempt. "Isn't that so, Master Suterbilt?"

The businessman grimaced. "There'll be no profit in anything for the best part of a year," he said. "It'll take at least that long to rebuild gage stocks. And what is the Delos cartel going to say?"

"There's no arrangement between Astra and the FDF," Coke said. "Zip. Nada. Do you have a chip projector here?"

He glanced over his shoulder. Ramon looked blank. "I can bring one," he offered.

"Here, you can use mine," Suterbilt said. He slid a palm-sized belt unit across the table to Coke.

The businessman was stocky and probably no older than Coke, now that the Frisian had time to focus on him. At the moment, Suterbilt wore a scowl that amplified the angry appearance of his ruddy complexion.

Coke looked at the projector, then unclipped the one from his own belt instead. "That's all right," he said. "Mine will do."

The Frisian unit was half the weight of the older Delian projector Suterbilt used. Coke had hoped for a console model—the equipment built into the table itself would have been perfect, if the cursed thing had worked—but it didn't really matter. Cantiluccans probably wouldn't feel comfortable with the sort of crystalline images which the civilized universe took for granted.

Coke dropped into the reader the chip he'd prepared. He turned up the gain. "This is why we have no deal with the Astras," he said.

The negotiations in Astra headquarters shimmered in a hologram a meter across.

The image had a gray translucence and there was considerable distortion toward the edges of the field, but it was both visible and audible.

"*A company of infantry and a company of combat cars,*" said Matthew Coke's image. The scene was assembled from recordings made by the commo helmets of the three Frisians present at the meeting.

The image cut forward a few seconds. Barbour had spliced the data into the continuous form Coke wanted, but that meant the visuals were choppy. "*Approximately three thousand Frisian thalers per day,*" the Coke hologram said, "*perhaps ten percent over.*"

Raul Luria was trembling with rage. His mouth worked, but no words came out. Ramon, who had moved to the side where he was visible out of the corner of Coke's eyes, wore a fixed smile. Suterbilt, the factor for Trans-Star Trading, simply frowned in puzzlement.

The Frisians vanished abruptly. The three Astra principals remained. Through the excellence of Barbour's editing, Adolpho Peres' lips moved in near synchrony with his words: "*So our Frisian visitors clean up our problem. They board the ship we provide, though they don't know the ship's ours. And the ship never gets home.*"

The bug Daun had left beneath the Astra conference table was audio only. You couldn't have told that when Barbour had finished mixing input from the bug with images culled during the two-party conference. When the Peres image "spoke" the final words, his face froze in a grin of murderous triumph… which was certainly true to the spirit of the plan the gigolo had outlined to his fellows.

Coke shut off the recorder and smiled at the L'Escorial leaders. "So," he said. "I've recommended to my superiors that we not do business with Astra. Shall my team and I go home, or… ?"

Raul Luria began to laugh. For the first moments, Coke thought the old man might be having a stroke instead. The paroxysm continued for nearly a minute.

Ramon pulled out a lace handkerchief and stepped to his father's side. He stood there, looking worried but unable to act. Raul hacked and wheezed and drooled from the corners of his mouth.

Suterbilt swallowed. His body tilted slightly away from the L'Escorial patriarch, and he was careful not to look to the side.

The old man finally regained his composure. "You're a right clever bastard, aren't you, boy?" he said. "What's your name? Coke, is it?"

Coke nodded.

"You planning to eavesdrop on us the way you did those Astra gutter-sweepings, then?" Raul demanded.

"No sir," Coke replied. "I am not."

Not in the same way, at any rate. The devices Daun and Margulies had emplaced all up and down Potosi's main street would keep an eye—and ear—on both syndicates.

Raul nodded. "That's good," he said. "So, that's your price for two companies of your Frisian Defense Forces?"

"That's an estimate," Coke said. "It's a good estimate, but the final figure will have to be determined at Camp Able."

Raul looked puzzled, glancing toward Suterbilt.

"FDF Command on Nieuw Friesland," Coke clarified. "Ah—and I gather it may not be possible to bring heavy vehicles like combat cars in through the port here without getting the Marvelan Confederacy concerned. The price would be comparable for three infantry companies."

"That's a *very* high price," Suterbilt said. He glared at the Frisian representative as though he'd like to throttle him. The factor's hands, Coke noticed, remained flat on the black surface of the table, spread wide and patently innocent.

"Compared to the losses you received last night?" Coke said. "Because your present personnel and equipment are of such low quality?"

Suterbilt tightened his lips. He gave a quick toss of his head. It could have implied either assent or disdain.

"Infantry and tanks is better than just infantry?" Ramon Luria asked. "And the price is the same?"

Coke nodded to the plump man. "Roughly the same daily rate," he agreed. "And combat cars aren't exactly tanks, but they're big. The folks down the street didn't think we could ship them in. If we could, the concentrated firepower would be better."

"*We* can bring in your combat cars," Raul said, looking at the factor beside him.

"There's excess capacity on all the TST ships that land on Cantilucca," Ramon amplified with a giggle. "Empty coming in, but it can be full if there's something we want to *bring* in."

"Don't talk about that!" Suterbilt snapped. He glanced from son to father, clearly angry but aware that the pair of gangsters didn't view the situation as he—a nominally honest businessman—did.

Quite obviously the factor was cooking Trans-Star Trading's records by showing lower cargo tonnage than the hulls' actual capacity. By so doing, he cheated his employers of shipping charges and—more important—permitted the L'Escorials to avoid port duties which should have been paid to the Marvelan Confederacy.

The ships that carried undeclared gage off Cantilucca traveled part-empty coming in. As Ramon had said, that unlisted volume could be filled with Frisian troops and equipment.

"If it's possible to bring in the cars, that would speed up the operation," Coke continued smoothly, as if the byplay among the locals meant nothing to him. "I'm estimating forty days with combat cars, but using infantry alone would add considerably to the completion time."

"A million-two in *thalers*," Suterbilt said, wincing. He stared at his hands.

"Roughly," Coke agreed. "With combat cars."

"The deal still has to be without the Bonding Authority," Raul said. "You know that, don't you?"

Coke gave a nod as tight and enigmatic as that of the factor a few moments before. "That does leave a problem, doesn't it?" he said.

Raul looked at Suterbilt. "Pay him," the old man said. "Pay him—"

He glanced back at Coke. "Ten days, that'll be enough, won't it? On account, an earnest of our good faith."

"I can't raise that—" Suterbilt objected.

"I can't commit my superiors," Coke warned. "I can only recommend by message capsule…."

The Old Man waved at Coke. "Yes, yes," he said, "but with the money in hand, there won't be any trouble about the deal."

Ramon giggled. "'Money talks, nobody walks,'" he said, quoting an aphorism old when Croesus struck the first coin.

"I don't have," Suterbilt said angrily toward Raul, "*we* don't have that kind of money available now. The warehouse *burned*, don't you remember?"

"It's still collateral so far as TST is concerned," Raul said. He waggled a wizened fist in Suterbilt's face to emphasize the point. "Borrow the money from the company accounts on Delos, that's easy enough."

"And we'll repay it out of the Astra stockpile," Ramon added complacently. "Nobody will know the difference."

The factor grimaced but did not speak.

"We'll be kings with Astra out of the way once and for all!" Raul snapped. "And there's no choice anyway. If we don't move now, how are we going to pay the men with the gage gone?"

Suterbilt raised his hands to his face. He gripped his cheeks with a trembling violence that Coke watched in concern, wondering what the factor was going to do next.

Suterbilt slammed his palms back down on the table. "All right," he said. "All right! I'll raise the money."

He glared viciously at Coke and continued, "But it will take five days, maybe six, because of transit time to Delos. I *can't* write you a valid draft out of the funds available here on Cantilucca!"

Matthew Coke nodded calmly. "I'll inform my superiors of the pending circumstances," he said.

Coke should have been enthusiastic at the success of his mission. True, a survey team leader couldn't *commit* the FDF; but this was a perfectly workable deal, a *good* deal. Cantilucca would provide live-fire experience for relatively green forces, just the thing Camp Able was looking for.

The trouble was, Coke kept seeing the red-clad thug with a powergun thrust against the cunt of the whore his fellows were beating. The gunman could have pulled the trigger as easily as not, *on whim*; and the next time, he or another of his sort likely would do just that.

Matthew Coke was making sure that the set of circumstances which made such behavior possible continued.

Angel's private cubicle was at the end of the bunk room filling most of the L'Escorial building's second floor. He paused with his hand on the doorknob.

"Look, El-Tee," he said, "it's not a palace I got here. Ah—maybe we could go somewhere else, find a bar or something."

Margulies snorted. "It could be pretty bad, Angel," she said, "and I'd still have lived in worse. You know that, because part of the time you were there."

"Yeah, well, this is no great shakes," the man repeated, but he opened the door.

She *had* seen worse. There'd been the militia barracks on Typer where the locals relieved themselves in one corner of the room in which they lived, slept, and ate. That was the only military installation Margulies could recall being dirtier than this room of Angel's.

She hadn't regarded the Typer Militia as being real soldiers. Neither, obviously, was her one-time comrade here.

No feces, and perhaps no urine. But the smell of sour vomit was overpowering, and the originally white sheets on the bed were so dirty that they had for the most part a gun-metal color. The common barracks from which Angel's room was set off was in far better shape, though the number of troops bunking in it had been doubled or tripled in the recent past.

"Look," Angel repeated. "We better—"

Margulies pushed him casually inside and followed. "You were going to get me a drink," she said as she closed the door behind them. "Stop dicking around, hey?"

"Yeah, I…" he said. This must have been the first time in quite a long while that he'd been straight enough to appreciate the reality of his existence. His shoulders slumped as he looked at the fetid ruin around him.

The back and one leg of a chair protruded from a pile of garments. Margulies lifted the chair and shook it, then kicked the filthy clothing aside to make room for her to sit down. "When we last talked," she said in a casual tone, "you were talking about buying a tract of land where you grew up."

"Aw, fuck it, Missie, I'm no farmer," Angel said. He seated himself on the edge of the bunk and met her eyes for the first time since they came upstairs. "I left here when I was fifteen. Engine wiper on a starship, then I did some soldiering on Wellbegone. Got in with the Slammers, then the FDF. I don't know what I was thinking when I said I was going to raise gage. I think I just wanted to be fifteen again."

He bent and groped first beneath the bunk, then within the bedding proper. He came up with a bottle. It was unlabeled. The ten centimeters' depth of fluid within had a pinkish tinge.

"Ah…" Angel said. "Do you really want a drink? I don't have glasses."

"No problem," Margulies said, taking the bottle from him. The liquor was harsh. The pink color suggested flavoring, but the only taste she noticed was that of raw alcohol. She returned the bottle, wiping her lips with the back of her free hand.

"Or there's gage, of course," Angel offered with false perkiness.

"Naw, not for me," Margulies said. "But you used to prefer it to booze, didn't you?"

Angel got up and rested his hands on the window ledge. The glass was painted black and reflected the light of the single fixture overhead.

"I really stepped on my dick, Mary," he whispered to the glass. "I went out, I looked at land, and it all came back to me, starving and scrabbling and bored, bored to fucking *tears* all the time I was a kid. That was why I left. And it's worse now, the syndicates take twice the bite they did when I left."

He turned and looked at his former lieutenant again. "And I looked around the security troops and I thought, these clowns, they're not fit to be *recruits* to the Slammers."

"You got that right," Margulies murmured. Her mouth was oily with the liquor's aftertaste.

"So I hired on, with the Lurias because my old village, it belonged to L'Escorial," Angel continued. "Not that it mattered. I thought I could make something out of them, give them some discipline. That'd make it better for everybody, you see that, don't you El-Tee? The farmers too, if it was just paying for protection they had to worry about. Via, what place doesn't have taxes?"

"You can't turn the lot out there into soldiers," Margulies said. "Any more than you can build a gun out of cat turds."

"Don't I know it," Angel whispered. He looked at the bottle in his hand, then drank greedily from it. His Adam's apple throbbed with three swallows, four, before he set the liquor down again.

"I tried, El-Tee," he whispered to the bottle. "But they wouldn't listen. I'd have had to shoot a couple of them to get their attention and Via, the rest would've greased me the next night. You've got to sleep sometime, and there wasn't anybody *but* me."

He looked up at her. She nodded, agreement without empathy. Angel had chosen, just as surely as the constant low-level pain in Margulies' rebuilt leg reflected choices she had made.

"The gage stopped working," Angel said. "I was using too much. The first dose would put me to sleep. My skin was crawling, I'd scratch myself bloody."

He swallowed. "So I switched to booze and that, you know, that helped some. And I found that mixed gage didn't put me to sleep the way the pure stuff did, so sometimes I used that."

"Refinery tailings are poison," Margulies said harshly. "The best you're going to do is grind down the nerve sheaths so that you're a spastic for the rest of your life. *Or* you'll go blind. Or you'll fry your brain and sit around drooling. Think your new buddies are going to want to change your diapers, Angel?"

"I know all that!" he shouted. "I said it was just a time or two with tailings, didn't I?"

He hadn't, and if he had said that, it would have been a lie. It was amazing that Angel had managed the effort of will required to get straight when he learned that an FDF survey team was on Cantilucca, but it was vanishingly improbable that he would be able to maintain that state for more than a few hours.

Angel sat heavily on the bed, clutching the liquor bottle to him as if it were the only warmth in a world of ice. "Look, El-Tee," he said to the wall, "I just want you to know I've got it under control now. I'm fine, and in a day or two I'll have all my gear strac. I just want you to know that."

"I'm glad to hear that, Angel," Mary Margulies said as she rose to her feet. "I'd better check on the major. I'll see you around."

Twenty-odd L'Escorial gunmen lounged in the open barracks, laughing and talking. The general volume lowered as Margulies left the cubicle, but she heard some pointed gibes.

She didn't look to either side as she walked to the stairs at the other end of the room. If she looked at the men, she would kill them all.

It wasn't the liquor or the stench of Angel's room that made Margulies want to vomit. It was the vision of what her driver had become….

And the warning of what might become of Mary Margulies herself, if she ever tried to reenter civilian life.

Wind kicked dust and litter down the street. The eastern horizon was a mass of cloud, though the late afternoon sun still shone onto Potosi.

Coke drove one of the rented jitneys to the street from the walled courtyard at the rear of Hathaway House. Margulies waited for him at the head of the alley. The angles of a weapon in a patrol sling distended her light cape.

Coke disengaged the torque converter and braked beside her. "I don't need a guard, Mary," he said. "I'm just going to run up to the port and send a capsule off."

Margulies squatted to put her face on a level with his. Her smile was crooked; she hadn't said much since the pair of them left the meeting in L'Escorial headquarters that morning.

"You could lower the top and squeeze your cyclo into the back of the port van," she said. "I guess that's what you're planning to do. But I could also drive it back myself and save you the trouble. What do you figure?"

Coke looked at the security lieutenant. "Yeah," he said. "That sounds like a good idea. Hop in."

The jitney had four seats in back, facing outward in pairs from the central spine. Margulies sat crossways, so that she looked forward over Coke's right shoulder.

"I felt like getting out of Potosi for a bit," she explained quietly. "This isn't much out, but it's out."

"What the hell is that?" Coke said. He had started to reengage the drive train. Instead, he took his hand from the knob and touched the 2-cm weapon he'd thrust muzzle-down between his seat and the spine in back.

Three red-painted vehicles drove down the road from the spaceport at 30 kph, their sirens blowing. The first and last were armored trucks of the sort the team had seen before. The convoy's pace was probably governed to their best speed.

An air-cushion limousine drove between the two escorts. The vehicle was fitted with appliqué armor—which couldn't have been very heavy or the battery-powered drive fans wouldn't have been able to keep the car floating on a bubble of air. A scarlet film darkened the windows so that they were nearly opaque from the outside, but

Coke thought the driver was the only occupant.

Coke switched his commo helmet to channel one, the command push. "Stand by," he ordered. "Over."

He didn't know what was happening. He didn't think it was an immediate problem, but by definition he couldn't be sure of that. There was a tiny click behind him as Margulies took her sub-machine gun off safe.

L'Escorial gunmen spilled out of the gateway, thronging the street from which the sirens had driven all civilian traffic. Engines started up in the courtyard of Astra headquarters, but none of the Guzman personnel showed themselves.

The wind gusted again, promising the storm would sweep over Potosi in a few minutes. The open-sided jitney wasn't much protection, but it wouldn't be the first time Coke got soaked in the line of duty.

He keyed the command channel again. "Bob," he ordered, sure that Barbour would be at the console. "Upper right quadrant, feed me a composite of what's going on across the street. Over."

"Roger," the intelligence officer replied. A quarter of Coke's faceshield brightened with the scene in front of L'Escorial HQ, viewed by miniature cameras Daun had emplaced on the other side of the convoy. "Audio?"

"Negative," said Coke, "but maybe later. Out."

The Lurias, father and son, walked stiffly through the gateway. Raul leaned on Ramon's arm and used a cane with his other hand.

The sirens wound down to silence. The leading armored car fired a warning burst up the street past Astra headquarters. The tribarrel functioned properly, chugging out twenty bolts of deep cyan before the gunner took his thumbs off the butterfly trigger.

The limousine's doors lifted simultaneously like gull wings. A slim man got out on the other side of the vehicle. Without being ordered to, Barbour manipulated the camera view to give Coke a close-up of the newcomer's face. The man was young and handsome, with features as fine-boned as those of a bird of prey.

"Pepe!" Ramon Luria called.

Raul walked/staggered two steps forward and embraced his grandson. "You've come at a good time, my boy," the Old Man said.

The sound of the wind rasped syllables away from the words the men across the street spoke. Lightning flashed behind the cloudbank, but there was as yet no audible thunder.

"Bob, patch in the audio," Coke directed in a whisper. "Out."

"Trouble with our neighbors?" said Pepe Luria with liltingly ironic tones that now came through Coke's helmet. "Well, it had to come sometime, didn't it? I brought some toys that may come in useful."

Pepe reached back inside the limousine. When he straightened again, the camera showed that he had buckled on a belly-pack controller. He was holding a sphere some twenty centimeters in diameter in his hands.

"Bloody *hell*," Margulies whispered. "That's a firefly. All we need is a few of *those* things flying around."

"Watch!" Pepe commanded triumphantly.

The sphere floated out of his hands. A corona of purple sparks bathed its lower surfaces. Coke's commo helmet crackled minusculely in response to the discharge. The crowd of gunmen let out a collective wheeze of surprise.

"They won't last long," Coke muttered. "Who are you going to get to maintain fireflies on Cantilucca?"

"They're six to a set," Margulies said "Do you suppose he'd have brought more than one set?"

"I can direct them…." Pepe continued. He worked one of the tiny joysticks on his belly pack. The firefly danced and staggered nervously.

"He's not very good at it," Margulies said.

"Nobody can use those stock control sets," Coke said. "Not even one bird at a time."

"Bet Barbour could thread needles with it if he had to," Margulies replied.

"Or I can let them act for themselves on programmed instructions!" Pepe said.

He took his hands away from the controls. The firefly sailed up the street at a smooth walking pace, two meters in the air. The sphere kept the same face forward at all times. It only appeared to rotate because of the spinning static discharge which supported it.

"I hate those bastards," Coke murmured. "With a man, you can watch his eyes or his hands. I always refused to serve around the fireflies in the field."

The device was now a hundred meters up the street. It stopped and began to turn very slowly on its axis.

Pepe's belly pack projected a holographic view of what the firefly "saw." "I can watch things with them," he announced. He poised his finger on the control lever.

"And I can do more than watch!"

He pressed the lever in. The firefly lighted the facades around it with the rapid-fire flashes of five pistol-caliber powergun bolts. The bar adjacent to where the device hovered was The Blue Ox, an Astra hangout. The sign over its armored door disintegrated in flame and molten plastic.

The firefly turned another ninety degrees and drifted purposefully back. A man stuck his head out of The Blue Ox, gaped up at the blasted sign, and ducked inside again.

Pepe Luria stood arms akimbo, facing up the street toward the returning firefly. "Widow Guzman!" he cried. "I have six of them, Widow! And I can tell them to attack men wearing any color I choose, just the color! Do you hear me, Widow?"

Only the wind answered.

Pepe linked arms with his father and grandfather. He walked with them into the L'Escorial courtyard, laughing with bubbling promise. A red-clad subordinate jumped into the limousine to drive it and its cargo within.

The firefly's ammunition was expended. It trailed along behind its master. The glow of its iridium barrel faded.

"Let's get to the port," Coke said, but he stepped off the driver's saddle and motioned Margulies to take his place. "You drive. I've got to make some additions in the message I'm sending home."

The first drops of the storm hit, cratering the dust. The temperature had dropped ten degrees, but Coke felt colder than the weather justified.

CANTILUCCA: DAY FIVE

The telephone in the Hathaways' private quarters rang. Coke, lying in a haze of almost-sleep directly above the sound, snapped awake.

Moments later someone hammered on the hotel's front door. "Quick, open up!" a man called from the street. "I have to see the Frisian major at once! The Old Man needs him!"

It was three hours before dawn. Coke pulled on his commo helmet and switched it to the command channel. "Stand to," he ordered, probably needlessly, as he slid his feet into his boots. "Out."

He keyed channel five, the push Barbour chose as a patch to Cantilucca's landline communications. The transceiver Niko Daun had placed in the Hathaways' handset was the size of a matchhead and far more reliable than the phone to which it was attached.

Coke already wore his trousers and tunic. The night before was the first time on Cantilucca he'd taken his boots off to sleep. He guessed he'd return to field SOP from here on out.

"Hello?" Georg Hathaway croaked into the phone receiver. The innkeeper sounded both nervous and disoriented.

"Quick, you old fool and don't start arguing about it!" ordered the voice on the other end of the line. "Tell that hireling Coke that he's to come at once to Astra headquarters. At once! This is Adolpho Peres. And I warn you, little man, if there's any delay in Coke arriving, I'll take it out of *your* hide!"

"But—" Hathaway gasped.

"At once!" Peres shouted. He broke the connection with a bang.

Barbour had been sleeping beside his console in the lobby. Coke met the rest of the team, armed and ready, in the upstairs corridor. Below, Mistress Hathaway was talking to the L'Escorial messenger through the viewport in the door.

"I'll take care of the Astras," Johann Vierziger volunteered. Like Coke, he wore a cape over his weapons. "Peres feels we're soulmates, after all."

His smile was as thin as the corona of a collapsed star.

Evie Hathaway ran up the stairs. "Major Coke!" she called. "Major Coke!"

"Right," said Coke. "I'll take L'Escorial. Sten, you're in charge here—"

He flicked a quick finger at Margulies, forestalling the comment poised between her open lips.

"—and no, I don't want company, I want a reaction force. If both sides are calling us, there's probably no immediate danger, but I want all of you ready to move as needed."

The Hathaways had stopped at the head of the stairs as they saw the Frisians were up and alert.

"Please, Major—" Georg began.

Coke waved his hand. "It'll be taken care of," he said. "We're on our way." He slid between the locals with more haste than courtesy, though that would have been the Hathaways' choice had they been asked.

"There's an envoy from Delos," Bob Barbour called as Coke and Vierziger passed him. "A Madame Yarnell from the gage cartel on Delos, and she is *not* amused. From the way the Astra leaders talk, she's the cartel's troubleshooter—with the emphasis on 'shooter.'"

"Why can't they do this stuff at a decent time of day?" Coke muttered as he helped the sergeant pull open the heavy door.

"Because they're not decent people, Matthew," Vierziger said. "Of course, neither are we."

"You're the major?" the L'Escorial messenger said as Vierziger pushed past him. Then to Coke, "*You're* the major."

"Right," Coke agreed, striding across the street. Vierziger headed for Astra HQ at a gliding pace, not quite a jog.

"What's he doing?" the L'Escorial bleated, running to catch up with Coke but glancing toward Vierziger.

"Minding his own business," Coke said. "Pray to the Lord that *you* never find yourself his business."

He'd expected to find the L'Escorial courtyard full of armed men. Instead, half-dressed L'Escorials were trying to back their armored trucks into the garage beneath the headquarters building. The second-floor barracks was lighted. Coke could hear Pepe Luria shouting for his gunmen to get out by the back way at once.

Ramon Luria stood in the building's doorway, looking alternately inside and out toward the courtyard. The messenger scampered up to him.

Ramon raised his hand to strike. "You idiot, Pierro!" he shouted. "I told you to bring the Frisian major!"

"He's—" Pierro shrieked.

"I'm here," Coke said. The courtyard was indifferently lighted, primarily by the headlights of the armored vehicles. The Frisian in his gray cape was a moving shadow.

"Coke!" Luria cried. "Thank the Lord you're here! Look, you have to stop your troops coming. At once! You have to hold them back until Madame Yarnell has left Cantilucca!"

"Nobody at Camp Able's going to make a decision until they have your money in hand, Luria," Coke said harshly. "According to your paymaster, Suterbilt, that's still several days. You needn't have kittens."

Despite his aggressive tone, Coke felt cold inside. His daily message capsules were shipped by first available transport to Nieuw Friesland, but there was at least a week between sending and receipt. Coke wondered what the Lurias would do to him if they knew he had recommended against taking the proffered contract, whether or not Suterbilt came through with the earnest money.

The Old Man lurched along the hallway toward his son. Gunmen, groggy with drink and gage, were being hastened onto the back stairs by their more alert fellows. Pepe Luria fought his way down the stairwell through them. He wore the firefly controller, but none of the spheres were themselves in evidence.

"She's coming!" a L'Escorial shouted from the courtyard gate. "She's coming!"

"Everybody into the basement!" Ramon screamed. He gripped the Frisian's arm, fiercely and apparently unaware of what he was doing. His hand bumped the muzzle of Coke's sub-machine gun.

"Oh my Lord!" Ramon cried. "You're carrying a gun! Are you mad? She said no weapons in sight, none! She'll—"

Pepe joined them. Ramon turned to his son and said, "He's carrying a gun, Pepe!"

The youngest Luria looked Coke up and down with the interest of a dog sniffing something dead. "So, you'd be the expensive Major Coke, would you?" he said. "I suppose I needed to meet you some time, since L'Escorial now employs you."

To his father Pepe added, "It isn't in sight. But"—Pepe's eyes were as black as cannel coal. They focused again on Coke.—"hold it so that it's less obvious nonetheless. I don't care what the good madame does to you, but she might mistakenly think L'Escorial was involved in your bad manners."

The last of the L'Escorial armored trucks collided with a wall. The vehicle stalled on the ramp into the garage. The driver tried to restart his engine.

Ramon scampered over to the vehicle. "Leave it!" he cried. "Shut it down! And get out, get out!"

A car with a slim, armored body and four metal-mesh wheels on wide-spread outriggers pulled up in front of the L'Escorial building. Coke had seen similar vehicles used for ground reconnaissance where for one reason or another hovercraft were contra-indicated.

Raul Luria reached the doorway. Pepe put an arm around the Old Man's shoulders, more for solidarity than for physical support. Ramon skipped back to join his father and son.

Matthew Coke stepped aside, flattening himself in the shadows across the wall. He held the sub-machine gun vertically against his body, covered by the folds of the cape. He glanced at Pepe Luria, but only for an instant; and there was no expression on his face.

The door of the reconnaissance car folded down; the female passenger got out. Though the car's interior was more luxuriously appointed than was normal for the type of vehicle, it was still cramped quarters for those within.

The woman wore a white jumpsuit trimmed with silver, and a short, lustrous cape of some natural fur. She was by no means young, but surgery and cosmetics prevented Coke from trying to guess her age within two decades. She halted in the gateway where the lights of the stalled truck lit her brilliantly.

Raul Luria began hobbling toward her with his descendants a half-pace behind to either side. "Madame Yarnell!" he wheezed. "You honor us with your presence."

"Don't bother, Luria," the woman ordered sharply. "I'm going to say what I have to and then go back and repeat it to the Astras, those *other* childish idiots. This must stop! Do you understand?"

"Madame—" Ramon said, "we of course—"

"No, it's not 'of course,'" Madame Yarnell snarled. "If anything were *obvious* to you morons, you'd get on with business instead of ruining it. Can you imagine how much trouble you've caused with your fighting already?"

"It wasn't us who—" Raul began.

"Shut *up*, old man!" the woman ordered. "I'm here to talk, not listen. The reason gage deliveries have dropped by thirty percent over the past two quarters, and the *reason* that the product my fellows and I need to fulfill contracts has burned to *ash*—the reason is that you and Astra are squabbling instead of doing business. That will stop, now! Do you understand?"

"Of course, we want nothing more than to do business ourselves, mistress," Pepe said with his eyes lowered.

"That's good," the Delian representative said, "because if there's any more trouble, *our* retailers will cancel contracts and find other sources of supply. Whereupon Cantilucca will become superfluous… and you *gentlemen* in particular will become superfluous. Do you understand me?"

Pepe's face tightened.

Raul laid a hand heavily on the youth's shoulder. "May we offer you the hospitality of L'Escorial during your stay on Cantilucca, madame?" the Old Man said.

"You may not," Madame Yarnell snapped. "I'll be staying in the cartel offices in the port reservation while I'm here. And if you're wondering how long that will be—it will be until I'm absolutely sure that you and your imbecile compatriots have heard my message and are acting on it. I regret to say that it may be *years* that I'll be stuck in this cesspool!"

She spun on her heel, whirling the cape out from her shoulders, and walked back to the recon car. As soon as the door latched, the driver slammed into a tight turn and headed back toward Astra HQ. Coke suspected that the cartel representative had bypassed the Astras initially because she feared that L'Escorial, as the more seriously aggrieved party, was likely to take the next escalating step.

The Lurias bent their heads together, all talking at once. Coke looked at them, pursed his lips, and sauntered across the street to Hathaway House.

He supposed he should have been pleased that peace might come to Cantilucca. The trouble was, he kept thinking that with the syndicates in unbroken control, the best ordinary citizens could hope for was the peace of the grave.

CANTILUCCA: DAY SIX

"The beer isn't any better than Hathaways," Sten Moden said. The logistics officer watched the afternoon traffic over Coke's shoulder, as Coke did over Moden's. "But it's good to get out anyway. With Madame Yarnell in town, you could almost imagine Potosi was a normal place, couldn't you?"

Niko Daun returned from the bar, clanking three more mugs down on the sidewalk table. "They've got a dancer in the back room," he said indignantly. "They let the johns poke at her with shock batons. I don't care if she's stoned, they shouldn't do that!"

"There's a lot of things on Cantilucca they shouldn't do," Coke said. He drained the last mouthful from his current mug and set the empty under his chair to get it out of the way. "Madame Yarnell stopped people who'd be better dead from killing each other. That's about it."

He didn't see any guns on the street. Syndicate colors were muted as well. A red beret, a blue neckerchief—rarely anything more overt. Widow Guzman and the Lurias had sent most of their gunmen back into the farming districts for the time being.

"I wonder how Esteban's father-in-law's doing," Sten Moden said. "I'm afraid that the thugs that were swaggering around Potosi'll be looking for something to keep them occupied out in the sticks."

A woman screamed in a broken voice from the cafe's back room. Shouts and laughter greeted the outburst. A pair of men wearing red armbands got up from the table beside the Frisians and walked toward the back. They were fumbling in their pockets for the cover charge.

"Sir," Niko blurted. "Are we really going to help these guys? I mean, both sides, they're—they're animals, sir! The least we ought to do is say 'no sale' and go on back to Friesland."

"That still leaves the same people here," Moden said. "It's not an answer."

He swizzled a sip of beer around his mouth. He didn't appear so much to be savoring as analyzing the fluid.

"Oh, the beer's not that bad," Coke said. Without changing his tone, he went on, "I think if we wanted to…"

He paused, looked at his companions in turn, and resumed: "I don't think it would require much pushing from behind the scenes to get Astra and L'Escorial to pretty well eliminate each other."

In Matthew Coke's mind, the response was:

Daun: *"Sir, your proposal is clearly against the interests of Nieuw Friesland!"*

Moden: *"Major, I regret that, in accordance with the provisions of the Defense Justice Code, I'm going to have to relieve you of command for that treasonous suggestion."*

Niko Daun's face split with a wide grin. "Lord, sir!" he said. "I was afraid you were going to burn me a new asshole for saying that."

"Yeah," agreed Sten Moden, setting his mug down hard enough in his enthusiasm to slosh. "We were all afraid to discuss it with you, Matthew. But I don't care what color their money is—*something* has to be done about these bastards, and the six of us are the only folks around who might be able to do it."

"We *all*?" Coke repeated. "You two talked to the others?"

Daun nodded. "Vierziger said that was what he was here for, he guessed."

"Johann said he *presumed*." Sten Moden corrected. He shrugged. "I don't know exactly what he meant by that. But Johann's willingness to shoot people isn't in doubt, is it?"

"Bob, he's not real comfortable with the business," Niko resumed. "He's not afraid of Camp Able, it's not that, but… Well, anyway, he finally said he was in."

The sensor tech shook his head. "He's a good guy, Bob is. I don't understand what's going on under the surface, but he's a *good* guy. And a fucking wizard with that console!"

"Yeah, he's good all right," Coke said. All five of his people were good, were about the best he'd ever seen. And he was talking about dropping them into the gears of a very powerful machine, in hopes that the machine would break before they did.

"Mary?" he added aloud.

"She's the one who brought it up," Moden said with a half-smile. "I suppose we'd all been thinking about it, but she said it aloud."

"She said," Niko amplified, "that this was sort of like wiping your ass with a broken beer bottle—sooner or later, you were going to wind up in a world of hurt. But if she survived, she didn't want to remember that she hadn't tried to change things on Cantilucca."

Coke drank half his beer in a series of smooth swallows. Nobody spoke again until he stopped to breathe and brush his mouth with the back of his hand. "I'll work up a plan of action," he said. "We'll have to wait for the cartel representative to leave, but that shouldn't take long."

Daun frowned. "She said she might stay here for years, sir," he said. "We aren't going to…?"

"No," Coke said. "No, Madame Yarnell isn't going to bury herself on Cantilucca for any longer than necessary. A few months at the outside. Her coming is actually better for our purposes. When she does leave, the lid's going to come off with a bang."

The red hovercraft Pepe Luria brought back from Delos whined slowly down the street. Its presence cleared a path through the mostly civilian traffic, even though the overt threat of guns and murder was held temporarily in abeyance. The vehicle stopped alongside the table where the three Frisians sat.

A red-veiled side window slid down. Pepe was in the driver's seat. His father and grandfather sat in back.

Ramon leaned forward to get a better view past Raul. "Come with us, Major Coke," he called. "We'll ride in my Pepe's fine new toy, shall we not? And we'll talk."

Sten Moden's face was blank. Niko Daun looked questioningly from the hovercraft to his commander, taut as the hammer spring of a cocked pistol. Moden, seeing the same danger that Coke did, put his hand firmly on the sensor tech's right wrist.

Niko was desperately eager to do the right thing, but he hadn't a clue as to what the right thing *was* under these circumstances. That was a bad combination….

"Glad to learn there's something to talk about," Coke said easily as he got to his feet.

"He'll be okay, then?" Daun murmured to Moden as the hovercraft drove away with the major.

"He's got as good a chance as any of the rest of us," the logistics officer said. He finished his beer in a single mighty draft, then banged the mug down. "Another?" he asked.

Daun shook his head with an impish smile. "I'm meeting a friend in twenty minutes," he said. His expression segued into a frown. "Unless you think, you know, with the major and all?"

Moden shrugged. "He'll call us if he needs us," he said. "Don't get yourself so fucked up you can't function, that's all. But you can't be a hundred percent *on* all day forever."

"Yeah, well, this is nothing serious," the younger man said casually. "She's a nice enough girl, but it's just passing the time."

He glanced at Moden from the corners of his eyes. "Suppose the major's getting anywhere with the lady from the port office, sir?"

The logistics officer looked at Daun hard. "Do you suppose that's any of our business?" he asked.

Daun laughed without embarrassment. So far as he was concerned, there was no rank when guys talked about women. "Not business at all, sir," he said. "Though the Lord knows Potosi isn't short of that kind of business establishment."

Moden laughed also. "Yeah, well, we could ask Bob," he said. "But I think we won't, okay?"

The big man got to his feet. "Twenty minutes is time enough for a beer, kid. Sounds like you need to be slowed down some anyhow."

Pepe had raised the hovercraft's window even before Coke could open the passenger door. The youngest Luria's feelings about Coke were a complex blend of disdain, the hostility of a dominating male for a rival, and fear. Pepe was smart enough to know that Matthew Coke was someone he should fear.

Coke's feelings about Pepe were much simpler: Pepe was a scorpion Coke had found in his boot, to be dealt with directly—in both senses of the word.

The hovercraft wallowed into a turn and proceeded north, toward the spaceport. The chassis was a standard civilian model. With the full four passengers aboard and the armor added by some custom shop on Delos, the vehicle was seriously underpowered. It was a toy, just as Ramon had said.

"Here's the earnest money," Raul said abruptly. He extended a quivering hand between the front seats to pass Coke a credit chip.

"Now, how quickly can you get your gunmen here?" Ramon asked. "Madame Yarnell will be leaving Cantilucca in six days, maybe seven."

Coke took the chip and held it in his hand.

A pair of jitneys was passing in opposite directions in the street ahead. There was room for the hovercraft to fit between them, but the vehicle's damping program hadn't been upgraded to take account of the weight of the armor.

Pepe steered left. The car had by now accelerated to 45, perhaps 50 kph. The back end swayed outward, continuing the vector of the directional change after the driver centered his wheel again.

The left-side jitney carried a farm family—two adults, four children, and a vast burden of produce piled on top. The hovercraft sideswiped it with a bang and screech of metal. Three-meter-long stalks of sugar cane slapped the car's windshield. They left syrupy blurs across the film-darkened glass.

Pepe cursed viciously. He continued to overcorrect for the next hundred meters. The car fishtailed up the street, its paint scarred beyond the capacity of anyone on Cantilucca to match.

"The times are the same they've always been," Coke said. "Seven sidereal days, plus or minus, to get the message to Nieuw Friesland. A day to load the companies. Five days to get them here since the troopship will come direct. Plus whatever time it takes Camp Able to decide whether or not to take the contract. If they take the contract."

"You'll send the message now," Pepe said in a rasping whisper. "We're carrying you to the port to do that. And you'll see to it that your mercenaries do arrive on schedule, Master Major, or it will be very unfortunate for you and your friends. You don't expect to leave before *all* the business with Astra is completed to our satisfaction, do you?"

"Now, Pepe," Ramon said nervously. "We don't want the major to think that we don't trust him."

"I trust him," Pepe sneered. "Because he knows he's a dead man if he doesn't do what he's promised to do."

"What the major has promised…" Coke said in a thin voice as his spirit floated out of his body to observe. "Is that he'll inform his superiors of the situation on Cantilucca. I doubt they'll act as you desire. There's every reason to expect your Delian mistress will summon a large force of her own as soon as the FDF arrives. Camp Able isn't going to send two companies into a ratfuck."

"Madame Yarnell is going to be recalled!" Ramon said.

They were beyond the outskirts of Potosi. The hovercraft had accelerated to about 75 kph, probably its best speed with this load. The vehicle pogoed over the bad surface, but the ride was more comfortable than it would have been in a jitney or the port van.

"I heard you before," Coke said. "When she leaves, I will immediately inform Camp Able of the fact."

Pepe gave him a look of boiling hatred. The flexible skirts of the car's plenum chamber brushed a treebole. Contact sent the vehicle in a slow carom toward the other side of the road.

"A bomb will go off in a consignment of Astra gage after it arrives on Delos," Raul Luria said in a voice as jagged as a crosscut saw.

"Grandpapa—" Pepe said.

"I will handle this," the Old Man retorted. "There will be a fire, perhaps great destruction. It will be far more important to the cartel than anything happening on Cantilucca is. When Madame Yarnell goes to Delos to investigate, *that* will be the moment to sweep Astra away forever."

"And by the time she comes back," Ramon added complacently, "there will be peace all across the planet, just as we all desire."

"I see…." said Coke as a placeholder while he thought. "You don't think the cartel might take a serious view of this bomb?"

The car was nearing the spaceport reservation. Warned by his previous control problems, Pepe started the braking process in good time.

The young man looked at Coke. "Do you think I'm a fool?" he said. "We have nothing to do with the business. It's Astra gage, and its not traveling on a TST hull. If they do trace the particular drum back, they'll find it was placed in the shipment by a port flunky."

"Not one of our people," Ramon chuckled. "He knows nothing about it. He thinks he's working a scam to substitute tailings for pure gage. Even the whore we're working through doesn't know more than that."

The hovercraft pulled up in front of the passenger operations building. The idled fans imparted a low-frequency wobble to the vehicle as it rested on its skirts.

"Now will you send your message?" Pepe demanded.

"You bet," Coke said. "You needn't wait around—I'll find my own way back."

Coke waited until he'd closed the car door behind him before he keyed his commo helmet. Pilar Ortega would be inside at the desk, and he didn't want her to overhear either. She'd be glad to see him, as she always was….

"Two and Four," he said, alerting Moden and Barbour. "I'm going to need information on a shipment of gage that went out yesterday or today. Somebody, probably a port official, doctored a manifest, and I need to know his name soonest."

Margulies stood at the front door, looking out through the triangular viewport. The evening traffic was somewhat lighter than it had been with a thousand more gunmen in town, but civilians had reappeared on the street in nearly a great enough number to balance the loss.

The two police huddled in a corner of the saloon. At another table, Georg Hathaway chatted morosely with his friend Larrinaga.

"There we go," said Sten Moden with satisfaction. He expanded the sidebar into the main screen. "There's the anomaly, sure enough."

Bob Barbour sat in a folding chair beside the console. Moden had handled the equipment enough in his presence that Barbour no longer hovered like a mother hen when the logistics officer used the console.

The intelligence officer leaned forward to check the line Moden highlighted. "Serial numbers out of sequence?" he said. His doubt was evident only in the perfect neutrality with which he stated the evidence he saw.

"Not the Astra serial number," Moden explained with satisfaction. "That wouldn't mean anything. This is the *transaction* number, the slug the port computer gave the drum at initial processing. That ought to be perfectly linear, but see—this one appears in a sequence of drums delivered three days later."

"I'll be hanged," Barbour said. "I didn't know there were transaction numbers different from the manifest serials."

He looked at Moden. "Sten," he said. "You just taught me something."

The big man grinned. "A lot of people think supply is boring," he said. "I didn't find it that way."

Still grinning, though the expression took on a certain stiffness, he patted the scar of his left shoulder and added, "Sometimes it's way *too* exciting."

"Nothing's boring if it's in your soul," the intelligence officer said. "All right, do you want to run the check on who was on duty or shall I? When we cross-check the time the drum dropped out and the time it reappeared, we ought to have our boy."

"I'm coming in," the console reported in the voice of Johann Vierziger.

Moden looked up at Margulies. "Was he out with the major?" he asked.

"Just out," Barbour murmured before the security lieutenant could respond. "The major's still at the port."

"Waiting for us to answer him," Moden realized aloud. He got up from the console. "Go ahead, Bob. Do the personnel check. Two hands'll get the data out quicker."

He grinned. "And anyway, you're going to have kittens if I don't let you play with your lady, here."

When Margulies pulled the door a crack open, Vierziger entered the lobby of Hathaway House wraith-swift. He looked at the men at the console. "You're succeeding?" he asked.

"So far, so good," Barbour murmured as his fingers danced over the keys. He didn't look up from his work, the two parallel half-screens of data which he was correlating.

"I'm glad somebody's doing something useful," Vierziger said in a voice of bridled fury. He walked into the saloon alcove.

Margulies turned so that her sergeant was within the arc of her vision, though she instinctively avoided focusing *on* Vierziger. Tonight he gave the impression of a door glowing white with the fire behind it, restrained until something happens to destroy the panel's integrity. After that—

"You!" Vierziger said. "Larrinaga. What are you doing here?"

The local man looked at the dapper Frisian. For a moment Mary Margulies thought Larrinaga was going to make a smart remark. She knew she wasn't fast enough to stop Vierziger if that happened, she didn't think *any* human being was fast enough.

Larrinaga swallowed and said, "Nothing, I suppose. That's all I've done for a long time."

"Get up," Vierziger said. Larrinaga blinked at him.

"Get up!" Vierziger repeated, his voice cutting like a bread knife honed to a wire edge. His left hand reached for Larrinaga's throat.

Georg Hathaway rose from his chair and backed away, mumbling to himself.

Larrinaga jumped to his feet. "Are you going to kill me?" he shouted. "Go on! That way maybe I'll see Suzette again!"

"Johann—" Mary Margulies said. Her arms were out to her sides; her hands spread wide.

Vierziger slapped the local man, an open-handed blow *only* to the cheek. It cracked like a pistol shot and knocked Larrinaga to the floor.

"Vierziger, slow down," Sten Moden said, stepping from the console into the bar alcove. His manner was neither threatening nor afraid. He moved like a storm blowing off the sea.

With the same hand he'd used to slap, his left, Vierziger reached into his purse. He tossed several credit chips onto Larrinaga's chest.

"There you go!" he said. "Three hundred thalers, enough to get you off this *cesspool* of a world and off to somewhere that you can be a man again. Do you want to do that? Do you *want* to be a man?"

Larrinaga got to his feet. "I am a man, Master Vierziger," he said in a raspy voice. He met Vierziger's eyes, and that took balls even if he really wanted to die. Margulies knew there were worse things than death, and she was pretty sure that Johann Vierziger had seen some of them.

Moden stood quietly, arm's length from the pair of men. The situation was under control. He didn't want to draw attention to himself by moving again.

Larrinaga gathered the credit chips in his hand and offered them back to the Frisian. Vierziger didn't move.

Larrinaga put the money on the table at which he'd been sitting. "Thank you for the offer," he said. "I don't choose to leave Cantilucca while… what remains of my wife is here. But I'm not going to buy our house back by sitting here and cadging drinks, am I?"

He stepped around Vierziger because the Frisian wouldn't shift to let him by. Larrinaga nodded to Moden and to Margulies. "Thank you for your hospitality, Georg," he called to Hathaway. "I won't return until I'm able to pay down my bill, though."

He pulled open the front door and was gone. The mark of Vierziger's hand on his sallow cheek blazed like a flag.

"Oh my goodness," mumbled Georg Hathaway. He set upright the chair that had fallen over. "Oh my goodness!"

Moden sat down beside Bob Barbour. When things were serious, the big man seemed more like a force of nature than a human being.

Margulies let out a deep sigh of relief. She looked at Vierziger and shook her head ruefully. "You know," she said, "I gotta hand it to you, Johann. You may just have saved that silly bastard."

Vierziger looked at her. She remembered what she'd thought about the things he'd seen. "Nobody can save another person," he said, so quietly that Margulies thought perhaps she'd imagined the words.

Vierziger walked to the staircase. "Niko!" he called. "Come down here, please, with your kit. We have work to do."

Sten Moden glanced at the security lieutenant. He raised an eyebrow. Margulies shrugged.

Daun appeared at the top of the stairs, trying to buckle his equipment belt one-handed. The other hand held his larger equipment case and the sling of his sub-machine gun.

"What's up?" he asked, jouncing down the steps.

"We're going to check out security for our new employers," Vierziger said. He opened the coat closet beside the front door and took out the attaché case he'd put there. The case was made of—at least covered with—reptile hide of some sort, black and shiny and as exquisite as every other part of Vierziger's ensemble.

The only weapon he carried was the pistol over his right hip.

"Driving or walking?" the sensor tech asked. He stopped in the lobby and fastened the belt properly.

"You're driving us," Vierziger answered. "I'll give you directions."

He nodded goodbye to the others as he closed the door behind him.

"Doesn't handle himself much like a sergeant, does he?" Sten Moden said to nobody in particular after the door closed.

"Yeah, I noticed that too," Margulies said dryly. "Sten, did you know Joachim Steuben? Colonel Hammer's hit man?"

Moden shrugged. "Saw him once, a long way away. I'd heard he was dead."

"He *is* dead," Margulies said. "I saw the incident report. Took a 2-cm bolt slap between the shoulder-blades. No trouble with the identification—head and limbs weren't touched. But there's *no* curst doubt he was dead—"

The two officers looked at the armored door without speaking further.

"Bingo!" said Barbour. He'd gone on with his search while everyone else was focused on Johann Vierziger. "I've got what the major's looking for!"

"Well, call it in to him," Sten Moden said. "Sounded like he meant it when he said ASAP."

Barbour touched the channel one button on the console.

Mary Margulies leaned over the intelligence officer's shoulder to see the highlighted name. "Cargo Supervisor Terence Ortega," she read aloud. She frowned. "The name's familiar for some reason."

"Now," said Johann Vierziger as the door to the underground garage quivered. Daun ran the jitney forward five meters, across the head of the ramp.

Suterbilt's armored four-wheeled van pulled halfway through the doorway. The driver slammed on his brakes in a panic when he realized the lighter vehicle was halted across his passage.

Vierziger stepped off the back of the jitney with the attaché case in his left hand and a bright smile on his face. The van's headlights fell across him. "Master Suterbilt!" he called in a cheerful voice. "Just the man we're looking for! We've identified a security problem."

The van's driver opened the door and stepped out onto his running board. He pointed a bell-mouthed mob gun through the crack at the Frisian. Vierziger walked over and extended his right hand to the driver. The local man aimed the mob gun skyward and shook hands, looking confused.

"Who are you?" Suterbilt called from inside the vehicle. After a moment, he got out and walked a step up the ramp.

"Johann Vierziger of the Frisian Defense Forces," Vierziger answered enthusiastically. "We've run a security check on L'Escorial—and yourself, of course, since you're really the most important—"

"I'm not a member of any local organization!" Suterbilt interrupted hastily. "I work for Trans-Star Trading."

"Of course you do," Vierziger agreed with a patently oily smile. "Of course. But—you can see how significant you are to us, to the FDF, surely?"

He waved his hand toward the street traffic. "That other lot, they're boobs with guns. They don't matter to professionals like ourselves, whatever color they happen to be wearing when we go to work. But *you*, Master Suterbilt… Anything that could affect our payment is a matter of serious concern."

The TST offices were on the second floor of the building Suterbilt was leaving on his way home. He glanced up at the block of lighted windows.

"We have a security system as well as guards," he said in dawning nervousness. "Do you think…?"

"It's not here that we foresee a problem," Vierziger explained. "After all, an attack on TST doesn't affect you personally. We're more concerned that the work of art you have in an outlying dwelling would be targeted. You have a Suzette, do you not? A psychic ambiance that's probably worth close to the value of the warehouse which Astra has already destroyed."

Except for the pistol on his hip, Vierziger looked like an unusually well-dressed businessman from a highly developed world. The reptile-skin case caught the light of passing vehicles as he gestured with it. The shimmer drew attention away from his right hand—gun hand—which moved scarcely at all.

"What could they possibly gain by damaging the ambiance?" the factor asked in amazement. "Anyway, I've thought of that. There's six guards in the house at all times. As thick as the walls are, they could hold out for days if there was trouble."

Suterbilt's driver settled back into his seat. He shifted his gaze between his principal, standing beside the van, and Niko Daun, seated in the saddle of the jitney with a vaguely positive expression.

"Precisely!" Vierziger said, leaving Suterbilt even more puzzled. "And what would you give to prevent the destruction of that valuable work of art, Master Suterbilt? Would you cancel the FDF's contract?"

"Well, I wouldn't—" the factor began.

"And more to the point," Vierziger said, steamrollering the reply, "does Astra *think* you might do that? They've struck unexpectedly once, you remember. That success will encourage them to choose the next weak point."

"There's nothing weak about it!" Suterbilt insisted. "I have guards and—"

"*And* an alarm system, just as the L'Escorial warehouse had!" Vierziger snapped. "If you don't mind, sir, why don't we finish this discussion in place—at the threatened location. I can point out the problems to you as well as the steps we'll take to solve them."

"I wasn't planning—"

Vierziger turned and gestured imperiously with the attaché case. "Specialist Daun!" he ordered. "Back up your cyclo, please. When the car pulls out of the drive you'll be able to park in the garage and get in with us. I want you along."

He looked at Suterbilt again. "That is all right, isn't it?" he said. "I'm concerned that Astra sympathizers or even mere vandals will deface the vehicle if it's not protected. Specialist Daun's expertise is quite important for our assessment."

Suterbilt swallowed. "Well, I—" he said. "Yes, of course, park your car in space twelve. I'll drop you off here again when we're done."

He frowned. "This isn't going to take very long, is it?"

"Tsk!" Vierziger said. "Ten minutes, fifteen at most. But if it's not done, the damage could be irreparable."

He slipped past Suterbilt and into the back of the van as though he'd been formally invited to do so. After a moment, Suterbilt sighed and got in beside the Frisian.

It would be simpler to carry out the inspection than to continue the discussion. Besides, Suterbilt got an uncomfortable feeling when he argued with the dapper stranger. It was as though he was eye to eye with a cobra, or perhaps a shark.

"Roger," Coke said, looking over the counter at Pilar Ortega as he spoke into the pickup of his commo helmet. "One out."

The artificial intelligence in the helmet disconnected the circuit at the word "out."

Pilar glanced up with a smile that faded when she saw the set of Matthew Coke's face. They'd spent long enough together during the time the Frisian had been on Cantilucca that she was beginning to read even expressions meant to be noncommittal.

"Bad news?" she asked. Her voice quivered on the second word. No one else was present in the passenger services building; Pilar had been in the process of shutting up for the evening.

Coke looked around, more to provide a moment to think than because he expected there would be anything to see. A freighter well across the field lifted in a rainbow of ionized atoms. Pilar had processed the two passengers, traveling salesmen in irrigation and cultivating machinery, through the boarding checks an hour before.

"Expected news," Coke said. He met the woman's eyes. "Bad news, yeah."

He took a deep breath. "Pilar," he said, "you've got to get off Cantilucca immediately. Pack a bag with enough clothes to wear, take any—"

She was staring at him in horror. Her right hand clasped the crucifix.

"—knickknacks that you absolutely have to have," Coke continued, plowing forward even though the woman looked as if he'd started to disrobe in the middle of the office. "You can go anywhere, except not Delos, and you've got to—"

"Matthew! Stop this!" Pilar said.

"—go *now*," Coke blurted. "Pilar, please, I don't want to say this—"

"*Stop*, Matthew!" she cried.

The rainbow curtain of light lifted rapidly. It raced across the terrazzo floor as the freighter climbed vertically from the port. The deep thrum of the starship's engines made the prefabricated building shudder with familiar vibrations.

Coke leaned across the counter. He hugged Pilar tightly to him so that he couldn't look at her face.

"Pilar," he said quickly, crisply. "Terry, your husband Terry, has screwed up really badly. He's done something that'll cost the Delos cartel millions of pesos, maybe tens of millions. When they investigate they'll spot him, just as my people did. They'll kill him and everybody close to him as slowly as they can make it happen. You've got to get out of the way now, before it happens."

He thought that Pilar would push him away, though they'd held each other past evenings in the privacy of her suite. Instead she pressed her hands against his shoulder blades. "Matthew," she said, "why are you saying this?"

"I'll give you money, money's not a problem," he said. "*Time* is a problem. If you're still around when the cartel comes looking, I don't know what, what your chances'll be no matter how I try."

"Please," Pilar said in a subdued tone. She straightened against his pull. He let her go.

"Matthew," she said. "Even if what you say is true, I can't abandon Terry. You know—"

"Pilar, he's abandoned you!" Coke shouted. "He hasn't been home to sleep for a week! Three days ago he picked up some of his clothes while you were—"

"Matthew! How did you know that?"

"While you were at *work*, curse it, and I know it because I'm having him watched, that's how I bloody know it!"

She turned her back. Her shoulders hunched over her sobs. "You don't understand," she cried. "What Terry does is between him and the Lord. *I* won't abandon him."

Coke threw open the gate in the counter and stepped inside. Pilar flinched away, but he grabbed her by the upper arms. "All right, Pilar," he said. "You won't go without your husband, so let's get him."

She didn't resist as the Frisian walked her toward the side door where the van was parked. The door opened ahead of them. A Marvelan, one of the clerks from the office next door, stuck his head in. "Hey, Pilar," he said. "Tomorrow will you cover for—"

He finally noticed Coke and Ortega in an apparent embrace. "Oh," he concluded.

Coke cleared the Marvelan out of their way by pointing a finger like a lance tip. "Go do your own job for a change!" the Frisian shouted. "Pretend you're good for something!"

He handed Pilar into the van and stepped around to the driver's side. The key was already in his pocket. He'd driven the pair of them ever since the first night he escorted Pilar home.

The freighter had vanished into orbit, preparatory to entering Transit space. The two moons were chips on the eastern horizon.

"Where are we going, Matthew?" the woman asked softly.

"I told you," he said. The diesel spun thirty seconds before it caught. He'd meant to have Sten's mechanic friend work the cursed thing over, but he didn't suppose it mattered any longer. "We're going to get your husband and I'll put both of you on the next ship *out* of here."

He revved the engine to keep it well above its lumpy idle while he dropped the transmission into gear. The van lurched forward. Only when they were twenty meters along the driveway did Coke add the load of the headlight to his demands on the stumbling engine.

"I hope the two of you will find a happy life in your new home," he added bitterly.

Suterbilt got out of the van in front of a one-story freestanding structure on the northern outskirts of Potosi. The walls were sheer and windowless, and the door would have done for a bank vault.

"You see?" the factor said with a sweep of his arm. "No common walls or floors to break in through. This is probably the safest place in the whole town. A fortress!"

"If it were a fortress," Johann Vierziger said as he followed Suterbilt from the vehicle, "it would have firing ports. That's the obvious first problem here."

He sauntered toward the door. Behind him, Suterbilt wore a look of dawning concern.

"Larrinaga must really have been in the money to afford this," Niko Daun observed as he brought up the rear. "You wouldn't guess that to see him now, would you?"

"What?" said Suterbilt. "Well, yes, I suppose he was doing rather well. It was Larrinaga's competition that drove that old fool Roberson to tie in with Astra, to tell the truth."

The factor laughed with cruel humor. "Out of the frying pan and into the fire, that was," he added. "If I'm feeling kindly after we've cleaned out the Astras, I'll let Roberson go off-planet alive."

He pressed the call button beside the door. A melodious chime sounded, blurred by the thickness of the walls. Nothing else happened for a moment

"*And*," Vierziger noted aloud, "none of the so-called guards are keeping a watch on the exterior display."

He nodded upward toward the miniature lens array above the door. The camera fed a surveillance display inside.

Suterbilt pursed his lips.

Locks within the panel chuckled liquidly as the mechanism drew them back. A man inside grunted and pushed the heavy door open. He wore a red headband and tried to stand at attention when he'd accomplished his task. Three other men stumbled into the entryway behind him, tucking in their clothes and checking weapons that they'd obviously just grabbed.

"Ah, g'day, sir," the guard with the headband said. "I, ah, we weren't expecting you tonight."

The last two guards appeared from the living area beyond. One of them was holding the other upright. The front of the latter man's tunic was stiff with dried vomit. His eyes were open, but they didn't focus.

"You normally call ahead, I gather," Vierziger said to the factor. A sneer was implicit in his dry tone.

"These gentlemen are security specialists," Suterbilt said harshly. "They're here to view the premises."

Vierziger walked into the house. "And to look at the ambiance itself," he said coolly.

He raised his attaché case, holding it between himself and the guard. The gesture was similar to that of a woman whisking her long skirt away as she passes dog droppings on the sidewalk. When he was clear, he set the case down beside the wall.

The interior of the house was pretty much of a pig sty. Liquor bottles and hundreds, perhaps thousands, of empty stim cones littered the floors. The building had a sophisticated environmental system to exchange outside air, but the filters had been unable to control the stench of human wastes, vomit, and unwashed bodies.

There was no sign of women, though. Apparently Suterbilt's orders that no outsiders should be admitted had been obeyed to the letter.

The factor rapped his knuckles on a wall to direct attention away from the state of housekeeping which he'd permitted. "See these?" he said. "The whole place is a ceramic monocasting, twenty centimeters thick on the outside. You could shoot straight into a wall and not so much as scar it!"

Vierziger sniffed. "Ceramics are all very well so long as you don't exceed their strength moduli," he said. He walked down the hall, deliberately shuffling his feet sideways to sweep litter out of his path. "One additional straw beyond *that* and you've got sand, not armor."

"Well, yes, but…" Suterbilt said. "Ah—the ambiance is at the end of the hall. It was the master bedroom."

"I assumed that," Vierziger sneered. "I'm glad you had sense enough to lock your guard *slugs* away from it. Otherwise there wouldn't be anything left for Astra to threaten, would there?"

Niko sniffed. "Not much of a lock," he said. It was an add-on, cemented to the panel and jamb. "I guess it's good enough, though."

The guards were restive and concerned. One of them had drunk enough to be obviously angry, but a pair of his fellows gripped his wrists. The group was armed with the assortment of shoulder weapons, pistols, and knives that had been typical street wear for the gangsters before Madame Yarnell arrived.

"I'll open it for you," Suterbilt said, stepping forward with an electronic key. Vierziger's sneering superiority had reduced the factor to nervous acquiescence with every demand, spoken or not.

The room illuminated itself softly when the door opened. The fixtures in the portion of the house which the guards occupied had been dimmed over the months by a grimy miasma. Here the light, though subdued, had the purity of evening over a meadow.

"*Nice* installation work," Niko said as he surveyed the bare room. "Some artists, they think the hardware is beneath them. Not her."

"What?" Suterbilt said. "Are you joking? I had the furniture removed. Quite a nice bed. I'm using it myself."

"No, no," the sensor tech said. "The ambiance, of course. Look at these heads."

Daun walked into the center of the room. His focus on the psychic ambiance burned through the layers of good humor which made him easy to get along with. Niko Daun liked to be alone when he was working… and people who'd been around him while he was in work mode didn't care to repeat the experience.

"There," he said, pointing to a glint in the ceiling, a rubidium-plated bead the size of a man's thumbnail. "There, there, there, there"—the sidewalls—"and the main board here"—he pointed to the shimmering fifteen-centimeter disk in the center of the floor—"where the bed would keep people from walking on it. Though I doubt that would have hurt the resolution, the way she's got the projectors bedded. Just *look* at the way she faired them into the matrix!"

"Yes, it can't be removed without destroying the whole thing," Suterbilt said. "And probably the house as well."

Daun turned on him with the casual prickliness of a cat. "Don't talk nonsense!" the technician snapped.

"Specialist Daun," Vierziger said smoothly, "we're here to—"

"Look," Daun said, the first time anybody who knew Johann Vierziger had interrupted him in a long while. "Since we're here, I'm going to try the ambiance. This is probably the only time I'll be around a genuine Suzette."

Nothing in the sensor tech's tone suggested he was willing to discuss the matter further. As he spoke, he took a flat, palm-sized device from his smaller toolkit and opened its keyboard.

Vierziger laid the tips of his left index and middle fingers on Daun's wrist. "Master Suterbilt will switch on the ambiance for us, I'm sure," Vierziger said.

"Yes, yes, but I'm in a hurry," the factor grumbled. He took another key from his wallet. He flicked the on switch in the air without result. "Let's see…"

"Stand over here," Daun said, gesturing Suterbilt to a point near where the head of the bed would have been.

Suterbilt frowned but obeyed.

"I could have turned it on easier," Daun grumbled under his breath to the other Frisian.

"You could remove the work so that it could be reconstructed?" Vierziger murmured back.

"Huh?" said Daun. "Course I could. Don't be an idiot. The adhesive'll powder at twenty-eight point nine kilohertz. Take about three seconds each. And realigning them afterward, *that's* no sw—"

The room shimmered out of the present and into a golden timelessness. Suterbilt had finally managed to trigger the ambiance with his low-powered key.

Vierziger was in an individual paradise. Foliage waved slowly in breezes the viewer could not feel, and the air was perfumed with life itself.

Movement was thought-swift and effortless. The trees mounted like towers holding the sky, far taller than was possible for normal vegetation which fed its branches by osmosis against the drag of gravity. The viewers' minds could ascend the roughness of the bark, feel the single-celled microflora which gave texture and color to the trunks, or exist as the entire world—plant, animal, and the supporting soil beneath.

The ambiance was more real than the sidereal universe to those within its pattern of impinging stimuli. Through it all, informing it all, was the single warm presence of its creator.

"*…what remains of my wife is here…*" Larrinaga had said. He was right, and he was perhaps right as well that Suzette was a saint.

That wasn't a subject on which Vierziger felt competent to judge.

The glow dimmed, vanished. Physical reality reasserted itself and memory of the ambiance sucked itself down a wormhole into the unconscious of the men who had experienced it.

Suterbilt shook himself. "I ought to come here more often," he said. "It relaxes me."

Niko Daun looked at the projection heads, shaking his head in delight. "Amazing," he said. "Absolutely amazing. I wish I could meet her."

"I think," said Vierziger, "that you just did."

The effect was no more than a mental hologram; not *life*, not even something alive. But Vierziger could understand why Larrinaga believed his wife was still present in the ambiance. He supposed that was all you really had of any artist, and perhaps of any human being: the things they had done.

"We can go now," Vierziger said aloud. His left hand gestured Daun and Suterbilt toward the bedroom door, as if he and not the factor were the host.

The guards had returned to the main living area of the house, an arc of floor raised three steps on one end to set off, without a vertical barrier, the kitchen/dining facilities from the relaxation area. A hologram display blared loud music to accompany a pornographic recording.

The furniture was cheap, obviously junk brought in for the guards when Suterbilt carried off the original furnishings. It had been wrecked—shot, slashed, and broken apart. Two of the men sprawled on the floor, filthy though it was. The man with the headband got up from a legless sofa when the factor reappeared.

"Sir?" the guard asked.

"Keep a better lookout, for one thing!" Suterbilt snapped. He looked over at Vierziger. "Do you have anything to add?"

"Not at the moment," Vierziger said coolly. "I'll make my recommendations in two days."

He looked around the mess and the men guarding it. "They will be expensive to carry out, *that* I can assure you. But necessary."

The three men walked outside. Suterbilt's driver switched on the pump which powered the van's four wheel-hub hydraulic motors.

Vierziger swung the house door almost to, then caught the panel just before it clanged home and locked. "Blood!" he snapped. "I've left my briefcase."

He pivoted back into the house, pulling the door closed behind him. The guard wearing the headband was halfway back to the hologram. He turned, opening his mouth to speak.

"I forgot—" Vierziger began.

The door rang against its jamb. The Frisian drew and fired his pistol eight times in a single flowing motion.

The man with the headband lurched backward, flinging his hands in the air. The first bolt had blown out the thin bones of his nose and emptied his eyesockets.

The chest of a burly, blond-haired guard vanished in a red flash and a deafening roar. Vierziger hadn't noticed the string of grenades the fellow was wearing beneath a light jumper. The bolt that should have ruptured the guard's aorta instead set off a secondary explosion.

The blast flung the remaining guards in four separate directions, complicating the Frisian's task. It saved the man still seated on the sofa—for the few hundredths of a second before a second bolt slapped his temple while the ceramic wall behind where his head *had* been glowed white from the previous round.

Each of the men sprawled on the floor before the shooting started took a round. One of them was faceless and screaming from the grenade blast. The bolt that ruptured his skull was a mercy.

The last guard—and it was all in a half-second punctuated by the grenade—was turning with a fully automatic shotgun. Centrifugal force made his long red hair stand out like a porcupine's quills. The cascade of hair caught the first bolt. It vanished in a red fireball, drinking the cyan plasma and dissipating its force.

Vierziger's trigger twitched a last time. His bolt punched the guard's scream back through his palate.

The shotgun fired three times before it jammed. Aerofoil projectiles, designed to spread wider than spherical pellets, zinged from the walls and ceiling. One traced a line as thin as a razor cut across the Frisian's right cheek.

The living area was bloody chaos.

A toolkit/ammo pouch on the left side of Vierziger's belt balanced the weight of the pistol he carried on the right. He took out a spanner and turned the white, shimmering barrel off the weapon's receiver and dropped it on the floor. Rapid fire had eroded the iridium to half its original thickness. The remainder of the refractory metal was so hot that it deformed when it bounced on the cast flooring.

Vierziger fitted a fresh barrel—the kit held two—and reloaded the pistol, then holstered it again. The process of replacing the shot-out barrel had taken less than thirty seconds.

The house stank of ozone and bodies ripped apart and half-burned. The plasticizer of the grenade had a pungent reek, unpleasant and probably poisonous in a confined space. Vierziger ignored it.

Some of the men's clothing was afire. An arc of garbage centered on the grenade explosion burned also, though all the fires seemed likely to smolder out rather than build into a major conflagration.

Vierziger's attaché case was just inside the living area, where he'd set it behind a pile of trash when he entered the house behind Suterbilt. He opened the case and took out a cylindrical blasting device twenty centimeters across and half that in depth. He peeled the protective layer off one end, stuck the charge on the front wall near the door, and twisted the dial of delay fuze to one hour.

Vierziger had printed a message on a card before he left Hathaway House. He stuck that to the wall just below the explosive device, then surveyed the room for one last time.

One of the bodies twitched like a decorticated frog. The burning clothes had smothered themselves in veils of bitter smoke. Behind the gray, the hologram danced, more enticing for the partial coverage than it had been when the performers' tired flesh was uncompromisingly revealed.

Vierziger opened the door. The card on the wall read:

REMOVE THE AMBIANCE AND GET BACK ASAP

"All right, I'll tell him!" the Frisian called over his shoulder as he stepped outside.

Standing with his hand on the door he held ajar, Vierziger said to the sensor tech, "Daun, they're having problems with the hue of their hologram projector. I told them you could fix it in three minutes at the outside."

He gestured Niko toward the doorway. "Get at it. I don't want to wait longer than I have to."

"Say!" said the factor. "*I* don't want to wait at all! I've already wasted half an hour."

Vierziger closed the door behind Daun and stood with his back to it. "Relax," he said. "Remember, you said you needed to use the ambiance more often anyway. Besides, if those turds don't have the projector to amuse them, who knows what they'll get up to?"

Suterbilt sighed. "Yes, I suppose there's that," he agreed.

He grimaced. The van's headlights were on. This far out of town, their sidescatter was the only illumination. "Do you really think expensive changes will be necessary?" the factor asked.

Vierziger shrugged. "It's really a pair of changes," he said. "Part of the guard force has to be outside. Not really to do anything—just to be a tripwire so that if they're killed, the men inside have warning of an attack. *But* you also have to provide firing ports for the guards inside."

"That's impossible!" Suterbilt said. "You can't cut holes in these walls!" He slapped one to underscore his point.

"It's not impossible," the Frisian said. The lighted half of his face drew up in a deliberate sneer. "It's simply very expensive—as I said. *And* necessary. I'll have a detailed plan for you in two days."

The door began to swing open. Vierziger stepped forward, moving Suterbilt back a pace. "Any trouble, Daun?" Vierziger asked over his shoulder.

Niko looked at his fellow Frisian. "No," he said. "No, I took care of my end."

He didn't say anything more during the drive back to the TST offices, and he only once looked directly at Johann Vierziger.

Vierziger smiled at him.

"Stay in the car," Coke ordered harshly. He thrust his sub-machine gun at Pilar. Her hands wouldn't close on the dense metal and plastic. The weapon slipped into her lap. "If anybody gives you trouble, shoot them. It's off safe and there's one up the spout. Just fucking *use* it."

He'd stopped the port operations van in front of a six-story structure on the space-port end of Potosi. Except for the location, the building was very similar to the one which held the Ortegas'—which held Pilar's—apartment. The ground floor was a club, The Red Rooster, which was beginning to get under way for the evening.

The doorman/bouncer realized that Coke intended to leave the vehicle parked in front while he went up the stairs beside the club's entrance. The doorman stepped toward Coke and shouted, "Hey dickhead!"

Coke pointed his left index finger at the man's face. His right hand hung out at his side. The hand was crooked on a level with the butt of his pistol.

"Don't even think about it," the Frisian warned. The flat assurance of his voice was more threatening than a snarl.

The doorman backed inside the club. Coke went up the stairs two at a time.

The door off the second-floor landing was metal-faced. The jamb was wood, however, and the interior wall didn't look particularly sturdy either.

Coke hammered on the panel with his knuckles. "Ortega!" he called. "Front and center! This is an emergency!"

"Hey bud!" somebody called from below. Coke looked down.

A man close to two meters tall, wearing an electric-green jumpsuit, had swung out of the club entrance. He held a combination weapon, a pneumatic gun firing explosive projectiles through a 30-cm long barrel with a shock baton of twice that length mounted beneath the muzzle like a bayonet.

"Serafina's busy!" he shouted as he pounded up the stairs toward Coke. "Now, buddy, you can wait or I can line you up with somebody just as sweet. But don't you go—"

Coke judged his moment. He kicked when the pimp was three steps below him. The gun was pointed up and to the left in rhythm with the tall man's strides. Coke's boot caught the pimp's jaw and flung him down the stairs, limbs flailing.

Coke turned to the door. Instead of knocking again, he took a flat ring charge from a pouch on his equipment belt, peeled off the protective layer, and pasted the charge around the door latch.

He pulled the igniter wire and jumped several steps down the stairs to get clear of the blast. "Fire in the hole!" he shouted from reflex.

The charge went off with a flat *whack!* A fragment of metal whined off the opposite wall. The door jounced on its hinges and stood ajar in a haze of gray smoke.

Coke pulled the panel fully open but kept his body behind the wall. A stunner needle snapped through the dissipating smoke. It sparkled minusculely against the opposite side of the stairwell.

"Ortega!" Coke shouted. "The drum you substituted in the gage going off yesterday on the *Tellurian Queen*—there's a bomb in it. The cartel's stocks on Delos are going up in smoke three days from now, and when they do people are going to be looking for you. You've got to get off-planet now!"

"Get out of here," a man called. "*Get out of here!* I don't know what you're talking about!"

A burst of a dozen stun needles hissed and popped through the opening.

Coke fumbled at his equipment belt, feeling for a smoke grenade. He'd go in with his visor on thermal—

"Matthew!" Pilar screamed. Her sub-machine gun ripped cyan runs in the night.

Coke drew as he turned. The street door's jamb and lintel were a shower of shattered concrete from the cyan bolts. The tall pimp had gotten safe to the shelter of the stairwell before Pilar fired.

The pimp aimed his weapon. Coke shot him in the chest and face.

The pimp jerked his trigger. The pneumatic gun coughed, recoiling out of the dying man's grip. The heavy shell hit three steps above the landing and burst, showering the stairwell with shrapnel and orange light.

Coke, startled by the blast and prickles from the shell, sprayed three more bolts. He hit the pimp only once—in the ankle as he fell backward. The fellow was dead already, or at least he would be in the next minute or two.

"Ortega!" Coke repeated. His ears were ringing. "Come on out. I won't hurt you, and you don't have a lot of time."

"Matthew, you mustn't kill him!" Pilar called. She was at the bottom of the staircase. She tried to step past the tall man. His thrashing arm struck her calf. She came up anyway, her face pale and her sub-machine gun's muzzle shimmering brighter than the stairwell glow-strip.

"Go back!" Coke ordered. She climbed toward him anyway.

The explosive shell had flung the room door shut again. Coke reached for it with his left hand. The panel opened from the inside. A naked woman stepped out onto the landing.

Her name—the name she went by, anyway—was Serafina Amoretta. Coke had seen her image, but that hadn't prepared him for her youth. She couldn't be more than fourteen standard years, though her breasts and hips were full.

"Who do you think you are?" she shouted in bright-eyed fury. Perhaps she was on gage or other drugs, though she seemed alert enough. "Do you think you'll get me by coming here like this? Well, you won't!"

Serafina stood with her fists on her hips, glaring at Coke on the step below her. There was no sign that the corpse of her pimp or the gun in the hand of his killer affected her in any way. She didn't shave or pluck her body, but there was only a halo of hair surrounding the lips of her vulva.

"I don't want you," Coke said. "I'm here for Terence Ortega, to keep him from being killed by your little game."

The pistol in his hand embarrassed him. He tried to holster it again. He was awkward now in the aftermath of the shooting. He managed to sear the side of his rib cage with the hot muzzle.

"You want Terry?" Serafina caroled in raucous delight. "So that's it, is it? His frigid wife sent you to get him back? Terry, come out here. Now!"

Coke risked a look over his shoulder. He prayed that Pilar would have returned to the van, but she hadn't, she was just below him. Her lips trembled, and her face had no expression.

The door behind Serafina moved. A man looked out nervously, then stepped the rest of the way. He carried a needle stunner in one hand and held his trousers before him as a veil. He hadn't managed to get his legs into the openings.

"See who's here, Terry?" Serafina said, cocking her head so that she could watch the man out of the corner of her eyes. "She's here to take you back with a gun!"

"That's nothing to do with it!" Coke said. "I tell you, there was a *bomb* in the drum you thought was refinery tailings. You've got to disappear before the folks on Delos learn what I already know."

"Lies!" Serafina cried. "All lies!"

Her gaze slipped past Coke to Pilar. "Do you want to shoot me, bitch? It won't get you Terry back, you know. He'll never go back to you now that he knows what it's like to fuck a real woman!"

Ortega had been a good-looking man once. He still had the face, but standing nude on the landing made his paunch and generally run-down appearance painfully evident. Part of Coke's mind found time to wonder at what Serafina Amoretta saw in the fellow.

"Look," the Frisian said desperately. "You can lie to me, but it won't do you a bit of good with the enforcers from Delos, you know that. And L'Escorial, it's L'Escorial that planned this, they'll be *curst* sure Delos learns who planted the bomb because they don't want suspicion falling on *them*."

"You can't have Terry and you can't have me!" Serafina cried. She groped behind her and caught the hand with which Ortega held up his trousers. She jerked the garment from him, tossed it down the steps, and then drew his hand forward to cup her breast. "Do you see! Your lies get you nothing. Nothing!"

There was a clatter behind Coke. He glanced back. Pilar had dropped the sub-machine gun. She was stumbling down the stairs.

"Wait!" he called.

"You see!" Serafina said. She jutted her hips backward against Ortega's groin and wriggled. "You see!"

Coke backed down the stairs. He didn't dare turn away from the needle stunner.

His boot jarred the sub-machine gun. He snatched the weapon up. For a moment he imagined blasting the couple on the landing to doll rags. *No, the cartel would take care of that. . . .*

He reached the bottom of the stairs. He heard the van's diesel roar to life. Serafina turned, drawing Ortega with her back into the room. Coke ran out into the street. He was too late. The van was a block and a half away, still accelerating. .

A crowd had gathered at a discreet distance, drawn by the shooting and the corpse lying half in, half out of the stairwell. The pimp's eyes were glazed below the ruin of his forehead.

"*One, this is Four,*" Coke's commo helmet announced in the voice of Lieutenant Barbour. "*Something's happened at what used to be Larrinaga's house. I think you'd better be present when L'Escorial gets to checking. Do you have transportation? Over.*"

"That's a negative, Four," Coke said, watching the port operations van disappear in the distance. "Over."

"*Roger, somebody'll pick you up on the way,*" Barbour said. "*Four out.*"

Matthew Coke stared into the night. Spectators shifted when his blank expression fell across them, but they were only blurs to his consciousness.

He tried to change the sub-machine gun's half-expended magazine for a full one. He had to give up the attempt, because his hands were trembling too badly.

Metal scraps and pieces of broken glass hung from an ankle-height string concealed in the broad-leafed ground cover. Despite his visor's light amplification, Vierziger would have missed the warning device if he hadn't been looking for something of the sort. He knelt and tugged the trip-line with his left hand, making the trash rattle.

The only response was greater stillness.

"Larrinaga," Vierziger called in a low voice.

There was a rustle from the bole of the fallen tree. "Who's there?" Larrinaga demanded.

Larrinaga was crouched in the opening, gripping a club with metal spikes. He wouldn't be able to make out Vierziger's crouching form against the background of the trees between him and the rear of Potosi's buildings.

"Vierziger," the Frisian said. He switched on the miniflood in his left hand.

Larrinaga jumped as abruptly as if Vierziger had shot him. His head knocked against the lip of his shelter, but the punky wood cushioned the blow.

Vierziger stood up. "Don't worry," he said with the touch of a sneer in his voice.

"I'm not here to put you out of your misery."

The local man scrambled to his feet. The intense light made him sneeze. Vierziger slid the control down, dimming the glare to a yellow glow.

"What do you want then?" Larrinaga said. He seemed to notice the club for the first time. He dropped it at his feet.

Vierziger's lips quirked with wry approval. He clipped the dimmed light to his belt, then slid the strap of his attaché case off his left shoulder. His right hand remained free at all times.

"Here," Vierziger said. "Take it and get to the port. You're booked on the *Argent Server* and she lifts in twenty minutes. You'd better be aboard, because I suspect it's going to be a while before any later ship gets clearance."

"I can't—" Larrinaga said.

"There's money in the case," the Frisian snarled. "And there's a cyclo in the alley that'll get you there in time. Get *going*."

"I—" said Larrinaga, and his face smoothed in dawning comprehension. He knelt and thumbed the latches of the reptile-skin case.

The six portions of a psychic ambiance gleamed from the bed of sprayfoam which cushioned them and held them in place.

Larrinaga carefully closed the case. He began to cry.

"You can find an expert to set it up again when you've settled," Vierziger said harshly. "I'm told that anybody good enough to do the job will be honored to work on it, on a Suzette. Now get out of here before it's too late!"

He grabbed Larrinaga by the shoulder and dragged him upright with fingers that could bend steel. "Get going!"

The local man stumbled toward the buildings of Potosi and the vehicle that would take him away from them forever. He turned at the edge of the lighted arc.

"Why are you doing this, Master Vierziger?" he asked.

"I'm damned if I know," the Frisian said. "But then, I'm damned anyway, not so?"

Vierziger began to laugh. The sound mounted swiftly to a register suggesting bats and madness.

The laughter, if it was laughter, broke off. "Shall I shoot you now?" Vierziger shouted. "Get going!"

"Thank you, sir," Larrinaga said. He turned and jogged off through the familiar darkness.

"I don't expect it'll make the least difference in the long run!" Vierziger called after him. "But try to make a life for yourself this time. There's that one chance in hell."

In a much softer voice he added, "Even in Hell."

One of the L'Escorial trucks mounted a bank of floodlights behind the armored cab instead of a heavy weapon. The floods weren't well aligned, but their glare made the former Larrinaga house stand out like the lead actor during curtain call.

The gap in the front of the building was a nearly perfect circle, about two meters in diameter. The mass of ceramic casting belonging there was a heap of black grit, trailing off both inside and outside the dwelling.

Suterbilt and the three generations of Lurias stared at the hole as Margulies drove up with Coke. Daun and Moden were already present. Thirty or forty L'Escorial gunmen and four armored trucks surrounded the site, and there were more men inside.

All six of the fireflies danced a complex pattern around the Lurias. Pepe wore the controller.

"How did it happen?" Ramon Luria demanded, shaking his fist at the hole. "How did they do this?"

"Either sonics…" Coke said as he walked through the line of L'Escorial guards unchallenged. "Which I doubt, because of the time it'd take, or—"

He pinched some of the shattered ceramic between his thumb and forefinger, then sniffed the vapors still clinging to the material. "Nope, that's what it was. A spalling charge. That's the danger with monocastings. You really need to have spaced layers to prevent this sort of thing from happening, though that degrades projectile resistance."

A four-wheeled L'Escorial patrol vehicle pulled up with two red-uniformed gunmen and Johann Vierziger aboard. The dapper Frisian sauntered over to the blast site.

Pepe Luria turned toward Coke. "Now tell me what spalling charge *means*," he said in a deadly voice. His hands gripped the edges of his controller. "Instantly!"

"It means a quantity of inhibited plasticized explosive," Sten Moden said calmly, "which is spread in a thin layer over the target surface by a precursor charge and detonated from the open face a microsecond later."

Moden ran his fingers carefully across the inner surface of the hole. The ceramic was rippled in a series of surflike conchoidal fractures.

"The shock waves," Moden continued, "reflect within the plate. A ceramic of this sort has virtually no elasticity. When the stresses peak, the material itself crumbles."

He raised a handful of the glittering black residue and let it dribble down through his fingers.

Niko Daun eased up beside Coke and whispered directly into the major's ear. Coke's eyes blanked. He carefully looked away from Johann Vierziger.

"I don't believe it," Suterbilt said. "The house is a fortress, a *fortress*."

"You should have hired the FDF sooner," Vierziger said coolly. "Or perhaps Master Suterbilt and I should have stayed longer when we visited earlier tonight."

"What would a few more men have mattered?" shouted Pepe Luria. "There must have been twenty Astras, more even! Look there!"

The house's interior lights were on. The guards' sprawled bodies looked more like cast-off clothes and lumber than they did a scene of carnage.

Pepe's hands twitched. One of the fireflies above him suddenly pirouetted, firing its powergun as it spun. One bolt glared from the roof coping. Three more blazed out into the uncleared forest, lighting small fires. The last round snapped back toward Potosi.

Raul put a shaky hand on his grandson's shoulder to calm him. "Not that," the Old Man said. "We don't want Madame Yarnell coming down on us."

Raul looked at Sten Moden. "If the bomb was outside the house," he said, "why didn't it blow the wall *in* instead of out?"

"It didn't *blow* in either direction," the logistics officer explained. "The structure vibrated itself apart."

He pointed. "The fragments fell in both directions, you see?"

As Moden said, as much of the shattered wall was in the slope across the living area floor as was outside the wall.

Daun drifted away. Coke motioned Vierziger over by crooking his finger.

"Is there something you want to tell me, Johann?" Coke asked in a low voice.

"No," said Vierziger, "there isn't. But thank you for asking, Matthew."

"All right, they've had their game," Pepe Luria cried. "Now we shall take the set. Tijuca! Tijuca! Where's the drunken bastard Tijuca!"

Pepe's expression was as furious as that of a weasel in a trap. "That's it, I'll—"

Mary Margulies stepped forward. "I told Angel I'd cover for him tonight," she said calmly. "We got used to trading off like that in the old days."

Pepe started to shout a curse in the Frisian's face. He looked at her more closely before the words came out. He settled back on his heels, then said, "Will you? All right then. We'll take eight men only, and two patrol cars."

"What are you going to do, Pepe?" Ramon asked nervously. He touched his son's wrist to draw the youth's attention. "We daren't anger the cartel."

Pepe's snarl melted into a smile even more cruel and terrifying. "In and out, gone before anyone knows there's been an attack, hey?" he said in a husky whisper. "That's the way the Astras do it, and they've had no trouble. We'll do the same."

"Their warehouse?" Raul asked, frowning.

"No, we'll kidnap Peres!" his grandson said. "And the price to get him back alive will be for him and the Widow to leave Cantilucca forever!"

CANTILUCCA: DAY SEVEN

A jitney filled with gunmen—Margulies thought they were L'Escorials, but the muted gang colors of the present didn't show up at night—rolled down the nearly empty street. The vehicle swayed from side to side. The passengers cursed and flung bottles. Before Madame Yarnell arrived on Cantilucca, they would have been shooting.

The L'Escorial acting as communications officer, still holding the radio handset to his ear, turned to face Pepe in the back seat with Margulies. "They've taken in another case of liquor. There's no chance she'll be moving before noon."

"Yarnell parties every night," Luria muttered angrily. "Imported food, wines from *Earth* to drink. And we pay for it! She acts like she's a queen."

"On Cantilucca," Margulies said, "she *is* a queen."

A pair of jitneys drove out of the garage beneath the building opposite. The structure's lower three stories were an Astra recreational center of varied capability. None of the men aboard noticed the pair of patrol cars in the alleys across the street.

"He'll be coming soon," Pepe said. He peered down at the firefly controller.

"No," Margulies said.

Pepe reached for the power switch anyway. The Frisian caught his hand.

"No," she said. "Fireflies are good for an area target—"

A lie as far as she was concerned, but the politic thing to say just now.

"—but this has to be precise. Let me handle the shooting."

Pepe's faced blanked in white fury, then relaxed again in a smile. The change was as sudden as a pair of eyeblinks. Margulies put her left hand back on the fore-end of the 2-cm weapon she'd brought for this operation.

"Area target," Pepe said. "Yes. But I've set them to attack blue, you see? They'll kill the guards, but Peres doesn't wear blue himself!"

"Peres *usually* doesn't wear blue," Margulies corrected. "You're betting that he won't come out of that whorehouse with his new girlfriend's blue bra around his neck."

She shrugged. "Likely so. But why risk it?"

The radio set crackled. "He's coming!" warned the commo officer.

Margulies stepped out of the car and took her position at the mouth of the alley. The wall against which she stood blurred her outline, but she had no real concealment beyond the darkness. She held her heavy shoulder weapon diagonally across the front of her body.

The garage's automatic door rose with a series of rhythmic bangs. The gigolo's newly repaired aircar howled up the ramp.

Peres himself was driving. He misjudged the slope and struck the street lip. The plastic landing skids flexed and bounced the nose high.

Margulies fired. Her 2-cm bolt stabbed the right front fan nacelle. The blue flash sent blades and fragments of the shorted windings in all directions, like shrapnel from a bomb burst.

The vehicle yawed right, hit the pavement at 30 kph, and cartwheeled.

The armored garage door started to close automatically. While the aircar was still spinning, flinging off bits of body panel, Margulies fired at where the edge of the door mated with the track along the jamb. The plasma bolt vaporized a section of the track and hammered the door panel like a collision with a speeding truck.

The door skewed in its frame and stuck. Nobody was going to get out of the garage to aid Peres unless they wanted to crawl through the twenty-five-centimeter gap beneath the lower edge of the jammed panel.

Both L'Escorial four-wheelers accelerated from their ambush positions. Pepe Luria stood, clinging to the back of the commo officer's seat. He held an automatic carbine in his free hand.

The aircar landed upside down. It continued to rotate slowly, driven by the vibration of the two fan nacelles still spinning at full revs. The right rear installation had torn itself apart when that corner of the vehicle slammed down violently and drove the side of the housing into the blade arc.

The L'Escorial cars skidded and stopped on opposite sides of Peres' vehicle. The roof of the aircar was compressed but not flattened to the level of the car's body.

A youth crawled from the passenger side. He, wore a blue posing suit, blue sandals, and nothing else. He was crying and the crash had bloodied his forehead.

Pepe Luria pointed his carbine from the hip and triggered a burst. The weapon fired large-bore explosive bullets, rocket-assisted to keep the recoil manageable. The rocket exhausts were red sparks across the night. Two of the projectiles hit the boy in the chest, blowing him backward into the wrecked aircar.

The quartet of L'Escorials from the other four-wheeler dragged open the driver's side door of the aircar. One of them smashed the warped support pillar with the butt of his 2-cm weapon to make it release.

Peres screamed in terror. Two of the men pulled him out. A third threw a restraint net over the prisoner, and the fourth L'Escorial—the man with the 2-cm weapon— swatted him with the flat of the gun butt to silence the blubbering cries. They tossed Peres facedown into the back of their vehicle and got in themselves.

Mary Margulies stood at the edge of the alley, looking down the street toward Astra headquarters and the jitneys full of gunmen who'd driven that way moments before. The only thing moving in the night was the aircar, quivering on its back like a half-crushed bug.

"Get in!" Pepe Luria called to her.

Margulies glanced aside at him. She waved. "Go on," she said. "I'll walk, thank you. You've got what you came for."

The pair of patrol cars made tight low-speed turns and accelerated together up the street. The L'Escorial gunmen shouted to one another in glee.

There was a brief squeal of metal from the underground garage. Somebody was trying to free the door with a prybar. An argument broke out inside, identifiable from the timbre of the voices though the words were inaudible.

Margulies changed her weapon's magazine for a fresh one. She set off toward Hathaway House, staying close to building fronts and trying to look in all directions. She was nearly home before she heard the wail of sirens from Astra headquarters.

The Roberson & Co. trading post in the hamlet of Veridad was separate from the Astra patrol base there, but loud music from the stockade housing a score of gunmen pulsed through the walls. Roberson shivered, clutched his arms around himself as if against a cold wind.

"He's not coming," he said to the Widow Guzman. "It's some sort of—"

The door at the back of the trading post gave onto a fenced storage area, inaccessible from the outside. The door opened. A tall, nervous-looking Frisian soldier, not a man the Astra leaders had met before, stepped out.

"Barbour?" the Widow said in surprise.

"How did you get there?" Roberson gasped.

"I'm Barbour," the Frisian said. "And don't worry about how I got through your fence, I *did*, that's all. Did you bring the money?"

The merchant glanced reflexively at the case on the floor beside him, behind the counter. They'd expected Barbour to arrive for the meeting he'd arranged by the post's front door.

There was a pistol in the case as well. To Roberson's surprise, the Frisian appeared to be unarmed.

"You claim you can free Adolpho," said the Widow Guzman. "If you can do that, you'll have your pay. You'll have any pay you ask."

"In open-remitter chips, so there's no way they can trace back where it came from?" Barbour warned. He looked as skittish as a roach when the lights come on.

"Yes, yes, just as you said," Roberson snapped. "Now, how are you going to release Peres?"

He couldn't keep the distaste from his tone as he spoke the gigolo's name, but he hadn't even attempted to argue with the Widow when the Frisian made his offer. Barbour had called on what was supposed to be a private direct line between Roberson's office and Astra HQ. That in itself lent credence to his proposition.

"I didn't say I'd get him out," Barbour said defensively. His gaze shifted quickly around the big room, but he didn't make eye contact with the Astra leaders. "I said you could get him with what I'd give you."

"Well go on, then, man!" the Widow said. "How? Tell us!"

She stepped close to the Frisian and caught his chin between her right thumb and forefinger. He jerked his face away. Her ornate silver rings traced glittering arcs as she slapped him hard.

"Tell us!" she shouted.

Barbour turned his head away. "Look, they'd kill me if they knew I was doing this," he whined. "The major would say it was treason!"

"Via, boy!" Roberson cried. "Where—"

"It's the TST offices, you see?" the Frisian blurted. "They aren't guarded like L'Escorial bases are. You go in there and pull the core from Suterbilt's private data bank, you see?"

They didn't see. Guzman and the merchant looked blankly from Barbour to one another, then back.

Barbour shook his head in disgust. "Don't you see?" he repeated. "Suterbilt's cheating both TST and the Confederacy, faking the amount of gage that goes out of here. If the Confederacy learns they're being done out of port duties, they'll clean L'Escorial out of here, right? And it's all there in Suterbilt's private data bank, it's *got* to be!"

The music from the patrol stockade paused. For a moment, the only sound within the trading post was the breathing of the three occupants.

Barbour had chosen the meeting place, an Astra-controlled village twelve klicks from Potosi. He'd demanded that no one be inside the post save himself and the two principals. The Widow agreed and held to her agreement, overruling Roberson on the point. It was now evident to the merchant also that the Frisian would have noticed guards, no matter how well concealed.

"He'll have the information coded," Roberson said cautiously. "We won't be able to read it, will we?"

"What does that matter, you fool?" Barbour snarled. He appeared to be a man clinging to the ragged edge of his sanity. "The Marvelans can decrypt it, can't they? And anyway, it doesn't matter—Suterbilt won't dare take the chance."

"We're not using the information," the Widow Guzman agreed in a distant voice. "We're trading the information for Adolpho. But if Adolpho's been harmed or they won't give him up—"

Her voice had been bleak. Now it became as cold as the heart of a comet.

"—then I will give it all to the Marvelans. And they will gut this planet when they learn how they've been cheated."

"Now, Stella," Roberson said nervously. "We don't want *that* to happen. If the Confederacy really takes direct control here, it'll put a crimp in our operations too. Or worse."

The Widow looked at him. "Do you think I care?" she whispered.

"Look, that won't be necessary," Barbour said. "Look, I've got to get out of here. I'll give you the codes to get through the TST security system and you give me the money."

His moods appeared to change as abruptly as a rat's did. He was whining again.

"No," said the Widow.

Roberson looked at her in surprise.

"What do you mean?" the Frisian said. "You need the codes or you won't be able to get into the offices without setting off alarms. If L'Escorial comes in, you've got a war!"

"You'll come with us," the woman said. Her combs shimmered. Glow-strips covering most of the ceiling illuminated the post's interior. The light was diffuse but considerable in total, like that of a clear sky as the sun sets.

"I can't!" Barbour whined. "Via, you'll have me killed to save the money!"

"We'll messenger the payment to Hathaway House in your name," the Widow continued in icy determination. "You understand the security system better than we do. You'll get us through it with less chance of a mistake."

"We?" Roberson said, hugging himself. "I'm not going on a *raid*."

"I am," said the Widow. She gestured in the direction of the music coming from the patrol stockade. "We'll take those men. Twenty should be sufficient. And we'll go now."

Barbour covered his face with his hands. "Oh Lord, oh Lord," he whimpered.

He looked up. "All right," he said. "Let's do it quickly before, before…"

He covered his face again. "Oh Lord, don't let the major learn about this!"

In the lobby of Hathaway House, Sten Moden looked up from the console. "Do you think Bob's going to need help, Matthew?" he asked.

Major Matthew Coke looked at the four soldiers waiting with him. All were fully kitted out with weapons and extra ammunition.

"If he does," Coke said, "then we're ready to give it to him."

CANTILUCCA: DAY EIGHT

Robert Barbour projected a hologram for Kuklar, the Astra chosen to remove the guard. The monochrome display was a schematic of the back of the building which held the TST offices. The building itself was a dark blob fifty meters away. Stella Guzman watched over his shoulder.

The night sandwiched them with human sounds from Potosi and, behind the Astra force, forest noises. Despite Barbour's desperate orders for them to keep silent, the gunmen talked, cursed the scrub they'd tramped through from where they left the vehicles, and injected stim cones.

The Frisian gestured with his light pen. "You see, there's only one guard at the back staircase," he whispered. His pen dabbed twice again. "There's two more inside, but they're asleep on the couches in the waiting room."

"Where?" demanded Kuklar. He looked from the display toward Barbour, then the Widow. "I don't see nobody."

Kuklar didn't understand that the icon Barbour pointed out on the display, a jagged lightning bolt that slowly pulsed, indicated an armed man. It wasn't certain that he understood what a *map* was. Barbour took a deep breath.

Somebody on the top floor tugged open a window.

"Hey!" shouted a voice from ground level. "Don't you—"

A bucket of waste slurped its way down anyway.

"Fucker!" the L'Escorial guard bawled. He fired his sub-machine gun upward.

A few of the bolts slapped the back of the building; most of them vanished as quivering sparks among the stars. The burst didn't hit whoever'd thrown the slops, because the window closed again a moment later.

"Oh, there he is," Kuklar muttered. "Why din't you say he was down there? I thought you said he was *here*."

Kuklar started to crawl forward. He unlimbered a weapon from his belt as he moved through the garbage and scrub. Barbour couldn't be sure of the sort of weapon, even with his visor amplifying the ambient light to daytime levels.

"Get a fucking move on, won't you?" a gunman said at nearly normal volume. "I'm supposed to be off duty tonight."

Barbour winced.

"They were the first men available!" the Widow Guzman said. "You were the one who chose Veridad!"

"I didn't say anything," the Frisian muttered.

"Hey?" called the L'Escorial guard.

There was a sound like a melon hitting from a height. Somebody squealed. Violent thrashing punctuated Kuklar's shout, "I got—come on—I got—"

Astras ran toward the building, jostling one another and cursing as they stumbled over garbage in the darkness. None of them had night viewing equipment, even though they were supposed to be a patrol unit.

Barbour shut off his projector and jogged along behind. He noticed that about half the score of gunmen *didn't* move forward until others had reached the scene of the fighting.

Guzman kept up with him, though she wore a dress and was as blind as her troops in this starlight. "Leave most of them down here to cover our retreat," the Frisian ordered her. At this stage in the proceedings, the task overrode his desire to appear a cowardly buffoon. "I'll take three with me. That'll be plenty. The guards upstairs probably won't wake up till long after we're gone."

Kuklar had used a brush knife with a hooked blade as long as his forearm. He was levering the hilt back and forth. The heavy blade was buried in the guard's skull, as deep as the orbit of his right eye.

Barbour swallowed as he started up the stairs. The staircase actually served the building's upper three floors, but it angled past a window at the back of the TST offices. Barbour felt the treads flex as Astra gunmen followed him.

It would have been easier simply to walk up to the L'Escorial guard and shoot him. The burst of shots the man had fired didn't arouse any attention.

Barbour was used to Frisian standards. He began to appreciate Niko Daun's bitter scorn of "indigs."

The window was locked, barred, and in the beam of a microlaser across the room. If the glass pane stopped reflecting a calibrated amount of laser light to the receptor above the tiny emitter, alarms would go off here, in Suterbilt's apartment, and in L'Escorial HQ. The system had a lifetime charge so that it remained independent of the buildings power supply.

Barbour knelt, placed the drill, and felt the diamond bit whine happily as it spun a one-centimeter disk out of the pane. Hands-on work wouldn't usually have been an intelligence officer's task, but the team had thought it might come to this. Daun had trained Barbour patiently until they were both convinced he could use the equipment successfully.

He replaced the drill in his borrowed belt kit and fitted the mimicking emitter to the hole. It was self-adjusting: when Barbour switched it on, the microlaser aimed and brought itself into sequence with the security sensor. The telltale at the back of the little unit glowed red, then amber as the Frisian bent over it.

Somebody's chin bumped Barbour's shoulder. Barbour whirled around, poising the laser's carrying case to strike. "Fucking *fool!*" he snarled. "Do you—"

The Widow Guzman started away from him. Kuklar stood behind her, idly wiping the hook of his knife with his shirt-tail.

Barbour swallowed. "Don't do that," he muttered. He set the case down and smoothed the top of it with his fingertips. "Please, you'll get us all killed."

"Yes," she said. "Yes, I see."

The telltale was green.

Barbour took the cutting bar out of his toolkit. Unlike that of a standard brush-clearing blade, this one was only ten centimeters long and a millimeter thick. The diamond teeth sang through each of the four vertical bars in a few seconds. When Barbour had the top severed, he cut the bottom of the first bar, holding the shaft as he did so.

"Here," he said, handing the bar to Guzman. She took it, then yipped as the friction-heated end touched the inside of her wrist.

Barbour ignored her. The powered blade gave a high-pitched whine as it spun into the steel. It was a tortured sound, certainly loud enough for the guards to hear through the closed door to the lobby. They must be in the throes of gage comas. Why did Suterbilt even bother having such *people* present?

The Frisian handed the last bar behind him. He hadn't been able to practice the next part, but Daun assured him it would work.

Barbour set the end of the cutting bar's blade at an upper corner of the window and pressed inward. There were sparks and an angry sputter from the wire-cored glass; then the blade was through. Barbour drew the bar across, shearing the reinforced pane like tissue paper. Flakes of glass pattered against his wrists and visor.

He cut the other three edges of the pane as easily. When he made the final cut, on the left side, he remembered to angle the cutting bar. The blade levered the glass out where the Frisian could catch it, rather than letting it drop onto the floor. He wasn't worried about the sound, particularly, but the glass would interrupt the mimicking laser if it fell across the beam.

"There," he said. He set the pane down. "There!"

As Barbour climbed through the opening, he happened to look over his shoulder. The Widow stared at him with a puzzled expression. He supposed his obvious competence had surprised her.

If it came to that, he'd surprised himself. Barbour had always been somebody who *helped* people who did things.

The locks on Suterbilt's desk were electronic biosensors. Rather than try to duplicate the patterns of the factor's brain activity, Barbour zeroed the settings, then changed the combination to his own patterns. It was childishly simple.

The owner was supposed to scramble the access codes after he or she set the locks. If Suterbilt had done that, even the computing power Barbour could call in through his commo helmet would have required ten minutes to get to this point. Most people, Suterbilt included, didn't bother to proof their locks properly. It was as if the equipment were a magic talisman which need only exist to be effective.

The desk popped open. Barbour leaned under it and began unhooking the computer itself.

Several Astras entered the office behind him. "Keep quiet," he whispered, "and keep away from the waiting room. Let them sl—"

He heard the anteroom door open quietly.

"Don't—" he rasped.

A sub-machine gun lighted the office cyan with reflected light. The gunman emptied his entire magazine into the sleeping L'Escorials. The air roiled with ozone, hot matrix from expended powergun ammunition, and fires the bolts started in the upholstery.

"Shut the door," the Widow Guzman ordered. "Keep the smoke out."

Barbour closed his eyes and whispered a prayer. Then he got back to work. He had the computer out in three minutes, but by then the stench of feces from the men disemboweled in the anteroom had oozed under the door to bathe him.

He sat up and handed the fist-sized unit to the Widow. "There," he said hoarsely. "They'll trade your friend back to you for this, never fear."

She nodded her head crisply. "Yes," she said. "The chips are waiting in your name at your hotel."

Gunmen were leaving the office through the window, as they'd come. The waiting room door was beginning to glow from the heat of the fire enclosed behind it.

Barbour looked at the door. Unwilling to speak but unable to help himself, he said, "Did you have to do that? They were asleep!"

The Widow frowned at him. "What does that matter?" she said. "It's better that they're dead, surely?"

Robert Barbour looked at her in a sudden epiphany. For the first time in his life he realized that there really were people who should better be dead.

It gave meaning to his life.

CANTILUCCA: DAY NINE

Matthew Coke and Johann Vierziger watched from chairs set on the sidewalk in front of Hathaway House. The breeze followed Madame Yarnell's reconnaissance vehicle up the street and out of Potosi. Bits of trash lifted as if waving goodbye for the evening.

It was midnight. If past practice continued, the cartel representative would remain in the spaceport compound for the remainder of the night.

The gangs began to come out. An armored gun truck maneuvered from the L'Escorial courtyard. Down the street, the converted bulldozer grunted forward to lead the Astra contingent.

Vierziger chuckled. "The best show in town," he said. "And we're the only ones interested in front row seats."

"They're watching, though," Coke said, glancing at the facades of the nearby buildings. "For that matter, we could get a better view at the main console inside."

All the windows were shuttered, curtained, or blocked with makeshifts like the side of a packing crate, but there were hidden viewslits in the screens. The citizens of Potosi didn't want to call attention to themselves, but they were afraid not to watch.

"Something I've noticed about war zones, Matthew," Vierziger said. "The people who live in them either act as if they're in danger always, or they act as if there's no danger at all."

Three more L'Escorial armored vehicles followed the first. They puffed and snarled as they lined up side by side to block the street. The same thing was happening in front of Astra headquarters.

The escape hatch in the back of one L'Escorial truck was open. Suterbilt huddled inside, mentally clinging to both armor protection and freedom of movement.

Coke glanced at his companion. "Look, I know it's dangerous," he said. "I just didn't want to be cooped up inside if something popped."

Somebody on the Astra side signaled with a bosun's whistle. The L'Escorial gunmen who followed the vehicles on foot stared goggle-eyed, looking for signs of an ambush.

"The rest of the team can handle security for Bob," Coke said. Vierziger's comment still rankled. It wasn't the whole truth, but… And nothing was the *whole* truth. "Via, I know we might get shot out here."

"The difficulty isn't in being killed, Matthew," Vierziger said. His smile was as unreadable as that of the *Mona Lisa*. "The difficulty's in what comes after."

Pepe Luria sauntered from the courtyard of the L'Escorial building. His galaxy of fireflies looped and spun ten meters above him, each outlined by the purple haze of the static discharge which supported it.

Adolpho Peres stumbled along behind his captor. A L'Escorial gunman walked a meter to either side of the gigolo, but from a distance Peres did not appear to be tethered.

Coke raised his visor's magnification to x40, then doubled it again. A glint joined Peres' face to the short batons which the men beside him held. Trickles of blood had dried on the back corners of his jaw.

The L'Escorials had poked a length of piano wire through the gigolo's cheeks. The men escorting Peres held the ends wrapped around their batons. If Peres tried to run—if he did *anything* except walk in precise unison with his escorts—the wire would rip his face open like a razor blade.

A L'Escorial with a handheld radio sat on the back deck of an armored car. He held his free hand over his ear as he spoke, then listened, to his radio. He looked up and waved to Pepe. Pepe waved back.

The four armored vehicles roared and staggered forward in clouds of black smoke. The men behind them followed, squinting through the dust and exhaust fumes. Overhead, the fireflies sailed in a figure-eight formation that advanced just ahead of the armored cars.

The breeze had died. The Astras moved up also, in a pall of their own raising.

Roberson clung to himself and shivered at the gates to Astra headquarters. The Widow Guzman walked behind the snorting armored vehicles. Kuklar was beside her, wearing a blank expression and carrying a drawstring sack. The bag held the data base looted from Suterbilt's private office.

Vierziger laughed. He leaned his chair back against the building wall. "What do you suppose they'd do if Madame Yarnell returned to town just now?" he asked.

"Both sides are watching her," Coke said. "They'd scurry to their holes like mice when the cat comes home. There'd be enough time."

The L'Escorial radioman kept the armored cupola between him and Astra guns while he watched Pepe. When the lines of opposing vehicles had advanced to within fifty meters of one another, Pepe pointed his index finger.

The radioman spoke into his mouthpiece, turned, and closed his eyes. He jumped upright in plain view of the Astras, waving his arms like a semaphore.

The armored lines halted. The radioman lurched forward. He almost slipped off the side of his mount. He caught himself to crouch again in the shelter of the cupola.

Pepe gestured forward the men holding Peres. They worked their way carefully between the flanks of two of the armored cars, paying more attention to the hot exhaust louvers than they did to the man whom they were escorting. The wire twitched and quivered, drawing drops of fresh blood at every motion. The gigolo was crying.

Kuklar stepped in front of the armored bulldozer. The vehicle's rocket launcher was depressed to sweep the street ahead. If Kuklar realized that, he didn't seem to care. He walked forward stolidly, the sheath of his hook-bladed knife swinging in synchrony with his right leg.

"You know?" said Vierziger idly. "If something went wrong right now, they might all kill each other."

Coke shook his head. "Not all of them," he said. "Besides, we'd likely catch something ourselves, you and me."

"There's that," his companion agreed.

Suterbilt got out of the armored car and scuttled forward behind Peres and his escort. The factor was terrified, but he was the only one who could identify the stolen data bank so that the exchange could be completed.

The banks of lights on the opposing vehicles cast multiple faint shadows from the men converging between the armored lines. The Widow Guzman stood with her left hand on the blade of the bulldozer. Her right was extended toward Peres as the gigolo approached haltingly. Her visage trembled between fear and longing.

The engine of an Astra vehicle stalled. The driver restarted with a roar. Men on both sides jumped. Pepe Luria raised his face to the sky and laughed.

When Kuklar was almost halfway between the lines, Suterbilt ran to him. The TST factor tugged open the bag holding the computer core while Kuklar continued to grip one of the drawstrings. Suterbilt nodded his head furiously toward the L'Escorial line, invisible behind the blaze of headlights.

Kuklar looked at the Widow. She waved. Kuklar let go of the drawstring.

Peres' escorts dropped their batons and ran to the armored vehicles. The gigolo, weeping with pain, staggered toward Widow Guzman. The ends of the wire trailed from his face like the barbels of a catfish.

The exchange was complete. Either side's gunmen on foot—Coke was unwilling to think of them as infantry—streamed toward the safety of their headquarters.

The armored cars backed with greater difficulty. Two of the L'Escorial vehicles crunched, fender to fender, as they swerved in opposite directions at the start of the maneuver. The drivers rose from their cabs and screamed curses at one another. In ten minutes, even the vehicles had vanished from the street, however…

"Show's over, I suppose," Vierziger said. He let his chair drop onto its front legs. "No excitement at all." He giggled. "Nobody killed."

Coke looked at the little man curiously. "Is that the only kind of excitement?" he asked.

Vierziger stood up. "Well, there's sex, I suppose," he said. "But that's a bad second for me." He smiled. "What do you think about that, Matthew?"

Coke rose to his feet. Backblast from the directional mines the day the team arrived had left black starbursts across the reinforced concrete. He opened his mouth to speak.

The door of Hathaway House opened. Georg peeked out, then stepped into full view. "Major Coke," he said. He cleared his throat. "There was just a message for you, a Mistress Ortega. She'd like you to call on her at your earliest convenience. She, ah, she said she was at home."

Johann Vierziger chuckled. "I'll give you a night to consider your answer, Matthew," he said.

Pilar's door opened as soon as Coke reached the landing. That meant not only that she'd been watching the surveillance screen for his arrival, but that she'd kept the door unlocked.

She shouldn't take chances like that. Coke didn't think she had a gun in the suite, not even a needle stunner like the one her husband carried.

He stepped inside. Pilar was wearing a strapless black dress with a mantilla of white lace over her bare shoulders. She closed the door without looking at him and began setting the multiple locks.

"You shouldn't take chances like that," Coke said. She turned and threw herself into his arms.

"Terry's gone," she said against Coke's shoulder. "He went off on the *ND Maru* this evening. I guess he listened to you after all. Or she did."

Coke tried to kiss her. She wouldn't lift her lips to him. Her arms clamped him fiercely.

"He came to see you before he left?" Coke asked. He stroked her auburn hair with his right hand; she'd let it down for the first time since he'd met her. It was amazingly thick and fell below the pinch of her waist.

"No," she whispered. "I—I recognized the number of the account to which the passage was charged. It was one of Terry's, I suppose one I wasn't supposed to know about."

She nuzzled Coke's shoulder for a moment before she added, "They traveled under the name Sanchez. Master and Mistress Sanchez."

"I'm sorry," Coke said softly. He *was* sorry. It surprised him. Sorry for her pain, though his body was very well aware of the implications of the new state of affairs.

"I need somebody to hold me, Matthew," Pilar said. As she drew him toward the bedroom, he noticed that tonight she was not wearing her crucifix.

CANTILUCCA: DAY TEN

Dawn was red with a promise of storm. The sky was bright enough to mute the lighted advertising signs, but too dim to bring out the color of paint.

At night Potosi looked tawdry. This morning the city was a dull waste; steel rusting on dirty sand.

Hundreds of men, all the members of both gage syndicates who remained in Potosi, lined opposite sides of the street. The gunmen looked sleepy, sickly, and sullen. Most of them would barely have gotten to bed when Madame Yarnell called, demanding that they be assembled to hear her.

The leaders of Astra and L'Escorial faced each other with only the width of the right-of-way between them. Both groups were nervous. Coke's magnified view of their faces suggested that while the Widow Guzman and her companions felt uncertain, an air of monstrous glee underlay the Lurias' twitchiness. The L'Escorial leaders knew, or they thought they knew….

The sound of Madame Yarnell's reconnaissance vehicle preceded the car itself. The driver was winding out his motors, and the active suspension set up an audible keening as it smoothed the high-speed ride over the spaceport highway.

"As pissed as she was to come to Cantilucca," Margulies said, squatting on the roof of Hathaway House beside the major, "you'd think she'd be happy to be going back to Delos. Doesn't seem like she is, though."

"There's folks that'd bitch if you hanged them with a golden rope," Coke said. He kept his tone light, but he knew that very shortly the survey team would have to fish or cut bait.

The Hathaways stored building materials on their roof. The team had converted the crates, lumber, and barrels into a temporary refuge against need, but it couldn't hide them for long.

Madame Yarnell's car didn't slow until it reached the center of town. It skidded to a halt from a hundred, hundred-and-ten, kph. Pebbles and a stoneware bottle, miraculously unshattered by the *poot!* the tire gave it, flew out like langrage from a cannon.

The charge pelted the gunmen who hadn't ducked away when they realized what was about to happen. The bottle dished in the sloped forehead of a L'Escorial gunman; two Astras leaped back with their hands to their faces, screaming that they'd been blinded.

The car's passenger door lifted while gravel from the crash stop still clicked and pattered. Madame Yarnell got out. Her headgear was similar in design and purpose to a Frisian commo helmet. She surveyed the crowd that had gathered at her orders.

"You filth!" she said at last. Her voice boomed from the omnidirectional speaker on top of her helmet. "You cretins, you hog feces!"

The cartel representative turned as she spoke, so that all those present could receive her direct contempt. Lightning traced the eastern clouds. A gunman injured by the gravel whimpered brokenly.

"I'm going off-planet now," Madame Yarnell announced abruptly.

Peres seemed alternately frightened and exultant. The face of the Widow Guzman didn't change, but she wrapped her arm around the gigolo's waist and held him tightly. Roberson simply looked terrified, as he had since he appeared in obedience to the summons.

The Lurias' suppressed glee suggested—correctly—that they knew more about Madame Yarnell's recall than she did herself. Coke guessed that the cartel representative was too furious at this moment to take much notice of the gangsters' expressions; but she wasn't stupid, and she wasn't the type to limit the basis of her judgments to hard facts.

When Madame Yarnell returned to Cantilucca it would be obvious who had gained by her absence. Coke believed it would be very, very bad for those same parties.

"You *will* keep the peace," Madame Yarnell said. "*While* I'm gone, *when* I return—forever! All of you!"

She looked around the segregated assembly. "If there's any problem, *any* problem with the supply of gage from Cantilucca, may the Lord have mercy on you! For I will have none."

"I wonder how much she knows about what's been going on while she's here?" Margulies said.

Coke shrugged. "Not a lot," he said. "She doesn't have any local sources she could trust, and she didn't bring the sort of hardware Barbour and Daun deployed for us. She's probably pretty frustrated with what she must guess."

Madame Yarnell threw herself into the reconnaissance vehicle. The driver began his hard turn before the passenger door had finished closing.

"How do you feel, boss?" Margulies asked. She lifted her eyebrow.

Coke smiled grimly. "A little antsy," he said. "Not frustrated, though. We may or may not be able to pull this off, but we sure as *hell* know what we're doing."

The Delian vehicle screamed up the street, shimmying as hard acceleration unloaded the front wheels. One of the electric drive motors sent occasional sparks quivering out into the night.

"Ramon Luria's coming this way," Margulies said as she peered over the roof coping.

"Yeah, he's probably wondering when the FDF is going to arrive on Cantilucca," Coke said.

"And?" Margulies asked.

"And the answer's, 'Never, if Camp Able takes my recommendation,'" Coke replied. "But I'll say something more neutral than that to hold him for the time being. Sooner or later, though…"

He started for the trap door and the ladder down into Hathaway House.

"Sooner or later," Mary Margulies said, "everybody dies. When that happens, I wouldn't want to remember that I helped keep either group of these bastards in power."

CANTILUCCA: DAY SEVENTEEN

The youth's facial make-up made him look like an actor in a Noh play. His body was slim, supple, and completely hairless. The room's score of mirrors reflected all angles of his perfect beauty as he stretched.

"I'll get some more wine," he said. "The same vintage?"

Johann Vierziger turned on the blue satin bed. "Yes," he said. "It wasn't bad."

Vierziger arched his chest upward, supporting himself on toes and the tips of his fingers extended backward. The mattress' resilient underlayer undulated softly in reaction.

"But don't be long," Vierziger added with a chuckle. .

The youth opened the door concealed behind one of the brothel's floor-to-ceiling mirrors. A pair of fireflies drifted in past him.

"Shall we have a friendly talk, Master Vierziger?" Pepe Luria called from the corridor. "You and me and my friends?"

The fireflies halted a meter to either side of the bed, balanced on their hissing violet spikes. Another pair followed them.

"Get out of here, boy!" Pepe snarled to the youth who'd frozen in the doorway. He struck backhanded.

The youth darted past Luria, whimpering. Blows thudded as he ran the gauntlet of Pepe's coterie further down the hallway.

"Would you mind if I relaxed, Luria?" the Frisian asked from the tight arc in which he balanced. His erection of moments before had subsided, but his voice was calm.

Pepe stepped into the room, flanked by the last pair of fireflies. He wore the belt-pack, but he held his left thumb down on a separate remote control. "Do you know what this is?" he asked in place of answering.

"A dead-man switch," Vierziger said.

Pepe giggled. "Just so you know," he said. "If I release the button, poof! My little darlings do—what I've directed them to do. Are you faster than an electronic switch, Frisian?"

"I'm faster than some of them," Vierziger said. There was no sign of strain or emotion in his voice.

"You're not faster than six at the same time!" Pepe snapped, obviously angry at the lack of response to his murderous banter. "All right, you can sit up."

Three L'Escorial gunmen followed Luria into the room. Two carried wide-mouthed mob guns, the third a sub-machine gun. They looked relieved to see the Frisian nude and unarmed.

Vierziger lowered himself flat, then turned to swing his feet onto the floor as he lifted his torso. His movement was smooth but not as quick as it would have been under normal circumstances. He didn't want to startle the L'Escorials.

"Something puzzled me when I went through Suterbilt's house," Pepe said. "The house he took from Larrinaga. The psychic ambiance was missing. And that night

Larrinaga, who didn't have a pot to piss in, lifted on a starship to Mahan. Interesting coincidence, no?"

Vierziger shrugged. "Maybe Larrinaga helped the Astras with their attack," he said. "You say it was his house, after all."

"I thought of that," Pepe agreed in a falsely reasonable tone. "But that didn't answer all the problems."

The Frisian's chased and carven pistol hung in its holster from a chair backed against the head of the bed. Pepe nodded toward the weapon.

The sub-machine gunner jumped as though prodded with a shock baton. He snatched the pistol away. The Frisian commo helmet continued to rest on the seat of the chair.

Johann Vierziger smiled faintly. He looked at the constellation of fireflies encircling him.

"Is that fellow Daun your gunsel?" Luria demanded sharply.

Vierziger shook his head. "Niko wouldn't be in the least interested," he said. "Even if I were a woman, I'd be too old for him."

He shrugged. "Besides," he added, "I prefer professionals."

Pepe reached into a pocket with his free hand. "But sometimes amateurs, isn't that so?" he snarled.

He held out his open right hand. On the palm was a shot-out pistol barrel. The iridium had been so hot when Vierziger dropped it inside the Larrinaga house that the cylinder had deformed when it hit the floor.

"I thought to myself," Pepe continued. "There were very few shots fired. All the guards *could* have been killed by a single man. But it would have had to be a particular man, isn't that so?"

He let the barrel fall toward Vierziger's shrunken genitals. Vierziger's right hand, flat on the mattress beside him, moved as a blur. When the motion ended, the iridium was a bump raising the knuckles of the Frisian's hand—palm-down again, beside him.

Vierziger's lips held the faintest quirk of a smile. He said nothing.

"Ass is cheap in Potosi!" Pepe Luria shouted angrily. "But I can't imagine why else you would have bothered to help a wretch like Larrinaga!"

Vierziger looked up at the L'Escorial leader. "No," he agreed. "You wouldn't be able to imagine it, Luria."

"Take him!" Pepe said.

Johann Vierziger didn't move or cease to smile, even as the butts of the mob guns swung toward his head from opposite sides.

"Scramble!" Bob Barbour shouted. "L'Escorial's picked up Johann!"

Margulies snatched the 2-cm weapon she'd slung from the back of the chair beside hers in the saloon alcove. She'd been ready to drive Coke on his normal evening run to the spaceport to send a message capsule.

Coke was on his way down to the lobby. He paused, midway on the stairs, and asked, "Are they coming here?"

"Not yet, the bloody fools," the intelligence officer said. "Either they're not that organized, or they don't realize that we're keeping an eye on things."

Barbour watched his console as he spoke. The main screen showed Johann Vierziger surrounded by L'Escorials and fireflies on a brothel bed, but graphic and numerical sidebars reduced the main image by sixty percent.

Barbour's shouted warning drew Georg Hathaway's head from the family apartment. Coke heard the door open beneath him.

"Hathaway!" he said, leaning over the balustrade to make eye contact. "Is anybody in the building but us, you, and Evie?"

"No sir," Hathaway said, staring at Margulies by the door. The security officer was pulling her armor on one-handed while she held the shoulder weapon with the other and looked out the peephole in the front door. "No sir, there's only you two gentlemen and the lady, that's all who are present in our establishment."

The innkeeper's voice singsonged, as if he were chanting to himself in private. He was so frightened that his hands were still rather than washing themselves.

Evie Hathaway appeared behind her husband. She laid a hand on his shoulder.

"Sten's on the way back," Barbour noted. "He's picking up Niko on the way."

"Via, they shouldn't risk it!" Margulies muttered from the doorway.

"They'll be all right," Barbour said. Tension clipped his tones, but his enunciation remained perfect. On the main screen, a pair of gunmen clubbed Vierziger unconscious. "Pepe guessed Johann sprang the ambiance for Larrinaga. There's no evidence it's occurred to him to come after the rest of us yet."

Coke walked down the stairs and turned to face the Hathaways. "Georg, Evie," he said. "If you can handle it, we'll go up to the hide on your roof now. If you can't, we'll head for the woods. Either way, tell Pepe or whoever comes looking that an Astra messenger came for us twenty minutes ago. We left with him. All right?"

"Sten and Niko're back," Margulies called. The whine of a jitney's motor came through the peephole and, faintly, through the building's thick walls. "They're going around to the lock-up."

"Go upstairs, then," Evie Hathaway said. "That's what you want, isn't it? Go!"

"Master Hathaway?" Coke said.

Georg finally met the Frisian commander's eyes. He patted his wife's hand on his shoulder. "Yes," he said. "You are our guests. We will do what we can for you, despite, despite…"

Hathaway's face settled into unexpectedly firm lines. "Your friend helped Pedro, returned Suzette to him and got him away from here. You'll want to do what you can for your friend. We'll hide you until you can."

"There's about forty men leaving L'Escorial HQ," Margulies warned from the peephole. "A couple armored cars are coming up from the garage, too."

"Sten and Niko have gone up the ladder to the back," Barbour said.

"Shut it down, Bob," Coke ordered, putting a hand for emphasis on the intelligence officer's arm. "Everybody up to the—"

He heard the trapdoor open. "Stay where you are!" he bawled to Moden and Daun, who'd climbed the rope ladder from the locked parking area behind Hathaway House. "We're on our way!"

Barbour blanked the console. His hesitation at abandoning his equipment was obvious in the longing glance he threw over his shoulder when Coke tugged him way.

"They're crossing the street!" Margulies warned. She hadn't moved from her position.

"Come *on!*" Coke shouted. He gave Barbour a push toward the stairs and skipped up after him, charging his sub-machine gun as he moved. The security lieutenant backed from the door, covering the rear.

"Twenty minutes ago!" Coke called from the top of the stairs.

The Hathaways couldn't hold out against torture—nobody could if the stress was properly applied, though Coke doubted any non-Frisian on Cantilucca was competent at *that* either. Whether or not the Hathaways would blurt something when L'Escorial gunmen knocked them around, as would inevitably happen, was an open ques—

"We will stand it!" Evie Hathaway called. "For your sake, and for Cantilucca!"

"Blow the fucking door down!" shouted a gaunt, one-eyed L'Escorial gunman at the front of Hathaway House. Georg Hathaway was already pulling the door open as quickly as its mass would allow.

The five Frisians waited silently beneath piled lumber and the barrels on the roof. Enough of the twilight leaked through cracks in their concealment that they could see one another as their eyes adapted.

So long as the console in the lobby operated as a base unit, the commo helmets could access sounds and images from any of the sensors Daun had placed—including those in the hotel. There were no peepholes to look out through directly.

Six gunmen bulled into the lobby, deliberately slamming the innkeeper against the wall. Evie Hathaway stood at the doorway to the family apartment, glaring at the L'Escorials.

Ramon Luria entered behind his men. He looked at Evie, then Georg. "Where are the Frisians?" he asked.

"They're gone—" Georg began.

Ramon nodded. Two of the gunmen grabbed Hathaway by the wrists.

"—twenty minutes ago when—" Georg said, his voice climbing a note with every syllable.

Ramon punched the innkeeper in the belly with all the strength of his pudgy body. Georg's breath whooped out; his face lost color.

"The Astras sent for them!" Evie cried. "They went to the Astras with nothing but their guns!"

Ramon turned from the husband and slapped the wife. It was a full-armed blow which Evie could have dodged had she wished to. Instead she accepted the *whack*, knowing that there was no escape but death from whatever Luria chose to do.

Three scarlet armored cars were in the street, their armament pointed at Hathaway House. Several score gunmen milled around the vehicles. If the tribarrels and rocket launcher ever opened up, shrapnel and fragments of the facade would kill more of the L'Escorials than the Frisians could in the first few seconds.

Evie's head rocked back. She put a hand to her cheek, then snatched it away as a sign of weakness.

"Go on," she said. "Go on! The Astras came for them twenty minutes ago. Hitting me won't change that!"

Ramon panted from his exertion. "Search the place," he ordered his men generally. "Search it all!"

Four men of the group who'd entered with him scattered. Three went upstairs while the last entered the kitchen with his sub-machine gun outstretched like a cattle prod.

More L'Escorials stamped through the outer doorway, multiplying the number of searchers without adding organization to the process. One gunman began opening the console's access panels, though only a child or a midget could have fit into the enclosed volume.

"Hey, there's a ladder up to the roof!" a man called from the top of the stairwell.

The Frisians faced the barrels that formed the side of their concealment nearest the trapdoor. Each of them but the intelligence officer held a weapon ready.

Barbour started to pick up the sub-machine gun on the floor beside him; Coke laid a hand on his and shook his head. Barbour nodded understanding and let the weapon lie. The chance that the intelligence officer would do something noisily wrong was greater than any help his unskilled shooting would provide if the situation blew up.

Sten Moden carried three shoulder weapons, two slung and the last in his hand where it looked like a pistol by comparison to his size. There wasn't room in the narrow hide for the rocket launcher he favored, and the big missiles would be useless in a point-blank shootout anyway.

Three L'Escorials came out onto the roof clumsily. Each of them climbed with one hand and waved his weapon through the trapdoor ahead of himself. The first man out shouted in alarm as the next prodded him in the back with a fléchette gun.

"They been up here," a L'Escorial noted. "Hey, look at this!"

He'd found the panoramic camera Daun glued to the coping of the facade weeks before. It was a relatively large unit, about the size of a clenched fist, and Niko hadn't tried to conceal it. The camera provided a view of the entire streetscape—distorted at the edges, but correctable into normal images by the console's processing power.

"It's a bomb!" cried the man with the fléchette gun. Why he thought so was beyond imagining, especially since the next thing he did was put the muzzle of his weapon against the camera and fire.

If it *had* been an explosive device, it would have detonated and killed all three L'Escorials. Instead, the gun's enormous muzzle blast blew the camera across the street in tiny fragments. The osmium fléchette left a split and a crater in the facade of L'Escorial headquarters.

"What's that?" a gunman in the street screamed. Another man emptied an automatic shotgun upward, scarring the reinforced concrete of Hathaway House. Dust and sparks flew past the coping.

"You bloody fool!" a L'Escorial snarled—correctly—at the man with the fléchette gun.

"Hey!" called a man through the trapdoor. "You dickheads up there? Come on back, we're moving!"

Two of the L'Escorials moved quickly to the trapdoor. The third demanded, "What do you mean, we're moving?"

"I mean we're going to take out the Astras once and for all!" cried the man below. "Pepe just gave the order!"

The last of the three gunmen jounced down the ladder. Coke waited another thirty seconds, then reached for the latch holding the side of the barrel closed. Bob Barbour touched his hand. "Not yet," the intelligence officer whispered. "I'll tell you when they're all clear of the building."

Barbour's faceshield would be taking the input of up to a dozen of the visual sensors in and around Hathaway House. Coke couldn't have kept that many locations straight, quite apart from needing a clear view of his immediate surroundings in the event of a firefight.

Coke grinned and nodded to his intelligence officer.

"Now," Barbour murmured. "They're gone."

Margulies swung open the door; Coke was out onto the roof first. He kept his head below the level of the roof coping. The sun had fully set, but the afterglow was vivid to eyes that had been covered within the hiding place.

"They took the weapons they found," Sten Moden said. "They carried my launcher and the reloads back across the street."

"We've got what we need," said Coke. "First we'll do something about Johann."

Mary Margulies looked at him. "We're going to take them all on, then?" she said.

"Yeah," Coke said. "All that're left after they get done with each other."

Margulies shrugged. "Suits me," she said, checking with her fingers the pouches of 2-cm ammo on her crossed bandoliers.

Niko Daun slapped another panoramic camera onto the coping, a centimeter from where the previous one had been blown to atoms.

Coke stared at him. "You carried an extra one of those when you ran for cover?" Coke asked.

The sensor tech looked defensive. "I've got two of them, sir. Well, they're real handy."

"It's all right," Barbour said, responding to a threat before his fellows were aware of it. He positioned himself so that his body was between the trap door and the other members of the team. "It's Hathaway."

Georg Hathaway stuck his head up through the opening. It certainly hadn't occurred to the innkeeper that without Barbour's warning, somebody—very likely Coke himself—would have blown him away.

"Sirs," he said. His normally pudgy cheeks looked sunken, though the fact he'd climbed the ladder spoke well of his general condition. "They've gone for now, all of them. They say they're going to attack Astra. You can escape now."

"I'm checking my equipment," Bob Barbour said, the last syllable spoken as he slipped past Hathaway. He let himself drop to the corridor since the innkeeper's body blocked the ladder. Hathaway recognized the problem and scurried down also, puffing and wheezing.

Coke started for the ladder. Margulies touched his arm. "Sir?" she said. "What's the drill? Do we break Johann out now?"

"We check the situation on the big screen," Coke said. "And then we break Johann out, yes."

Wild gunfire erupted from the street.

Both syndicates had moved gunmen back into Potosi as soon as Madame Yarnell left, though the gangs kept a lower presence than before. Instead of loitering in opposing groups at every corner, men of the two sides kept generally to one end of town or the other—spaceport side for Astra, the eastern half for the L'Escorials.

Though the Lurias were acting on the spur of the moment, Pepe's sudden decision was tactically ideal. Three red-painted armored cars were already in the street. The remaining vehicles rumbled out of the garage beneath L'Escorial HQ even as the first phase of the battle began.

The gateway into the Astra compound was blocked, as usual, by the converted bulldozer. As the L'Escorials swept unexpectedly toward their rival's headquarters, the blue-clad guards started the dozer's engine.

Pepe's fireflies stooped like hawks with violet pinions. The short powergun barrel in each firefly spat cyan death at the startled guards. The side hatch to the cab of the converted bulldozer was open. A firefly slid in, lighted the vehicle's interior with its five-round magazine, and curved out again.

The bulldozer stalled in a cloud of black smoke. The Astra guards sprawled on or around the vehicle, mangled by concentrated gunfire. The fireflies hissed back toward their controller. Pepe had told off a pair of his henchmen as assistants to reload the fireflies' magazines when they returned.

Civilians vanished from sight. A few Astra gunmen opened fire on the advancing L'Escorials. The Lurias' armored cars raked the street with their tribarrels and a salvo of 10-cm bombardment rockets. The latter blew up on building fronts with huge red flashes, hurling shrapnel and broken concrete in every direction.

Astras dived for cover in doorways and alleys. Counterfire stopped instantly, though only a handful of Astras were hit by the wild volley. The sheer volume of fire which the vehicles put down was too much for undisciplined troops to face. As more armored cars joined the initial trio, the gunmen who'd been chased to cover tore off their blue accoutrements and disappeared into the night.

The only Astras still fighting after the first exchange were those in the headquarters building with their leaders—and they were trapped like mice in a bucket of water. By taking the initiative, Pepe had won the battle.

A pair of L'Escorials, stoned on gage and bold to the point of lunacy, leaped aboard the converted bulldozer. Astras fired wildly from ports in the headquarters building, but most of the shots were aimed at fireflies which existed only in the gunmen's minds.

Powergun bolts traced magenta afterimages across unprotected retinas; terror turned the shudder of color into the fireflies' static suspension system, though all the little devices were at the moment being reloaded.

The bulldozer grunted to life. One of the L'Escorials jumped from the hatch again. He was immediately shot in half by gunmen from both syndicates. The remaining man backed the converted vehicle with a skill that its regular driver couldn't have managed with leisure and full daylight.

The door to the underground garage was open; an armored truck was driving up the ramp. The bulldozer crashed into the flimsier armored vehicle, blocking the exit completely.

The L'Escorial driver jumped out and scampered away, miraculously unhurt by the sleet of bolts and bullets which pursued him. A L'Escorial armored car nosed through the opened gateway. Its three tribarrels fired point-blank at the rocket pod mounted on the converted bulldozer.

The dozer was armed with hypervelocity rockets which didn't have explosive warheads. The rocket fuel deflagrated with what was only technically a fire rather than an explosion.

A ball of yellow light enveloped the front of Astra headquarters and the vehicles in the garage beneath the building. More fuel and munitions went off in a second blast a heartbeat after the first. The building's protective facade lifted as a piece, then settled again in slabs and pieces that crumbled away.

A L'Escorial armored car raked the courtyard wall with fléchette rockets. Almost all the hundreds of osmium penetrators punched through the cast concrete, each drilling a finger-sized hole on entry and blowing a divot the size of a soup plate from the inner face as the projectile keyholed out. Backblast from the powerful rockets incinerated dozens of L'Escorials who had sheltered behind the launcher.

Wreathed in smoke from its rocket exhausts, the vehicle that fired the salvo drove into the weakened portion of concrete. Metal shrieked, but a ten-meter stretch of wall collapsed inward.

A cloud of white dust enveloped Astra headquarters. Scores of L'Escorial guns fired with no target beyond the silent building itself. Another armored car rumbled through the gap. Its sole functioning tribarrel ripped a rich cyan line across and through the building's inner fabric. There was no return fire, but ricocheting projectiles spun several of the red-clad gunmen.

"About now, I'd say," Mary Margulies prompted. She gripped the large hasp to open the unlocked front door.

"Not yet!" Coke ordered. His mind tried to fill the immediate future, encompassing every possible event and side effect. The task was beyond his conscious intellect, but instinct told him that the moment was not—

A white flag—a scrap of sheet—waved from a hole on the ground floor of Astra headquarters. Bob Barbour gestured minusculely to the keyboard of the console at which he sat.

The holographic screen split. The lower half showed the interior of the building. Audio was from one of the laminar bugs Daun set during the initial visit to Astra HQ. Visuals came through miniature cameras at roof level across the street, processed to an illusory slickness by the console's artificial intelligence.

"Luria!" the Widow Guzman shouted through a bullhorn, toward a hole torn into the wall by powergun bolts. "We surrender! We're coming out!"

Three Astra gunmen and Adolpho Peres crouched with the Widow in what had been her private office. In the outer area, another gunman stood behind the thickest remaining portion of the building's facade, waving the white flag. There were dozens of bodies around him, most of them mangled beyond recognition of their species.

The fireflies, their magazines reloaded, curved toward the riddled building like swarming hornets.

"Bob, you're control," said Matthew Coke as he stepped to the door of Hathaway House. "The rest of us—now!"

Margulies put her weight against the inertia of the door, then stepped out behind her commander.

The Lurias had left a six-man guard at the gate to their headquarters. By this stage in the fighting the gunmen stood in the middle of the street to watch the battle in the near distance.

Coke didn't make the mistake of using his sub-machine gun as an area weapon when he had individual targets. Three-round bursts spun two of the L'Escorials an instant before Margulies blew a third nearly in half with her 2-cm weapon. The last three syndicate gunmen went down in a ripple of cyan as all four Frisians fired simultaneously.

The brief fusillade didn't arouse the attention of the fighters half a kilometer away, locked in the death throes of the Astra syndicate. Coke and his team sprinted across the street and through the open door into L'Escorial headquarters.

The smoldering body of Angel Tijuca lay faceup in the center of the entryway. He'd been shot in the chest, twenty or thirty times at close range. The 1-cm powergun bolts had burned most of his torso away. He still held the pistol he'd managed to draw in the last instants of his life.

"Fireflies," Margulies said softly. "He wouldn't have liked it when Pepe brought Johann in."

"I'm sorry, Mary," Coke said.

She looked at him. Her face was freckled by the overlay in one quadrant of her visor, echoing the image from Barbour's console. "Don't be," she said. "We all die. He didn't—die a bad way after all."

Coke nodded. "Sten," he said, "Niko—check the barracks upstairs and rejoin when it's clear. Mary, Johann ought to be—"

Margulies had already swung herself into position beside the heavy door to the right of the anteroom. It was ajar, though it had a lock.

"Go," said Coke. He had the automatic weapon, so he would be first through.

Margulies pulled the door open. The room beyond was the armory. Weapons lockers lined the walls, most of them emptied or nearly so for the sudden attack. The cases of Frisian equipment that Ramon's men had taken from Hathaway House lay on the floor among the remains of the L'Escorial hardware.

A restraint cage stood against the far wall. Johann Vierziger was in it. The probes touched his nude body at a dozen points including his genitals, sending fluctuating currents through his nerve pathways.

A fat man, naked to the waist, sat on an ammunition case beside the prisoner. He was mopping sweat from his face with the red bandanna tied around his throat. He jumped halfway to his feet between the time the door opened and the moment Coke's long burst disemboweled him.

Margulies fired into the control box at the top of the cage. The electronics disintegrated under the jolt of plasma. Droplets of metal and silicon shards sprayed a wide area. Some splashed on Vierziger as the cage released him to topple forward, but the prickles were nothing to the pain from which he'd been freed.

Coke started toward Vierziger. A young L'Escorial, scarcely a boy, stepped into the room behind the Frisians. He was buttoning his trousers. "*Wha—*" he cried as Margulies turned, bringing her heavy weapon to bear less than arm's length from the gunman's breastbone.

He didn't have a gun. That wouldn't matter, but as her finger took up slack on the trigger she recognized—

"Emilio!" she said. "Your name's Emilio and you come from Silva Blanca."

The muzzle of the 2-cm weapon shimmered yellow. The iridium was cooling slowly from the five rounds she'd put through it in the street a moment ago. Coke glanced back at the lieutenant, but his real attention was on Vierziger. Margulies' situation was under control, though he wasn't sure what she meant to do.

The young L'Escorial swallowed. He leaned back, afraid to move his feet and unable to take his eyes from the 2-cm mouth that would swallow his life with another millimeter of trigger travel. "How did you know?" he whispered. "How did you know me?"

An automatic carbine leaned against the wall by the doorway, probably Emilio's weapon. Margulies doubted the boy would have been able to grip it if she picked it up and put it in his hands.

"Go home to your parents, Emilio," Margulies said. The boy wore a red armband. She ripped it off while her right hand continued to steady her weapon on the youth's chest. "Farming's better than dying. You've got *no* talent for this business."

"You'll shoot me if I turn," Emilio whimpered. Tears dribbled down his cheeks. "Oh, Mama, Mama…"

Margulies thrust the 2-cm weapon toward Emilio's face. The heat of the muzzle made him flinch away. He turned and ran into the night, still crying.

Moden and Daun strode into the armory. "All clear," Niko called. He was bright, spiky with hormones and eagerness.

The logistics officer lifted the triple rocket launcher and checked it with a critical eye. "Who was that?" he asked Margulies in a low voice.

Margulies grimaced. "A civilian," she said. "Somebody who didn't have any business here."

Coke helped Vierziger rise cautiously from the floor where he'd fallen. The little gunman waved him away.

"Find me some clothes," Vierziger said. His eyes were open. He looked straight ahead and held himself stiffly. "They cut mine off me when they put me in there."

Niko Daun turned and sprinted up the stairs to the barracks without formal orders from anyone. The dead torturer's pants wouldn't have fit, even if they'd been in better condition than the corpse which wore them.

"They had the cage's power turned all the way up," Coke said in a quiet voice. "They put him through hell."

Vierziger looked at Coke and managed a shaky smile. "No, Matthew," he said. The lilting insouciance was back in his tone. "That was somebody else entirely. And it can't have been Hell, can it? Because I still have a chance to do penance."

He flexed his hands with apparent approval.

"Here you go!" Niko Daun called as he returned with boots, a pair of gray trousers, and a camouflaged tunic. The items were all small enough to fit Vierziger. If they weren't particularly clean, they at least offered the spiritual protection which clothing gives a civilized man.

Coke frowned as Vierziger drew the garments on. "I don't understand, Johann," he said.

Vierziger chuckled. "Neither do I, Matthew," he replied. "But we're not required to understand, you realize."

Heavy fire roared from down the street. Coke switched his visor to give him a quarter overlay view of the console display. He chose another sub-machine gun from the selection available in the armory.

The three Astra gunmen in the office with the Widow and Peres stumbled out through a hole torn in the facade by L'Escorial fire. They'd thrown away their weapons. One of the Astras had even stripped so that he didn't show any blue garments in the lights bathing the battered headquarters.

Fireflies dropped from the night sky, circled the men, and stabbed them with multiple cyan bolts. The Astras screamed and died in the rubble of their fortress. One man flung out his arm to fend death away. Bolts blew the limb off at the shoulder before another round finished him.

"Come out, Widow!" Pepe Luria called. His father and grandfather crouched behind the courtyard wall, but Pepe stood in the gap between two L'Escorial armored vehicles. "We'll treat you with full honors!"

"I'll take the roof," Sten Moden said, hefting his launcher and a case holding three additional missiles. "Niko, will you load for me?"

"The roof?" Coke said. "That's not great if you've got to displace."

Moden shrugged despite the enormous weight he carried on his one arm. "A good vantage point," he said. "And the backblast of these—it'd be almost as bad in an alley as inside. The cost of power, you know."

"Go on," Coke said. "But be careful."

L'Escorials had refilled the tubes of the car mounting fléchette rockets. Pepe stepped to the side. This time his henchmen were careful to avoid the lethal wedge of exhaust behind the vehicle.

The gunner inside closed the firing contacts. The twelve rockets rippled off in four nearly simultaneous trios. A fraction of a second after they left the launching tubes, the casings split open and unleashed hundreds of dense arrows, finned to spread slightly along their trajectory.

The fléchettes hit the facade of Astra headquarters like osmium sleet. The pillar sheltering the flag-waving gunman disintegrated, as did what remained of the wall of the office beyond. Dust rose, dazzlingly white in the lights of L'Escorial vehicles.

"Come out, Widow!" Pepe shouted gleefully as he stepped into view again.

Johann Vierziger draped himself with bandoliers and two slung weapons, a submachine gun and a 2-cm powergun. He slid a pistol into the pocket of the tunic he wore.

"Pepe must have kept my rig," he said wryly. "Well, it's only a tool. Like the flesh itself. The tools aren't what matter."

"You and Margulies stick together," Coke ordered. "I'll take the opposite side of the street myself."

Vierziger shook his head and smiled. "The two of you take the other side," he said/ordered. "I prefer to work alone."

Vierziger began dropping grenade clusters into various pockets of his garments. His body armor lay where it had been dumped with the other Frisian suits.

Coke looked at the little man, then said, "Okay, Mary, let's get into position. It'll be party time any moment now."

They stepped from the building and crossed the courtyard, covering one another's movements alternately. Fires lighted the interior of a dust pall to mark Astra headquarters and the street before it. Hundreds of L'Escorial gunmen capered about the site, silhouetted like insects by a lamp.

Adolpho Peres, an overlay on one corner of Coke's visor, bawled, "I surrender! I surrender! I'm coming out!"

The gigolo staggered through the curtain of dust and smoke. Debris fouled his outfit, a ruffed doublet and tights of black velvet. His eyes were slitted.

Peres negotiated the rubble of the protective facade without falling, only to trip over the riddled bodies of the gunmen who'd preceded him from the building. He tumbled to his knees and clasped his hands in prayer. "Oh, dear Lord in heaven Luria I'm your friend you mustn't—"

The fireflies drifted within a meter of Peres before they one at a time emptied their magazines into him. When the last unit fired, only scraps of bone remained of what had been the gigolo's muscular torso.

"*Four to team,*" Lieutenant Barbour said through the silence on the scene his console projected. "*Are any of you wearing visible red garments? Report ASAP, repeat ASAP! Over.*"

Coke sprinted across the street under cover of Margulies' shoulder weapon. He took cover at the corner of the next building up from Hathaway House to avoid involving Barbour and the Hathaways themselves. "One negative," he called

"*Two negative,*" from the logistics officer, breathing heavily with the exertion of his climb to the roof of the L'Escorial building.

"*Three nega—Five negative,*" Niko Daun stepping on Margulies' report, but they were both clear and that was what mattered.

"*Six negative,*" said Sergeant Johann Vierziger, by pay grade the lowest-ranking member of the survey team. "*And it is time that we act, Matthew. Out.*"

"*Negative!*" Bob Barbour snapped. The command was as unexpected as seeing a nun aim a rocket launcher. "*This is Four. I'll tell you when I'm ready, but do nothing till then. Four out.*"

"Roger that," Coke said, crouching at the corner of the building. He wasn't sure what the intelligence officer had in mind, but he knew Bob well enough now to trust his judgment. Hell, he trusted every member of his team. "One out."

The town of Potosi was locked and unlighted. Civilians huddled beneath furniture, praying that their homes would be spared by the heavy weapons that could shatter walls and bring down upper stories in an avalanche of brick and timber.

On Coke's faceshield, the image of Stella Guzman stepped through the curtain of dust. Her combs gleamed in the glaring lights. She stood like a wraith. The ruin of her fortress wound a shroud about her.

"Luria!" she cried. Her eyes stared straight before her, as though she were unaware of her lover's corpse at her feet. "I will wait for you in Hell, Luria. You'll join me this night! Do you hear me? *You'll join me this night!*"

Pepe's assistants were still reloading the fireflies' magazines. The youngest Luria let his controller hang at his belt and rose to face the Widow. "Why, Stella!" he called. "How shameless! Making an assignation and your lover's body still—"

He drew a pistol and pointed it. From the purple highlights it was indeed Vierziger's weapon.

"—warm!"

"I'll wait for you in—"

Pepe shot her in the face. The Widow turned. Luria continued shooting as the body spun onto the rubble and bounced. The Widow's hand was outstretched toward Peres, but their dead fingers did not touch.

The last of the fireflies rose from the hands of the attendant servicing it. The six deadly constructs wove a violet corona above the L'Escorial leadership.

"*Now,*" the intelligence officer said. "*But don't harm the fireflies, they're mine. Four out.*"

Pepe Luria noticed that his constellation of fireflies moved without his ordering them to do so. He reacted instantly, diving to cover under one of the armored cars flanking him.

"*Take them!*" said Major Matthew Coke, and the darkness ignited.

Vierziger fired his 2-cm weapon into the side of the vehicle. Even at a range of nearly 500 meters, the powerful charge turned a chunk of steel armor into vapor and white flame rupturing outward.

Molten and gaseous metal sprayed Pepe beneath the opposite car. Luria jumped up screaming, his hair and clothing afire. Vierziger's second bolt blew his head off in a cyan flash.

Sten Moden launched a missile. The roof of L'Escorial headquarters reflected some of the backblast straight up, so the building itself appeared to have exploded in red flames.

Before the launcher operator fired, he locked a missile on by snapping an image with his guidance laser, then designated it as a point or object target. In the latter case—a maneuvering armored vehicle, for example—the missile guided itself to the target without updates from the operator.

The missiles had a ten-kilometer range, or even farther if they were launched from a level higher than the chosen target. Here, at half a klick, unburned rocket fuel added to the already cataclysmic effect of the powerful warhead.

An armored car disintegrated in a flash so bright that it seemed to shine through the steel. A red-orange mushroom mounted a hundred meters in the air, raining debris. The blast stove in the side of the car nearest the target vehicle and set it afire. The spray of fragments killed scores of L'Escorial gunmen, shredding some of them from knee height upward.

Matthew Coke chose targets—anybody moving on the street this night—and spun them down with short bursts. Margulies fired her 2-cm weapon from a door alcove five meters ahead of Coke, and Vierziger's weapons slapped with mechanical precision from the alley west of L'Escorial headquarters.

On targets so distant, a sub-machine gun's 1-cm bolts were near the low end of their effectiveness. Coke preferred an automatic weapon to the wallop of a 2-cm powergun, particularly at the short ranges he expected before this night was over. He could have carried weapons of both styles, as Vierziger did, but when he got tired he might have grabbed the wrong ammo for the gun he was trying to reload. Even the most experienced veteran could screw up that way....

Part of Coke's mind wondered if Johann Vierziger ever screwed up. Not when it involved killing something, he supposed.

The second missile hit. The launcher was intended for vehicular use. The thrust of exhaust against the sides of a launching tube pushed even a man as big and strong as Sten Moden a pace backward, so it took a moment to recenter the sights between rounds.

This time the target was the vehicle which carried bombardment rockets. The launching rack was empty, but Moden guessed there might be reloads within the armored hull. He must have been right, because the secondary explosion shattered the concrete facade protecting the building across the street and swept away all the external staircases.

The carnage among L'Escorials still stunned by the first blast was immense. The gunmen literally didn't know what had hit them.

Coke changed magazines, then slung the first sub-machine gun to cool while he fired the backup weapon. Anything moving was a target. They weren't human, they weren't even *alive;* they were merely motions in his holographic gunsights. He supposed a few of his bursts missed, but he was carrying over 2,000 rounds of ammunition....

"Three, cover my advance!" he ordered. He sprinted past Margulies to the alcove that had served a ground-floor brothel at the west end of the building. The strapped and plated door was firmly closed.

Gunmen—L'Escorials now, like the Astras before them—would be seeking shelter in the buildings. There was none. Those inside would not open their doors to the violence beyond, and the lawlessness of Potosi in past days meant the locked portals would withstand the efforts of panicked thugs to break in.

There was only the forest; and, for those who stayed in Potosi, death.

Two figures—a pudgy man and the aged one clinging to his arm—staggered toward the armored cars straddling the hole in the wall before the Astra compound. A tribarrel on one vehicle raked the night, but its bolts slashed at mid-height across the facades across the street.

The gunner didn't have a target despite the flaring backblast of Moden's launcher, which Coke thought would have fingered the rocket team across a five-kilometer radius. The fellow was blind with fear, shooting the way a devotee of Krishna might have chanted to bring himself closer to God in a crisis.

Coke aimed at Raul Luria. If he shot Ramon first, the Old Man would fall out of the sight picture as the son who supported him twisted down in death.

Moden's third rocket hit the armored car as Coke took up the slack on his trigger. The gunner found whatever god he worshipped, and the expanding fireball engulfed the Lurias.

Something tapped Coke's helmet. He spun, slashing empty air with the butt of his weapon. Shock from the blast had flung bits from the wall above him, nothing more.

The L'Escorial vehicles were all out of action, either hit by missiles or wrecked by the explosion of neighboring vehicles. Fuel fires spread a lurid illumination across the scene in place of the harshness of headlights a few minutes before. The wreckage of Astra headquarters was ablaze also, a pulsing, bloody glow that erupted from among the fallen walls.

Fireflies coursed the alleys, working outward from the killing ground about Astra headquarters. Occasionally the little machines dipped and stabbed the darkness with a single shot. They had been under Barbour's direction since he broke, then changed, Pepe's control codes.

A violet spark trundled purposefully down the street at a hundred-meter altitude, then dived to waist height directly in front of Matthew Coke. A hatch in the rear of the hovering device popped open. The firefly had expended its ammunition on L'Escorial gunmen and needed refilling.

Coke thumbed five rounds from a sub-machine gun magazine and fed them into the firefly. The hatch closed and the device curved back into action. *Better machines clear the alleys like ferrets in a rabbit warren than that men should have to do so....*

The fireflies weren't armored, and their corona discharges marked them for hostile gunmen. Like tanks, however, the machines had a psychological impact on untrained troops that went far beyond the physical threat they posed. Thugs ran screaming or closed their eyes and sprayed the sky blindly.

The fireflies put their pistol bolts into the center of mass. They dropped each target with the cool precision of hunting wasps stabbing the nerve ganglia of the prey that will feed their larvae.

Coke and Margulies advanced past one another twice more. There were few targets for their guns now.

Moden put a missile into the center of the Astra courtyard, blasting a crater in the scattered rubble, and flushed several figures. One of them sent a short burst of automatic fire in the direction of the launcher's signature. Coke, Margulies, and Vierziger all spiked the L'Escorial shooter; Niko Daun's sub-machine gun spattered the vicinity of the target a moment later.

Coke paused just short of an alley mouth. *"Cover my—"* Margulies began.

"Three, this is Four," Barbour broke in. *"Don't advance just yet, I want to run the alley. Over."*

"What do you—" Coke said.

A blast of shots and powergun bolts glanced from within the alley. A man screamed. Three gunmen—an Astra and two L'Escorials, each unaware of the others' presence until that moment, burst onto the street. Coke cut them down arm's length from his muzzle in a single long burst.

Two fireflies which had expended their magazines but were still lethally threatening drifted into sight above the men they had chased to their deaths. The devices' static suspension sputtered faintly, like hot grease.

Across the street, Vierziger's bolts lit a gunman who'd been similarly chased into sight. The fireflies turned and rose to comb the next pair of alleys in similar fashion.

"Two to One," Sten Moden reported. *"We've run out of missile targets, so we figured we'd work east from where you started. Is that a roger? Over."*

"One to Two," Coke said. "Roger, but use the fireflies for the action, keep them loaded. Break. Four, put half the fireflies at Two's disposal. One out."

Neither Daun nor Moden was properly combat material, but Sten was right: a few

L'Escorials would have kept away from the battle on their end of town. They weren't the hardcore gunmen, obviously. Nonetheless, they couldn't be simply ignored.

The trio on the ground were nearing what had been Astra headquarters. The stench of blood and death was overpowering. Heat from a burning vehicle—plastics and the rubber tires blazed long after the fuel had been consumed—drove Coke into the center of the street. His boots slipped on blood and flesh pureed by the explosions.

A man who breathed in rhythmic gasps tried to stuff coils of intestine back into his belly. Coke sighted on the dying man's head, then shifted his weapon back to the search for possible threats.

He knew it would have been kinder to finish off the L'Escorial. He just didn't have the stomach for that particular mercy on top of so much other killing.

A figure running, its limbs jerking like those of a wind-whipped scarecrow.

The man turned as Coke fired. Coke moved on. At every further step, his mind flashed the terrified visage which his bolts had lighted and blown apart.

Coke and Margulies leapfrogged again. Across the street Vierziger kept pace. Coke's bare hands prickled. Ozone and flakes of matrix plastic, spattered molten from the guns' ejection ports, had eaten away the outer layer of skin. Thirst was a red furnace within him, and his feet dragged with the effort of walking.

A man in a red vest with a leather fringe, kneeling and moaning a prayer at a locked doorway as a firefly made passes toward him.

Coke shot, then shot again as his bolts flung the man into the door and the corpse caromed back. *Not men, not things; merely motion.*

One of Coke's sub-machine guns jammed. He'd replaced the barrel twice, but the light-metal receiver warped from the heat of continuous firing. He threw it away and picked up a similar weapon which lay beside a man Margulies had decapitated.

The weight of Coke's ammunition had lessened. He'd emptied the pouches of two of the three bandoliers he'd belted on before the start of the action.…

The three Frisians reached the western end of Potosi. There were no more targets. Coke didn't know how much time had passed. His hands were swollen. They felt as though they were twice their normal size.

"Pretty well does it, s-s-Matthew," Margulies croaked. "I was wrong about fireflies. They come in handy s-sometimes."

Two of the fireflies had vanished while working the alleys ahead of Coke and his partners. Hit by lucky shots or mechanical failure, it didn't matter; they'd served their purpose.

The remaining unit hung close above the Frisians, hissing like a restive cobra. Coke hated the fireflies even more than he had before he'd operated with them. It was as bad as being allied to people who ate the men they killed.

Cyan flashes quivered across the forest in the direction of the spaceport. A moment after the shots, the Frisians heard the blat of a diesel engine being pushed.

The port operations van, its headlight flicking up and down like a conductor's baton as the vehicle flew over the washboard surface, raced toward Potosi. A circle of cooling metal on a quarter panel indicated that a fleeing gunman had hit the van when it failed to stop for him.

"Bloody *hell!*" Coke said as he lurched into the middle of the roadway. "Why did she take a chance like that? She could have been killed!"

"Sir!" Margulies warned. She dropped to a kneeling position with her back braced against the building as she aimed her 2-cm weapon. "That may not be your friend!"

Coke waved the sub-machine gun in his right hand. It felt immensely heavy, as if he were waggling a full-sized tree to get attention. The sky behind him was bright enough to cast his fuzzy shadow toward the oncoming vehicle.

The van fishtailed to a halt. The engine lugged but caught itself again without dying.

Pilar stuck her head out the side window. "Matthew!" she called. "Madame Yarnell's back, and she's come with a regiment of mercenaries! She says they're going to clear the syndicates off Cantilucca and set up new factors before Marvela has time to react. Matthew, get in! They'll kill you too, I'm sure of it!"

"*Bloody hell!*" Lieutenant Barbour blurted over the commo net. "*One, this is Four and she's right, I wasn't monitoring the port. Four transports have set down and there's another requesting landing instructions. It's the Heliodorus Regiment and I'd estimate—*"

A pause for instant mental synthesis of data that a normal interpretation team would have required an hour to complete.

"*—over two thousand troops. I don't know the equipment standard; it isn't in my data base. Over.*"

"Mary, you drive," Coke ordered as he got in on the passenger side of the van. "Pilar, get into the back, it'll be safer. How much fuel is there in the tank?"

"*Matthew, I'm really sorry,*" Barbour added. The needless and unprofessional comment showed how nervous he was. "*I should have been watching the port. Four over.*"

Barbour had run up to six fireflies simultaneously from a console that hadn't been built for the purpose. Who did he think he was? The Lord God Almighty, that he should be omniscient?

"The Heliodorus Regiment's light infantry," Johann Vierziger said as he swung open the van's rear door and sat, cradling his 2-cm weapon. The van now had a sting in its tail. "Wheeled transport, no fighting vehicles; coil guns with explosive bullets."

"The tank's about half full," Pilar said. Instead of getting into the back as ordered, she slid to the middle of the front seat where her thigh pressed Coke's. "The gauge doesn't work, but there should be enough fuel to go a hundred kilometers or more."

"And there're about three thousand bodies on the TO and E," Coke said to Vierziger as Margulies gunned the van forward. Data that hadn't been downloaded into the intelligence officer's console for lack of need bubbled to the surface of the combat veterans' minds. "Not that anybody ever landed with his complete table of organization strength."

Verbally keying the AI in his helmet, he continued, "Four, this is One. We'll pick up you and the eastern element, then keep going as far as we've got fuel for. Which apparently isn't very fucking far, the roads being what they are, but maybe we can improve our transport on the way. Break. Two and Five, do you copy? One over."

"One, this is Two," Sten Moden replied. His voice was breathy. *"We'll join you at L'Escorial HQ. We left the launcher there, and we may need the rounds we've got left. Over."*

"One, this is Four," Barbour said. *"I'm packing the console for travel now. Out."*

The intelligence officer shouldn't have been able to override his commanding officer's transmission—which is what he'd done, stepping on Coke's attempt to protest about Moden's plan. On the other hand, if Barbour couldn't control the net, he wouldn't have been as good as he'd repeatedly proved himself.

Coke sighed. "Roger both of you," he said. "One out."

He'd intended to run with a minimum of equipment. They would hide in the forest—if possible—until the situation changed or at least became more clear. If the survey team dropped off the map, Camp Able would send a follow-up mission.

In three weeks or a month, the FDF would send a follow-up mission. And while the Heliodorus Regiment was an organization of professionals, they were low-end professionals and the Cantilucca operation had to be handled without Bonding Authority oversight.

The Heliodorans just *might* carry out an order to execute captured Frisians. And there was no question in Coke's mind that Madame Yarnell would give such an order.

Pilar's hand lay beside his on their joined thighs. Coke squeezed it, then resumed compulsively counting the loaded magazines in his remaining bandolier. A moment before the van came in sight, Coke had wanted to find a hole and curl up in it for a week of sleep. Now he had a second wind, but he felt as though something could snap at any moment and leave him a pile of constituent atoms....

Margulies stopped in front of the L'Escorial building without killing the van's engine. Daun and Barbour ran from Hathaway House across the street. Both men were heavily laden. The intelligence officer carried his console, packed again into its integral case, while Niko staggered along ahead of the lieutenant with a wicker hamper.

"Daun, we don't have room for your..." Coke called. *Clothing? Housewares? What in hell* did *the kid have in the basket?*

"Beer!" Niko shouted as he slammed the hamper down in back of the van. "Master Hathaway's best! And if you're as dry as I am, it's better than ammo!"

Sten Moden, carrying so much equipment that he looked like a forklift, waddled from what had been L'Escorial's courtyard. Besides the launcher with two tubes ready, his hand gripped a pair of ammunition boxes. He'd slung additional weapons from his shoulder.

Coke jumped out to help his logistics officer. The team was going to need all the munitions, all Barbour's electronics, and mere thought of the beer was a cleansing shower for Coke's mind. But they were going to *need* a hundred times anything they could bring, so loading the van to the point of breakdown was bad tactics.

Particularly they were going to need troops. And the troops didn't exist on Cantilucca.

The beer was in earthenware bottles. Daun handed Coke one which he'd opened by digging the wax stopper out with a screwdriver blade. The cool lager slipped through the major's being like a blessing from the Lord.

"Let's get going," Coke said as he seated himself again beside the white-faced Pilar. He dropped the empty bottle out the window and took the fresh one Daun offered.

Margulies accelerated with care, but the vehicle wallowed anyway. It would be worse when they reached what passed for rural roads on Cantilucca.

The team couldn't run far enough on a planet where it had no friends, any more than the six of them could successfully fight a regiment. But they would run as far as they could; and then they would fight, because sometimes a bad choice is the only choice there is.

Coke reached an arm around Pilar. His hands were black with smoke, ammunition matrix, and iridium redeposited when plasma charges sublimed it from the bores of his weapons. Pilar snuggled close anyway.

Coke started to laugh. Margulies glanced over, and he felt Pilar stiffen. "It's not over yet, friends," Coke said in partial explanation.

Dawn was beginning to break over Potosi. The intelligence officer switched channels on his commo helmet intently, using its limited resources while his console was in traveling mode. He saw Coke looking back at him and flashed his commander a tight smile.

It was a hell of a thing to think under the circumstances, but Major Matthew Coke was glad to be alive.

The van rumbled eastward out of Potosi. According to the map Coke momentarily overlaid on his visor, the nearest hamlet had been owned by L'Escorial. The Lord only knew what the situation in the sticks was now, since both syndicates had lost their command groups and much of their rank and file.

Coke took only a glimpse at the map overlay, because he still had to watch for possible ambushers. Most of the gunmen who'd escaped Potosi alive would hide in panic when they heard a vehicle approaching, but a few might take potshots at strangers lucky enough to have transport.

Of course, bushwhackers would probably wait for the van to pass. That meant they'd be trying conclusions with Johann Vierziger.

"Heliodorus is just now putting out patrols," Bob Barbour reported. Niko had placed a variety of sensors throughout the spaceport one evening after driving Coke to the terminal. "Madame Yarnell is furious. She's told Colonel Shirazi that they should have been moving an hour ago."

"If she wanted professionals…" said Sten Moden. He was picking with a knifepoint at matrix congealed around the ejection port of a 2-cm weapon. "…she should have hired us."

"Direct rule by the Delos cartel's probably more efficient than leaving it to local thugs," Margulies said. "More of the locals might starve to death, but they wouldn't be as likely to be shot for the hell of it by some yo-yo having a night on the town."

"*Frisian Vessel* Obadiah *to FDF commander Cantilucca*," crackled an unfamiliar voice through Coke's commo helmet. "*Come in FDF Cantilucca. Over.*"

The members of the survey team stared at one another in surprise. Pilar didn't have a commo helmet. She clutched Coke fiercely, then snatched her hand away lest she interfere with his movements. She knew something had happened to startle her companions, but she couldn't imagine what it might be.

"It's coming from orbit," Barbour reported.

"*Frisian vessel* Obadiah *to FDF commander—*" the voice repeated. Coke cut the signal off so that it didn't interfere with his thinking.

"The Heliodorans?" Niko Daun suggested.

"Negative, they couldn't crash our frequencies," Barbour insisted. "This is on a general purpose push, but it's encrypted normally."

"The Heliodorans are trying to get us to give away our position," Margulies insisted stubbornly. They'll home on the transmission if we respond."

"There is an *Obadiah*," said Johann Vierziger as he watched the rear and sides of the van for possible dangers, "on the FDF naval list. She's a Class III combat transport."

Coke stared at the back of Vierziger's neck. The information Vierziger just stated wasn't secret—but it wasn't something Coke knew, or that a newbie sergeant was likely to have known. Coke didn't doubt that the statement was true, however.

Sten Moden released the blade catch and slid his knife back into the sheath on his belt. "I don't see that there's a downside to responding, Matthew," he said. "If the Heliodorans are good enough to mimic our codes, then they've got us anyway."

"The Heliodorans," Johann Vierziger said toward the landscape rumbling past the back of the van, "aren't good enough to hit the floor with their hats. Though numbers count for something."

Coke grimaced. "Bob," he said, "will my helmet raise them, or do we need to put up a beam?"

"You'll do better if you're out of the van," replied the intelligence officer. "But if they've got their antenna array extended, and I'm sure they do, they'll pick it up anyway."

"Pull off—" Coke began. Margulies swung the wheel and braked before he got to: "—the road, Mary."

Coke was out the door before the vehicle had come to a complete halt. The immediate area had been cleared around a shack now tumbled to moss and ruin. The van's other doors opened as suddenly as Coke's, the guns of his team facing the chance of attack. Even Margulies was scarcely a heartbeat slower than her commander in jumping from the vehicle she drove.

"—*FDF Cantilucca. Over,*" as Coke switched on the transmission from orbit again.

"Survey team commander to FDF vessel *Obadiah,*" Coke said. "We're glad to hear from you, boys, because we've got the Heliodorus Regiment looking for our scalps. Can you drop a boat to pick us up? The Heliodorans have secured the spaceport. Over."

Margulies had shut down the diesel when she stopped. Either she didn't choose to run further, or she was more optimistic about chances of restarting the beast in a hurry than Coke was. Metal pinged as the engine cooled.

"Obadiah *to FDF Cantilucca,*" the helmet responded. "*You bet we'll drop a boat. Hold what you've got, troopers. Help is coming in figures one-five minutes.* Obadiah *out.*"

"Well I'll be hanged!" Niko Daun said in pleased amazement.

"That depends on whether the extraction boat reaches us before Madame Yarnell does, kid," Moden said, but the big logistics officer was smiling also as he pointed his missile launcher back down the road toward dawn and the Heliodorus Regiment.

"Thirteen point six," Bob Barbour said with satisfaction. "Minutes, that is."

The intelligence officer's hearing must have been that much better than that of his commander, because it was another five or six seconds before Coke heard the first whisper of the vessel's landing motors.

Pilar stood beside him, a hand on his hip beneath the edge of his body armor. She didn't have armor of her own. Via, he should have grabbed Vierziger's suit for her since the sergeant wasn't using it. They brought every other cursed thing from Hathaway House when they—

Niko Daun looked up, toward the sound of the incoming boat. Coke, suddenly fearful that Pilar would follow the direction of Daun's gaze, shot his hand over her unprotected eyes. "His visor will darken automatically," Coke said.

Pilar pulled his hand down with a firm motion. "I've worked in spaceports for twelve years, Matthew," she said. "I know that plasma exhausts can be dangerous to my eyesight."

In a slightly sharper tone she added, "And I'm *not* fragile."

She squeezed him to take the edge off the rebuke. He remembered that in previous times of crisis she clutched her crucifix. She no longer wore that symbol.

"Sorry," he muttered, meaning more than his conscious mind really wanted to dwell on.

"Blood and martyrs, sir!" Niko said. "It's not a boat, it's the whole *ship!* They're coming straight in and there's no *port* here!"

"Class *III?*" Coke snapped to Vierziger as the penny dropped.

The little gunman smiled, though his eyes continued their ceaseless quest for a threat—or a target, it was all the same thing. He was holding a sub-machine gun now.

"That's right, Matthew," Vierziger agreed. "The *Obadiah*'s a battalion-capacity combat lander. She's got pontoon outriggers, so she doesn't require a stabilized surface to set down. And armor, in case the landing zone's hot."

The transport swept overhead at a steep angle. The roar and glare of her engines were mind-numbing,. Foliage at the tips of trees beneath her track curled and yellowed.

The vessel's exhaust was a rainbow flag waved at Madame Yarnell and the Heliodorans, some ten klicks to the west. Either the *Obadiah*'s commander expected to lift again before anyone could react, or—

Or the commander didn't care what a regiment of light infantry might attempt. The *Obadiah* was coming in with her landing doors open. The troops she carried were ready to un-ass the vessel as soon as the skids touched, or maybe a hair sooner.

"Bloody hell!" Mary Margulies shouted over the landing roar. "She's coming in loaded! She's coming in with troops!"

The *Obadiah* landed a hundred meters away, like a bomb going off in the forest. Her exhaust and armored belly plates cleared their own LZ. Dirt and shattered trees flew away from the shock. Coke caressed Pilar's head closer to his chest to protect her from the falling debris.

Lift fans howled through the shutdown sizzle of the landing engines. The rounded prow of a combat car burst through the fringe of forest which remained between the survey team and the LZ. The vehicle's wing tribarrels covered the sides, but the commander's weapon forward pointed straight at the van.

Coke stepped clear of the others, waving his sub-machine gun butt-upward. The combat car dropped to idle a meter from his feet. The legend on its scarred bow read *Cutting Edge*.

More vehicles deployed through the forest to either side. They were accompanied by squads of infantry riding one-man skimmers.

The commander of the leading car tilted up his tribarrel and raised his visor so that he could face Coke directly. "I'm Captain Garmin," he announced, "with my C Troop, First of the First and L Troop, Third of the First for infantry. I'm in acting command, but I'm supposed to turn the force over to Major Coke if he hasn't been incapacitated when we land. Are you Coke?"

You're supposed to fucking what?

Aloud Coke said, "I'm Coke, but what are you *doing* here?" *With a company of combat cars and a company of FDF infantry!*

Garmin grinned broadly. Coke remembered him vaguely from back in the days of the Slammers, a non-com who'd gotten a field commission.

"The colonel took your initial reports and cut a deal with the Marvelan Confederacy," Garmin explained. "We're to clean a couple gangs off Cantilucca for them. Orders didn't say anything about the Heliodorus Regiment, but I don't guess that'll change anything important."

"I'll be…" Coke muttered. He didn't finish the thought because he didn't know what the finish should be. "You've got just the two companies?"

"Yessir, but we're not cadre and trainees," Garmin said. "Most everybody in both troops wears the pin."

The captain tapped the left side of his breast with an index finger. His clamshell armor didn't show citations, but his meaning was clear: the expeditionary force was made up of Slammers veterans and soldiers with whom the veterans felt comfortable to serve. That was still true for much of the 1st Brigade of the Frisian Defense Forces.

"Right," said Coke as the next sequence of actions cascaded through his mind. "Your troopers are ready to go, Captain?"

"My troopers are gone, Major," Garmin corrected with justifiable pride. "Both troops have completed disembarking."

He coughed and added, "The *Obadiah* is armed and has her own security element, sir. I'd figured to get to work with my entire force—if you hadn't been around."

"Right, hit them before they get organized," Coke agreed. "Bob, set up in—"

He looked to his side. The intelligence officer had already re-erected his console, backing it against the parked van.

Barbour glanced up from a display of the Potosi area including the spaceport. Mauve icons denoted the Heliodoran forces. A platoon-sized Heliodoran detachment was probing Potosi, but the bulk of the regiment milled around the vessels on which it had landed.

"This'll do, sir," Barbour said. "I'm already patching data to the main com room of the ship. You can access it from there."

He nodded up to Captain Garmin. "We've got sensors throughout the area of operations," Barbour explained to the newcomer. "I'll hand you targets on a plate."

Garmin blinked in surprise. The officer who'd unloaded two troops inside of three minutes could appreciate professionalism in another man too.

"Niko, stay with Bob as security and a gofer," Coke ordered. "The rest of us'll need a car."

Who ever heard of running central intel from a shade tree? But Barbour was right, so long as he had a link to the nearby ship, it was as good a place as the next. "You others—"

"I'll drive," said Johann Vierziger. "It's not my favorite slot, but I'm good enough at it."

"I'll give you my XO's command car," Captain Garmin said. "It's—"

"Negative, Captain," Coke interrupted. "You will give me a *combat* car. The one you're in will do fine. If you want to ride into a firefight closed up in a can, be my guest—but I don't."

Coke hopped onto the skirts of *Cutting Edge*. "ASAP, Captain!" he prodded. Moden and Margulies were beside him—the logistics officer still shouldering his brace of heavy missiles. Vierziger mounted the bow slope and thumbed out the car's surprised driver.

"I—" Garmin began, then swallowed a protest that he knew wasn't going to do the least bit of good. "Yes *sir*," he said as he swung over the far side of the fighting compartment. He took with him only his personal weapon—a grenade launcher—and an AWOL bag of possessions.

A good man. And willing to be a good subordinate.

Niko Daun looked up in disappointment as the team's combat veterans crewed their new vehicle. Somebody had to keep an eye on the immediate surroundings while Barbour concentrated on his console. The sensor tech was the right person for the job… but he'd rather have been going along.

Coke checked the action of his tribarrel. It moved slickly on its gimbals, and the multifunction display beside it already glowed with enemy dispositions as reported by the survey team's sensor array. The Heliodorans flat wouldn't know what hit them.

Coke used the attached light pen to sketch the plan of action onto the display screen, from which it was echoed to every vehicle and helmet visor in his command. "C Troop, First and Second Platoons, north of Potosi. Flank speed, you'll hit the port from the east. Third Platoon and HQ element, south of the town to the south side of the port. Bypass the town! We don't want fighting there."

He was setting up a dynamic version of an L-shaped ambush, in which the attacking elements moved against a static target. Fields of fire shouldn't endanger friendly troops… much.

Coke rubbed his forehead before he continued. The only way to do this was headlong. If the Heliodorans had time to spread, it'd be the devil's own job winkling out each squad with their buzzbombs and explosive bullets. He was afraid to *think* beyond the level of reflex, so he'd go with reflex.

"Infantry commander"—Coke didn't even know that officer's name—"leave a squad in blocking position at either end of town on the east-west road. Remainder of your forces, conform to the movements of their opposite numbers in C Troop. Captain Garmin, take operational control of the eastern element. I'll handle the south."

Via, he didn't even have a callsign!

"Team One, that's Tony One, over."

"*Charlie One, confirm, out,*" said Garmin's voice. Coke wondered where the cars' CO had taken himself. Another combat car, he supposed.

"*Lima One, confirm,*" said a female stranger. "*Do you want the mortars here, where the ship provides a base of fire, or shall I put them on line? Over.*"

Bloody good question.

"Bring them along, Lima," Coke decided aloud. Ten klicks was within the effective range of the troop's pair of 10-cm automatic mortars, but he might want to use shellfire to prevent the Heliodorans from displacing west when the nutcracker of powergun bolts started to close. He'd best keep them near the target area. "Team out."

He looked around at the vehicles and mounted infantry already in line with his car. "Let's roll!" he ordered—

And noticed that Pilar Ortega squatted against the bulkhead of the fighting compartment, between Coke and Moden who manned the starboard tribarrel.

Vierziger poured power to the fans. He had as certain a touch with the fifty-tonne combat car as he did with a pistol's trigger.

"Not you, Pilar!" Coke said. "Blood and martyrs, not you!"

"Me," the auburn-haired woman said coolly. "I won't stay behind, Matthew."

She was holding a sub-machine gun, one of those Moden had brought aboard. She'd proved in Potosi that she could use one, would pull the trigger at least…

C Troop's Headquarters Squad—*Cutting Edge* and the XO's enclosed command car which carried additional commo in place of weapons and munitions—fell into line behind the five cars of 3d Platoon. Ten-man squads of infantry, each accompanied by a two-place gun jeep mounting a tribarrel, followed as the armor blazed a path through the scrub forest. Map data downloaded from the orbital scans provided a course for the lead driver, and the sensors Barbour monitored kept close watch on the Heliodorans.

"Bloody hell," Coke repeated. He couldn't very well throw her over the side of the car, could he?

Garmin's crew had left two suits of back-and-breast armor behind when they evacuated the car so suddenly. Coke sighed.

"Sten, show her how to get into her armor," he said, and he went back to planning the imminent battle.

The port's facilities—maintenance sheds and the terminal buildings; thank the *Lord* Pilar had gotten herself clear—were on the north side of the fenced reservation. The south was unobstructed, though there were twelve ships scattered over the ground in addition to the five from which the Heliodorus Regiment was slowly disembarking.

Coke had put the weight of his main thrust on the side toward which the newly landed regiment was moving, but the shock of ten combat cars and two infantry platoons was likely to drive the Heliodorans back. When they realized their south flank was being raked by a lesser force, they'd fight like raging hell to blow a way clear.

It was going to be interesting.

Coke's helmet AI filtered out all but Priority 1 messages. Margulies leaned close to him and said, loudly enough to be heard if her commander wanted to, "Barbour's told Madame Yarnell that the *Obadiah*'s a freighter that lost gyro control during normal set-down."

"She's not going to believe that, is she?" Coke said in surprise.

"Via, no!" Margulies agreed. Overlays projected across the inner surface of the security lieutenant's visor distorted her hard smile. "From what they're saying through the bugs in the terminal building, they're sure we're smugglers who picked a bad time to land and try to undercut the Delos cartel. Yarnell figures to take care of us smugglers just as soon as she's got Potosi secured."

Matthew Coke's mind flamed with blood and cyan light. He laughed. The sound made Pilar's face go blank in an expression closely akin to fear.

The south column burst from scrub into bottom land planted with gage. The leading car boosted its speed to 60 kph, three times the rate at which it had picked its way through the heavy growth. The combat cars were capable of doubling that in open terrain, but the infantry wouldn't have been able to keep up.

The gage crop was a month or so short of harvest. The reedy stems were a full meter tall, but the heads where the drug concentrated hadn't taken on the orangish tinge of full ripeness.

At Captain Garmin's orders, the cars spread from line-ahead formation to line abreast. As directed, Vierziger placed *Cutting Edge* on the left of the formation while the platoon leader took the right. There was an officer in position if the force had to displace suddenly toward either flank, and Coke was at the hinge of the attack.

"There's shooting in town," Margulies murmured, relaying data from the intelligence officer. "The Heliodorans ran into a couple dozen Astras who'd gone to ground and came out as the patrol arrived. The Astras just want to surrender to somebody, but the patrol leader's calling for heavy backup."

"I'd as soon," Sten Moden said, "if there wasn't fighting in Potosi. Civilians are bound to get hurt."

"When we take the main force," Coke said, "the rest—Heliodorans and syndicate both—the rest'll die on the vine."

Civilians weren't his concern at the moment. His task was to defeat hostile troops....

The column blasted by a dozen farmers' huts in fenced courtyards. Occasionally a shiver of movement indicated someone watching through the palings or from a shuttered window.

A squad of infantry dropped off to cover the community until the force was safely clear, but there was no real threat. A syndicate garrison might still occupy the loopholed stone building, but the flag was gone from the pole on the roof peak. Surviving gunmen didn't want to be identified with either of the losing parties.

"If there's ever to be peace on Cantilucca," said Pilar Ortega with a harshness at variance with the soldiers' professional calm, "it'll come the way you're bringing it. No other way."

Coke's eyes danced from the actual terrain to dots crawling across the combiner screen of his multifunction display. "Team One to Team elements," he ordered. "Take preliminary attack positions with at least five meters of screening between you and the perimeter fence. Out."

The south column was back in brush again, uncultivated country that was too dry to raise healthy gage. Vierziger slowed their car and pulled it off the general line of advance. The spaceport perimeter and all the structures within it were directly north of them but out of sight.

The local vegetation averaged three meters tall. A few trees rose half again as high before they flared out like golf tees. The trees had whippy, thin trunks, but their crowns were of straw-colored foliage which provided a complete visual screen. Someone in the spaceport tower could conceivably notice that the vegetation waved with the passage of the armored vehicles, but the chance of anybody being that alert was vanishingly slight.

Besides, the Frisians weren't going to be waiting very long.

A squad of infantry dropped off its skimmers and wormed its individual way into the scrub. The infantry could get much closer to the start line than the combat cars without risk of being observed. The squads air-cushion gun jeep halted back with the cars.

The mortars were jeep-mounted also. By themselves they could keep up with the infantry easily, but the jeeps carried only two 4-round ammo chargers. The remainder of the ammunition supply rode in a wheeled caisson behind each jeep.

Pulling a trailer with an air-cushion vehicle wasn't a great deal of fun on surfaced roads. Dragging wheels through brush and plowed fields, as this crew had been doing, was like trying to swim with a boat anchor. The company commander had wisely unloaded the pair of mortars as soon as she could.

"Charlie element in position," Captain Garmin reported. His platoons had a shorter route than Coke's, though there'd been a delay as many of the troops and cars crossed the road cautiously to reach their attack positions. *"Charlie out."*

Coke frowned at his display. Eight Heliodoran vehicles were moving away from the terminal building. Twelve more were in the final stages of loading soldiers from an early landed transport. A battalion headed toward Potosi to reinforce the patrol engaged there. The squad of infantry he'd left in a blocking position could at best slow them with a hit-and-run ambush, and that would be extremely risky.

On the southern perimeter, three of the combat cars and their associated infantry were short of where he'd wanted them to be able to enfilade the westernmost of the Heliodoran transports. Coke gave the order anyway: "All Team elements. Move into final attack positions."

Johann Vierziger eased *Cutting Edge* forward. His seat was raised so that he looked out of the hatch in the bow slope instead of through the vision displays within the driver's compartment.

"Wait for my command to fire," Coke continued, "unless the enemy engages you first. In the latter case, fire at will. Mortars, when the shooting starts, drop your rounds on concentrations shielded from direct fire. Team One out."

Some troopers felt claustrophobic when they were buttoned up in a vehicle. Coke was pretty sure that Vierziger just wanted to be able to add his own increment to the skein of fire which would shortly enwrap the Heliodorus Regiment.

The bow of *Cutting Edge* nosed up to the perimeter fence. Beside the vehicle, an infantryman was slicing a hole in the fence so that the wire didn't obstruct his line of fire.

The nearest starship—a freighter in the gage trade—was 200 meters away, north-ward and to the right. The terminal buildings were almost 800 meters distant.

The column of Heliodoran transport, lightly armored ten-wheeled trucks, drove toward the gate and Potosi beyond. Soldiers leaned on the waist-height panels of the cargo boxes, looking like sightseers rather than combat troops.

"Barbour says we've been seen!" Margulies shouted.

"Fire at will!" Coke ordered. He squeezed his thumb trigger as three red flares lifted from the terminal building.

Coke aimed at a detail of soldiers horsing crates from the cargo bay of a Heliodoran transport. The figures went down like bowling pins. A case ruptured, spewing out multicolored smoke from the marking grenades within.

Sten Moden launched one, then the other, of his missiles from the starboard wing of the fighting compartment toward targets far to the left. The backblast cleared swathes of empty scrub.

Coke needn't have worried about the most distant transports. A missile detonated on the boarding ramp of each.

Coke shifted his point of aim to the cargo hold of his chosen freighter. The inertia of the spinning iridium barrels fought the weapon's powered traverse, giving the motion a greasy dynamism.

The open hatch was a foreshortened trapezoid in his sight picture. Coke squeezed the butterfly again. The stream of 2-cm bolts reflected within the starship's dark interior like the pulses of a short circuit.

Ammunition detonated in a series of quivering yellow puffs. The orange flash that followed ripped the vessel apart, blowing the middle third across the port as jagged shrapnel.

The blast hurled Coke back from his tribarrel. The concussion set off stacked munitions previously unloaded from other ships. The shock wave skidded the eight Heliodoran trucks, already racked and burning from the eastern element's gunfire, into a single piled inferno.

Coke got up. He'd lost his helmet. Pilar, white and as stiff-featured as a skull, handed it to him.

A black mushroom mounted a thousand meters from the crater where the center of the starship had been. The two ends of the vessel lay crumpled, thirty meters from where they rested before the explosion.

Gunfire ceased for an instant. The shock had flattened potential targets as well as stunned the FDF gunners.

The initial eight-round salvo of mortar shells landed amidst the unloaded cargo. The white flashes and blasts would have seemed devastating had they not just followed a cataclysm.

Loudspeakers throughout the terminal buildings blared, "Invading forces, you have been surrounded by soldiers of the Marvelan Confederacy. Throw down your arms and surrender. You are surrounded by troops of the Marvelan Confederacy. There is no escape but surrender!"

Bob Barbour again, using the patches into the PA system he'd prepared weeks earlier. Coke had never doubted the value of intelligence and electronic warfare, but Barbour would make a believer of the most hardened grunt.

A Heliodoran crew-served weapon raked the southern perimeter from a position far enough to the west to have been shielded from the exploding starship. They were using a coil gun, a scaled-up version of the Heliodorans' personal weapons. The gun managed to cough out a dozen half-kg shells. One round lifted a Frisian infantryman twenty meters in the air, shedding limbs as he tumbled.

A storm of fire erased the weapon and its crew. Some of the shots came from nearby Heliodorans who knew their best chance of survival lay in surrender.

Partial silence returned, striated by the crackle of flames and the screams of those injured too badly to crawl from the spreading fires. Bits of cloth fluttered above whatever sparse cover the Heliodoran survivors had found. Some of the makeshift flags were white, but the intention was clear regardless.

"Colonel Shirazi to Marvelan Command!" a voice cried over one of the commo helmet's open channels. *"We're laying down our arms! I repeat, we're laying down our arms! We claim the right of exchange under Bonding Authority regulations! We're laying d—"*

Coke cut away from the Heliodoran commanders bleating. "Team One to all Team elements," he ordered. His throat felt as though somebody'd scaled it with a wood rasp. "Cease fire, but hold your positions. When the other side's sorted itself out a little better, I'll have them leave their weapons in place and march to the west end of the port reservation. Cease fire unless you're in danger. One out."

Coke switched to a general push to contact Colonel Shirazi. Sudden dizziness made him sag against the receiver of his tribarrel. The air above the glowing iridium shimmered. Through the heat waves, Coke saw Johann Vierziger looking back at him anxiously.

Pilar gripped Coke's shoulder, trying to keep him from falling. Silent tears cleared tracks across the grime on her face.

Sten Moden stared out at the barren killing field. There was no telling how many people had died. There would never be a certain figure: the secondary explosions had been too general and too powerful. Hundreds, perhaps over a thousand; in as little time as it takes to open a poached egg....

"It could have been worse," the logistics officer said. "It could have been us."

Niko Daun was talking sixteen to the dozen in the light of a lantern hanging over the nearby mess table. He wasn't bragging. In fact, he didn't seem to be aware of the presence of the members of the expeditionary force seated with him.

Many of the ex-Slammers were veterans of a score of incidents as hot as the one the young technician had just survived. They listened tolerantly as they ate.

"He's coming along, Matthew," Johann Vierziger said with mild amusement. "And the next time he won't make the mistake of pointing his gun at a pair of thugs and telling them to surrender."

The lantern illuminated only half of Vierziger's face. Shadows hollowed the killer's perfect features into the agony of a fourteenth century *Pietà*.

"Is mercy a mistake, Johann?" Coke asked. They sat on an empty mortar case near the edge of the expeditionary force's Night Defensive Position.

"I used to think so," Vierziger said. He smiled. "Thinking a gun's a magic wand that you wave—that is a mistake. When those Astra stragglers stumbled onto the van, he should have cut them down immediately."

The wired-in southwest corner of the port reservation was ablaze with floodlights. The Heliodorus Regiment, disarmed and under the guard of four combat cars, would be repatriated as soon as possible.

One of the transports the regiment landed in was still operable. Several days of work were necessary to repair two more, however.

Three transports would suffice to carry all the survivors comfortably.

"Niko did all right," Coke said. "A lot of veterans would have frozen when somebody shot them square in the chest. Thank the Lord for body armor."

Vierziger stretched his slim, hard form, still smiling. "It has its uses," he said, rather than agreeing.

Coke turned toward the eastern horizon, though there was nothing immediately visible save dark forest which had so recently flamed with the directed lightning of powerguns. "Thanks for taking over organizing a citizens' watch in Potosi," he said. "I've got a platoon backing them up as a reaction force, but the gunmen seem pretty much willing to come in peacefully."

Vierziger nodded. "Sten had some friends in town," he said. "Solid people, for civilians. It's not hard to set a structure up if you've got good material. And the locals want a structure."

Matthew Coke's spirit osmosed through the flesh and hovered above the scene. He was aware of sensory stimuli—the laughter of troops relaxing after an action of exceptionally concentrated violence; long-molecule soot from smoldering plastic, masking but not completely hiding the stench of burned flesh; the touch of a breeze on a night that was beginning to turn cool—the way he would have been aware of readings on a console display.

"The Marvelans should've sent along a civil administration unit with the troops," his voice said.

"They didn't have time," Vierziger said. "Alois wasn't going to wait for civilians to get their end together when he already had clearance to deal with the military side."

Vierziger spoke with almost proprietary satisfaction; the tone of a long-time veteran or even friend of President Alois Hammer. Coke looked at the sergeant and said nothing.

"I think, Matthew," Vierziger added mildly, "that you have a visitor coming."

Coke's mind was one again with his body, aches and stresses complete. Pilar's solid figure walked toward the NDP from the terminal building. She'd insisted on trying to put the facilities to rights immediately. It was hard to see that being possible, given the disruption the Heliodorans had caused and the damage from the exploding starship.

They had decisions to make in the near future, both of them.

Coke stood up. "Johann?" he said. "It's quiet now, but the Marvelans will pull us out of here in a few weeks at the longest. Do you think the civilians here will do any better the next time?"

"That's up to them, Matthew," Vierziger said. "The only thing that matters to our souls is what we've done ourselves."

"*You* believe in souls, then?" Coke snapped.

Vierziger nodded. His smile reminded Coke that Lucifer was a fallen angel. "Oh, yes," the little killer said. "*I* believe in souls."

Matthew Coke turned and walked to meet Pilar at the guardpost. By his own orders as Commanding Officer, troops of the Cantilucca Expedition were required to carry weapons with them at all times.

Coke's sub-machine gun and holstered pistol remained on the crate where he'd been sitting.

M9A7 COMBAT CAR WITH LONG RANGE AERIAL DEPLOYED

DEDICATION

To Larry Barnthouse, who long ago as another 96C2L94 was missed by all the same bullets that missed me.

ACKNOWLEDGMENTS

This book involved computer adventures unusual even for me, The Man Who Kills Computers. (Three dead within two weeks.) My son Jonathan, Mark Van Name, Karen Zimmerman, Allyn Vogel, and my wife Jo, were of particular importance in making it possible for me to continue working.

This book required a lot of attention by Dan Breen, my first reader. I'm very fortunate to have him.

PAYING THE PIPER

A BACKGROUND NOTE

I've always found it easier to use real settings and cultures than to invent my own. No matter how good a writer's imagination, the six or seven millennia of available human history can do a better job of creating backgrounds.

More than ten years ago I finally took the advice my friends Jim Baen and Mark Van Name had been giving me and did an afterword, explaining where I got the details of the book I'd just completed. I'd resisted this, feeling that it was bad art—the book should explain itself—and anyway, it was unnecessary. It was obvious to any reader that I was using historical and mythological backgrounds, so why should I bother to tell them?

It still may be bad art, and I may have been correct about readers in general seeing what I was doing without me telling them explicitly, but reviewers suddenly discovered that my fiction utilizes literary, historical and mythological material. I've kept up the practice, though generally not with straight Military SF like the Hammer series—but in this case I thought it might be useful, because the background I've used is from a backwater of history.

The Eastern Mediterranean at the end of the third century BC was a very complex region. The three empires founded by the successors of Alexander the Great were collapsing. They were locally powerful, but none was a superpower. Usurpers and secessionists complicated their politics.

Leagues of city states—the Achaeans and Aetolians in Greece proper, others in Asia Minor—had their own interests. New kingdoms, particularly that of Pergamum, were growing at the expense of their neighbors, and barbarians—both Celtic and Illyrian—were becoming regional powers instead of merely raiding and moving on.

Rome was still in the wings but the violent morass would shortly draw her in, ending both the chaos and her own status as a republic. (The region's enormous wealth and complexity, in my opinion, inexorably turned Rome into an empire.)

I adapted this setting for *Paying the Piper*. The general background is that of the war between Rhodes and Byzantium, ostensibly over freedom of navigation. It was about as stupid a conflict as you're likely to find, during which the real principals licked their lips and chuckled while well-meaning idealists wrecked their own societies in pursuit of unobtainable goals by improper means. Much of the military detail is drawn from the campaigns of Philip the Fifth and his allies against the Aetolian League, particularly the campaign of 219 BC which culminated in Philip's capture of Psophis.

I guess it isn't out of place to add one comment about the study of history. Knowing a good deal about how cultures interacted in the past allows one to predict how they will interact in the present, so I'm rarely surprised by the daily news. But I regret to say that this understanding doesn't appear to make me happier.

CHOOSING SIDES

The driver of the lead combat car revved his fans to lift the bow when he reached the bottom of the starship's steep boarding ramp. The gale whirling from under the car's skirts rocked Lieutenant Arne Huber forward into the second vehicle—his own *Fencing Master*, still locked to the deck because a turnbuckle had kinked when the ship unexpectedly tilted on the soft ground.

Huber was twenty-five standard years old, shorter than average and fit without being impressively muscular. He wore a commo helmet now, but the short-cropped hair beneath it was as black as the pupils of his eyes.

Sighing, he pushed himself up from *Fencing Master*'s bow slope. His head hurt the way it always did just after star travel—which meant worse than it did any other time in his life. Even without the howling fans of *Foghorn*, the lead car, his ears would be roaring in time with his pulse.

None of the troopers in Huber's platoon were in much better shape, and he didn't guess the starship's crew were more than nominal themselves. The disorientation from star travel, like a hangover, didn't stop hurting just because it'd become familiar.

"Look!" said Sergeant Deseau, shouting so that the three starship crewmen could hear him over the fans' screaming. "If you don't have us free in a minute flat, starting *now*, I'm going to shoot the cursed thing off and you can worry about the damage to your cursed deck without me to watch you. Do you understand?"

Two more spacers were squeezing through the maze of vehicles and equipment in the hold, carrying a power tool between them. This sort of problem can't have been unique to *Fencing Master*.

Huber put his hand on Deseau's shoulder. "Let's get out of the way and let them fix this, Sarge," he said, speaking through the helmet intercom so that he didn't have to raise his voice. Shouting put people's backs up, even if you didn't mean anything by it except that it was hard to hear. "Let's take a look at Plattner's World."

They turned together and walked to the open hatch. Deseau was glad enough to step away from the problem.

The freighter which had brought platoon F-3, Arne Huber's command, to Plattner's World had a number rather than a name: KPZ 9719. It was much smaller than the vessels which usually carried the men and vehicles of Hammer's Regiment, but even so it virtually overwhelmed the facilities here at Rhodesville. The ship had set down normally, but one of the outriggers then sank an additional meter into the soil. The lurch had flung everybody who'd already unstrapped against the bulkheads and jammed *Fencing Master* in place, blocking two additional combat cars behind it in the hold.

Huber chuckled. That made his head throb, but it throbbed already. Deseau gave him a sour look.

"It's a good thing we hadn't freed the cars before the outrigger gave," Huber explained. "Bad enough people bouncing off the walls; at least we didn't have thirty-tonne combat cars doing it too."

"I don't see why we're landing in a cow pasture anyway," Deseau muttered. "Isn't there a real spaceport somewhere on this bloody tree-farm of a planet?"

"Yeah, there is," Huber said dryly. "The trouble is, it's in Solace. The people the United Cities are hiring us to fight."

The briefing cubes were available to everybody in the Slammers, but Sergeant Deseau was like most of the enlisted personnel—and no few of the officers—in spending the time between deployments finding other ways to entertain himself. It was a reasonable enough attitude. Mercenaries tended to be pragmatists. Knowledge of the local culture wasn't a factor when a planet hired mercenary soldiers, nor did it increase the gunmen's chances of survival.

Deseau spit toward the ground, either a comment or just a way of clearing phlegm from his throat. Huber's mouth felt like somebody'd scrubbed a rusty pot, then used the same wad of steel wool to scour his mouth and tongue.

"Let's hope we capture Solace fast so we don't lose half our supplies in the mud," Deseau said. "This place'll be a swamp the first time it rains."

KPZ 9719 had come down on the field serving the dirigibles which connected Rhodesville with the other communities on Plattner's World—and particularly with the spaceport at Solace in the central highlands. The field's surface was graveled, but there were more soft spots than the one the starship's outrigger had stabbed down through. Deseau was right about what wet weather would bring.

The starship sat on the southern edge of the kilometer-square field. On the north side opposite them were a one-story brick terminal with an attached control tower and a dozen warehouses with walls and trusses of plastic extrusion. Those few buildings comprised the entire port facilities.

Tractors were positioning lowboys under the corrugated metal shipping containers slung beneath the 300-meter-long dirigible now unloading at the east end of the field. A second dirigible had dropped its incoming cargo and was easing westward against a mild breeze, heading for the mooring mast where it would tether. The rank of outbound shipping containers there waited to be slung in place of the food and merchandise the United Cities imported. The containers had been painted a variety of colors, but rust now provided the most uniform livery.

A third dirigible was in the center of the field, its props turning just fast enough to hold it steady. The four shipping containers hanging from its belly occasionally kicked up dust as they touched the ground. A port official stood in an open-topped jitney with a flashing red light. He was screaming through a bullhorn at the dirigible's forward cockpit, but the crew there seemed to be ignoring him.

Trooper Learoyd, *Fencing Master*'s right wing gunner—Huber chose to ride at the left gun, with Deseau in the vehicle commander's post in the center—joined them at the hatch. He was stocky, pale, and almost bald even though he was younger than Huber by several years. He looked out and said, "What's worth having a war about this place?"

"There's people on it," Deseau said with a sharp laugh. "That's all the reason you need for a war, snake. You ought to know that by now."

According to the briefing cubes, Rhodesville had a permanent population of 50,000; the residents provided light manufacturing and services for the Moss-hunters coursing thousands of square kilometers of the surrounding forest. Only a few houses were visible from the port. The community wound through the forest, constructed under the trees instead of clearing them for construction. The forest was the wealth of Plattner's World, and the settlers acted as though they understood that fact.

"There's a fungus that's a parasite on the trees here," Huber explained. "They call it Moss because it grows in patches of gray tendrils from the trunks. It's the source of an anti-aging drug. The processing's done off-world, but there's enough money in the business that even the rangers who gather the Moss have aircars and better holodecks than you'd find in most homes on Friesland."

"Well I'll be," Learoyd said, though he didn't sound excited. He rubbed his temples, as if trying to squeeze the pain out through his eyesockets.

Deseau spat again. "So long as they've got enough set by to pay our wages," he said. "I'd like a good, long war this time, because if I never board a ship again it'll be too soon."

The third dirigible was drifting sideways. Huber wouldn't have been sure except for the official in the jitney; he suddenly dropped back into his seat and drove forward to keep from being crushed by the underslung cargo containers. The official stopped again and got out of his vehicle, running back toward the dirigible with his fists raised overhead in fury.

Huber looked over his shoulder to see how the spacers were making out with the turnbuckle. The tool they'd brought, a cart with chucks on extensible arms, wasn't working. Well, that was par for the course.

Trooper Kolbe sat in the driver's compartment, his chin bar resting on the hatch coaming. His faceshield was down, presenting an opaque surface to the outside world. Kolbe could have been using the helmet's infrared, light-amplification, or sonic imaging to improve his view of the dimly lit hold, but Huber suspected the driver was simply hiding the fact that his eyes were closed.

Kolbe needn't have been so discreet. If Huber hadn't thought he ought to set an example, he'd have been leaning his forehead against *Fencing Master*'s cool iridium bow slope and wishing he didn't hurt so much.

Platoon Sergeant Jellicoe was at the arms locker, issuing troopers their personal weapons. Jellicoe seemed as dispassionate as the hull of her combat car, but Trooper Coblentz, handing out the weapons as the sergeant checked them off, looked like he'd died several weeks ago.

Unless and until Colonel Hammer ordered otherwise, troopers on a contract world were required to go armed at all times. Revised orders were generally issued within hours of landing; troopers barhopping in rear areas with sub-machine guns and 2-cm shoulder weapons made the Regiment's local employers nervous, and rightly so.

On Plattner's World the Slammers had to land at six sites scattered across the United Cities, a nation that was mostly forest. None of the available landing fields was large enough to take the monster starships on which the Regiment preferred to travel, and only the administrative capital, Benjamin, could handle more than one twenty-vehicle company at a time. Chances were that even off-duty troopers would be operating in full combat gear for longer than usual.

"What's that gas-bag doing?" Deseau asked. "What do they fill 'em with here, anyway? If it's hydrogen and it usually is…"

Foghorn had shut down, well clear of the starship's ramp. Her four crewmen were shifting their gear out of the open-topped fighting compartment and onto the splinter shield of beryllium net overhead. A Slammers' vehicle on combat deployment looked like a bag lady's cart; the crew knew that the only things they could count on having were what they carried with them. Tanks and combat cars could shift position by over 500 klicks in a day, smashing the flank or rear of an enemy who didn't even know he was threatened; but logistics support couldn't follow the fighting vehicles as they stabbed through hostile territory.

"Aide, unit," Huber said, cueing his commo helmet's AI to the band all F-3 used in common. "Tatzig, pull around where that dirigible isn't going to hit you. Something's wrong with the bloody thing and the locals aren't doing much of a job of sorting it out."

Sergeant Tatzig looked up. He grunted an order to his driver, then replied over the unit push, "*Roger, will do.*"

There was a clang from the hold. A spacer had just hit the turnbuckle with a heavy hammer.

A huge, hollow metallic racket sounded from the field; the dirigible had dropped its four shipping containers. The instant the big metal boxes hit the ground, the sides facing the starship fell open. Three of them did, anyway: the fourth container opened halfway, then stuck.

The containers were full of armed men wearing uniforms of chameleon cloth that mimicked the hue of whatever it was close to. The troops looked like pools of shadow from which slugthrowers and anti-armor missiles protruded.

"Incoming!" Huber screamed. "We're under attack!"

One of the attacking soldiers had a buzzbomb, a shoulder-launched missile, already aimed at Huber's face. He fired. Huber reacted by instinct, grabbing his two companions and throwing himself down the ramp instead of back into the open hold.

The missile howled overhead and detonated on *Fencing Master*'s bow. White fire filled the universe for an instant. The blast made the ramp jump, flipping Huber from his belly to his right side. He got up. He was seeing double, but he could see; details didn't matter at times like this.

The attack had obviously been carefully planned, but things went wrong for the hostiles as sure as they had for Huber and his troopers. The buzzbomber had launched early instead of stepping away from the shipping container as he should've done. The steel box caught the missile's backblast and reflected it onto the shooter and those of his fellows who hadn't jumped clear. They spun out of the container, screaming as flames licked from their tattered uniforms.

A dozen automatic weapons raked *Foghorn*, killing Tatzig and his crewmen instantly. The attackers' weapons used electromagnets to accelerate heavy-metal slugs down the bore at hypersonic velocity. When slugs hit the car's iridium armor, they ricocheted as neon streaks that were brilliant even in sunlight.

Slugs that hit troopers chewed their bodies into a mist of blood and bone.

The starship's hold was full of roiling white smoke, harsh as a wood rasp on the back of Huber's throat in the instant before his helmet slapped filters down over his nostrils. The buzzbomb had hit *Fencing Master*'s bow slope at an angle. Its shaped-charge warhead had gouged a long trough across the armor instead of punching through into the car's vitals. There was no sign of Kolbe.

The tie-down, jammed turnbuckle and all, had vanished in the explosion. Two pairs of legs lay beside the vehicle. They'd probably belonged to spacers rather than Huber's troopers, but the blast had blown the victims' clothing off at the same time it pureed their heads and torsos.

Slugs snapped through the starship's hatchway, clanging and howling as they ricocheted deeper into the hold. Huber mounted *Fencing Master*'s bow slope with a jump and a quick step. He dabbed a hand down and the blast-heated armor burned him. He'd have blisters in the morning, if he lived that long.

Huber thought the driver's compartment was empty, but Kolbe's body from the shoulders on down had slumped onto the floor. Huber bent through the hatch and grabbed him. The driver's right arm came off when Huber tugged.

Huber screamed in frustration and threw the limb out of the vehicle, then got a double grip on Kolbe's equipment belt and hauled him up by it. Bracing his elbows for leverage, Huber pulled the driver's torso and thighs over the coaming and let gravity do the rest. The body slithered down the bow, making room for Huber inside. The compartment was too tight to share with a corpse and still be able to drive.

Kolbe had raised the seat so that he could sit with his head out of the vehicle. Huber dropped it because he wanted the compartment's full-sized displays instead of the miniature versions his faceshield would provide. The slugs whipping around the hold would've been a consideration if he'd had time to think about it, but right now he had more important things on his mind than whether he was going to be alive in the next millisecond.

"All Fox elements!" he shouted, his helmet still cued to the unit push. Half a dozen troopers were talking at the same time; Huber didn't know if anybody would hear the order, but they were mostly veterans and ought to react the right way without a lieutenant telling them what that was. "Bring your cars on line and engage the enemy!"

Arne Huber was F-3's platoon leader, not a driver, but right now the most critical task the platoon faced was getting the damaged, crewless, combat car out of the way of the two vehicles behind it. With *Fencing Master* blocking the hatch, the attackers would wipe out the platoon like so many bugs in a killing bottle. Huber was the closest trooper to the job, so he was doing it.

The fusion bottle that powered the vehicle was on line. Eight powerful fans in nacelles under *Fencing Master*'s hull sucked in outside air and filled the steel-skirted plenum chamber at pressure sufficient to lift the car's thirty tonnes. Kolbe had switched the fans on but left them spinning at idle, their blades set at zero incidence, while the spacers freed the turnbuckle.

Huber palmed the combined throttles forward while his thumb adjusted blade incidence in concert. As the fusion bottle fed more power to the nacelles, the blades tilted on their axes so that they drove the air rather than merely cutting it. Fan speed remained roughly constant, but *Fencing Master* shifted greasily as her skirts began to lift from the freighter's deck.

A second buzzbomb hit the bow.

For an instant, Huber's mind went as blank as the white glare of the blast. The shock curtains in the driver's compartment expanded, and his helmet did as much as physics allowed to save his head. Despite that, his brain sloshed in his skull.

He came around as the shock curtains shrank back to their ready state. He didn't know who or where he was. The display screen before him was a gray, roiling mass. He switched the control to thermal imaging by trained reflex and saw armed figures rising from the ground to rush the open hatch.

I'm Arne Huber. We're being attacked.

His right hand was on the throttles; the fans were howling. He twisted the grip, angling the nacelles back so that their thrust pushed the combat car instead of just lifting it. *Fencing Master*'s bow skirt screeched on the deck, braking the vehicle's forward motion beyond the ability of the fans to drive it.

The second warhead had opened the plenum chamber like a ration packet. The fan-driven air rushed out through the hole instead of raising the vehicle as it was meant to do.

The attackers had thrown themselves flat so that the missile wouldn't scythe them down also. Three of them reached the base of the ramp, then paused and opened fire. Dazzling streaks crisscrossed the hold, and the *whang* of slugs hitting the *Fencing Master*'s iridium armor was loud even over the roar of the fans.

Huber decoupled the front four nacelles and tilted them vertical again. He shoved the throttle through the gate, feeding full emergency power to the fans. The windings would burn out in a few minutes under this overload, but right now Huber wouldn't bet he or anybody in his platoon would be alive then to know.

Fencing Master's ruined bow lifted on thrust alone. Not high, not even a finger's breadth, but enough to free the skirt from the decking and allow the rear nacelles to shove her forward. Staggering like a drunken ox, the car lurched from the hold and onto the ramp. Her bow dragged again, but this time the fans had gravity to aid them. She accelerated toward the field, scraping up a fountain of red sparks from either side of her hull.

The attackers tried to jump out of the way. Huber didn't know and didn't much care what happened to them when they disappeared below the level of the sensor pickups feeding *Fencing Master*'s main screen. A few gunmen more or less didn't matter; Huber's problem was to get this car clear of the ramp so that *Flame Farter* and *Floosie*, still aboard the freighter, could deploy and deal with the enemy.

Fencing Master reached the bottom of the ramp and drove a trench through the gravel before shuddering to a halt. The shock curtains swathed Huber again; he'd have disengaged the system if he'd had time for nonessentials after the machine's well-meant swaddling clothes freed him. Skewing the stern nacelles slightly to port, he pivoted *Fencing Master* around her bow and rocked free of the rut.

The air above him sizzled with ozone and cyan light: two of the tribarrels in the car's fighting compartment had opened up on the enemy. Somebody'd managed to board while Huber was putting the vehicle in motion. *Fencing Master* was a combat unit again.

There must've been about forty of the attackers all told, ten to each of the shipping containers. Half were now bunched near *Foghorn* or between that car and the starship's ramp. Huber switched *Fencing Master*'s Automatic Defense System live, then used the manual override to trigger three segments.

The ADS was a groove around the car's hull, just above the skirts. It was packed with plastic explosive and faced with barrel-shaped osmium pellets. When the system was engaged, sensors triggered segments of the explosive to send blasts of pellets out to meet and disrupt an incoming missile.

Fired manually, each segment acted as a huge shotgun. The clanging explosions chopped into cat food everyone who stood within ten meters of *Fencing Master*. Huber got a whiff of sweetly poisonous explosive residues as his nose filters closed again. The screaming fans sucked away the smoke before he could switch back to thermal imaging.

An attacker aboard *Foghorn* had seen the danger in time to duck into the fighting compartment; the pellets scarred the car's armor but didn't penetrate it. The attacker rose, pointing his slugthrower down at the hatch Huber hadn't had time to close. A tribarrel from *Fencing Master* decapitated the hostile.

A powergun converted a few precisely aligned copper atoms into energy which it directed down the weapon's mirror-polished iridium bore. Each light-swift bolt continued in a straight line to its target, however distant, and released its energy as heat in a cyan flash. A 2-cm round like those the tribarrels fired could turn a man's torso into steam and fire; the 20-cm bolt from a tank's main gun could split a mountain.

One of the shipping containers was still jammed halfway open. Soldiers were climbing out like worms squirming up the sides of a bait can. Two raised their weapons when they saw a tribarrel slewing in their direction. Ravening light slashed across them, flinging their maimed bodies into the air. The steel container flashed into white fireballs every time a bolt hit it.

Huber's ears were numb. It looked like the fighting was over, but he was afraid to shut down *Fencing Master's* fans just in case he was wrong; it was easier to keep the car up than it'd be to raise her again from a dead halt. He did back off the throttles slightly to bring the fans down out of the red zone, though. The bow skirt tapped and rose repeatedly, like a chicken drinking.

Flame Farter pulled into the freighter's hatchway and dipped to slide down the ramp under full control. Platoon Sergeant Jellicoe was behind the central tribarrel. She'd commandeered the leading car when the shooting started rather than wait for her own *Floosie* to follow out of the hold.

Jellicoe fired at something out of sight beyond the shipping containers. Huber touched the menu, importing the view from Jellicoe's gunsight and expanding it to a quarter of his screen.

Three attackers stood with their hands in the air; their weapons were on the gravel behind them. Jellicoe had plowed up the ground alongside to make sure they weren't going to change their minds.

Mercenaries fought for money, not principle. The Slammers and their peers took prisoners as a matter of policy, encouraging their opponents toward the same professional ideal.

Enemies who killed captured Slammers could expect to be slaughtered man, woman and child; down to the last kitten that mewled in their burning homes.

"Bloody Hell…" Huber muttered. He raised the seat to look out at the shattered landscape with his own eyes, though the filters still muffled his nostrils.

Haze blurred the landing field. It was a mix of ozone from powergun bolts and the coils of the slug-throwers, burning paint and burning uniforms, and gases from superheated disks that had held the copper atoms in alignment: empties ejected from the tribarrels. Some of the victims were fat enough that their flesh burned also.

The dirigible that'd carried the attackers into position now fled north as fast as the dozen engines podded on outriggers could push it. That wasn't very fast, even with the help of the breeze to swing the big vessel's bow; they couldn't possibly escape.

Huber wondered for a moment how he could contact the dirigible's crew and order them to set down or be destroyed. Plattner's World probably had emergency frequencies, but the data hadn't been downloaded to F-3's data banks yet.

Sergeant Jellicoe raked the dirigible's cabin with her tribarrel. The light-metal structure went up like fireworks in the cyan bolts. An instant later all eight gunners in the platoon were firing, and the driver of *Floosie* was shooting a pistol with one hand as he steered his car down the ramp with the other.

"Cease fire!" Huber shouted, not that it was going to make the Devil's bit of difference. "Unit, cease fire *now!*"

The dirigible was too big for the powerguns to destroy instantly, but the bolts had stripped away swathes of the outer shell and ruptured the ballonets within. Deseau had guessed right: the dirigible got its lift from hydrogen, the lightest gas and cheap enough to dump and replace after every voyage so that the ballonets didn't fill with condensed water over time.

The downside was the way it burned.

Flames as pale and blue as a drowned woman's flesh licked from the ballonets, engulfing the middle of the great vessel. The motors continued to drive forward, but the stern started to swing down as fire sawed the airship in half. The skeleton of open girders showed momentarily, then burned away.

"Oh bloody buggering Hell!" Huber said. He idled *Fencing Master*'s fans and stood up on the seat. "*Hell!*"

"What's the matter, sir?" Learoyd asked. He'd lost his helmet, but he and Sergeant Deseau both were at their combat stations. The tribarrels spun in use, rotating a fresh bore up to fire while the other two cooled. Even so the barrels still glowed yellow from their long bursts. "They were hostiles too, the good Lord knows."

"*They* were," Huber said grimly. "But the folks living around here are the ones who've hired us."

The remaining ballonets in the dirigible's bow exploded simultaneously, flinging blobs of burning metal hundreds of meters away. Fires sprang up from the treetops, crackling and spewing further showers of sparks.

Huber heard a siren wind from somewhere deep in the forest community. It wasn't going to do a lot of good.

The dirigible's stern, roaring like a blast furnace, struck the terminal building. Some of those inside ran out; they were probably screaming, but Huber couldn't hear them over the sound of the inferno. One fellow had actually gotten twenty meters from the door when the mass of airship and building exploded, engulfing him in flames. He was a carbonized husk when they sucked back an instant later.

Huber sighed. That pretty well put a cap on the day, he figured.

Base Alpha—regimental headquarters on every world that hired the Slammers was Base Alpha—was a raw wasteland bulldozed from several hectares of forest. The clay was deep red when freshly turned, russet when it dried by itself to a form of porous rock, and oddly purple when mixed with plasticizer to form the roadways and building foundations of the camp.

The aircar and driver that'd brought Huber from Rhodesville to Base Alpha were both local, though the woman driving had a cap with a red ball insignia and the words:

Logistics Section

Hammer's Regiment

marking her as a Slammers' contract employee. Colonel Hammer brought his own combat personnel and equipment to each deployment, but much of the Regiment's logistics tail was procured for the operation. Supplies and the infrastructure to transport them usually came from what the hiring state had available.

Huber stopped in front of the building marked PROVOST MARSHAL and straightened his equipment belt. The guards, one of them in a gun jeep mounting a tribarrel, watched him in the anonymity of mirrored faceshields. The tribarrel remained centered on Huber's midriff as he approached.

The orders recalling Lieutenant Arne Huber from F-3 directed him to report to the Provost Marshal's office on arrival at Base Alpha. Huber had left his gear with the clerk at the Transient Barracks—he wasn't going to report to the Regiment's hatchetman with a dufflebag and two footlockers—but he hadn't taken time to be assigned a billet. There was a good chance—fifty-fifty, Huber guessed—that he wouldn't be a member of the Slammers when the present interview concluded.

He felt cold inside. He'd known the possibilities the instant he saw the first bolts rake the dirigible, but the terse recall message that followed his report had still made his guts churn.

Nothing to be done about it now. Nothing to be done about it since Sergeant Jellicoe shifted her aim to the dirigible and thumbed her butterfly trigger.

"Lieutenant Huber reporting to the Provost Marshal, as ordered," he said to the sergeant commanding the squad of guards.

"You're on the list," the sergeant said without inflexion. He and the rest of his squad were from A Company; they were the Regiment's police, wearing a stylized gorget as their collar flash. In some mercenary outfits the field police were called Chain Dogs from the gorget; in the Slammers they were the White Mice. "You can leave your weapons with me and go on in."

"Right," said Huber, though the order surprised him. He unslung his belt with the holstered pistol, then handed over the powerknife clipped to a trouser pocket as well.

"He's clean," said a guard standing at the readout from a detection frame. The sergeant nodded Huber forward.

The Slammers were used to people wanting to kill them. Major Joachim Steuben, the Regiment's Provost Marshal, was obviously used to the Slammers themselves wanting to kill *him*.

Huber opened the door and entered. The building was a standard one-story newbuild with walls of stabilized earth and a roof of plastic extrusion. It was a temporary structure so far as the Slammers were concerned, but it'd still be here generations later unless the locals chose to knock it down.

It was crude, ugly, and as solid as bedrock. You could use it as an analogy for the Slammers' methods, if you wanted to.

The door facing the end of the hallway was open. A trim, boyishly handsome man sat at a console there; he was looking toward Huber through his holographic display. If it weren't for the eyes, you might have guessed the fellow was a clerk....

Huber strode down the hall, staring straight ahead. Some of the side doors were open also, but he didn't look into them. He wondered if this was how it felt to be a rabbit facing a snake.

I'm not a rabbit. But if half the stories told about him were true, Joachim Steuben was a snake for sure.

Before Huber could raise his hand to knock on the door jamb, the man behind the desk said, "Come in, Lieutenant; and close it behind you."

A holographic landscape covered the walls of Joachim Steuben's office; flowers poked through brightly lit snow, with rugged slopes in the background. The illusion was seamless and probably very expensive.

"You know why you're here, Huber?" Steuben asked. Everything about the little man was expensive: his manicure, his tailored uniform of natural silk, and the richly chased pistol in a cut-away holster high on his right hip.

The only chair in the office was the one behind Steuben's console.

"I'm here because of the ratfuck at Rhodesville, sir," Huber said. He held himself at attention, though the major's attitude wasn't so much formal as playfully catlike.

Instead of staring at the wall over Steuben's shoulder, Huber met the major's eyes directly. If he hadn't, he'd have been giving in to fear. Because Major Joachim Steuben scared the crap out of him.

"Close enough," Steuben said as though he didn't much care. "What's your excuse?"

"Sir!" Huber said, truly shocked this time. "No excuse, *sir.*"

It was the Nieuw Friesland Military Academy answer, and it was the right answer this time beyond question. Platoon F-3's commander had started to disembark his unit without waiting to issue sidearms and to cycle ammunition for the vehicles' tribarrels up from their storage magazines. Five troopers had died, a sixth had lost her left arm to a ricocheting slug, and it was the Lord's mercy alone that kept the damage from being worse.

Steuben raised an eyebrow and smiled faintly. His console's holographic display was only a shimmer of light from the back side, so Huber didn't know whether the major was really viewing something—Huber's file? A stress readout?—or if he just left it up to make the interviewee more uncomfortable.

Which would be a pretty good trick, as uncomfortable as Huber felt even before he entered the office.

"A fair number of people in the United Cities think it'd be a mistake to go to war with Solace, Huber," Steuben said calmly. "They want to use the way you gutted Rhodesville as an excuse to cancel the Regiment's contract and go back to peaceful negotiation with Solace over port fees. Do you have any comment about that?"

Huber licked his lips. "Sir," he said, "everything my platoon did at Rhodesville was by my direct order. No blame whatever should attach to any of my troopers."

Steuben laughed. It was a horrible sound, a madman's titter. "Goodness," he said. "An officer who has complete control of his troops while he's driving a damaged combat car? You're quite a paragon, Lieutenant."

Huber licked his lips again. He had to pull his eyes back to meet Steuben's. *Like looking at a cobra....*

"For the time being," the major continued, suddenly businesslike and almost bored, "you've been transferred to command of Logistics Section, Lieutenant Huber. Your office is in Benjamin proper, not Base Alpha here, because most of your personnel are locals. You have a cadre of six or so troopers, all of them deadlined for one reason or another."

He laughed again. "None of the others have burned down a friendly community, however," he added.

"Yes sir," Huber said. He felt dizzy with relief. He'd thought he was out. He'd been pretending he didn't, but he'd walked into this office believing he'd suddenly become a civilian again, with no friends and no future.

Major Steuben shut down his display and stood. He was a small man with broad shoulders for his size and a wasp waist. From any distance, the word "pretty" was the one you'd pick to describe him. Only if you were close enough to see Steuben's eyes did you think of snakes and death walking on two legs....

"I don't have any problem with what you did in Rhodesville, Lieutenant," Steuben said quietly. "But I don't have a problem with a lot of things that seem to bother other people. If the Colonel told me to, I'd shoot you down where you stand instead of transferring you to Log Section. And it wouldn't bother me at all."

He smiled. "Do you understand?"

"Yes sir," Huber said. "I understand."

"Lieutenant Basime was a friend of yours at the Academy, I believe," Steuben said with another of his changes of direction. "She's acting head of our signals liaison with the UC now. Drop in and see her before you report to Log Section. She can fill you in on the background you'll need to operate here in the rear."

He waved a negligent hand. "You're dismissed, Lieutenant," he said. "Close the door behind you."

Huber swung the panel hard—too hard. It slipped out of his hands and slammed.

Major Steuben's terrible laugh followed him back down the hallway.

The ten-place aircar that ferried Huber into Benjamin had six other passengers aboard when it left Base Alpha: three troopers going into town on leave, and three local citizens returning from business dealings with the Regiment. Each trio kept to itself, which was fine with Arne Huber. He wasn't sure what'd happened in Joachim Steuben's office, whether it had all been playacting or if Steuben had really been testing him.

A test Huber'd passed, in that case; seeing as he was not only alive, he'd been transferred into a slot that normally went to a captain. But he wasn't sure, of that or anything else.

He was the only passenger remaining when the car reached its depot, what had been a public school with a sports arena in back. The freshly painted sign out front read:

Benjamin Liaison Office
HAMMER'S REGIMENT

with a red lion rampant on a gold field. The driver set the car down by the sign, then lifted away to the arena to shut down as soon as Huber had gotten his luggage off the seat beside him.

Would the local have been more helpfully polite if he'd known Huber was his new boss? Huber smiled faintly. He was too wrung out, from the firefight and now from the interview with Major Steuben, to really care that a direct subordinate had just dumped him out on the pavement.

He bent to shoulder the dufflebag's strap. "We'll watch it for you, sir!" called one of the guards on the front steps. They were alert and fully armed, but they seemed relaxed compared to the White Mice guarding the Provost Marshal's office at Base Alpha.

The troopers of F-3 had been relaxed when they started to disembark, too. Huber winced, wondering how long he was going to remember the feel of Kolbe's body slipping through his fingers like a half-filled waterbed. For the rest of his life, he supposed.

Gratefully he left his gear behind as he mounted the stone steps to the front doors. The four troopers were from G Company, wearing their dismounted kit and carrying 2-cm shoulder weapons. Their two combat cars and the remaining crew members were parked at opposite ends of the arena with their tribarrels elevated on air-defense duty. They'd track anything that came over the horizon, whether aircraft or artillery shell, and blast it if required.

"Where's the signals office, Sergeant?" Huber asked the trooper who'd offered to watch his gear.

"All the way down and to the left, ground floor," the fellow said. "Ah, sir? You're Lieutenant Huber?"

"Yeah, I am," Huber said, suddenly cold. The name tape above his left breast pocket was too faded to read; the fellow must have recognized his face.

"It's an honor to meet you, sir," the sergeant said. "You saved everybody's ass at Rhodesville. We all watched the imagery."

For a moment Huber frowned, thinking that the man was being sarcastic. But he wasn't, and the other troopers were nodding agreement.

"Thank you, Sergeant," he said. His voice wanted to tremble, but he didn't let it. "That isn't the way it looked from where I was sitting, but I appreciate your viewpoint on the business."

Huber went inside quickly, before anybody else could speak. He was as shocked as if the guards had suddenly stripped off their uniforms and started dancing around him. Their words didn't belong in the world of Arne Huber's mind.

Dungaree-clad locals under the direction of a Slammers sergeant were bringing cartloads of files up the back stairs, two on each cart. When they got inside, they rolled them down the hallway to the big room on the right marked CAFETERIA. It was a clerical office now; the tables were arranged back to back and held data consoles manned by locals.

Huber moved to the left to let the carts get past. The sergeant turned from shouting at somebody in the six-wheeled truck outside and saw him. He looked like he was going to speak, but Huber ducked into the door with the recent SIGNALS LIAISON sign before he could.

Huber could have understood it if troopers turned their backs on him and whispered: five dead in a matter of seconds was a heavy loss for a single platoon. That wasn't what was happening.

Lieutenant Adria Basime—Doll to her friends—was bent over the desk of a warrant leader by the door, pointing out something on his console. She saw Huber and brightened. "Arne!" she said. "Come back to my office! My broom closet, more like, but it's got a door. Tory, have me those numbers when I come out, right?"

"Right, El-Tee," agreed the warrant leader. Even Huber, who'd never seen the fellow before, could read the relief in his expression. "Just a couple minutes, that's all I need."

There were a dozen consoles in the outer office, only half of them occupied. Three of the personnel present were Slammers, the others locals.

"I've got ten more people under me," Doll explained as she closed the door of the inner office behind her. "They're out trying to set up nets that we can at least pretend are secure. Plattner's World has a curst good commo network—they'd just about have to, as spread out as the population is. The trouble is, it *all* goes through Solace."

Doll's office wasn't huge, but it compared favorably with the enclosed box of a command car, let alone the amount of space there was in the fighting compartment of a combat car like *Fencing Master*. All a matter of what you've gotten used to, Huber supposed. Doll gestured him to a chair and took the one beside it instead of seating herself behind the console.

"What're you here for, Arne?" she asked. "Did you debrief to the Colonel in person?"

"I thought they were pulling me back to cashier me," Huber said carefully. "I didn't need Major Steuben to tell me how much damage we did to Rhodesville in the firefight. Apparently the locals want to void our contract for that."

Doll frowned. She was petite and strikingly pretty, even in a service uniform. She wore her hair short, but it fluffed like a dazzle of blonde sunlight when she wasn't wearing a commo helmet.

"Some of them maybe do," she said. "The government's in it all the way now, though. They can't back down unless they want to risk not only losing their places but likely being tried for treason if the peace party gets into power."

"Well, I'm transferred to run local transport," Huber said. He felt better already for talking to Doll. She came from a powerful family on Nieuw Friesland and had a keen political sense. If she said Huber hadn't jeopardized the Regiment's contract, that was the gospel truth. "They had to get me out of the field after the way I screwed up, after all."

"Screwed up?" Doll said in surprise. "You guys got ambushed by a company of Harris's Commando while you were still aboard the ship that brought you. You not only saved your platoon, you wiped out the kill team pretty much single-handedly, the way *I* heard it."

"That's not—" Huber said; and as he spoke, his mind flashed him a shard of memory, his finger selecting three segments of the Automatic Defense System and the *Whang!* as they fired simultaneously. He hadn't been thinking of the bunched infantry as human beings, just as a problem to be solved like the jammed turnbuckle. They were figures on his display; and after he'd fired the ADS, they were no longer a problem.

"Via," he whispered. "There must've been twenty of them...."

Huber had killed before, but he hadn't thought of what he'd done in Rhodesville as killing until Doll stated the obvious. He'd been thinking of other things.

"Yeah, well..." he said, looking toward the window. "Given the way they caught us with our pants down, things went as well as they could. But we *were* caught. *I* was caught."

Huber shrugged, forced a smile, and looked at his friend. "Major Steuben said you could give me a rundown on my new section, Doll. The people, I mean. I called up the roster on my helmet on the way here, but they were mostly locals and there's nothing beyond date of hire."

"I can tell you about Hera Graciano," Doll said with a grin. "She's your deputy, and she put the section together before the Regiment's combat assets started to arrive. For what it's worth, it seemed to me she was running things by herself even on the days Captain Cassutt was in the office."

The grin grew broader. She went on, "That wasn't many days, from what I saw. And he's on administrative leave right now."

"I'm glad there'll be one of us who knows the job, then," Huber said, feeling a rush of relief that surprised him. Apparently while his conscious mind was telling him how lucky he was to be alive and still a member of the Regiment, his guts were worried about handling a rear echelon job in which his only background was a three-month rotation in the Academy four years earlier.

"Her father's Agis Graciano," Doll said. "He's Minister of Trade for the UC at the moment, but the ruling party shifts ministries around without changing anything important. He was Chief Lawgiver when the motion to hire the Slammers passed, and he's very much the head of the war party."

Huber frowned as he ran through the possibilities. It was good to have a competent deputy, but a deputy who'd gotten in the habit of running things herself *and* who had political connections could be a problem in herself. And there was one more thing....

"Does the lady get along with her father?" he asked. "Because I know sometimes that can be a worse problem than strangers ever thought of having."

Doll laughed cheerfully. "Hera lives with her father," she said. "They're very close. It's the elder brother, Patroklos, who's the problem. He's in the Senate too, and he'd say it was midnight if his father claimed it was noon."

Her face hardened as she added, "Patroklos is somebody I'd be looking at if I wanted to know how Harris's Commando learned exactly when a single platoon was going to land at Rhodesville, but that's not my job. You shouldn't have any trouble with him now that you're in Log Section."

"Thanks, Doll," Huber said as he rose to his feet. "I guess I'd better check the section out myself now. They're on the second floor?"

"Right," Doll said as she stood up also. "Two things more, though. Your senior non-com, Sergeant Tranter? He's a technical specialist and he's curst good at it. He's helped me a couple times here, finding equipment and getting it to work. The only reason he's not still in field maintenance is he lost a leg when a jack slipped and the new one spasms anytime the temperature gets below minus five."

"That's good to know," Huber said. "And the other thing?"

Doll's grin was back, broader than ever before. "Mistress Graciano is a real stunner, trooper," she said. "And she wasn't a bit interested when *I* tried to chat her up, so I figure that means a handsome young hero like you is in with a chance."

Huber gave his buddy a hug. They were both laughing as they walked back into the outer office.

Instead of a stenciled legend, the words LOGISTICS SECTION over the doorway were of brass letters on a background of bleached hardwood. Huber heard shuffling within the room as he reached the top of the stairs, then silence. He frowned and had to resist the impulse to fold back the flap of his pistol holster before he opened the door.

"All rise for Lieutenant Huber!" bellowed the non-com standing in front of the console nearest the doorway. He had curly red hair and a fluffy moustache the full width of his face. There wasn't a boot on his mechanical left leg, so Huber didn't need the name tape over the man's left breast to identify him as Sergeant Tranter.

There were ten consoles in the main room but almost a score of people, and they'd been standing before Tranter gave his order. Beside Tranter stood a wispy Slammers trooper; his left arm below the sleeve of his khakis was covered with a rash which Huber hoped to the good Lord's mercy wasn't contagious. The others were local civilians, and the black-haired young woman who stepped forward offering her hand was just as impressive as Adria said she was.

"I'm glad you made it, Lieutenant Huber," she said in a voice as pleasantly sexy as the rest of her. "I'm your deputy, Hera Graciano."

"Ma'am," Huber said, shaking the woman's hand gingerly. Was he supposed to have kissed it? There might be something in the briefing cubes that he'd missed, but he doubted they went into local culture at this social level. It wasn't the sort of thing the commander of a line platoon was likely to need.

"Sergeant Tranter, sir," said the non-com. He didn't salute; saluting wasn't part of the Slammers' protocol, where all deployments were to combat zones and the main thing a salute did was target the recipient for any snipers in the vicinity. "This is Trooper Bayes, he's helping me go over the vehicles we're offered for hire."

Hera looked ready to step in and introduce her staff too. Huber raised his hand to forestall her.

"Please?" he said to get attention. "Before I try to memorize names, Deputy Graciano, could you give me a quick rundown of where the section is and where it's supposed to be?"

He flashed the roomful of people an embarrassed smile. "I intend to carry my weight, but an hour ago I couldn't have told you anything about Log Section beyond that there probably was one."

"Of course," Hera said. "We can use your office—" she nodded to a connecting door "—or mine," this time indicating a cubicle set off from the rest of the room by waist-high paneling.

"We'll use yours," Huber said, because he was pretty sure from what he'd heard about Captain Cassutt that useful information was going to be in the deputy's office instead. "Oh—and I don't have quarters, yet. Is there a billeting officer here or—?"

"I'll take care of it, sir," Tranter said. "Do we need to go pick up your baggage too?"

"It's out in front of the building," Huber said. "I—"

"Right," said Tranter. "Come on, Bayes. Sir, you'll be in Building Five in back of the vehicle park. They're temporaries but they're pretty nice, and engineering threw us up a nice bulletproof wall around the whole compound. Just in case—which I guess I *don't* have to explain to you."

Chuckling at the reference to Rhodesville, the two troopers left the room. Huber smiled too. It was gallows humor, sure; but if you couldn't laugh at grim jokes, you weren't going to laugh very much on service with the Slammers.

And it wasn't that Tranter didn't have personal experience with disaster. The non-skid sole of his mechanical foot thumped the floor with a note distinct from that of the boot on his right foot.

"I'm impressed by Sergeant Tranter," Hera said in a low voice as she stepped into her alcove after Huber. Though it seemed open to the rest of the room, a sonic distorter kept conversations within the cubicle private by canceling any sounds that crossed the invisible barrier. "As a matter of fact, I'm impressed by all the, ah, soldiers assigned to this section. I'd assumed that because they weren't fit for regular duties...."

"Ma'am," Huber said, hearing the unmeant chill in his voice. "We're the Slammers. It's not just that everybody in the Regiment's a volunteer—that's true of a lot of merc outfits. We're the best. We've got the best equipment, we get the best pay, and we've got our pick of recruits. People who don't do the job they're assigned to because they don't feel like it, they go someplace else. By their choice or by the Colonel's."

"I'm sorry," the woman said. "I didn't mean…"

Her voice trailed off. She *had* meant she expected people on medical profile to slack off while they were on temporary assignment to ash and trash jobs.

Huber gave an embarrassed chuckle. He felt like an idiot to've come on like a regimental recruiter to somebody who was trying to offer praise.

"Ma'am," he said, "I was out of line. I just mean the folks who stay in the Slammers are professionals. Sergeant Tranter, now—he could retire on full pay. If he didn't, it's because he wants to stay with the Regiment. And I'd venture a guess—"

Made more vivid by Huber's own sudden vision of being cast out of the Slammers.

"—that it's because he's grown to like being around other professionals, other people who do their job *because* it's their job. You don't find a lot of that in the outside world."

She looked at him without expression. "No," she said, "you don't. Well, Lieutenant Huber, again I'm glad for your arrival. And if it's agreeable to you, I prefer 'Hera' to 'ma'am' or 'Deputy Graciano.' But of course it's up to you as section head to decide on the etiquette."

"Hera's fine and so's Arne," Huber said in relief. "And ah—Hera? About Captain Cassutt?"

She gestured to affect disinterest.

"No, you deserve to hear," Huber said, "after the way I got up on my haunches. Cassutt had a bad time the deployment before this one. It wasn't his fault, mostly at any rate, but he got pulled out of the line."

The same way I did, but Huber didn't say that.

"He's off on leave, now," he continued. "He'll either dry out or he'll *be* out. If he's forcibly retired, his pension will keep him in booze as long as his liver lasts—but he won't be anywhere he's going to screw up the business of the Regiment."

"I…" Hera said. There was no way of telling what the thought she'd smothered unspoken was. "I see that. Ah, here's the transport that I've either purchased or contracted for, based on volume requirements sent me by the regimental prep section. If you'd like to go over them…?"

She'd set her holographic projector on a 360-degree display so that they both could read the data from their different angles. Huber checked the list of tonnage per unit per day, in combat and in reserve, then the parallel columns giving vehicles and payloads. Those last figures floored him.

"Ma'am?" he said, careting the anomaly with his light wand. "Hera, I mean, these numbers—oh! They're dirigibles?"

She nodded warily. "Yes, we use dirigibles for most heavy lifting," she explained. "They're as fast as ground vehicles even on good roads, and we don't have many good surface roads on Plattner's World."

She frowned and corrected herself, "In the Outer States, that is. Solace has roads and a monorail system for collecting farm produce."

"I don't have anything against dirigibles in general," Huber said, then said with the emphasis of having remembered, "*Hera*. But in a war zone they're—"

He kept his voice steady with effort as his mind replayed a vision of the dirigible crashing into Rhodesville's brick-faced terminal building and erupting like a volcano.

"—too vulnerable. We'll need ground transport, or—how about surface effect cargo carriers? Do you have them here? They look like airplanes, but their wings just compress the air between them and the ground instead of really flying."

"I don't see how that could work over a forest," Hera said tartly—and neither did Huber, when he thought about it. "And as for vulnerable, trucks are vulnerable too if they're attacked, aren't they?"

"A truck isn't carrying five hundred tonnes for a single powergun bolt to light up," Huber said, careful to keep his voice neutral. "And it's not chugging along fifty or a hundred meters in the air where it's a target for a gunner clear in the next state if he knows what he's doing."

He shook his head in memory. "Which some of them will," he added. "If Solace hired Harris's Commando, they'll get a good outfit for air defense too."

Hera didn't move for a moment. Her hands on the display controller in her lap could've been carved from a grainless wood. Then she said, "Yes, if we…"

Her fingers caressed the controller. The display shifted like a waterfall; Huber could watch the data, but they meant nothing to him at the speed they cascaded across the air-projected holograms.

"Yes…" Hera repeated, then looked up beaming. "There isn't anything like enough ground transport available in the UC alone, but if the other Outer States send us what *they* have, we should be able to meet your needs. Though roads…"

"We can use dirigibles to stage supplies to forward depots," Huber said, leaning forward reflexively though the data still didn't mean a cursed thing to him. "We'll need a topo display and for that matter a battle plan to know where, but—"

"Can you do that?" Hera said, also excited by breaking through a barrier she hadn't known of a few moments before. "The map and the battle plan?"

Huber laughed out loud—for the first time since Rhodesville, he guessed. "The topo display's easy," he said, "but lieutenants don't plan regimental operations by themselves. I'll forward what we have to the S-3, the Operations Officer, and his shop'll fill us in when they know more."

He locked his faceshield down and used the helmet's internal processor to sort for the address of the Log Section Deputy's console, then transfer the Regiment's full topographic file on Plattner's World to it. The commo helmet had both the storage and processing power to handle the task alone, but given where they were and the size of the file, Huber let Central in Base Alpha do the job.

He raised his faceshield and saw Hera disconnecting from a voice call. "Oh!" he said. "I'm sorry, I didn't explain—"

"I assumed you were doing your job," she said with a smile that exalted a face already beautiful. "And I can't tell you how reassuring it is to, ah, work for someone who can do that."

She gestured to the phone. "That's what I've been doing too," she said. "I just talked to my father. He's…"

She waved a hand in a small circle as if churning a pile of words.

"I've been told who he is," Huber said, saving Hera the embarrassment of explaining that Agis Graciano was the most important single person in the state which had employed the Slammers.

"Good," Hera said with a grateful nod. "When I said we can get ground transport from the other Outer States, I didn't mean that I could commandeer it myself. Father has connections; he'll use them. It'll have to be made to look like a business transaction, even though the other states are helping to fund the UC's stand against the tyranny of Solace."

Huber nodded acknowledgment. He knew better than to discuss politics with anybody, especially a local like Hera Graciano. It wasn't that he didn't understand political science and history: the Academy had an extensive mandatory curriculum in both subjects.

The problem was that the locals always wanted to talk about the rightness of their position. By the time they'd hired Hammer's Slammers, the only right that mattered rode behind iridium armor.

"Ah, Arne?" Hera said. "It's going to be two hours, maybe three, before Father gets back to me. We've certainly got enough work to occupy us till then—"

Their wry grins mirrored one another.

"—but do you have dinner plans for tonight?"

"Ma'am," Huber said in surprise, "I don't know any more about rations than I did about billeting."

The thought made him turn his head. Sergeant Tranter was back; he gave Huber the high sign. The locals still in the office buried their expressions quickly in their consoles; they'd obviously been covertly watching Hera and their new chief the instant before.

"As a matter of fact, I haven't eaten anything yet today," Huber continued to his deputy. "Hera. I didn't have an appetite before my meeting with Major Steuben."

Hera's face changed. "I've met Major Steuben," she said without expression.

Huber nodded understandingly. "I told you we were the best the UC could hire," he said. "Joachim Steuben is better at his job than anybody else I've heard of. But because of what his job is, he's an uncomfortable person to be around for most people."

For everybody who wasn't a conscienceless killer; but Huber didn't say that aloud.

"Yes," Hera said, agreeing with more than the spoken words. "Well, what I was saying—can I take you out to dinner tonight, Lieutenant? You've kept me from making a terrible mistake with the dirigibles, and I'd like to thank you."

"I'd be honored," Huber said, perfectly truthful and for a wonder suppressing his urge to explain he was just doing his job. She knew that, and if she wanted to go to dinner with him, that was fine. He didn't guess it much mattered who paid, not judging from the off-planet dress suit she was wearing even here at work.

"When you say 'trucks,'" he resumed, "what're we talking about? Five-tonners or little utility haulers?"

Hera Graciano was *very* attractive. And if Arne Huber didn't keep his mind on his business, he was going to start blushing.

The restaurant was quite obviously expensive. Huber could afford to eat here on his salary, but he probably wouldn't have chosen to.

"Well, I suppose you could say there was significant opposition to confronting Solace," Hera said, frowning toward a point beyond Huber's shoulder as she concentrated on the past. "Some people are always afraid to stand up for their rights, that's inevitable. But the vote in our Senate to hire your Regiment was overwhelming as soon as we determined that the other Outer States would contribute to the charges. My brother's faction only mustered nineteen votes out of the hundred, with seven abstentions."

Wooden beams supported the restaurant's domed ceiling. Their curves were natural, and the polished branches which carried the light fixtures seemed to grow from the wall paneling. The food was excellent—boned rabbit in a bed of pungent leaves, Huber thought, but he'd learned on his first deployment never to ask what went into a dish he found tasty.

His only quibble was with the music: to him it sounded like the wind blowing over a roof missing a number of tiles. The muted keening didn't get in the way of him talking with Hera, and her voice was just as pleasant as the rest of the package.

"And all your income, the income of the Outer States," Huber said, "comes from gathering the raw Moss? There's no diversification?"

"The factories refining the *Pseudofistus thalopsis* extract into Thalderol base are in Solace," she said, gesturing with her left hand as she held her glass poised in her right. "That isn't the problem, though: we could build refineries in the Outer States quite easily. We'd have to import technicians for the first few years, but there'd be plenty of other planets ready to help us."

"But…?" said Huber, sipping his own wine. It was pale yellow, though that might have been a product of the beads of light on the branch tips which illuminated the room. They pulsed slowly and were color-balanced to mimic candleflames.

"But we couldn't build a spaceport capable of handling starships the size of those that now land at Solace," Hera explained. "It's not just the expense, though that's bad enough. The port at Solace is built on a sandstone plate. There's no comparable expanse of bedrock anywhere in the Outer States. An artificial substrate that could support three-hundred kilotonne freighters is beyond possibility."

"I've seen the problems of bringing even small ships down in the UC," Huber said with studied calm. "Though I suppose there's better ports than Rhodesville's."

Hera sniffed. "Better," she said, "but not much better. And of course even the refined base is a high-volume cargo, so transportation costs go up steeply on small hulls."

The dining room had about twenty tables, most of them occupied by expensively dressed locals. The aircar Hera'd brought him here in was built on Nonesuch; it had an agate-faced dashboard and showed a number of other luxury details. She'd parked adjacent to the restaurant, in a tree-shaded lot where the other vehicles were of comparable quality.

Huber wore his newest service uniform, one of three he'd brought on the deployment. The Regiment had a dress uniform, but he'd never bothered to invest in one. Even if he *had* owned such a thing it'd be back in his permanent billet on Nieuw Friesland, since a platoon leader in the field had less space for personal effects than he had formal dinner occasions.

Huber's commo helmet was in his quarters, but his holstered pistol knocked against the arm of the chair he sat in. The Colonel hadn't issued a revised weapons policy for Plattner's World yet; and even if he had, Huber would probably have stuck his

1-cm powergun in a cargo pocket even if he couldn't carry it openly. He'd felt naked in Rhodesville when he saw the buzzbomb swing in his direction and he couldn't do anything but duck.

"Ten months ago…" Hera went on. "Ah, that's seven months standard. Ten months ago, Solace raised landing fees five percent. The buyers, Nonesuch and the other planets buying our base and processing it to Thalderol, refused to raise the price they'd pay. We in the Outer States, the people who actually do the work, were left to make up the difference out of our pockets!"

It didn't look like Hera had spent much of her life ranging the forest and gathering Moss, but Huber wouldn't have needed his history courses to know that politicians generally said "we" when they meant "you." The funny thing was, they generally didn't see there was a difference.

That wasn't a point a Slammers officer raised with a well-placed member of the state which had hired the Regiment. Aloud he said, "But you do have multiple markets for your drugs? For your base, I mean?"

"Nonesuch takes about half the total," Hera said, nodding agreement. "The rest goes to about a dozen other planets, some more than others. The final processing takes temperature and vibration control beyond anything we could do on Plattner's World. Building a second spaceport would be easier."

She paused, looking at her wine, then across at Huber again. "The government of Nonesuch has been very supportive," she said carefully. "They couldn't get directly involved, but they helped to make the arrangements that led to our hiring Hammer's Regiment."

"But they wouldn't simply raise their payments for Thalderol base?" Huber said, keeping his tone empty of everything but mild curiosity.

"Where would it stop?" Hera blazed. "If those vultures on Solace learn that they can get away with extortion, they'll keep turning the screws!"

Based on what Huber knew about the price of anti-aging drugs, he didn't think a five-percent boost in the cost of raw materials was going to make a lot of difference, but he didn't need to get into that. There was more going on than he saw; more going on than Hera was willing to tell him, that was obvious; and probably a lot more going on than even she knew.

None of that mattered. The result of all those unseen wheels whirling was that Colonel Hammer had a lucrative contract, and Lieutenant Arne Huber was spending the evening with a very attractive woman.

"My brother claims that even with other states defraying the costs, the UC is taking all the military risk itself," Hera continued. "But somebody has to have the courage to take a stand! When the other states see Solace back down, they'll be quick enough to step up beside us and claim credit!"

"It didn't seem when I arrived…" Huber said, the chill in his guts cooling his tone more than he'd intended. "That backing down was the way Solace was planning to play it."

He smiled, hoping that would make his words sound less like the flat disagreement that he felt. Hera was smart and competent, but she was turning her face from the reality the ambush at Rhodesville would've proved to a half-wit. It wasn't what she wanted to believe, so she was using her fine intellect to prove a lie.

"Well then, if they persist—" she said, but broke off as the waiter approached the table.

"More wine, sir and madam?" he asked. "Or perhaps you've changed your mind about dessert?"

The outside door opened, drawing Huber's eyes and those of the waiter. It was late for customers, though the restaurant hadn't started dimming the lights.

"Patroklos!" Hera said, her head turning because Huber's had. "What are you doing here?"

Not coming for dinner, that was for sure. Senator Patroklos Graciano was a good twenty years older than his sister. He was a beefy man, not fat but heavier than he'd have been if he were a manual laborer. His features were regular, handsome even, but they showed no resemblance whatever to Hera's.

Huber wondered if the two children had different mothers, but that wasn't the question at the top of his mind just this instant. He got to his feet; smoothly, he thought, but he heard the chair go over behind him with a crash on the hardwood floor and he didn't care about *that* either.

"What am I doing here?" Patroklos said. He had a trained voice; he used its volume to fill the domed restaurant. "I'm not entertaining the butcher who destroyed Rhodesville, that's one thing! Are you part of the mercenaries' price, dear sister? Your body as an earnest for the bodies of all the women of the United Cities?"

Chairs were scuffling all over the room; a pair of diners edged toward the service area since Patroklos stood in front of the outside door. There were two waiters and the female manager looking on, but they'd obviously decided to leave the business to the principals involved for now.

Huber was as sure as he could be that there wasn't going to be trouble—worse trouble—here unless something went badly wrong. Patroklos wasn't nearly as angry as he sounded, and he'd come into the restaurant by himself. If his bodyguards had been with him—Patroklos was the sort who had bodyguards—it would've been a different matter.

"Patroklos, you're drunk!" Hera said. He wasn't drunk, but maybe Hera didn't see her brother's real plan. "Get out of here and stop degrading the family name!"

She hadn't gotten up at the first shouting. Now that Patroklos was only arm's length away, she was trapped between the table and her brother's presence.

Huber thought of walking around to join her, but that might start things moving in the wrong direction. From the corners of his eyes he could see that others of the remaining customers were eyeing him with hard faces. The "butcher of Rhodesville" line had probably struck a chord even with people who didn't support Patroklos' position on the Regiment as a whole.

"Degrade the family name?" Patroklos shouted. "A fine concern for a camp follower!"

Huber scraped the table back and toward his left side, spilling a wine glass and some flatware onto the floor. Freed from its presence, Hera jumped to her feet and retreated to where Huber stood. He swung her behind him with his left arm.

That wasn't entirely chivalry. Huber wasn't worried about her brother, but the chance of somebody throwing a bottle at him from behind was another matter.

If I'd known there was going to be a brawl, I'd have asked for a table by the wall. He grinned at the thought; and that was probably the right thing to do, because Patroklos' mouth—open for another bellow—closed abruptly.

The Slammers didn't spend a lot of training time on unarmed combat: people didn't hire the Regiment for special operations, they wanted an armored spearhead that could punch through any shield the other guy raised. Huber wasn't sure that barehanded he could put this older, less fit man away since the fellow outweighed him by double, but he wasn't going to try. Huber would use a chair with the four legs out like spearpoints and then finish the job with his boots....

"Fine, hide behind your murderer for now, you whore!" Patroklos said, but his voice wasn't as forceful as before. He eased his body backward though as yet without shifting his feet. "You'll have nowhere to hide when the citizens of our glorious state realize the madness into which you and our father have thrown them!"

Patroklos backed quickly, then jerked the door open and stomped out into the night. The last glance he threw over his shoulder seemed more speculative than angry or afraid.

"Ma'am!" Huber said, turning his head a few degrees to face the manager without ever letting his eyes leave the empty doorway. "Get our bill ready ASAP, will you?"

"Maria, put it on my account!" Hera said. She swept the room with her gaze. In the same clear, cold voice she went on, "I won't bother apologizing for my brother, but I hope his display won't encourage others into drunken boorishness!"

She's noticed the temper of the onlookers too, Huber thought. Stepping quickly, he led the girl between tables Patroklos had emptied with his advance. They went out the front door.

The night air was warm and full of unfamiliar scents. A track of dust along the street and the howl of an aircar accelerating—though by now out of sight—indicated how and where Patroklos had departed. There were no pedestrians or other vehicles; the buildings across the street were offices over stores, closed and dark at this hour.

Huber sneezed. Hera whirled with a stark expression.

"Just dust," he explained. He rubbed the back of his hand over his eyes. "Or maybe the tree pollen, that's all. Nothing important."

He felt like a puppeteer pulling the strings of a body that'd once been his but was now an empty shell. The thing that walked and talked like Arne Huber didn't have a soul for the moment; that'd been burned out by the adrenaline flooding him in the restaurant a few moments ago. The emotionless intellect floating over Huber's quivering body was bemused by the world it observed.

"I can't explain my brother's behavior!" Hera said. She walked with her head down, snarling the words to her feet. "He's angry because father remarried—there's no other reason for what he does!”

Huber didn't speak. He didn't care about the internal politics of the Graciano clan, and the girl was only vaguely aware of his presence anyway. She was working out her emotions while he dealt with his. They were different people, so their methods were different.

It hadn't been a lucky night, but things could've been worse. Just as at Rhodesville…

They stepped around the corner of the building into the parking lot. Things got worse.

There were at least a dozen of them, maybe more, waiting among the cars. They started forward when Huber and the girl appeared. They had clubs; maybe some of them had guns besides. The light on the pole overhead concealed features instead of revealing them.

“Who are you?” Hera called in a voice of clear command. “Attendant! Where's the lot attendant?”

“Get back into the restaurant,” Huber said. “*Now!*”

He grabbed the girl's shoulder with his left hand and swung her behind him, a more brutal repetition of what he'd done with her earlier. Patroklos had been posturing in the restaurant. These thugs of his, though—this was meant for real.

Huber thumbed open his holster flap and drew his pistol. He held it muzzle-down by his thigh for the moment.

“He's got a gun!” said one of the shadowy figures in a rising whisper. That was a good sign; it meant they hadn't figured on their victim being armed.

“Shut up, Lefty!” another voice snarled.

The pistol had a ten-round magazine. Huber knew how to use the weapon, but if these guys were really serious he wouldn't be able to put down more than two or three of them before it turned into work for clubs and knives.…

Huber backed a step, hoping Hera had done as he ordered; hoping also that there wasn't another gang of them waiting at the restaurant door to close the escape route. If Huber got around the corner again, he could either wait and shoot every face that appeared or he could run like Hell was on his heels. Running was the better choice, but he didn't think—

“Easy now,” said the second voice. “Now, all to—”

A big aircar—it might've been the one that ferried Huber from Base Alpha to Benjamin—came down the street in a scream of fans. It hit hard, lifting a doughnut of dust from the unpaved surface. That wasn't a bad landing, it was a combat insertion where speed counted and grace just got you killed.

Half the score of men filling the back of the vehicle wore khaki uniforms; they unassed the bouncing aircar with the ease of training and experience. The civilians were clumsier, but they were only a step or two behind when the Slammers tore into the local thugs with pipes, wrenches, and lengths of reinforcing rod.

“Run for it!” shouted the voice that'd given the orders before. He was preaching to the converted; none of his gang had stayed around to argue with the rescue party.

Huber stood where he was, now holding the pistol beside his ear.

"Arne!" Doll Basime called. "This way, fast!"

She stood in the vehicle's open cab, her sub-machine gun ready but not pointed. Sergeant Tranter was at the rear of the aircar; he had a 2-cm shoulder weapon. Both wore their faceshields down, probably using light-enhanced viewing. If a thug had decided to turn it into a gunfight, he and his buddies were going to learn what a *real* gunfight was like.

Huber ran for the truck. He heard screams from the parking lot; thumps followed by crackling meant that some of the expensive aircars were going to have body damage from being used as trampolines by troops in combat boots.

That didn't even begin to bother Huber. He remembered the eyes on him in the restaurant.

"Recall! Recall! Recall!" bellowed the loudspeaker built into Tranter's commo helmet. The other troopers had helmet intercoms, but the civilians didn't.

"How'd you get the word, Doll?" Huber said as he jumped into the back of the vehicle, just behind Basime. Another of the party had been driving; the cab would be crowded even with two.

Doll was too busy doing her job to answer him. Her throat worked as she snarled an order over the intercom, though with the faceshield down her helmet muted the words to a shadow.

Sirens sounded from several directions. They were coming closer.

The rescue party piled into the back of the truck. Two Slammers and a civilian remained in the parking lot, putting the boot in with methodical savagery. Their victim was out of sight behind the parked cars. One of the thugs must've tried to make a fight out of it—that, or he'd hit somebody while flailing about in panic.

"Move it, Bayes!" Tranter called.

Huber pointed his pistol skyward and fired. The *thump!* and blue flash both reflected from overhanging foliage. For a moment the bolt was as striking as the blast from a tank's main gun. The three stragglers looked up in palpable shock, then ran to join their fellows.

Huber hung over the truck's sidewall to make sure Hera was all right. She wasn't in sight, so she'd probably gotten back into the restaurant. If she hadn't, well, better the local cops look into it than that the cops spend their energy discussing matters with the rescue party. *That* was a situation that could go really wrong fast.

The fans roared. Kelso, a civilian clerk from Log Section, was in the driver's seat. From the way the vehicle'd nosed in, Huber'd guessed a trooper was at the controls.

The aircar slid forward, gathering speed but staying within a centimeter of the gravel. Faces staring from the restaurant's front windows vanished as the car roared by in cascades of dust and pebbles.

Only when the vehicle had reached ninety kph and the end of the block did Kelso lift it out of ground effect. He banked *hard* through a stand of towering trees.

Huber could still hear sirens, but they didn't seem to be approaching nearly as fast as a moment before. Witnesses being what they were, Huber's single pistol shot had probably been described as a tank battle.

Doll put her hand on Huber's shoulder. Raising her faceshield she shouted over the windrush, "That was a little too close on the timing, Arne. Sorry about that."

"It was perfect, Doll," he shouted back. The aircar was racketing along at the best speed it could manage with the present overload. That was too fast for comfort in an open vehicle, but torn metal showed where the folding top had been ripped off in a hurry to lower the gross weight. "Perfect execution, too. What brought you?"

They were heading in the direction of the Liaison Office, staying just over the treetops. Kelso had his running lights off. Red strobes high in the sky marked the emergency vehicles easing gingerly toward the summons.

"That's a funny thing," Doll said, her pretty face scrunched into a frown. "Every trooper billeted at Base Benjamin got an alert, saying a trooper needed help—and if there was shooting, the best result would be courts martial for everybody involved. It gave coordinates that turned out to be you. We hauled ass till we got here."

She shrugged. "Sergeant Tranter invited some civilian drivers from Log Section, too. I guess there was a card game going when the call came."

"But who gave the alert?" Huber said. "Did the—"

He'd started to ask if the restaurant manager had called it in; that was dumb, so he swallowed the final words. There hadn't been time for a civilian to get an alarm through the regimental net.

"There was no attribution," Basime said. She lifted her helmet and ran a hand through her short hair; it was gleaming with sweat. "That means it had to come from Base Alpha; and it had to be a secure sector besides, not the regular Signals Office."

"The White Mice?" Huber said. That was the only possible source, but… "But if it was them, why didn't they respond themselves?"

"You're asking me?" Doll said. She grinned, but the released strain had aged her by years. She'd known she was risking her career—and life—to respond to the call.

"I will say, though," she added quietly, "that whoever put out the alarm seems to be a friend of yours. And that's better than having him for an enemy."

"Yeah," said Huber. Through the windscreen he could see the converted school and the temporary buildings behind it. Kelso throttled back.

Much better to have him for a friend; because the people whom Joachim Steuben considered enemies usually didn't live long enough to worry about it.

This time Huber had his equipment belt unbuckled and his knife in his hand before he stepped out of the four-place aircar in which Sergeant Tranter had brought him to the Provost Marshal's office. The sky of Plattner's World had an omnipresent high overcast; it muted what would otherwise be an unpleasantly brilliant sun and was turning the present dawn above Base Alpha into gorgeous pastels.

Tranter had shut down the car in the street. He sat with his arms crossed, staring into the mirrored faceshields of the White Mice on guard.

The guards didn't care, but the trivial defiance made Tranter feel better; and Huber felt a little better also. He wasn't completely alone this time as he reported as ordered to Major Steuben.

"Go on through, Lieutenant," said the faceless guard who took Huber's weapons. "He's waiting for you."

Huber walked down the hall to the office at the end. The door was open again, but this time Steuben dimmed his holographic display as Huber approached. The major even smiled, though that was one of those things that you didn't necessarily want to take as a good omen.

"Close the door behind you, Lieutenant," Steuben said as Huber raised his hand to knock. "I want to discuss what happened last night. How would you—"

He waited till the panel closed behind Huber's weight; it was a much sturdier door than it looked from the thin plastic sheathing on the outside.

"—describe the event?"

"Sir," Huber said. He didn't know what Steuben expected him to say. The truth might get some good people into difficulties, so in a flat voice he lied, "I was eating with my deputy in a restaurant she'd chosen. When we went out to get into her aircar, we were set on by thugs who'd been breaking into cars. Fortunately some off-duty troopers were passing nearby and came to our aid. My deputy went home in her own vehicle—"

He sure hoped she had. He didn't have a home number to call Hera at, and the summons waiting at Huber's billets to see the Provost Marshal at 0600 precluded Huber from waiting to meet Hera when she arrived at the office.

"—and I returned to my quarters with the fellows who'd rescued us."

"Want to comment on the shooting?" Steuben asked with a raised eyebrow. "The use of powerguns in the middle of Benjamin?"

"Sir," Huber said, looking straight into the hard brown eyes of Colonel Hammer's hatchetman, "I didn't notice any shooting. I believe the business was handled with fists alone, though some of the thugs may have had clubs."

Steuben reached into his shirt pocket and came out with a thin plastic disk. He flipped it to Huber, who snatched it out of the air. It was the pitted gray matrix which had held copper atoms in place in a powergun's bore; a 1-cm empty, fired by a pistol or sub-machine gun.

Specifically, fired from Huber's pistol.

"Sir, I don't have anything useful to say about this," Huber said. The bastard across the desk could only kill him once, so there wasn't any point in going back now. "If it came from the scene of the fight, it must have been fired after we left there."

"It's old news, Lieutenant," Steuben said, "and we won't worry about it. If there had been a shooting incident… let's say, if you'd shot one or more citizens of the UC, you'd have been dismissed from the Regiment. It's very possible that you'd have been turned over to the local authorities for trial. Our contract with the UC really *is* in the balance as a result of what happened at Rhodesville."

"Then I'm glad there wasn't any shooting, sir," Huber said. "I intend to stay inside the Liaison Office for the foreseeable future so that there won't be a repetition."

The holographic scenes on the major's wall weren't still images as Huber had thought the first time he'd seen them. What had initially been a tiny dot above the horizon had grown during the interview to a creature flying at a great height above the snowfields.

Steuben giggled. Huber felt his face freeze in a rictus of horror.

"Aren't you going to tell me it isn't fair, Lieutenant?" the major said. "Or perhaps you'd like to tell me that you're an innocent victim whom I'm making the scapegoat for political reasons?"

For the first time since the ambush at Rhodesville, Huber felt angry instead of being frightened or sick to his stomach. "Sir, you know it's not fair," he said, much louder than he'd allowed his voice to range before in this room. "Why should I waste my breath or your time? And why should you waste *my* time?"

"I take your point, Lieutenant," the major said. He rose to his feet; gracefully as everything he did was graceful. He was a small man, almost childlike; he was smiling now with the same curved lips as a serpent's. "You're dismissed to your duties—unless perhaps there's something you'd like to ask me?"

Huber started to turn to the door, then paused with a frown. "Sir?" he said. "How many people could have given Harris's Commando—given Solace—accurate information as to when a single platoon was landing at Rhodesville?"

"Besides members of the Regiment itself?" Steuben said, his reptilian smile a trifle wider. Huber nodded tersely. He wasn't sure if the question was serious, so he treated it as though it was.

"A handful of people within the UC government certainly knew," the major said. "A larger number, also people within the government or with connections to it, could probably have gotten the information unattributably. But it wasn't something that was being discussed on the streets of Rhodesville, if that's what you meant."

"Yes sir," said Huber. "That's what I meant."

He went out the door, closing it behind him as he'd been told to do the first time he'd left Major Steuben's presence. It was good to have the heavy panel between him and the man in that room.

He walked quickly. There was a lot of work waiting in Log Section; and there was another job as well, a task for the officer who'd been commanding platoon F-3 when it landed at Rhodesville.

Huber hadn't forgotten Kolbe or the crew of *Foghorn*; and he hadn't forgotten what he owed their memory.

Hera Graciano arrived at Log Section half an hour after Huber and the sergeant got back from Base Alpha, well before the staff was expected to show up for work. She stepped in, looking surprised to find the Slammers at their consoles.

"I rearranged things a bit." Huber said with a grin. "I moved my desk into the main office here; I figure we can use Captain Cassutt's office for a break room or something, hey?"

"Well, if you like…" Hera said. "But I don't think…"

"If they see me…" Huber explained quietly. Sergeant Tranter watched with the care of an enlisted man who knows that the whims of his superiors may mean his job or his life. "Then it's easier for them to believe we're all part of the same team. Given the number of factions in the UC right at the moment, I'd like there to be a core of locals who figure I'm on whatever their side is."

"I'm very sorry about last night!" Hera said, bowing her head in the first real confusion Huber had noticed in her demeanor. She crossed the room quickly without glancing at Tranter by the door. "That isn't normal, even for my brother. I think something's gone wrong with him, badly wrong."

"Any one you walk away from," Huber said brightly. He was immensely relieved to learn that Hera was all right, but he *really* didn't want to discuss either last night or the wider situation with her. "I'm paid to take risks, after all. Let's let it drop, shall we?"

"Yes," she said, settling herself behind her desk. Her expression was a mixture of relief and puzzlement. "Yes, of course."

Hera hadn't powered up the privacy shield as yet, so Huber could add smilingly, "By the way—does the UC have a central population registry? An office that tracks everybody?"

"What?" Hera said in amazement. "No, of course not! I mean, do other planets have that sort of thing? We have a voter's list, is that what you mean?"

"Some places are more centralized, yeah," Huber said, thinking of the cradle to grave oversight that the Frisian government kept on its citizens. Those who stayed on the planet, at least; which was maybe a reason to join a mercenary company, though the Colonel kept a pretty close eye on his troopers as well.

Through the White Mice...

"No matter," he continued. "Would you download a list of all the Regiment's local employees and their home addresses to me before you get onto your own work, Hera? It may be in this console I inherited from the good captain, but I sure haven't been able to locate it."

"Yes, of course..." she said, bringing her console live. She seemed grateful for an excuse to look away from Huber. Last night had been a real embarrassment to her.

One more thing to thank her brother for. It was pretty minor compared to the rest of what Huber suspected Patroklos was involved in, though.

Other clerks were coming in to the office; perhaps merely to make a good impression on the new director, but maybe they'd heard about the business last night and hoped to get more gossip. Huber grinned blandly and set to work with the file that appeared in his transfer box.

The business of the day proceeded. Log Section had been running perfectly well without Huber for the past three weeks, but as more starships landed—three in one mad hour at the relatively large field here in Benjamin, and four more during the day at other members of the United Cities—there were frequent calls to the Officer in Command of Log Section. None of the Slammers calling wanted to talk to a wog: they wanted a *real* officer wearing the lion rampant of the Regiment. They were fresh out of stardrive, with headaches and tempers to match.

Huber fielded the calls. He almost never knew the answer to the angry questions himself, but he dumped quick summaries to Hera through his console while holding the speaker on the line. As a general rule she had the answer for him—a vehicle dispatched, a storage warehouse located, or a staff member on the way to the scene—in a minute or less. When it was going to take longer, that warning appeared on Huber's console and he calmed the caller down as best he could.

Not everybody wanted to calm down. An artillery lieutenant shouted, "Look, are you going to stop being a dickheaded pissant and get my bloody hog out of the marsh you had us land in?"

Huber shouted back, "Look, redleg, when my platoon drove out of the ship there was a kill-team from Harris's Commando waiting for us. We managed. If you fools can't avoid a hole in the ground, then don't expect a lot of sympathy here! Now, I say again—there's a maintenance and recovery platoon due in Youngblood's Vale tomorrow and I'll vector the recovery vehicle to you people in Henessey ASAP. If you'd prefer to keep saying you want me to drag heavy equipment out of my ass because your driver's blind, you can talk to an open line!"

There was a pause, then, "Roger, we'll wait. Two-Ay-Six out."

One thing a soldier learns by surviving any length of time in a war zone is that you use whatever you've got available. Huber smiled grimly.

In between the work of the Log Section, he played with the data he was gathering on his other job. Huber didn't have the sort of mind that leaped instantly to the right answer to complex questions. He worked things over mentally, turning the bits and fitting them first this way, then another. It was a lot like doing jigsaw puzzles. At the end of the process there was an answer, and he guessed he'd be working on it till he found what the answer was.

Hera left for lunch. She invited Huber but didn't argue when he turned her down, and she didn't argue either when he insisted she go on as she'd planned instead of staying in the office because he was staying. Huber knew as well as the next guy how important it was to get some time away from the place you were working; otherwise you could lock yourself down tighter than happened to most prisoners.

It didn't apply to him, of course. He was too busy to worry about where his butt happened to be located at the moment.

The Regiment already employed more than three hundred UC citizens. There'd be over a thousand by the time the deployment was complete, and that was without counting the number of recreation personnel hired to deal with the off-duty requirements of the combat troopers. On a place like Plattner's World most of that last group would be freelance, but the Colonel would set up and staff official brothels if the free market didn't appear to him to be up to the job.

Central Repair was one of the larger employers of local personnel. CR was where heavily damaged vehicles were brought: for repair if possible, for stripping and scrapping if they weren't. Line maintenance was mostly done at company level, but at battalion in the case of major drive-train components; Central Repair dealt with more serious or complex problems.

Fencing Master was thus far the Regiment's only serious battle damage on Plattner's

World, but there were plenty of things that could go wrong with complex vehicles transiting between star systems. Furthermore, there were a dozen blowers deadlined from the previous contract. They'd been shipped to Plattner's World for repair instead of being held behind and repaired in place.

Late in the day, Huber got around to checking addresses. There were many groupings of employees who gave the same home address. That didn't concern him. Besides members of the same family all working in the booming new industry, war, many of the personnel came into Benjamin from outlying locations. Those transients lived in apartments or rooming houses here in the city.

Three of the mechanics in Central Repair lived at what the voter registration records—forwarded to Huber by Doll Basime; he didn't go through Hera to get them—listed as the address of Senator Patroklos Graciano. *That* was a matter for concern.

Huber looked around the office. Hera was out of the room; off to the latrine, he supposed. That made things a little simpler. Kelso, the local who'd driven the rescue vehicle the night before, looked up and caught his eye. Huber gestured him over, into the area of the privacy screen.

"Sir?" Kelso said brightly. His thin blond hair made him look younger than he probably was; close up Huber guessed the fellow was thirty standard years old. Kelso dressed a little more formally than most of the staff and he seemed to want very much to please. *Looking for a permanent billet with the Regiment,* Huber guessed; which was all right with Huber, and just might work out.

"I've got three names and lists of former employers here," Huber said, running hardcopy of the employment applications as he spoke. "I want you to check these out—just go around to the listed employers and ask about the people. I'm not looking for anything formal. If the boss isn't in—"

He handed the three flimsies to Kelso.

"—but the desk clerk remembers them, that's fine. Take one of the section jeeps, and I'd rather have the information sooner than later."

"Sir, it's pretty late…" Kelso said with a concerned expression. "Should I chase people down at their homes if the business is closed, or—"

Huber thought for a moment, then laughed. "No, nothing like that," he said. "But if you can get me the data before tomorrow midday, I'd appreciate it."

"You can count on me, sir!" the fellow said. Holding the hardcopy in his hand, he trotted past the consoles—some of them empty; it *was* getting late—and out the door just as Hera returned.

They passed; she glanced questioningly from the disappearing local and then to Huber. Huber waved cheerfully and immediately bent to his console, calling up information on the Officer in Charge of Central Repair. Hera might have asked what was going on with Kelso if Huber hadn't made it pointedly clear that he was busy.

Which he was, of course, but it bothered him to treat her this way. Well, it'd bother her worse if he told her what he was doing; and there was also the risk that…

Say it: the risk that this bright, competent woman, attractive in all respects—would be loyal to her brother if push came to shove, instead of being loyal to the regiment of off-planet killers she happened to be working for at the moment. Surviving in a combat environment meant taking as few risks as possible, because the ones you couldn't avoid were plenty bad enough.

CR was at present under the command of Senior Warrant Leader Edlinger; Buck Edlinger to his friends, and Huber knew him well enough from previous deployments to be in that number. Instead of doing a data transmission through the console, Huber made a voice call. It took a moment for Edlinger to answer; he didn't sound pleased as he snarled, "Edlinger, and who couldn't bloody wait for me to call back, tell me!"

"Arne Huber, Buck," Huber replied calmly. He'd been shouted at before—and worse. Edlinger'd been squeezed into a place too tight for him to wear his commo helmet, and he wasn't best pleased to be dragged out of there to take a voice call slugged Urgent. "I've got a problem that may turn out to be your problem too. Are your people working round the clock right now?"

"Via!" Edlinger said. "No, not by a long ways. You're in Log Section now, Huber? What're you about to drop on us? Did a shipload of blowers come down hard?"

"Nothing like that, Buck," Huber said. Edlinger must have checked Huber's status when *Fencing Master* came in for repair. "I want to check what three of your locals've been working on, and I want to check it when the locals and their friends aren't around."

"What d'ye know about maintenance oversight, Huber?" Edlinger said; not exactly hostile, but not as friendly as he'd have been if it hadn't seemed an outsider was moving in on his territory.

"I know squat," Huber said, "but I've got a tech here, Sergeant Tranter, who you gave curst good fitness reports to back when, when he worked for you. And you can help, Buck—I'd just as soon you did. But this isn't a joke."

That was the Lord's truth. This could be much worse than a company of armored vehicles getting bent in a starship crash.

"You got Tranter?" Edlinger said. "Oh, that's okay, then. Look, Huber, I can have everybody out of here by twenty hundred hours if that suits you. Okay?"

"That's great, Buck," Huber said, nodding in an enthusiasm that Edlinger couldn't see over a standard regimental voice-only transmission. "We'll be there at twenty hundred hours."

"Hey Huber?" Edlinger added as he started to break the connection.

"Right?"

"Can you tell me who you're worried about, or do I have to guess?"

That was a fair question. "Their names are Galieni, Osorio, and Triulski," Huber said, reading them off the display in front of him. "Do they ring a bell?"

Edlinger snorted something between disgust and real concern. "Ring a bell?" he said. "You bet they do. They're the best wrenches I've been able to find. I'd recommend them all for permanent status in the Regiment if they wanted to join."

Huber grimaced. "Yeah, I thought it might be like that," he said.

"And Huber?" Edlinger added. "One more thing. You wanted to know what they're working on? That's easy. They're putting your old blower, *Fencing Master,* back together. She'll go out late tomorrow the way things are getting on."

When Tranter came in with Bayes, the sergeant laughing as the trooper gestured in the air, Huber cued his helmet intercom and said, "Sarge? Come talk to me in my little garden of silence, will you?"

A console with regimental programming like Hera Graciano's could eavesdrop on intercom transmissions unless Huber went to more effort on encryption than he wanted to. It was simpler and less obtrusive to use voice and the privacy screen that was already in place around his area of the office.

Tranter patted Bayes on the shoulder and sauntered over to the lieutenant as though the idea was his alone rather than a response to a summons. Huber was becoming more and more impressed with the way Tranter picked up on things without need for them to be said. Sometimes Huber wasn't sure exactly what he'd say if he did have to explain.

"Do we have a problem, El-Tee?" Tranter asked as he bent over the console, resting his knuckles on the flat surface beside the holographic display.

Huber noticed the "we." He grinned. "We're going maybe to solve one before it crops up, Sarge," he said. "Are you up to poking around in a combat car tonight?"

"I guess," Tranter said, unexpectedly guarded. "Ah—what would it be we're looking for, El-Tee? Booze? Drugs?"

Huber burst out laughing when he understood Tranter's concern. "Via, Sarge!" he said. "You've been on field deployments, haven't you? All that stuff belongs, and so does anything else that helps a trooper get through the nights he's not going to get through any other way. No, I'm looking for stuff that our people didn't put there. I don't know what it'll be; but I do know that if something's there, I want to know what it is. Okay?"

Tranter beamed as he straightened up. "Hey, a chance to be a wrench again instead of pushing electrons? You got it, boss!"

"Pick me up at the front of the building at a quarter of eight, then," Huber said. "We need to be at Central Repair on the hour—I've cleared it with the chief. Oh, and Tranter?"

"Sir?" The sergeant looked… not worried exactly, but wary. He wasn't going to ask what was going on; but something was and though he seemed to trust Huber, a veteran non-com knows just how disastrously wrong officers' bright ideas are capable of going.

"Don't talk about it," Huber said. "And you know that gun you were holding last night? Think you could look one up for me?"

"Roger that, sir!" Tranter said, perfectly cheerful again. "Or if you'd rather have a sub-machine gun?"

Huber shook his head. "I want something with authority," he explained. "I don't think there's a chance in a million we'll have somebody try to pull something while we're flying between here and Central Repair tonight… but I do think that if it happens, I'm going to make sure we're the car still in the air at the end of it."

Chuckling in bright good humor, the sergeant returned to his console. The other clerks looked at him, but Hera was watching Huber instead.

Huber cued his intercom and said, "What's the latest on the ground transport situation, Hera? Did your father come through?"

The best way to conceal the rest of what was going on was to bury it in the work of Log Section; and the fact that quite a lot of work was getting done that way was a nice bonus.

Central Repair was a block of six warehouses in the north-central district of Benjamin. Engineer Section had thrown up a wall of plasticized earth around the complex as a basic precaution, but the location was neither secure nor really defensible despite the infantry company and platoon of combat cars stationed there.

Tranter brought the four-place aircar down at CR's entrance gate. They were tracked all the way by a tribarrel of the combat car there—*Flesh Hook*, another F Company vehicle—and, for as long as the aircar was above the horizon, by the guns of two more cars within the compound. Huber would've been just as happy to ride to Repair in a regimental-standard air-cushion jeep, but Tranter was proud of being able to drive an aircar. There were plenty of them in Log Section's inventory since they were the normal means of civilian transportation on Plattner's World.

Tranter wasn't a good aircar driver—he was too heavy-handed, trying to outguess the AI—and there was always the chance that a trooper on guard would decide the car wobbling toward the compound was hostile despite Huber's extreme care to check in with detachment control. Still, Tranter was investing his time and maybe more to satisfy his section leader's whim; the least the section leader could do was let him show off what he fondly imagined were his talents.

The car bumped hard on the gravel apron in front of Central Repair. The gate was open, but *Flesh Hook* had parked to block the entrance. Huber raised his faceshield and said, "Lieutenant Huber, Log Section, to see Chief Edlinger. He's expecting me."

"Good to see you, El-Tee," called the trooper behind the front tribarrel. The driver watched from his hatch, but the two wing guns were unmanned; they continued to search the sky in air defense mode under detachment control. "You guys earned your pay at Rhodesville, didn't you? Curst glad it was you and not us in F-2."

"I don't know that I feel the same way," Huber said; but even if he'd shouted, he couldn't have been heard over the rising howl of drive fans as the combat car shifted sideways to open the passage. Tranter drove through the gate in surface effect.

Central Repair would've been much safer against external attack if it had been located within Base Alpha. It remained separate because of the greater risk of having so many local personnel—well over a hundred if combat operations persisted for any length of time—inside the Regimental HQ. Losing Central Repair would be a serious blow to the Regiment; the sort of damage a saboteur could do within Base Alpha wouldn't be survivable.

The warehouses had been placed following the curve of the land instead of being aligned on a grid pattern. Tranter followed the access road meandering past the front of the buildings. Three of them were empty, held against future need. The sliding doors of the fourth from the gate were closed, but light streamed out of the pedestrian entrance set beside them.

Three troopers looked down from the warehouse roof as Tranter pulled the aircar over. Huber waved at them with his left hand; he held the 2-cm powergun in his right.

Chief Edlinger met them at the door. "Good to see you again, Huber," he said. "Tranter, you need a hand?"

"I haven't forgotten how to carry a toolchest, Chief," the sergeant said, lifting his equipment out of the back of the car with a grunt. And of course he hadn't, but his mechanical leg didn't bend the way the one he'd been born with had; balance was tricky with such a heavy weight.

Huber had offered help when they got into the car. If Tranter wanted to prove he could move a toolchest or do any other curst thing he wanted without help, then more power to him.

"I appreciate this, Buck," Huber said as he entered the warehouse. The air within was chilly and had overtones of lubricant and ozone; it was a place which only tolerated human beings. "I'd like there not to be a problem, but—"

"But you think there is," Edlinger completed grimly. He was a wiry little man whose sandy hair was more gray than not; he'd rolled his sleeves up, showing the tattoos covering both arms. Time and ingrained grease had blurred their patterns. If even the chief could identify the designs, he'd have to do it from memory.

Huber laughed wryly. "I think so enough that if we don't find something, I'll worry more," he admitted. "I won't believe it isn't there, just that we didn't find it."

"That looks like the lady," Tranter said, striding purposefully across the cracked concrete floor. There were two other combat cars in the workshop, but *Fencing Master* wore like a flag across her bow slope the marks of the buzzbomb and the welding repairs. Iridium was named for Iris, the goddess of the rainbow, because of the range of beautiful colors that heat spread across the metal.

Tranter and the chief spent the next two hours taking off panels, running diagnostics, and sending fiber optic filaments up passages that Huber hadn't known were parts of a combat car's structure. He stayed clear, sitting mostly on an empty forty-liter lubricant container. The techs worked with the natural rhythm of men who'd worked together often in the past; they spoke in a verbal shorthand, and they never got in one another's way.

It struck Huber that the chief must really have regretted losing Tranter from his section. Huber hadn't known the sergeant very long, and *he'd* bloody well miss him if something happened.

"Hel-*lo,* what have we here?" Tranter called, his voice echoing out of the iridium cavern into which he'd crawled. He'd removed a hull access plate beneath the driver's compartment; only his feet showed outside the opening. "Chief, what d'ye make of this? I'm sending it on channel seven."

Huber locked his faceshield down and cued it to the imagery Tranter's probe was picking up. He had no context for what he was looking at: a series of chips were set in a board bracketed between iridium bulkheads. On the bottom of the board was an additional chip, attached to the circuits on the other side with hair-fine wires.

"Hang on, I've got the catalog," Edlinger replied. They were using lapel mikes because their commo helmets were too bulky for some of the spaces they were slipping into. "Can you give me more magnification? Are those two reds, a blue and a…"

"Purple and white, Chief," Tranter said. "The fourth line's a purple and white."

"Roger that," said Edlinger. "A simple control circuit, sonny. Probably made on Sonderby, wouldn't you say?"

A dozen chips flashed up on Huber's faceshield beside the real-time image, matches that the chief's AI had found in a catalog of parts and equipment. They could've been many mirror images as far as Huber could tell, but the techs and their electronics apparently found minute differences among them.

"Galieni said he'd been trained on Sonderby," Edlinger added in a somber voice. "I don't doubt that he was, but I'd be willing to bet that it wasn't Southern Cross Spacelines that hired him when he left school."

The original image blanked as Sergeant Tranter squirmed back out of the equipment bay. Huber raised his faceshield as the chief walked around from the other side of the car.

"All right," said Huber. "What does it do? Is it a bomb?"

"It isn't a bomb, El-Tee," Tranter said, squatting for a moment before he got to his feet. "It's a control circuit, and it's been added to the air defense board. It's got an antenna wire out through the channel for the running lights—that's how I noticed it."

"They could've set it to switch off the guns when somebody sent a coded radio signal, Huber," Edlinger added. "That's the most likely plan, though it depends on exactly where on the board they were plugged in. I'm not sure we can tell with just the maintenance manuals I've got here."

"I've got a better guess than that, Buck," Huber said, standing and feeling his gut contract. "Shutting the guns off wouldn't be a disaster if it just affected one car in a platoon. What if that chip locked all three tribarrels on full automatic fire in the middle of Benjamin? What do you suppose would happen to the houses for a klick in every direction?"

"Bloody hell," Tranter muttered.

Huber nodded. "Yeah, that's exactly what would happen: bloody hell. And coming on top of Rhodesville, the UC government'd cancel the Regiment's contract so fast we'd be off-planet with our heads swimming before we knew what happened."

The technicians looked at one another, then back to Huber. "What do we do now, El-Tee?" Tranter asked.

"Have you disconnected the chip?" Huber asked.

"You bet!" Tranter said with a frown of amazement. "I cut both leads as soon as I saw them. Whatever the thing was, I knew it didn't belong."

"Then we shut things up and I go talk to Major Steuben in the morning," Huber said. "I'd do it now, but—"

He grinned with wry honesty.

"—not only do I think it'll keep, I *don't* think I'm in any shape to talk to the major before I've had a good night's sleep."

Sergeant Tranter rubbed the back of his neck with his knuckles. "And maybe a stiff drink or two, hey El-Tee?" he said. "Which I'm going to share with you, if you don't mind."

"I'm buying for both of you for what you've done tonight," Huber said, thinking of the coming interview. "And I just wish you could carry it the rest of the way with the major, but that's my job...."

Major Steuben wasn't available through the regimental net at dawn plus thirty, at noon, or at any of the other times Huber checked for him into mid-afternoon. Huber didn't leave a message—he was sure Steuben would learn about the calls as soon as he wanted to know—and it didn't even cross his mind to talk to some other member of the White Mice. Little as Huber liked the major, this was no time to bring a subordinate up to speed on the problem. He began to wonder if he was going to reach Steuben before 1800 hours, close of business for the regular staff.

Huber smiled at his own presumption; he'd gotten to think that Steuben would be there any time he wanted him—because the major had been in his office the times he summoned Huber. Why his mind should've reversed the pattern was just one of those mysteries of human arrogance, Huber supposed. It wasn't like Log Section didn't have work to do, after all.

Now that more crews and vehicles were on the ground, the Regiment was setting up a second operations base outside Arbor Palisades, the second-largest of the United Cities and located on the northeast border with Solace. Two platoons from L Troop plus support vehicles would be leaving Base Alpha tonight for the new location. Huber with the approval of the S-3 shop had decided to send a column of thirty wheeled vehicles along with them. The civilian trucks could've moved on their own—the UC and Solace weren't at war despite the level of tension—but it gave both the troopers and the civilian drivers practice in convoy techniques.

"Via, El-Tee," Sergeant Tranter said, shaking his head in amusement. "You better not let anybody in L Troop catch you in a dark alley. The trip'll take 'em four times as long and be about that much rougher per hour besides."

"Right," said Huber. "And nobody's shooting at them. Which won't be the case if we have to do it for real, as we bloody well will when those trucks start supplying forward bases inside Solace territory as soon as the balloon goes up."

Huber didn't take lunch, though he gnawed ration bars at his desk. Most people claimed the bars tasted like compressed sawdust, but Huber found them to have a series of subtle flavors. They were bland, sure, but bland wasn't such a bad thing. The commander of a line platoon had enough excitement in his life without needing it in his food.

At random moments throughout the day, Huber checked in with the Provost Marshal's office. At 1530 hours instead of a machine voice announcing, "Unavailable," Major Steuben himself said, "Go ahead."

"Sir!" Huber said. His brain disconnected but he'd rehearsed his approach often enough in his head to blurt it out now: "May I see you ASAP with some information about the Rhodesville ambush?"

"If by 'as soon as possible' you mean in fifteen minutes, Lieutenant…" Steuben said. He had a pleasant voice, a modulated tenor as smooth and civilized as his appearance; and as deceptive, of course. "Then you may, yes."

"Sir, on the way, sir!" Huber said, standing and breaking the connection.

"Tranter!" he shouted across the room as he rounded his console; he snatched the 2-cm powergun slung from the back of his chair. "I need to be in front of Major Steuben in fifteen minutes! That means an aircar, and I don't even pretend to drive the cursed things."

Huber waved at Hera as he followed the sergeant out the door. "I'll be back when I'm back," he said. "I don't expect to be long."

The good Lord knew he *hoped* it wouldn't be long.

He and Tranter didn't talk much on the short flight from Benjamin to Base Alpha. The sergeant turned his head toward his passenger a couple times, but he didn't speak. Huber was concentrating on the open triangle formed by his hands lying in his lap. He was aware of Tranter's regard, but he really needed to compose himself before he brought this to Major Steuben.

This time when Huber got out of the car in front of the Provost Marshal's, he reflexively scooped the 2-cm shoulder weapon from the butt-cup holding it upright beside his seat. If he'd been thinking he'd have left the heavy weapon in the vehicle, but since he was holding it anyway he passed it to the watching guard along with his pistol and knife.

"Expecting some excitement, Lieutenant?" said the man behind the mirrored faceshield as he took the weapons.

"What would a desk jockey like me know about excitement?" Huber said cheerfully as he opened the main door.

He wondered about his comment as he strode down the hallway. It struck him that it was the first interaction he'd had with the guards that wasn't strictly professional. As with so much of his life since he'd landed on Plattner's World, Huber had the feeling that he was running downhill in the darkness and the only thing that was going to save him was pure dumb luck.

Major Steuben nodded him into the office. Huber closed the door behind him and without preamble said, "Sir! Three of the techs in Central Repair are living at Senator Graciano's townhouse. That is, Patroklos Graciano, the—"

"I know who Patroklos Graciano is," Steuben said through his cold smile. "Continue."

"Right," said Huber. He was blurting what he knew in the baldest fashion possible. He understood Major Steuben too well to want to exchange empty pleasantries with the man. "We checked—Chief Edlinger and a former tech in my section, that is—checked the combat car they were working on. There's an extra control chip in the air defense board with an antenna for external inputs. I think it was meant to send the tribarrels berserk while the car was in the middle of Benjamin."

"You've disconnected the chip?" Steuben said. For a moment there was a spark from something very hard glinting in his voice.

"Yes sir, but that's all we've done thus far," Huber said. His muscles were tight across his rib cage and his tongue seemed to be chipping out the words. In a firefight he wouldn't have been this tense, because he'd have known the rules....

"Good," said the major, smoothly unconcerned again. "You've properly reported the matter and your suspicions, Lieutenant. Now go back to your duties in Logistics and take no more action on the matter. Do you understand?"

Huber felt the anger rise in his throat. "No sir," he said. He spoke in a normal voice, maybe even a little quieter than usual. "I don't understand at all. Senator Graciano is certainly a traitor, probably the traitor who set up me and my platoon at Rhodesville. We can't leave him out there, looking for another place to slide the knife into us. One more chance may be just the one he needed!"

Steuben didn't rise, but he leaned forward very slightly in his seat. He wore his 1-cm pistol in a cutaway holster high on his right hip. Inlays of platinum, gold, and rich violet gold-uranium alloy decorated the weapon's receiver, but the pistol was still as deadly as the service weapon Huber had left with the guards outside the building.

And the dapper little man who wore it was far more deadly than Huber had ever thought of being.

"You've shown initiative, Lieutenant," Steuben said. "Because of that, I'm going to politely point something out to you instead of treating your insolence as I normally would: even if everything you believe regarding Senator Graciano is true, he remains *Senator* Graciano. He has a large following in the United Cities and is in some ways more influential in the remainder of the Outer States than any other UC politician, his father included. Probably the best way to boost his standing still further would be for off-planet mercenaries to accuse him of being a traitor."

"Sir, I lost friends at Rhodesville!" Huber said.

"Then you were lucky to have friends to begin with, Lieutenant," the major said, rising to his feet. "Friendship is an experience I've never shared. Now *get* back to Log Section and your duties. Or submit your resignation from the Regiment, which I assure you will be accepted at the moment you offer it."

Huber's lips were dry. He didn't speak.

"I asked you before if you understood," Steuben said, his left fingertips resting lightly on the desk top. "You chose to discuss the matter. Now the only thing for you to understand is this: you will go back to your duties in Log Section, or you will resign. *Do* you understand?"

"Sir!" Huber said. "May I return to my duties now?"

"Dismissed, Lieutenant," the major said. "And Lieutenant? I don't expect to see you again until I summon you."

As Huber walked down the hallway, his back to the door he'd closed behind him, he kept thinking, *It's in the hands of the people who ought to be handling it. It's none of my business anymore.*

The trouble was, he knew that at the level of Steuben and Colonel Hammer it was a political problem. Political problems were generally best solved by compromise and quiet neglect.

Huber didn't think he'd ever be able to chalk up the sound of Kolbe's body squishing down *Fencing Master*'s bow slope to political expedience, though.

"Got any plans for tonight, El-Tee?" Sergeant Tranter asked as he followed Huber up the stairs to Log Section. "There's a game on in the maintenance shed."

The paint on the stairwell walls had been rubbed at the height of children's shoulders; it was a reminder of what the building had been. Whether it'd ever be a school again depended on how well the Slammers performed. If things went wrong, the Outer States—at least the United Cities—would be paying reparations to Solace that'd preclude luxuries like public schooling.

"I'm thinking about throwing darts into a target," Huber muttered. "And don't ask whose picture I'm thinking of using for the target!"

Hera wasn't at her desk. In her absence and Huber's, a senior clerk named Farinelli was in titular charge—and he obviously had no idea of how to deal with the two armed Slammers who stood before his console. Their backs were to the door and the remainder of the staring locals.

"Can I help you gentle—" Huber began, politely but with a sharp undertone. A stranger listening could have guessed that he didn't much like aggrieved troopers making personal visits to Log Section when a call or data transmission would get the facts into his hands without disrupting the office. Midway in Huber's question, the troopers turned.

"Deseau!" Huber said. "And you, Learoyd! Say, they didn't reassign you guys too, did they?"

The troopers smiled gratefully, though Learoyd knuckled his bald scalp in embarrassment and wouldn't meet Huber's eyes. "Nothing like that, Lieutenant," the sergeant said. "We're here to take *Fencing Master* back to the unit as soon as they assign us a couple bodies from the Replacement Depot. I figured you wouldn't mind if we stopped in and saw how you were making out."

From the way Deseau spoke and Learoyd acted, they weren't at all sure that Huber *wouldn't* mind. They were line troopers, neither of them with any formal education; the only civilians they were comfortable with were whores and bartenders. It must have been a shock to come looking for the lieutenant who'd been one of them and find themselves in an office full of well-dressed locals who stared as if they were poisonous snakes.

Huber thought suddenly of the ropes of 2-cm bolts sending the dirigible down in fiery destruction over Rhodesville. There was never a poisonous snake as dangerous as either of these two men; or as Arne Huber, who *was* after all one of them.

"Mind?" he said. "I'm delighted! Sergeant Tranter—"

Huber took his men by either hand and raised his voice as his eyes swept the office. "Everybody? These are two of the people who kept me alive at the sharp end: my blower captain Sergeant Deseau and Trooper Learoyd, my right wing gunner. That won't mean much to you civilians, but you can understand when I say I wouldn't have survived landing on Plattner's World if it weren't for these men!"

Learoyd muttered something to his shoes, but he looked pleased. Deseau's expression didn't change, but he didn't seem to mind either.

"Do you have plans for tonight?" Huber asked. "Ah, Sergeant Tranter? Do you think we could find these men a billet here in the compound?" He switched his eyes back to Deseau and Learoyd, continuing, "There's usually a card game, and I think I can promise something to drink."

"And if he couldn't get you booze, I can," Tranter said cheerfully. "Sure, we can put you guys up. It's best the El-Tee not go wandering around, but you won't miss Benjamin."

"If I never see Warrant Leader Niscombe," Learoyd said to his boots, "it'll be too soon."

"Niscombe runs the enlisted side of Transient Depot, sir," Deseau explained. "He figures that something bad'll happen if he lets folks passing through from field duty just rest and relax. He'll find a lot of little jobs for us if we bunk there."

"Something bad'll happen to Niscombe if he ever shows his face out in the field," Learoyd muttered with a venom Huber hadn't expected to hear in that trooper's voice. "Which he won't do, you can be sure of that."

"Right," said Huber. "I'll send a temporary duty request for the two of you through channels, but for now consider yourselves at liberty."

He glanced at Hera's empty desk. "Ah, does anybody know when Deputy Graciano's due back?" he asked the room in a raised voice.

Everybody stared at him; nobody answered the question, though. It struck Huber that all this was out of the locals' previous experience with the Slammers. When Captain Cassutt was director, there hadn't been troopers with personal weapons standing in the middle of the office.

"Sir?" said Kelso from the back of the room.

"What?" said Huber. "Via, if you know something, spit it out!"

"Yessir," said Kelso, swallowing. "Ah, I don't know when the deputy's coming back, but she went out as soon as I gave her the information you requested, sir."

"Information?" Huber repeated. For a moment he didn't know what the local was talking about; nonetheless his stomach slid toward the bottom of an icy pit.

Then he remembered. "You mean the previous employment data."

"Yessir!" said Kelso, more brightly this time. "None of those techs had worked at the places they put down. Not a soul remembered any one of the three!"

Huber opened his mouth to ask another question, but he really didn't have to. He'd given Kelso the full applications including the applicants' home addresses. That's what Hera had seen, and she wouldn't have had to check to recognize the address of her brother's townhouse. The fact that the men's listed employment records were phony would be a red flag to anybody with brains enough to feed themselves.

"What's the matter, sir?" Tranter said.

"I screwed up," Huber said. His face must've gone white; he felt cold all over. "It's nobody's fault but mine."

Hera could've gone to her father with the information; she could've gone to the civil authorities—though Huber wasn't sure the United Cities had security police in the fashion that larger states generally did; or she could even have gone to Colonel Hammer. Any of those choices would have been fine. The possibility that scared Huber, though, was that instead—

His helmet pinged him with an Urgent call. Huber wasn't in a platoon and company net, so the sound was unexpected. He locked down his faceshield to mute the conversation and said, "Fox Three-six, go ahead!"

In his surprise—and fear—he'd given his old call signal. Somebody else was leader of platoon F-3 nowadays.

"*Arne, this is Doll,*" said Lieutenant Basime's voice. "*We don't exactly monitor the civil police here, but we are a signals liaison section. Ah—*"

"Say it!" Huber snapped.

"*There was a police call just now,*" Doll said mildly. She was a solid lady, well able to stand up for her rights and smart enough to know when that wasn't the best choice. "*There's an aircar down west of town. The driver and sole occupant is dead. Initial report is that it's your deputy, Hera Graciano.*"

"Right," said Huber. He felt calm again, much as he'd been as he watched the stern of the blazing dirigible slide slowly into the terminal building. The past was the past; now there were only the consequences to deal with. "Can you download the coordinates of the crash site?"

"*You've got 'em,*" Doll said. There was an icon Huber hadn't noticed in the terrain box on his faceshield. "*Anything more I can do, Snake?*"

"Negative, Doll," Huber said. "I'll take it from here. Three-six out."

He broke the connection and raised his faceshield. "Trouble, El-Tee?" said Sergeant Tranter. Tranter had been in the field, but he didn't have a line trooper's instincts. Deseau and Learoyd stood facing outward from their former platoon leader; their feet were spread and their sub-machine guns slanted in front of them. They weren't aiming at anything, not threatening anybody; but they hadn't had to ask if there was trouble, and they were ready to deal in their own way with anything that showed itself.

The civilian clerks looked terrified, as they well should have been.

"Tranter, I need a ride," Huber said. "West of town there's been an aircar crash. I'll transfer the coordinates to the car's navigation system."

"We're coming along," Deseau said. He continued to watch half the room and the doorway, while the trooper watched the clerks on the other side. "Learoyd and me."

"You go relax," Huber said in a tight voice. "This is Log Section business, not yours."

"Fuck that," said Deseau. "You said we're at liberty. Fine, we're at liberty to come with you."

"Right," said Huber. He was still holding his big shoulder weapon; he hadn't had time to put it down since he entered the office. "You—Farinelli? You're in charge till I get back." He thought for a moment and added, "Or you hear that I've been replaced."

"But Director Huber!" the clerk said. "What if Deputy Graciano comes back?"

"She won't," Huber snarled. Then to his men he added, "Come on, troopers. Let's roll!"

"She was up about a thousand meters," said the cop. He was a young fellow in a blue jacket and red trousers with a blue stripe down the seam. For all that he was determined not to be cowed by the heavily armed mercenaries, he behaved politely instead of blustering to show his authority. "She had the top down and wasn't belted in, so she came out the first time the car tumbled."

It was probably chance then that the body and the vehicle had hit the ground within fifty meters of one another, Huber realized. Hera had gone through tree-branches face-first, hit the ground, and then bounced over to lie on her back. Her features were distorted, but he could've identified her easily if the UC policeman had been concerned about that; he wasn't.

There was almost no blood. The dent in the center of her forehead had spilled considerable gore over Hera's face, but that had been dry when the branches slashed her and wiped much of it off. Huber was no pathologist, but he'd seen death often and in a variety of forms. Hera Graciano had been dead for some length of time before her body hit the ground.

"Why did the car tumble?" Tranter said, kneeling to check the underside of the crumpled vehicle. It'd nosed in, then fallen back on its underside with its broken frame cocked up like an inverted V. "There's an air turbine that deploys when you run outa fuel. It generates enough juice to keep your control gyro spinning."

"You're friends of the lady?" the cop asked. He was expecting backup, but the Slammers had arrived almost as soon as he did himself. He seemed puzzled, which Huber was willing to grant him the right to be.

But it was a really good thing for the cop that he hadn't decided to throw his weight around. Huber wasn't in a mood for it; and while he wasn't sure how Sergeant Tranter would react, he knew that the two troopers from *Fencing Master* would obey without question if their lieutenant told them to blow the local's brains out.

"She was my deputy," Huber said. "She worked for the Regiment in a civilian capacity."

"Somebody whacked the turbine with a heavy hammer," Tranter said, rising from where he knelt. "That's why it's still stuck in the cradle."

He pulled at an access plate on the wreck's quarter panel. It didn't come till he took a multitool from his belt and gave the warped plastic a calculated blow.

The local policeman looked at the sky again and fingered his lapel communicator. He didn't try to prod the dispatcher, though. "There was an anonymous call that the car had been circling up here and just dropped outa the sky," he explained. "D'ye suppose it was maybe, well… suicide?"

"No," said Huber. "I don't think that."

"That's good," said the cop, misunderstanding completely. "Because you guys might not know it, but this lady was from a bloody important family here in the UC. I don't want to get caught in some kinda scandal, if you see what I mean."

"I see what you mean," Huber said. His eyes drifted across Tranter for a moment, then resumed scanning their surroundings. They were within ten klicks of the center of Benjamin, but the forest was unbroken. Trees on Plattner's World had enough chlorophyll in their bark to look deep green from a distance. Their branches twisted like snakes, but the leaves were individually tiny and stuck on the twigs like a child's drawing.

The cop grimaced. "I wish the Commander Miltianas would get the lead outa his pants and take over here," he went on. "Of course, he probably doesn't want to be mixed up in this either—but curse it, it's what they're paying him the big bucks for, right?"

"There's four fuel cells in this model," Tranter said, his head inside the vehicle's stern section. "The back three are disconnected and there's a puncture in the forward cell."

He straightened, looking puzzled and concerned. "El-Tee," he said. "It looks to me like—"

"Drop the subject for now, Sergeant," Huber said. He gestured to their own vehicle, a ten-place bus rather than the little runabout Tranter had used to ferry Huber alone. Four troopers in combat gear would've been a crowd and a burden for the smaller car. "We'll talk on the way back to the office."

"But—" said Tranter.

Deseau rapped the side of Tranter's commo helmet with his knuckles. "Hey!" Deseau said. "He's the man, right? He just gave you an order!"

Tranter looked startled, then nodded in embarrassment and trotted for the bus. There were three aircars approaching fast from Benjamin. Two had red strobe lights flashing, but they weren't running their sirens.

Huber turned to the cop. "Thanks for letting us look over the site," he said. "We'll leave you to your business now. And we'll get back to our own."

"Yeah, right," said the local man with a worried frown. "I sure hope I don't wind up holding the bucket on this one. A death like this can be a lot of trouble!"

"You got that right," Huber muttered as he got into the cab with Tranter. The tech already had the fans live; now he boosted power and wobbled into the air, narrowly missing a line of trees.

Kelso would have done a better job driving, but this was no longer business for civilians. Huber locked his faceshield down.

"Unit, switch to intercom," he ordered. Nobody but the three men in the car with him could hear the discussion without a lot of decryption equipment and skill. "Tranter, I'm leaving you in the circuit, but I'm not expecting you to get involved. You'll have to keep your mouth shut, that's all. Can you handle that?"

"*Fuck not being involved,*" Tranter said. His hands were tight on the control yoke and his eyes were straight ahead; a degree of hurt sounded in his voice. "*I knew the deputy better than you did, sir. She was a good boss; and anyway, she was one of ours even if she didn't wear the uniform. Which I do.*"

"Right," said Huber. "Deseau and Learoyd, you don't know the background. I figure her brother killed her or one of his thugs did. It was probably an accident, but maybe not. She'd have gone to see him, threatening to tell the world he was an agent for Solace. She maybe even guessed he'd set up the ambush at Rhodesville."

Sergeant Deseau made a sound loud enough to trip the intercom. In something like a normal voice he went on, "*We gonna take care of him, then?*"

"He's got a lot of pull," Huber warned. "I went to Major Steuben about him and got told to mind my own business. It's going to make real waves if somebody from the Regiment takes him out. *Real* waves, about as bad as it gets."

"*El-Tee?*" Learoyd said, frustration so evident in his tone that Huber could visualize the trooper trying to knuckle his bald scalp through his commo helmet. "*Just tell us what to do, right? That's your job. Don't worry about me and Frenchie doing ours.*"

Learoyd was correct, of course. He had a simple approach of necessity, and he cut through all the nonsense that smarter people wrapped themselves up with.

"Right," Huber repeated. "There'll be a gang of thugs at the guy's townhouse, and they'll have guns available even if they aren't going out on the street with them just yet. It could be that he'd got a squad of Harris's Commando on premises. I doubt it because of the risk to him if it comes out, but we've got to figure we're going up against people who know what they're doing."

He paused, arranging his next words. The aircar was over Benjamin now, but Tranter was taking them in a wide circuit of the suburbs where the tree cover was almost as complete as over the virgin forest beyond.

"For that reason," Huber said, "I figure to borrow *Fencing Master* for the operation. There's a detachment leaving Central Repair for Base Alpha tonight. We'll tag onto the back and trail off when we're close to the bastard's compound. If we can, we'll duck back to CR when we're done—but I *don't* expect to get away with this, troops."

"*I been shot at before,*" Deseau said calmly. "*I can't see anything worse'n that that's going to happen if they catch us.*"

Learoyd didn't bother to speak. Huber heard the *clack* as the trooper withdrew his sub-machine gun's loading tube, then locked it back home in the receiver. Like he'd said, he was getting ready to do his part of the job.

"Sergeant Tranter," Huber said, turning to the tech beside him. "Now that you know what we're talking about, I think it'd be a good night for you to spend playing cards back at the billets. You're a curst good man, but this really isn't your line of work."

Tranter's face was red with suppressed emotion. "*Guess you'll need a driver, right?*" he snapped. "*Guess I've driven the Lord's great plenty of combat cars, shifting them around for repair. I guess it bloody well is my line of work. Sir.*"

"Well in that case, troopers…" Huber said. "We'll leave our billets for Central Repair at twenty hundred. Start time for the draft is twenty-one hundred, but they'll be late.

That'll make the timing about right."

Tranter muttered, "*Roger*," Deseau grunted, and Learoyd said as little as he usually did. There wasn't a lot *to* say at this point.

Huber wasn't frightened; it was all over but the consequences.

Senator Patroklos Graciano was about to learn the consequences of fucking with Hammer's Slammers.

The racket of drive fans made every joint in the girder-framed warehouse rattle and sing. There were two other combat cars besides *Fencing Master*; all three thirty-tonne monsters were powered up, their fans supporting them on bubbles of pressurized air. From the way the interior lights danced, some of the overhead fixtures were likely to be sucked down into the intakes unless the cars either shut down or drove out shortly.

"Are they going to get this bloody show on the road?" Sergeant Deseau muttered. His faceshield was raised and he wasn't using intercom. Huber wouldn't have understood the words had he not been looking into Deseau's face and watching his lips move.

"Can it!" Huber snapped. "Take care of your own end and keep your mouth shut."

Deseau grimaced agreement and faced front again. They were all nervous. Well, three of them were, at any rate; Learoyd seemed about as calm as he'd been a couple hours before, when he'd been methodically loading spare magazines for his sub-machine gun.

"*Seven Red, this is Green One,*" ordered the detachment commander—an artillery captain who happened to be the senior officer in the temporary unit. If the move had been more serious than the five kilometers between Central Repair and Base Alpha, the detachment would've been under the control of a line officer regardless of rank. "*Pull into place behind Five Blue. Eight Red, follow Seven. Unit, prepare to move out. Green One out.*"

"Tranter, slide in behind the second blower," Huber ordered. "Don't push up their ass, just keep normal interval so it looks like we belong."

Chief Edlinger had put Huber and his men on the list for admission to Central Repair, but that was easily explained if it needed to be. The chief didn't know what Huber planned—just that it wasn't something he *ought* to know more about. The detachment commander didn't know even that: he was in the self-propelled gun at the head of the column. The eight vehicles leaving for Base Alpha included two tanks, four combat cars, the detachment commander's hog, and a repair vehicle with a crane and a powered bed that could lift a combat car. The crews didn't know one another, and nobody would wonder or even notice that a fifth car had joined the procession.

The lead car jerked toward the open door. The driver, inexperienced or jumpy from the long wait, canted his nacelles too suddenly. The bow skirt dipped and scraped a shrieking line of sparks along the concrete floor until the car bounced over the threshold and into the open air.

The second car followed with greater care but the same lack of skill, rising nearly a hand's breadth above the ground. The skirts spilled air in a roar around their whole circuit. The car wallowed; when the driver nudged his controls forward Huber thought for a moment the vehicle was going to slide into the jamb of the sliding door.

"They've got newbie crews," Tranter said scornfully. *"Via, I could do better than that with my eyes closed!"*

"I'll settle for you keeping your eyes open and not attracting attention," Huber said tightly. "Move out, Trooper."

Fencing Master slid gracefully through the doorway and into the warm night. The skirts ticked once on the door track, but that wasn't worth mentioning.

"Let's keep him, El-Tee," Deseau said with a chuckle. *"He's as good as Kolbe was, and a curst sight better than I ever thought of being as a driver."*

"Keep your mind on the present job, didn't I tell you?" Huber snapped. "I don't think any of us need to plan for a future much beyond tonight."

Deseau laughed. Huber supposed that was as good a response as any.

Plattner's World had seen moons, but none of them were big enough to provide useful illumination. The pole lights placed for security when these were warehouses threw bright pools at the front of each building, but that just made the night darker when *Fencing Master* moved between them. Huber locked down his faceshield and switched to light enhancement, though he knew he lost depth perception that way.

The rocket howitzer at the head of the column started to negotiate the gate to the compound, then stopped. The tank immediately following very nearly drove up its stern.

There was something wrong with the response of the hog's drive fans, or at any rate the captain thought there was. He began arguing off-net with Repair's Charge of Quarters, a senior sergeant who replied calmly, *"Sir, you can bring it back and park it in the shop if you like, but I don't have authority to roust a technician at this hour on a non-emergency problem."*

The CQ kept saying the same thing. So did the captain, though he varied the words a bit.

Huber listened for a moment to make sure that what was going on didn't affect him, then switched to intercom. "They'll get it sorted out in a bit," he said to his crew. "The blowers are straight out of the shops and half the crews are newbies. Nothing to worry about."

"Who's worried?" Deseau said. He stretched at his central gun station, then turned and grinned at Huber.

They were all wearing body armor, even Tranter. The bulky ceramic clamshells crowded the fighting compartment even without the personal gear and extra ammo that'd pack the vehicle on a line deployment.

Learoyd could've been a statue placed at the right wing gun. He didn't fidget with the weapon or with the sub-machine gun slung across his chest. Though his body was motionless, his helmet would be scanning the terrain and careting movement onto his lowered faceshield. If one of the highlights was a hostile pointing a weapon in the direction of *Fencing Master*—and anybody pointing a weapon at *Fencing Master* was hostile, in Learoyd's opinion and Huber's as well—his tribarrel would light the night with cyan destruction.

"*Unit, we're moving,*" the captain announced in a disgruntled tone. As he spoke, the hog shifted forward again. Metal rang as the drivers of other vehicles in the column struggled to react to the sudden change from stasis to movement. Skirts were stuttering up and down on the roadway of stabilized earth. *You get lulled into patterns in no time at all.…*

Huber brought up a terrain display in the box welded to the pintle supporting his tribarrel. *Fencing Master* didn't have the sensor and communications suite of a proper command car, but it did have an additional package that allowed the platoon leader to project displays instead of taking all his information through the visor of his commo helmet.

The column got moving in fits and starts; a combat car *did* run into the back of the tank preceding it. Huber's helmet damped the sound, but the whole fabric of *Fencing Master* shivered in sympathy to the impact of a thirty-tonne hammer hitting a hundred-and-seventy-tonne anvil.

"*Via, that'll hold us up for the next three hours!*" Sergeant Deseau snarled. "*We'll be lucky if we get away before bloody dawn!*"

Huber thought the same. Instead the detachment commander just growled, "*Unit, hold your intervals,*" as his vehicle proceeded down the road on the set course.

"*Dumb bastard,*" Deseau muttered. "*Dicked around all that time for nothing, and now he's going to put the hammer down and string the column out to make up the time he lost.*"

That was close enough to Huber's appreciation of what was going on that he didn't bother telling the sergeant to shut up. He grinned beneath his faceshield. Under the circumstances, a lieutenant couldn't claim to have any authority over the enlisted men with him except what they chose to give him freely.

The tank got moving again smoothly; *its* driver at least knew how to handle his massive vehicle. Tanks weren't really clumsy, and given the right terrain and enough time they were hellaciously fast; but the inertia of so many tonnes of metal required the driver to plan her maneuvers a very long way ahead.

The collision hadn't sprung the skirts of the following combat car, so it was able to proceed also. Its driver kept a good hundred and fifty meters between his vehicle's dented bow slope and the tank's stern. The rest of the column trailed the three leaders out of Central Repair and into the nighted city beyond.

Tranter lifted *Fencing Master*'s skirts with a greasy wobble, then set the car sliding forward. They passed the guard blower at the gate and turned left. Huber waved at the trooper in the fighting compartment; he—or she—waved back, more bored than not.

"Tranter, when we make the corner up ahead," Huber ordered, "cut your headlights and running lights. Can you drive using just your visor's enhancement?"

"*Roger,*" the driver said calmly. Behind them the guard vehicle was pulling back across the compound's gateway; ahead, the last of the cars in the detachment proper slid awkwardly around an elbow in the broad freight road leading west and eventually out of Benjamin.

Even here in the center of the administrative capital of the UC, there were more trees than houses. The locals built narrow structures three or four stories high, with parking for aircars either beneath the support pilings or on rooftop landing pads. Most of the windows were dark, but occasionally they lighted as armored vehicles howled slowly by on columns of air.

Even without lights, *Fencing Master* wasn't going to pass unnoticed in Senator Graciano's neighborhood of expensive residences. This'd have to be a quick in and out; or at least a quick in.

Tranter was keeping a rock-solid fifty-meter interval between him and the stern of Red Eight. He seemed to judge what the driver ahead would do well before that fellow acted.

"Start opening the distance, Tranter," Huber said, judging their position on the terrain display against the quivering running lights of Red Eight. "We'll peel off to the right at the intersection half a kay west of our present position. As soon as Red Eight's out of sight, goose it hard. We've got eighteen hundred meters to cover, and I want to be there before they have time to react to the sound of our fans."

"*Roger*," Tranter said. He still didn't sound nervous; maybe he was concentrating on his driving.

And maybe the technician didn't really understand what was about to happen. Well, there were a lot of cases where intellectual understanding fell well short of emotional realities.

Fencing Master slowed almost imperceptibly; the fan note didn't change, but Tranter cocked the nacelles toward the vertical so that their thrust was spent more on lifting the car than driving it forward. Red Eight ahead had gained another fifty meters by the time its lights shifted angle, then glittered randomly through the trees of a grove that the road twisted behind.

"Here we go, Tranter," Huber warned, though the driver obviously had everything under control. "Easy right turn, then get on—"

Fencing Master was already swinging; Tranter dragged the right skirt, not in error but because the direct friction of steel against gravel was hugely more effective at transferring momentum than a fluid coupling of compressed air. As the combat car straightened onto a much narrower street than the route they'd been following from Repair, the headlights of four ten-wheeled trucks flooded over them. An air-cushion jeep pulled out squarely in front of the combat car.

"*Blood and bleeding Martyrs!*" somebody screamed over the intercom, and the voice might've been Huber's own. Tranter lifted *Fencing Master*'s bow, dumping air and dropping the skirts back onto the road. The bang jolted the teeth of everybody aboard and rattled the transoms of nearby houses.

The combat car hopped forward despite the impact. They'd have overrun the jeep sure as sunrise if its driver hadn't been a real pro as well. The lighter vehicle lifted on the gust from *Fencing Master*'s plenum chamber, surfing the bow wave and bouncing down the other side on its own flexible skirts.

A trim figure stood beside the jeep's driver, touching the top of the windscreen for balance but not locked to it in a deathgrip the way most people would've been while riding a bucking jeep upright. The fellow's faceshield was raised; to make himself easy to identify, Huber assumed, but the glittering pistol in his cutaway holster was enough to do that.

"Lock your tribarrels in carry position!" Huber shouted to his men. As he spoke, he slapped the pintle catch with his left hand and rotated the barrels of his heavy automatic weapon skyward. "That's Major Steuben, and we won't get two mistakes!"

Tranter never quite lost control of *Fencing Master*, but it wasn't till the third jounce that he actually brought the car to rest. Each impact blasted a doughnut of dust and grit from the road; Huber's nose filters swung down and saved him from the worst of it, but his eyes watered. The jeep stayed just ahead of them, then curved back when the bigger vehicle halted.

The trucks—they had civilian markings and weren't from the Logistics Section inventory—moved up on either side of the combat car, two and two. They were stake-beds; a dozen troopers lined the back of each, their weapons ready for anybody in *Fencing Master* to make the wrong move.

That wasn't going to happen: Huber and his men were veterans; they knew what was survivable.

"*Bloody fucking hell*," Deseau whispered. He kept his hands in sight and raised at his sides.

"*Get out, all four of you*," Major Steuben ordered through the commo helmets. He sounded amused. "*Leave your guns behind.*"

Huber slung his 2-cm weapon over the raised tribarrel, then unbuckled his equipment belt and hung it on the big gun also. He paused and looked, really *looked*, at the White Mice watching *Fencing Master* and her crew through the sights of their weapons. They wore ordinary Slammers combat gear—helmets, body armor, and uniforms—but the only powergun in the whole platoon was the pistol on Major Steuben's hip. The rest of the unit carried electromagnetic slug-throwers and buzz-bombs.

"Unit," Huber ordered, "let me do the talking."

He raised himself to the edge of the fighting compartment's armor, then swung his legs over in a practiced motion. His boots clanged down on the top of the plenum chamber. Starting with the coaming as a hand-hold, he let himself slide along the curve of the skirts to the ground.

Deseau and Learoyd were dismounting with similar ease, but Tranter—awkward in body armor—was having more difficulty in the bow. The technician also hadn't taken off his holstered pistol; he'd probably forgotten he was wearing it.

Huber opened his mouth to call a warning. Before he could, Steuben said, "*Sergeant Tranter, I'd appreciate it if you'd drop your equipment belt before you step to the ground. It'll save me the trouble of shooting you.*"

He tittered and added, "*Not that it would be a great deal of trouble.*"

Startled, Tranter undid the belt. He wobbled on the hatch coaming, then lost his balance. He and the belt slipped down the bow in opposite directions, though Tranter was able to keep from landing on his face by dabbing a hand to the ground.

Huber stepped briskly toward the jeep, stopping two paces away. He threw what was as close to an Academy salute as he could come after five years in the field.

"Sir!" he said. Steuben stood above him by the height of the jeep's plenum chamber. "The men with me had no idea what was going on. I ordered them to accompany me on a test drive of the repaired vehicle."

"Fuck that," Deseau said, swaggering to Huber's side. "We were going to put paid to the bastards that set us up and got our buddies killed. Somebody in the Regiment's got to show some balls, after all."

He spit into the dust beside him. Deseau had the bravado of a lot of little men; his pride was worth more to him than his life just now.

Joachim Steuben, no taller than Deseau flat-footed, giggled at him.

Learoyd walked up on Deseau's other side. He'd taken his helmet off and was rubbing his scalp. Sergeant Tranter, his eyes wide open and unblinking, joined Learoyd at the end of the rank.

"What did you think was going to happen when a Slammers combat car killed a senior UC official and destroyed his house, Lieutenant?" Steuben asked. The anger in his tone was all the more terrible because his eyes were utterly dispassionate. "Didn't it occur to you that other officials, even those who opposed the victim, would decide that Hammer's Regiment was more dangerous to its employers than it was to the enemy?"

"I'm not a politician, sir," Huber said. He was trembling, not with fear—he was beyond fear—but with hope. "I don't know what would happen afterward."

"Not a politician?" Steuben's voice sneered while his eyes laughed with anticipation. "You were about to carry out a political act, weren't you? You do understand that, don't you?"

"Yes sir, I do understand," Huber said. The four trucks that surrounded *Fencing Master* had turned off their lights, though their diesel engines rattled at idle. The jeep's headlights fell on Huber and his men, then reflected from the combat car's iridium armor; they stood in almost shadowless illumination.

"Is there anything you want to say before I decide what I'm going to do with you, Lieutenant?" Steuben said with a lilt like the curve of a cat's tongue.

"Sir," Huber said. His muscles were trembling and his mind hung outside his body, watching what was going on with detached interest. "I'd like to accompany you and your troops on the operation you've planned. It may not be necessary to discipline me afterward."

"You mean it won't be possible to discipline you if you get your head blown off," the major said. He laughed again with a terrible humor that had nothing human in it. "Yes, that's a point."

"El-Tee?" said Learoyd. "Where are you going? Can I come?"

Huber looked toward the trooper. "They're carrying non-issue weapons, Learoyd," he said. He didn't know if he was explaining to Deseau and Tranter at the same time. "Probably the hardware we captured at Rhodesville. They're going to take out Graciano just like we planned, but they're going to do it in a way that doesn't point straight back at the Regiment."

"I shot off my mouth when I shouldn't've, Major," Deseau said. "I do that a lot. I'm sorry."

Huber blinked. He couldn't have been more surprised if his sergeant had started chanting nursery rhymes.

Deseau cleared his throat and added, "Ah, Major? We carried an EM slugthrower in the car for a while till we ran out of ammo for it. The penetration was handy sometimes. Anyway, we're checked out on hardware like what I see there in the back of your jeep."

"So," Steuben said very softly. "You understand the situation, *gentlemen*, but do you also understand the rules of an operation like this? There will be no prisoners, and there will be no survivors in the target location."

"I understand," Huber said; because he did.

"Works for me," said Deseau. Learoyd knuckled his skull again; he probably didn't realize he'd been asked a question.

"We're going to kill everybody in the senator's house, Learoyd," Huber said, leaning forward to catch the trooper's eyes.

"Right," said Learoyd. He put his helmet back on.

"Caxton," Major Steuben said to his driver, "issue slug-throwers to these three troopers. Sergeant Tranter?"

Tranter stiffened to attention.

"You'll drive the combat car here back to Central Repair," Steuben said. "And forget completely about what's happened tonight."

"Sir!" said Tranter. His eyes were focused into the empty night past Steuben's pistol holster. "I can drive a truck, and I guess you got people here—"

He nodded to the truck beside him, its bed lined with blank-faced troopers.

"—who can drive *Fencing Master*. Sir, I deserve to be in on this!"

Joachim Steuben giggled again. "Deserve?" he said. "The only thing any of us deserve, Sergeant, is to die; which I'm sure we all will before long."

He looked toward the cab of an idling truck and said in a whipcrack voice, "Gieseking, Sergeant Tranter here is going to drive your vehicle. Take the combat car back to Central Repair and wait there for someone to pick you up."

Huber took the weapon Steuben's driver handed him. It was a sub-machine gun, lighter than its powergun equivalent but longer as well. It'd do for the job, though.

And so would Arne Huber.

Major Steuben's jeep led two trucks down the street at the speed of a fast walk. Their lights were out, and sound of their idling engines was slight enough to be lost in the breeze to those sleeping in the houses to either side.

Huber and the men from *Fencing Master* rode in the bed of the first truck; Sergeant Tranter was driving. The only difference between the line troopers and the White

Mice around them was that the latter wore no insignia; Huber, Deseau, and Learoyd had rank and branch buttons on the collars. Everyone's faceshield was down and opaque.

In this wealthy suburb, the individual structures—houses and outbuildings—were of the same tall, narrow design as those of lesser districts, but these were grouped within compounds. Road transport in Benjamin was almost completely limited to delivery vehicles, so the two-meter walls were for privacy rather than protection. Most were wooden, but the one surrounding the residence of Patroklos Graciano was brick on a stone foundation like the main house.

Huber muttered a command to the AI in his helmet, cueing the situation map in a fifty percent overlay. He could still see—or aim—through the faceshield on which terrain features and icons of the forty-six men in the combat team were projected.

The other two trucks had gone around to the back street—not really parallel, the way things were laid out in Benjamin, but still a route that permitted those squads to approach the compound from the rear. They were already in position, waiting for anybody who tried to escape in that direction. The squads in front would carry out the assault by themselves unless something went badly wrong.

Few lights were on in the houses the trucks crawled past; the Graciano compound was an exception. The whole fourth floor of the main building was bright, and the separate structure where the servants lived had many lighted windows as well.

The gate to the Graciano compound was of steel or wrought iron, three meters high and wide enough to pass even trucks the size of those carrying the assault force if the leaves were open. As they very shortly would be…

An alert flashed red at the upper right-hand corner of Huber's visor; the truck braked to a gentle halt. The light went green.

Huber and all but three of the troopers ducked, leaning the tops of their helmets against the side of the truck. The three still standing launched buzzbombs with snarling roars that ended with white flashes. The hollow *bang*s would've been deafening were it not for the helmets' damping. Gusts of hot exhaust buffeted the kneeling men, but they were out of the direct backblast. The second truck loosed a similar volley.

Two missiles hit the gate pillars, shattering them into clouds of mortar and pulverized brick. The leaves dangled crazily, their weight barely supported by the lowest of the three sets of hinges on either side. Tranter cramped his steering wheel and accelerated as hard as the truck's big diesel would allow.

The rest of the buzzbombs had gone through lighted windows of both structures and exploded within. The servants' quarters were wood. A gush of red flames followed the initial blast at the ground floor, a sign that the fuel for the oven in the kitchen had ignited.

Tranter hit the leaning gates and smashed them down. He roared into the courtyard, knocking over a fountain on the way, and pulled up screeching in front of the ornamental porch.

The truck's tailgate was already open. Huber was the first man out, leaping to the gravel with Deseau beside him and Learoyd following with the first of the squad of

White Mice. The ground glittered with shards of glass blown from all the windows.

A buzzbomb had hit the front door; the missile must've been fired moments after the initial volley or the gate would've been in the way. The doorpanel was wood veneer over a steel core, but a shaped-charge warhead designed to punch through a tank's turret had blown it off its hinges.

Scores of fires burned in the entrance hall. White-hot metal had sprayed the big room, overwhelming the retardant which impregnated the paneling. Huber's nose filters flipped into place as he ran for the staircase; his faceshield was already on infrared, displaying his surroundings in false color. If fire raised the background temperature too high for infrared to discriminate properly, he'd switch to sonic imaging—but he wasn't coming out till he'd completed his mission.…

There were two bodies in the hall. Parts of two bodies, at any rate; the bigger chunks of door armor had spun through them like buzzsaws. They were wearing uniforms of some sort; guards, Huber assumed. One of them had a slugthrower but the other's severed right arm still gripped a 2-cm powergun.

The stairs curved from both sides of the entrance to a railed mezzanine at the top. Huber's visor careted movement as he started up. Before he could swing his sub-machine gun onto the target, a trooper behind him with a better angle shredded it and several balustrades with a short burst.

The staircase was for show; the owner and guests used the elevator running in a filigree shaft in the center of the dwelling. It started down from the top floor when Huber reached the mezzanine, which was appointed for formal entertainments. He couldn't see anything but the solid bottom of the cage. He put a burst into it, chewing the embossed design, but he didn't think his sub-machine gun's light pellets were penetrating.

One of the White Mice standing at the outside door put seven slugs from his heavy shoulder weapon through the cage the long way. One of them hit the drive motor and ricocheted, flinging parts up through the floor at an angle complementary to that of the projectile. The elevator stopped; a woman's arm flopped out of the metal lacework.

Huber jerked open the door to the narrow stairwell leading upward from the mezzanine. A pudgy servant in garishly patterned pajamas almost ran into him. Huber shot the fellow through the body and shoved him out of the way. The servant continued screaming for the moment until Deseau, a step behind his lieutenant, ripped a burst through the dying man's head.

Huber ran up the stairs, feeling the weight and constriction of his body armor and also the filters that kept him from breathing freely. Platoon leaders in the combat car companies didn't spend a lot of time climbing stairwells in the normal course of their business, but he'd asked for the job.

The door to the third floor was closed. Huber ignored it as he rounded the landing and started up the last flight. Teams of White Mice would clear the lower floors and the basement; the men from F-3 were tasked with the senator's suite at the top of the building.

The door at the stairhead was ajar. Huber fired through the gap while he was still below the level of the floor. As he'd expected, that drew a pistol shot—from a powergun—though it hit the inside of the panel instead of slapping the stairwell.

"Learoyd!" Huber shouted. He crouched, swapping his sub-machine gun's magazine for a full one from his bandolier. Deseau would cover him if somebody burst out of the door. "Gren—"

Before he finished the word, Learoyd spun a bomb the size of a walnut up through the narrow opening. Huber had seen the trooper knock birds off limbs ten meters high; this was no test at all for him.

The grenade blew the door shut with a bright flash that to the naked eye would've been blue. The bomb's capacitors dumped their charge through an osmium wire. Electrical grenades had very little fragmentation effect, but their sudden energy release was both physically and mentally shattering for anybody close to the blast. Huber rose to his feet, leaped the final steps to the landing, and kicked the door open again. He went in shooting.

For the first instant he didn't have a target, just the need to disconcert anybody who hadn't lost his nerve when the grenade went off. The carpet of the sitting room beyond was on fire. A man lay in the middle of it, screaming and beating the floor with the butt of his pistol. Huber's burst stitched him from the middle of one shoulderblade to the other. The man flopped like a fish on dry land, then shuddered silent.

There was a doorway ahead of Huber and another to the right, toward the back of the building. Huber went straight, into a small foyer around the elevator shaft. The top of the cage remained just above floor level.

Huber jerked open the door across the foyer. The room beyond was a mass of flame. It'd been a bedroom, and the buzzbomb had ignited all the fabric. Huber slammed the door again. His hands were singed; and only his faceshield had saved his eyes and lungs from the fire's shriveling touch.

At the back of the foyer was a window onto the grounds; concussion from the warhead going off in the bedroom had blown out the casement an instant before it slammed the connecting door. Through the empty window, Huber heard the lift fans of an aircar spin up.

He jumped to the opening. To his right a closed car with polarized windows sat on a pad cantilevered off the back of the building, trembling as its driver built up speed in the fan blades. It was a large vehicle, capable of carrying six in comfort. The front passenger door was open and a uniformed man leaned out of it, firing a heavy slugthrower back toward the sitting room. The aluminum skirts that propelled the osmium projectiles vaporized in the dense magnetic flux, blazing as white muzzle flashes in Huber's thermal vision.

Huber aimed between the hinge side of the car door and the jamb, then shot the guard in the neck and head. The fellow sprang forward like a headless chicken, flinging his gun away with nerveless hands.

The aircar lifted, the door swinging closed from momentum. Huber fired, starring the windscreen but not penetrating it. Deseau and Learoyd were in the doorway now, pocking the car's thick plastic side-panels; their sub-machine guns couldn't do real damage.

The car half-pivoted as its driver prepared to dive off the edge of the platform and use gravity to speed his escape. A buzzbomb detonated on the underside of the bow, flipping the vehicle over onto its back. The instant the warhead hit, Huber saw a spear of molten metal stab through the car's roof in a white dazzle. The driver would've been in direct line with the explosion-formed hypersonic jet.

The blast rocked Huber away from the window, but the car had taken the direct impact and the building had protected him from the worst of the remainder. Deseau and Learoyd, running toward the vehicle when the warhead went off, bounced into the wall behind them and now lay sprawled on the deck. Learoyd had managed to hang onto his sub-machine gun; Deseau patted the tiles numbly, trying to find his again.

A man crawled out of the overturned car. The right side of his face was bloody, but Huber recognized Senator Patroklos Graciano.

The senator stood with a look of desperation on his face. Huber braced his left elbow on the window opening and laid his ring sight at the base of Graciano's throat. He fired a short burst, flinging the man backward. Tufts of beard trimmed by the pellets swirled in the air, falling more slowly than the corpse.

There were figures still moving in the car. A stunningly beautiful woman tried to squirm out, hampered by the necklaces and jewel-glittering rings she clutched to her breasts with both hands. She wore a diaphanous shift that accentuated rather than hid her body, but on her a gunnysack would've been provocative.

Huber aimed. She looked up at him, her elbows on the chest of her lover so freshly dead that his corpse still shuddered. A powergun bolt blew out her left eyesocket and lifted the top of her skull. Her arms straightened convulsively, scattering the jewelry across the landing platform.

Major Steuben stood in the doorway from the sitting room, his pistol in his delicate right hand. His faceshield was raised and he was smiling.

The girl still in the car was probably a maid. She opened her mouth to scream when she saw her mistress die. The second pistol bolt snapped between her perfect teeth and nearly decapitated her. Her body thrashed wildly in the passenger compartment.

Learoyd was getting to his feet. Steuben grabbed the collar of Deseau's clamshell armor and jerked the sergeant upright; the major must have muscles like steel cables under his trim exterior. The muzzle of the powergun in his other hand was a white-hot circle.

He turned toward Huber, looking out of the adjacent window, and shouted, "Come along, Lieutenant. We've taken care of our little problem and it's time to leave now."

Huber met them in the sitting room. Steuben waved him toward the stairwell. Sergeant Deseau still walked like a drunk, so Huber grabbed his arm in a fireman's carry and half-lifted, half-dragged the man to the trucks. Every floor of the building was burning. The major was the last man out.

In all the cacophony—the screams and the blasts and the weeping desperation—

that Arne Huber had heard in the past few minutes, there was only one sound that would haunt his future nightmares. That was Joachim Steuben's laughter as he blew a girl's head off.

If I buy the farm here on Plattner's World, Huber thought as he walked toward the open door of Major Steuben's office, *they're going to have to name this the Lieutenant Arne C. Huber Memorial Hallway.*

There's never a bad time for humor in a war zone. This was a better time than most.

"Come in and close the door, Lieutenant," Steuben said as Huber raised his hand to knock on the jamb. "And *don't,* if you please, attempt to salute me ever again. You're not very good at it."

Huber obeyed meekly. The major was working behind a live display, entering data on the touchpad lying on his wooden desk. It wasn't a game this time: Steuben was finishing a task before he got on to the business who'd just walked in his door.

He shut down the display and met Huber's eyes. He smiled; Huber didn't try to smile back.

"This will be brief, Lieutenant," Steuben said. "The United Cities are in a state of war with Solace, or will be when the Senate meets in a few hours. There's been a second attack within UC territory by mercenaries in Solace pay. This one was directed against Senator Patroklos Graciano here in Benjamin."

Steuben quirked a smile. "It was quite a horrific scene, according to reports of the event," he went on. "Graciano and his whole household were killed."

Huber looked at the man across the desk, remembering the same smile lighted by the flash of a powergun. "If I may ask, sir?" he said. "Why did the, ah, mercenaries attack that particular senator?"

"It's believed that the Solace authorities had made an attempt to turn the poor fellow against his own people," the major said blandly. "Graciano had gathered a great deal of information about Solace plans and was about to make a full report to the Senate. The attack forestalled him, but as a result of such blatant aggression even the former peace party in the Senate is unanimous in supporting military action against Solace."

I wonder how many of the senators believe the official story, Huber thought, *and how many are afraid they'll go the same way as Patroklos Graciano if they continue to get in the way of the Regiment's contract?*

Well, it didn't really matter. Like he'd told Major Steuben last night, he wasn't a politician. Aloud he said, "I see, sir."

"None of that matters to you, of course," Steuben continued. "I called you here to say that a review of your actions at Rhodesville the day you landed has determined that you behaved properly and in accordance with the best traditions of the Regiment."

He giggled. "You may even get a medal out of it, Lieutenant."

Huber's mouth was dry; for a moment he didn't trust himself to speak. Then he said, "Ah, sir? Does this mean that I'm being returned to my platoon?"

Steuben looked up at Huber. He smiled. "Well, Lieutenant," he said, "that's the reason I called you here in person instead of just informing you of the investigation outcome through channels. How would you like a transfer to A Company? You'd stay at the same rank, but you probably know already that the pay in A Company is better than the same grade levels in line units."

"A Company?" Huber repeated. He couldn't have heard right. "The White Mice, you mean?"

"Yes, Lieutenant," Steuben said. His face didn't change in a definable way, but his smile was suddenly very hard. "The White Mice. The company under my personal command."

"I don't…" Huber said, then realized that among the things he didn't know was how to end the sentence he'd begun. He let his voice trail off.

"Recent events have demonstrated that you're smart and that you're willing to use your initiative," the major said. His fingers were tented before him, but his wrists didn't quite rest on the touchpad beneath them.

The smile became amused again. He added, "Also, you can handle a gun. You'll have ample opportunity to exercise all these abilities in A Company, I assure you."

"Sir…" said Huber's lips. He was watching from outside himself again. "I don't think I have enough…"

This time he stopped, not because he didn't know how to finish the sentence but because he thought of Steuben's hell-lit smile the night before. The words choked in his throat.

"Ruthlessness, you were perhaps going to say, Lieutenant?" the major said with his cat's-tongue lilt. "Oh, I think you'll do. I'm a good judge of that sort of thing, you know."

He giggled again. "You're dismissed for now," Steuben said. "Go back to Logistics—you'll have to break in your replacement no matter what you decide. But rest assured, you'll be hearing from me again."

Arne Huber's soul watched his body walking back down the hallway. Even his mind was numb, and despite the closed door behind him he continued to hear laughter.

THE POLITICAL PROCESS

The air above *Fencing Master* sizzled just beyond the visual range; some of the farm's defenders were using lasers that operated in the low-ultraviolet. Lieutenant Arne Huber sighted his tribarrel through his visor's thirty percent mask of the battlefield terrain and the units engaged. He swung the muzzles forward to aim past Sergeant Deseau's left elbow and gunshield.

If Huber fired at the present angle, the powerful 2-cm bolts would singe Deseau's sleeve and his neck below the flare of his commo helmet. He wouldn't do that unless the risk to his sergeant was worth it—though worse things had happened to Deseau during his fifteen years in Hammer's Slammers.

"Fox Three-one," Huber said; his helmet's artificial intelligence cued *Foghorn*, another of the four combat cars in platoon F-3. "Ready to go? Fox Six over."

A rocket gun from somewhere in the Solace defenses fired three times, its coughing ignition followed an instant later by the *snap-p-p!* of the multiple projectiles going supersonic. At least one of the heavy-metal slugs punched more than a hole in the air: the *clang* against armor would have been audible kilometers away. No way to tell who'd been hit or how badly; and no time to worry about it now anyway.

"*Roger, Six, we're ready!*" cried Sergeant Nagano, *Foghorn*'s commander. He didn't sound scared, but his voice was an octave higher than usual with excitement. "*Three-one out!*"

Huber figured Nagano had a right to be excited. Via, he had a right to be scared.

"Costunna, pull forward," Huber ordered his own driver, a newbie who'd replaced the man whom a buzzbomb had decapitated. "Three-one, rush 'em!"

The Northern Star Farm was a network of cornfields crisscrossed by concrete-lined irrigation canals. In the center were more than twenty single-story buildings: barns, equipment sheds, and barracks for the work force. The layout was typical of the large agricultural complexes with which the nation of Solace produced food not only for her own citizens but for all the residents of Plattner's World—when Solace wasn't at war with the Outer States, at any rate.

Technically, only the United Cities were at war with Solace at the moment. Everybody knew that the other five Outer States were helping fund the cost of hiring Hammer's Regiment, but Solace couldn't afford not to look the other way.

The civilians had fled, driving off in wagons pulled by the farm's tractors. The buildings and canals remained as a strongpoint where a battalion of Solace Militia and a company of off-planet mercenaries defended howitzers with the range to loft shells deep into the UC. Colonel Hammer had sent Task Force Sangrela, one platoon each of tanks, combat cars, and infantry, to eliminate the problem.

Fencing Master began to vibrate as Costunna brought up the speed of the eight powerful fans which pressurized the plenum chamber and lifted the combat car for frictionless passage over the ground. The thirty-tonne vehicle didn't slide forward, however. "Go, Costunna!" Huber screamed. "Go! Go! G—"

Finally *Fencing Master* pulled up from the swale in which she'd sheltered during her approach to the target. Huber's helmet careted movement all along the canal slanting across their front at thirty degrees to their course: Solace Militiamen rising to fire at *Foghorn*, which was already in plain sight.

If the two cars had broken cover together as Huber planned, *Foghorn* wouldn't have looked like the lone target in a shooting gallery. Swearing desperately, he hosed the lip of the canal with his tribarrel. Deseau, Learoyd at *Fencing Master*'s right wing gun, and *Foghorn*'s three gunners fired also, but the other car sparkled like a short circuit as slugs struck her iridium armor.

In Huber's holographic sight picture, dark-uniformed Militiamen turned with horrified looks as they tried to shift the heavy rocket guns they wore harnessed to their shoulders. They'd been so focused on *Foghorn* that the appearance of another combat car two hundred meters away took them completely by surprise.

Fencing Master's forward motion and the angle of the canal helped Huber traverse the target simply by holding his thumbs on the tribarrel's trigger. The two-centimeter weapon's barrel cluster rotated as it sent copper ions blasting at the speed of light down each iridium bore in turn. The bolts burned metal, shattered concrete in flares of glass and white-hot quicklime, and blew humans apart in gushes of steam. An arm spun thirty meters into the air, trailing smoke from its burning sleeve.

One of the D Company tanks on overwatch to the west fired its main gun twice, not toward the canal but into the interior of the farm where anti-armor weapons were showing themselves to engage the combat cars. An orange flash blew out the sidewalls of a barn; three seconds later, the shock of that enormous secondary explosion made water dance in the irrigation canals.

The surviving Militiamen ducked to cover. *Foghorn* had stalled for a moment, but she was bucking forward again now. Huber cleared the terrain mask from his faceshield to let his eyes and the helmet AI concentrate on nearby motion, his potential targets. He didn't worry about the heavier weapons that might be locking in on *Fencing Master* from long range; that was the business of the tanks—and of the Gods, if you believed in them, which right at the moment Huber couldn't even pretend to do.

A slug penetrated the plenum chamber on the right side of the bow, struck a nacelle inside—the fan howled momentarily, then died; blue sparks sprayed from a portside intake duct and the hair on Huber's arm stood up—and punched out from the left rear in a flash of burning steel. Costunna screamed, "*Port three's out!*"

The air was sharp with ozone. Huber's nose filters kept the ions from searing his lungs, but the skin of his throat and wrists prickled.

"Drive on!" Huber shouted.

You didn't have to believe in Gods to believe in Hell.

Instead of a square grid, Northern Star's canal system formed a honeycomb of hexagons three hundred meters across each flat. *Fencing Master* slid to where three canals joined and halted as planned. Costunna had adequate mechanical skills and took orders well enough, he just seemed to lack an instinct for what was important. Huber had a straight view down the length of the shallow trough slanting north-northeast from his side. Solace Militiamen—some of them dead, some of them hunching in terror; a few raising weapons to confront the howling monster that had driven down on them—were dark blurs against the white concrete and the trickle of sunbright water.

Huber fired, his bolts shredding targets and glancing from the canal walls in white gouts. Deseau was firing also, and from *Fencing Master*'s starboard wing Learoyd ripped the canal intersecting at a southeastern angle. *Foghorn*'s left gun was raking that canal in the opposite direction.

It was dangerous having two cars firing pretty much toward one another—if either of the gunners raised his muzzles too far, he'd blow divots out of the friendly vehicle—but this was a battle. If safety'd been the Slammers' first concern, they'd all have stayed in bed this morning.

A bullet from the central complex ricocheted off *Fencing Master*'s bow slope, denting the armor and impact-heating it to a shimmering rainbow. Further rounds clipped cornstalks and spewed up little geysers of black dirt.

Sergeant Deseau shouted a curse and grabbed his right wrist momentarily, but he had his hands back on the tribarrel's spade grips before Huber could ask if he was all right. The slug that hit the bow had probably sprayed him with bits of white-hot iridium; nothing serious.

The two automatic mortars accompanying the infantry chugged a salvo of white phosphorus from the swale where *Fencing Master* had waited among the knee-high corn. The Willy Pete lifted in ragged mushrooms above the courtyard building where the farm's workforce ate and gathered for social events.

The roofs slanted down toward the interior; Militiamen with automatic weapons had been using the inner slopes as firing positions. The shellbursts trailed tendrils up, then downward. From a distance they had a glowing white beauty, but Huber knew what a rain of blazing phosphorous did where it landed. Bits continued burning all the way through a human body unless somebody picked them out of the flesh one at a time.

Solace troops leaped to their feet, desperate to escape the shower of death. The other two-car section of Huber's platoon, *Floosie* and *Flame Farter* under Platoon Sergeant Jellicoe, were waiting to the south of the complex for those targets to appear. Their tribarrels lashed the Militiamen, killing most and completely breaking the survivors' will to resist.

"Costunna, get us across the canal!" Huber ordered. He didn't feel the instant response he'd expected—the driver should've been tense on his throttles, ready to angle the car down this side of the channel and up the other with his fans on emergency power—so he added in a snarl, "Move it, man! Move it *now!*"

The tanks were firing methodically, punching holes in the sides of buildings with each 20-cm bolt from their main guns. Walls blew up and inward at every cyan impact, leaving openings more than a meter in diameter. The tanks weren't trying to destroy the structures—a pile of broken concrete made a better nest for enemy snipers than a standing building—but they were providing entrances for infantry assault.

The infantry, twenty-seven troopers under Captain Sangrela himself—the task force commander wasn't going to hang back when his own people were at the sharp end—were belly-down on their one-man skimmers, making the final rush toward the complex from the south. A heavy laser lifted above the wall of a cow byre to the southeast and started to track them. Two D Company tanks on overwatch had been waiting for it. The laser vanished in a cyan crossfire before it could rake the infantry line.

Costunna shoved his control yoke forward. *Fencing Master* scraped and sparked her skirts over the lip of the canal, then down into the watercourse, spraying water in a fog to either side. Instead of building speed and quickly angling up the opposite wall, the driver continued to roar along the main channel.

"Costunna!" Huber screamed. He leaned forward, trying to see the man, but the driver's hatch was closed. "Via, man! Cut right! Get us up out of here!"

Foghorn was stalled, unable to climb up from the canal. Her fans and skirts had taken a serious hammering while she advanced alone toward the Solace position. *Fencing Master* was nowhere near that badly damaged, but Costunna seemed unwilling or emotionally unable to turn back toward the guns that'd targeted him before.

And until he did, neither of the cars in Huber's section could support the infantry at the moment they needed it most. The tribarrels were unable to shoot through the haze surrounding *Fencing Master;* the water droplets would absorb the bolts as surely as a brick wall or a meter of armor plate could do.

Captain Sangrela was bellowing furious orders over the command channel, but Huber didn't need to be told there was a problem. He opened his mouth to shout at Costunna again because he couldn't think of anything else to do. Before he got the words out, Deseau snarled over the intercom, "*Costunna, get us the fuck outa this ditch or I'll stick my gun up your ass before I pull the trigger!*"

Maybe it was the threat, maybe it was realizing that the car's bumping was its skirts hitting the bodies of Militiamen before smearing them into the concrete. Whatever the reason, Costunna twisted his yoke convulsively. *Fencing Master* lurched from the canal, her plenum chamber shrieking over the concrete coping.

Three white flares burst over the central complex, a signal that the surviving mercenaries wanted to surrender. They were probably broadcasting on one of the general-purpose frequencies as well, but you couldn't trust radio in a battle. Powerguns and drive fans both kicked out seas of RF trash, so even commands could be lost or distorted in the middle of a battle. A moment after the flares went up, four soldiers in mottled battledress came out of a smoldering barn with their hands in the air.

"Fox Three elements cease fire!" Huber ordered. He didn't raise the muzzles of his tribarrel, but he took his hands off the grips. If some trooper got trigger happy now with those easy targets, it'd be the difference between peaceful surrender and a last-ditch defense that meant a lot more Slammers' casualties before it was over. "Stop shooting *now!* Three-six out."

Captain Sangrela was shouting much the same thing over the common task force push also, and Huber figured Lieutenant Mitzi Trogon echoed the words to her four D Company tanks. A powergun snapped a single shot into the bright sky: an infantryman trying to put his weapon on safe while he steered his tiny skimmer had managed to shoot instead.

No serious harm done: the rest of the mercenary company emerged from dug-outs and the concrete buildings. They'd been armed with crew-served lasers, bulky weapons but effective even against tanks when they were close enough. Rather than bull straight in, Captain Sangrela had used F-3's combat cars to draw the lasers into sight where the tanks could vaporize them from a safe three kilometers away. Arne Huber understood the logic and he trusted the skill of Mitzi's gunners about as far as he trusted anybody, but he'd known who was going to catch it if something went wrong.

"Costunna, pull around to the tramhead," he ordered, frowning. The main thing that'd gone wrong this time had been with *Fencing Master*'s driver, and that was Arne Huber's responsibility.

Most of the single continent of Plattner's World was accessible only by aircar or dirigible. The trees covering the coastal lowlands were parasitized by "Moss," a fungus which in turn was the source of an anti-aging drug. The forests were therefore more valuable than almost anything that would have replaced them on other planets, highways and railroads included.

The exception was Solace, the state comprising the central highlands. There the soil supported Terran grains and produce, but native trees which grew in the drier climate were stunted and free of the Moss. Solace had become the granary of Plattner's World, and its bedrock supported the only starport on the planet which could accept the largest interstellar freighters.

A network of monorail tramways connected Solace's collective farms with Bezant, the capital, from which giant dirigibles distributed food and manufactured goods to the Outer States. They brought back Moss, *Pseudofistus thalopsis*, which factories on Solace turned into Thalderol base and shipped off-planet for final processing.

In theory one might have thought that the huge profits from Thalderol meant that the inhabitants of Plattner's World lived with one another in wealthy harmony. Mercenary soldiers, even Academy-trained officers like Arne Huber, learned about human nature in a practical school: the riches of Plattner's World just meant people could hire better talent to fight for them. When Solace raised port dues by five percent and the buyers refused to pay more for Thalderol base, the Outer States had hired Hammer's Slammers to reverse the increase.

"Fox Three-six, this is Charlie Six!" Captain Sangrela called abruptly. *"The mercs have surrendered but the locals are planning to break out to the north in their aircars. Cut 'em off, will you? I don't want a massacre, but I'm curst if I want to fight 'em again either! Six out."*

Sangrela was obviously using signals intelligence; it was probably forwarded to him as task force commander by Central, Slammers headquarters at Base Alpha far to the rear. The locals didn't understand what they were up against, of course. The tanks on high ground to the south could track and vaporize even fast-moving aircars at a greater distance than the eye could see: there was no escape from a battlefield they overwatched.

But a volley of 20-cm bolts wasn't a threat, it was a massacre just as Sangrela had said. The Slammers took prisoners wherever possible: that encouraged their opponents to do the same. Needlessly converting several hundred locals into steam and carbonized bone, on the other hand, was likely to have a bad result the next time a trooper got in over his head and wanted to surrender.

"Cancel that, Costunna!" Huber said, setting his faceshield left-handed to caret the electromagnetic signatures of aircar fans revving up. Two equipment sheds on the north side of the complex became a forest of red highlights as the AI obeyed. If they were as full of vehicles as the carets implied, there was a score of large aircars in each. "Get us around north of the buildings—but stay away from the canal, right?

Goose it!"

The sheds were aligned east-west and had overhead doors the length of both long sides. As Huber spoke, all twelve of the north-side doors began to rise.

"Guns!" Huber shouted over the intercom to the men with him in the fighting compartment. "Aim low, don't kill anybody you don't have to! Costunna, get *on* it!"

Fencing Master finally started to accelerate. The car was five hundred meters from the west sidewall of the nearer shed, almost twice that from the far end of the other one. The tribarrels were effective at many times that distance, but it was beyond the range at which you could expect delicate shooting from a moving vehicle. It'd be what it'd be.

An aircar with room for twenty soldiers or two tonnes of cargo nosed out of the nearer shed. Huber laid his holographic sights on it, letting the aircar's forward motion pull it through his rope of vividly cyan bolts. The plastic quarterpanel exploded in a red fireball, flipping the car onto its right side in the path of the identical vehicle pulling out of the adjacent bay. They collided, and the second car also overturned.

A third truck started from the near end of the shed and pitched nose-high as the driver tried to vault the line of powergun bolts. He didn't have enough speed. The bow slammed back into the ground, breaking the vehicle's frame and hurling passengers twenty meters from the wreck.

If Costunna had known his job better, he'd have slewed *Fencing Master* so that her bow pointed thirty degrees to starboard of her axis of movement. Because he didn't—*and Via! Sure, he was a newbie but didn't he know* any *cursed thing?*—Huber stopped firing when Sergant Deseau's gunshield masked his point of aim.

Deseau and Learoyd didn't need help anyway. The gunners punched three-round bursts into each truck that showed its bow past the side of the sheds. Though the bolts couldn't penetrate even an aircar's light body, the energy they liberated vaporized the sheathing in blasts with the impact of falling anvils, slamming the targets in the opposite direction. Aircars skidded, bounced, and overturned. None of them got properly airborne.

Huber swung his tribarrel onto the canal half a klick to the north, intending to cover the troops who'd been using it as a trench like their fellows in the stretch Huber's section had overrun. None of them showed themselves, let alone fired at *Fencing Master*.

A pair of gleaming troughs reaching from the south to just short of the canal's inner lip indicated why: while Huber concentrated on the equipment sheds, two D Company tanks had warned the hidden Militiamen of what'd happen to them if they continued to make a fight of it. The main-gun bolts had converted all the silica in the ground they struck to molten glass, spraying it over those huddled in the canal. The flashes and concussion must have been enormous, but Huber hadn't been aware of it while it was happening.

Huber glanced to his right, past the two gunners hunched over their tribarrels. The crown of red markers on his faceshield collapsed as he looked. The surviving vehicles were shutting down; the only fan motors still racing were in the wrecks whose drivers weren't able to obey the order to switch off.

Deseau fired into the bow of a motionless truck, visible now because *Fencing Master* was crossing the front of the nearer shed. The molded plastic flared red, blooming into a meters-wide bubble that hung shimmering for several seconds in front of the building.

"Guns, cease fire!" Huber ordered. "They're surrendering, boys. Cease fire!"

Via! He hoped he was right because there was the Lord's own plenty of locals, coming out of the equipment sheds and rising from the canals on the other side of *Fencing Master.* The troops in the sheds must've been the crews for the howitzers dug into pits in the center of the complex. There the guns were safe from the sniping tanks, but they hadn't been able to threaten the assault force with direct fire either. The commander must have pulled the crews under cover, knowing the artillerymen would've been no better than targets if he'd tried to use them as infantry against the oncoming mercenaries.

The nearest friendly unit was *Foghorn,* just managing to work out of the channel where she'd been stuck. Maybe some of Captain Sangrela's troopers were still advancing from the south, but Huber guessed most of those figured to let *Fencing Master* learn what the locals intended before putting themselves in the middle of things. Huber couldn't say he blamed them.

Costunna slowed the car, then brought it to a halt with the fans idling. Huber'd been about to order him to do that, but the driver shouldn't have made the decision on his own. Well, Costunna was business for another time—though the time was going to come pretty cursed soon.

A middle-aged man limped toward *Fencing Master* with his helmet in his left hand. He looked haggard, and the left side of his face and shoulder were covered with soot. A younger man hovered at his side. The glowing muzzles of Learoyd's tribarrel terrified the aide, but the older officer didn't appear to notice the gun aimed point blank at them.

"I am Colonel Apollonio Priamedes," he said. His voice was raw with emotion and the mix of ozone and combustion products that fouled the atmosphere; the Solace Militia didn't have nose filters or gas masks that Huber could see. "I was in command here. I have ordered my men to lay down their weapons and surrender. May I expect that we will be treated honorably as prisoners of war?"

Huber raised his faceshield. His fingers were claws, cramping from their grip on his tribarrel.

"Yes sir," Huber said, "you sure can."

And the Solace colonel couldn't possibly be more relieved by the end of this business than Lieutenant Arne Huber was.

When the resupply and maintenance convoy radioed, they'd estimated they were still fifteen minutes out from Northern Star. If they'd get on the stick they could cut their arrival time by two-thirds. Huber supposed the commander was afraid stragglers from the garrison would ambush his mostly soft-skinned vehicles. That was a reasonable concern—*if* you hadn't seen how completely the assault had broken the Solace Militiamen.

When the convoy arrived Task Force Sangrela could stand down and let the new-comers take care of security, but right now everybody was on alert. The eight combat vehicles were just west of the building complex, laagered bows-outward so that their weapons threatened all points of the compass. The jeep-mounted mortars were dug in at the center. Two infantry squads were in pits between the vehicles, while the remainder of the platoon was spread in fire teams around the two relatively undam-aged buildings into which the prisoners had been herded.

Sangrela had ordered each car to send a man to help guard the prisoners. Normally Huber would've complained—F-3 had carried out the assault pretty much by itself, after all—but he was just as glad for an excuse to send Costunna off. Learoyd was in the driver's compartment now with the fans on idle. The squat, balding trooper wasn't the Regiment's best driver, but you never had to worry about his instincts in a firefight.

Nights here on the edge of the highlands were clearer than under the hazy atmo-sphere of the United Cities. Arne Huber could see the stars for the first time since he'd landed on Plattner's World.

They made him feel more lonely, of course. The one thing that hadn't changed during Huber's childhood on Nieuw Friesland was the general pattern of the night sky. Since he'd joined the Slammers, he couldn't even count on that.

He smiled wryly. "El-Tee?" Sergeant Deseau said, catching the expression.

"Change is growth, Frenchie," Huber said. "Have you ever been told that?"

"Not so's I recall," the sergeant said, rubbing the side of his neck with his knuckles. "Think they're going to leave us here to garrison the place?"

The slug that splashed the bow slope had peppered Deseau between the bottom of his faceshield and the top of his clamshell body armor. He knew that a slightly bigger chunk might have ripped his throat out, just as he knew that he was going to be sweating in the plenum chamber tomorrow, when he helped Maintenance replace the fan that'd been shot away. Both facts were part of the job.

Huber could hear the convoy now over *Fencing Master*'s humming nacelles. The incoming vehicles, mostly air-cushion trucks but with a section of combat cars for escort, kept their fans spinning at high speed in case they had to move fast.

"*Charlie Six to all units,*" said a tense voice on the common task force channel. "*Eleven vehicles, I repeat one-one vehicles, entering the perimeter at vector one-seven-zero. They will show—*"

A pause during which the signals officer waited for Captain Sangrela's last-instant decision.

"*—blue. Charlie Six out.*"

As he spoke, the darkness to the southeast of the laager lit with quivering azure spikes: static discharges from the antennas of the incoming convoy. Huber didn't bother to count them: there'd be eleven. Electronic identification was foolproof or almost foolproof; but soldiers were humans, not machines, and they liked to have confirmation from their own eyes as well as from a readout.

Captain Sangrela walked forward, holding a blue marker wand in his left hand. The troops between the armored vehicles rose and moved to the center of the laager where they wouldn't be driven over. The newcomers would be parking between the vehicles of Task Force Sangrela.

If the units spent the night in two separate laagers they risked a mutual firefight, especially if the enemy was smart enough to slip into the gap and shoot toward both camps in turn. The Solace Militia probably didn't have that standard of skill, but some of mercenaries Solace had hired certainly did. Soldiers, even the Slammers, could get killed easily enough without taking needless chances.

The convoy came in, lighted only by its static discharges. Huber could've switched his faceshield to thermal imaging or light-amplification if he'd wanted to see clearly—that's how the drivers were maneuvering their big vehicles into place—but he was afraid he'd drop into a reverie if he surrounded himself with an electronic cocoon. He still felt numb from reaction to the assault.

"El-Tee, that combat car's from A Company," Deseau said, one hand resting idly on the grip of his tribarrel. He was using helmet intercom because the howls of incoming vehicles would've overwhelmed his voice even if he'd shouted at the top of his lungs. *"So's the infantry riding on the back of them wrenchmobiles. When did the White Mice start pulling convoy security?"*

Huber's mind kept playing back the moment *Fencing Master* had lurched into position above the canal so he could rake it with his tribarrel. In his memory there was only equipment and empty uniforms in the sun-struck channel. No men at all…

"You've got me, Frenchie," Huber said. He should've noticed that himself.

A Company—the White Mice, though Huber didn't know where the name came from—was the Regiment's field police, under the command of Major Joachim Steuben. The White Mice weren't all murderous sociopaths; but Major Steuben was, and the troopers of A Company who still had consciences didn't let them get in the way of carrying out the orders Steuben gave.

"Officers to the command car ASAP," a female voice ordered without bothering to identify herself. *"All units shut down, maintaining sensor watch and normal guard rosters. Regiment Three-three out."*

Huber felt his face freeze. Regiment Three-three was the signalman for the Slammers' S-3, the operations officer. What was Major Pritchard doing out here?

Though his presence explained why the White Mice were escorting the convoy, that was for sure.

Resupply was aboard six air-cushion trucks. They could keep up with the combat vehicles on any terrain, but their only armor was thin plating around the cab. Besides them the convoy included two combat cars for escort and two recovery vehicles—wrenchmobiles—which could lift a crippled car in the bed between their fore and aft nacelles. For this run the beds had been screened with woven-wire fencing, so that the twenty A Company infantrymen aboard each wouldn't bounce out no matter how rough the ride.

The last member of the convoy was a command vehicle. Its high, thinly armored box replaced the fighting compartment and held more signal and sensor equipment than would fit in a standard combat car. It backed between *Fencing Master* and the tank to Huber's left, then shut down; the rear wall lowered to form a ramp with a whine of hydraulic pumps.

"Well, you don't got far to go, El-Tee," Deseau said judiciously. He rubbed his neck again. *"What d'ye suppose is going on?"*

"I'll let you know," Huber said as he swung his legs out of the fighting compartment and stood for a moment on the bulge of the plenum chamber. He gripped the frame of the bustle rack left-handed, then slid down the steel skirt with the skill of long practice.

His right hand held a sub-machine gun, the butt resting on his pelvis. It fired the same 1-cm charges as the Slammers' pistols, but it was fully automatic.

Deseau sounded like he didn't expect to like the answer his lieutenant came back with. That was fair, because Huber didn't think he was going to like it either.

Captain Sangrela, looking older than Huber remembered him being at the start of the operation, had just shaken hands with Pritchard at the bottom of the ramp. Mitzi Trogon, built like one of her tanks and at least as hard, was climbing down from *Dinkybob* on the other side of the command track from *Fencing Master*. She was a good officer to serve with—*if* you were able to do your job to her standards.

"Lieutenant Myers's on the way from the prisoner guard in the farm buildings," Sangrela explained to Pritchard as Huber joined them. The buzz of a skimmer was faintly audible, wavering with the breeze but seeming to come closer. "I moved us half a klick out before laagering for the night so we wouldn't have hostiles in the middle of us if they got loose or some curst thing."

This was the first time Huber had seen Major Danny Pritchard in the field; body armor made the S-3 seem bigger than he did addressing the Regiment from a podium. His normal expression was a smile, so he looked younger than his probable real age of thirty-eight or so standard years. He'd come up through the ranks, and the pistol he wore over his clamshell in a shoulder rig wasn't just for show.

A woman wearing a jumpsuit uniform of a style Huber hadn't seen before—it wasn't United Cities garb, and it *sure* wasn't Slammers—had arrived in the car with Pritchard but now waited at the top of the ramp. She responded to Huber's grin with a guarded nod. She was trimly attractive, very alert, and—if Arne Huber was any judge of people—plenty tough as well.

Pritchard looked to his right and said, "Good to see you again, Mitzi," in a cheerful voice. Turning to Huber he went on, warmly enough but with the touch of reserve proper between near strangers, "Lieutenant Huber? Good to meet you."

Lieutenant Myers' skimmer buzzed to a halt beside them, kicking dirt over everybody's feet. Sangrela glared at the infantry platoon leader who now acted as the task force's executive officer.

"Sorry," Myers muttered as he got to his feet. He was a lanky, nervous man who seemed to do his job all right but never would let well enough alone. "I was, I mean—"

"Can it, Lieutenant!" Sangrela said in a tone Huber wouldn't have wanted anyone using to him. To Pritchard he continued apologetically, "Sir, all my officers are now present."

Pritchard quirked a smile. "I guess we'll fit inside," he said, stepping back into the command car and gesturing the others to follow. The roof hatch forward was open; from the inside, all Huber could see of Pritchard's signals officer was the lower half of her body standing on the full-function seat now acting as a firing step. "Not for privacy, but the imagery's going to be sharper if we use the car."

Huber unlatched his body armor and shrugged it off before he climbed into the compartment. Mitzi wasn't wearing hers anyway—she said she bumped often enough in a tank turret as it was. Lieutenant Myers saw Huber strip, started to follow suit, then froze for a moment with the expression of a bunny in the headlights. He was the last to enter, and even then only when Sangrela gestured him angrily forward.

The compartment was smaller than it looked from the outside because the sidewalls were fifteen centimeters thick with electronics. There were fold-down seats at the three touchplate consoles on each side, blandly neutral at this moment because nobody'd chosen the function they were to control.

"Right," said Pritchard when they were all inside. "Officially the government of United Cities has hired the Regiment to support it in its tariff discussions with the government of Solace. Unofficially, everybody on the planet knows that the other five of the Outer States are helping the UC pay our hire."

Huber suspected that not all the Slammers—and not even all the officers here in the S-3's command car—knew or cared who was paying the Slammers. It wasn't their job to know, and a lot of the troopers didn't want to clutter up their minds with things that didn't matter. It might get in the way of stuff that helped them stay alive....

"The government of the Point," Pritchard continued, "that's the state on the north of the continent—"

A map of the sole continent of Plattner's World bloomed in front of Huber. Everyone in the compartment would see an identical image, no matter where they stood. Though an air-projected hologram, it was as sharp as if it had been carved from agate.

A pale beige overlay identified UC territory on the contour display; as Pritchard spoke, an elongated diamond of the map went greenish: a promontory in the north balanced by a southward-tapering wedge which ended at the central mass of Solace. The Point and the United Cities were directly across the continent from one another.

"—is fully supportive of the UC position. Melinda Riker Grayle, a politician who's not in the government but who has a considerable following among the Moss rangers who collect the raw material for the anti-aging drug—"

The image of a stern-looking woman, well into middle age, replaced the map. She wouldn't have been beautiful even thirty years before, but she was handsome in her way and she glared out at the world with a strength that was evident even in hologram.

"—opposes the government in this. She argues that supporting the Regiment lays the Point open to Solace attack, and that the Regiment couldn't do anything to help the Point in such an event."

Huber nodded. It seemed to him that the only thing protecting the "neutral" Outer States from Solace attack was the fact that Solace needed both the Moss they shipped to Solace for processing and the market they provided for Solace produce. For that matter, everybody knew that part of the Moss shipped from the neutral states came from the UC, and that food and manufactures from Solace found their way back to the UC by the same route.

Pritchard grinned. He had a pleasant face, but his expression now made Huber realize that Colonel Hammer's operations officer had to be just as ruthless as Joachim Steuben in his different way.

"Task Force Sangrela's going to prove Grayle's wrong," he said. "You're going to run from here straight to the Point and be in the capital, Midway, before any civilians even know you're coming."

His grin tightened fractionally. "I wish I could say the same about the Solace military," he added, "but their surveillance equipment's better than that. We're all leaving the satellites up because our employers need them. We can hope they won't have time to mount a real counter to the move, though."

"Blood and Martyrs!" Lieutenant Myers muttered.

"How's my infantry supposed to keep up?" asked Captain Sangrela in a more reasoned version of what was probably the same concern. "That's fourteen hundred kilometers by the shortest practical route—"

Either he'd cued his helmet AI with the question, or he was a better off-the-cuff estimator than Huber ever thought of being.

"—and we're not going to do that in skimmers without taking breaks the cars 'n panzers won't need."

Slammers infantry could travel long distances on their skimmers, recharging their batteries on the move by hooking up to the fusion bottles of the armored fighting vehicles. What they couldn't do was change off drivers the way their heavy brethren would.

Pritchard nodded. "The recovery vehicles that just arrived will go along with you on the run," he said. "Off-duty troops'll ride in the boxes the A Company infantry arrived in. There'll be a convoy of wheeled trucks here tomorrow for the prisoners; the White Mice will ride back in them as guards and escort."

Huber frowned. "What happens if a car's too badly damaged to move under its own power, though?" he asked. Battle damage wasn't the only thing that could cripple a vehicle on a long run over rough country, but a montage of explosions and dazzling flashes danced through Huber's memory as he spoke the words. "The wrenchmobiles can't carry twenty troops and a car besides."

"If a car's damaged that bad," Pritchard said, "you blow her in place, report a combat loss, and move on."

He turned to Mitzi Trogon and continued, "You do the same thing if it's a tank. No hauling cripples along, no leaving other units behind to guard the ones that have to drop out. This mission is more important than the hardware. Understood?"

Everybody nodded grimly.

What Arne Huber understood was that on a mission of this priority, the troops involved were items of hardware also. Colonel Hammer wouldn't throw them away, but their personal wellbeing and survival weren't his first concern either.

"My people plotted a route for you," the S-3 resumed. The electronics projected a yellow line—more jagged than snaky—across the holographic continent. More than a third of the route was within the russet central block of Solace territory, though that probably didn't matter: the task force was going to be a target anywhere the enemy could catch it, whether or not that was in theoretically neutral territory.

Captain Sangrela's face went even bleaker than it'd been a moment before. Pritchard saw the expression and grinned reassuringly. "No, you're not required to follow it," he said. "I know as well as the next guy that what looks like a good idea from satellite imagery isn't necessarily something I want to drive a tank over. Make any modifications you see fit to—but this is a starting point, in more ways than one."

Sangrela nodded, relaxing noticeably. Huber did too, though he was only fully conscious of the momentary knot in his guts when it released. It was good to know that despite the political importance of this mission, the troops on the ground wouldn't have Regimental Command trying to run things from Base Alpha. That'd have been a sure way to get killed.

Mind, if Solace reacted as quickly as the Slammers themselves would respond to a similar opportunity, the mission was still a recipe for disaster.

"What're we going to find when we get to the Point?" Lieutenant Myers asked. "You say there's opposition in the backwoods. Are we going to have to look out for local snipers when we get to—"

He grinned harshly.

"—friendly territory?"

"I'll let our guest field that one," Pritchard said with a tip of his hand toward the woman in the jumpsuit beside him. "Troops, this is Captain Mauricia Orichos of the Point Gendarmery, their army. Captain Orichos?"

"We're not an army," Orichos said. Her pleasant, throaty voice complemented her cheerfully cynical smile. "The job of the Gendarmery is primarily to prevent outsiders from harvesting our Moss. Without paying taxes on it, that is."

She let that sink in for a moment, then continued, "My own job is a little different, however. You might say that I'm head of the state security section. I contacted my opposite number in your regiment—"

Which means Joachim Steuben. Huber hoped he kept his reaction from reaching his facial muscles.

"—and asked for help. The situation is beyond what the Gendarmery, what the Point, can handle by itself."

The map had vanished when Orichos began to speak. Now in its place the car projected first the close-up of Melinda Grayle speaking, then drew back to an image of her audience—a long plaza holding several thousand people: mostly male, mostly armed. Mostly drunk as well, or Huber missed his bet.

"Generally," Orichos continued, "Grayle's supporters—they call themselves the Freedom Party—have stayed in the backlands. They've got a base and supposedly stores of heavy weapons on Bulstrode Bay—"

The map returned briefly, this time with a caret noting an indentation on the west coast of the peninsula, near the tip.

"—which is completely illegal, of course, but we—the government—weren't in any position to investigate it thoroughly." Her smile quirked again. "It seemed to me that most members of the government were concerned that we'd find the rumors were true and they wouldn't be able to stick their heads in the sand anymore."

Huber and the other Slammers smiled back at her. Cynicism about official cowardice was cheap, but mercenary soldiers gathered more supporting evidence for the belief than many people did.

The image of Grayle appeared again, but this time the point of view drew back even farther than before. The crowd itself shrank to the center of the field. On all sides were the two- and three-story buildings typical of Plattner's World, set within a forest which had been thinned but not cleared. This was a city. It was larger by far than Benjamin, the administrative capital of the UC.

"Two weeks ago," Orichos said, "Grayle ordered her followers to join her in Midway—and come armed. Her Freedom Party has its headquarters directly across the Axis, Midway's central boulevard, from the Assembly Building. They've been holding rallies every day in the street. This was the first, but they've gotten bigger."

"And you can't stop them?" Captain Sangrela asked. He tried to keep his voice neutral, but Huber could hear the tone of disapproval.

Orichos had probably heard it also, because she replied with noticeable sharpness, "Apart from the ordinary members of the Freedom Party, Captain, there are some ten thousand so-called Volunteers who train in military tactics and who're considerably better armed than the Gendarmery—as well as outnumbering us two to one. I *am* doing something about them: I'm calling in your Regiment to aid the Point with a show of force."

"Captain Sangrela was merely curious, Mauricia," Pritchard said mildly, though his smile wasn't so much mild as dismissive of anything as trivial as status and honor. "Task Force Sangrela's arrival in Midway will prove Mistress Grayle was wrong about the Slammers being unable to reach the Point in a hurry… and if a more robust show turns out to be necessary, that's possible as well."

The imagery vanished. Pritchard looked across the arc of officers, his eyes meeting those of each in turn. In that moment he reminded Huber of a bird of prey.

"Troopers," he said, "route and intelligence assessments have been downloaded to all members of your force. The resupply convoy brought a full maintenance platoon; they'll be working on your equipment overnight so you can get some sleep. I recommend you brief your personnel and turn in immediately. You've got quite a run ahead of you starting tomorrow."

"Blood and Martyrs!" Lieutenant Myers repeated. "That's not *half* the truth!"

Huber waited for Sangrela and Myers to clear the doorway, then started out. Offering politely to let Mitzi precede him would've at best been a joke—at worst she'd have kicked him in the balls—and he didn't feel much like joking.

"Lieutenant Huber?" Pritchard called. He turned his head. "Walk with me for a moment, will you?"

"Sir," Huber said in muted agreement. He stepped down the ramp and put his clamshell on as he waited for the major to follow Mitzi out of the command car. For a moment his eyes started to adapt to darkness; then the first of several banks of lights lit the Night Defensive Position. The scarred iridium hulls reflected ghostly shadows in all directions.

Huber didn't know why the S-3 wanted to talk to him out of Captain Orichos' hearing; the thought made him uncomfortable. Things a soldier doesn't know are very likely to kill him.

Pritchard gestured them into the passage between his command car and Mitzi's tank, *Dinkybob*. He didn't speak till they were past the bows of the outward-facing blowers. A crew was already at work on *Fencing Master;* across the laager, a recovery vehicle had winched *Foghorn*'s bow up at a thirty-degree angle so that a squad of mechanics could start switching out the several damaged nacelles for new ones. Power wrenches and occasionally a diamond saw tore the night like sonic lightning.

"Two things, Lieutenant," Pritchard said when they were beyond the bright pool from the floodlights. He faced the night, his back to the NDP. "First, I was surprised to see you were back with F-3. I had the impression that you'd applied for a transfer?"

Ah. "No sir," Huber said, looking toward the horizon instead of turning toward the major. "Major Steuben offered me a position in A Company. I considered it, but I decided to turn him down."

"I see," said Pritchard. "May I ask why? Because I'll tell you frankly, I don't know of a single case in which Joachim offered an officer's slot to someone who didn't prove capable of doing the job."

"I'm not surprised, sir," Huber said, smiling faintly. "It was because I was pretty sure I *could* handle the work that I passed. I decided that I didn't want to live with the person I'd be then."

Pritchard laughed. "I can't say I'm sorry to hear that, Huber," he said. "What are your ambitions then? Because I've looked at your record—"

He faced Huber, drawing the younger man's eyes toward him. They couldn't see one another's expressions in the darkness, but the gesture was significant.

"—and I don't believe you're *not* ambitious."

"Sir…" Huber said. He was willing to tell the truth, but right in this moment he wasn't sure what the truth *was*. "Sir, I figure to stay with F-3 and do a good job until a captaincy opens up in one of the line companies. Or I buy the farm, of course. And after that, we'll see."

Pritchard laughed again. Huber thought there was wistfulness in the sound along with the humor, but he didn't know the S-3 well enough to judge his moods. "Let's go back to your car and get you settled in," he said.

"Yes, sir," Huber said, turning obediently. "But you said there were two things, sir?"

"Hey, there you are, El-Tee!" Sergeant Deseau bellowed as he saw Huber reentering the haze of light. "Come look what the cat dragged in! It's Tranter, and he says he's back with us for the operation!"

"I saw from the after-action review that you were going to need a replacement driver," Pritchard said in a low voice. "You've worked with Sergeant Tranter before and I believe you found him a satisfactory driver—"

"Frenchie says he's the best driver he ever served with," Huber said. "I say that too, but Frenchie's got a hell of a lot more experience than I do."

"—so I had him transferred from Logistics Section to F-3."

Huber strode forward to greet the red-haired sergeant he knew from his brief stint in Log Section. Suddenly remembering where he was—and who he'd just turned his back on—he stopped and faced the major again.

"Sorry, sir," he muttered. "I—I mean, I've been sweating making the run tomorrow short a crewman, and there was no way I was going to have Costunna on my car or in my platoon. I was… Well, thank you, I really appreciate it."

"Colonel Hammer and I are asking you and the rest of the task force to do a difficult job, Lieutenant," Major Danny Pritchard said. This time his smile was simple and genuine. "I hope you can depend on us to do whatever we can to help you."

He clasped Huber's right hand and added, "Now, go give your troopers a pep talk and then get some rest. It's going to be your last chance to do that for a bloody long time."

Unless I buy the farm, Huber repeated mentally; but he didn't worry near as much about dying as he had about carrying out tomorrow's operation with his car a crewman short.

The Command and Control module housed in the box welded to Huber's gun mount projected ten holographic beads above *Fencing Master*'s fighting compartment. Call-Sign Sierra—the four tanks, four combat cars, and two recovery vehicles of Task Force Sangrela—was ready to roll.

If Huber'd wanted to go up an increment, the display would've added separate dots for the vehicle crews, the infantry platoon, and the air-cushion jeep carrying the task force commander with additional signals and sensor equipment. He didn't need that now, though he'd raise the sensitivity when the scout section—one car and a fire-team of infantry on skimmers—moved out ahead.

Huber gestured to the display and said over the two-way link he'd set with Captain Orichos' borrowed commo helmet, "We're on track, Captain. Another two minutes."

Sergeant Tranter ran up his fans, keeping the blade incidence fine so that they didn't develop any lift. Huber heard the note change minusculely as the driver adjusted settings, bringing the replacement nacelle into perfect balance with the other seven.

Sergeant Deseau nodded approvingly, chopping the lip of the armor with his hand and then pointing forward to indicate the driver's compartment. Trooper Learoyd didn't react. He usually didn't react, except to do his job; which he did very well, though Huber had met cocker spaniels he guessed had greater intellectual capacity than Learoyd.

The fighting compartment was crowded with Orichos sharing the space with the three men of the combat crew, but Via! it was always crowded. A slim woman who wasn't wearing body armor—her choice, and Huber thought it was a bad one—didn't take up as much room as the cooler of beer they'd strapped onto the back of the bustle rack when they took her aboard. They weren't using overhead cover for the combat cars here on Plattner's World because they were generally operating in heavy forest.

"*Wouldn't your helmet show that information?*" Orichos asked, tapping the side of the one Huber had borrowed for her from a mechanic when he learned she'd be traveling in his car. She didn't need it so much for communications as for the sound damping it provided. A run like the one planned would jelly the brains of anybody making it without protection from all the shrieks, hums, and roars they'd get in an open combat car.

"*Sierra Six to Sierra,*" Captain Sangrela. "*White Section—*" the scouts "*—move out. Over.*"

The lead car, *Foghorn*, was already off the ground on fan thrust. Its driver nudged his control yoke forward, sending the thirty-tonne vehicle toward the northwest in a billow of dust. *Foghorn*'s skirts plowed a broad path through the young corn.

Four infantrymen on skimmers lifted when the combat car moved. For a moment they flew parallel to the bigger vehicle, just out of the turbulent air squirting beneath the plenum chamber; then they moved out ahead by 150 meters, spreading to cover a half-klick frontage. *Foghorn*'s sensor suite covered the infantry while they ranged ahead on their light mounts to discover the sort of terrain problems that didn't show up on satellite.

"I can access everything Central's got in its data banks here on my faceshield," Huber replied to Orichos, thinking about her gray eyes behind her faceshield. She'd smiled at him when he offered her the helmet. "I like to keep it for stuff with immediate combat significance, though."

He grinned through his visor and added, "Sometimes it's more important that I'm *Fencing Master*'s left wing gunner than that I command platoon F-3."

The scouts patrolled a klick ahead of whichever vehicle was leading the main body. The combat cars and infantry would rotate through White Section every hour under the present conditions, more frequently if the terrain got challenging.

Huber had picked Sergeant Nagano's car to start out in the lead because it'd been so badly battered at Northern Star. If last night's massive repairs weren't going to hold up, Huber wanted to know about it now—by daylight and long before the enemy started reacting to Task Force Sangrela.

"*Sierra Six to Sierra*," Sangrela ordered in a hoarsely taut voice. "*Red Section—*" the main body, with *Fencing Master* leading two tanks, followed by the recovery vehicles and the last two tanks "*—move out. Over.*"

"That's us, Tranter," Huber ordered on the intercom channel. "Hold us at thirty kph until the whole section's under way, got that?"

They planned to average sixty kph on the run, putting them in Midway exactly twenty-four hours from this moment, including breaks to switch drivers and the stretches of bad terrain that'd hold down their speed. Ordinarily on this sort of smooth ground they'd have belted along at the best speed the infantry could manage on skimmers, close to 100 kph. Sierra had to build speed gradually, however, or the vehicles would scatter themselves too widely to support each other in event of enemy action.

Which was certain to come; more certain than any trooper in Task Force Sangrela could be of seeing the next sunrise.

Sergeant Tranter brought *Fencing Master* up from a dead halt as smoothly as if he were twisting a rheostat. He'd been a maintenance technician, so he'd learned to drive armored vehicles by shifting them—frequently badly damaged—around one another in the tight confines of maintenance parks. He'd stopped being a tech when a hydraulic jack blew out, dropping a tank's skirts to a concrete pad and pinching his right leg off as suddenly as lightning.

The mechanical leg was in most respects as good as the original one, but in serious cold the organic/electrical interface degraded enough to send the limb into spasms. The Regiment had offered Tranter the choice of retirement on full pay or a rear-echelon job he could do in a heated building. He'd chosen the latter, a berth in Logistics Section.

Summer temperatures on Plattner's World never dropped below the level of mildly chilly. If Regimental Command was willing to make an exception, there was nobody Arne Huber would've preferred driving his car than Tranter.

Huber looked over his shoulder, twisting his body at the waist because the clamshell armor stiffened his neck and upper torso. The lead tank, *Dinkybob*, lifted to follow thirty meters behind *Fencing Master*. Mitzi's driver echeloned the big vehicle slightly to the right of Tranter's line to stay out of the combat car's dust. That was fine on a grain field like this, but pretty soon Task Force Sangrela would be winding through hillside scrub where the big vehicles'd feel lucky to have one route.

Well, troopers got used to dust pretty quick. The only thing they knew better was mud.… The commo helmets had nose filters that dropped down automatically and static charges to keep their faceshields clear, but on a run like this Huber knew to expect a faintly gritty feeling every time he blinked. The ration bars he ate on the move would crunch, too.

The tribarrels were sealed against dust—until you had to use them. It didn't take much grit seeping down the ejection port to jam mechanisms as precise as those in the interior of an automatic weapon.

Captain Orichos swayed awkwardly, uncertain of what she could safely grab or sit on. She was familiar with aircars and thought this would be the same. She hadn't realized that terrain affected the ride of air-cushion vehicles—not as much as it affected wheels and treads, but still a great deal.

She caught Huber's glance and waved a hand in frustration. *"I'd expected the floor to vibrate,"* she said. *"But the jolting—what does that? I didn't feel anything like that when I rode here with Major Pritchard."*

Huber grinned. "You rode here in a convoy traveling at the speed of heavily loaded supply vehicles, with the number two man in the Slammers aboard. Sierra has different priorities. Even on these fields, the front skirt digs in every time there's a little dip or rise in the ground. It'll get a lot worse when we start working along the sides of the foothills we're scheduled to hit pretty soon."

"Then it's always like this?" she asked. Deliberately she lifted her faceshield, squinting slightly against the wind blast. She quirked the wry smile he'd seen the night before as she discussed the moral courage of elected officials.

"No, not always," Huber said, raising his own shield to give Orichos a much broader smile than the one he'd been wearing before. "Sometimes they're shooting at us, Captain."

"Sierra Six to Sierra," Captain Sangrela said. *"Blue Section, move out."*

Blue Section was the two remaining combat cars under Platoon Sergeant Jellicoe. They'd follow the main body at a kilometer's distance, extending the column's sensor range to the rear by that much. There wasn't a high likelihood that the enemy would sweep up on the task force from behind, but some of the mercenary units Solace was known to have hired had equipment with sufficient performance to manage it.

The cars in Blue Section would rotate at the same intervals as the scouts did. Either Huber or Jellicoe would be at the front or rear of the column—but never both at the same end.

"Then I guess I'd better get used to it, hadn't I?" Orichos said. She spread her left hand over her eyes to shield them as she surveyed the terrain. She added, *"Have you been with Hammer's Slammers long, Lieutenant?"*

"Five years," Huber said, facing forward and lowering his faceshield so that Orichos could do the same. "I entered the Military Academy on Nieuw Friesland with the intention of enlisting in the Regiment when I graduated... and I did."

The scouts were already into the gullied scrubland that the task force would grind through for the first half of the route. Central had timed the departure from Northern Star so that Sierra would be in pitch darkness while it navigated the last of the foothills south of Point territory where forests resumed.

Until the task force set off, the enemy would assume the Slammers intended to return to UC territory after capturing Northern Star. It'd take Solace Command time to react when they realized the Slammers' real intent. The most dangerous ambush sites were in the foothills; by waiting till noon to set off, the task force would have the advantage of the Regiment's more sophisticated night vision equipment in that last stretch which the enemy might reach in time to block them.

Huber hoped the Colonel was right; but then, he hoped a lot of things, and his tribarrel was ready to take care of whatever reality threw at them. You couldn't always blast your way through problems, but the ability to out-slug the other fellow never stopped being an advantage.

"Do you know much about the political structure of the Point, Lieutenant?" Orichos asked. Since her voice came through the commo helmet, she could've been standing anywhere on the planet—but Huber was very much aware of her presence beside and just behind him.

"Not a thing, ma'am," he admitted. "I studied the United Cities some from the briefing cubes because they were hiring us, but I didn't look at the rest of you folks."

He touched the controller with his left hand, projecting an image remoted from *Foghorn* into the air before him. The scout car was bulling through brush already. The stems were wiry enough to spring back after *Foghorn* passed, but they were too thin to be a barrier to a thirty-tonne vehicle.

He hoped what he'd just said didn't sound too much like, "I'm not interested in you dumb wogs;" which wasn't true for Arne Huber himself but pretty well summed up the attitude of a lot of Slammers, officers as well as line troopers like Sergeant Deseau. Trooper Learoyd wasn't likely to have thoughts so abstract.

"Midway's the only city in the Point," Orichos said. *"We're not like Trenchard or the UC where there's half a dozen places each as big as the next. There's a quarter million people in Midway, and no town as big as a thousand in all the rest of the country."*

"So about a third of your population's in the one city," Huber said. He hadn't *studied* the Point, not like you'd really mean studied; but he'd checked the basic statistics on Plattner's World, sure. "I guess there's a lot of trouble between people in Midway and the rest of the country, then?"

"There wasn't any trouble at all before Melinda Grayle came along!" snapped Captain Orichos, her very vehemence proving that she was lying. *"She started stirring up the Moss rangers ten years ago. All she's interested in is power for herself."*

Not unlikely, Arne Huber thought. Of course, Melinda Grayle wasn't the only politician you could say that about; and she maybe wasn't the only politician in the Point you could say it about, either.

"Grayle claims that the votes in the last election were falsified and that she should've been elected Speaker of the Assembly," Orichos went on. *"She's threatening to take by force what she claims her Freedom Party lost by fraud. Everybody knows that the reason most Assemblymen are residents of Midway is because Moss rangers can't be bothered to vote!"*

"Ma'am," said Arne Huber, "I wouldn't know about that. But if the lady thinks she's going to use force while we're in Midway—"

He turned his head toward her again and patted the receiver of his tribarrel.

"—then she'll have another thing coming. Because force is something I do know about."

"Amen to that, El-Tee," said Frenchie Deseau. He didn't raise his voice on the intercom, but his words had the timbre of feeding time in the lion house.

It was four hours to dawn; the sky was a hazy overcast through which only the brightest stars winked. The car's vibration and buffeting wind of passage—seventy kph, a little more or a little less—drew the strength out of the troopers who'd been subjected to it for the past half-day.

Huber sat cross-legged beside the left gun, watching the shimmering holographic display. He was too low to look out of the fighting compartment from here, but the range of inputs from *Fencing Master*'s sensors should provide more warning than his eyes could even during daylight.

Body heat, CO_2 exhalations, and even the bioelectrical field which every living creature created were grist for the sensors to process. They scanned the gullied slopes a full three kilometers ahead, noting small animals sleeping in burrows and the scaly, warm-blooded night-flyers of Plattner's World which curvetted in the skies above.

Tranter was sleeping—was curled up, anyway—under the right wing gun on a layer of ammo boxes. Orichos squatted behind him with her back to the armor, looking as miserable as a drenched kitten. Learoyd had just taken over the driving chores from Deseau, awake but barely as he hunched over the forward tribarrel. Huber didn't worry about how the sergeant'd react to an alarm—Deseau was enough of a veteran and a warrior both to lay fire on a target in a sound sleep—but he certainly wasn't going to *raise* the alarm.

That would be Arne Huber's job. As platoon leader he wasn't taking a turn driving, but neither did he catch catnaps like the rest of the crew between stints in the driver's compartment. *Fencing Master* was the combat car in White Section during this leg, so Huber had the sensor suite on high sensitivity.

Task Force Sangrela was running the part of the route which Solace forces might have been able to reach for an ambush. Central hadn't warned of enemy movement, but there could've been troops already in place in the region. Technically they were still within Solace territory, not that anybody was likely to stand on a technicality during wartime.

"Bloody fuckin' hell," Sergeant Deseau growled over the intercom. He clung to the grips of his tribarrel as though he'd have fallen without them to hold onto… which he might well have done. High-speed driving over rough terrain at night was a ten-tenths activity, many times worse than the grueling business of surviving the ride in the fighting compartment. *"I wish somebody'd just shoot at us for a break from this bloody grind."*

"There's nobody around to shoot, Frenchie," Huber said; and as he spoke, he saw he was wrong.

Keying the emergency channel with the manual controller he'd been using to switch between sensor modes, Huber said, "White Six to Sierra, we've got locals waiting for us ahead. It's six-three, repeat six-three—" the display threw up the numbers in the corner; he sure wasn't going to have counted the blips overlaying the terrain map that fast "—personnel, no equipment signatures. Looks like dispersed infantry with personal weapons only."

A company of infantry with small arms would be plenty to wipe out White Section if they'd driven straight into the ambush. Mind, knowing about the ambush didn't mean there was no risk remaining, especially to the scouts on point.

"*Sierra, this is Sierra Six,*" Captain Sangrela snapped. His voice sounded sleep-strangled, but he'd responded instantly to the alert. "*Throttle back to twenty, repeat two-zero, kay-pee-aitch. Charlie Four-six—*" The sergeant commanding the infantry of White Section "*—take your team ahead while they're listening to the cars and see if you can get a sight of what we're dealing with. Six out.*"

Deseau, now wakeful as a stooping hawk, stretched his right leg backward without looking. He kicked Tranter hard on the buttocks, bringing him out of the fetal doze as the alarm call had failed to do.

Swaying, drunk with fatigue, Tranter took his place behind the right gun. He didn't look confident there.

"*Charlie Four-six,*" responded a female voice without a lot of obvious enthusiasm. On Huber's display, the four beads of the skimmer-mounted fire team curved to the right, up the slope the column was paralleling. "*Roger.*"

Instead of throttling back when Sangrela ordered them to cut speed, Learoyd adjusted his nacelles toward the vertical. The fans' sonic signature remained the same, but the blades were spending most of their effort in lifting *Fencing Master*'s skirts off the ground instead of driving her forward. The car slowed without informing the listening enemy of the change.

Huber rose to his feet and gripped the tribarrel. The task force commander had taken operational control of White Section, so Huber's primary task was to lay fire on any hostiles who showed themselves in his sector.

"Fox Three-one, come up to my starboard side," he ordered. Sergeant Tranter was a fine driver and a first-rate mechanic, but he may never have fired a tribarrel since his basic combat qualification course in recruit school. Huber wanted more than two guns on line if they were about to go into action against an infantry company.

"*Roger, Three-six,*" Sergeant Nagano responded. The display icon indicating his combat car disengaged from the front of the main body and began to close the kilometer gap separating it from *Fencing Master*.

Captain Sangrela must have seen *Foghorn* move as well as overhearing Huber's order on the command channel; he chose to say nothing. Sensibly, he was leaving the immediate tactical disposition to the man on the ground.

Mauricia Orichos stood erect, her back against the rear coaming of the fighting compartment. She didn't ask questions when the troopers around her obviously needed to focus on other things, but she looked about her alertly, like a grackle in a grain field.

Huber noticed that she didn't draw the pistol from her belt holster. To Orichos' mind it was an insignia of rank, not a weapon.

Huber switched his faceshield to thermal imaging. It wouldn't give him as good a general picture of his surroundings, but it was better for targeting at night than light amplification would be. He couldn't see the cold light of the holographic display, so he projected the data as a thirty percent mask over the faceshield's ghostly infrared landscape.

The dots representing the mounted infantrymen approached the upper end of a ravine in which the combat car's sensors saw more than a dozen hostiles waiting under cover. From their angle, the four Slammers would be able to rake the gully and turn it into an abattoir. The enemy gave no indication of being aware of the troopers.

When *Fencing Master* slowed, the dust her fans had been raising caught up with her. Yellow-gray grit swirled down the intake gratings on top of the plenum chamber and settled over the troops in the fighting compartment; the back of Huber's neck tickled.

He felt taut. He wasn't nervous, but he was trying to spread his mind to cover everything around him. The task was beyond human ability, as part of Arne Huber's soap-bubble thin consciousness was well aware.

The fire team leader started laughing over the command push. The sound was wholly unexpected—and because of that, more disconcerting than a burst of shots.

"*Charlie Four-six, report!*" Captain Sangrela snarled. He sounded angry enough to have slapped his subordinate if she'd been within arm's length. Huber wouldn't have blamed him....

"*Imagery coming, sir,*" the sergeant replied; suppressing her laughter, but only barely.

Huber raised his visor and used the Command and Control box to project the view from the sergeant's helmet where everybody in the car could see it. The hologram of a sheep stared quizzically at him. Behind the nearest animal stretched a hillside panorama of sheep turning their heads and a startled boy holding a long bamboo pole.

"*Sierra Six to Sierra,*" Captain Sangrela said in a neutral tone. "*Resume previous order of march. Out.*"

Fencing Master lurched as Learoyd adjusted his nacelles again. The bow skirts gouged a divot of the loose soil, but the car's forward motion blew it behind them.

"*Blood and Martyrs!*" said Sergeant Deseau. "*Curst if I'm not ready to blast a few a' them sheep just for the fright they give me!*"

"Save your ammo, Frenchie," Huber said. "I guess we'll have plenty of things to kill before this mission's over."

The sun was an hour above the horizon, Task Force Sangrela had been in the fringe forest for longer than that. *Fencing Master* was in the trail position, last of the ten vehicles. *Foghorn* was a hundred meters ahead where Huber could've caught glimpses of her iridium hull if he'd tried.

He didn't bother. His job was to check the sensor suite, oriented now to the rear, and that was more than enough to occupy the few brain cells still working in his numb mind.

Tranter was driving again; the ride was noticeably smoother than either of the troopers could've managed, even when they were fresh. Learoyd was curled beneath his tribarrel, asleep and apparently as comfortable as he'd have been back in barracks.

Because they were in the drag position in the column, Deseau wasn't at his forward-facing tribarrel. Instead he crouched in the corner behind Huber, cradling a 2-cm shoulder weapon in the crook of his arm. It fired the same round as the tribarrels, but it was self-loading instead of being fully automatic. A single 2-cm charge in the right place was enough to put paid to most targets.

Mauricia Orichos had sunk into herself, seated between Learoyd's head and Deseau across the rear of the fighting compartment. She didn't look any more animated than a lichen on a rock. Huber knew how she felt: the constant vibration reduced mind and body alike to jelly.

This run'd get over, or Arne Huber would die. Either'd be an acceptable change.

A red light pulsed at the upper left corner of the display. Fully alert, Huber straightened and locked his faceshield down. "Frenchie," he snapped. "Take over on the sensors!"

Huber cued the summons, turning his faceshield into a virtual conference room. He sat at a holographic plotting table with the other task force officers—Mitzi Trogon blinked into the net an instant after Huber did; Myers and Captain Sangrela were already there—and Colonel Hammer himself.

The imagery wavered. It was never fuzzy, but often it had a certain over-sharpness as the computer called up stock visuals when the transmitted data were insufficient.

To prevent jamming and possible corruption, Central was communicating with the task force in tight-beam transmissions bounced from cosmic ray ionization tracks. The Regiment's signals equipment used the most advanced processors and algorithms in the human universe to adjust for breaks and distortion. Even so, links to vehicles moving at speed beneath scattered vegetation were bound to be flawed.

"There's a battalion of the Wolverines on the way to block you," the Colonel said without preamble. "We operated alongside them once—Sangrela, you probably remember on Redwood?"

"Roger that," Sangrela said, rubbing his chin with the knuckles of his left fist. "Anti-tank specialists, aren't they?"

"Right, and they're good," Hammer agreed. The only time Huber'd seen the small, stocky man without his helmet, he'd been surprised that the sandy hair was thinning; nothing else about the Colonel's face and smooth, muscular movements hinted at age. "They're tasked to set up a hedge of gunpits across our route."

Imagery on the plotting table—a holographic representation of a holographic representation, indistinct but adequate for this moment—showed a terrain map. Red dots blinked across a ten-kilometer stretch to form a serrated line: a rank of interlocking strong points.

Hammer smiled grimly. "We couldn't have broken the Wolverines' encryption any more than they could break ours," he said. "But they passed the information to the Solace authorities, and that's a different matter."

The smile—and it'd never been one of enthusiastic joy—froze back into the previous hard lines. "Which doesn't solve our problem. Your problem in particular, since each of those positions is a 5-cm high intensity weapon with ten men for crew and close-in defense. They aren't mobile—the teams're being lifted in by air, two to a cargo hauler. The trucks have light armor but they won't dare come anywhere close to point of contact. I'm doing the briefing because Operations is looking for alternative routes so you can skirt them. Shooting your way through would take too long and cost too much."

"Sir?" said Huber. His mind was working on a glacially smooth surface divorced from the vibration he still felt through his separated body. "They're still en route, aren't they?"

"Roger," the Colonel said, his eyes pinning Huber like a pair of calipers. He had a presence, even in virtual reality, far beyond what his small form should've projected.

"If I put one or two of my cars on high ground, the hostiles'll have to land short of where they plan to set up," Huber said. "We can hold 'em down until the rest of Sierra's clear, then catch up."

Without poring over a terrain map Huber couldn't have determined where to site his cars, and even then there were plenty of people better at that sort of thing than he was. The principle of it, though, and the certainty that there was a way to do it—that he had. His tribarrels would be effective against thin-skinned aircars at twenty klicks or even greater range. The hostiles wouldn't dare try to bull through the combat cars.

What the Wolverines *would* do, almost certainly, was surround the detached cars and eliminate them in default of the bigger catch they'd hoped to make. They'd be willing to accept the detachment's surrender, but Huber figured he'd try to break out. He could hope that at least one of the two cars—he had to use two, he couldn't be sure of driving the hostiles to the ground with only one—would get clear.

A 5-cm high-intensity round could penetrate even a tank's frontal armor. A hit on a combat car would vaporize the front half of the vehicle.

"No!" said Mitzi Trogon unexpectedly. "Huber's got a good idea, but we don't want to send his little fellows to do the job. Sir, find a firing position for my panzers and screw this business of scaring the hostiles to ground. I'll blow 'em to hell 'n gone before they know they've been targeted!"

"By the *Lord*," Colonel Hammer said in a tone of rasping delight. "Roger that! Go back to your duties, troopers. I'll be back with you as soon as I've brought Operations up to speed."

The virtual conference room vanished so suddenly that Huber jumped with the shock. The change made him feel as though he'd dropped into ice water instead of just returning to the world in which his body rode a combat car toward a powerful enemy.

"*What's the word, El-Tee?*" Deseau said, his voice sharp. He sat cross-legged at Huber's feet with his 2-cm weapon upright, its butt on his left knee. His eyes were on the sensor display.

"Fox Three, this is Fox Three-six," Huber said, cueing the platoon push instead of answering Frenchie on the intercom channel. "There's an anti-tank battalion headed out to block us. They probably figure to hold us while Solace Command comes up with a way to do a more permanent job. Lieutenant Trogon and Central between 'em are planning to put the hostiles in touch with some 20-cm bolts before they get anywhere close to the rest of us. Hold what you got for now, and keep your fingers crossed. Out."

"*Is there going to be a battle, then, Lieutenant?*" a voice asked. Gears slipped a moment before meshing in Huber's mind. Captain Orichos had spoken; she was standing upright with her eyes on him, her faceshield raised. Orichos looked calm but alert. Vibrant as her face now was, she seemed brightly attractive instead of the haggard, aged derelict she'd looked before the alarm.

Learoyd stood at his tribarrel, scanning the scattered forest to starboard. None of the trees were more than wrist-thick, though the tufts of flowers at the tips of some branches showed they were adults. The leading vehicles, the tanks and especially the broad-beamed recovery vehicles, had to break a path where the stunted forest was densest.

Closer to the coast where the soil and rainfall were better, the overarching canopy would keep the understory clear. The task force'd have to skirt the trees there, however; not even a tank could smash down a meter-thick trunk without damaging itself in the process....

"Not a battle, no," Huber said over the intercom. "If things work out, the hostiles won't get anywhere near us. If things don't, we'll still go around them rather than shooting our way through. That may mean worse problems down the road, but we'll deal with that when it happens."

As Huber spoke, he cued his AI to project a terrain and status map in a seventy percent mask across the upper left quadrant of his faceshield. His helmet with all Central's resources on tap could provide him with whatever information he might need. What electronics *couldn't* do was to stop time while he tried to absorb all that maybe-necessary information.

In a crisis, making no decision is the worst possible decision. A shrunken map that he could see through to shoot if he had to was a better choice than trying to know everything.

"*Is it gonna work, El-Tee?*" Deseau asked, still watching the sensor display. He cocked his head to the left so that he could scratch his neck with his right little finger.

Instead of saying, "Who the fuck knows?" which a sudden rush of fatigue brought to his mind, Huber treated the question as a classroom exercise at the Academy.

"Yeah," he said, "I think it maybe will, Frenchie. The Wolverines, that's who's coming, they know what a big powergun can do as well as we do—but knowing it and *knowing* it, that's different. If Sierra just keeps rolling along, they're going to forget that a tank can hit 'em any time there's a line of sight between them and a main gun's bore. A surprise like that's likely to make the survivors sit tight and take stock for long enough that we can get by the place they planned to hold us."

"*That's good,*" Deseau said. "*Because I saw what a battery of the Wolverines did to a government armored regiment on Redwood. Bugger me if I want to fight 'em if we can get by without it.*"

"*Sierra, this is Sierra Six,*" said Captain Sangrela, sounding hoarse but animated. "*Delta elements, execute the orders downloaded to you from Central. Remaining Sierra elements, hold to the march plan. We're not going to do anything to alert the other side. Estimated time to action is thirty-nine, that's three-niner, minutes. Six out.*"

"Fox Three-six, roger," Huber said, his words merging with the responses of Sierra's other two platoon leaders.

He stretched his arms, over his head and then behind him, bending forward at the waist. It was going to feel good to get the clamshell off; it itched like an ant colony had taken up residence.

Always assuming he lived long enough to get to a place he didn't need body armor, of course. But he did assume that, soldiers always assumed that.

Arne Huber grinned behind his faceshield. And it was always true—until the day it wasn't true.

The task force had slowed again to switch assignments. *Fencing Master* was now at the head of the main body, *Foghorn* and a fire team of infantry who'd jumped their skimmers off the maintenance vehicle where they'd been resting were scouting a klick in the lead, and Sergeant Jellicoe's section trailed to the rear.

Huber smiled grimly behind the anonymity of his faceshield. "Resting" wasn't a good word to describe what the infantry was going through, jolting around in the back of a wrenchmobile. Though this was a hard ride for the troops in the armored vehicles, it was a lot worse for the infantry. But Via! every soul in the Slammers was a volunteer.

They were climbing a slope of harder rock than most of the surroundings—a spine of sandstone from which time had worn away the limestone overburden. The top was bald except for patches of wiry grass and a few saplings whose roots had found purchase in a crack. A fresh scar across the stone showed where *Foghorn* had dragged her skirts.

"*Sierra, thirty seconds to execute!*" snapped Captain Sangrela over the general push.

Huber rested his left hand on the receiver of his tribarrel and looked over his shoulder. Fifty meters behind *Fencing Master, Dinkybob,* a massive iridium tortoise, snorted up the slight rise. The tank's hatches were buttoned up; as Huber watched, the turret swung to starboard. The squat 20-cm main gun elevated very slightly.

Mauricia Orichos raised her faceshield to watch the tank. Huber reached over her shoulder and clicked the protection back over her eyes. "Not now!" he said sharply. "Aide—"

As Huber voice-cued his AI, he manually keyed the pad over Orichos' right ear to link her helmet to his.

"—import targeting from Delta Two-six."

With the final word, Huber viewed not his immediate surroundings but the sight picture from the gunnery screen of the huge tank just behind him. It was at high magnification, so high that it had the glassy smoothness of images heavily retouched by the computer to sharpen them.

Five waves of large aircars skimmed undulating, almost barren, terrain. There were four vehicles in the leading ranks and three in the final, all echeloned right. They'd just crossed a ridgeline and were nosing down to cross a shallow valley.

Dinkybob's sight pipper settled over the lead vehicle in the left file. Instead of being a solid orange ball, the reticle was crosshatched to indicate that the fire-control computer was auto-targeting just as it would do in air defense mode.

The cyan flash of the main gun stabbed across Huber's bare skin like a separate needle every millimeter. It would've been instantly blinding to anyone looking toward it without a faceshield's polarizing protection. The crash of heated air—louder than an equally close thunderbolt—shook *Fencing Master*. Deseau, jounced from his squat, sprawled across Huber's feet.

The center of the targeted aircar erupted in blue flame. The bow and a fragment of the stern tumbled out of the sky, spilling such of the contents as hadn't been carbonized by the blast.

Dinkybob continued to fire, ripping the formation as quickly as her gun mechanism could cycle fresh loads into the chamber. Trogon was burning out her barrel by shooting without giving the bore time to cool between rounds. For the people in *Fencing Master*'s fighting compartment, the volley was like being whipped by a scorpion's tail.

For the Wolverines at the other end, it was a brief glimpse of Hell.

A tank hit at that range—eighty-one kilometers distant—might have shrugged off the bolt with damage only to its external sensors and its running gear. It was impossible for a vehicle that had to fly with a heavy cargo the way the Wolverines' trucks did to be armored like a tank. Each bolt scattered its target in a fireball of its own burning structure.

Dinkybob was nearing the edge of the bald patch, but *Doomsayer* was immediately behind. For an instant both 20-cm guns fired in tight syncopation; then *Fencing Master* drove into heavy forest, *Dinkybob* passed out of its targeting window, and even *Doomsayer*'s main gun ceased firing. Huber's heartbeat throbbed in the silence.

The summons wobbled at the corner of Huber's faceshield. He cued it, dropping into the virtual conference room again.

Colonel Hammer looked around the circle of Sierra officers. "That's fourteen out of nineteen trucks destroyed," he said, "and two of the others grounded hard enough to break as best we can tell by satellite."

Hammer grinned like a shark. "Task accomplished, troopers. Complete the rest of the mission the same way and there'll be a lot of promotions out of this business. Dismissed!"

Arne Huber swayed in the rumbling fighting compartment of his combat car, thinking about what the Colonel had just said. Promotion—maybe.

But if they didn't complete the mission, very probably death. Well, the Slammers were all volunteers....

The muzzle of *Dinkybob*'s main gun had cooled from white to a red so deep it was mostly a shimmer in the air around the hot metal. Mitzi's turret hatch was open, dribbling a trail of gray haze. A plastic matrix held the copper atoms in alignment for release as plasma down the powergun's bore; the smoke was the last of the breakdown products from the recent shooting.

An alert wobbled on the upper right corner of Huber's faceshield. He crooked his left little finger, one of six ways he could cue the icon. It was a download-only channel, information from Central for Sierra Six. Huber and the other task force officers were brought into the circuit to listen but not to comment.

"Sierra, this is Operations Three-four-one," said the voice from somewhere back in Base Alpha. *"Solace Command is pissed about what you did to the Wolverines. They've ordered a fire mission by all batteries that can range you. You'll have to take care of your own air defense. Any questions? Over."*

Though voice-only, the increasingly thick foliage overhead attenuated the transmission to sexlessness. On this side of the ridge, the task force was descending into healthy coastal forest.

"What do you mean 'all batteries'?" Captain Sangrela asked. He sounded more irritable than concerned. *"Is this a real problem? Over."*

"Negative on a real problem," Central replied calmly. It was easy to be calm in Base Alpha, of course. *"There's two, maybe three off-planet batteries with rocket howitzers and carrier shells. We'll get you time and vector data as soon as they fire, but you'll have plenty of room to pop them before the carriers separate. Besides that, the Solace Militia has thirty or forty conventional tubes that can range you with rocket assisted rounds, but they won't have any payload to speak of after what the booster rocket requires. I repeat, you'll have full data soonest. Over"*

"Roger, Sierra out," Sangrela said. *"Break, Fox Three-six—"*

The signal now was coming through the task force command channel.

"—that puts it on your cars. Is there going to be any problem? Over."

"No problem, Six," Huber said curtly. "Just give me a minute to plan. Out."

He raised his faceshield and brought up a terrain display through the Command and Control box. On cue the AI highlighted the locations on or near Sierra's forward track which provided a line of sight toward the arc of territory where the hostile guns might be sited.

The display used a violet overlay to mark ranges of thirty klicks and above; the hue moved down the spectrum as the range closed. Points from which a tribarrel could reach out five kilometers—as close as Huber was willing to let the sophisticated carrier shells get—were green.

A single carrier shell held a load of between three and several scores of bomblets, each with its own target-seeking head. When the carrier round opened to release them, the difficulties of defense went up by an order of magnitude.

Sergeant Tranter had traded jobs with Deseau. He turned from the forward tribarrel and asked, "*Whatcha got, El-Tee?*"

"Watch your sector!" Huber snapped in a blaze of frustration.

He'd apologize later. Tranter was a good driver and a great man to have on your team, but he was a technician and not—till this run—a combat crewman. He didn't know by reflex that Huber was busy with something that likely meant all their lives if he did it wrong. Had Tranter realized that, he'd have kept his mouth shut.

The display showed what Huber expected but didn't like to see: there were very few places along Sierra's planned route that would let the tribarrels range out ten klicks, and even those were points. The combat cars wouldn't be able to protect the column on the fly. They'd have to set up on the few patches where the ground was higher and relatively clear of vegetation.

Huber straightened. Learoyd scanned the car's starboard flank with the bored certainty of a machine; Sergeant Tranter was as rigid as a statue at the forward gun—*Via! I didn't mean to bite his head off*—and Captain Orichos was trying to watch all directions like a bird who's heard a cat she can't see.

"Sierra, this is Fox Three-six," Huber said. "When Central gives us an alert, the C&C box'll choose the best overwatch position and direct the nearest car to it. The rest of Sierra'll bypass that car, which'll leapfrog forward when it comes out of air defense mode. It may be that there'll be more than one car at a time out of the column. Three-six out."

There was a series of *Rogers* from the other officers. Huber hadn't bothered to run the plan by Sierra Six before delivering it to the whole unit. Sangrela'd tasked him with the solution of the problem, and it was something that an infantry officer didn't have much experience with anyway.

"*What happens if the bad guys're waiting out in the woods, El-Tee?*" Deseau asked over the intercom from the driver's compartment. He had the hatch open so that he could drive with his head out in the breeze. "*With the guns locked on air defense, a lone car's pretty much dead meat, right?*"

"The same thing that happens if you fall out a window drunk, Frenchie," Huber said with a quiver of irritation. Did Deseau think that hadn't occurred to him? But there wasn't any choice. With only four cars, he couldn't detach a second unit to guard the one on air defense. "Either you get up and go on, or you don't."

"*Yeah, that's about what I figured,*" Deseau said. He sighed. "*You don't suppose me 'n Tranter could trade off again, do you?*"

"Negative," said Huber. "We've got to keep moving."

He too would like to have Frenchie in the fighting compartment, watching their surroundings with his shoulder weapon while the gunnery computer aimed the tribarrels skyward. Huber'd like a lot of things, but he was a veteran. He'd make do with what he had.

The alert from Central overrode F-3's helmet AIs, filling ninety percent of each faceshield with fire control data and relegating previous tasks to a box in the center.

Huber flicked his helmet back to Sierra status in a thirty percent mask over the forest around him and ordered, "Fox Three-three, execute."

Not that Sergeant Jellicoe needed his okay. Her car, *Floosie*, had already steered to the right of the column's track and was pulling up a rise. *Flame Farter* would be alone in the drag position until *Floosie* rejoined, and *Floosie* would be very much alone.

"A Rangemaster battery's sent us a salvo of 200-mm shells," Huber explained over the intercom. "The battery's sited at one-thirty degrees from us, so Jellicoe's breaking out of line for a moment to take care of the incoming. The Rangemasters're a good enough outfit, but there's next to no chance that anything'll get past *Floosie*."

He was speaking mostly for Orichos' benefit; *Fencing Master*'s crew probably understood the situation as well as their lieutenant did. Well, Deseau and Tranter understood; Learoyd understood the little he needed to understand.

Mauricia Orichos nodded appreciatively, then quirked Huber a smile. *"It's like being a baby again,"* she said. *"I know there's a lot going on, but I don't understand any of it."*

Her smile grew marginally harder; she no longer looked haggard. She added, *"We'll be back in my element soon."*

Huber switched his helmet to remote, importing fire control imagery from *Floosie*. As an afterthought, he restored the link to Orichos' helmet also.

The display was blank until Huber stuttered up three orders of magnitude. At such high gain there was a tiny quiver that even the Slammers' electronics couldn't fully damp.

The shell, twenty centimeters in diameter and almost two meters long, was a blurred dash in the four-bar reticle to which Jellicoe had set her sights. The image jumped minusculely as a tribarrel's recoil jiggled the platform. Several cyan dots, vivid even at that range, intersected the shell.

The target ruptured in a red flash and a puff of dirty black smoke. Two more shells exploded into black rags in the sky around it; a fourth followed an instant later as one of the car's tribarrels made a double. Bomblets from the last shell detonated around the initial burst in a white sparkle.

Huber thought he heard the distance-delayed thumping of *Floosie*'s guns, but he was probably wrong. Loud though they were up close, the sound of 2-cm discharges several klicks away would've been lost in *Fencing Master*'s intake roar. As for the shellbursts, they wouldn't have been visible to unaided eyes even if the column had a clear view of the sky to the southeast.

Huber cleared his and Orichos' faceshield. "They'll keep on firing for a while," he said, speaking through the intercom but keeping eye contact with the local, the only person in the car who'd be interested. "The thing is, cargo shells're expensive to make and they have to be brought in from off-planet. If Solace Command wants to waste them like this, they can be our guests. There could be a time the tribarrels'd have their usual work to do, and we wouldn't want to worry then about firecracker rounds going off overhead."

"Fox Three-three rejoining column," Jellicoe said in a tone of mild satisfaction. Sure

it was shooting fish in a barrel; and true, neither she nor her crew had touched their triggers while the gunnery computer took care of business… but it was still a nice bag of fish. "*Out.*"

"*Three indig batteries have opened fire,*" Central announced. "*Seventeen tubes. None of the rounds are going to come close enough to worry about, so proceed on course as planned. Over.*"

Tranter straightened, stretched, and then turned enough to meet Huber's eyes. He ventured a weak grin; Huber clasped Tranter's arm, closing the file on their previous short exchange.

From the driver's compartment Deseau called, "*Hey El-Tee? See if you can find us something t' shoot at, will you? I don't want my tribarrel growing shut like an old maid's cunt.*"

He laughed.

Before Huber could speak, Central broke in with, "*Six rounds incoming from vector oh-nine-three. Fox Three-six respond. Over.*"

A terrain display appeared on the upper left quadrant of his faceshield with a short, crooked red line reaching left toward the spot Central had picked for *Fencing Master*'s firing position.

"Roger, Central," Huber said, swaying as Deseau pulled into a ravine. It was filled with feathery bushes that crumpled beneath *Fencing Master*'s bow skirts. The car rocked violently on the rough climb.

"*Well, it's a start,*" said Frenchie. He kept his voice bright, but Huber could hear the strain; this wasn't easy driving, not for anybody. "*But you know, it's been a bitch of a run. I'm looking forward to getting back behind my gun where I can maybe kill some of the bastards who put us through it.*"

Deseau laughed. Huber didn't join him, but he noticed that Captain Orichos wore a broad, grim smile.

"*Sierra, we got buildings up here!*" called an unfamiliar voice. Huber's AI slugged the speaker as one of the scouting infantry. "*By the Lord, we do! There's more of 'em! We finally made it!*"

"*Ermanez, get off the push!*" Captain Sangrela snapped. They were all punchy, fatigued in mind and body alike. "*White Section, hold in place. Blue Section, close up as soon as you can without running any civilians down. These're friendlies, remember! Six out.*"

"Six, this is Fox Three-six," Huber said. He twisted and leaned sideways to look off the stern of the car, past Captain Orichos. As he expected, the commander's jeep was on its way forward. The light vehicle wobbled furiously in the turbulent air spurting beneath the skirts of the wrenchmobiles and tanks it was passing. "I'm moving into the lead in place of Sergeant Nagano. All right? Over."

"*Roger, Three-six,*" Sangrela said. Huber watched the jeep lift airborne and plop down again hard enough to pogo on its flexible skirts. The message paused for a grunt. Sangrela went on, "*Three-six, I'm dismounting all the infantry. I'm putting two squads up front with you for outriders. Out."*

"Fox Three-one," Huber said, cueing *Foghorn* ahead of him with the scouts, "halt at a wide spot and let me in ahead of you. Three-six out."

He could see *Foghorn.* For nearly eight hundred kilometers the column had been picking its way through trees. Suddenly they'd exited the forest onto a boulevard broad enough that even the wide recovery vehicles could've driven down it two abreast. The buildings to either side were three- and four-story wood-framed structures, but they had much wider street frontage than those of the United Cities. In the UC, Huber'd had the feeling he was standing in a field of towers rather than houses.

A few pedestrians walked between buildings and a scattering of high-wheeled jitneys bounced and wavered along the street. There was no other traffic. Despite its width the road wasn't surfaced. At the moment it was rutted and dusty, but a rainstorm would turn it into a sea of mud.

Captain Orichos took a hand-held communicator from a belt pouch, stuck a throat mike against her larynx—it adhered to the skin of her neck, but it hadn't clung to her fingers—and lifted the commo helmet enough to slip earphones under. As she entered codes on the handset, her eyes remained on the road ahead.

The scouts waited as ordered, the four infantrymen beside their skimmers to the left of *Foghorn.* They looked ragged and filthy—Huber glanced down at himself, his jacket sleeves a rusty color from the road grime, and grinned wearily—but they held their weapons with the easy care of veterans ready for whatever happened next.

Tranter throttled back and adjusted his nacelles to slow gently to a halt. He steered to bring *Fencing Master* up on *Foghorn's* starboard side without fishtailing or dragging a jolting dust storm with the skirts.

The thought made Huber look over his shoulder. He trusted Sergeant Tranter to be able to drive safely, no matter how tired. The tank immediately behind them weighed 170 tonnes and its driver had probably had less rest than the car crewmen. Some of the infantry could drive and had been spelling the two-man crews of the tanks, but there was still a real chance that whoever was at *Dinkybob's* control yoke wouldn't notice that the vehicles ahead were stopped.

Orichos lowered her communicator and looked at Huber. *"You'll be camping on the grounds of the Assembly Building straight ahead,"* she said over the intercom. *"I informed my superiors that you were on the way. We can proceed immediately."*

Can we indeed? Huber thought. He didn't let the irritation reach his face; it'd been a hard run for all of them. Instead of responding to Orichos, he said, "Sierra Six, this is Fox Three-six. The indig officer riding with me says that that we can go straight on in to the Assembly Building and set up around it. Do you have any direction for me? Over."

The jeep pulled alongside *Fencing Master.* Captain Sangrela sat braced in the passenger seat, his holographic display a shimmer before him as he looked up at Huber. *"Via, yes!"* he snarled. *"Let's get to where we're going so we can bloody dismount! Move out, Three-six. Sierra Six out."*

Dinkybob had managed to slow to a halt. So did the vehicles following, though as

Huber looked back he noticed one of the later tanks swing wide to the left when its driver awoke to the fact that he was in danger of overrunning whoever was stopped ahead of him.

"Roger, Six," Huber said, keeping his tone even. "Three-six out. Break. Tranter, start on up the street. Keep it at twenty kph and—"

"And don't run over any locals," he'd started to say, but there wasn't any risk of that. The words would've done nothing but shown his own ill-temper.

"—and maybe we'll have a chance to rest pretty quick."

Huber's muscles were so wobbly that he wasn't sure he'd be able to walk any distance when he got down from the combat car. The clamshell had chafed him over the shoulders, his hip bones, and at several points on his rib cage. He itched everywhere, especially the skin of his hands and throat; they'd been exposed to the ozone, cartridge gases, and iridium vaporized from the gunbores when the tribarrels raked incoming shells from the sky.

Fencing Master lifted and started forward, building speed to an easy lope. The roadway was smooth, a welcome relief from the slopes and outcrops they'd been navigating for the last long while. Dust billowed from beneath the skirts, a vast gulp initially but settling into a wake that rolled out to either side.

Even before the recovery vehicles had halted, the infantrymen pitched off to port and starboard on their skimmers. The infantry platoon, C-1, had left the jeep-mounted tribarrels of its Heavy Weapons Squad behind in Base Alpha. The gun jeeps weren't needed for the original mission, the capture of Northern Star Farm, because there the infantry was to operate in close conjunction with combat cars in open country. The soft-skinned jeeps would be easy targets for an enemy and wouldn't add appreciably to the firepower of the task force.

Here in a city, gun jeeps would look a lot more useful than the pair of automatic mortars Sierra *did* have along; but they'd make do. They always did.

More aircars appeared, circling above the column instead of buzzing from place to place across the sky. The Slammers' sudden appearance had taken the city by surprise, but now the citizens were reacting like wasps around an opened hive.

Deseau looked up and muttered a curse. His hand tightened on his tribarrel's grip, raising the muzzles minutely before Huber touched his arm.

Huber leaned close and said, "They're friendly, Frenchie."

"Says you!" Deseau snarled, but he lowered the big gun again.

Huber coughed. "I'm surprised the streets here are so wide, Captain Orichos," he said, looking at the local officer again. With *Fencing Master* idling along like this he could've spoken to her also without using the intercom, but he didn't see any reason to. "In the United Cities, even the boulevards twist around under the trees."

"This street—the Axis—is wide," Orichos explained. *"We don't have a separate landing ground here at Midway. The warehouses where the rangers sell their Moss are on both sides—"*

She gestured.

"—here, so the dirigibles from Solace set down in front of the establishment they're

trading with. They unload goods, mostly from the spaceport, of course—then they lift off again with the bales of Moss."

Now that Orichos had told him the adjacent buildings were warehouses, Huber could see the outside elevators on each one and the doors at each story wide enough to take corrugated steel shipping containers which would then be shifted within by an overhead suspension system. The windows were narrow, providing light and ventilation, but with no concern for the view out them.

Orichos' face blanked. She turned her head away from Huber and began talking into her communicator again.

Huber locked his faceshield down and concentrated on the terrain to the left front of his vehicle. That was the area his tribarrel'd be responsible for if the task force was suddenly ambushed… which they wouldn't be, of course, but his irritation with the local officer cooled when he thought about a hose of cyan bolts lashing the buildings *Fencing Master* slid past.

Chances were Orichos would inform him of whatever crisis had called her attention away. Besides, it was a near certainty that the signals equipment in Sangrela's jeep could break whatever encryption system the Point Gendarmery was using if Huber really thought the task force needed to know.…

Which he didn't. He was just in a bad mood from the long run.

Captain Orichos lowered the communicator and said, *"Lieutenant Huber, there's a problem. Grayle's gotten word of your arrival. She's ordered her supporters to gather in the Axis in front of the Freedom Party offices. There's already hundreds of them there, blocking the street. There may be thousands by the time we arrive."*

Even if there'd been no previous contact between Solace and the Freedom Party, somebody there had certainly given Grayle a heads-up when they realized where Task Force Sangrela was bound. Grayle probably wasn't pro Solace, but they were both opposed to the Point's present government.

At the word "problem," Huber had cut Sierra Six into the intercom channel. Orichos looked startled when Sangrela rather than Huber replied, *"Are they armed, then? Do we have to shoot our way through? Six over."*

"Via, no!" Orichos cried in horror. *"A bloodbath would do exactly what Grayle hopes! Everybody'd turn against you mercenaries and the government! These are just people standing in the street!"*

In the distance ahead of *Fencing Master* stood the stone Assembly Building on a terraced hillside. A quick flash of Huber's map display showed him that the Axis circled the building and continued its broad way northward.

Huber's eyes narrowed. The map also emphasized that Midway was a large city compared to most of the places the Slammers operated. A company-sized task force would drown in a place this big if it turned hostile. And gunning down a few hundred citizens in the street would be a good way to make the hundreds of *thousands* of survivors hostile.…

"Well, bloody Hell, woman!" Captain Sangrela said. His jeep had pulled alongside Fencing Master and he was glaring up at Orichos. *"If it's a job for the police, get your*

bloody police on it, will you? You don't expect us to idle here in the middle of the bloody street, do you? Or do you? Six over."

"Captain Sangrela, I'm very sorry for the delay but we're working on it," Orichos said. *Fencing Master* continued to rumble on, twenty meters behind the screen of skimmer-mounted infantry. *"We didn't expect Grayle to react so quickly. Most of the crowd in the street are the Freedom Volunteers, the party's militia, and there's too many of them for the Gendarmery manpower we've got available at the moment. Over."*

She realizes she's on a net, not the car's intercom, and she's following proper commo protocol, Huber noticed with a grin.

"Well, what use will waiting do, Captain?" Sangrela demanded. *"Look, is there a back way around? Because if the idea was for the Regiment to make a show of force, having a bunch of yahoos stop us in our tracks is going to send a bloody wrong signal! What about us putting a few shots over their heads? Six over."*

Huber touched Orichos' arm to silence her before she could answer. He said, "Six, this is Fox Three-six. Put me out front and the panzers right behind me. Get the infantry outa the way, back on the recovery vehicles'd be the best place—they can't do any good without shooting and that's what we're trying to avoid. Three-six over."

"You can handle this, Three-six?" Sangrela said. Captain Orichos was searching Huber's face, her expression blankly concerned. *"Because if you can, go with it. Six over."*

"I've got a driver who can handle it, sir," Huber said. "Three-six out. Break—" cutting Captain Sangrela out of the circuit again "—Tranter, on a road surface like this, I'll bet my left nut you can spray enough rock and grit off the bow to clear us a path and still keep us moving forward. What d'ye say?"

"I'd say you needn't worry about disappointing your girlfriend, El-Tee," Tranter replied cheerfully. He laughed. *"Just watch our dust!"*

The infantry ahead of *Fencing Master* turned and circled back, obeying Sangrela's command on the C-1 unit push. Lieutenant Myers was on one of the skimmers; he looked at Huber as he slid past. *Dinkybob* closed up so that the gap between the tank and *Fencing Master's* rear skirt was only about five meters. That'd probably be safe when both vehicles were moving at a slow walk—but if something *did* go wrong, the tank'd send Huber's car cannoning forward like a billiard ball.

Huber could easily see the mob filling the street without raising his faceshield's magnification. He didn't want to do that: he needed all the peripheral vision he had and probably then some.

Aircars kept arriving at the back of the crowd, adding to the numbers already present. Many were big vehicles marked in red with the logo of a broken chain, capable of carrying twenty passengers. It looked to Huber as though they were ferrying people from outlying locations and going back empty for more.

Sergeant Deseau must've thought the same thing, because he leaned back from his tribarrel and shouted, "Hey El-Tee? I bet I could scatter those jokers right fast if I popped a couple of trucks while they was overhead."

"That's a big negative, Sergeant," Huber said, hoping he sounded sufficiently disapproving. He'd been thinking the same thing himself, and Deseau probably knew him well enough to be sure of that.

Though that did raise another thought. The sky above Task Force Sangrela was full of aircars jockeying for position. So far as Huber could tell they were simply civilians who wanted to watch what was going on, but some might be members of Grayle's militia with guns or grenades.

Besides, there was a fair chance that cars might collide and crash down on the column. The trees bordering the Axis constrained the aerial spectators into a relatively narrow channel, so they kept dropping lower to get a good view.

"Captain Orichos," Huber said. "I understand you can't deal with the mob on the ground, but can't you Gendarmes do something about the idiots buzzing around overhead? ASAP."

Orichos gave him a hard look, then nodded and spoke into her communicator. A pair of gun-metal gray aircars with blue triangles bow and stern had been paralleling the column at the fringes of the civilian vehicles. They immediately began bellowing through loudspeakers. The words were unintelligible over the intake roar of *Fencing Master*'s fans, but the aircars overhead edged away reluctantly.

Apparently to speed the process, a Gendarme aimed his electromagnetic carbine skyward and fired a burst. The civilian cars dived away in a panic.

That was bad enough, though the actual collisions were minor and didn't knock anybody out of the air. It would've been much worse if Huber hadn't caught Deseau as the sergeant reacted to *shots fired* in the fashion any bloody fool should've expected, by swinging his tribarrel onto the threat.

"Captain Orichos?" Huber said. "Shooting is a really bad idea. No matter who's doing it. All right?"

Orichos nodded with a guarded expression; she didn't like the implied reprimand, but it was obviously well-founded. She snapped a further series of orders into the communicator.

Two men in jumpsuits like the one Orichos wore—hers was now gray/yellow/red from grit it'd picked up during the run—looked over the side of the aircar to the right of the column. Deseau gave them the finger. The face of the cop who'd fired the carbine went black with anger. Orichos shouted into her communicator and the police vehicle rose quickly to a hundred meters.

"Sorry," Orichos muttered over the intercom. Huber shrugged noncommittally.

Fencing Master's bow slope was well within half a klick of the mob. Looking forward, his left hand on the tribarrel's receiver and his right at his side instead of on the spade grip, Deseau said, "*Some a' them got guns, El-Tee. What do we do if they start shooting? Just take it?*"

"Crew," Huber said, "Nobody shoots till I do. Break. Six, this is Fox Three-six. If we start taking serious fire, my people aren't going to stand here and be targets. Are we clear on that? Over."

"*Roger Three-six,*" Sangrela said. "*Delta Two-six—*" Lieutenant Trogon "*—if Fox Three-six opens fire, put a couple main gun rounds at his point of aim. Break. Sierra, Fox*

Three-six and Delta Two-six will do all the shooting till I tell you otherwise. Six out."

"Roger, Three-six out," Huber said. He was keyed up and felt as though he should be standing on the balls of his feet. Myers and Mitzi Trogon responded curtly as well.

Dinkybob slid to the left of *Fencing Master*'s track. Trogon was buttoned up in the turret. She'd elevated the 20-cm main gun to forty-five degrees for safety when the column entered an inhabited area; now she lowered it in line with the mob ahead. A crust of iridium redeposited from the bore made the muzzle look grimy.

If *Dinkybob* fired from close behind, the side-scatter from the burned-out gun was going to be curst uncomfortable in *Fencing Master*'s fighting compartment. But then, it was going to be curst uncomfortable regardless if this turned into a firefight.

The mob watched the column come on. Tranter closed the driver's hatch. He'd been throttling back gradually, so by now *Fencing Master* was advancing no faster than a promenading couple. Huber and the troopers with him in the fighting compartment looked out through polarized faceshields as they aimed their forward-facing tribarrels. Normally the wing gunners'd be covering the flanks—and the good Lord knew, there might be snipers in the buildings, tall dwellings now instead of warehouses, to either side. The rest of the task force was going to have to deal with that threat, because *Fencing Master* had really immediate problems to her front.

Huber'd hoped the crowd'd scatter when the shouting civilians saw the huge vehicles coming at them, but they were holding steady. The front rank was of rough-looking men—almost all of them were men—with clubs. They didn't have uniforms, but each of them and many of those behind wore red sweatbands. Banners with the red logo on a black ground waved from several places in the midst of the group.

Huber's eyes narrowed. Those in front didn't have guns, but many of the ones standing at the back of the crowd carried short-barreled slugthrowers much like the Gendarmery's. You wouldn't often have call for a long-range weapon in the forests of Plattner's World, but at anything up to two hundred meters those carbines were as deadly as a powergun.

The trucks which'd been ferrying people in now landed in line across the Axis, forming a barrier behind the crowd. Grayle was doing everything she could to prevent her demonstration from melting away before the roaring bulk of the armored vehicles.

A good half of the mob was shouting and waving their fists in the air, often holding a club or a bludgeon. The other half seemed more scared than not, but they were in it now and knew there was no easy way out.

"*What d'ye guess, El-Tee?*" Deseau said. "*Maybe three thousand of 'em?*"

"Maybe more," Huber said. "Just stay calm and let Tranter do the work. Ready, Sarge?"

"*Roger that, sir,*" Sergeant Tranter said, brightly cheerful. "*Any time you say.*"

It'd been a worse run for Tranter than for the line troopers—they were used to the hammering, or at least to some degree of it. Now at last Tranter was in his element, moving a combat car in precise, minuscule increments. As a repair technician, he'd regularly shifted cars and tanks in crowded maintenance parks where the tolerances were much tighter than anything combat troops dealt with in the field.

"Execute, then!" Huber said.

Huber felt the fans speed up through the soles of his feet; *Fencing Master* shivered. The crowd was shouting in unison, "*Free-dom! Free-dom!*" Compared to the intake roar, the sound of so many voices was no more than bird cries against the boom of the surf.

A dozen meters from the crowd, Tranter tilted the nacelles vertical and brought the fans up to maximum output so that the car drifted to a quivering halt. *Dinkybob* continued sliding forward till its bow slope overlapped *Fencing Master*'s stern. If they'd been directly in line, there'd have been a collision.

While *Fencing Master* balanced in place, dust and grit billowed out all around beneath her lifted skirts. Some flew toward the crowd, forcing the thugs in the front rank to cover their faces or turn their heads away.

"Watch the guys in the back!" Huber ordered, gripping the tribarrel with his thumbs deliberately lifted clear of the butterfly trigger. "Watch for anybody aiming at us!"

With the skill of a ballerina, Tranter cocked the two bow nacelles forward at the same time as he angled the six other fans slightly to the rear. The blast from the bow nacelles dug like a firehose into the gravel roadway, then sprayed the spoil into the crowd with the energy required to float thirty tonnes of combat vehicle.

The crowd broke. Those in the direct blast could no more stand against it than they could've swum through an avalanche. Spun away, battered away—some of the gravel was the size of a clenched fist—frightened away; blind from the dust and deafened by the howling air, they drove against those behind them.

The rout was as sudden and certain as the collapse of a house of cards. Tranter adjusted his throttles with the care of a chemist titrating a solution. The thugs at the front and the gunmen at the rear were no threat compared to the iridium sandstorm that ground forward, minutely but inexorably.

Dinkybob held station at *Fencing Master*'s left flank, her mass even more of a threat than the gape of her main gun's pitted bore. She and the tank echeloned to the right behind her, *Doomsayer*, were buttoned up. There was nothing human about any of them, not even the mirrored facelessness of the gunners behind the combat car's tribarrels.

When panic started the crowd running, it continued till there was nothing left but the sort of detritus a flood throws up at the edge of its channel: clothing, clubs, papers of all manner and fashions, whirling in the wind from beneath *Fencing Master*'s steel skirts. A few bodies lay in the street as well: people who'd been trampled, people who'd been squeezed breathless; probably a few who'd fainted.

Tranter cut his fan speed, adjusting the nacelles in parallel again to bring *Fencing Master* back into normal operation. They resumed forward movement at a walking pace.

Arne Huber relaxed for the first time in… well, he wasn't sure how long. He raised his faceshield and rubbed his eyes with the back of his hand.

"Good job, Tranter," he said. "Now, park us in the grounds of that building up there on the mound."

"Roger, El-Tee," the driver said. *"Ah, how about the landscaping, sir?"*

"Fuck the landscaping!" said Sergeant Deseau.

Huber looked over his shoulder at Captain Orichos. She stood with the communicator in her hand but she wasn't speaking into it. Huber grinned and said, "Frenchie's right, Tranter. The bushes can take their chances."

He took a deep breath and looked at the dust and debris in front of them. "The good Lord knows the rest of us just did," he added.

The second recovery vehicle backed carefully into position between *Fencing Master* and a tank, grunting and whining through her intake ducts. Her rear skirts pinched up turf which her fans fired forward out of the plenum chamber in a black spray. The driver shut down, and for the first time since Task Force Sangrela's arrival, there was relative peace in the center of Midway.

"Can we stand down now, El-Tee?" Deseau asked, turning to face Huber. People in the street were staring up at the mercenaries while others looked down from circling aircars, but they were simply interested spectators. Some onlookers might have belonged to the mob that scattered half an hour earlier, but if so they'd thrown away their weapons and hidden their red headbands. Certainly they were no present threat.

"Fox, this is Fox Three-six," Huber said, making a general answer to Frenchie's personal question. "Stand down, troopers. One man in the fighting compartment, the rest on thirty-second standby. I don't know how long we'll be halting here, but at least break out the shelter tarps. Three-six out."

"Learoyd, you've got first watch," Frenchie said. "In two hours I'll relieve you. Tranter, give me a hand with the tarp and the coolers."

Captain Orichos had vanished into the Assembly Building as soon as *Fencing Master* settled onto the terraced mound. To Huber's surprise, a stream of chauffeured aircars had begun to arrive while Task Force Sangrela was setting up a defensive position around the pillared stone building. The civilian vehicles landed in the street and disgorged one or two expensively dressed passengers apiece, then lifted away in a flurry of dust.

The new arrivals walked up the steps—three flights with landings between on the terraces—and entered the building. Some eyed the armored vehicles with obvious interest; others, just as obviously, averted their eyes as if from dung or a corpse.

Captain Sangrela had spaced his vehicles bows outward like spokes on a wheel. Because there were only ten vehicles, they had to back onto the uppermost terrace in order to be close enough for mutual support; even so there was a twenty-meter gap between the flank of one unit and the next. The infantry were using power augers to dig two-man pits above and behind the armored circle.

Huber unlatched his body armor to loosen it, but he didn't strip it off quite yet. Tranter and Deseau stood behind *Fencing Master*, releasing the tie-downs that held gear to the bustle rack. Huber leaned out of the fighting compartment to steady a beer cooler with his hand till the troopers on the ground were ready to take the weight.

Trooper Learoyd raised his helmet and rubbed his scalp; he was in his early twenties but already nearly bald. "Hey El-Tee?" he said. "Are all them people behind us friendlies? Because if they're not…?"

"I don't think they're going to shoot at us, Learoyd," Huber said. "I won't say I think they're friendly, though."

That was particularly true of the group now walking across the Axis toward where *Fencing Master* was grounded. There were three principals, a woman with two men flanking her at a half-step behind to either side. Each wore a white blouse and kilt with a bright red sash and cummerbund. Before and behind that trio were squads of toughs with red sweatbands, some of those who'd been at the front and rear of the mob half an hour before. Now they weren't carrying weapons, at least openly.

They'd come from a walled compound across the Axis where it circled the Assembly Building. The outer walls were plasticized earth cast with a dye that Huber supposed was meant to be bright red. Because the soil was yellowish, the mixture had the bilious color of a sunburned Han.

There were two four-story buildings within—wood-sheathed and painted red—and two more domed roofs which the three-meter walls would've hidden from ground level. *Fencing Master* had a good view down into the compound, however.

Mauricia Orichos came out of the Assembly Building, pausing briefly to speak with a man entering. His cape of gossamer fabric shimmered repeatedly up through the spectrum on a three-minute cycle.

The conversation over, Orichos walked purposefully toward Captain Sangrela who was bent over the commo unit on the back of his jeep. His driver was inflating a two-man tent.

"El-Tee?" Learoyd said. "Is that the woman who's making all the trouble?"

He meant the head of the three dignitaries in white and red, now climbing the steps. "Right," Huber said, a little surprised that Learoyd had volunteered what amounted to a political observation. "That's Melinda Riker Grayle."

Grayle moved with an athleticism that hadn't come through in the hologram of her haranguing the crowd. Those images must have been taken right here: Grayle speaking from the steps of the Assembly Building to a crowd larger than the one *Fencing Master* had just scattered.

"But I still shouldn't shoot her, that's right?" Learoyd said, his voice troubled.

"Blood and Martyrs!" Huber said. "Negative, don't shoot her, Learoyd!"

Grayle wasn't one of those who averted her eyes from the armored vehicles. She noticed Huber's attention and glared back at him like a bird of prey. Her hair was in short curls. Judging from Grayle's complexion she'd once been a redhead, but she'd let her hair go naturally gray.

She and her companions—including the escort—stalked through the tall doors of embossed bronze into the Assembly Building. Learoyd sighed and said, "Yeah, that's what I figured."

Huber looked at him hard. Nobody but Learoyd would've considered shooting the leader of the opposition dead in the middle of the city, with the whole country watching through video links. Nobody but simple-minded Herbert Learoyd; but you know, it might not have been such a bad idea after all....

"Fox Three-six to me ASAP!" Captain Sangrela ordered. Huber glanced over. Beside Sangrela stood Orichos, wearing a gray beret in place of the commo helmet she'd left behind on *Fencing Master*. She looked very cool and alert: her hands were crossed behind her at the waist. *"Six out."*

"No rest for the wicked," Huber murmured, but he couldn't say he was sorry for the summons. "Fox, this is Fox Three-six. Sergeant Jellicoe will take acting command of the platoon till I return. Three-six out."

Huber snugged the sling of his 2-cm weapon, then swung out of the fighting compartment. He balanced for a moment on the bulging plenum chamber before half jumping, half sliding to the ground. The landing was softer than he'd expected because his boots dug into the black loam of what had been a flowerbed.

"You gonna be all right, El-Tee?" Sergeant Tranter asked. Despite the hard run they'd just completed, Tranter managed to look as though he'd stepped off a recruiting poster.

"Sure he is!" said Deseau who'd by contrast be scruffy the day they buried him in an open coffin. Right now you might guess he'd been dragged behind *Fencing Master* instead of riding in her. "Hey, there's nobody around this place that the Slammers need to worry about, right?"

"I'll let you know, Frenchie," Huber said. He walked toward the captain wearing a grin, wry but genuine.

Now that Huber's world no longer quivered with the harmonics of the drive fans, he was coming alive again. He guessed he knew how a toad felt when the first rains of autumn allowed it to break out of the summer-baked clay of a water hole.

"Sir?" he said to Sangrela. Huber hadn't known the captain well before the operation began, but he'd been impressed by what he'd seen thus far. A lot of times infantry officers didn't have much feel for how to use armored vehicles. Officers from the vehicle companies probably didn't do any better with infantry, but that wasn't Huber's problem.

"Captain Orichos wants you with her inside there," Sangrela said, indicating the Assembly Building with a curt jerk of his head. He didn't look happy about the situation. "Our orders are to cooperate with the Point authorities, so that's what you're going to do."

"The Speaker's called an extraordinary meeting of the Assembly to deal with the crisis," Captain Orichos said, sounding conciliatory if not apologetic. "I'm to address them. I'd like you with me, Lieutenant, as a representative of Hammer's Regiment."

Me rather than Sangrela, Huber thought. "Sure," he said aloud. "Do I need to say anything?"

"No, Lieutenant," Orichos said. "Your presence really says all that's necessary. Your armed presence."

Well, that's clear enough, Huber thought. He said, "All right, I'm ready when you are."

Orichos turned, nodding him to follow. "When we get inside, the ushers will direct us to the gallery upstairs," she said. "Ignore them; we'll wait in the ante-room until Speaker Nestilrode recognizes me. When he does, you'll come with me to the podium."

Huber shrugged. Parliamentary procedure, especially on somebody else's planet, wasn't a matter of great concern to him. "Who all's going to be in there?" he said, gesturing left-handed to the approaching doorway. The stairway up from the street was limestone, but the building's plinth and the attached steps were of dense black granite.

"Most assemblymen will be present," Orichos said. "Many are afraid, but they've been warned that this is the government's only chance of safety and that they won't be allowed to compromise it. If necessary—"

She looked sidelong at Huber.

"—members of the Gendarmery would escort a sufficient number of assemblymen here to make up a quorum. Whether they wanted to come or not."

Huber grinned, then sobered again. It was easy—and satisfying—to mock cowardly politicians, but in fairness they weren't people who'd signed on for armed conflict. You could be brave enough in the ordinary sense and still not want to enter a building surrounded by tanks and professional killers.

"The only people in the gallery…" Orichos continued. "Will be the goons, the so-called Volunteers, who you saw enter with Grayle and her Freedom Party colleagues. Those few are just bodyguards, but there'd have been hundreds packing the seats if it weren't for your arrival."

A porch of the same hard black stone as the plinth loomed above them. Just inside the doorway stood a man and a woman in embroidered tunics, presumably the ushers.

A mural on the wall of the semi-circular anteroom depicted an idealized Moss ranger on the right and an equally heroic female mechanic on the left. Stairs slanted upward from either side.

"We'll wait here," Orichos said curtly to the male usher. He and his colleague looked doubtful, but they didn't argue. Huber's big powergun drew their quick glances the way the view of a nude woman might have tempted a modest man, but they said nothing about the weapon.

Huber stood beside the jamb and looked through the inner doorway. Save for the anteroom, the ground floor of the Assembly Building was given over to a single chamber paneled in carved wood. Desks in ranks curved around three sides, each row rising above the one before it. It didn't look to Huber as though half of the places were occupied, but presumably enough assemblymen for the purpose were present.

The entrance was on the fourth side. Facing the desks to the right of the doorway was a railed enclosure with seats for a dozen members; all but one of them were filled. To the left was a raised lectern at which an old man in a black robe was saying, "By virtue of the powers granted me as Speaker, I have called this extraordinary session.…"

Orichos leaned close to Huber. "The cabinet," she whispered, nodding toward the enclosure.

The ordinary assemblymen sitting in the arcs of desks were staring at Huber and Orichos instead of watching the Speaker. Even some of the cabinet members stole furtive glances over their shoulders, though they faced front quickly when they caught Huber's eye.

Melinda Grayle and her two companions were almost alone on the Speaker's side of the room. The men appeared ill at ease, but Grayle's expression was sneeringly dismissive as she eyed the doorway.

Huber couldn't see the gallery from where he stood; that meant it must be directly overhead. The Volunteers'd be staring at his back if he went to the podium with Orichos. Staring at, and maybe aiming…

Well, Huber hadn't joined the Slammers because he was looking for a risk-free life. He grinned; but he also latched his clamshell again.

The Speaker continued reading from a lighted screen set into the lectern before him. He stumbled frequently over the words. This may have been the first time he'd had occasion to invoke these emergency powers, and he was probably just as nervous as most of the assemblymen.

"I'd think some of the public would want to watch," Huber said into Captain Orichos' ear. "Is everybody in the Point afraid of his shadow?"

Orichos looked at him sharply. "Of course not!" she said. "The proceedings are broadcast to the whole country by satellite! The gallery only holds a few hundred people; it'd be full normally, but by citizens indulging their whim rather than because they needed to be present to know what the Assembly was doing. Half the population lives in individual households scattered throughout the forest anyway."

Huber nodded, his eyes on the Assembly beyond. He hadn't meant to step on the woman's toes, but he should've known his comment would do just that. He must be nervous too.

"Therefore…" the Speaker said, his voice gaining new life as he reached the end of the set formula; the constitutions of most colonies had been drafted by settlers with little education but a fierce desire to make things "sound right" by using high-flown language. "Invoking the special powers granted the Speaker in the present emergency, I hereby call Captain Mauricia Orichos of the Gendarmery to address the Assembly."

Melinda Riker Grayle rose to her feet. "I protest!" she said. She filled the hall as effectively with her unamplified voice as the Speaker had moments before using a concealed public address system. "This is a business for the citizens of the Point, not for the self-serving bureaucracy which rigged the last—"

Speaker Nestilrode stabbed a control on the lectern with his bony index finger.

"—elec—" Grayle said. Her voice cut off abruptly; her lips continued to move. The Assembly Building had a *very* sophisticated audio system. The Speaker had clamped a sonic distorter around Grayle, not for privacy as it'd be used in an office but to shut her up.

"The member from Bulstrode Borough is out of order," Nestilrode said with a touch of venom in his dry voice. "The chair recognizes Captain Orichos."

Orichos stepped forward purposefully. Huber followed at her heel like a well-trained dog. The patrol sling held his 2-cm weapon muzzle-forward. His hand was on the grip, though his index finger lay along the receiver instead of through the trigger guard.

His faceshield was down. For the moment he left it clear instead of polarizing the surface to those trying to look at him.

Orichos mounted the podium. The Speaker edged sideways to let her by, but there wasn't even possibly room for Huber wearing his body armor. He stood below the Gendarmery officer instead, surveying the Assembly.

"Honored Personages," Orichos said in a tone that combined dignity with considerable forcefulness. "As many of you know, my department is responsible for information about our foreign enemies and potential enemies. While pursuing sources in the Solace government, we came upon conclusive proof that Assemblyman Grayle of Bulstrode Borough takes the pay of Solace in exchange for sowing discord within the Point."

Grayle jumped to her feet, shouting silently. The older of her male colleagues rose also, but the younger man—a blond fellow in his thirties with a neat moustache and goatee—was noticeably slower to get up. His eyes flicked from Orichos to Grayle, as nervous when they rested on his own leader as when he looked at the Gendarmery officer.

"Based on this report," Orichos continued as though oblivious of the capering Freedom Party officials, "I have applied for and been granted a warrant by the Chief Justice of the High Court to search the premises of the Freedom Party in order to corroborate our information. Due to the delicacy of the situation, I'm informing the Assembly before taking action."

Grayle's older colleague was a rougher sort than the handsome blond on her other side. She extended an arm to keep him from climbing over his desk to reach the floor. Grayle's blue eyes never left Orichos and the Speaker on the podium.

She sat down again, gesturing her colleagues with her. Her face was red, but she stared at Orichos with sneering contempt, not anger. She touched a button in her desk; a spiral of coherent orange light appeared above her head.

Orichos nodded meaningfully to the Speaker. Nestilrode leaned forward, touched the muting switch, and said, "The chair recognizes the member from Bulstrode."

Still seated, Grayle said, "That's not just a lie but a bloody lie. As Captain Orichos knows well, my party is funded entirely by the contributions of the Moss rangers on whom the nation's economy is based. There are no documents in our party headquarters or anywhere else to support these lies!"

Grayle turned so that her gaze swept the hostile assemblymen to her left and behind her. Some met her eyes; most did not. "I will not have the machinery of the law perverted to allow lying bureaucrats to plant false documents in our party offices. The so-called search has no other purpose. If that's what you intend, *Captain*, you'll have to shoot your way in—or use the mercenaries you've hired at a true cost equal to the national budget for three full years!"

Her eyes locked Huber's with almost physical force. The blond man to her left was cringing back in his chair, looking at an empty corner of the chamber with an anguished expression.

Captain Orichos gestured the Speaker aside again. "We have no desire to plant anything in the Freedom Party files," she said, "nor would we even need to disturb the normal office routine. Will the member from Bulstrode permit me and one aide to search her files in her presence, with the entire exercise being broadcast live to the citizens of the Point?"

The older man snarled something toward Grayle. She shushed him with a gesture, though the chamber's electronics had swallowed the words.

Grayle stood. She pointed her index finger at Orichos. "You'll be showing this live over the regular governmental channel?" she said. "And you'll search in the presence of me and my fellow party members?"

"Yes," said Orichos, nodding without expression. "The only concern I and my department have is that the truth come out. If our sources in Solace have misled us, then I will be the first to apologize to you and your colleagues."

Grayle slammed her fist down on her desk. "By the Lord's bleeding wounds!" she said. "That's *just* what you'll do."

She stepped sideways toward the aisle leading out. "Come on, then," she added. "We'll take care of that now—and then we'll discuss the cost of these alien murderers you've saddled the Point with!"

"You'll come with me into the Freedom Party headquarters, Lieutenant," Orichos murmured as they watched Melinda Grayle and her henchmen stride out of the chamber. Their bodyguards were trampling down the stairs from the gallery to join them. The remaining assemblymen were either rigid in their seats or whispering in small cliques.

"All right," said Huber. "Sierra, this is Fox Three-six. I'll be accompanying the liaison officer into the red buildings across the way. If anything pops, you'll know where to come and get me. Three-six out."

"*Roger that, Three-six,*" growled Captain Sangrela. "*Six out.*"

Huber looked at the Gendarmery captain. "Why me?" he said.

"Let's go," Orichos said, nodding to the doorway. "A recording team from the Speaker's staff is joining us outside."

They went out. The ushers were backed against the walls, watching Huber and Orichos with silent concern.

"I want you rather than someone from the Point…" Orichos said, showing that she wasn't ignoring Huber's question after all. "Because Grayle knows that her Volunteers outnumber the Gendarmery by several times. Your regiment's an unknown quantity, so she'll be less inclined to resort to violence."

Huber noticed that she said "…the Gendarmery…" rather than "…from my organization…." Orichos was a member of the police force only as a matter of administrative convenience. In their own self-image, intelligence personnel are a breed apart—and generally a law unto themselves as well.

Two black-haired young women waited on the porch with lens wands and satchels of recording equipment. One technician was plumpish with a broad mouth, the other razor-thin with three vertical blue lines on her right cheek. Huber couldn't tell whether the marks were tattoos or makeup.

Grayle and her entourage were walking back across the Axis to their compound. The older male was speaking into a hand communicator as he gestured forcefully with the other arm. The compound gates were open; the squad waiting there wore red headbands and carried carbines openly.

"Come along," Orichos said to the recording technicians as she strode past and started down the steps. They fell in behind obediently, looking excited but not frightened. They obviously didn't have any conception of what they were about to get into.

Trooper Learoyd waved from *Fencing Master;* Huber nodded in response. He was operating on trained reflex now. His intellect had dug itself a hole from which it viewed its surroundings in puling terror, but the part of him that was a soldier remained fully functional.

If things broke wrong, Task Force Sangrela couldn't get Huber out of the Freedom Party headquarters. The whole Regiment in line couldn't do that, though it could pulverize the buildings and everybody in them easily enough.

That wouldn't help Huber while he *was* inside. He wasn't going to fight his way out through the hundreds—at least—of armed Volunteers inside with him, either. Well, it'd be what it'd be….

On the lowest of the three terrace landings, Orichos turned her head and said, "This is of course dangerous, Lieutenant; but I don't want you to imagine that it's a suicide mission."

Huber shrugged. "It doesn't matter what I think," he said. "It's my job."

Oddly enough, the words brought him a degree of comfort. They reminded him that he was here by choice, however dangerous "here" turned out to be. And by the Lord—Arne Huber couldn't clear out the compound alone, but if push came to shove the Volunteers who took him down'd know they'd been in a fight.

The road surface was more irregular than it'd seemed while Huber was riding over it in a combat car; repeatedly his foot slipped in a rut or scuffed a ridge he hadn't noticed because his attention was where it belonged, on the armed guards waiting for him in the gateway. He imagined taking this same route while mounted on *Fencing Master.* The thought made him grin, and maybe because of that expression the solid phalanx of Volunteers parted to let Huber and his companions through without jostling.

Orichos looked over her shoulder and said, "Begin recording now," to the technicians.

The thin one sniffed and replied tartly, "We've been recording since you came out of the building, ma'am. We have orders from our supervisor."

Orichos nodded without evident emotion. Huber wondered if she were nervous or if like him she was following by rote the path she'd planned while there was time for cool reflection.

They entered the compound. Melinda Grayle stood with the older male assembly-man in the doorway of the building ten meters ahead of them. Grayle was still in the white and red outfit she'd come from the Assembly with, but her companion had changed into black battledress set off by a red headband; he carried a carbine and wore a powergun in a belt holster.

Huber didn't see the blond assemblyman. He might be inside the building, of course. Aircars, mostly battered-looking private vehicles—the large trucks were garaged in an annex outside the walls—filled the grounds within the compound. They were parked so tightly that except for the path between the gate and the central building, anyone walking across the tract would have to worm his way through and sometimes over cars.

The people they'd flown into the city watched Orichos and her companions from the buildings and from the cars themselves. Everyone Huber saw was armed, and they were trying to look tough. For most of them, that didn't require a great deal of effort.

"All right, madam snoop," Grayle said to Orichos. "You're here now. How do you intend to proceed?"

"We'll go directly to the file room adjacent to your personal office on the fourth floor, Assemblyman Grayle," Orichos said calmly. "If there's no record of wrongdoing there, you'll have my apologies and we'll leave immediately."

Grayle's eyes narrowed; she looked angry but not, if Huber read her correctly, afraid. "I'll have your apology *and* your resignation, Captain," she said. "And you'll be lucky if there's not a libel suit as well!"

"Just as you please," Orichos said. She didn't look concerned either.

Grayle turned on her heel and strode into the building. Orichos followed immedi-ately instead of waiting for the permission that wasn't going to come. Huber gestured the recorders ahead of him and brought up the rear. He didn't bother trying to watch behind him; he knew he'd see an armed mob, and it wasn't going to make him feel any more comfortable.

The two girls now looked nervous. They were walking so close together so that they occasionally bumped elbows. They'd started to understand....

There were two elevators in the wall to the right of the doorway. Grayle gestured to them with her left hand and said sardonically, "Take your pick, snooper."

"We'll take the one that goes to the fourth floor," Orichos replied in a mild tone, stepping in front of Grayle and pressing the call button for the cage farther from the door.

Grayle's face went carefully neutral, but the male assemblyman with her said, "Hey, how does she—"

"Shut up, Fewsett!" Grayle said. Her voice didn't rise, but the snarl in it brought a look of surprise and anger to her subordinate's face. He cocked his right hand back, then gaped in blank horror at what he'd been about to do.

Grayle ignored him, pushing past Orichos to enter the elevator before the delega-tion from the Assembly could do so. Fewsett followed; other Volunteers would have done so as well, but there simply wasn't room on what was meant as a private car for the highest officials.

Huber grinned without humor. He didn't doubt that there'd be a sufficiency of gunmen already waiting for them upstairs.

The elevator rose smoothly but with a repetitive squeak to which the plump recording technician winced in synchrony. The thinner girl took her hand and squeezed it tightly. The contact seemed to help; at any rate, the twitches immediately became less pronounced.

The elevator stopped. What had been the back of the cage opened into an office appointed like a throne room. A large stuffed chair with gilt upholstery stood on a dais behind an agate-topped desk. Behind it was a wood-framed triptych of heroic figures created not by an artist but by a technician using stock imagery. Highlights on the pictures' glossy surface veiled them; a good result.

Even urban structures on Plattner's World tended to be tall and narrow, slipped in among the trees that were the source of the planet's considerable income. This high-ceilinged office was half the building's top floor; even so, another dozen people besides the six waiting gunmen would've filled the space left over by the desk and throne. They'd have had to stand, because there was no other chair in the room.

Grayle and her henchman got out first as they had entered. Fewsett immediately began to talk in a guttural whisper to the leader of the waiting squad, a slender man with tattoos and a serpentine copper bracelet.

Captain Orichos led the way to the small door at the side of the throne room; Huber brought up the rear. Through it was a paneled hallway with a stairwell at the far end and a doorway on the left side. Another squad of guards waited in the hall.

"Back, if you please!" Orichos said, gesturing at the guards. She opened the side door and entered the file room beyond.

Huber gave the gunmen a wry smile. They didn't know what was going on any better than he himself did. That didn't make him and the Volunteers brothers, but it was a good enough illustration of a soldier's life to amuse him.

There was no one in the file room; five-drawer cabinets circled the walls, leaving only an aisle in the middle. Though the Freedom Party was as technically advanced as the rest of Plattner's World, hardcopy remained a necessary backup to electronic files and ultimately more secure than any form of information linked directly to the outside world.

"Assemblyman Grayle?" Orichos said to the woman watching from the doorway. "Would you or a deputy please join us before I begin examining your files? Although the whole nation is witness to the proceedings—"

The thin technician's face was frozen, her mouth slightly open; she held her wand rigidly upright where it recorded events in a sphere around her. The other technician huddled against a back corner, leaning on her wand as though it were a cane. Huber supposed it was doing an adequate job of recording the parts of the file room that were blocked from her companion's lenses.

"—I'd like someone in whom you have confidence to be present to ensure that I'm merely examining files, not adding anything to them."

"By the Lord, you'd *better* not be adding stuff!" Fewsett growled. He added, presumably to some of the gunmen, "Come on, boys."

Grayle stepped in herself. Huber squeezed against the cabinets behind him to allow her to get by if she wanted, but she merely gave him a sneer. "Go ahead!" she said. "You'll find nothing because there's nothing to find."

Fewsett crowded in behind Grayle and touched her shoulder to move her back. She slapped his hand without looking around. More Volunteers stacked into the doorway; those in front pushed back against their fellows to the rear to keep from being shoved into Fewsett's massive figure.

Orichos nodded, then turned to a cabinet midway down the row. "Let the record show that I am at a cabinet marked Finance," she said, and opened the second drawer from the top.

Huber stood with his head cocked so that though he mainly faced the Freedom Party officials, he could still watch Orichos out of the corner of his eye. Grayle's expression was one of iron disdain; Fewsett glared past her with a mixture of anger and frustration.

"Bring the wand closer," Orichos snapped to the plump recorder. When there was no reaction, Orichos lifted the girl's arm and placed the lens wand on the edge of the drawer. In a dry, mechanical voice Orichos continued, "I am removing a file marked Special."

"What is this?" Grayle said on a rising note. She tried to look behind her but the way was filled with gunmen. "Where's Patronus? Why isn't he here?"

Orichos displayed her empty right hand to the lens wand, then reached into the drawer and brought out a folder with a red tab. She spread her left hand in plain sight also, then opened the folder.

Fewsett turned and bellowed, "Get that bastard Patronus here now! He's the fucking party treasurer. We need him *now!*"

Huber didn't move except to slide his finger into the trigger guard. He'd figured how the business was going to play out, but he didn't know quite the exact time.

Or whether he'd survive it.

"The folder holds a list of amounts and dates," Orichos said. "It purports to be records—"

The lens wand slipped off the drawer; the plump technician had curled her arms around herself, sunk into a personal world light-years away from this terror. In a sudden break from her detached calm, Orichos looked at the girl and screamed, "Hold that bloody thing up or I'll have you executed for treason!"

The thin technician tilted her wand closer to the open drawer. She didn't look toward Orichos.

"This is fake!" Grayle said. "It's been planted! There's no—"

"Purports to be a record," Orichos resumed in a louder voice, "of payments—"

"—truth in it at all!"

"—by the Interior Ministry of the Government of Solace to the Freedom Party!"

Grayle turned to get out of the file room. Fewsett knocked her back accidentally as he raised his carbine. Huber fired from the hip. His 2-cm bolt hit Fewsett in the upper chest, vaporizing most of the big man's torso in a thunderclap. The shockwave slammed Huber against a file cabinet and knocked the Volunteers in the doorway off their feet.

A Volunteer tried to aim his carbine, or maybe he was just flailing his arms for support. The powergun's cyan flash would've blinded anybody seeing it close-up without the protection of a polarizing faceshield like Huber's. He fired twice more, clearing the doorway save for a scatter of body parts. A blast-severed head flew past Huber, driven by vaporized body fluids.

The thin technician screamed and flung down her wand. It wobbled behind her on its flex as she sprang through the doorway Huber was trying to slam shut with his left hand. Two or more gunmen riddled her before she took a second step into the hallway. She thrashed backward, but Huber threw all his weight against the panel. It latched despite the obstructions.

A burst of shots whanged into the door from the outside. The panel was metal-cored, but concentrated gunfire would peck through it before long. For that matter there must be somebody in the gang outside with the key to the door's snap lock.

"Don't shoot, you idiots!" Melinda Riker Grayle screamed. "Don't shoot or you'll kill me!"

Huber glanced behind him. Grayle sprawled on the floor. Captain Orichos lay on top of her, twisting back her left arm and holding a pistol to Grayle's neck.

The plump technician sat on the floor with her legs splayed, crying uncontrollably. The room was hot—oven hot, heated by the three heavy-caliber powergun discharges in its narrow confines.

When a bolt liberated its energy in a human body, it turned the tissues to steam with explosive suddenness. The file room's walls, the ceiling, and the people within were all covered with a mist of blood. Huber's hands were red, and there was a sticky film across his faceshield that the static charge hadn't been able to repel. He flipped the shield up and out of the way.

The stench of cooked flesh and of the wastes voided when Fewsett's sphincters spasmed in death was stomach-churning, even for Huber who'd smelled it before. Some things you never get used to....

Captain Orichos raised herself to her knees, still pointing her pistol at the assembly-man. She patted the floor with her left hand till she found the lens wand and raised it vertical again. Grayle twisted to look back into the bore of the pistol.

"Assemblyman Grayle!" Orichos said. "You stand convicted of treason by your own records and by your failed attempt to use force against the agents of the Assembly!"

"That's a lie!" Grayle said in a hoarse voice. "You planted that file!"

Several voices were jabbering at Huber through his commo helmet; at least one of them seemed to be from Base Alpha. He locked out all incoming channels and concentrated on the door in case the Volunteers tried to rush it. The muzzle of his powergun was cooling from yellow to bright orange.

"In order to prevent bloodshed among citizens…" Orichos continued as though her prisoner hadn't spoken. She was facing Grayle over the gunsights, but Huber noted that her eyes weren't focused anywhere in this world. "I'm offering you, in the name of the citizens of the Point, a chance to go into exile. You and all your fellow conspirators will have one hour to leave Midway and six hours to leave the Point. After that time, you will be considered criminals and dealt with according to law."

"You faked that so-called evidence," Grayle said, "and you faked the vote count to steal the last election from the Freedom Party! You're the criminals! You're thieves, and you're bankrupting the state by hiring these mercenaries!"

"Assemblyman Grayle!" Orichos said. She jerked her weight backward to balance her as she stood. She held the wand in her left hand like a torch, and the pistol slanted down toward her prisoner's face. "Do you accept my offer, made in the presence of the entire citizenry of the Point?"

"Better take the offer, lady," Huber said. Ozone from the 2-cm bolts had flayed his throat, making his voice a rasp that he wouldn't have recognized himself. "Whatever else happens, I guarantee you're not going to leave here alive any other way."

Grayle looked at him. Her eyes slid downward to the floor on which she lay. Fewsett's head, severed when his chest exploded, stared back at her from a hand's breadth away. She jumped to her feet, forgetting the threat of Orichos' pistol.

"It's all a lie!" Grayle said. She got control of her breathing and went on, "But I don't have any choice. All right—we'll leave Midway, but I'm agreeing under duress. You have no legal right to expel us!"

"You out there in the hall?" Huber shouted. He figured the Volunteers, a lot of them anyway, would be watching the broadcast along with the rest of the citizens, but the gunmen just outside the door might be an exception. "I'm going to open the door. The first one through it's going to be your leader, Assemblyman Grayle. But be clear on this—you've got a deal with your government and your Gendarmery. You don't have a deal with me personally. If anybody sticks his head into this room, I'm going to blow him to atoms just like I did a lot of his buddies a moment ago. Got it?"

Nobody answered. Huber thought he heard the sound of boots running down the staircase. Grayle was poised like a roach caught by the light, momentarily frozen.

"Captain Orichos?" Huber said.

"Yes, open the door," Orichos said.

Instead of reaching, Huber kicked out with his right boot and sprung the latch. The panel bounced open. The hallway was empty.

Grayle jumped through so quickly that she slid on the blood pooling from the dead technician's body. She caught herself on the wall and ran toward the stairs, leaving a handprint on the wall behind her.

Nothing else moved for over a minute.

Huber let out his breath. He switched his helmet back to RECEIVE mode and said, "Fox Three-six to Sierra. We're holding our present position on the fourth floor of the Freedom Party headquarters until somebody comes to fetch us out. And give me plenty of warning before you show yourselves, people, because I'm as jumpy as I've ever been in my life!"

Captain Sangrela's driver had bounced his jeep up the Assembly Building steps and parked it under the porch. The officers and senior sergeants of Task Force Sangrela stood on the patterned stone, listening to the holographic image of Danny Pritchard speaking from Base Alpha.

Around them the citizens of Midway noisily celebrated their release from Freedom Party domination. In the street below whirled a round dance with hundreds of participants. A fiddler stood on a raised platform in the middle of the circle; beside him, occasionally crowding his elbow, gyrated a young woman wearing only briefs. Huber didn't think she was professional—just exuberant and very happy. As far up and down the Axis as Huber could see there were similar dances as well as free buffets, speakers on makeshift podiums, and crowds of people drinking and singing in good fellowship.

"The Volunteers are gathering at their base on Bulstrode Bay on the northern coast," said Danny Pritchard's holographic image. "They call it Fort Freedom, and it's going to be a tough nut to crack."

Aircars spun and swooped overhead, often with sirens blaring. The drivers were as excited and as generally drunk as the people in the street. Huber had seen two collisions and heard a worse one that sent a car crashing to the ground on the other side of the Mound.

"Why us, sir?" Captain Sangrela asked. His voice was calm, but the way his hands tightly gripped the opposite elbows indicated his tension.

"Because you can, Captain," Pritchard said simply. "Because we can't leave ten thousand armed enemies in a state whose support we need. And because the locals can't do it themselves—"

He grinned harshly.

"—which is generally why people hire the Slammers, right?"

The Gendarmery had been conspicuous by its absence during the events of the afternoon. Now the Point's gray-uniformed police were out in force, though they seemed more to be showing themselves than making an effort to control the good-natured partying that was going on. The Gendarmes on foot patrol carried only pistols; those in the cruising aircars may have had carbines but they weren't showing them.

"Ten *thousand* of 'em, sir?" said C-1's platoon sergeant, a rangy man named Dunsterville. He sounded incredulous rather than afraid at what he'd heard. "You mean the guys with red sweatbands?"

"The Volunteers, yes," Pritchard agreed with a grim nod. "You won't have to deal with all of them—indeed, that's why we've decided to move on Fort Freedom immediately. We expect that at least half of Grayle's Volunteers will decide to stay home in the woods if they know that joining her means facing tanks. If we withdraw from the Point and the Volunteers don't have anybody to worry about except the locals, then they'll everyone of them march back into Midway and this time loot the place."

When Pritchard said "we've decided," he meant Colonel Hammer and his Regimental Command group. The "we" who'd be carrying out the operation meant Call-Sign Sierra, ten vehicles and less than a hundred troopers under Captain Sangrela. Huber was a volunteer, and he knew that the senior officers had all been at the sharp end in their day too… but Via! Fifty to one was curst long odds!

"Here's a plan of Fort Freedom," Pritchard continued. The image of his body disappeared, leaving his head hovering above a sharply circular embayment viewed from the south at an apparent downward angle of forty-five degrees. The sea had cut away the northern third of the rock walls and filled the interior. "Bulstrode Bay's an ancient volcano. The walls average a hundred meters high and are about that thick at the base. There's normal housing inside of the crater, but the Volunteers have also tunneled extensively into the walls."

"Have they got artillery?" Huber asked. He was still trying to get his head around the notion of going up against five *thousand* armed hostiles… or maybe ten thousand after all, because staff estimates were just that, estimates, and Sierra would be facing real guns.

"The Volunteers don't have an indirect fire capacity so far as we can tell," Pritchard said, nodding at a good question. "Not even mortars. What they *do* have—"

The holographic image transformed itself into a gun carriage mounting eight stubby iridium barrels locked together in two banks; each tube had its own ammo feed. The chassis was on two wheels with a trail for towing the weapon rather than being self-powered.

"—are calliopes. We've traced a lot of twenty purchased by Grayle's agents nine months ago, and it's possible that there've been others besides."

Calliopes, multi-barreled 2- or 3-cm powerguns, provided many mercenary units with the air defense that the Slammers handled through their own armored vehicles. The weapons were extremely effective against ground targets as well. A short burst from a calliope could shred a combat car and turn its crew into cat's meat.…

Pritchard's full figure replaced the image of the calliope. "I'm not making light of the job you face," he said. "But I do want to emphasize that the Volunteers are *not* soldiers. Most of them have only small arms, they aren't disciplined, and they've never faced real firepower. If you hit them hard and fast they'll break, troopers. You'll break them to pieces."

"Calliopes cost money," Mitzi Trogon said. "More money than I'd expect from a bunch of hicks in the sticks."

Pritchard nodded again. "Whatever you think of the documents the Point security police found," he said with a grin, "we have evidence that the government of Solace is indeed supporting the Freedom Party."

Solace would be insane not to, Huber thought. Arming the internal enemies of a hostile government was about the cheapest way to reduce its threat.

In the street and sky, the citizens of Midway danced and sang. They were the rulers, the people who split among themselves the wealth and the status and the political power of the Point. They were right to fear Melinda Grayle, a demagogue who'd united the Moss rangers against the urban elite who lorded it over them.

Captain Sangrela rubbed the back of his neck. "We're going cross-country, I suppose?" he said. "There isn't much *but* cross-country on this bloody planet."

"Not exactly," Pritchard said as the image of a terrain map replaced that of his body. "The direct route'd take you through ancient forest. The trees are too thick and grow too densely for your vehicles to push through or maneuver through either one. We've plotted you a course down the valley of the River Fiorno. It won't be fast, but the vegetation there's thin enough that even the cars can break trail."

The red line of the planned course dotted its way along the solid blue of a watercourse. Not far from the coast, the red diverged straight northward for some fifty kilometers to reach Bulstrode Bay.

"The last part of the route, we'll clear for you with incendiary rounds. We estimate it'll take you nearly two days to reach the point you'll leave the Fiorno. The fire should've burned itself out by then, so you can make the last part of your run relatively quickly."

Pritchard smiled again. "The fire should also limit the risk of ambush," he said; then he sobered and added, "But that'll be a very real possibility while you're following the river. We'll do what we can from Base Alpha, but you'll have to proceed with scouts and a full sensor watch the same as you did on the way here."

Pritchard's image looked around the gathering. "Any questions?" he asked.

"I don't like to complain, Major…" said Sergeant Jellicoe, lacing her fingers in front of her. "But do you suppose after this, somebody else in the bloody regiment can get a little action too?"

Everybody laughed; but everybody, Pritchard included, knew that the comment hadn't entirely been a joke. "I'll see what I can do," he said.

On the fiddler's platform below, the woman dancing had stripped off her panties as well. Huber glanced down at her… and turned his head away.

He was going to need his rest. The next part of the operation sounded like it was going to be even rougher than what it'd taken to get Task Force Sangrela this far.

Huber called up a remote from *Flame Farter*, on the move with White Section for the past ten minutes. The Fiorno River was only thirty meters wide and almost shallow enough to wade where it curved around the north and east of Midway. The scouts' skimmers danced in rainbows of spray out in the channel to avoid the reeds along the margins; the combat car was chuffing down the bank, spewing mud and fragments of soft vegetation from beneath her skirts.

"*Red Section, move out!*" Captain Sangrela ordered. The main body with Jellicoe's *Floosie* in the lead was already lined up on the Axis north of the Assembly Building. Dust puffed beneath their skirts as they lifted from the gravel. One at a time, carefully because objects so powerful must move carefully if they're not to destroy themselves and everything around them, the seven vehicles of the main body started down the avenue. The doughnuts of dust spread into wakes on either side.

Sergeant Nagano glanced over from *Foghorn*'s fighting compartment; Huber was keeping his section on the Mound till the main body had cleared the road beneath. Huber gave Nagano a thumbs-up. Nagano hadn't commanded a car before the operations against Northern Star, and he was doing a good job.

"How'd you make out last night, El-Tee?" Sergeant Deseau asked, stretching like a cat behind the forward gun.

"I slept like a baby," Huber said. "I never sleep that well on leave when I'm in a bed."

The Assembly had offered the Slammers any kind of billets they wanted, but Captain Sangrela had decided to keep his troopers beside their vehicles for the night. Nobody'd argued with him. The weather wasn't unpleasant, and chances were some Freedom Party supporters had stayed in Midway. The risks of going off by yourself were a lot greater than any benefit a bed in an unfamiliar room was going to bring.

"Not me," said Deseau, grinning even broader. "The people here are *real* grateful, let me tell you."

Learoyd looked around from his gun. Shyly he said, "The girls didn't charge nothing, El-Tee. I never been a place before that the girls didn't charge."

A Gendarmery aircar came up the Axis from the south, flying low and slow. Huber caught the motion in the corner of his eye, then cranked the image up to x32 as an inset on his faceshield. As he'd thought, Captain Orichos was in the passenger seat.

The fourth D Company tank pulled out at the back of the main body, accelerating with the slow majesty that its mass demanded. *Floosie* was out of sight beyond the northern end of the Axis, into the mixture of forest and scattered houses that constituted the city's suburbs.

"Fox Three-six to Three-one," Huber said to Sergeant Nagano. "Move into the street. We'll follow you down and bring up the rear. Three-six out."

Foghorn lurched from its berth and ground through a hedge that'd survived Task Force Sangrela's arrival. *Whoever was driving for Nagano today must be keyed tighter than a lute string,* Huber thought; he grinned faintly. *Which showed the driver understands what we're about to get into.*

"*Sir, shall I shift us now?*" Sergeant Tranter prodded from the driver's compartment.

"Give me a moment, Tranter," Huber replied. "I think I've got a visitor."

"Hey, it's your girlfriend, El-Tee," Deseau said cheerfully. He waved at the aircar swinging in along *Fencing Master*'s port side.

"Not *my* girlfriend," Huber said as he lifted himself out of the fighting compartment to stand on the plenum chamber. And probably not even a friend, to Arne Huber or to any member of the Slammers. Orichos had other priorities, and Huber had only the vaguest notion of what they might be.

As the aircar hovered beside them, the Gendarmery captain tossed Huber a satchel no larger than the personal kit of a trooper on active deployment. "I hope you don't mind, Lieutenant…" she called over the thrum of the aircar and the whine of *Fencing Master*'s idled fans. "But I'm going to join you again."

Huber thrust the satchel behind him for Deseau to take. He extended his right hand while his left anchored him to the fighting compartment's coaming.

"Welcome aboard, Captain," he said, swinging Orichos across to the combat car. She was surprisingly light; his subconscious expected the weight of a figure wearing body armor, of course.

Mauricia Orichos wasn't welcome, but she was part of Huber's job so he'd make the best of it. And he really had more important things on his mind just now....

Huber heard a coarse *ripping* as three more rounds from batteries far to the south streaked overhead. To give the shells sufficient range from the Slammers' gun positions in the UC, a considerable part of what would normally be payload was given over to the booster rockets.

"*What's that?*" asked Mauricia Orichos, pointing upward. The shells' boron fluoride exhaust unrolled broad, poisonous ribbons at high altitude, spreading as she watched. "*Are we under attack?*"

"No, that's outgoing," Huber explained, mildly surprised that their passenger had picked up the sound of artillery over *Fencing Master*'s intake howl. Orichos noticed quite a lot, he realized, and she had the knack for absorbing what was normal in a new situation so that she could quickly identify change. "They're prepping the route for us."

He wasn't sure how much Orichos knew about the plan, and he wasn't going to be the one to tell her anything Base Alpha hadn't already explained. If it'd been up to Arne Huber, he'd have told the Point authorities an amount precisely equal to the part Point forces were taking in the reduction of Fort Freedom: zip.

He glanced up at the path the shells had taken northward. For this use, the reduced payloads didn't matter. The shells would spill their incendiary bomblets at very high altitude to get maximum dispersion. The target wasn't a single facility but rather a fifty-kilometer swathe of forest, and there was plenty of time for the widely-spread ignition points to grow together into a massive firestorm.

Which wasn't the sort of thing a local from Plattner's World, where the forest was preserved with almost religious fervor, could be expected to like. Colonel Hammer put his troopers' lives first, though, and Colonel Hammer was calling the shots on this one.

The vehicles ahead of *Fencing Master* had mown and gouged the riverbank into a muddy wasteland. Wherever possible the lead car had chosen a route that kept its skirts on solid ground, but occasionally an outcrop or a deep inlet forced the column partly into the water. Each *thrum!* as plenum-chamber pressure beat the river echoed for kilometers up and down the channel.

Huber grinned. Orichos misread his expression, for she smiled back ruefully and said, "*I suppose I do sound like a Nervous Nellie. Sorry.*"

"What?" said Huber. "Oh, not at all. I was just thinking that there's never been an armored column in human history that sneaked up on anybody, and this time isn't going to be the exception."

"El-Tee?" said Learoyd, staring dutifully into the holographic display. "*Take a look *at this, will you?"*

Huber'd put his right wing gunner on the first sensor watch of the run because he hadn't expected anything to show up so early. He'd manually notched out *Fencing Master* and the other vehicles in the column during the run from Northern Star, so that they wouldn't hide the more distant, hostile, signals. Unlike a quicker mind, Learoyd's wouldn't be lulled into daydreams by the minute changes in pearly emptiness that was probably all that he'd see in the display, but Huber feared that Learoyd might not notice subtleties that really had meaning.

Except that the trooper'd done just that. Huber frowned at the display in dawning comprehension, then said, "Sierra Six, this is Fox Three-six. We've got an aircar, probably a small one, following us about a kilometer back. I figure if it was just civilian sightseers, they'd be, well, in sight. Over."

"Roger, Three-six," Captain Sangrela said. *"We leave a broad enough track that the Volunteers figure they can follow us without coming so close we spot them. Good work, Huber. I'll drop off a fire team to take care of it. Six out."*

"Three-six out," Huber said. "Break. Blue Section, some infantry's staying behind to clean off our tail. Don't run 'em over, and get ready to back 'em up when the music starts. Three-six out."

"We gonna get a chance to pop somebody, El-Tee?" Deseau asked, turning hopefully to meet Huber's eyes.

"Not a chance, Frenchie," Huber said. "But we're going to follow the drill anyway."

A thought struck him and he went on, "Captain Orichos? Is there any chance that a Gendarmery aircar is trailing the column? If there is, tell me now. You won't get a second chance."

Orichos frowned. *"One of ours?"* she said. *"Not unless somebody's disregarded my clear instructions. And if that's happened, Lieutenant—"*

She smiled. Frenchie Deseau couldn't have bettered the cruel surmise in her expression.

"—then the sort of lesson I assume you propose will bring the survivors to a better appreciation of the authority granted me by the Assembly."

Huber nodded and returned his attention to his tribarrel's sector forward. He didn't have a problem with ruthlessness, but he found disquieting the gusto with which people like the Gendarmery captain did what was necessary.

"Three-six, watch the pedestrians!" Nagano warned from *Foghorn* fifty meters ahead. Four infantrymen had hopped their skimmers off one of the maintenance vehicles; now they were positioning themselves behind treeboles where they'd have good fields of fire for their 2-cm weapons as soon as the aircar came in sight above the water. Huber nodded in salute, but the infantrymen were wholly focused on what was about to happen.

The ambush team had shut down their skimmers immediately upon hitting the ground. The Volunteers weren't likely to have sensors that'd pick up a skimmer's small fans more than a stone's throw away, but regimental training emphasized that you didn't assume any more than you had to. Plenty of stuff that you couldn't control was going to go wrong, so you made doubly sure on the rest.

"*How long, Lieutenant?*" Orichos asked. Not what: how long. She was a sharp one, no mistake.

"About a minute and a half," Huber explained. "We're traveling at about forty kph in this salad—"

He gestured to the soft vegetation just outside the track, where the previous vehicles hadn't ground it to green slime.

"—and our Volunteer friends back there'll be holding to the same speed. The last thing they want's to fly up on our tail."

He smiled. Which was just what they were about to do.

Orichos nodded and turned to watch the route behind *Fencing Master*. There wasn't anything to see but mud and muddy water, of course. Sight distances close to the ground were at most a hundred meters in the few places the river flowed straight, and generally much less where vegetation arched over the curving banks.

Huber imported to the lower left quadrant of his faceshield the view from the sergeant commanding the ambush team; it wouldn't interfere with his sight picture in the unlikely event that *Fencing Master* ran into trouble. After a moment's hesitation, he touched Orichos' shoulder. When she turned, he linked their helmets as he had while *Floosie* raked incoming shells from the sky. Orichos nodded appreciatively.

It took ten seconds longer than Huber'd estimated before an open aircar with four men aboard loitered into sight. Sangrela had chosen the ambush site well: the car slowed, dipping beneath a branch draped with air plants which crossed the river only three meters above the purling surface.

The lift fans flung a rainbow of spray through the sunlight, momentarily blinding the two men in the front. As the car started to rise again, three cyan bolts hit the driver, vaporizing his torso, and a fourth took off the head of the gunman in the passenger seat.

The driver jerked the control yoke convulsively, throwing the car belly forward and spilling the remaining gunman off the stern. The sergeant shot the falling man before he hit the water; the three troopers blew the car's underside into fireballs of plastic paneling superheated into a mixture that exploded in the air.

"Blue Section, reverse!" Huber screamed. Sergeant Tranter was a trifle slower to spin *Fencing Master* than he should've been; Huber'd forgotten the driver didn't have reflexes ingrained by combat like the rest of them did. "Move it! Move it! Move it!"

The ambush team didn't need help. The aircar crashed edgewise onto a spine of rock sticking up from the water; it broke apart. The fourth Volunteer had been concentrating on detector apparatus feeding through a bulky helmet. He must've been strapped in; his arms flailed, but he didn't get out of the car even when the wreckage slipped off the rocks and started to sink.

The river geysered as at least four and maybe twice that many 2-cm bolts hit the man and the water nearby. A bolt hit an upthrust rock; it burst like a grenade, shredding foliage on the bank with sharp fragments.

I guess the poor bastard's not going to drown after all, Huber thought.

When *Fencing Master* reached the ambush site a few seconds later, the infantrymen had remounted their skimmers. Huber gestured them forward to put the combat car in drag position again.

"*You were right, El-Tee,*" said Deseau regretfully. "*Not a bloody thing for us.*"

One of the infantrymen waved back as he passed *Fencing Master*. He was now wearing a helical copper bracelet, its ends shaped like snakeheads.

Apparently the leader of the squad Huber shot it out with in Freedom Party headquarters hadn't learned from that experience. Huber smiled coldly. The Slammers didn't give anybody a third chance.

The alert signal brought Huber out of a doze; it was like swimming upward through hot sand. He'd jumped to his feet and had the tribarrel's grips in his hands, straining for a target in his faceshield's light-amplified imagery, before his conscious mind took over and he realized why he'd awakened.

Learoyd was driving. Sergeant Deseau was at the forward gun, as rested as anybody could be after eighteen hours of slogging through river-bottom vegetation. Huber wouldn't have been able to drop off if he hadn't been sure Frenchie was there to take up the slack. He'd needed the mental down-time badly, though. The shoot-out in Freedom Party headquarters had drained him more than he'd realized right after it happened.

But that was part of the past, a different world, and now the present was calling. "Fox Three-six acknowledging!" Huber said, and his helmet dropped him into the virtual meeting room with Colonel Hammer himself and the other officers of Task Force Sangrela. He'd been the last to arrive, but from the look of Mitzi Trogon—her mouth was half-open and her eyes looked like they were staring into oncoming headlights—she was in at least as bad a shape as he was.

"Troopers," Hammer said, acknowledging his four subordinates with a glance that swept the table. The imagery was sharper than it'd been in the forest south of Midway; the sky above the Fiorno was fairly open. "There's Volunteers setting up a blocking position on an island three hours ahead of you. There's about two hundred men with buzzbombs and six calliopes if they're not further reinforced."

Hammer's torso vanished into a slant view of a roughly oval island; it covered about as much of the river valley as the channels flowing to north and south of it. From the scale at the bottom of the image, the heavily wooded surface between the streams was on the order of a square kilometer.

"They've been flying in from Bulstrode Bay over the past hour," Hammer said with a disbelieving shake of his head. "They apparently don't realize that here at Base Alpha we can follow everything they're doing, right down to who had grits for breakfast."

Icons of red light marked hostile positions: calliopes on the forward curve of the island, and squads of infantry both on the island itself and on the north bank of the floodway. The Volunteers probably intended the mainland element to halt the task force in line along the shore where the calliopes could rake the Slammers from the flank.

Sangrela laughed in derision. "You want us to go through 'em or around 'em, sir?" he asked. "For choice we'll go through."

"Neither," said Hammer with a spreading smile. "I'm just telling you what the situation is. We're going to handle it from here with artillery."

"Why in hell would you want to do that?" Mitzi Trogon snarled. She must've heard her own tone; she snapped fully awake at last. "Ah, *sir*, that is," she added with a grimace of embarrassment.

Hammer looked at Trogon without expression for a moment, then lifted his chin minutely to show that the incident was closed—if not forgotten. "Right," he said with a mildness that deceived nobody. "This ambush isn't a problem, but Fort Freedom is likely to be more of one. Here the Volunteers have their calliopes tasked for ground use, waiting for your column to come into their killing zone. They aren't professional enough to redirect the guns for artillery defense in the amount of time they'll have. Follow?"

Because Huber understood and none of his fellow officers were in a hurry to speak after Mitzi'd stepped on her dick, he said, "When a salvo takes out the whole ambush party, Volunteer Command is going to decide it's our shells they ought to be worrying about. When we get to Bulstrode Bay, their calliopes are going to be aimed up for artillery defense and we'll take 'em with direct fire."

"Roger that, troopers," Hammer said, his face minusculely softer than it'd been a moment before. "This won't be a milk run for you, there's no way it's going to be that. But I told you from the beginning that you'd have all the support we could give you. Any questions?"

"Support" this time didn't mean the artillery, not really, Huber realized. It was the planning, the misdirection; the thinking two steps ahead of his own troops and at least six steps ahead of the enemy, that the Colonel was providing here.

"What orders do you have for us, sir?" Captain Sangrela asked, the burr of warmth in his tone suggesting that he was thinking along the same lines as Huber was.

"Keep on with what you're doing, that's all," Hammer said. His grin spread. "Which is plenty, I know that. We'll time the stonk for thirty seconds before you come into sight of the target. Hit anybody that shows himself, but keep going as fast as you can. That'll make more of an impression on what passes for a Volunteer Command group than we would by digging out a couple shell-shocked wogs and blasting them. Clear?"

"Clear," said Sangrela, nodding, and Huber added his "Clear" to the muttered "Roger," and "Clear," from his fellow lieutenants.

That'd save gun bores for the real fight at Bulstrode Bay as well. Maintenance had replaced the barrels burned out at Northern Star, but there probably wouldn't be time for another refit before Sierra slammed into Fort Freedom and the Volunteers' main body....

Hammer gave a crisp nod. "Let me stick it to the bastards this time, troopers," he said. "There'll be plenty of opportunity for you up north."

The Colonel's image dissolved, returning Huber to *Fencing Master*'s jouncing fighting compartment. His mind and senses were as sharp as they'd ever been in his life. To the watchful expressions of his troopers and Captain Orichos, he began, "In about three hours…"

What looked like a streak of sparse vegetation at right angles to the river was a dike of impermeable clay channeling water into the softer soil beyond. The scout section infantry slid across without being aware of the change, but *Fencing Master* came down on algae-covered soup instead of the expected solid ground. A gout of mud spewed higher than the armored sides, drenching Huber and the others in the fighting compartment.

Tranter boosted power and adjusted the nacelles vertical for maximum lift. *Fencing Master* pogoed back onto an even keel and wallowed slowly across the basin.

"Fox Three-six to Sierra," Huber warned. "There's quicksand here. The panzers had better swing wide or they'll sink to wherever the bottom turns out to be. Three-six out."

By rights, *Foghorn* would've been the leading car if they'd gone by the preplanned rotation. Sergeant Nagano hadn't been pleased when Huber exercised his command prerogative to put *Fencing Master* in the lead as the column prepared to run the Volunteer ambush, but Huber was doubly glad he'd done it now. Only a driver as able as Sergeant Tranter would've kept from bogging or simply sinking out of sight in this soft spot, and there were bloody few drivers that good.

"Roger Three-six," Captain Sangrela said. "*Delta units, follow the contour lines north. Looks to me like two hundred meters will let you cross safely. Six out.*"

Fencing Master lifted itself with a jerk onto higher, harder ground. Tranter paused a moment before readjusting the fans, checking to be sure that mud and water plants hadn't choked any of the intake ducts. The combat car built up speed again, shedding weed and watery mud like a dog emerging from a pond.

Mauricia Orichos dabbed at the muck staining her uniform, managing only to spread the stain until she gave up the pointless exercise. She noticed Huber's glance and smiled faintly.

"*I suppose it doesn't matter,*" she said. "*I'm used to thinking in… urban terms, I suppose.*"

"It doesn't matter," Huber agreed. *Especially if we're all dead in the next thirty seconds,* but he didn't let that last thought reach his tongue.

He heard the incoming shells at first as a distant friction in the sky. With shocking suddenness their howl filled the whole world and still grew louder. Sergeant Deseau hunched over the forward gun, aware that it was friendly fire aimed to impact half a klick ahead of *Fencing Master;* aware also that mistakes happen, that even the most technologically advanced shells land short occasionally, and that no fire is friendly when it's coming in on your position.

The Gendarmery captain's face went blank; her eyes opened wide. For a moment Huber thought she was going to throw herself as close to flat as she could get in the crowded fighting compartment, but she recovered her composure when she noticed he wasn't taking any action.

"It's all right," he explained. "This is the prep that's—"

The shells burst directly overhead with four distinct pops. The opened casings spilled the separate white streaks of over a thousand bomblets toward the ground ahead of *Fencing Master*. They whistled like a symphony for chalk on blackboards.

"—going to land on the—"

The timing was slightly off: *Fencing Master* tore through the last screen of feather-fronded vegetation a second before instead of a few seconds after the bomblets struck the Volunteer positions. The mid-channel island was a green mass against the tannin-black water. Near the shore the foliage was the same sort of lush shrubbery that Task Force Sangrela had ground through on the route from Midway, but there were some sizeable trees a hundred meters back from the bank.

The landscape disintegrated in crackling white flashes, snarling and sparkling for almost five seconds. A pall of mud and shredded greenery lifted several meters high, then settled back on a barren wasteland. Only memory could say that eastern half of the island and the spit of riverbank to the north of it had been covered by dense vegetation a moment before.

A cyan flash blew a temporary crater in the mud: a calliope's ammunition had detonated. A wheel spun skyward, then fell back and splashed into the river.

The scout infantry had grounded their skimmers at the moment of impact. Now they lifted again and resumed their course, four fingers feeling Sierra's path across the trackless terrain. *Fencing Master* snorted a hundred meters behind, the iridium fist ready to punch if the infantry touched anything.

"Not a bloody thing for us, El-Tee," Deseau said. *"Not a bloody thing."*

The firecracker rounds had left a haze of explosive residue and finely divided soil above the island, blurring its shape, but Huber knew there'd have been little more to see even without that blanket. The rolling blasts had pulped everything in the impact area. Except for the single wheel, there'd been no sign of two hundred enemy soldiers and their equipment.

His nose wrinkled. That wasn't quite true. Besides the prickle of ozone and the sickening sweetness of explosive, the air had a tinge of burned flesh.

Fencing Master bucked into the undisturbed vegetation beyond the line which shell fragments had scythed. When the professionals sat down to the table, war stopped being a game for street thugs wearing uniforms. The Volunteers at ground zero here hadn't had time to learn that, but the folks who'd given them their orders must be thinking hard about the future by now.

Because the prevailing winds were from the northwest, Huber had been smelling the fire for almost three hours before the infantry sergeant with the scouting section called over the command channel, *"Blood and Martyrs, Captain! This is Charlie One-three-four. Are we supposed to go through this on skimmers? Over."*

Huber switched a quadrant of his faceshield to the view from *Floosie*, the combat car attached to White Section at the moment. It was like looking into the maw of Hell.

Regimental rocket howitzers hundreds of kilometers to the south in United Cities' territory had seeded the forest with incendiaries. Each time-fuzed zirconium pellet was capable of burning though light armor. When one landed in old growth forest, the likelihood of it igniting even green timber was three out of five… and there were tens of thousands of pellets in the shells, raining down over hundreds of square kilometers. The myriad simultaneous fires had spread till they joined in a firestorm, a towering conflagration that drove its column of smoke through the stratosphere and sucked air to feed it from all sides in a torrent at hurricane velocities.

Everything combustible within the core of the blaze had burned, including the loam. Silica in the clay substrate ran liquid before cooling into slabs of glass colored like the rainbow by trace minerals.

Though the first flush of the fire had burned to a glowing shadow of itself, what remained still shimmered. The boles of the largest trees smoldered, stripped to pillars of carbonized heartwood. Monstrous pythons of smoke and ash eddied, the ghosts of a forest dancing among its bones.

"One-three-four, recover to your carrier vehicle," Sangrela responded without hesitation. *"ASAP, troopers, don't get into that! There won't be an ambush in that stuff, not from anything these Volunteers have available."*

He paused, then resumed, *"Break. Sierra, button up all hatches. Drivers switch to microwave radar, and exposed personnel lock down your faceshields. Make sure your filters are working before we get into it. We'll form an echelon perpendicular to the prevailing winds so—"*

A route map clicked as an imposed overlay on the lower right corner of Huber's faceshield. Every trooper in the task force had the same image.

"—that we're not all driving through the trash the leaders stir up. Six out."

Floosie must've entered the burned area just as Sangrela spoke, because a plume of ash shot skyward two kilometers ahead of *Fencing Master*. It was like watching the first puff of a volcano gathering its strength.

The fire'd been set to clear the forest between Fort Freedom and the Fiorno Valley at its closest approach, some twenty klicks west of where the river entered the Northern Sea. The tract was well-watered and the foliage was in the green lushness of late spring, so the fire had generally burned itself out to either side of the kilometer-wide swathe seeded with incendiaries. Nothing organic could've resisted that dense rain of exothermic metal.

Deseau was driving; Huber heard the hatch cover close over him. Learoyd checked his faceshield and filters with his left hand, then drew up the throat closure of his blouse to get the maximum protection possible without donning an environmental suit.

Tranter was curled up asleep under the forward gun; his head rested on his commo helmet. Huber shook him awake and leaned close to shout, "Get your gear on and locked down, Sarge. There's going to be a lot of ash and sparks for the next hour or so."

As Tranter slipped his helmet on with a grin of embarrassment, Huber turned to Captain Orichos. She'd been watching the troopers, but she wasn't on the Sierra net and didn't know what was happening. Her expression was neutral, with just enough quirk to the lips to prevent it from being grim.

"We're going to be going through a burned-out area," he explained to Orichos over the intercom. He mimed locking down his faceshield rather than touch hers, at present raised. "Your nose filters ought to come down automatically when we hit the smoke, but you might want to push this button here—"

He touched the hinge of his faceshield; the filters dropped over his nostrils.

"—and deploy them manually right now."

"*Burned area?*" Orichos said. Her hand stopped halfway to her faceshield, then finished the movement. "*Have those animals set the forest on fire?*"

All the vehicles of the main body were out of the floodway now, striking north toward their goal. Eight separate ribbons of smoke and ash trailed downwind, spreading till they merged into a broad miasma that settled slowly back to the ravaged forest.

"Whatever happened," Huber said, "it's going to be hot going till we reach the marshes this side of Bulstrode Bay. Get your filters in place now, all right?"

Fencing Master had reached the point at which Sierra's route left the river; Deseau boosted fan speed and adjusted his nacelle angles. The previous vehicles, particularly the tanks, had battered the bank into a slope of glistening mud. Skirts had dragged chunks of buried quartz up with them in deep gouges through the clay.

Fencing Master roared, bursting over the top of the bank at over thirty kph. Huber realized what was about to happen in time to brace his left hand against the coaming and clasp Orichos to his chest with the other arm. The Gendarmery officer didn't have the instincts to react correctly even if he'd had a chance to warn her instead of acting.

The car's nose skirts spilled air and dropped, slamming down onto the charred soil. Despite being prepared, Huber's own weight and that of Captain Orichos threw him hard against the coaming. The rigid clamshell armor spread the shock, but he'd still have bruises along the side of his ribcage by the morning.

If he was alive in the morning, of course. Well, civilians could die at any moment too.

Deseau took them into the hell-lit wasteland. Smoke was a gray pall; sometimes dense enough to seem solid, sometimes hiding objects that were solid in all truth. Huber tried light-amplified viewing but decided the lack of depth perception would be too dangerous at their present high speed. Infrared—thermal imaging—wasn't ideal at the ambient temperatures of the burning forest, but the helmet AI had enough discrimination to make it the choice.

"*Vandals!*" snarled Captain Orichos. "*Stupid vandal bastards! What did they think they'd accomplish by this destruction?*"

There was no point in telling her how the blaze had really started. Not when she and Arne Huber shared a crowded combat car on the verge of action with an entrenched enemy.

Hot spots—open flames and sparks the skirts plowed up from fires banked in the ashes—were white highlights in the faceshield. The AI coded cooler objects through the spectrum from violet to dark reds that verged on black, though little in this expanse was colored below green. A suited human would be visible in outline against the brighter background, but nobody expected to find Volunteers waiting *here* in ambush.

Fencing Master bumped and racketed across the landscape, scraping its skirts frequently and often hurling up gouts of fire. Deseau was being careful—too careful. He was trying to avoid every possible stump and cavity instead of taking a line and holding it till a major obstacle interposed. The combat car repeatedly sideswiped the skeletons of fallen trees, blasting them into sparks, or grounded when the skirts swayed over the edge of a pit left when a toppling giant had dragged its root ball out of the soil. Sergeant Tranter gripped the coaming to either side of his gun pintle with a set look on his face.

Huber touched Tranter's shoulder to get his attention, then leaned close to shout into his ear instead of using the intercom circuit and including Deseau: "Don't worry, Sarge—you and Frenchie will switch positions when we form up for the attack."

Tranter nodded gratefully. He might or might not understand that Huber was even more interested in getting Deseau behind the forward tribarrel than he was to have Tranter's expertise in the driver's compartment. Horses for courses…

"*Vandals!*" Mauricia Orichos repeated as she stared across the flame-ravaged bleakness. Sparks whirled from the skirts and spun down again into the fan intakes, dusting those in the fighting compartment. Slammers' uniforms were flame resistant, but Huber stuck his hands under the opposite armpits and wished he had gauntlets.

Did Orichos think that Colonel Hammer cared about trees when the lives of his troopers were at stake? And if there'd been a thousand civilians in the corridor before the incendiaries fell, that wouldn't have changed the Colonel's plan either.

This was war. If the government of the Point hadn't known what it meant to hire the Slammers to do their fighting for them, then they were in the process of learning.

Fencing Master slowed, wobbled drunkenly, and finally came to rest on a south-facing backslope with her fans at idle. Deseau rotated the driver's hatch open; Tranter was already climbing off the right side of the fighting compartment.

Huber raised his faceshield, then lifted the commo helmet for a moment to scratch his scalp. He grinned at Captain Orichos and said, "We're getting ready for the final run-up, Captain. If there's anything you need to do while we're halted, do it now. We won't stop again until the shooting's over."

He smiled more broadly and added, "At least over for us, I mean."

Huber was keyed up, but it was in a good way. The drive had been physically and mentally fatiguing. It had blotted out the past and future, turning even his immediate surroundings into a gray blur. Now adrenaline coursed through him, bringing the fire-swept wasteland into bright focus and shuffling a series of possible outcomes through his mind.

Arne Huber was alive again. He might die in the next ten minutes, but a lot of people never *really* lived for even that short time.

"No, I'm ready," Orichos said. She rubbed her hands together, then wiped her palms on the breast of her jumpsuit. If she was trying to clean the ash and grit off them, she failed. "What do you want me to do? In the battle, that is."

Frenchie climbed into the fighting compartment past his tribarrel; Tranter was walking forward on the steel bulge of the plenum chamber. The thirty-degree slope was awkwardly steep for the exchange, but the relatively sparse vegetation here had left fewer smoldering remains than the flatter, better-watered stretches the task force had been crossing.

"Keep out of the way," Huber said. "Keep your head down unless one of us buys it. If that happens, take over his gun and try not to shoot friendlies."

He grinned, feeling a degree of genuine amusement to talk about his own death in such a matter-of-fact way. He'd chosen the line of work, of course.

Huber really would've preferred to get the Gendarmery officer off his combat car, but that wasn't a practical solution in this landscape. Orichos was smart and quick both, so he could at least hope that she'd jump clear if he or a trooper needed one of the ammo boxes stacked behind her.

Frenchie slid behind his gun and spun the mechanism, ejecting the round from the loaded chamber in a spurt of liquid nitrogen. As he did so, Tranter spun the idling fans up one at a time so that he could listen to the note of each individually. Both men were veterans and experts; they didn't trust their tools to be the way they'd left them until they'd made sure for themselves.

Barely visible eighty meters eastward, *Foghorn*'s crew were giving their car and weapons a final check. Sierra's remaining six combat vehicles waited still further to the east, out of sight from *Fencing Master* behind undulations of the ground.

Despite hotspots in the terrain, the infantry had deployed from the wrenchmobiles; they'd advance on their skimmers to avoid the risk of losing two squads to a single lucky hit. Besides, the recovery vehicles might shortly be needed for their original purpose.

"*Central, this is Sierra Six,*" Captain Sangrela reported over the command channel. "*Sierra is in position. Over.*"

"*Roger, Sierra,*" Base Alpha replied. Despite the compression and stuttering created when the transmission bounced from one ionization track to another, Huber would've been willing to swear the voice was Major Pritchard's. "*Hold two, I repeat, figures two, minutes while we prepare things for you from this end. Central out.*"

Though the transmission closed, an icon on the corner of Huber's faceshield indicated there was view-only information available if he wanted to tap it. He did, tonguing the controller instead of voice-activating the helmet AI.

A crystalline, satellite-relayed voice announced, "*Freedom command, this is Solace Intelligence! Emergency! Emergency! Slammers artillery is launching a maximum effort barrage on your positions! We will relay shell trajectories to you as they leave the guns!*"

The voice transmission ended without a signoff. A data feed which the AI courteously translated into a schematic of lines curving from south to north across the continent replaced it. The tracks shown as emanating from all three of the Regiment's six-gun batteries were initially blue but turned red at a rate scaled to 880 meters per second: the velocity of 200-mm shells launched from the Slammers' rocket howitzers.

Learoyd clicked the loading tube into his backup weapon, a sub-machine gun, and turned to Huber. "Are we just mopping up again, El-Tee?" he said.

"No, Learoyd," Huber said. He was explaining to Captain Orichos as well. Deseau'd been on the net and would've understood the implications of the way the artillery smashed the Volunteer ambush. Learoyd hadn't understood, and Orichos hadn't heard. "Central's broken into the Solace net to send a false transmission to make the Volunteers think our enemies are helping them. There isn't really any artillery—"

As he spoke, the Regiment's Signals Section followed the graph of "shell trajectories" with computer-generated images of hogs firing at their maximum rate of ten rounds per minute. The gun carriages jounced from the backblast of each heavy rocket. Doughnuts of dust lifted around the self-propelled chassis and a bright spark of exhaust spiked skyward for the seven seconds before burnout. Real shells would ignite sustainer motors in the stratosphere to range from firebases in the UC to the northern tip of the Point, but there was no need to simulate that here.

"—but if the Volunteers think there is, they'll switch their calliopes to high-angle use. They won't be waiting to hit us when we come into sight."

"This's what we've been waiting for, Learoyd," Deseau said, murderously cheerful. "We get to blow away a bunch of civilians in uniform!"

"Oh," said Learoyd. He turned again and swung his tribarrel stop to stop, just making sure it'd work when he needed it. Huber didn't recall ever hearing the trooper sound enthusiastic. "All right."

Herbert Learoyd wasn't the brightest trooper in the Regiment, but you could do worse than have him manning the right wing gun of your combat car. In fact Huber wasn't sure he could've done better.

It was time to be a platoon leader again. Huber cleared his faceshield and replaced the phony transmission with a fifty-degree mask of the terrain map. It showed the planned routes that would take the four combat cars toward the outlying Volunteer positions and Fort Freedom itself. Colored bands connected each course to the segment of hostile terrain for which that car's guns were responsible.

"Fox Three-six to Fox," Huber said. "We'll be executing in a minute or less. If there's any questions, let's hear them now, troopers. Three-six over."

None of his vehicle commanders responded. He'd have been amazed if one had. Four green beads along the top of his faceshield indicated that the cars themselves were within field-service parameters. That could've meant they'd have been deadlined for maintenance on stand-down, but unless there'd been serious damage since the last halt Huber figured they'd all pass even rear-area inspection.

"Central to Sierra Six," the command channel announced. *"You're clear to go. Out."*

"Sierra Six to Sierra," said Captain Sangrela. *"Execute, troopers!"*

"Go, Tranter!" Huber shouted, thinking that the former technician was waiting for his direct superior to relay the force commander's order.

Fencing Master was already moving. Tranter had fooled him by the skill with which he coaxed the nacelles into a smooth delivery of power, balancing acceleration against blade angle so perfectly that the speed of the eight fans didn't drop below optimum. *Fencing Master* lifted from the clay and climbed the hillside as slickly as a raindrop slides down a windowpane.

They shot over the brow of the hill. Bright verticals on Huber's faceshield framed the sector *Fencing Master* was responsible for, the left post on the western spur of the ancient cinder cone fifteen kilometers away.

To the right *Foghorn* blasted into view measurable seconds later, its bow skirts nearly a meter above the ground for the instant before gravity reasserted itself. *That'll rattle their back teeth*, Huber thought, but he had more immediate problems of his own.

A cyan bolt split the smoke-streaked gloom, whirling helices of ash as it snapped toward the volcano. A gout of white-hot rock spurted from a cave mouth prepared as a firing position.

Two tanks were hanging back on overwatch while the infantry and the other six armored vehicles charged Fort Freedom at the best speed their fans could drive them. The second tank's bolt lit a secondary explosion, munitions detonating at the ravening touch of a 20-cm powergun. Even at this range, the main guns were capable of destroying anything short of another tank.

Fencing Master's path across the terrain was as smooth as a flowing river—not straight, but never diverging much from the line Tranter had chosen. The other cars and the two advancing tanks were plumes of ash streaking the sky to eastward; they were falling behind *Fencing Master,* though not by so much that Huber worried about it. Somebody had to lead the advance, after all, and he guessed that was what he was being paid for.

The tanks on overwatch, now well to the rear, continued firing, one and then the other. They could hit on the move, but they'd halted so that irregularities of terrain wouldn't mask their fire at some instant it was critically needed. Even the best soldiers and best equipment in the universe—and most of Hammer's troopers would say that meant the Slammers—couldn't keep things from going wrong in battle, but good planning limited the number of opportunities Fate got to screw things up.

Floosie raked the volcano's eastern margin with two tribarrels. The streams of 2-cm bolts interlaced like jets from a fountain—now crossing, now fanning apart. The impacts sparkled against the lava like dustmotes caught in a shaft of sunlight. At twelve kilometers' range the tribarrels weren't likely to be effective, but Jellicoe always claimed that keeping the other guy's head down was the first rule of survival.

The platoon sergeant was a twenty-year veteran so she must know something, but Huber didn't want to burn out his barrels now when in a matter of minutes he'd be at knife range with several thousand hostiles. There wasn't a right way to do it. If suppressing fire was the rabbit's foot Jellicoe used to get through hard times, Huber wasn't going to order her to stop.

Not that he thought she'd obey him anyway.

A geyser of cyan light—powergun ammunition gang-firing—lit the side of the volcano. Blast-gouged rock gleamed white, fading toward red in the instant before the shattered slope caved in to hide it. The tanks were first hitting positions which Central believed were occupied, though they'd shortly hammer the locations where the Volunteers planned to move their guns after the first exchange of fire.

The bloody *civilians* didn't understand that none of their guns would survive its first shot at the Slammers.

A calliope opened up, one of those dug so deep into the forward slope that Volunteer Command couldn't retask it to air defense. Its dense volley of 30-mm bolts was probably aimed at *Flame Farter*, which'd already raced past the narrow window through which the calliope fired. The rounds instead came dangerously close to the infantry following. Calcium in the clay soil blazed white in the center of gouting ash; the skimmers maneuvered wildly to avoid the track of shots.

Two 20-cm bolts hit the firing slit in quick succession. The calliope might have been deep enough that neither tank had a direct line on the weapon itself, but the amount of energy the main guns liberated in the tunnel would be enough to cook the crew in a bath of gaseous rock. The hillside burped, then slumped as it rearranged itself.

Fort Freedom loomed above the plain five klicks ahead like a sullen monument. Where the eastern sun angled across ravines, shadows streaked the cinder cone. Speckles against the lava indicated a few Volunteers were firing their personal weapons. At this range the electromagnetic carbines were harmless; the slugs probably wouldn't carry to the oncoming Slammers. Though the attempt showed bad fire discipline, it also meant that not all—not quite all—of the enemy were cowed by the sight of the iridium hammers about to fall on them.

The ground rose slightly into a ridge paralleling the base of the cone and changed from clay to a friable soil that must have been mostly volcanic ash. The forest here had been of tall trees spaced more widely than those of the stretch the task force had just traversed, but the firestorm had reduced them to much the same litter of ash and cinders.

The two tanks accompanying the combat cars halted on the ridge; the wake of debris they'd raised during their passage continued to roll outward under its own inertia. They immediately began punching Volunteer positions with their main guns. The panzers now far to the rear began to advance, accelerating as quickly as their mass allowed. They'd each shot off the twenty-round basic load in their ready magazines and couldn't use their main guns until a fresh supply had cycled up from storage in their bellies.

Mercenary artillery in Solace might weigh in at any time. The tanks' tribarrels were tasked to air defense. With the wide sight distances here, that should be a sufficient deterrent. If it wasn't, well, Huber had more pressing concerns right now.

His faceshield careted movement at the top of the cinder cone: the Volunteers were shifting calliopes from air defense sites in the interior of the ancient volcano to notches cut in the rim from which they could bear on the advancing armored vehicles. Huber adjusted his sight picture onto the leftmost caret, enlarging the central portion around the pipper while the surrounding field remained one-to-one so that he wouldn't be blindsided by an unglimpsed danger.

The gun crew had rolled their multi-barrel weapon into position and were depressing their eight muzzles at the mechanism's maximum rate. Huber locked his tribarrel's stabilizer on the glinting target and squeezed the trigger.

Huber's AI blacked out the 2-cm bolts from the magnified image to save his retinas. Instead of a smooth *Thump! Thump! Thump!* as the tribarrel cycled at 500 rounds per minute, it stuttered *Thump!* and a moment later *Thump! Thump!* again. The stabilizer adjusted the weapon within broad parameters, but *Fencing Master* was jolting over broken terrain with a violence beyond what the servos were meant to control. The software simply interrupted the burst until the gun bore again on its assigned target.

The calliope in the holographic sight picture—its iridium barrels gleaming against the frame of baked-finish steel and the taut-faced Volunteers crewing it—slumped like a sand castle in the tide. The impacts were smears of emptiness, but the image cleared in snapshots of destruction, headless bodies falling and white-glowing cavities eaten from the carriage and gun tubes.

The target's magazines detonated. The flash scooped the square-bottomed firing notch into a crescent five meters across. A mushroom of vaporized rock lifted from the site. Nothing remained of the calliope and its crew.

Blasts and gouts of lava spurted from a dozen places on the crater's rim as combat cars raked the enemy with their tribarrels. Deseau and Learoyd both fired at the turret of an armored car which the Volunteers had held beneath the crater rim until the Slammers were within range of whatever weapon it mounted. Satellite imagery from Central cued the troopers' AIs, so they were waiting with their thumbs on their triggers at the instant the armored car's crew drove up a ramp into firing position.

The turret of high maraging steel blazed in a red inferno before its gun could swing on target. Internal explosions must have killed the whole crew, because they didn't attempt to back the vehicle or bail out of it.

Deseau and Learoyd continued firing, eating away the rock to get to the car's hull. They didn't have a better target—other tribarrels had cleared the rest of the Volunteer positions—and they saw no reason to stop shooting at something that might possibly be useful to the enemy. A fireball of exploding fuel finally ended their fun.

Fencing Master bucked onto humped, barren ridges of hard rock. Layers of ash blown from the vent had formed most of the nearby landscape, but here magma had rolled out of cracks in the base of the cone and solidified. The steel skirts clanged and squealed, scraping showers of red sparks.

Huber grabbed the coaming with his left hand. Captain Orichos shouted as the car bounced her forward into Deseau. Frenchie snarled a vivid curse, but he didn't lose his grip on the tribarrel.

"*They're running!*" somebody shouted over the general channel. From the voice and the way the AI let it cut through the chatter of a dozen or more excited soldiers, Huber figured it was Captain Sangrela. "*Get the bastards! Get 'em all!*"

The Volunteers had spent years building Fort Freedom. In addition to tunnels carved through the cone, they'd dug hundreds of bunkers on the volcano's outer face. The squads and fire teams placed there hadn't run earlier because there was no way out except up a bare slope; by the time they'd had a good enough look at what was coming toward them, they were more afraid to show themselves than they were to stay.

The shriek as combat cars crossed rock and the nearing intake howl of the fans changed the equation. First a few, then many scores of Militiamen clambered out of their holes to dash for the rim and what they hoped was safety. It was near suicide, but with the tanks continuing methodically to pulverize bunkers, running may still have been the better option even so.

The Volunteers' black uniforms would've blended well with the slopes of compacted ash, but the Slammers' helmets keyed on motion. A forest of translucent red carets lit on Huber's faceshield. All he had to do was swing his sight picture onto the thickest clumps and squeeze his trigger, letting *Fencing Master*'s movement hose the burst across running victims. Bodies and severed limbs bounced against the rock, shrouded in smoke from burning uniforms.

"Get the bastards before they grow their spines back!" Captain Sangrela screamed. *"Get 'em all!"*

Some Volunteers fired from their bunkers or turned to fight like cornered rats as cyan bolts slaughtered their comrades. A burst hit *Fencing Master*'s bow slope and ricocheted in dazzling violet streaks. The car's armor rang like a trip hammer working, but that was just a fact of life. Huber's skin prickled and his throat was as raw as if he'd drunk lye.

Fencing Master reached the cone. It was steep, forty degrees on average and occasionally almost vertical where weather had sheared the concreted ash. Tranter fought his controls, fishtailing the car so that they mounted the slope in a series of switchbacks instead of fighting gravity head on. The combat cars had a higher power to weight ratio than the massively armored tanks did so they could climb the cone, but it still took finesse to do it well.

A powergun bolt stabbed over the rim of the fighting compartment's armor, splashing the interior. The cyan brilliance blew a chunk of iridium into a white-hot bubble between Huber and Deseau.

The gas flung Huber backward, tearing his hands from the tribarrel. He felt as though he'd been slammed in the crotch by a medicine ball.

Heat penetrated a moment later. The fabric of his uniform was temperature resistant, but the metal resolidifying as a black crust over the khaki had vaporized at something over 4800 degrees. *I'll worry about it later....*

Frenchie'd gone down also. He was still holding his tribarrel's left grip, but that was the way a drowning man clutches flotsam. Litter on the floor of the compartment had ignited, twigs and leaves which had whirled into the vehicle during the march as well as plastic wrappers and similar human trash.

Learoyd ripped short bursts toward what was now blank hillside above them: the Volunteer sniper had ducked into his foxhole after firing, and the slope itself concealed the opening. The shooter must've been lucky to hit a target he couldn't see till he showed himself, but he was also good. If he thought he was safe because he was out of sight again, though—

The rock Learoyd's 2-cm bolts was splashing into fist-sized divots of glass suddenly erupted as though the volcano had gone active again. Two tanks hit it, then doubled the initial impacts as soon as their main guns could cycle. Each bolt lifted a truck-sized volume of compacted ash which strinkled down again on the breeze.

There was no sign of the shooter. If his ammunition had gone off, its flash was lost in the immense violence of 20-cm bolts.

Huber's legs were splayed before him; his hands waved in the air. Captain Orichos caught his right wrist and bent close. "Should I take your gun?" she shouted. "Can you—"

"I'm all right," Huber said, forcing the words out. The shock had numbed his diaphragm; breathing was one agony among many. He braced his left arm against the side armor, then let the car's lurch help Orichos lift him to his feet again.

On his feet but not upright; he was still half doubled over and he was pretty sure that he'd vomit if he tried to straighten fully. Via! but he hurt.

Deseau's gun thumped a burst toward the top of the cone. Huber didn't see a target there; Frenchie was probably just proving to himself and others that he was alive and functioning… which is what Huber was doing, after all.

"I'm all right!" he repeated, forcefully and with more truth this time. He took his tribarrel's grips in his hands as *Fencing Master* lurched to the top of the ridge, the western battlements of the Volunteer fortress. Below was the interior of the partial cone, and beyond that the sea.

Aircars ranging from the big trucks that could haul twenty or more armed men to hoppers with one seat and room for a sack of groceries were mixed indiscriminately on the crater floor. The drivers had squeezed in wherever they'd seen a place to set down. The Volunteers had left Midway in a near panic; they probably hadn't landed here in much better emotional condition.

There wasn't room in the tunnels to conceal so many vehicles, so the calliopes had been the Volunteers' only means of protecting their hope of escape if things went wrong—as they were certainly going wrong now. Those calliopes were molten ruin, but there was no need to waste shells on the aircars. They were perfect targets for *Fencing Master*'s tribarrels.

A few minutes ago there'd have been only a handful of Volunteers in the open. The maze of tunnels would've seemed safety until those inside realized that the Slammers would with certainty penetrate the outer defenses and so control the tunnel entrances. Now several of the armored doors had swung back; black-uniformed figures were running for vehicles. Huber's view was like a child's of a stirred-up anthill.

A Volunteer drew a holstered powergun and fired in the direction of *Fencing Master* as he ran. One of the bolts snapped only twenty meters overhead, but that was dumb luck: nobody was that good, not with a pistol. Learoyd's short burst vaporized everything between the Volunteer's neck and his knees without any need for luck. He was an expert using a stabilized weapon with holographic sights. Learoyd could've put a round into his target's left nostril if he'd wanted to.

The accompanying infantry squads spaced out to either side of *Fencing Master*, taking firing positions along the ridge. *Foghorn* still labored a hundred meters down the slope. Huber didn't have leisure to see how Jellicoe's section was doing on the eastern edge of the cone where a deep gully complicated the approach, but he knew she'd get them into action as quick as anybody could.

An aircar lifted. Huber fired as he tracked it, his bolts splashing behind the accelerating vehicle for a moment before three flashes walked up the fuselage from the back. The car, a luxury model, flipped over and crashed under power. Ruptured fuel cells sprayed their contents over a dozen other vehicles, some of which also started to burn.

"Cue aircar motors!" Huber shouted, shifting his AI to mark the electromagnetic rhythms of fan motors spinning. "Gunners—"

Going to intercom.

"—hit the moving cars, not the men!"

Three more vehicles tried to take off. One didn't have enough altitude and collided immediately with the truck parked ahead of it. As it tumbled, Learoyd's burst chopped the car's belly open.

The infantry were shooting at individual targets. Though their weapons were semi-automatic, a single 2-cm bolt was enough to disable an aircar—let alone kill the driver.

One and then both cars of Jellicoe's section opened fire from the other side of the crater. *Foghorn* finally not only mounted the rim but started down the steeper inner slope, wreathed in the grit its steel skirts rasped from the soft rock. Solid cyan streams lashed from its guns.

Deseau either didn't hear Huber's order or ignored it, instead laying his sights onto an entrance. He squeezed his trigger till a blast within spurted a cloud of smoke and yellow flame into the sunlight; the tunnel collapsed.

Three Volunteers rose together behind the bed of a truck, aiming at *Foghorn* for the split second before Huber shot them down. One's carbine fired skyward as his head exploded. Huber'd been swinging his gun onto the car behind the men; its driver leaped out and flattened on the ground. The empty vehicle started to loop before falling sideways and crashing.

Fuel fires and the foul black plumes of burning plastic rose from dozens of vehicles. Nobody was coming out of the tunnels anymore, and the Volunteers surviving on the crater floor either huddled beside cars—there was no "behind" to the crossfire from the rim—or raised their hands in surrender. Many of the latter had their eyes closed as if they were afraid they'd see death coming for them.

"*Sierra, cease fire!*" Captain Sangrela called. "*The enemy's radioed to surrender! Cease fire!*"

A carbine fired. The *whack* of the electromagnetic coils might've gone unnoticed in the chaos, but the *clang!* of the slug ricocheting from *Foghorn*'s armor was unmistakable. Some Volunteer hadn't gotten the word....

Huber hadn't seen the shooter, but Deseau did: his tribarrel was one of five or six guns which spiked the closed cab of an aircar. That car and three more nearby erupted in fireballs. A body panel fluttered skyward, deforming in the heat of the blast that lifted it.

"*Cease fire!*" Sangrela repeated angrily. His jeep was so heavy with electronics that he hadn't been able to reach the rim, so he didn't know the reason for the additional gunfire. "*Cease fire!*"

The shooting stopped. Arne Huber took his hands from the tribarrel grips and flexed them cautiously, afraid they'd cramp. He might need to use them if things got hot again. The underside of his chin was as stiff and painful as if it'd been flayed. The skin there'd caught some of the iridium vaporized when the bolt hit inside the fighting compartment.

"*Cease fire!*" said Captain Sangrela, but nobody was firing anymore.

"*Blood and Martyrs!*" Deseau wheezed, raising his faceshield. "*I'm as dry as that rock out there!*"

Huber'd had the same thought. In turning toward the cooler that still should have a few beers in it, he caught sight of Captain Orichos' expression: she looked as though she'd just been told she was Master of the Universe.

It shouldn't have disturbed Huber, but it did.

It'd been pouring rain. Now that the afternoon sun was out, the tents steamed and the clay had already started to bake to laterite. Ash lay as a slimy gray coating over ridges in the soil, but the sides of the rain-carved gullies were the color of rust. Dead treetrunks stood like tombstones for the forest that had once grown here.

"What a bloody fucking awful fucking place!" Deseau snarled, flipping up the front of his poncho without taking it off; the rain could resume any moment. "Learoyd, did you ever see such a bloody fucking awful fucking place?"

"Sure, Frenchie," Learoyd said, frowning as he tried to puzzle sense out of the question. "Remember Passacaglia, where the dust got in everything and we kept burning out drive fans? And that swamp the place before that? And where was it everybody got skin fungus if they didn't wear their gas suits all the time? Was that—"

"Yeah, well, this's still a crummy place," Deseau muttered. He saw Huber smiling and grimaced, turning his head away. Frenchie'd been around Learoyd long enough to know the trooper had too much trouble with the literal truth to make a good audience for a figure of speech—even a figure as simple as rhetorical exaggeration.

Looking eastward toward a dirigible unloading what seemed to be empty shipping containers, Deseau went on, "I wish to hell they'd let us go when the local cops arrived. They can handle anything that's left, can't they?"

Dirigibles full of Gendarmes and the supplies needed for an open-air prison had begun arriving within a few hours of the collapse of Volunteer resistance. Huber, *and* Captain Sangrela, *and* probably every other trooper in the task force, had thought Sierra would be released immediately. The optimists had even hoped they'd be sent back by way of Midway, with a few days of leave as a reward.

Surviving a major engagement like the one just completed made even level-headed troopers optimistic.

Central hadn't felt that way. Sierra had stayed where it was for the three days it took for a column from Base Alpha to reach them.

"It won't be long, Frenchie," Huber said. He quirked a smile. "It shouldn't be long, anyhow."

There were worse places, just as Learoyd said, but this was bad enough in all truth. The Slammers had snagged tents from the loads brought in to house the prisoners, but they didn't help much. You could keep the rain from falling on you, but the ditches the troopers dug around the tents hadn't been enough to stop streams of ash-clogged water from finding their way in from below and soaking everything.

Huber looked over at the POW camp which lay between Task Force Sangrela's defensive circle and the slopes of what had for a short time been Fort Freedom; it was now Mount Bulstrode again. The prisoners had it worse than the troopers did, of course. There wouldn't have been enough tents to go around even if the Slammers hadn't imposed their tax on defeat, but accommodations weren't what was probably worrying the former Volunteers. The Slammers knew they'd be leaving within a few days, maybe even a few hours. The prisoners weren't sure they'd be alive in a few hours.

"*Sierra,*" said Huber's commo helmet in the voice of the signals officer of the approaching column, "*this is Flamingo Six-three. We'll be in sight in figures two, I say again, two, minutes. Don't get anxious. Flamingo out.*"

"Stupid bitch," Deseau muttered. "The only thing I'm anxious about is getting away from this bloody place. And if they'd got the lead outa their pants, that could've happened yesterday."

Huber's opinion was similar enough that he didn't bother telling Frenchie to cool it. You never get relieved as quickly as you want to be....

He wondered if Sierra would be allowed to pick its own route back through the unburned forest, or if in the interests of speed they'd have to return across the fire-swept wasteland. The downpour would've quenched the hotspots, but the filthy sludge the vehicles'd be kicking up in its place wouldn't be much of an improvement.

Huber chuckled. Deseau gave him a sour look.

"Don't mind me, Frenchie," he said. "I'm just thinking that I went into the wrong line of work if I wanted luxury travel arrangements."

"Guess they had to keep us," Learoyd said, nodding toward the waste of mud and tents and captured Volunteers. "I mean, if them guys tried to break out, what was the cops gonna do about it?"

Learoyd was right, as he usually was when he offered an opinion. Squads of Gendarmes patrolled the perimeter of the vast razor-ribbon cage. Six or eight strands of wire were strung on flimsy poles only two meters out of the ground; all things considered, it wasn't much of a barrier. The Point didn't have the resources to deal with the sudden influx of over five thousand prisoners.

The Gendarmes had carbines and pistols. If they'd hoped to supplement those with automatic weapons captured from the Volunteers, they were out of luck. Every crew-served weapon in Fort Freedom had been brought out to face the Slammers, and none of them had survived. For the most part, the sharp-shooting tanks had destroyed the emplacements before the Slammers were in range of the defenders' return fire.

If the prisoners, many of whom were rightly desperate, made a concerted rush on the fence, a few hundred Gendarmes weren't going to stop them. The Slammers' massed fire would, and the certainty the powerguns would hose the camp indiscriminately meant that prisoners who *didn't* want to try a breakout were going to be bloody determined to keep their wilder fellows in line also.

"Via, where's there to run to?" Deseau said. He spat toward the camp a hundred meters away, then started to shrug out of his poncho after all.

"Back into the tunnels, for one thing," Huber said. "There might be enough guns down there to equip a division. It won't be safe till the support column comes up with the gas cylinders."

"That what they're doing, El-Tee?" Deseau said, his tone bright with interest. "Pump the place full of gas?"

Huber shrugged. "Nobody's appointed me to the staff," he said, "but that'd be standard operating procedure: fill the tunnels with KD1 or another of the persistent agents and forget about 'em."

Sledges had been ringing on iron posts as prisoners constructed a narrow chute from the eastern end of the camp. An off-key *whang* indicated a hammer'd hit skew and broken the helve. A Gendarme shouted in a tone of anger tinged with fear, drawing the three troopers' attention.

"Naw, nothing," Deseau muttered, lifting the muzzles of his tribarrel a safe fifteen degrees again so that the weapon wouldn't hit anything in the vicinity if it fired accidentally. "Them cops, they're ready to piss their pants they're so scared."

Twenty Gendarmes guarded a crew of no more than fifty prisoners driving posts and stringing the wire. They seemed nervous to Huber, also. Maybe they knew what was planned and were afraid of what would happen when the prisoners learned also.

"*Sierra, this is Flamingo Six-three,*" the voice said. "*We're coming into sight. Flamingo out.*"

The vehicles of the task force were bows-out in a defensive circle, though the formation was looser than it'd have been if there were a real likelihood of attack. Instead of turning his head, Huber switched the upper left quadrant of his faceshield to the view from *Floosie* at the opposite side of the formation.

A combat car slid over the ridgeline where Sierra had launched its assault on Fort Freedom. Three similar vehicles followed, then a dozen air-cushion trucks, and after them two wrenchmobiles modified to carry troops. The last vehicle in line was a command car.

"It's the White Mice," Deseau said. From the tone of his voice, Huber thought he might be about to spit. "You know, I was kinda hoping I wouldn't see them again for a while."

"If they're relieving us," Learoyd said, "I don't care who they are."

"Yeah, I guess that's right," Deseau said; but Huber wasn't sure he agreed.

Some prisoners drifted toward the south edge of their camp, interested in the column as a break in their miserable routine and probably also concerned about what it might mean. Huber noticed that others of the former Volunteers were disappearing into tents. He didn't know what they expected to gain by that, but he understood the impulse.

A dozen civilians had come in by aircar a few hours before. They wore hooded raincapes even now that the sun was out, but Huber had raised his faceshield's magnification until he was sure of what he'd suspected: one of the newcomers was Speaker Nestilrode, and he recognized two others as cabinet ministers he'd seen when he entered the Assembly with Captain Orichos.

Now they came out of Orichos' tent. She and the Speaker shook hands; then the civilians strode quickly to their car without a backward glance.

Orichos sauntered toward the chute of razor ribbon. Perhaps she felt Huber's eyes on her because she turned her head and waved before she walked on.

Deseau snickered. "She fancies you, El-Tee," he said.

"Balls," Huber muttered. Orichos had been running the operation ever since enough Gendarmes had arrived to take primary responsibility from Task Force Sierra. The route march had been just as hard on her as on the Slammers, and so far as Huber'd seen she hadn't had a moment's downtime since. Despite that, Orichos looked as coolly fresh as she'd been the night a lifetime ago when Joachim Steuben introduced her at Northern Star.

Learoyd looked over his shoulder at Huber. "He's right, El-Tee," he said. "She does."

Huber shrugged rather than speaking. He didn't know what to say because he didn't know what he thought. He figured if he pretended not to care, they'd drop the subject.

There was motion in the near distance eastward. "Hey, what d'ye suppose that's all about?" Frenchie said, swinging his tribarrel both as a pointer and out of judicious concern.

Six dirigibles hovered a half-kilometer east of the enclosure. Slung beneath them were bar-sided containers like those Huber had seen transporting livestock from the feedlots of Solace to the United Cities where they'd be slaughtered. The props of one of the big airships began to turn at a slightly faster rate than what was necessary to hold position against the breeze. It crawled closer to the camp, its empty containers bonging occasionally when they touched the ground.

Instead of halting to coordinate with Task Force Sangrela, the A Company combat cars drove past the defensive circle and continued around the east side of the prisoner cage. Their skirts squirted water and gray sludge in jets punctuated by the furrows in the soil. Prisoners putting the finishing touches on the chute dropped their tools and scuttled away from the spray.

"Fox Three-six to Sierra Six," Huber said. "Any word what we're supposed to be doing? Over."

The cars' passage splashed the guards as well. A Gendarme officer retrieved the hat that'd been blown into a puddle and shook his fist at the big vehicles. Deseau snickered and said, "Bad move. Could've been a *real* bad move if the dumb bastard'd decided to wave his gun instead."

"Sierra, this is Six," Captain Sangrela said, replying to the whole unit. *"I've been told we're to hold ourselves in readiness to support Flamingo as required. If that sounds to you like, 'Go play, kiddies, while the big boys get on with business,' then you've got company thinking that. Six out!"*

The incoming infantry drove their skimmers off while the wrenchmobiles were still slowing. Huber noticed with some amusement that they didn't perform the operation as smoothly as Captain Sangrela's troopers had. The White Mice were real soldiers as well as being the Regiment's police and enforcers, but they didn't use skimmers nearly as much as the line infantry did.

The newcomers began to deploy along the southern length of the cage. There were only forty of them, so that meant almost ten meters between individuals. They carried 1-cm sub-machine guns rather than a mix of the automatic weapons with 2-cm shoulder weapons.

Deseau must've been thinking along the same lines as Huber was, because he said, "Blow apart the first man who moves with one a' these—"

He patted the receiver of the 2-cm weapon wedged muzzle-down beside his position between two ammo boxes and the armor.

"—and you quiet a mob a lot faster than spraying it with a buzz-gun."

Learoyd looked at him. "Did you ever do that, Frenchie?" he said. "To a mob?"

Huber kept his frown inside his head. You didn't generally ask another trooper about his past. Learoyd had an utter, undoubted innocence that allowed him to say things nobody else could get away with… and a lack of mental wattage that made it very likely he would.

Deseau said nothing for a moment, then shrugged. He nodded to Huber, explicitly including him, and said, "Naw, that was back on Helpmeet when I was a kid, Learoyd. I was on the other side of the powergun, you see. So when things quieted down, I joined the Regiment before they shipped out again."

The moving dirigible settled so that all three containers dragged, then detached them. The center box stuck momentarily. The airship bounced upward when the weight of the other two released, so the third clanged loudly to the ground when it finally dropped. It hit on a corner which bent upward, kinking the bars.

"Good thing it wasn't full of cattle," Huber muttered, frowning at the thought of broken legs and beasts bellowing in pain and terror. Now that he'd seen dirigibles in operation, he realized that they were about as unwieldy a form of transportation as humans had come up with. Useful here on Plattner's World, though.

"The cows're gonna be killed anyway, El-Tee," Deseau said. "It don't matter much, right?"

"Maybe not," Huber said; not agreeing, just ending a discussion that didn't have anywhere useful to go. Maybe nothing at all mattered, but on a good day Arne Huber didn't feel that way.

The command car pulled up alongside the chute, making a half turn so that its bow angled toward the camp proper. Though it was an hour short of sunset and the clouds had cleared, the driver switched on his headlights. In their beams the strands of razor ribbon glittered like jagged icicles. Two troopers with sub-machine guns got out of the vehicle and walked over to the wire.

"Prisoners of Hammer's Regiment!" a voice boomed through the command car's loudspeakers. "You will walk in line through the passage at the southeast corner of this camp. As you pass my vehicle—"

The whip antenna on top of the car glowed, becoming a wand of soft red light.

"—you will turn to face it. Then you will walk on to the containers in which you'll be transported to Midway. There you'll be released."

The words were being repeated on the north side of the POW encampment. It wasn't an echo from the volcano, as Huber thought for a moment. The A Company combat cars were relaying the speech through their public address systems.

"Who's that in the car?" Deseau said. From the way his eyes were narrowed, he already knew the answer to his question.

"It sounds like Major Steuben," Huber said. "As you'd expect."

A full company of Gendarmes stood by the shipping containers. Mauricia Orichos was among them, her hands linked behind her back. Huber had been watching her as Steuben spoke. Orichos hadn't been best pleased at the words "prisoners of Hammer's Regiment."

That was tough. She knew she'd been the only member of the Point forces present when Fort Freedom fell. The Slammers had taken these prisoners, and if the Gendarmery wanted to get snooty about it, the Slammers could take the prisoners away from their present guards any time they wanted to.

A prisoner bellowed something toward the car. Though he made a megaphone of his hands, Huber couldn't catch the word or brief phrase.

Steuben did, however. The loudspeakers boomed, "A gentleman has expressed doubt that you will actually be released. Let me assure you, mesdames and sirs, that if I wished to kill you all I would not bother with play acting. When you get to Midway, you will be told to sin no more and be released."

The trucks had unloaded their pallets of black-banded gas cylinders. Five of them shut down. The sixth lifted and lumbered past Task Force Sangrela to settle again beside the command car. The driver opened the cab door and stood on his mounting step, looking at the camp. Another squad of White Mice dismounted from the back and walked over to the chute.

"Very well," the PA system thundered. Amplification softened Steuben's clipped tones, making his words sound pompous. Huber found the contrast with the real man chilling. "Start coming through. The sooner you get moving, the sooner we can all get on to more congenial tasks."

A prisoner near the front looked around, then shambled into the chute. One of the White Mice reached an arm over the wire to halt the man in the headlights. His head rose in surprise and sudden fear.

"Keep going!" the amplified voice ordered.

The trooper's arm dropped; the prisoner jogged the rest of the way to where Gendarmes herded him into the first container. Several more prisoners followed, shuffling forward in a mixture of desperation and apathy.

"I suggest reconsideration on the part of anyone who thinks he'll remain in the tents," Steuben continued, the catlike humor of his tone coming through despite mechanical distortion. "We're going to destroy the entire site, starting at the north side. We can see you through cloth as surely as we'll be able to see you in the dead of night, so don't be foolish."

There was a hollow *boop,* then a second later a white flash and a shattering crash. A second *boop, Wham!* followed immediately. Troopers in the combat cars on the north side were firing grenade launchers into the tents.

Thermal viewing would show any holdouts, so there was no need for the grenades. Major Steuben was just making a point, to the Gendarmes as surely as to the captive Volunteers.

"Sierra, this is Flamingo Six-three," said the A Company signals officer. *"Fox Three-six is to report to the command car ASAP. Out."*

Deseau and Learoyd both looked at Huber. From the driver's compartment, Sergeant Tranter said over the intercom, *"El-Tee? What's going on?"*

Huber cued his intercom and said, "Curst if I know, Sarge. I'll tell you when I get back. Assuming."

He swung his left leg over the armor, then paused. He unclipped the sling of his 2-cm weapon from the epaulet and offered the big gun to Learoyd, saying, "Trade me, will you, Herbert?"

"Sure, sir," the trooper said. He took the 2-cm weapon and slapped the butt of his sub-machine gun into Huber's palm.

Deseau cackled like a demon. "Handier inside a car, eh, El-Tee?" he said.

Huber climbed the rest of the way out of the fighting compartment, then hopped from the plenum chamber to the ground. He started grinning also. You might as well see the humor in the screwed-up way things worked. It didn't change things; but then, nothing *did* change them.

He started toward the command car, his boots squelching and tossing mud up his pants leg with each stride. He didn't look over his shoulder to see the troopers of Task Force Sangrela watching him, but the Gendarmes watched and the driver of the big air-cushion truck stared down from the cab with a puzzled expression.

Grenades continued to crash on the north side of the camp. They'd started several fires; the sluggish flames gave off curls of black smoke.

Enough prisoners had passed through the chute that the cage meant for twenty cattle was what Huber would've called full. The Gendarmes seemed happy to pack more in. Well, if the former Volunteers had nothing worse in their future than an uncomfortable airship ride, they were luckier than they deserved to be.

"That one," the loudspeaker ordered crisply. A low-intensity laser stabbed from the mount of the command car's tribarrel. Its yellow dot quivered like a suppurating boil on the cheek of the bald-headed man nearing the end of the chute.

The fellow looked up in startled horror. One of the waiting troopers grabbed him left-handed by the shoulder, holding the sub-machine gun back like a pistol in his right where the prisoner couldn't reach it.

The trooper walked the fellow out of the chute. Instead of leaving him for the Gendarmes, he handed him over to another of the White Mice who led him in turn to the back of the air-cushion truck.

The prisoners had been moving with something like the docility of the cattle normally loaded into the shipping containers. Now they paused; the woman two places behind the fellow who'd been taken away tried to go back.

"Move it!" the other trooper at the chute snarled, waggling his weapon.

The woman resumed her way down the chute—and out the other end to the Gendarmes, ignored by the voice from the command car. A man who'd been waiting in the crowd turned and started to force his way back through his fellows.

"Halt!" called the trooper nearest to him along the fenceline as he leveled his sub-machine gun. The prisoner tried to run, pushing at others who were trying desperately to get out of the line of fire. The sub-machine gun stuttered a short burst into the man's legs, one bolt into the left calf and two more at the back of the right knee.

The prisoner fell, screaming with surprise. It was too soon yet for the pain to have reached him; though that'd come, it'd surely come. Only a tag of skin and one tendon connected his right thigh and lower leg.

"Two of you carry him through," ordered the loudspeaker. "Make sure to turn his face toward me."

The wounded man continued to scream. He tried to stand but slipped onto his right side.

From the command car, Joachim Steuben giggled. Amplified, the sound was even more gut-wrenching than it'd seemed when Huber heard it from across the major's desk.

The prisoners nearest the fallen man stood frozen till the trooper waggled the glowing muzzle of his sub-machine gun. Then they grabbed his arms convulsively and stumbled through the chute as he screamed even louder. One brushed the razor ribbon, leaving much of his sleeve on the wire and blood dripping from his torn arm. The wounded man's legs didn't bleed; the powergun bolts had cauterized the wounds.

"A moment of your time, Lieutenant Huber," said Captain Orichos. He jumped. She'd walked over to him while his attention was on the byplay in the camp.

"Ma'am?" he said. Without thinking about it, he stiffened to parade rest. "That is, Captain?"

"Mauricia, I hope," Orichos said. After the battle she'd resumed wearing her beret instead of a Slammers commo helmet. She took it off now and shook her short hair loose before replacing the cap. "I suppose you know your unit will be routed back with a stopover in Midway?"

"No ma'am," Huber said with a faint grin. "There were rumors, but we're line soldiers. Nobody tells us anything."

"Well, I'm telling you," Orichos said with a mixture of crispness and challenge. "I'll be flying back by car shortly; there are some things to clear up in the capital now that the threat's been dealt with."

She cleared her throat and looked away. "What I'm saying, Arne, is that I hope when you arrive in Midway, you'll get in touch with me. I'll have some free time by then, and I'd really like to repay you for all you've done for the Point and for me."

Orichos smiled. It softened and transformed her face to a remarkable degree.

"I think I can guarantee you a good time," she said. She touched the back of Huber's wrist, then turned and went back to her fellows.

Huber rubbed his wrist with the fingers of his other hand as he walked on, thinking about Orichos and about the shooting he'd just watched.

It'd taken skill to hit the running man and not nail a couple of the bystanders. Though it could as easily have been dumb luck: he didn't suppose either the trooper or Major Steuben would've cared if some of the other prisoners had lost limbs.

Huber reached the hatch in the rear of the command car. It opened before he rapped it with the barrel of his powergun. The two men inside had their backs to him as they watched a high-resolution image of prisoners moving steadily through the chute to the shipping containers.

Joachim Steuben was as dapper as if he'd spent the past three days in Base Alpha instead of making a thousand kilometer run over difficult terrain. His companion was blond and in his thirties; Grayle's chief civil aide, Huber recalled, the one who'd disappeared between the Assembly meeting and the time Captain Orichos found incriminating papers in the files that had been under the aide's control.

"That one!" the aide said. What was his name? Patronus; *that* was it. "He's Gerd Danilew. He was in charge of off-planet weapons purchases!"

"That one," Steuben said, his amplified voice damped to silence when the hatch closed behind Huber. The pipper of the cab-mounted tribarrel framed the face of the sallow, moustached prisoner walking nervously between the barriers of razor ribbon.

The man looked up. Instead of trying to run, he fell in a faint as limp as if the tribarrel had decapitated him—as the slightest additional pressure of Steuben's finger on the trigger control would've made it do.

"Well, carry him, then," Steuben ordered into the pickup for the external speakers. He looked over his shoulder at Huber and raised an eyebrow in delighted amusement, then turned back and added, "Now!"

The procession resumed. Patronus kept his face rigidly forward as if he thought that by refusing to acknowledge Huber, he could deny what was going on.

Steuben rotated his full-function chair to smile at Huber. "So, Lieutenant," he said. "I thought I'd use this opportunity to see if you're still happy with a line command."

Instead of the slot in the White Mice that he offered me three weeks ago, Huber thought.

He shrugged and said, "Yeah, I'm happy. We did a good job here."

He guessed he'd made that sound like a challenge, which wasn't the smartest sort of attitude to show when you were talking to a weasel like Joachim Steuben. Huber didn't care much at the moment.

"Indeed you did," Steuben said, nothing in his tone but mild approval. "Both the task force and you personally… which is why my offer is still open."

He cocked an eyebrow.

"I said I was happy!" Huber said. Via, he was going to have to watch himself. It'd be a hell of a note to come through a mission like this one and then be shot because he mouthed off to a stone killer like Joachim Steuben.

He smiled—at himself, but it was probably the right thing to do because the major giggled in response.

"That one!" Patronus said, pointing at the image. His hands were clean but he'd chewed his fingernails ragged.

Major Steuben's right hand moved minutely, then clicked the switch that controlled the laser marker. Huber didn't see him look around, not even a quick glance, but the pipper was centered on the forehead of the grim-looking man who'd brushed his full moustache in an attempt to cover the scar on his cheek. "That one," Steuben repeated into the PA system.

In a quick voice, bobbing his head to his words, Patronus continued, "That's Commander Halcleides, he took over after Commander Fewsett—that is, when he died."

"What happens next?" Huber asked. He didn't exactly care, but he knew Deseau'd ask when he got back to *Fencing Master* and he wanted to have an answer. "You'll shoot them?"

Patronus turned with a furious expression. "They're traitors!" he snarled. "They deserve to die!"

Steuben made a peremptory gesture with his left hand. His head didn't turn, but Huber saw his eyes flick toward the former aide.

"Master Patronus," Steuben said without raising his voice, "I'd appreciate it if you'd attend to your duties while the lieutenant and I speak like the gentlemen we are. I don't want the bother of replacing you."

He giggled again. To Huber he added, "Though shooting him would be no bother at all, eh, Lieutenant? For either of us, I suspect."

Patronus was on a seat that folded down from the sidewall. He turned again to face the screen across the front of the compartment, pointedly concentrating on the prisoners shambling through the identification parade. His face flushed, then went white.

Huber looked at the man who'd first planted evidence on his friends and now was fingering his closest colleagues for probable execution. In a good cause, of course: the Regiment's cause. But still…

"No, Major," Huber said. "It wouldn't be much bother."

"But to answer your question," Steuben continued, "no, we're not going to shoot them, Lieutenant. They'll be shipped off-planet to a detention center; an asteroid in the Nieuw Friesland system, as a matter of fact. The Colonel believes they'll be a useful… reminder, shall we say, to the government of the Point as to what might happen if it suddenly decided to back away from its support for the war with Solace."

"Th-the-there," Patronus said, pointing at the strikingly attractive woman going through the chute. His outstretched hand trembled. "Talia Mandrakora, she was in charge of propaganda."

"That one," Steuben said, highlighting the woman. To Huber he added, "Do you fancy her, Lieutenant? I dare say you could convince her that the only chance she has to survive would involve pleasing you."

Huber felt his lip curl. "No thanks," he said. "I don't have trouble finding company for the night."

"I'm sure that's true," Steuben said with a smirk. He rotated his chair toward the screen again. His posture didn't change in any definable way, but he was no longer the man who'd been joking with catlike cruelty. "And now, I think, we have the personage we've been waiting for."

The prisoners waiting to walk through the chute parted, glancing over their shoulders and then lowering their faces as they pushed clear. Melinda Riker Grayle strode through the gap which fear rather than respect had opened for her. She was no longer the woman who'd cowed her colleagues in the Assembly. She wore a white uniform but the right sleeve had been singed and at least some of the stain on her trousers was blood. Nonetheless she walked with her back straight, glaring toward the command car.

"Invite Assemblyman Grayle to join her associates in our van, if you please, Sergeant Kuiper," Steuben said into the pickup.

Grayle walked alone into the chute. The trooper there hesitated, his arm raised but not fully extended.

"Keep your filthy hands off me!" Grayle said. Steuben must've switched on the external microphones, for the assemblyman's voice sounded as clear as if she'd been in the compartment with them.

She turned to face the car and shouted, "You in there, whoever you are! Hired killers! You know the election was rigged! And *you* know that you're charging ten times what the citizens think they're paying for your services! Tell them!"

"Take her away, Kuiper," Steuben said, sounding vaguely bored. "I'd rather you not shoot her in the legs so that she has to be carried, but do that if she won't come peaceably."

"You know it's true!" Grayle screamed. When the trooper reached for her shoulder she slapped his hand away, but instead of resisting further she marched down the chute and turned toward the truck where her aides were being held. Her head was high, and she didn't look around.

Steuben smirked at Huber. "She's right, you know," he said conversationally. "The election was rigged. The Freedom Party would've taken forty-four percent of the seats if your friend Captain Orichos hadn't manipulated the vote count."

Huber looked sharply at the smaller display above the big screen, a 360-degree panorama from the command car. Mauricia Orichos stood watching the parade with three other Gendarmery officers, a few meters behind the White Mice who did the sorting. They followed Grayle with their eyes until she'd disappeared into the box of the truck.

"Orichos did that?" Huber said.

"She asked us for technical help so it could be done without detection," Steuben said, looking up at the panorama with a faint smile. "I provided someone from my signals section. It would've been extremely awkward if Grayle had become Speaker and tried to take the Point out of the war."

As Steuben spoke Patronus turned slowly toward him, like a rat hypnotized by the slowly waving hood of a cobra. Steuben focused his ice-colored eyes on the traitor and said, "I believe I told you—"

He broke off in the middle of the passionless threat for another giggle. "But then," he continued, "with Mistress Grayle in hand, we don't have to worry about other threats to hold over our friends, do we? I suppose we could just dismiss the rest of the prisoners… though I don't believe we will for the moment."

He gestured Patronus back to the screen and the line of prisoners resuming their procession through the chute. Patronus obeyed with the slow, jerky motion of an ill-made automaton.

"Was the rest of it true too?" Huber asked harshly. His throat hadn't recovered from the ozone he'd breathed during the battle, but he and the major both knew there was more to his tone than that. "About the costs being higher than they know?"

Steuben shrugged. "In a manner of speaking," he said. "The governments of the Outer States believe the Regiment's price is only about twenty percent of the real figure.… But don't worry: our fees *are* being paid, and line lieutenants don't have to worry about where the money comes from."

"I suppose not," Huber said. He tried to make his mind go blank, but he couldn't manage it. "Sir, if you don't have any further duties for me here…?"

"You don't like our company?" Steuben said, his smile flashing on and off like a strobe light. "All right, Lieutenant. You're free to leave."

Major Steuben rotated his chair toward Huber again. His face, too pretty to be handsome in a man, was suddenly as hard as chilled steel. "The offer remains open, Lieutenant," he said. "You should feel flattered, you know."

"I appreciate your confidence, sir," Huber said. He turned to the hatch; it opened before he could touch the control plate.

Huber stepped into the gathering darkness. Grenade launchers continued to work, the choonk/*wham!* choonk/*wham!* punctuating the sound of drive fans and power tools. Troopers were pulling maintenance on their vehicles with spares the column had brought from Base Alpha. The white flashes of the bombs were quick speckles through the fabric of tents bulging outward before they collapsed.

Mauricia Orichos saw Huber come out of the command car. She stepped away from the group she was with and waved to him.

Huber looked at her, then slipped his faceshield down and quickened his stride in the direction of *Fencing Master*. As he'd told Major Steuben, he could find his own company. And he wasn't going to find it there.

NECK OR NOTHING

"Red Section, pull back two hundred meters!" Lieutenant Arne Huber ordered over the platoon channel. A laser from one of the hostile hovertanks touched a tree to the right, blasting a ten-meter strip off the trunk. Fragments of bark and sapwood stung Huber and the two gunners with him in the combat car's open fighting compartment. "Blue, we'll hold till Red's in position! Six out."

The artificial intelligence in Huber's commo helmet imposed a translucent red caret on his faceshield, warning of movement to the left. Huber was *Fencing Master*'s left wing gunner as well as commander of platoon F-3. At the moment, swinging his tribarrel onto the threat took precedence over controlling the platoon's other five cars.

The motion was the hull of a hovertank from a mercenary unit hired by Solace in its war with the Outer States. The vehicle was three hundred meters away, much farther than you could generally see in the forests of Plattner's World, and the tank's two crewmen probably weren't aware of *Fencing Master* as they drove across the battlefront hoping to take F-3 in the flank.

The target quivered in Huber's holographic sight picture. He settled his weapon and squeezed the butterfly trigger with both thumbs. The cluster of iridium barrels rotated as they fired, giving each tube a moment to cool after spewing a bolt of ionized copper downrange at the speed of light.

The narrow window didn't allow Huber to choose a particular spot on his target, but the energy a 2-cm powergun packed made most things vulnerable. The compartment holding the hovertank's crew was armored with ceramic layered in ablative sheets, proof against single bolts or even a short burst, but the skirts enclosing the plenum chamber were light plastic to keep the weight down. Huber raked the bulge where the two joined.

A fireball erupted from the tank's port side: the cyan plasma had converted the plastic into its constituent elements—which recombined explosively. The flash ignited even the loam of the forest floor.

"I can't see it!" screamed Frenchie Deseau at *Fencing Master*'s bow gun. "Padova, pull up, for Hell's sake! I can't see the target!"

The hostile was directly ahead of *Fencing Master*, so by rights it should've been Deseau's target while Huber watched the left flank the way Trooper Learoyd was doing the right from the other wing gun. It was a chance of visibility that made the tank Huber's prey while the trees concealed it from Deseau.

The tank rocked to the right, then slewed to a halt because Huber'd ripped its skirts wide open. The tank's gunner tried to rotate his roof-mounted laser, but Huber's tribarrel blew the weapon to fiery slag an instant before rupturing the crew compartment itself.

What mattered was that *some*body got the tank before it took F-3 from the rear; but if F-3 didn't fall back quickly, another tank or tanks *were* going to circle them. There were too many hostiles for a single platoon of combat cars to deal with for long. Where the bloody hell was Ander's Legion, the combined arms battalion that was supposed to follow when F-3 seized the knoll in the face of the advancing Solace column?

"Three-six, this is Three-three!" crackled the voice of Platoon Sergeant Jellicoe, commanding the three cars of Red Section. For this operation Huber would rather have operated in three two-car sections, but two of his vehicles were crewed with replacements. The newbies had been trained and may well have been veterans of other units before they joined Hammer's Slammers, but Huber didn't want to risk anybody operating alone until he'd personally seen how they held up in combat. *"We're in position! Over!"*

"Blue Section," Huber ordered, "pull—"

Fencing Master was already starting to reverse. Although she'd just been transferred to F-3, Padova'd already shown an ability to anticipate orders—sometimes the difference between life and death in combat. As the car grunted backward, Deseau and Learoyd fired simultaneously.

For an instant, saplings ranging from thumb-thick to thigh-thick blazed. When the blue-green bolts had sawn through the undergrowth, they flashed and cascaded from the sloping armor of the hovertank coming up from a swale less than twenty meters away.

"*Via!*" Huber shouted. The tank was well to starboard, but *Fencing Master* shimmied as Padova backed so there was a chance the stern would swing enough to give Huber a shot. He tried to bring his tribarrel to bear as he cursed himself for not keeping better tabs on the sensor readouts. Because Huber was the platoon leader, *Fencing Master* carried a Command and Control box whose holographic display would show the heat, noise, and radio-frequency signatures of a fifty-tonne tank charging to within stone's throw. He just hadn't taken—hadn't *had*—time to glance at it.

The tank's sloping armor reflected a portion of the bolts' energy as a haze of cyan light, searing the leaves from overhanging trees. The glare was so intense that Huber's faceshield blacked it out to save his eyesight.

Despite the hits, capacitors feeding the tank's laser screamed twice. The first pulse fried the air close enough overhead that Huber might've lost his hand if he'd raised it at the wrong time. That was probably a chance shot, though, because the second charge ripped empty forest twenty meters to the left, and then the tank's ceramic armor failed under the tribarrels' hammering.

At the temperature of copper plasma, almost everything burns. The gulp of orange flame from the tank's interior was partly plastic, partly fabric, and partly the flesh of the crew.

Padova kept backing away from the line of contact. Flat-screen displays provided a combat car's driver with just as good a view to the rear as forward, but driving through dense woodland in reverse required considerable skill. *Fencing Master*'s skirts struck only one tree too thick to shear off. Even that was a glancing blow, though it threw the troopers hard against the fighting compartment's armor.

"Blue Section, pull back!" Huber said, completing the interrupted order as he checked his display. The other two cars were already retreating up the forested ridgeline; their commanders must have filled in the obvious if their drivers had needed the prodding. You didn't have to be a military genius to know that F-3's position wasn't survivable for long, when at least a company of hostile tanks was advancing and there was no bloody sign of Ander's Legion.

The woods were afire in a dozen places, ignited by energy weapons and the violent destruction of several vehicles—all of them hostile so far, the Lord be thanked, but that couldn't last forever. Besides the wall of trees, smoke obscured normal vision. That gave F-3 an advantage because the Slammers' sensors were better than those of their opponents, but in the confusion of battle there were too many inputs for anybody to use them all. Quick reactions, not technology, had saved *Fencing Master* when the hovertank roared up at them from less than pistol range.

Red Section waited hull-down over the reverse slope of the ridge from which F-3 had advanced twenty minutes before. Huber had expected to form a skirmish line while Ander's Legion dug in to ambush the oncoming Solace column. Ander hadn't come and the hostiles had—*very* aggressively.

Padova brought *Fencing Master* back to where they'd started their advance, in the shelter of smooth-barked trees whose foliage was a golden contrast to the deep green of most of the species around them. The economy of Plattner's World was based on gathering the so-called Moss, a fungus that parasitized the native trees and which could be processed into the anti-aging drug Thalderol. In normal times here, the wanton destruction of forest was a serious crime.

War imposed different standards. The recent engagement had turned a kilometer of woodland into a spreading blaze where munitions occasionally exploded. The hostiles, elements of the West Riding Yeomanry hired by Solace, had halted to regroup to the west of the fiery barrier. The tanks would come on in a moment, buttoned up and using their numbers to envelope the Slammers on both flanks even though Huber had stretched F-3 with forty meters between combat cars.

That was far too great an interval in forest where normal sight distance was only half that. *Foghorn*, immediately to the right of *Fencing Master*, was an occasional glint of iridium through the foliage. Skilled infantry could slip through the line to do all manner of damage before the troopers knew what was happening.

The long burst had heated *Fencing Master*'s right tribarrel till it jammed. A smear of the plastic matrix that held copper atoms in alignment in the chamber clogged the ejection port instead of spitting out cleanly. Learoyd was chipping at the mess with his knife while Deseau covered both front and starboard with quick jerks of his head and a tense expression.

"Fox Three," Huber ordered; it was time and past time to cut and run. "We'll withdraw in line behind Three-six on the plotted track."

As he spoke, he entered EXECUTE on the manual controller of the C&C box, transmitting to all the troopers of his platoon the course the AI had chosen to his directions. They'd retreat parallel to the line on which they'd advanced, but not over the same track in case Solace forces had laid artillery on it in the interim.

"I'm going to start at forty kph and I'll raise our speed if I can," Huber continued. "If you've got trouble keeping interval let me know, but I don't want these bloody tanks up our ass. Over."

"*Three-six, this is Three-three!*" Jellicoe called from the north end of the line. "*I've got movement to my rear, El-Tee! D'ye suppose Ander's got his thumb outa his butt finally? Over.*"

"Fox Three," Huber ordered as he switched his display to give the readout from *Floosie*, Jellicoe's car. "Hold in place! Three-six out."

Everything takes time.… F-3 couldn't sit long on a hillside in the face of flames and a hostile armored column, but Huber *had* to process information before he made a decision on which turned a battle and the lives of all his troopers. Beside him, Lear-oyd spun his barrel cluster a third of a turn to charge the weapon. Deseau slewed his tribarrel to the left; the bearing squealed faintly. Now Frenchie was covering the port side while his lieutenant concentrated on sensor readouts.

For a moment Huber thought they might pull this off after all: Ander's Legion was late, but the delay would've convinced the hostiles that the Slammers had been left hanging. When F-3 pulled back, the Yeomanry were likely to follow without keeping a proper lookout. With any kind of luck, Ander's force could take them in the flank and hammer them good while Huber brought his cars around to block the Solace line of retreat.

Except—

"Bloody fucking Hell!" Huber shouted.

He didn't want it to be true, but there was no question in the world that it was. Sergeant Jellicoe wasn't at fault: all the cars carried the same sensor pack, but the additional sorting power in *Fencing Master*'s Command and Control box made the difference.

There was an armored column coming up fast from F-3's rear, all right, but it wasn't Ander's Legion which rode on *tracked* armored personnel carriers. These twenty-three vehicles, a mix of APCs and gun carriers, ran on six or eight wheels. The AI gave a ninety-three percent probability that they were a company of the Apex Dragoons, another of the units in Solace pay.

F-3 was trapped.

"Fox Three, this is Three-six," Huber said, his voice calm. He was speaking notice-ably slower than he usually would have. Every syllable was precise, a reaction to stress rather than a conscious attempt to be clear in a crisis. "The vehicles approaching from the east are hostile also. We'll charge through them in line abreast instead of withdrawing to the southeast as planned."

As Huber spoke, his right hand laid out routes and targets in the C&C display for immediate transmission to the helmets of his troopers. There were more enemy vehicles than there were guns in F-3, almost four targets per car, so he had to overlap the assignments.

That was if everything went right, of course. As soon as F-3 started taking casualties, its suppressing firepower went down and with it everybody's chance of survival.

"Hit anything you see, troopers, but remember job one is to save our asses," Huber said. "Drivers, keep your foot in it. Don't slow for anything, get through and get out, that's the only way we're going to be around to talk about this afterward."

Beneath Huber, Padova was rotating *Fencing Master* on its axis to align its bow for the coming attack. Huber was conscious of the change only as vibration and a blur in his peripheral vision; his focus was utterly on the holographic landscape of six blue dots and the hornet's nest of red hostiles through which F-3's commander had to lead them.

"We'll execute on the command," Huber said, giving the display a last searching glance as he prepared to exchange it for the view through his tribarrel's sights. "And the Lord help us, troopers, because there sure as hell isn't anybody else on our side today. Fox Three, *execute!*"

Padova had *Fencing Master*'s drive fans whining at full power. Instead of setting the blades to zero incidence, she'd chosen to cock the nacelles against one another in pairs so that they were already flowing maximum air and wouldn't have to accelerate against a fluid mass when it came time to move. *Fencing Master* pogoed minusculely as it slid downhill through the undergrowth. The Dragoons, approaching in line abreast, were within half a klick but still on the other side of rising ground.

Fencing Master's skirts crumbled a low overhang into a flat-bottomed swale. There must've been a watercourse here in season, but now the leaves the fans stirred were dust-dry. Huber watched his sector, his tribarrel slanted slightly upward to cover the crest of the ridge beyond the concealing undergrowth.

The soil on the slope must not have been as good as that in most of the region, because the trees were sparser and averaged twenty meters in height instead of the twenty-five or thirty normal for adult specimens of the same species elsewhere. More light reached the understory and low brush grew thicker.

Huber ignored the C&C display to focus on the portion of *Fencing Master*'s surroundings for which he was personally responsible. The Slammers' faceshields used sensor data to caret the most probable vectors from which targets might appear. He'd directed the AI to screen out hostiles to the rear. In the unlikely event the pursuing tanks caught up with F-3, Huber and his troopers were dead with absolute certainty: there was no point in worrying about what couldn't be changed.

The vehicles' electronics suites meant the Slammers had a huge amount of information. Unless they were careful, they could drown in information instead of making the instant decisions a battle demanded of anyone who hoped to survive.

Arne Huber wouldn't allow his mind to lose itself in data instead of action, but the sensors' warning had saved F-3 from stumbling unaware into a superior enemy. The Apex Dragoons were a respectable force, but they didn't have electronics of comparable discrimination and might not even know the combat cars were heading toward them. Though Huber couldn't kid himself that the Solace forces had mousetrapped his platoon by pure accident....

"*Wait for it...*" Deseau warned over the intercom; talking to himself mostly, because they were all veterans and knew what was about to happen.

Padova tweaked her fan nacelles expertly, lifting *Fencing Master* over the crest on nearly an even keel. Below, zigzagging because their power-to-weight ratio didn't allow them to climb the steeper reverse slope straight on, were three armored personnel carriers with a pair of anti-tank missiles on a cupola mounting an automatic cannon. Far to *Fencing Master*'s right was a larger vehicle with a long electrochemical cannon in its turret. Huber squeezed his trigger as his tribarrel settled on the nearer of the two APCs on his side.

The APC's commander had his head out of the cupola hatch to conn his vehicle. He'd started to duck, but Huber's first bolt decapitated him in a cyan flash. The rest of the burst splashed on the cupola, setting off an anti-tank missile in a gushing yellow low-order explosion.

Huber'd pulled the APC's teeth by wrecking the turret. Without spending more rounds—*Fencing Master* would be through the Dragoons and gone before the infantry in the rear compartment could unass their vehicle and start shooting—he swung his gun toward the APC that he'd assigned both to himself and the car to the left, Sergeant Nagano's *Foghorn*. Deseau and Learoyd were firing, and the forest echoed with the snarling thump of powerguns punctuated by the blast of the Dragoons' weapons.

When Huber saw black exhaust puff from the far side of his target's cupola, he knew he'd been too late to keep the gunner from loosing a missile. Though the cupola hadn't rotated onto *Fencing Master* yet, as the missile came off the launch rails it made a hard angle toward the combat car on the thrust of its attitude jets.

"*Via!*" Huber screamed, knowing that now survival was in the hands of the Lord and *Fencing Master*'s Automatic Defense System. A segment of the ADS tripped, blasting a charge of osmium pellets from the explosive-filled groove where the car's hull armor joined the plenum chamber skirts.

Fencing Master jumped and clanged. The pellets met the incoming missile, shoving it aside and tearing off pieces. The warhead didn't detonate—a good thing, because this close it still would've been dangerous—but a shred of tailfin slashed Huber's gunshield, leaving a bright scar across the oxidized surface.

Learoyd's target, a forty-tonne guncarrier, went off like a huge bomb. The concussion spun *Fencing Master* like a top, slamming Huber against the side of the fighting compartment. Despite the helmet's active shock cushioning, his vision shrank momentarily to a bright vertical line.

The guns of the Apex Dragoons used liquid propellant set off by a jolt of high current through tungsten wire. Besides adding electrical energy to the chemical charge, the method ignited the propellant instantly and maximized efficiency for any bore that could accept the pressures.

Learoyd's burst had detonated the reservoir holding the charges for perhaps a hundred main-gun rounds. The explosion left a crater where the vehicle had been and a cloud of smoke mushrooming hundreds of meters in the air.

Fencing Master grounded twice, sucked down when the wave of low pressure followed the shock front. Padova fought her controls straight, then tried to steer the car back in the original direction; they'd spun more than a full turn counterclockwise and were now headed well to the left of the planned course.

The shockwave rocked the Dragoon APC up on its three starboard wheels. The vehicle didn't spin because it was some distance farther from the blast and its tires provided more stability than the fluid coupling of pressurized air linking the combat car to the ground.

Huber's eyesight cleared; his tribarrel already bore on the APC's rear hull. He fired, working his burst forward while bolts from Deseau's weapon crossed his. Their plasma shattered the light aluminum/ceramic sandwich armoring the APC's side. The hatches blew open in geysers of black smoke which sucked in, then gushed as crimson flames.

Learoyd lay huddled on the floor of the fighting compartment. His left hand twitched, so at least he was alive. There was no time to worry about him now, not with all F-3 in danger.

Fencing Master drove between the two APCs, both oozing flames, and roared down the steep slope. Explosions thundered in the near distance. Huber glanced to his left as a ball of orange flame bubbled over the treetops. It had vanished some seconds before the ground rippled and the walls of the valley channeled a wave of dust and leaf litter past *Fencing Master* and on.

Huber pivoted his tribarrel to cover the rear. In shifting, he banged his right side on the coaming. The unexpected pain made him gasp. The blast had bruised him badly and maybe cracked some ribs.

Deseau took over the right wing gun. Learoyd had managed to get to his hands and knees, but it'd be a while before he was able to man his weapon again.

Or maybe it wouldn't, come to think. Bert Learoyd had the tenacity of an earthworm, though perhaps coupled with an earthworm's intellectual capacity.

Huber checked his C&C display. All six cars were still in action, though the icons for *Foghorn* and *Farsi's Fancy*—car Three-seven in Jellicoe's section—showed they were reporting battle damage.

Even the Slammers' electronics couldn't discriminate between the signatures of vehicles with some systems running though the crews were dead, and those which were fully functional. Apart from the occasional catastrophic explosion like that of Learoyd's target, there was no way to be sure of how much of the hostile mechanized company remained dangerous. They'd taken a hammering, no mistake, but right now all Huber was concerned about was F-3's survival. Thanks to Ander's inaction, the Slammers had lost this battle before the first shot was fired.

The United Cities government had employed many small units of mercenaries instead of a few large formations, because no place on the planet except Port Plattner in Solace could land a starship big enough to hold a battalion and its equipment. Hammer's Regiment was one of the largest units in UC pay, and some of the others were only platoons.

There would've been coordination problems even at best, but the real trouble arose because neither the UC nor any of the other Outer States had a military staff capable of planning and executing a war on the present scale. Colonel Hammer and his team at Base Alpha had taken over the duties because there was no one else to do it, but that caused further delays and confusion. Everything had to be relayed through UC officers who often didn't understand the words they were parroting, and even so other mercenary captains dragged their feet on orders they knew were given by a peer.

Some UC units were incompetently led; that might well be the case with Ander's Legion. Their communications systems varied radically; Central at Base Alpha could communicate with all of them, but many couldn't talk to one another. And some mercenary captains, especially those who commanded only a company or platoon, were less concerned with winning wars than they were with protecting the soldiers who were their entire capital.

Those were staff problems, but they became the concern of line lieutenants like Arne Huber when they meant that his combat cars were left swinging in the breeze. Ander hadn't gotten the word, or he hadn't obeyed orders, or he was simply too bumbling to advance when he was supposed to.

There was an obvious risk of further Solace units following close behind the initial company of Dragoons, but despite that Huber had a bad feeling about continuing on his plotted course to the southeast. He'd already asked his AI to assess alternate routes, but before he got the answers the C&C display threw sensor data across the terrain in a red emergency mask. It was worse than he'd feared.

"Three-six to Fox Three," Huber said in a tone from which previous crises had burned all emotion. "Hostile hovertanks have gotten around us to the south. Fox Three-three—" Sergeant Jellicoe in *Floosie* "—leads on the new course at nine-seven degrees true. Three-six out. Break—"

His voice caught. He thought for a moment that he was going to vomit over the inside of his faceshield, but the spasm passed. There'd been too much; too much stress and pain and stench, even for a veteran.

"—Padova, throttle back so that we stay on the crest after the rest are clear. We may need the sensor range."

The Solace commander had reacted fast by sending part of the Yeomanry around the Slammers' left flank at the same time as the mechanized company circled their right. Huber'd held F-3 too long as he waited for supports that never came, but there was still a chance. The crews of the hovertanks wouldn't be in a hurry to come to close quarters with the cars that had bloodied their vanguard so badly at the first shock.

Fencing Master growled onto the ridge line. The rise would separate the combat cars from the units they'd already engaged, though the tanks approaching from the south were in the same shallow valley. The forest was somewhat of a shield for F-3, maybe enough of one.

Learoyd was on the forward gun now, swaying as though the grips were all that kept him upright. Deseau scanned the trees to the right, the direction the tanks would come from. Undergrowth was sparse here, but the treeboles allowed only occasional glimpses of anything as much as a hundred meters away.

F-3 was in line with the flanks echeloned back. The four cars in the center were across the ridge and proceeding downslope, but Jellicoe had slowed *Floosie* also. The additional ten seconds of sensor data hadn't brought any new surprises, so Huber said, "Padova, goose it and—"

The clang of a slug penetrating iridium echoed through the forest. The icon for Fox Three-three went cross-hatched and stopped moving across the holographic terrain of the C&C display.

"Padova, get us to *Floosie* soonest!" Huber shouted. "Break! Fox Three, follow the plotted course. Three-one, you're in charge till I rejoin with the crew of Three-five! Three-six out!"

Huber hadn't thought, hadn't had time to think, but he knew as Padova jerked *Fencing Master* hard left that instinct had led him to the right decision. Though two other combat cars were nearer *Floosie* than *Fencing Master* was, they'd have to reverse and climb the slope to reach the disabled vehicle. Gravity was more of a handicap than an extra hundred meters on level ground when you were riding a thirty-tonne mass.

Sergeant Nagano—Fox Three-one—was a few months junior in grade to Three-seven's Sergeant Mullion, but Nagano'd been in F-3 when Huber took command a year ago while Mullion had been posted into the platoon only a few days before. Mullion might turn out to be a real crackerjack, and if so Huber would apologize to him at a suitable time. Right now there was enough else going wrong that Huber wasn't about to trust his troopers to an unknown quantity besides.

Fencing Master wove between the trunks of massive trees. Learoyd slid the fingers of his left hand under his helmet to rub his scalp and forehead, but his right never left the grip of his tribarrel. He seemed to be back to normal now, or anyway what passed as normal for a trooper in the middle of a firefight.

Chatter filled the platoon push, but none of it came from Jellicoe and her crew. Huber tuned out the empty noise—anybody was likely to babble in the stress of a battle, no matter how well-trained and experienced they might be—and concentrated on what wasn't there.

The icon for Three-three continued to pulse sullenly. Huber imported a remote image from Jellicoe's gunsight to the corner of his faceshield. He got only a motionless view of treetops, but at least that was better than the black emptiness of an open channel.

"*There's* Floosie!" Learoyd said. "*El-Tee, they been hit from your side!*"

Floosie was tilted against the west side of a huge tree, spun there by the first of the two rounds which'd hit her. The slug had struck the back of the fighting compartment and penetrated cleanly, angling slightly left to right and exiting above the driver's hatch.

Floosie'd stalled at the impact. The second shot had slammed into the plenum chamber before the driver could restart his vehicle. That wasn't his fault: the combined shock of the slug and collision with a three-meter-thick treebole was more anybody could've shrugged off instantly, even protected by the automatic restraint system of the driver's compartment. The follow-up round had put paid to *Floosie*: there was a gaping hole in the skirts and at least half the fan nacelles would've been damaged or destroyed.

The tank that had knocked out the combat car was sited on the high ground a kilometer to the west. The hostile gunner had been lucky to get a sight line through the trees, but he'd been bloody good to react to the unexpected target and then to punch out a second round to finish the job. With so many shots ripping through the forest, one of them was bound to connect with something....

"Padova, get us—" Huber said, but his driver was already slewing *Fencing Master* to the right, putting the tree and the bulk of the disabled car between them and the Solace gunner. The tank might've moved forward after it fired; but its commander just might have decided that he was better off where he was than he'd be if he came to close quarters with the Slammers' tribarrels.

Deseau braced himself against the coaming beside Huber, cursing a blue streak. He'd grabbed Learoyd's backup 1-cm sub-machine gun from its sling on a tie-down beside the right tribarrel. It wasn't much of a weapon to threaten tanks with, but at least Deseau could point it toward the probable dangers.

Fencing Master slewed around the tree and grounded hard, its port quarter almost in contact with *Floosie*'s damaged bow skirt. The ragged exit hole was bigger than an access port.

Jellicoe's driver climbed out of his hatch. He'd lost his helmet and his mouth hung open. A bitter haze of burned insulation lay over the fighting compartment, but as *Fencing Master* stopped, Huber saw a hand reach up to grip the coaming: Sergeant Jellicoe was still alive, if only just.

"Get aboard!" Huber screamed to the driver. As he spoke, he lifted his right foot to the top of *Fencing Master*'s armor and leaped into the disabled car. If anybody'd asked him a moment before, he'd have said he was so exhausted he had trouble just breathing. Deseau, continuing to curse, took over the left wing gun.

Floosie's fighting compartment was an abattoir. The guns that hit her fired frangible shot that broke into a hypersonic spray on the other side of the penetration. Jellicoe had been manning the left wing gun and out of the direct blast, but the sleet of heavy-metal granules had splashed the thighs and torsos of her crewmen across the interior of the armor. Huber's boots slipped when they hit the floor.

He fell with a dizzying shock. He was up again in a moment, but his right side was numb.

He lifted Sergeant Jellicoe. She was a stocky woman, still wearing the body armor that'd saved her life. Huber didn't try to strip the ceramic clamshell off her now because he wasn't sure his fingers could manipulate the catches. He stepped back and bent, throwing Jellicoe's torso over his shoulders, then stumbled forward.

Learoyd and Deseau fired past Huber to either side; his faceshield blacked out the vivid cyan of their bolts. *Via!* there was no way in hell he was going to get aboard *Fencing Master*. He couldn't carry Jellicoe and he sure couldn't throw her into—

"*Gotcha, El-Tee!*" Frenchie said, bracing his left hand on the tribarrel's receiver as he prepared to cross to help. "*We're golden!*"

Huber didn't hear the shot that struck *Floosie*'s bow slope, but he felt the car buck upward in the middle of a white flash.

Then he felt nothing. Nothing at all.

… he should be coming around very shortly… some part of the cosmos said to some other part of the cosmos.

Awareness—not consciousness, not yet—returned with the awkward jerkiness of a butterfly opening its wings as it poises on the edge of its cocoon. *My name is Arne Huber. I'm—*

Huber's eyes opened. He saw three faces, anxious despite their hard features. Then the pain hit him and he blacked out.

He regained consciousness. The world was white, pulsing, and oven-hot—but he was alert, waiting for his vision to steady. He knew from experience that he hadn't been out long this time, but how long he'd been *here*, in the main infirmary at Base Alpha… He must've been hurt bad.

"How's Jellicoe?" he said. Huber'd heard rusty hinges with better tone than he had now, but he got the words out. "How's my platoon sergeant?"

The technician adjusted his controls, his attention on the display of his medical computer. He nodded in self-satisfaction. Huber felt a quivering numbness in all his nerve endings.

The other men in the room were Major Danny Pritchard and—Blood and Martyrs—Colonel Hammer himself.

"She didn't make it," Hammer said flatly. "If you hadn't had her over your back, you wouldn't have made it either. The shot that hit Three-three's bow slope splashed upward. The good part of it is that the impact pretty well threw you aboard your own car. Your people were able to bug out after the rest of the platoon with no further casualties."

"It was quick for her," said Major Pritchard. He smiled wryly. "This time that's the truth."

You always told civilian dependents that their trooper's death had been quick, even if you knew she'd been screaming in agony, unable to open a jammed hatch as her vehicle burned. You didn't lie to other troopers, though, because it was a waste of breath.

Huber nodded. Pain washed over him; he closed his eyes. The technician muttered and made adjustments. Huber felt the pain vanish as though a series of switches were being tripped in sequence.

The Slammers used pain drugs only as first aid. Once a trooper was removed to a central facility, direct neural stimulation provided analgesis without the negative side effects of chemicals. The Medicomp had kept Huber unconscious while he healed, exercising his muscles group by group to prevent atrophy and bed sores. He'd been awakened only when he should be able to walk on his own. The technician was smoothing out the vestiges of pain while Huber lay in a cocoon of induced inputs.

Huber opened his eyes. His brain was still collecting itself; direct neural stimulation tended to separate memory into discrete facets which reintegrated jarringly as consciousness returned. Part of Arne Huber understood it was remarkable that the Regiment's commander and deputy commander stood beside his pallet, but *everything* was new and remarkable to him now.

"How long's it been?" he said aloud, marvelling at the sound of his voice. "How long've I been out?"

"Four days," Danny Pritchard said. "Going on five if you count the time before we got you back to Base Alpha by aircar."

"Right," said Huber. "Well, I'm ready to go back to my platoon now. Are we still in the field?"

As he spoke, he braced his hands on the edges of the pallet and with careful determination began to lever his torso up from the mattress. A spasm knotted his muscles; his vision went briefly monochrome. The technician clicked his tongue.

"F-3 ought to be out of the line," Hammer said in a gravelly voice, "but we can't afford that luxury just now. We've assigned a car from Central Repair and personnel from the depot to bring them up to strength. I've put in a lieutenant named Algren as CO. He's green as grass, but he was top of his class at the Academy."

"I'm the fucking CO of F-3!" Huber said, swinging his legs over the side of the bed. "I can—"

He lurched to his feet. His knees buckled. Hammer caught him expertly and lifted him onto the pallet. Huber gasped, hoping he wouldn't vomit. There was nothing in his stomach, but acid boiled against the back of his throat while the technician's fingers danced on his keypad.

"No, you can't," Major Pritchard said. "We need the troopers we've got too badly to let you get a bunch of them killed to prove you're superman, which you're not. Besides, I want you in Operations."

"Right," said Hammer. "Bad as things are in the field, just now I need experienced officers on my staff worse than I do line commanders. I might transfer you to Operations even if you were fit to go back to F-3."

Huber glared at the Colonel, then let himself relax on the pallet. "Yeah, well," he said. "I'm not fit, you've got that right. But…"

"But when you are," Hammer said, "then I guess you've earned your choice of assignments. You did a good job getting your people out of that ratfuck. I won't bother saying I'm sorry for the way you got left hanging, but sure—I owe you one."

"For now you can do the most good to F-3 and the whole Regiment just by helping ride herd on what passes for the military forces of the United Cities," Pritchard said. "If we don't get them working together, it's going to be…"

His voice trailed off. He shook his head, suddenly looking drawn and gray with despair.

"The first thing you can help with," said Hammer, "is coming up with a platoon sergeant. I don't want to bring in somebody new, not with a newbie CO. I offered the job to your blower captain, Sergeant Deseau, and he turned it down; the others aren't seasoned enough on paper, and I don't know any of them personally."

"Frenchie'd hate the job…" Huber said, his mind settling into professional mode instead of focusing on his body and its weakness. "He could do it, but…"

"I can put the arm on him," the Colonel said. "Tell him it's take the job or out—and I wouldn't be bluffing."

"No," said Huber. "There's a sergeant in Log Section now, Jack Tranter. He's worked with us before. He isn't a line trooper, but he's seen the elephant. He's got the rank and organizational skills, and he's got the judgment to balance some young fire-eater straight out of the Academy."

"I remember him," said Pritchard with a frown. "He's a good man, but he's missing his right leg."

"The way things are right at the moment, Danny," said the Colonel with a piercing look at his subordinate, "he could be stone blind and I'd give him a trial if Huber here vouched for him. We don't have a lot of margin, you know."

Pritchard nodded with a grim smile. "Yeah," he said. "There's that."

Hammer turned to Huber again. The movement was very slight, but his gaze had unexpected weight. Huber felt the sort of shock he would if he'd been playing soccer and caught a medicine ball instead.

"So, Lieutenant?" he said. "Are you going to do what I tell you, or are you going to keep telling me what *you'll* do?"

"Sir!" said Huber, sitting up. He didn't feel the waves of nausea and weakness that'd crumpled him moments before, but neither did he push his luck by swinging his feet over the side of the bed. "You're the Colonel. I'll do the best job I can wherever you put me."

Hammer nodded, a lift of his chin as tiny as the smile that touched his thin lips. Huber wondered vaguely what would've happened if he'd been too bullheaded to face reality. Hard to tell, but the chances were he'd be looking for a civilian job when he got out of the infirmary instead of arguing about where he belonged in the Regimental Table of Organization.

Danny Pritchard looked at the technician and said, "When'll he be able to move? Sit in front of a console in the Operations shop I mean, not humping through the boonies."

The technician shrugged. "I can have him over there by jeep in maybe three hours. It's not how brave you are or how many pushups you can do, it's just the neural pathways reconnecting. D'ye want me to requisition a uniform or did his own gear come in with him?"

All three men looked reflexively at Huber. Huber gulped out a laugh and felt better by an order of magnitude to have broken his own tension that way.

"Hey, when I came here the only thing I had on my mind was my hair," he said. "Draw me a medium/regular and I'll worry about my field kit later."

"Roger that," said Hammer, ending the discussion. His glance toward Huber was shrouded by layers of concerns that had nothing to do with the man on the bed. "You'll report to Operations as soon as you can, Lieutenant, and Major Pritchard'll bring you up to speed."

Hammer started out of the room. Pritchard put a hand on the Colonel's shoulder and said, "Sir? You might tell him about Ander."

Hammer looked from his Operations Officer to Huber. "Yeah," he said, "I might do that. Lieutenant, the UC government ordered General Ander's arrest after his failure to execute their lawful orders. While he was in a cell pending his hearing before the Bonding Authority representative, he committed suicide."

Huber frowned, trying to take in the information. "The UC arrested him?" he said. "Sir, how in hell did they do that? Ander's Legion may not be the best outfit on the planet, but the UC doesn't have anything more than a few forest guards with carbines."

"I suggested they deputize a platoon of the White Mice for the job," Hammer said. "I believe Major Steuben chose to lead the team himself."

"Ah," said Huber. He didn't say, "Why would Ander kill himself?" because obviously Ander hadn't killed himself. Huber'd turned down a chance to serve in the White Mice, the Regiment's field police and enforcers; but he understood why they existed, and this was one of the times he was *glad* they existed.

"Right," he said. "Ah… thank you, sir, though I hadn't been going to ask. I know we're in a complicated situation here on Plattner's World."

"You just *think* you know," said Pritchard over his shoulder as he followed the Colonel out of the room. "After a day in Operations, Lieutenant, you'll know bloody well."

Like every other line soldier throughout history, Arne Huber had cursed because his superiors expected him to follow orders without having a clue as to what was really going on. Transferred now to the operations staff, he found himself in a situation he liked even less: he knew the Big Picture, and the reality was much worse than he'd believed when he had only a platoon to worry about.

Even more frustrating, there was nothing he could do to change the situation. It was like trying to push spaghetti uphill.

Huber cut the present connection, watching the image of a dark-skinned officer in a rainbow turban shrink down to a bead and vanish. Colonel Sipaji swore that his troops were already in position outside Jonesburg, save for the few support units which were still en route from the spaceport at Rhodesville. Jonesburg's own spaceport had been closed because of the danger from Solace energy weapons. Like all the ports in the United Cities, it was only a dirigible landing field which small starships could use with care.

Sipaji commanded the Sons of Mangala, a battalion-sized infantry unit, not very mobile but potentially useful when dug in at the right place. Satellite imagery showed that not only were they not in Jonesburg, they were halted only two kilometers outside Rhodesville. The visuals were good enough that with a modicum of enhancement

Huber had been able to see the cluster of officers outside the trailer that served as Colonel Sipaji's Tactical Operations Center. They were sitting on camp stools with their legs crossed, drinking from teacups.

And that knowledge didn't make the least bit of difference, because Colonel Sipaji was going to stick to his lie with the bland assurance of a man who knows what the truth ought to be and isn't affected by consensus reality. Sipaji wasn't a coward and if his battalion ever got into position it would be a very cost-effective way of protecting the northern approaches to Jonesburg; but it *wasn't* going to get there before Solace forces had closed the route from Rhodesville. Intent was reality to Sipaji, and he truly intended to go to Jonesburg… soon.

Huber stood. He was at one of a dozen consoles under a peaked roof of extruded plastic whose trusses were supported by posts along each of the long sides. This annex to the Regimental Operations Center was located in the parking lot of the Bureau of Public Works for the City of Benjamin, the administrative capital of the United Cities.

The portable toilet within the chain-link fencing hadn't been emptied in too long, which was pretty much the way life had been going for Huber during the week since he got out of the infirmary. He turned, then swayed and had to catch himself by the back of the console's seat. He'd been planning to go inside the wood-frame Bureau HQ itself, but now he wasn't sure that he'd bother.

"Lieutenant Huber," said the officer who'd come down the aisle behind him. "Take a break. I don't want to see you for the rest of the day and I mean it."

Huber jumped in surprise. He'd been so lost in his frustration that he hadn't seen the section chief, Captain Dillard, coming toward him. Dillard was a spare man with one eye, one arm, and a uniform whose creases you could shave with. Huber respected the man, but he didn't imagine the captain had been anyone he could've warmed to even before the blast of a directional mine had ended Dillard's career as a line officer.

"Sir," said Huber, "I can't get the Sons of Mangala to move. I thought if I took an aircar to where they're camped, maybe—"

"Get out of here, Lieutenant," Dillard said in the tone he'd have used to a whining child. "If you went to see Colonel Sipaji, his troops still wouldn't move. I don't care to risk the chance that you'd shoot him. That'd cause an incident with the Bonding Authority and delay the deployment even longer. Get a meal, get some sleep, and don't return before ten hundred hours tomorrow."

"But—"

"I mean it!" Dillard snapped. "Get out of here or you'll leave under escort!"

"Yessir," Huber muttered. He was angry—at the order, at Sipaji, and at himself for behaving like a little boy on the verge of a tantrum.

The troopers at the occupied consoles pretended to be lost in their work. Three of the eight were on the disabled list like Huber; the remainder had been culled from other rear-echelon slots to fill the present need to coordinate the mercenary fragments of the UC forces. Text and graphics were more efficient ways to transfer data to the other units, but face-to-face contact had a better chance of getting a result on the other end of the line of communication.

Huber gurgled a laugh, surprising Captain Dillard more than the snarl he'd probably expected. Huber's stomach was fluttery—he did need food—and if he was letting anger run him like that, he needed rest besides.

"Captain," he said, "it looks to me like we're hosed on this one. The UC's hosed, I mean, so we ought to advise 'em to make peace with Solace on whatever terms they can get. Solace has columns moving on Simpliche and Jonesburg both. We can—the Regiment can—block either one, I guess, but I don't see any way Solace won't capture one place or the other unless the units we're operating with get their act together. And when the core cities of the UC start to fall—it's over, the rest of the Outer States'll cut off their financing, and then everybody goes home. Which we may as well do right now, hadn't we?"

"That's not my decision, Lieutenant," Dillard said impatiently, "nor yours either. Get some food and rest, report at ten hundred hours."

He made a brusque gesture with his hand. So far as Huber had been able to tell during his week's contact with Captain Dillard, the man genuinely didn't care whether or not what he was doing had any purpose. Maybe to Dillard, *nothing* had purpose… which wasn't a bad attitude for a professional soldier. Anyway, it didn't keep Dillard from being efficient at his present job.

Huber walked out of the lot and stumped up the stairs to the back of the HQ building. His quarters were in a barracks within the Central Repair compound in the warehouse district. It was walled and guarded by a platoon of combat cars, making security less of a problem than it would've been elsewhere in the city. There'd be an aircar driven by a contract employee, a UC citizen, in front of the Bureau HQ, or if there wasn't the receptionist in the entranceway would call one.

After he took a leak…

"Lieutenant Huber?" called the receptionist as he pushed open the door to the rest room. Huber ignored him. To his surprise, the door opened again as he settled himself before the urinal. The receptionist, a middle-aged warrant officer with signals flashes on his epaulets, had followed him in.

"Sir?" the fellow said. "There's a woman out front to see you. She's been waiting, but I told her nobody disturbed the personnel on duty."

"I've been disturbed ever since I was assigned here," Huber muttered, "but that's nothing new. Who is she and what's she want?"

His tension and frustration drained away as he emptied his bladder. Was it that simple? All the trouble in life was just a matter of physical discomfort?

No, there were still the Colonel Sipajis of this world. They might have no more value than a bladderful of urine, but they weren't as easy to void.

"Her name's Daphne Priamedes, sir," the receptionist said. "I don't know what she's got in mind, but she's a looker, *that* I know."

She must be, to get a plump, balding veteran this excited. Well, the receptionist hadn't spent the past fourteen hours talking to the commanders of mercenary units who had an amazing number of variations on the theme of, "No, I think I should do something else instead."

"Never heard of her," Huber said. Right now the only thing that was going through his mind was that if he let her, she'd slow him down on his way back to the barracks and a bed. He didn't plan to let her. He turned, closing his fly. "There a car out front to take me home?"

"She's got a car, sir," the receptionist said. "A big one, brand new."

Huber started to swear and realized he didn't have the energy for it. The receptionist got out of the way as Huber lurched toward the doorway and down the hall.

Huber hadn't been able to find a comfortable position to sleep in, and being tired made his left leg drag worse than it would've anyway. Slivers of metal from both the frangible shot and the bits it'd gouged from *Floosie*'s bow armor had spattered him from knee to pelvis, and even the most expert nanosurgery did additional damage in removing the tiny missiles.

A striking black-haired woman stood between Huber and the outside door. She was within a centimeter of his height; her gaze was as direct as it could be without being hostile.

"Lieutenant Huber?" she said in a pleasant contralto. "I heard you tell Chief Warrant Leader Saskovich that you needed a ride. I have a car, and if you'll permit me I'll also buy you a better meal than you're likely to get on your own."

"Ma'am…" said Huber. He wondered if she was going to jump out of his way like the receptionist—Saskovich, apparently, and this woman had not only noticed the fellow's name but she'd gotten his rank right—or whether Huber would shoulder her aside on his way to the door. "The *only* bloody thing I know is that my job doesn't include talking to civilians. Find somebody in the public affairs section or talk to your own government; I don't have the time or the interest."

Through the glass front door of the building Huber could see a combat car on guard—there were no unit numbers stenciled on the skirts; it was an unassigned vehicle from Central Repair—and two aircars. One was a battered ten-place van with a Logistics Section logo on the side; a local contract employee chewing tobacco in the cab. The other was a luxury vehicle.

"*My* government is the Republic of Solace," the woman said. She stiff-armed open the swinging door and held it for him. "My father is Colonel Apollonio Priamedes. You saved his life at Northern Star Farms where he'd been in command when you attacked. I want to thank you in person before I accompany him back to Solace in tomorrow's prisoner exchange."

Huber's mouth opened, then closed as he realized that all the several things he'd started to say were a waste of breath. He remembered the Solace colonel limping out of the smoke to surrender, just as straight-backed as this woman who said she was his daughter.

Huber knew now what that erect posture had cost Priamedes. Because of that, and because Daphne Priamedes really *was* a stunner, he said, "Ma'am, I don't want company for dinner. But if you'll run me back to my barracks down in the warehouse district, I'll buy you a drink on the way."

"Yes, of course, Lieutenant," the woman said. "And I'd appreciate it if you'd call me Daphne, but I understand that you may prefer a more formal posture. Perhaps you're uncomfortable with the attitude toward hostilities we have on Plattner's World."

She strode past and opened the limousine's passenger door for him. That was a little embarrassing, but there wasn't a lot Huber could do about it in his present condition. Walking upright was about as much as he could manage at the moment. He braced his hands on the door and side of the vehicle to swing himself onto the seat, noticing the inlays of wood and animal products on the interior panels.

"I'm not uncomfortable, ah, Daphne," he said, "since it's the same attitude we mercenaries have toward each other: we may be enemies today and fighting on the same side tomorrow, or the other way around. Either way the relationship's professional rather than emotional. But I didn't expect to see a Solace citizen traveling openly in the UC capital when there's a war on."

Daphne Priamedes got in behind the control yoke and brought the car live. The vehicle had six small drive fans on each side instead of the normal one at either end; it was noticeably quieter than others Huber had ridden in.

Aircars were uncommon on most planets, but special circumstances on Plattner's World made them the normal means of personal transportation. The per capita income here was high, the population dispersed, and the preservation of the forests so much a religion—the attitude went beyond awareness of the economic benefit—that people found the notion of cutting roadways through the trees profoundly offensive.

Only in the Solace highlands where trees were sparse and not parasitized by Moss was there a developed system of ground transportation. There a monorail network shifted bulky agricultural produce from the farms to collection centers from which dirigibles flew it to the Outer States and returned with containers of Moss.

"There's ten generations of intercourse between Solace and the Outer States," Priamedes said. "This trouble—this war—is only during the past six months. We *need* each other on Plattner's World."

Her eyes were on the holographic instrument display she'd called up when she started the motors; it blinked off when she was comfortable with the readouts. She twisted the throttle in a quick, precise movement.

As the car lifted, she glanced over at Huber and went on, "Besides, for the most part it's you mercenaries fighting—not citizens. We in Solace tried to fight with our own forces at the beginning, but we learned that wasn't a satisfactory idea."

She smiled. Her expression as bright and emotionless as the glint of cut crystal.

"War's a specialist job," Huber said, keeping his tone flat. The car was enclosed and its drive fans were only a hum through his bootsoles. "At least it is if you've got specialists on the other side. We are, the Slammers are, and the other merc units are too even if they don't necessarily have our hardware."

He paused, then added, "Or our skill level."

"As I said, we recognized that," Priamedes said. "A disaster like Northern Star Farms rather drives the point home, particularly since it was obvious that things could have gone very much worse than even they did. Instead we're mortgaging ten years of our future hiring off-planet professionals to do what the Solace Militia couldn't."

Huber didn't speak. He regretted getting into the car with this woman, but he regretted a lot of things in life. This wasn't his worst mistake by any means.

Northern Star was a collective farm that'd been turned into a firebase under Colonel Priamedes. He commanded an infantry battalion and an artillery battery from the Solace Militia, with a company of mercenaries whose high-power lasers were supposed to be the anti-armor component of the force.

Huber'd led the combat cars in the company-sized Slammers task force that had punctured the defenses like a bullet into a balloon. The Militia were brave enough and even well trained, but they weren't veterans. The cars' concentrated firepower had literally stunned them, and the mercenary lasers were too clumsy to stand a chance against 20-cm tank guns which had virtually unlimited range across flat cornfields.

In retrospect it hadn't been much of a battle, though it'd seemed real enough to Arne Huber as he watched scores of Militiamen rise from a trench and aim at his oncoming combat cars. And all it takes is one bullet in the wrong place and you're dead as dirt, no matter how great your side's victory looks to whoever writes the history books.

Priamedes shook her head in inward directed anger, then turned a genuinely warm smile toward Huber. "I'm sorry," she said. "The situation frustrates me, but that isn't your fault and it's not what I came to see you about. Will this place do for our drink? I like it myself."

She banked the car slightly and gestured through her window. On Plattner's World, there was forest even in the cities. She was pointing toward a three-story structure shaded by trees on all sides. On the roof were open-air tables, half empty at this hour, and a service kiosk in one corner with an outside elevator rising beside it. Above, a holographic sign, visible from any angle, read GUSTAV'S. The letters changed from dark to light green and back in slow waves.

"That's fine," Huber said. "Anywhere's fine. I don't know much about Benjamin."

He'd been on seven planets besides Nieuw Friesland where he was born, and he didn't know much about any of them. He remembered the way powergun bolts glinted among the ice walls on Humboldt and the way the whores on Dar es-Sharia dyed their breasts and genitalia blue; those things and scores of similar things, little anecdotes of existence with nothing connecting them but the fact they were fragments from the life of Lieutenant Arne Huber.

Priamedes brought them around in a tight reverse instead of angling the fans forward to slow them. The car dropped between the treetops to level out just above the gravel roadway. The elevator was descending with a pair of well-dressed men in the glass cage.

Dust puffed as Priamedes landed smoothly in a line of similar cars. City streets in the Outer States were for parking and delivery vehicles. They were almost never paved, because that would speed storm-water runoff and decrease the amount of water that penetrated the soil to nourish vegetation.

Huber reached for his door release; parts of his body decided to protest, cramping when they were directed to move. He gasped with pain, then tried to cover his weakness with a blistering curse.

"Wait, I'll—" Priamedes said.

Snarling under his breath, Huber shoved the door open before his hostess could get around the vehicle to help him. He hopped out, forcing his left leg to work even though it felt as if somebody had turned a blowtorch on the hip joint.

She paused, turning her head away politely, and waited for Huber to join her so that they could walk to the waiting elevator together. "My father was injured in the fighting before he was captured," she said in a neutral tone. "He got off crutches a few days ago and should make a full recovery."

Huber laughed as the cage rose. "So will I," he said, more cheerfully than he felt. "Look, mostly I'm just stiff from sitting at a console all day. I'm not used to desk duty, that's all."

That was part of why he was stumbling around, all right; and he was tense from frustration at the people he had to deal with, which was another part of the problem. But at the back of Huber's mind was the awareness that the fragments he'd caught when the shot struck might have done damage that even time and the best medical treatment couldn't quite repair. That he might never again be fit for a field command....

"Lieutenant?" the black-haired woman said in concern.

Via, what had his expression been like? "Sorry," Huber said, forcing a smile. "I was klicks away, just thinking of the work I've got to do in the morning."

He must have sounded convincing, because Priamedes' features softened with relief. To keep away from the subject of his health, Huber made his way to a table near the wickerwork railing and pulled out a chair for the woman. It was with considerable relief that he settled across from her, though.

A waitress approached with an expectant look. The dozen other customers were glancing covertly at them as well, their eyes probably drawn by Huber's uniform and possibly his limp. There were a lot of mercenaries in Benjamin now, but the Slammers' khaki and rampant lion patch were the trappings of nobility to those who were knowledgeable. On a planet as wealthy and interconnected as Plattner's World, that meant most people.

Because of that perfectly accurate perception and because of the perfectly normal human resentment it engendered in other mercenaries, the United Cities were going to lose the war. A single armored regiment couldn't defeat several divisions worth of enemies, many of whom were themselves highly sophisticated; and the other UC mercenaries weren't cooperating with the Slammers the way they'd need to do to win.

"Lieutenant?" said Daphne Priamedes, loudly enough to penetrate Huber's brown study. They were waiting for his order, of course.…

He swore in embarrassment. "Ah, there's corn whiskey? I don't remember the name for it here, but my sergeant when I was in Log Section…?"

Priamedes nodded understanding and said to the waitress, "Zapotec—and water, I believe, unless…?"

"That's fine," Huber said in reply to her raised eyebrow. "Anything's fine, really."

He didn't know whether Zapotec was generic or a brand name; if the latter, it was probably the best available unless he'd misjudged Daphne Priamedes. Huber suddenly realized that he knew very little about anything beyond what he needed to do his job well. He and his fellow troopers wouldn't have been nearly as effective if they hadn't focused so completely on their jobs, but when he thought about it he felt lonely.

The waitress trotted away. Priamedes glanced around the covered patio, slapping the eyes of the others back to their own proper concerns. When she and Huber were as private as one ever is in open air, she said, "My father told me what happened at Northern Star, Lieutenant. At the end, I mean. He said it would've been much easier for you to kill him and his men than to capture them, but you took a considerable risk to spare their lives."

The waitress came back with the drinks. Priamedes entered her credit chip in the reader before Huber even thought to take his out of its pouch. Via! Maybe it was a good thing he wasn't in the field right now, because he was dropping too bloody many stitches.

Though… in the field he knew what he was doing reflexively. This was civilian life, and that was another matter. Arne Huber hadn't been a civilian for a long time.

He took a swig of the liquor; it cleaned the gumminess from his mouth and tongue and focused his mind like a leap into cold water. "Ma'am," he said, "I guess I've done worse things than shooting civilians who didn't have sense enough to give up, but only by mistake or when I had to."

He drank again; too much. He'd supposed he'd made his opinion of the Solace Militia clearer than he should've to an officer's daughter. The whiskey was good but it was strong as well, even cut with water; the big slug made his throat spasm and he had to cough.

Covering his embarrassment, Huber went on, "Ma'am, I can give you policy reasons why my commanding officer didn't want to blow away your father's men when they made a break for it. The truth is, though, neither I nor Captain Sangrela really likes to kill people. I'm a soldier, not a sociopath."

"I see that," she said, smiling faintly. "And I still prefer Daphne, Lieutenant."

"It's the booze talking," Huber said, smiling back. It was warm in his stomach, though and it felt good. "Look, Daphne, I appreciate the drink, but I really need to get to a bunk."

"Very well," she said, tossing off the rest of the fizzy, light green concoction she was drinking over ice. "If I can't offer you dinner…?"

"No ma—no *Daphne*," Huber said, rising more easily than he'd sat down. "I'll eat some rations, but right now I need sleep more than company—even company as nice as you."

"Then I'll just thank you again for sparing my father," she said, standing also. "And I hope we'll see one another again in the future when you're better rested—Arne?"

"Arne," Huber agreed. "And I hope that too."

"I'll expect your report in three hours, then, General Rubens," Huber said and broke the connection. He adjusted the little fan playing on him from the console as he thought about the next call he had to make. The day'd started out cool, but now by midmorning it was unseasonably hot for Plattner's World.

Parts of Base Alpha were climate controlled, but mostly the Regiment's machines and personnel were expected to operate under whatever conditions nature offered. You weren't going to win many battles from inside a sealed room, and the Colonel tried to discourage people from thinking you could.

As a break from talking to people he didn't like and didn't trust—he knew they probably felt the same way—Huber called up the Solace Order of Battle. He wasn't sure he was really supposed to have the information, but he'd found that his retina pattern was on Central's validation list. A benefit of being assigned to Operations…

As he viewed the latest information, his gut told him that he'd have been better off staying ignorant. Sure, things could've gotten worse—things can always get worse—but he hadn't really expected them to go this bad. Daphne'd said Solace was mortgaging its next ten years to hire mercenaries. Huber knew now that she'd been understating the real costs.

He looked out through the fence, trying to settle his mind. An aircar with Log Section markings had landed in the street under the guns of the combat car on guard. The driver, one of the locals the Regiment had hired for non-combat work, waited in the cab. A tall civilian in an expensive-looking pearl-gray outfit got out, stalked to the gate, and said, "I am Sigmund Lindeyar. Take me to Colonel Hammer at once!"

Instead of snapping to attention obediently, Captain Dillard turned his back to the furious man on the other side of the fence. He was frowning as he called Central on his commo helmet.

The fellow ought to be more thankful than he seemed. Dillard was treating him a lot better than some troopers would've done to a civilian who raised his voice to them.

Dillard grimaced minusculely as he signed off. When he focused again on his present surroundings, he caught Huber's eye. "Lieutenant Huber?" he called. "Will you join us, please?"

Huber cut the power to his console manually instead of trusting it to turn itself off when he rose from the attached seat. He didn't want anybody else to see what he'd just learned. *Blood and Martyrs, a brigade of armored cavalry in addition to what Solace was already fielding!*

"Sir?" said Huber crisply to Captain Dillard. He stood at parade rest, trying to look like what a civilian expected a professional soldier to be. He'd picked up from Dillard's expression that Central had confirmed the civilian's high self-opinion, so a little theater was called for.

Huber's rumpled fatigues weren't what a rear-echelon soldier would've called "professional appearance," but Huber *wasn't* a rear-echelon soldier.

Huber'd thought Lindeyar was an old man; viewing him closely, he wasn't sure. The hair beneath the fellow's natty beret was pale blond, not white, and his face was unlined; despite that, his blue eyes had age in them as well as a present snapping fury.

"Lieutenant," Dillard said, turning to include both Huber and the civilian, "Mr. Lindeyar is the Nonesuch trade representative. His driver brought him here rather than to the Tactical Operations Center at Base Alpha, where he's to meet Colonel Hammer. I'd like you to escort Mr. Lindeyar to the correct location."

"Yessir!" Huber said, his back straight. He thought about saluting, but that'd come through as obvious caricature if Lindeyar knew *anything* about the way the Slammers operated. Besides, Huber was lousy at it.

"Mr. Lindeyar," Dillard said, shifting his eyes slightly, "Lieutenant Huber is my second in command. He'll see to it that there isn't a repetition of the error that brought you here in the first place."

"He'd better," said the civilian, his eyes flicking over Huber with the sort of attention one gives to a zoo animal. "Your colonel is expecting me. Expecting me before now!"

"We'll get you there, sir," Huber said as Dillard opened the gate. He was the only officer in the annex besides Dillard himself, but "second in command" was more theater. If one of the warrant officers or enlisted men had caught Dillard's eye at the moment he needed a warm body to cover somebody else's screwup, that trooper would have become "my most trusted subordinate" as sure as day dawns.

And screwup it'd been. The driver had a navigational pod, but he or it had chosen the coordinates for the operations annex instead of the TOC. A soldier wouldn't have made that mistake, but to the contract driver it was simply a destination. That probably wasn't the fault of anybody in the Regiment—and it certainly wasn't Captain Dillard's fault—but Lindeyar didn't seem like the sort of man who worried about justice when he was angry.

They walked toward the street together. The path was gravel and Huber's left knee didn't want to bend. He tensed his abdomen to keep from gasping in pain as he kept up with the long-legged civilian.

"I want you to drive," Lindeyar said as they reached the aircar—a ten-seat utility vehicle that'd seen a lot of use. "I don't trust this fool not to get lost again."

"Negative!" said the scruffy driver—who turned out to be female, though Huber couldn't imagine anyone to whom the difference would matter. "I own this truck and I'm not letting any soldier-boy play games with it!"

"No sir," said Huber, letting himself breathe now that he didn't have to match strides with Lindeyar, "I can't drive an aircar. We won't get lost."

He got into the cab, motioning the driver aside. She opened her mouth for another protest. "Shut up," Huber said, not loudly but not making any attempt to hide how he felt.

He was pissed at quite a number of things and people right at the moment, and the driver was somebody he could unload on safely if she pushed him just a hair farther. Huber didn't know how to drive an aircar, that was true; but he was in a mood to give himself some on-the-job training with this civilian prick along for the ride.

The driver shut her mouth. Huber switched on the dashboard navigational pod, synched it with his helmet AI, and downloaded the new destination. Lindeyar climbed into the back, looking tautly angry but keeping silent for now.

"All right," Huber said to the driver, more mildly than before. "I'll check as we go, but you shouldn't have any trouble now. Let's get going."

She nodded warily and fed power to her fans. The drive motors were in better shape than the truck's body, which was something. They lifted smoothly, sending back a billow of dust before they transitioned from ground effect to free flight.

Why did a trade representative figure he could give orders to the Slammers? And being pretty close to right in the assumption, given the way Captain Dillard had hopped to attention after checking with Central. Nonesuch bought half the Thalderol base which Plattner's World exported, but that was no concern of the Regiment's.

Except that it obviously was a concern, if Hammer himself took time to meet with the fellow while the war was going to hell in a handbasket. Huber chuckled.

"You find something funny in this, Lieutenant?" Lindeyar said in a voice that could've frozen a pond.

"I'd been thinking earlier this morning that things can always get worse, sir," Huber said calmly. When you've spent a significant fraction of your life with other people shooting at you, it's easy to stay calm in situations where the potential downside doesn't include a bullet in your guts. "I won't say I'm glad to've been right, but I guess I do find it amusing, yes."

Lindeyar didn't reply, not so that he could be heard over the fans at any rate. Huber'd called up a topo map as a thirty percent mask on his faceshield. Base Alpha lay just beyond the city's eastern outskirts. The driver was holding them on a direct course toward it, the only variations being those imposed by traffic regulations which were completely opaque to an outsider like Huber.

As well as five dirigibles hauling heavy cargoes, there were hundreds of aircars in sight. That in itself was a good reason to leave the driving to a local.

Base Alpha was a scar on the landscape, a twelve-hectare tract scraped bare of forest. There was nothing else like it in the Outer States. Even the dirigible fields where starships now landed were smaller. The soil had a yellow tinge and was already baking to coarse limestone. A two-meter berm of dirt stabilized with a plasticizer surrounded the perimeter; the TOC complex was a cruciform pattern dug in at the center.

The clearing wasn't just to house the vehicles and temporary buildings required for the headquarters of an armored regiment: Hammer also demanded sight distances for the powerguns that defended the base against incoming aircraft and artillery fire. The UC government had protested, but that didn't matter. The Colonel didn't compromise on military necessities; he and his troops were the sole judges of what war made necessary.

One or more guns had been tracking the aircar ever since it came over the horizon on a course for the base. An icon quivered in the right corner of Huber's faceshield, indicating that his AI had received and replied to Central's authentication signal.

A kilometer from the base, the driver slowed her vehicle to a hover. Lindeyar leaned forward and said, "Why are we stopping?" in a louder voice than the fan roar demanded.

Huber tapped the green light on top of the navigational pod and said to the driver, "Go on in, we're cleared."

"No, I've got to call in," the driver said. "Otherwise they'll shoot us out of the air. It's happened!"

"I told you, we're cleared!" Huber said. "Do as I tell you or I'll shoot you myself!"

Most of that was for Lindeyar's benefit—but he wasn't in a good mood, that was the bloody truth. Not that he'd have shot the woman while they were a hundred meters in the air and she was driving…

The driver obeyed with a desperate look, though they flew into the compound at a noticeably slower pace than they'd crossed Benjamin proper. The navigation pod directed her to a ten-by-ten meter square just outside the gate through the razor ribbon surrounding the TOC. The troopers on guard in a gun jeep watched with bored interest rather than concern, but their tribarrel tracked the car all the way in.

Huber hopped out immediately and offered Lindeyar his arm for support; the open truck didn't have doors in back, though the sidewalls weren't high. The civilian ignored the offer with the studied discourtesy that Huber'd expected.

A staff lieutenant—an aide, Huber supposed, but he didn't know the fellow—trotted up the ramp from the TOC entrance as Huber and the civilian got out of the aircar. The driver kept her fans spinning, so grit swirled around their ankles and made Huber blink. He didn't bother snarling at her.

"Mr. Lindeyar?" the aide called as he swung open the wire-wrapped gate. "Please step this way. The Colonel's waiting for you."

Well, I guess that's "mission accomplished" for me, Huber thought. He turned to get back into the aircar. His helmet filters slapped down as the driver took off without him in a spray of dust. Some of it got under his collar, sticking to the sweat and making the cloth feel like sandpaper when he moved.

Lindeyar and his new escort were already entering the TOC, four buried climate-controlled trailers. Corrugated planking roofed the hub, and there was a layer of dirt over the whole. It wouldn't do much against a direct hit by artillery, but the air defense tribarrels took care of that threat. A sniper with a 2-cm powergun could be dangerous from an aircar many kilometers away, though; burying the TOC avoided possible disruption.

Rather than call Log Section for another ride, Huber nodded to the troopers on guard and walked toward a temporary building a few hundred meters away. He wasn't in a hurry to get back to the operations annex. The Lord knew, he'd always tried to do his job; but it was hard to see what good he was doing there, or what good he or anybody else *could* do in a ratfuck like Plattner's World was turning into.

A combat car drove slowly along the clearing outside the berm; Huber could see only the upper edge of the armor. The trooper in the fighting compartment was part of the training cadre, giving a newbie driver some practice. The car was either worn out or a vehicle straight from Central Repair, being tested before it was released to a field troop.

Either way, the car and both troopers were going to be in combat very shortly—unless the UC faced reality and surrendered. The Colonel'd have to throw everything in to stop the Solace juggernaut, and it wouldn't be enough.

The building's open window had screens whose static charge repelled dust. The door with the stenciled sign SIGNALS 2 wasn't screened, so Huber stepped inside quickly and closed it behind him. Three troopers looked at him through the displays of their specialized consoles.

"Is Lieutenant Basime here?" Huber asked. "I was told—"

Doll Basime stepped out of a side office, looking elfin although she wore issue fatigues without the tailoring some rear-echelon officers affected. "Arne! Come on in. Yeah, I've been at Central the past three weeks. Are you okay, because from what I'd heard…?"

"Hey, I'm walking around," Huber said with a laugh. "That'll do for now."

Doll's office was really a cubicle, but it had a door as a concession to her rank. She closed it behind Huber and motioned him to the chair behind the console, taking the flip-down seat on the wall for herself.

"You're going to be a REMF like me from now on, Arne?" she asked, smiling but obviously concerned. She and Huber had been good friends at the Academy, a relationship simplified by the fact that neither had any sexual interest in men.

"Just for now," he said as he sat down carefully. "I'm getting movement back day by day, and it doesn't hurt much anymore."

He shrugged, wishing he could truthfully say more. It felt *really* good to take the weight off his left leg, and that scared him. "A trade representative arrived from Nonesuch for a meeting with the Colonel and wound up in the wrong place. I got to bring him back here."

Doll's face went grim. "Do you know anything about what's going on, Arne?" she asked. She patted her console. "Because I wasn't about to eavesdrop on the Colonel's private meetings."

"Could you?" Huber said, interested.

She grinned, a more familiar expression. "Yeah," she said, "but I couldn't do it without leaving a trail that the counterintelligence people could follow. I don't want to discuss that with Joachim Steuben."

"It'd be a short discussion," Huber said, also with a smile of sorts. Major Steuben was as *pretty* as Doll herself. Frequently his duties involved killing somebody, a task at which Steuben was remarkably good. Inhumanly good, you might say.

"I don't know anything about Lindeyar except he seemed to expect a red carpet and wasn't best pleased not to have one," Huber said. He rubbed his neck; Doll gestured to the box of tissues on the console.

"Doll?" he went on, meeting her eyes. "Do you know how bad it is out there?"

She shrugged in turn. "I know it's not good," she said. "My section's job is to keep up the links with friendly units, so I see all the traffic whether I want to or not."

"Solace is pushing us everywhere," Huber said. He was glad to talk to somebody. Misery wanting company, he supposed, and he knew he could trust Doll. "We're just trying to block their advances."

He shrugged again and went on, "The Waldheim Dragoons are landing at Port Plattner in a day's time. They're mechanized and brigade strength, maybe a thousand combat vehicles. They've got powerguns and there's three 5-cm cannon in each platoon. Those'll take out a tank at short range, and a combat car's toast any time they hit it."

Doll made a moue and patted her tight black hair with her fingertips as she absorbed the information. "I can tell you," she said, staring toward the bulldozed wasteland past the slanting louvers, "that the UC isn't expecting the arrival of any significant reinforcements in the next ten days. I'd have been warned to make sure there'd be circuits clear."

"It wouldn't matter," Huber explained. "Solace is landing the Dragoons in a single lift. In a week or less they'll be organized and move out. It'd take a month to unload a brigade in what passes for spaceports in the UC, and it'd take longer than that to put the dribs and drabs together as a fighting force. Via, what we've got *now* isn't a coherent force except for the Regiment!"

"Could Nonesuch do anything?" Doll asked. "They're the major player in this arm of the galaxy."

"Lindeyar isn't somebody whose good will I'd want to depend on," Huber said. He chuckled at the thought. "But I sure don't see a better hope."

He was still wearing his commo helmet out of habit. The faceshield was raised, so the attention signal chimed in his ear instead of being a flashing icon. At the same time Doll's switched-off console lit under Central's control.

Colonel Hammer's face coalesced out of pearly light. He looked grim, though that was normal for the few times Huber had seen the Colonel make a Regiment-wide announcement.

"Listen up, troopers," Hammer said. Huber and Basime stared at the display. Hammer's hard gray eyes were locked with theirs, despite the varied angles, and with those of everyone else who viewed the transmitted image. "Orders'll be coming down in two hours. Be ready to move with your field kit. This means *everybody*. There'll be reassignments of rear echelon personnel to line slots where they need to be filled."

The Colonel rubbed his forehead; for a moment he looked very tired. His expression hardened again and he went on, "You've been the best soldiers every place you've fought. It's no different here. Do your jobs, troopers; and if I do mine as well as you've always done yours, we're going to pull this off yet!"

The image shrank and vanished; the memory of the Colonel's words hung a moment longer in the small office. Huber got to his feet.

"Going to get your kit together, Arne?" Doll said as she squeezed aside to let him past.

"That's next," Huber said. "First I'm going to see the Colonel."

He grinned at Doll as he opened the door. He felt numb, and there was a glowing wall in his mind that blocked off all the future except the next five minutes or so.

"First…" Huber said as he stepped into the outer office. "I've got to make sure I'm going back to the line!"

Huber strode toward the TOC entrance, his left leg stiff but not slowing him up a bit. He didn't know how he was going to bluff his way through the guards, but as it chanced he didn't have to. They'd heard the Colonel also, and they knew a lot of people were going to be moving fast on Regiment business.

Half a dozen figures came up the ramp from the TOC at the same time as Huber reached the wire going the other way. He unhooked the gate and pulled it open, then closed it behind him when they'd passed.

The last one through was the civilian, Lindeyar. He reached back and caught Huber's arm over the wire. "You, Lieutenant!" he cried. "There's to be a vehicle to carry me to Benjamin!"

Huber hooked the wire loop to the gate's frame. He pulled his arm away, suppressing a momentary desire to slap the civilian back on his haunches with the same movement. He nodded to the guards and shuffled down the ramp, keeping to the right side as three more officers came out of the buried trailers with set expressions. They were on their way to duties that weren't limited to staring at a display as other people fought a war.…

Huber grabbed the door before it closed; the air puffing from the interior was cool. The man coming out *now* was Colonel Hammer himself, with Major Kreutzer—the S-4 Personnel Officer—just behind him. Kreutzer's arm was raised; he was in an agony of wishing he dared to physically restrain his commanding officer.

"Sir!" said Huber, stepping in front of Hammer.

"Not bloody now!" the Colonel snarled. He looked as though he might bull past. Huber braced himself, but there was no contact.

"Sir, you said you owe me," Huber said, pitching his voice loudly enough to be heard over the sound of vehicles spinning up all around the base. "I'm collecting now. I want to go back to the field."

Behind Kreutzer were three other officers, trying to catch Hammer before he went off without answering their questions. Warrant officers sat at consoles to either side of the narrow aisle, immersed in their displays.

"Huber?" Hammer said. His face thawed like ice breaking up on the surface of a river. "Via, yeah, you're going back if you're able to walk."

He looked over his shoulder at the personnel officer. "Kreutzer, you wanted a CO for L Company?" he said. "All right, put Huber in the slot. And brevet him captain when you get a chance."

"No sir!" Huber said. He'd expected the fury in Hammer's expression, so it didn't slow him down as he continued, "Sir, I've never commanded infantry and this is no time for on-the-job training. Send me back to F-3."

"You only get away with crossing me if you're right, Lieutenant!" Hammer said; and smiled again, minusculely. "Which you are this time. Kreutzer, got any suggestions?"

"Yancy in L-2's senior enough," Kreutzer said. He shrugged. "We'll see if she can handle it. There's not a lot of choice, not now."

"Not a bloody lot," Hammer agreed. "All right, and we'll transfer—Algren, isn't it? The newbie we put in F-3 to L-2. Get on with it."

He pushed past Huber. The S-4 locked down his faceshield and passed the orders on, his voice muffled by his helmet's sonic cancellation field. Huber fell in behind the Colonel, heading back to the surface and an aircar to take him to wherever platoon F-3 was while the movement orders were being cut.

Lieutenant Arne Huber was going home.

Huber could've held a virtual meeting, but for his first contact with F-3 since his medevac he preferred face-to-face. The platoon could still scramble in thirty seconds if they had to; as they well *might* have to....

Fox Three-eight was straight out of Central Repair and hadn't been named yet. Until this moment Huber hadn't seen either the vehicle or its crew, three newbies commanded by a former tank driver named Gabinus who'd just been promoted to sergeant.

Its forward tribarrel, tasked to sector air defense, ripped a burst skyward. One of the newbies jumped.

"Relax, trooper," Sergeant Deseau said, making a point of being the blasé veteran. "They're just sending over a round every couple hours to keep us honest. If one ever gets through, then they'll start shelling us for real."

Nothing would get through while elements of the Slammers were stiffening the defenses of Benjamin. This shell popped above the northern horizon, leaving behind a flag of dirty black smoke. The sun was low above the trees, though it'd be three hours before full dark. Three hours before the start of the mission.

"For those of you who don't know me…" Huber said. Because Three-three had been knocked out in his absence, eight of the wary faces were new to him. "I've been at Central for the past three weeks, and I'm glad to be back with F-3 where I belong."

"And we're bloody lucky to have you back, El-Tee," Deseau muttered. "It's going to be tough enough as it is."

It's going to be tougher than that, Frenchie, Huber thought, but aloud he said, "We're part of Task Force Highball—" the whole Regiment had been broken up into task forces for this operation; Captain Holcott of M Company was leading Task Force Hotel "—with F-2, Battery Alpha, and the infantry of G-1 riding the hogs and ammo haulers. We'll have a tank recovery vehicle, but it'll be carrying a heavy excavator. If a car's hit or breaks down so it can't be fixed ASAP, we combat loss it and proceed with the mission. Got that?"

A couple of the veterans swore under their breath; they got it, all right. An operation important enough that damaged vehicles were blown in place instead of being guarded for repair meant the personnel involved couldn't expect a lot of attention if they were hit, either.

"I'm in command of the task force," Huber continued. "Lieutenant Messeman of F-2 is XO. We've got six cars running, they've got four. There'll be six hogs—" self-propelled 200-mm rocket howitzers "—and eleven ammo vehicles in the battery, and G-1 has thirty-five troops under Sergeant Marano."

"Thirty-five?" Sergeant Tranter said. "I'd heard they were down to two squads after the holding action at Beecher's Creek."

"Sergeant Marano got a draft from Base Alpha an hour ago," Huber said grimly. "They've all had combat training even if they've been punching keys for the past while. They're Slammers, they'll do all right."

"So what's the mission, El-Tee?" Deseau said. "We're going to hit the hostiles that're pushing Benjamin?"

"Come full dark, we're going to break through the Solace positions around Benjamin," Huber said. "Other units will continue to defend the city. When we're clear, we'll strike north as fast as we can run."

"What d'ye mean, 'north'?" asked a sergeant Huber didn't know. He was a grizzled veteran with a limp, probably transferred back to a line slot under the same spur of necessity that had returned Huber to F-3. "How far north?"

"All the way to the middle of Solace," Huber said flatly. "We're going to take Port Plattner before Solace gets its latest hires into action. We'll cut all Solace forces off from their base and leave them without a prayer of resupply."

"Blood and Martyrs," the sergeant said; Deseau was one of several who muttered some version of "Amen to that!"

"That's what we're going to do, troopers," Huber said. The left side of his body was trembling with adrenaline and weakness. The future spun in a montage of bright shards, no single one pausing long enough to be called a hope or a nightmare.

"That's what we're going to do," he repeated, "or we'll die trying."

He laughed, and half the veterans around him joined in the laughter.

A battalion of UC militia held the portion of the Benjamin defenses a klick to F-3's southwest. From there scores of automatic carbines snarled unrestrainedly. The electromagnetic weapons used by all the Outer States fired with a sharper, more spiteful sound than chemical propellants; the fusillade sounded like a pack of Chihuahuas trying to pull down an elephant. Occasionally a ricochet bounced skyward, a tiny red spark among the gathering stars.

"*What've they got to shoot at?*" asked Padova from the driver's compartment. Rita Padova had proved solid when it came down to cases, but she didn't like twiddling her thumbs and waiting for the green light. "*Did somebody jump the gun, d'ye think?*"

"They're nervous, they're shooting at shadows," Huber said. "Keep the channel clear, trooper."

He frowned to hear himself. If he hadn't been wound too tight also, he wouldn't have jumped on Padova that way. With careful calm, Huber went on, "Wait for it, troopers, because it ought to be happening right about—"

The sky flickered soundlessly to the northwest: not heat lightning but a 20-cm bolt from one of the tanks holding high ground at Wanchese, thirty kilometers from Benjamin. A moment later there was an even fainter shimmer from far to the east. The panzers were shooting Solace reconnaissance and communication satellites out of orbit. Until now the warring parties hadn't touched the satellites, a mutual decision to allow the enemy benefits that friendly forces were unwilling to surrender.

The Slammers had just changed the rules. The war was no longer between Solace and the Outer States but rather between Hammer's Slammers and the rest of the planet. If the disruption from Solace's certain retaliation caused problems for the UC, that was too bloody bad. To pull this off, the Slammers had to hide what they were doing for as long as possible.

An instant after the big powerguns fired, the rocket howitzers of Battery Alpha cut loose with three rounds per tube from their position near Central Repair in the heart of Benjamin. Backblast reflected briefly orange from wispy clouds in mid-sky before the bright sparks of rocket exhaust pierced them and vanished in the direction of Simpliche.

"Blue element," Huber said, "the batteries in Jonesburg and Simpliche'll be scratching our backs in about eighty seconds. You've all got the plan, you all know your jobs. In and out, shake 'em up but *don't* stick around, then reform on at grid Yankee Tango Four-four-three, Two-one-four where the Red element will be waiting."

Red element was Messeman with F-2 and the artillery. The guns couldn't move till they'd fired the salvo that would rip the Solace units which threatened Simpliche.

Besides the Slammers' Battery Alpha, there were ten mercenary batteries in Benjamin. It would've been simpler to delegate the preparatory barrage to the others so that Battery Alpha could move instantly, but there was the risk the orders would be intercepted—or ignored.

Central chose to add a minute and a half delay to the Red element rather than chance much worse problems. Huber's combat cars would be delayed much longer than that while they shot up the firebase that anchored the Solace forces facing Benjamin.

"On the word," Huber said, "we'll—"

The sky to the east and west popped minusculely. If Huber had been looking in just the right direction, he might have seen tiny red flashes as bursting charges opened cargo shells several kilometers short of their targets. Calliopes, multi-barreled powerguns, began to raven from the Solace positions. They directed their cyan lightning toward the sub-munitions incoming from both Jonesburg and Simpliche.

The initial shells were packed with jammers—chaff and active transmitters across the electro-optical spectrum. The second and third salvos burst much closer, spewing thousands of anti-personnel bomblets with contact fuzes and a time backup to explode duds three minutes after they left the cargo shell.

"Blue element, execute!" Huber ordered, feeling *Fencing Master* lift beneath him as Padova anticipated the order by an eyelash.

The six combat cars reversed out of the semi-circular berms protecting them from direct fire and advanced through the open woodland in line abreast. Solace troops weren't in contact with the Benjamin defenses anywhere that the Slammers stiffened the line. Hostiles couldn't conceal themselves from the Regiment's sensors, and anybody who could be seen vanished in a fireball in the time it took a trooper to squeeze the thumb trigger of his tribarrel.

Nevertheless Learoyd fired as *Fencing Master* rounded its fighting position, his blue-green bolts raking trees and leaf-litter forty meters from the car. Flames blazed yellow-orange from a shattered treetrunk. If anybody else had shot, Huber would've thought they were jumpy; Learoyd was as unlikely to be jumpy as he was to start lecturing on quantum mechanics.

The artillery impact zone was out of Huber's sight, but the sky flickered white with reflected hellfire. At least one round of the second salvo escaped the calliopes' desperate attempt to sweep the cargo shells out of the sky before they opened. The calliopes stopped firing when the glass-fiber shrapnel scythed down the gunners who hadn't thrown themselves under cover.

As the crackling snarl of the single previous round reached Huber, all six shells of the third salvo burst over the target. The sky beyond the branches was bright as daylight, and the blast remained louder than the car's intake howl for nearly a minute.

The bomblets were anti-personnel, but several must have hit fuel or munitions. Secondary explosions, red and orange and once the cyan dazzle of ionized copper, punctuated the ongoing white glare.

Huber swore softly. He knew he should've felt pleased. The firecracker rounds were landing on the enemy, clearing a path so that Task Force Huber had a chance of surviving the next ten minutes. Sometimes, though, Huber found it hard to forget that the hostiles were human beings also, soldiers very like his own troopers.

And maybe Huber wasn't alone in his reaction. Frenchie Deseau, nobody's choice for Mr. Sensitive, pounded the coaming with the edge of his left hand. His right was still on the grip of his tribarrel, though.

Stray bomblets had lit scores of small fires outside the main impact area. That and the continuing roar had confused the troops in the ring of Solace bunkers outside the firebase berm. Huber's faceshield alerted him for the oncoming target for thirty seconds before *Fencing Master* wheeled around a giant tree and got a clear view of a low log-covered bunker some sixty meters away. The defenders had cut three firing lanes through the undergrowth to give them several hundred meters of range along those axes, but Padova had split a pair of them and *Foghorn* to *Fencing Master*'s right had done the same.

Huber aimed at the bunker's firing slit. The car's jouncing advance through the forest made perfect accuracy impossible but he didn't need perfection, not with the amount of energy in a 2-cm bolt.

Cyan flashes caved in the bunker's thick face and shattered the collapsing roof despite the layers of sandbags overhead. Ammunition inside blew the wreckage into the air a moment later. The shockwave shoved Huber hard against the side of the fighting compartment and slewed *Fencing Master* against a treebole.

Padova recovered with a savage thrust of her fan nacelles. *Fencing Master* charged through the line of trees into the hundred-meter clearing around the Solace perimeter.

There were bunkers built into the berm, but the troops within them still had their heads down when F-3 roared into the open. The bunker roofs were proof against the anti-personnel bomblets which had carpeted the firebase, but the thunder of multiple explosions was literally stunning. The main blast had ended, but duds continued to go off with occasional vicious *cracks* that were almost equally nerve-shattering.

Huber's helmet picked targets for him, coordinating its choices with the AIs of the platoon's other gunners. *Fencing Master* was on the left of the line, so Huber raked a sandbagged watchtower several meters above the western curve of the berm. The wooden roof—a shelter, not ballistic protection—already smoldered where a bomblet had hit it. Huber's burst was low, but his bolts blew apart two of the support posts. The structure twisted and collapsed under the weight of its armor, spilling sandbags, weapons, and several screaming soldiers.

The night sizzled with the blue-green glare of tribarrels. Every gun in the platoon was firing as the combat cars charged the firebase. Huber switched his point of aim to a bunker and held his trigger down for three seconds. A red flash lifted the roof before dropping it back into the blast-scoured interior.

Coils of barbed wire crisscrossed the cleared area. *Fencing Master* hit a post and slid over it, dragging the tangles of wire under the skirts. If Padova had gotten the wrong angle, the wire would've scraped up the bow slope and decapitated any gunner who hadn't ducked quickly enough.

The pressure of the air in the plenum chamber was enough to detonate anti-personnel mines even when the skirts didn't touch the ground. Several went off in quick succession, *Whang! Whang! Whang!* like hammers striking the car's underside. Huber jumped at each blast though his conscious mind knew the worst harm a few ounces of high explosive beneath *Fencing Master* could do was maybe fling stones into a fan blade.

Padova canted the rear nacelles, swinging *Fencing Master*'s stern out to starboard without changing the car's direction of movement. They bumped down into the shallow ditch where Solace engineers had scraped up dirt to raise the two-meter berm. The earth wasn't compacted; it lay at the angle of repose, about forty-five degrees.

Padova shoved the throttles to their gates, giving the fans as much power as they could take without overheating. *Fencing Master* mounted the berm at a slant, wallowing but never bogging. Soft dirt sprayed in all directions. She reversed the cant of her nacelles; the combat car roared down the other side and into the Solace firebase.

A heavy electromagnetic slugthrower opened up just as the combat car tipped downslope. The gun was only thirty meters away, mounted on the cab of the tracked prime mover parked beside the nearest of the dug-in howitzers. Heavy-metal slugs spurted dirt to starboard, then clanged into *Fencing Master*'s skirts and hull as the gunner walked his burst onto them.

Learoyd's tribarrel tore apart the cab; the metal shutters on the windows flopped open a moment before the plastics and fabric of the interior gushed red flame. The vehicle's light armor had shrugged off shrapnel, but it wasn't meant for trading shots point blank with a combat car.

There was a line of tents along the inside of the berm. Bomblets had torn and flattened many of them, but Huber raked his tribarrel across the row anyway. Treated canvas burst into ugly red flames with billows of smoke, a good way to confuse and disrupt the defenders. Midway through Huber's burst, a crate of flares erupted in red, green and magnesium white sprays, setting alight tents that the tribarrel hadn't reached yet.

Everything was shouting and chaos. *Fencing Master* drove between gunpits, firing with all three tribarrels. Huber aimed down at a howitzer, hitting the recoil mechanism. Hydraulic fluid sprayed, then exploded as the car swept past.

It was impossible to pick targets but there was no need to choose: every bolt served F-3's purpose, to throw the Solace forces off-balance so that they'd be unable to react as the thin-skinned, highly vulnerable vehicles of Battery Alpha drove through the siege lines, blacked-out and at moderate speed. If Lieutenant Messeman's escorting combat cars had to shoot, then the plan had failed. All F-3's gunners had to worry about was not hitting friendly vehicles, and their helmet AIs kept them from doing that.

Deseau's tribarrel jammed. Instead of clearing the sludge of melted matrix material from the ejection port, he grabbed his backup 2-cm shoulder weapon and slammed aimed shots at men running in terror.

"Blue section, withdraw!" Huber shouted, hosing a group of trailers around a latticework communications mast. Their light-metal sheathing burned when the plasma lashed it. "All units, withdraw!"

An orange flash lit the base of the clouds. Huber ducked instinctively, but the shockwave followed only a heartbeat later. The blast shoved *Fencing Master* forward in a leap, then grounded them hard. The skirts plowed a broad ditch till the car stalled. The gunners bounced against the forward coaming, and the shock curtains in the driver's compartment must've deployed around Padova.

A red-hot ball shot skyward and had just started to curve back when it exploded as a coda to the greater blast that'd flung it into the heavens. Somebody'd hit an ammo truck or a dump of artillery shells offloaded for use.

Huber hadn't been trying to keep control of his platoon in the middle of a point-blank firefight, but now one of the five green dots along the top of his faceshield pulsed red. At the same instant a voice cried, "*Somebody help us! This is Three-seven and our skirts are clean fucking gone! Get us out!*"

The man shouting on the emergency channel was Three-seven's commander, Sergeant Bielsky—the retread with the limp—but he was squeaking his words an octave higher than Huber had heard from him in the past.

"*Fox, this is Three-five!*" Sergeant Tranter said, his transmission stepping on Bielsky's. "*We've got them, we're getting them out, but cover us!*"

Padova had lifted *Fencing Master* and started to turn clockwise to take them back over the berm where they'd entered: if they left the firebase by the opposite side, the north-facing bunkers might rip them as they crossed the cleared stretch. Now instead of continuing her turn, the driver straightened again and accelerated to where Three-seven lay disabled in the center of the compound. Huber fired short bursts into a line of shelters that the huge explosion had knocked down. Hostiles might be hiding in the piles of debris, clutching weapons that they'd use if they thought it was safe to.

Another orange flash erupted, this time near the eastern edge of the compound. It wasn't as loud, especially to senses numbed by the previous explosion, but two more blasts stuttered upward at intervals of a few seconds.

Fencing Master rounded a line of wrecked trucks, several of them burning fitfully. Car Three-seven lay canted on its starboard side beyond. Bielsky hadn't been exaggerating: the blast that shook *Fencing Master* had torn the port half of Three-seven's plenum chamber wide open. The gunners were clambering aboard Tranter's *Fancy Pants* as that car sawed the darkness. It was a wonder that they'd survived; they must've had enough warning to flatten themselves on the floor of the fighting compartment.

Huber's faceshield warned him of motion to his left rear. He pivoted the tribarrel. A pair of Solace soldiers knelt on a ramp slanting up from an underground bunker Huber hadn't noticed until that moment. The muzzles of their sub-machine guns quivered with witchlight, light-metal driving bands ionized by the dense magnetic flux that accelerated slugs down the bore. Three-seven's armor sparkled and one of the escaping crewmen flung his arms up with a cry.

Huber blew the men apart with a dozen rounds before *Fencing Master*'s motion carried him beyond the bunker entrance. Something flew over Huber's head and bounced down the ramp, then exploded: Frenchie'd emptied his powergun and was throwing grenades.

"*Three-five clear!*" Tranter shouted as *Fancy Pants* shifted away from the wrecked vehicle, accelerating as fast as fans could push its thirty tonnes. Ropes of 2-cm bolts snapped past *Fencing Master* to either side, other cars keeping the defenders' heads down.

"Blue element, withdraw!" Huber shouted as he raked the camp. "Go! Go! Go!"

Padova fell in behind *Fancy Pants*; Deseau'd reloaded and was leaning out the back of the fighting compartment, punching the night dead astern. The tunnel mouth burped a red fireball. It hung in the air for measurable seconds before sucking in as the bunker collapsed.

Fancy Pants drove through a waste of shelters destroyed when F-3 entered the camp; the car's fans whirled smoldering canvas and scantlings into a sea of flame. Preceding vehicles had scraped the berm to a low hump for which Tranter's driver didn't bother to slow. *Fancy Pants* lifted, then vanished into the night with *Fencing Master* close behind her.

Huber took his thumbs off the trigger as they crossed the berm. Shooting now would call attention to the escaping cars for any of the defenders who'd kept their composure.

That wasn't a serious danger. Huber took a last view of the firebase as *Fencing Master* returned to the forest's concealment. Scores of fires within the compound silhouetted the furrowed berm. Another explosion flung sparks a hundred meters into the sky.

Huber took a deep breath and almost choked. Struggling not to vomit in reaction to the adrenaline that had burned through his body for the past several minutes, he said, "Red element, this is Highball Six. Blue element will rendezvous as planned in—"

His AI prompted him with a time display on the upper left quadrant of his faceshield.

"—three, that's figures three, minutes. Six out."

Deseau had his tribarrel's receiver open to chip at the buildup of matrix material. It was a wonder that Huber's gun hadn't jammed also: its iridium barrels still glowed yellow. They'd been white hot when *Fencing Master* crossed the berm.

Frenchie glanced back. "*Not bad, El-Tee,*" he said over the intercom. "*About time we showed 'em who's boss!*"

Another explosion rocked the night. Solace forces around Benjamin weren't going to be worrying any time soon about the breakout from the city.

But there was a long road still ahead, for the Slammers and especially for Task Force Huber....

Sergeant Nagano in *Foghorn* led the column. Huber'd decided to run without a scouting element a kilometer in the lead. He was more afraid that Solace units would stumble onto Task Force Huber by accident than he was of driving into hostiles with their signatures masked against the Slammers' sensors.

Even with the drivers trying to keep minimum separations, the line of twenty-seven vehicles stretched nearly half a klick back through the forest. A single aircar flying between Solace positions could see the column and end the secrecy that was their greatest protection.

Deseau slept curled up on the floor of the fighting compartment. The surest mark of a veteran was that he could sleep any time, any place. On Estoril Huber had awakened one night only when the level of cold rainwater in his bunker had risen to his nose and he started to drown. Soldiering was a hell of a life, a *Hell* of a life, and Arne Huber and every other trooper in the Regiment was a volunteer.

Learoyd braced his right boot on an ammo box to raise his crotch over the coaming of the fighting compartment, then emptied his bladder into the night. He stepped down again, sealing his fly, and said, "Is Frenchie going to take the next shift driving, El-Tee, or d'ye want me to do it?"

He'd spoken directly instead of using the intercom that might've awakened Deseau. *Fencing Master* was driving between the massive trees at a steady, moderate pace, and experienced troopers could hear one another over the intake noise.

Bert Learoyd sometimes made Huber think of a social insect: he seemed to have almost no intellectual capacity, but through rote learning alone he'd become capable of quite complex activities. It was bad to wake up your buddies unnecessarily, so Learoyd didn't do that.

"I'll put Deseau in next," Huber said aloud. Frenchie was too active to be a good driver; he kept overcorrecting, second-guessing himself. Learoyd didn't have Padova's genius for anticipating the terrain, but his stolid temperament was well suited to controlling a thirty-tonne vehicle in tight quarters. "He'll be all right on this stretch; it's pretty open."

Pretty open compared to much of the forest on Plattner's World, but light amplification didn't make driving a combat car at night through the woods a piece of cake. Huber'd been hoping to raise the column's speed to forty kph, but that didn't seem likely now that the whole task force was assembled. The combat cars might be able to make it, but the hogs' high center of gravity made them dangerously unstable while running cross-country. As for the recovery vehicle, it was a full meter wider than the cars whose drivers were choosing the route.

Another thought struck Huber. "Learoyd?" he said. "Have you seen Padova manning a gun? In action, I mean—I know she's checked out in training."

Learoyd shrugged. "She's okay," he said, flicking regular glances toward his side of the car just in case there was something besides treeboles there. "She was on night-watch when them wog sappers tried to creep up on us a couple weeks ago. She didn't freeze up or something."

Good enough. On this run there'd be no halts except to change drivers. There was no way of telling who'd be in the fighting compartment if the task force ran into hostiles—as they surely would, later if not sooner. The best driver in the Regiment was a liability if she panicked when she needed to be shooting.

"El-Tee?" Learoyd said. He was talkative tonight; by his standards, that is. "What's going to happen back at Benjamin when we're not there? The wogs'll waltz right in, won't they?"

"There's enough other mercs in the garrison to hold the place," Huber said. "The Poplar Regiment and Bartel's Armor, they're troops as good as anything Solace has close by."

He grimaced. Benjamin was all right, sure, but Solace hadn't been making a real effort on the UC administrative capital yet. Jonesburg and Simpliche were in serious danger even before the Slammers there abandoned the defenses they'd been stiffening to run north at the same time Task Force Huber did.

"Look, Learoyd, we've got to hope for the best," he said. "Chances are Solace Command's going to take a while to figure out what's going on. With luck they still think we withdrew back into Benjamin instead of breaking out."

Learoyd shrugged. "I just wondered, El-Tee," he said. "I don't think them other lots're worth much, but if you do…"

The trouble was, Huber didn't.

He suddenly laughed and clapped Learoyd on the shoulder. "What *I* think, trooper," he said, "is that everybody in Task Force Huber does his job as well as you've always done yours, then we're going to come through this just fine. The other guys, they have to take care of themselves."

He realized as he spoke that he was more or less echoing Colonel Hammer. Well, he didn't guess the Colonel had lied to the Regiment, and the Lord knew Huber wasn't lying to Learoyd either.

And because of that, just maybe the Slammers were going to pull this off after all.

According to the topo display, the Salamanca River was shallow at present though it regularly flooded its valley when the rains came in autumn. Huber hadn't expected much difficulty in crossing it until Lieutenant Messeman—F-2 was in front for the moment—radioed, "*Six, this is Fox Two-six. Take a look at these sensor inputs from—*"

Huber was already bringing up the data transmitted from Messeman's lead car.

"*—my Two-five unit. Over.*"

"This is Six!" Huber said. He couldn't fully understand the data without a little time to digest it, but it was *bloody* obvious that Task Force Huber wasn't crossing at the ford Central had picked for its planned route. "All Highball units, halt in place!"

Learoyd obeyed the orders literally: instead of canting all eight nacelles forward for dynamic braking, he feathered the fan blades to drop their thrust to zero. Gravity slammed *Fencing Master* down, chopping the skirts into the soil like a giant cookie cutter.

The car hopped forward, grounded again, and skidded to a complete stop in a cascade of dust and grit. They'd halted within five meters of the point Learoyd got the order.

Huber'd braced himself on his gun pintle when he realized what was about to happen. He swore viciously and he glanced astern to see if *Flame Farter*, the next car back, was going to slam into them. It didn't, partly from the driver's skill and partly because he angled his bow into a stand of saplings growing up in place of a giant tree that'd fallen a few years previous.

I'm *the bloody fool who said "Halt in place,"* Huber thought. *It's nobody's fault but my own.*

"Highball," he resumed aloud, "keep a low profile. There's an enemy battalion on the other side of the bluffs across the river we were going to cross. They don't act like they know we're here—this is just bad luck. We'll head southwest, that's upstream—"

His hand controller drew a line on the terrain display of his Command and Control box, transmitting it automatically to the helmets of his troopers.

"—and cross—"

The C&C box provided Huber with both a graphic and a tabular description of the hostiles arriving on the other side of the river. The data base identified them as an elite unit of the Solace Militia, the 1st Cavalry Squadron, fully professional and equipped with nearly a hundred air-cushion armored vehicles mounting powerguns.

Instead of driving overland, Solace Command had airlifted the squadron to a landing zone in the valley paralleling the Salamanca to the northwest. The terrain made the location safe from sniping by the Slammers' tanks, and it was as close to the fighting as a dirigible could approach.

"—seven klicks down, there's another ford there, and we're on our way again. Fox Three-zero leads until further notice. Six out."

If Task Force Huber had arrived six hours sooner, they'd have been past before the Solace squadron landed; two hours later they'd have fought a meeting engagement as the hostile vehicles—which mounted twin 3-cm powerguns as well as carrying an infantry fire team in the rear compartment—came over the bluffs on the south side of the river. As it was, it just meant the Slammers had to detour and add an hour or so to their travel time.

Flame Farter lifted and started to reverse in its own length. Deseau—who was blower captain, commanding *Fencing Master* while Huber's duties were for the whole task force—said over the intercom, "*Turn us around, Learoyd. We're following Three-zero up the river, now.*"

Padova slapped the receiver of the right wing gun in frustration. She was a slight, dark woman and smart enough to be an officer some day if she learned to curb her impatience. Padova thought Learoyd should've understood Huber's unit order as meaning he should rotate *Fencing Master*… and so he should've, but—

Before Huber could speak, Deseau took Padova by the arm and turned her so they were facing. Both were short, but Frenchie had an hourglass figure and the shoulders of a wrestler.

"I'll tell you, Padova…" he said, shouting over the howl as the fans accelerated under load instead of using the intercom. "When you can make headshots every time at five klicks downrange, then maybe you'll be ready to give Bert lessons on being a soldier. Got it, trooper?"

Padova glanced at Huber, perhaps expecting support. Huber gave the driver a hard grin and said, "Saves me telling you the same thing. You're good at your job, but you're still the newbie in this car."

Padova forced a smile and turned her palms up; Frenchie nodded and let her go. *A first-rate driver, and apparently smart enough to learn…*

Huber went back to the display as the combat car shifted beneath him. *Fencing Master* was another world, one he didn't have to worry about right at the moment.

He had plenty of other worries. Reversing the order of march put three ammunition haulers immediately behind the two combat cars in the lead. He'd interspersed F-3's remaining three cars among the artillery vehicles, with all of F-2 in the lead to deal with trouble in the most likely direction. He could reorganize the order of march, but first they had to get away from the Solace cavalry.

The problem wasn't anybody's fault. This Solace deployment must've been planned weeks in the past, but the dirigibles wouldn't've lifted off until after the reconnaissance satellites went down at the start of the breakout. Central couldn't have extrapolated the appearance of an armored cavalry squadron across Task Force Huber's line of march. It'd been close, but close only counts in horseshoes—

"*Bloody hell, Six!*" Lieutenant Messeman shouted over the command channel. "*There's a couple aircars coming over! They're going to spot us sure!*"

—and hand grenades.

Huber opened his mouth to order the task force to hold its fire; the Slammers' discipline was good enough that his troops would probably have obeyed, though the gunners with a clear shot at the aircars would've cursed him.

But secrecy was screwed regardless. Unless the Solace scouts were stone blind, they weren't going to miss a company's worth of thirty- and forty-tonne armored vehicles on the route they'd been sent to reconnoiter.

"All Highball elements!" Huber ordered. "Slap 'em down as soon as you can get both at the same time! All Fox units, form below the ridgeline—"

His controller drew another line across the terrain map.

"—in line abreast, five meter intervals between cars, and wait for the command to attack. Fox Two-six has the right flank. India elements—"

The infantry platoon under Sergeant Marano, and Lord help them if the influx of rear-echelon troopers weren't up to the job.

"—on your skimmers and prepare to follow the cars over the ridge."

Fencing Master grounded again, not as hard because they weren't scrubbing off the inertia of thirty kph this time. Huber was barely aware they'd halted, but from the corner of his eye he saw Padova climb out of the fighting compartment. A moment later Learoyd clambered in and seized the grips of his tribarrel. Frenchie was giving the orders Huber would've wanted if he'd had time to think about car Three-six at this juncture.

Tribarrels, at least a dozen of them, snarled from the head of the column. Huber couldn't see the targets from where he was, but an orange flash briefly filled interstices in the foliage to the north. The aircars were chemically powered, and the multiple plasma bolts had atomized their fuel cells into bombs.

The C&C box had converted Huber's orders to a graphic of routes and positions for the nine combat cars. Huber could've overruled the computer but there was no reason to. He'd planned to put *Fencing Master* on the left end of the line, but that would mean changing position with *Flame Farter* when there wasn't much room or time for either one. Sergeant Coolidge and his crew could handle the flank.

Fencing Master was moving again without the bobbling usual when a combat car lifted from the ground. That was good, but having Learoyd on the right wing was better yet....

"X-Ray elements—"

The vehicles seconded to the task force from Regimental Command: the artillery, transport, maintenance, and engineers that the line elements were escorting.

"—hold what you got, we'll be back for you."

Huber drew a deep breath and raised his head from the holographic display. *Fencing Master* was passing to the left of an ammo hauler with about the thickness of the paint to spare. Huber would've liked more clearance, but he wasn't going to second-guess Padova.

"Troopers," Huber resumed, his eyes on the trees jolting past, "on the command the combat cars are going over the hill to shoot up all the hostiles we can in thirty seconds. We're going to make it look like we're trying to force the crossing, but we'll pull back, I repeat, pull back in thirty seconds. The infantry follows the cars over the ridge line ten seconds later but grounds and conceals itself on the downslope instead of withdrawing."

Lord, Lord…. He was counting on the hostiles being fooled by a fake withdrawal, counting on them not spotting the infantry ambush, counting on not losing every car in the task force in the initial attack which *had* to look real if this had a prayer of working.

And there was no choice.

"When the wogs're moving up from the river," Huber continued aloud, "the by-passed India elements will hit their flanks and rear, then Fox comes back over the hill and finishes the job. It'll be a turkey shoot, troopers! Six out."

Huber rubbed his face with both hands. The trouble was that these turkeys would be shooting back.

The combat cars were just below the crest of the reverse slope but still out of sight from across the river. The Solace sensors weren't good enough to pinpoint them, although the Slammers weren't making any real effort to suppress their signatures. They couldn't, not and balance on a twenty-degree slope.

Mercenaries wouldn't've tried to use aircars to scout against the Slammers, but the Solace Militia hadn't yet come to terms with what it meant when the other side had powerguns and sensors good enough to tell them exactly when you were going to come in sight. The Solace scout crossed the river three klicks upstream, then rose above the forested hills to see what Task Force Huber was doing.

Flame Farter's forward tribarrel snarled out six shots, every one of them a hit. The scout disintegrated like sugar dropped into flashing cyan water. It didn't explode in the air, but a fiery mushroom rose over the trees where the wreckage landed.

Frenchie muttered something, to himself or Learoyd. Solace gunners across the Salamanca opened fire, raking the ridgeline and the tops of the trees growing on the southern side. A pair of 3-cm bolts hit the thick trunk to *Fencing Master*'s immediate right, shearing it ten meters above the ground. The blasts showered flaming splinters which drew smoke trails behind them. The Solace vehicles mounted high-intensity weapons, slow-firing compared to the Slammers' tribarrels but round for round far more powerful.

The upper three-quarters of the treebole toppled downslope and hit with a crash, igniting the undergrowth. Despite recent rains, there'd be a major forest fire on this side of the river shortly. That didn't matter to Huber, because shortly he and his troopers would either be well north of here or dead.

Learoyd took one hand from his tribarrel's grips and brushed burning debris from the other arm and shoulder. His face had no more expression than a Buddha's.

"Fox elements…" said Huber, his eyes on the C&C display. Three Solace armored cars started down the slope toward the river, moving cautiously instead of trying to outrace the bolts that might come slashing toward them. A dozen similar vehicles were settled on the ridge behind them to overwatch. Their twin guns ripped and snarled, blasting only trees and rocky soil because the Slammers were still sheltered by the high ground.

All the troopers in the task force could watch the situation map on their helmet displays if they wanted to. Most of them wouldn't, avoiding distractions that didn't have much to do with their jobs. Knowing too much is a handicap when instant decisions mean life or death. Their AIs would pick targets for them and they'd hose those targets with their tribarrels; that's all that would matter in the next minute and a half.

"The wogs 've taken the bait," Huber went on, speaking calmly and distinctly as he timed his words with the order to come. "We'll go over in thirty, that's three-zero, seconds. Six out."

Huber shut down the C&C display and straightened behind his tribarrel. The simple choices made by Huber's eye and trigger finger would be a relief after the sorts of imponderables he'd been balancing for way too long....

A haze of dust and leaf litter swirled about *Fencing Master* and the other cars spaced along the forested slope. Their fans were spinning at high output, wasting their energy beneath their raised skirts. When the drivers tilted their nacelles forward, the cars would drop into ground effect and lurch into action on the thrust of those fans.

Infantrymen hunched on their skimmers in groups of three and four a little below the big vehicles. Their nose filters were down so that they could breathe despite the fan blast and the smoke from the scores of fires lit by the Solace powerguns. They must be miserably uncomfortable, but they were still better off than they'd be in the next few seconds. That was a risk that came with the uniform.

"Fox units, execute!" Huber shouted. "In and out, troopers! In and out!"

Fencing Master roared up the remaining slope, moving against gravity with glacial deliberation though their fans spun on overload power. Padova angled the car to the right where an instant before a pair of 3-cm bolts had grazed the crest, spraying fans of molten rock and organic material southward.

Huber swung his sight picture onto the opposite ridgeline. Deseau fired a heartbeat before the two wing gunners. Huber thumbed his trigger, sending a rope of cyan bolts into the humped shape of a Solace armored car. Its twin guns were mounted on top of the hull in an unmanned barbette. The muzzles already glowed white from firing before the Slammers gave them a target. They fired again, a quick SLAM/SLAM of bolts so fiercely powerful that the slope to Huber's left erupted like a volcano under their released energy.

Padova had allowed for the fact the Solace car was traversing its weapons as it raked the hill. By lifting over the crest where bolts had just struck, *Fencing Master* survived when the gunner twitched his trigger reflexively instead of swinging back to where his target really was.

Huber's burst struck the car's bow slope, the first bolt or two splashing reflected radiance before the thin armor ruptured. The forward compartment bulged; then the fuel tanks on the underside of the hull exploded, sending fiery debris in all directions. The twin powerguns lifted toward the river, tumbling over and over.

The Salamanca Valley was shallow and a kilometer wide from crest to crest, but frequent floods had scoured all but scrub vegetation from its slopes. The foliage was almost maroon rather than the vivid green of the forests elsewhere in the lowlands.

The world to Huber's left flashed white as *Flame Farter* took a direct hit. The high-intensity bolt vaporized the right side of the bow armor, swinging the car counterclockwise in reaction.

Flame Farter staggered forward, out of control though its running gear was still whole. Two figures rolled out of the fighting compartment as more bolts struck the vehicle broadside. The spray of molten iridium ignited the coarse shrubs in a ten-meter semi-circle below the destroyed vehicle.

Huber's bolts merged with those from Deseau's gun, raking the Solace car that had fired. Powergun ammunition detonated in an intense blue flash devoured the target.

The Slammers infantry had come over the crest and vanished downslope as planned. The brush grew three meters high; it would've seemed sparse from directly above, but its knitted branches provided good cover from eyes at the height of an armored car's viewslits.

Huber shifted his sights onto another Solace vehicle. It exploded before he could squeeze the trigger. Flames and black, roiling smoke marked the opposite ridgeline, each the pyre of an armored car and most of its crew.

A car of the advance party near the river was still firing, its bolts gouging the hillside; the panicked gunner was shooting low. His bad aim had kept him from being an immediate threat—and therefore target—but now half a dozen tribarrels converged on the car. The rear hatch flew open. Three black-clad Solace Militiamen sprang out, throwing themselves into the brush to hide as their vehicle sank into a sea of fire behind them.

For a moment Huber thought they were going to survive, at least for now, but one of Messeman's gunners switched to thermal imaging that let him see through the thin brush. The third man ran into the open after short bursts incinerated his companions; the single shot that decapitated him was bragging.

"Fox units withdraw!" Huber ordered. "All units withdraw at speed!"

It was war; those three desperate Militiamen were enemies who'd wanted to kill Huber and his troopers. But Huber'd still just as soon they'd been allowed to hide....

Fencing Master shuddered as Padova cranked the nacelles forward. Once *Fencing Master*'d gotten over the crest, she'd let inertia and gravity take them downslope with the fans vertical, supplying lift but no thrust. It was time to get the hell out; in a firefight that meant backing so that the thicker bow armor and all three tribarrels continued to face the enemy.

Their skirts touched, a jar but not a disorienting crash. Padova got control again and *Fencing Master* began to slide backward up the hill again.

Huber fired a short burst over the opposite crest. He didn't have a target at the moment, but his faceshield indicated a Solace armored car was driving up the reverse slope. He wanted the hostile driver to hesitate until the Slammers were back under cover.

There were vehicles advancing behind the whole length of the opposite ridge. At least fifty Solace armored cars were in line, and there were others forming behind to replace casualties. The Solace commander might not have a subtle grasp of tactics, but there was nothing to fault in his courage or that of his troops. And with odds of ten to one in favor of the Militia, they'd win a slugging match against eight surviving combat cars if Huber were dumb enough to try one.

Fencing Master snorted and scraped, reaching the ridgeline and then dropping with more enthusiasm than control onto the reverse slope. Huber checked his icons; all the cars had made it back except Three-zero, *Flame Farter*. He'd seen two men bail out. The driver was surely dead, but maybe the fourth crewman—

Reality returned, smothering hope like clouds covering the moon. The fourth crewman was dead also, dead when the follow-up bolts had vaporized the fighting compartment even if the initial hit hadn't killed him. The survivors must've gone to ground with the infantry. For now that was a better choice than trying to scramble back over the crest while a lot of very angry Solace gunners were looking for targets.

Learoyd was unfastening his clamshell armor, moving awkwardly because his right arm didn't seem to be working. Deseau turned to help. What in hell had happened to Learoyd?

But that was a problem for later; first Huber had to make sure there'd *be* a later. A storm of 3-cm bolts ripped from the other side of the river, blasting trees twenty meters above the concealed combat cars. The Solace commander had decided to take no chances whatever: his gunners started shooting before they could see the crest, let alone the Slammers below it.

"All Highball units," Huber ordered. He'd have liked to transmit in clear so that the Militia commander might hear him, but that would be too obviously phony to risk. "Withdraw to the southwest along the plotted course. X-Ray elements lead, Fox elements follow as rear guard in present order. Six out!"

The forest was already burning fiercely. There were fires in the Salamanca Valley also, but the brush was green and the flood-swept slopes weren't covered with leaf litter and humus to get a real blaze going in the next half-hour. The smoke and sluggish flames would help conceal the infantry in ambush; or at least Huber prayed they would.

Crossing at an upstream ford wasn't a real option now that the Solace forces knew the location of Task Force Huber. By the time the Slammers could grind seven kilometers through forest and rough terrain, the enemy would've flown in at least a platoon of infantry. The availability of aircars here on Plattner's World meant that light forces could be shifted very quickly; light forces with buzzbombs and 2-cm powerguns were quite sufficient to turn a truckload of artillery ammunition into an explosion that'd clear everything in a half-klick radius.

The withdrawal would *look* real, though; a maneuver forced by desperation on Slammers who had to cross the river and who'd failed to shoot their way through at their first attempt. The Solace commander would certainly have sent a report and request for support back to his superiors, but he'd also be looking for revenge. The 1st Cavalry Squadron would follow the retreating Slammers—cautiously, because the Militiamen had learned how dangerous the combat cars could be—in hopes of closing the door behind them when other Solace troops had blocked the way forward.

Of course for Huber's plan to work, the Solace commander had to know what the Slammers appeared to be doing.

"All Highball units," Huber said. "When enemy scouts appear, shoot to miss, I repeat, *miss* them. We want the wogs to know that we've cut and run. Six out."

His helmet buzzed with a series of callsigns followed by "Roger." The ball was in the Solace court. Huber could only hope his opposite number would act sooner rather than later; which was a pretty fair likelihood, given the way he'd responded to the initial exchange.

The artillery vehicles were taking longer to get turned around than they would've done if this had been a real change of plan, but the delays and seeming clumsiness were perfectly believable. The hogs were bloody awkward under the best conditions, and the ammunition haulers rarely operated very far off a road. The maintenance vehicle was larger and heavier still, but its driver was used to maneuvering anywhere a combat vehicle could go—and become disabled.

Huber brought up the C&C display again to check the location of his vehicles. "Padova," Huber ordered, "get us moving but not fast."

The X-Ray portion of the task force was half a klick south and west of the combat cars. The last hog in line wasn't moving yet, but it would be before *Fencing Master* closed up. The forest fire was getting serious enough to pose a danger, especially to Lieutenant Messeman's cars at the end of the line.

Padova eased *Fencing Master* into motion, picking a line close to the crest. The fire was bloody serious, but more so downslope where Solace bolts had flung most of the flaming debris.

Huber looked at his gunners again. Learoyd's body armor lay on the ammo boxes at the back of the compartment. Deseau'd sliced off Learoyd's sleeve with his belt knife and was covering the shoulder with bright pink SpraySeal, a combination of replacement skin with antiseptic and topical anesthetic. Learoyd tried to watch, but because of the angle his eyes couldn't both focus on something so close.

"Bert's all right!" Frenchie said over the intake noise. He gestured with the can of SpraySeal. "Make a fist, Bert! Show him!"

Learoyd obediently clenched his right fist. His thumb didn't double over the way it should have. Frowning, he bent it into place with his left hand.

"A chunk of *Flame Farter* spattered him," Deseau explained. "It was still a bit hot, but Bert's just fine. A little bad luck is all."

Learoyd opened his hand again. This time the thumb worked on its own, pretty well. The molten iridium had hit mostly on the back of his clamshell, but some splashed his upper arm where nothing but a tunic sleeve protected the flesh.

Frenchie *needed* to believe Learoyd wasn't seriously injured. Learoyd being who he was, that was probably true: another man who'd been slammed by a quarter-kilo of liquid metal might well have gone into shock, but apart from stiffness and the fact his shoulder was swelling, Learoyd seemed to be about what he always was.

"Learoyd," Huber asked. He nodded toward the clamshell behind him. "Can you get your armor back on over that?"

"I guess," Learoyd said. He worked his fist again; the thumb still didn't want to close. Doubtfully he went on, "Frenchie, will you help me?"

"Sure, Bert, sure!" Deseau said, his voice as brittle as chipped glass.

He snatched up the armor, holding the halves apart for Learoyd to fit his torso into. The fabric covering the right shoulder flare had been melted down to the ceramic core; in its place was a wash of rainbow-hued iridium, finally cool after flying from *Flame Farter*'s hull to strike Learoyd thirty meters away.

"Good," said Huber as he turned deliberately back to the C&C display. "Because we've still got work to do today, and I want you dressed for it."

That blob of white-hot metal could as easily have hit Huber himself between helmet and body armor, burning through his neck… or it could've missed *Fencing Master* and her crew entirely. You never knew till it was over.

Task Force Huber was moving at last. Padova held *Fencing Master* twenty meters off the stern of the last hog in line. More debris flew from beneath the skirts of a self-propelled howitzer than even a combat car threw up.

Huber grinned. It could be worse: following a tank closely was a good way to get your bow slope sandblasted to a high sheen. Of course if Huber had a platoon of tanks with him right now, he'd be dealing with the Solace cavalry squadron in a quicker fashion….

The C&C display warned of new movement on the Solace side of the river. "Fox elements!" Huber said. "Four wog aircars are lifting; it looks like they're going to swing around us to east and west in pairs. Remember, shoot to miss."

A thought struck him, almost too late, and he added, "And make sure your guns aren't in Air Defense Mode! Put your guns on manual, for the Lord's sake! Six out."

The cars' gunnery computers couldn't be programmed to miss. If a gun was on air defense—and one on each combat car normally would be while the column was in march order—then the Solace scouts were going to vanish as quickly as they appeared. That'd almost certainly be before they could report back.

Frenchie and Learoyd lifted the muzzles of their tribarrels, tracking blips on the inside of their faceshields. *Fencing Master* was now weaving through forest that hadn't been cleared by plasma bolts and the fires they ignited. The gunners were tracking on the basis of sensor data because the low-flying aircars were screened by bluffs and undamaged treeboles. When metal finally showed through a gap in the foliage, they were going to be ready.

The hog immediately ahead wobbled through the forest, moving at about twenty kph but seeming even slower than that. The leading vehicles had rubbed the bark to either side of the route, leaving white blazes a meter high on the treetrunks. Often their skirts had gouged brushes of splinters from deep into the sapwood.

Tribarrels volleyed from the tail of the column; an instant later Deseau and Learoyd fired together, their guns startling Huber out of his concentration on the display of sensor data overlaid on a terrain map. He jerked his head up as the upper half of a tree thirty meters toward the northwest burst into red-orange flames. The blasts of plasma had shattered the trunk, blowing it into spheres of superheated organic fragments which exploded when they mixed with oxygen-rich air a few meters distant.

In the sky a kilometer away, a diving aircar flashed its belly toward the column. Deseau sent another burst into empty sky; some of the artillerymen were firing submachine guns from the cabs of their hogs.

Huber checked his display again. Three of the scouts had flattened themselves close to the Salamanca's surface. The fourth—

"Six, this is Two-six," Lieutenant Messeman reported in a clipped, cold voice. *"I regret to report that we hit one of the aircars. The other should've gotten a good look at us before it escaped, though. Two-six over."*

"Roger, Two-six," Huber said. "Proceed as planned."

This was even better than if all the scouts had gotten away: it made the Slammers' response look real. Messeman would be talking to the shooter when things had quieted down, though. Hitting the car had been a screwup, and a battle at these odds was dangerous enough even when all your people executed perfectly.

Huber's gunners had blown apart a tree in order not to hit their pretended target. It now finished toppling to the ground with a crash and ball of flaming debris. Undergrowth ignited immediately, reminding Huber that his cars would be driving back through a full-fledged forest fire. That couldn't be helped.

And a forest fire was a hell of a lot less dangerous than what came next, anyway.

"All Highball elements," Huber said, "reverse and hold until ordered to take assault positions."

He'd have liked to put his cars under the hillcrest right now, but he didn't dare do so with the fire so bad on the slope where they'd have to wait. It was one thing to drive through the inferno at speed, trusting nose filters and the temperature-stable fabric of the Slammers' uniforms. Those weren't enough protection that troopers could twiddle their thumbs in Hell and still be ready for action, though.

"And troopers?" he added. "Those scouts had their only free pass. If they come back for another look at us, shoot fast and shoot to kill! Six out."

Fencing Master slowed to a halt, then rotated deliberately on its axis without touching the ground. Huber wasn't sure whether Padova was showing off or if she was simply so good that she executed the difficult maneuver without thinking about it.

"Six, this is Two-six!" Lieutenant Messeman said excitedly on the command channel. *"They took the bait! They're coming, it looks like four waves! Two-six over!"*

Messeman's *Fandancer* was a half-kilometer closer to the enemy than *Fencing Master*, so its sensors provided a sharper picture than Huber's of what was going on across the river. The Command and Control unit synthesized inputs from every vehicle in the task force, though, so Messeman's report—while proper—wasn't news to Highball Six.

"Roger," Huber said, feeling a familiar curtain fall between him and his present surroundings. His hands were trembling, but that'd stop as soon as he placed them back on his tribarrel's grips. "Break. All Highball units, reduce speed to ten kay-pee-aitch but continue on the plotted course. The wogs must have *some* kind of sensors, and I want any data they get to show we're still moving southwest for as long as possible."

He took a deep breath and continued, "They're coming, troopers. India elements, we're depending on you—but you can count on the rest of us to help as soon as you stick it to them. Six out."

He grimaced and rubbed his palms on his body armor. He wanted to grab the tribarrel, but it wasn't time yet. Lord! he was keyed up.

"*Hey El-Tee,*" Deseau said over the intercom. "*Learoyd and me got a bet on who gets the most wogs this time. You want a piece of it? A case of beer to the winner.*"

"Hell, yes!" Huber said, grinning with the release of tension. "Though one case isn't going to cut the thirst I'm working up on this run."

He turned his gaze back on the C&C display. Nineteen armored cars had driven down the slope and were crossing the Salamanca, in some confusion because the ford wasn't wide enough to take them all in a single passage.

Huber'd expected the Solace hovercraft to be able to skitter across the water's surface, but though they weighed much less than his combat cars, their power-to-weight ratio wasn't as high either. They needed to be able to touch their skirts to the bottom. When two on the upstream end had gotten deeper than that, they'd stalled.

A second line of twenty-three armored cars had just pulled over the crest to follow. The remainder of the squadron, forty vehicles—a mixture of armored cars and headquarters vehicles—lined the far ridgeline with only a meter or two between their bulging skirts.

Under other circumstances Huber would've kept his combat cars where they were and delightedly called in artillery, but the target was too close for Battery Alpha and Central's movement orders had made it clear that every task force was on its own. The operation was more important than the problems of any individual element.

The first wave of armored cars started up the southern slope. For the most part they advanced at the speed of a walking man, but several of the drivers seemed to think speed was protection and drew ahead. They were wrong, of course, but their timid fellows weren't going to survive the morning either if things went the way Huber planned.

"All Fox units," he ordered, "reverse course and take up attack positions. X-Ray units, reverse but hold in place till ordered. Execute. Six out!"

Fencing Master rotated smoothly. Padova dipped the skirts to the ground this time so that she wouldn't run *Fencing Master* up the stern of *Foghorn* whose driver had bobbled the maneuver.

Huber wrung his hands together, wishing he had real-time imagery from the other side of the ridge. Red beads moving on a landscape of green contour lines didn't give him the feel of big vehicles shouldering their way through the scrub, their fans whirling sluggish fires to new life as their paired 3-cm cannon probed the crest above them. The Solace gunners would be ready to shoot if a cloud blew across their sight picture; they'd remember the way a dozen cars like their own had been reduced to flaming wreckage a few minutes before.

Fencing Master began to accelerate, holding interval. Both platoons were returning to the positions they'd held on the reverse slope before the initial skirmish. *Foghorn* roared through what had been a burning treetop before the six cars ahead had driven over it. Now it was a swirl of sparks, eddying out from beneath her skirts and curling back through the intakes into the plenum chamber again. Sergeant Nagano and his crew hunched over their guns, their hands clamped into their armpits for protection.

Fencing Master followed into a surge of heat with occasional prickles where sparks found bare skin. It was like being in a swamp full of biting insects, frustrating and unpleasant but not life-threatening, not unless you let it drive the real dangers out of your mind. Beyond the first obstacle was what had been a glade and now was so many vertical pillars of flame; they drove through that also. In another thirty seconds, it would be time.

Huber kept his attention on the C&C display, pretending to ignore the distortions that flying debris threw across the holographic imagery. The Solace headquarters group, twelve vehicles armed with only light weapons, left the slope. The second wave was mostly across the Salamanca, and the first was nearing—

The flicker of a plasma bolt through gaps in the blazing forest could've been overlooked, but the *zzt!* of RF interference through the commo helmet was familiar to any veteran. A moment later a column of burning hydrocarbon fuel mushroomed from the other side of the ridge, vividly orange and much brighter than the smoky red flames of the well-watered forest.

One of the Slammers infantry had fired his 2-cm weapon into an armored car, picking his spot. At point blank range the powerful bolt had burst the car's fuel tank and turned the vehicle into a firebomb. Huber hoped the shooter hadn't been caught in his own secondary explosion, but he had more important concerns just now.

"Fox elements, do not engage!" he shouted. "Hold in your attack positions! Do not—"

Though the combat cars weren't back to their start positions, Huber was afraid that one or more of his vehicle commanders would react to the shooting across the crest by piling into it instantly. That was a good general response for any trooper in the Regiment, but right now timing would be the difference between survival and not.

"—cross the ridgeline!"

At least a hundred 3-cm powerguns fired at or over the quarter kilometer of hillcrest which was already scarred and glazed by previous bolts. The lighter *crack!* of infantry weapons was lost in the roar of cannons volleying at where the gunners thought the enemy must be. Another fuel tank detonated, lifting ten square meters of glass-cored aluminum armor with it; the magazine explosion a heartbeat later burned so vividly cyan that the light seemed to seep through solid rock.

Fencing Master reached its start position and rotated ninety degrees counterclockwise, putting its bow to the ridgeline and the enemy. Flames licked up behind and beside the car, but the trees close by had been burned and blasted into a bed of coals rather than towers that might topple.

The Solace cavalrymen were shouting over at least six channels. Huber'd set his

C&C box to give him a graph of the number of Solace transmissions. He could've listened to them as well—most of the hostiles were too panicked to bother with encryption—but Huber already knew what they'd be saying: "*Help!*" and "*Where?*" and "*You're shooting at us, you idiots! Cease fire!*"

Especially "*Cease fire!*" from the armored cars on the south slope who *knew* there was nobody on the ridge immediately above them. Therefore the shots that'd destroyed their fellows had to be bolts misaimed by the cars blazing away from across the river.

The storm of bolts fired at empty rock slowed, then ceased. Apart from anything else, the Solace cars must've exhausted their ready magazines and heated their guns dangerously hot by sustained fire. The squadron commander would be starting to reassert control; in a moment somebody would realize how the leading wave had been ambushed.

"Fox elements…" ordered Arne Huber as his hands settled on his tribarrel's familiar grips. "Charge! Take 'em out, troopers!"

Fencing Master lifted with the ease of a balloon slipping its tether. By judicious adjustment of nacelle angles Padova kept the hull nearly horizontal despite the slope, so that all three tribarrels came over the ridge together.

Huber squeezed his trigger as his muzzles aligned with an armored car on the opposite ridgeline, its twin guns glowing white. Huber's burst walked down the barbette and blew the glacis plate inward. Fire and black smoke burst from the car's seams; the hull settled into the plenum chamber and began to burn.

Huber's faceshield careted his next target, also an overwatching armored car, but before he could fire it blew up on the skewer of Learoyd's gun. There'd been more Solace vehicles on the far ridge than there were tribarrels in Huber's two understrength platoons, but the combat cars had destroyed both their primary and secondary targets without taking a single additional casualty. Some of the Solace cannon had burst in vivid rainbows even before Huber counterattacked; they'd been fired so fast and so often that the overheated bores finally gave way.

The timing worked the way Huber'd hoped and prayed. The Solace gunners, confused and half-disarmed by the number of rounds they'd fired into emptiness, couldn't react to the sudden appearance of real targets; and the Slammers didn't miss.

Fencing Master continued forward and over the hill. An armored car was stalled ten meters ahead, its guns traversed to the right. The gunner had tried to reply to the pair of troopers with shoulder weapons lying belly-down on the slope as they blew holes in the thin-walled plenum chamber. The vehicle's cannon couldn't depress low enough to hit them, and the five Solace infantrymen who'd leaped out of the rear compartment lay in a bloody tangle just beyond the hatch. This close, a 2-cm bolt vaporized a human torso and flung the head and limbs in separate parabolas.

Huber put a three-round burst into the car's barbette; 3-cm ammunition in the loading tray gang-fired, devouring the breeches and mountings.

The cannon barrels tilted down. He didn't bother firing into the hull. The

Solace driver and gunner might well be unharmed, but they were no longer a danger to the task force.

Arne Huber didn't kill people for pleasure: that was simply an aspect of his business.

His faceshield careted the smoke-shrouded net of air roots supporting a copse of thin trunks. He didn't see a target—maybe he would've in infrared—but he mashed his trigger with both thumbs. His chain of cyan bolts reached out, spinning eddies in the white haze. A Solace armored car drove out, its hatches blown open and spewing oily black smoke. Huber's nose filters were in place, but he nonetheless smelled cooking flesh as *Fencing Master* passed downwind of the target.

The smoke grew thicker. He switched from normal optics to thermal imaging.

An armored car stood broadside and motionless; had its crew already bailed out, hoping to be ignored and to survive? The AI called the vehicle a target, so Huber's bolts punched at the forward compartment until something shorted and the car started to burn.

A man in a black Solace uniform ran in front of *Fencing Master*. Huber didn't shoot him but somebody did, a single bolt; probably an infantryman who didn't see any reason to quit just because the combat cars had joined the fight. Vehicles blew up, some of them so violently that the smoke now covering the valley surged and rippled like a pond in a hailstorm.

Fencing Master reached the river, its bank broken down by the armored cars which had recently crossed. At least a dozen were burning in the water or just beyond it. Huber's faceshield cued the far slope. He elevated his tribarrel, noticing that the muzzles glowed white though he'd been trying to keep his bursts short.

Some of the Solace Command vehicles were trying to escape. They couldn't be allowed to. This battle had been a victory for Task Force Huber by anybody's standards, but the fragments of the Solace squadron were still sufficient to do serious damage to the artillery vehicles if anybody got them organized.

Fencing Master plunged into the Salamanca, bucking forward in a rainbow of mist. Even drops of water could dissipate a powergun's jet of plasma. Huber waited for the car to lift, concurrently flattening the curtain of spray, before he squeezed the trigger.

His burst struck the squared rear end of a communications van. The plating was so thin that the second round ignited the interior through the hole the first had blown; the three bolts that followed were probably overkill.

There was still shooting, some of it probably at real targets, but Huber's faceshield didn't highlight anything for his gun. Strung out to the right of the commo van, other headquarters vehicles belched smoke and flame. Tribarrels had ripped them open even more easily than they did the armored cars.

Via! That one was an ambulance. Well, worse things happen in wartime....

"X-Ray elements, proceed across the ford at your best speed," Huber ordered. He was panting and for a moment his vision blurred. "Fox Three elements, take overwatch positions on the north ridge. Fox Two elements, wait on the south side and escort X-Ray. India elements, recover to the X-Ray vehicles and mount up. You did a hell of a job."

Fencing Master swerved right, then left, to avoid a pair of burning vehicles. Something *whumped* inside one; a crimson geyser blew debris out of the driver's hatch. It would've been attractive in its way if Huber hadn't realized the tumbling object was a shriveled human hand.

"Via, troopers…" he said, looking back across the valley as his combat car swung into position on the crest. Despite the filters, his eyes watered and the back of his throat felt raw. "We *all* did a hell of a job! Six out."

Smoke, gray and becoming black, blanketed the ford. In some places it bubbled above a particular vehicle, but for the most part it hung silently. Because Huber's faceshield was still set for thermal imaging, he could see through the pall to the wreckage littering the valley. The smoke would make a good screen against sniping by Solace survivors, in the unlikely event that any of those survivors wanted to continue the battle.

The tank recovery vehicle carrying the excavator in its bed grunted over the south crest and drove slowly into the smoke. It was the first of the X-Ray units, but a hog was close behind and then two ammo haulers. Infantry swung aboard the big vehicles, dragging their skimmers up behind them.

Tribarrels continued to snarl, and once Huber thought he heard the sharp hiss of a Solace rocket gun. The ford wasn't perfectly safe, but this was a war and nothing was perfect. Better to run the non-combat vehicles through immediately than wait to completely clear the area and give the enemy time to respond.

Huber eyed the flame-shot wasteland again. "A hell of a job," he repeated.

And a job of Hell.

"*Six, this is Three-five,*" reported Sergeant Tranter; he was pulling drag on this leg of the run, while *Fencing Master* was in the center of the column between a pair of ammo haulers. "*We've got three aircars incoming just like planned, all copacetic. Three-five over.*"

Huber examined the data from *Fancy Pants* on his C&C box. Three-five's sensors had picked up the aircars while they were still over the southern horizon. Their identification transponders indicated they were the resupply mission which Central's transmission had said to expect, and they were within ninety seconds—early—of the estimated time of arrival, but still…

"Highball elements," Huber said, "we'll laager for ammo resupply for ten minutes at point—"

The AI threw up an option, a knob half a klick ahead and close to the planned route. It wasn't quite bald, but the trees there were stunted and would allow the tribarrels enough range for air defense.

"—Victor Tango Four-one-two, Five-five-one. Take your guns off automatic but keep alert. The wogs could've captured aircars with the IFF transponders and they might just've gotten lucky on the timing. Six out."

Fencing Master bumped a tree hard enough to throw those in the fighting compartment forward. Padova'd gotten over the reflex of growling every time the driver—Deseau was in front at the moment—didn't meet her standards, but this one made her wince.

"*It'll be good to stand on the ground again,*" Padova said, bending forward to massage her calf muscles. She looked up at Huber in concern. "*Ah—we will be dismounting, won't we?*"

"We'll have to," Huber said, forcing himself to grin. "Those ammo boxes aren't going to fly out of the aircars. We'll be humping 'em."

He was bone tired, but he wasn't going to take another popper just now. Task Force Huber had a long way to go, and he'd need the stimulant worse later on.

The C&C box projected halt locations in the temporary laager to all the drivers. *Fencing Master* growled up the slight rise, then pulled into scrub forest which the bigger X-Ray vehicles ahead in the column were scraping clear. The place the AI had chosen for *Fencing Master* was across the circle of outward-facing vehicles. They brushed the massive wrenchmobile closer than Huber would've liked, but it was all right. Frenchie wasn't a great driver and it was near the end of his two-hour stint anyway. They hadn't collided, and this wasn't a day Arne Huber needed to borrow trouble.

Deseau set them down and almost immediately climbed out the driver's hatch. He wasn't under any illusions about his driving, though he didn't complain about the duty. Learoyd ought to take the next session, but…

Huber looked at Padova. "You up for another shift?" he asked. "It's not your turn, I know."

"You bet I am," she said, nodding briskly. "You bet your ass!"

"*Highball, we're coming in,*" an unfamiliar female voice said. "*Three aircars at vector one-one-nine degrees to your position. Action Four-two out.*"

"Roger, Action," Huber said. "Highball elements, hold your fire. Six out."

He knew he was frowning. He'd expected the resupply to be carried out by Log Section, maybe even UC civilians under contract to the Regiment. "Action" was a callsign of the White Mice.

The recovery vehicle had ground the brush in the center of the laager to matchsticks, then shoved the debris into a crude berm. The aircars came low over the treetops, circled a moment to pick locations, and landed. All showed bullet scars. They each carried two troopers, but the guard on one lay across the ammo boxes amidships, either dead or drugged comatose.

"*Fox elements,*" ordered Sergeant Tranter, acting as first sergeant for the task force, "*each car send two men to pick up your requirements. India elements, two men per squad. Also we'll transfer the dead and wounded to the aircars. Three-five out.*"

"Frenchie," Huber said, "hold the fort. I'm going to learn what's going on back at Base Alpha."

He swung his legs over the coaming, paused on the bulge of the plenum chamber, and slid to the ground. He almost crumpled under the weight of his clamshell when he landed. Via! he was woozy.

The troopers in the aircars were loosing the cargo nets over their loads; they looked as tired as Huber and his personnel. The woman with sergeant's pips on her collar was working one-handed because the other arm was in a sling.

"Tough run?" Huber asked, sliding out a case of 2-cm ammo for Learoyd, who took it left-handed. There were spare barrels too, thank the Lord and the foresight of somebody back at Central.

"Tough enough," she said, not quite curt enough to be called hostile.

"How are things at Base Alpha?" Huber asked, passing the next case to Padova. He didn't know who was defending the base with so many of the combat-fit Slammers running north. He was sure it wasn't a situation anybody was happy about.

"We'll worry about fucking Base Alpha," the sergeant snarled. She met his eyes; she looked like an animal in a trap, desperate and furious. "You worry about your job, all right?"

"Roger that," Huber said evenly, taking a case of twelve 2-cm gunbarrels to empty the belly of the car. "Good luck, Sergeant."

"Yeah," the woman said. "Yeah, same to you, Lieutenant."

The three dead infantrymen and the incapacitated—three more infantry and *Flame Farter*'s left wing gunner—had been placed in the aircars. *Flame Farter*'s driver and commander were ash in the remains of their vehicle.

The sergeant settled back behind the controls and muttered something on her unit push, the words muffled by circuitry in her commo helmet. Nodding, she and the other drivers brought their fans up to flying speed again.

"*Action Four-two outbound*," crackled her voice through Huber's commo helmet. The White Mice took off again, their vector fifteen degrees east of the way they'd arrived. Their approach might've been tracked, so they weren't taking a chance on overflying an ambush prepared in the interim.

"Bitch," said Padova, who'd been close enough to hear the exchange.

Huber stepped to *Fencing Master* and paused before swinging the spare barrels to Deseau waiting on the plenum chamber. The case of fat iridium cylinders was heavy enough in all truth; in Huber's present shape, it felt as if he were trying to lift a whole combat car.

"Got it, El-Tee," Learoyd said, taking the barrels one-handed before Huber had a chance to protest. He shoved them up to his partner in a movement that was closer to shot-putting than weight lifting.

Huber stretched, then quirked a grin to Padova. "I guess even the White Mice are human," he said, grinning more broadly. "We all do the best we can. Some days—"

He held his right arm out straight so that she could see he was trembling with fatigue.

"—that's not as good as we'd like."

"*Mount up, troopers*," Sergeant Tranter ordered. He gave Huber a thumbs-up from *Fancy Pants*' fighting compartment. "*Fox Three leads on this leg*."

Padova scrambled down the driver's hatch. Huber climbed the curve of the skirts and lifted himself into the fighting compartment without Deseau's offered hand. He seemed to have gotten his second wind.

As the fans lifted *Fencing Master* in preparation to resume the march, Deseau said, "Glad they brought the barrels, El-Tee. We were down to two sets after what we replaced after that last fracas. I don't guess that's the last shooting we'll do this operation."

"I don't guess so either, Frenchie," Huber said. For a moment he tried to visualize the future, but all his mind would let him see was forest and stabbing cyan plasma discharges.

"Hey El-Tee?" Learoyd said. Huber looked at the diffidently waiting trooper and nodded.

"What about the panzers, El-Tee?" Learoyd asked. "Aircars can't carry the barrel for a main gun, and even if they could it takes three hours and the presses on a wrench-mobile to switch barrels on a tank."

"I don't know, Learoyd," Huber said. *Fencing Master* reentered the unbroken forest, the second vehicle in the column this leg. "I guess they'll just make do like the rest of us."

Or not, of course; but he didn't say that aloud.

The trees in this stretch had thick trunks and wide-spread branches. That made the driving easier, especially now in deep darkness. Of course if a car hit one of them squarely, it wasn't going to be the tree that was smashed to bits.

A red bead pulsing twice in the center of Huber's faceshield gave him a minimal warning before Central crashed the task force net with, *"Highball, this is Chaser Three-one. You will halt for an artillery fire mission in figures three-zero seconds. Mission data is being downloaded now. You will resume your march after firing a battery three. Chaser Three-one over."*

The voice on the other end of the transmission was broken and attenuated to the verge of being inaudible. Central was bouncing the message in micropackets off cosmic ray ionization tracks, the Regiment's normal expedient on planets where security was the first priority or there weren't communications satellites. Even so—and despite interference from the foliage overhead, a screen if not a solid ceiling—the transmission would normally have been crisper than this.

What the hell was going on at Base Alpha?

But like the A Company sergeant said, it wasn't Arne Huber's job to worry about Base Alpha. Nor to ask questions when Central's orders were brusque because there was no time to give any other kind.

"Roger, Chaser Three-one," Huber said. "Highball Six out."

"Chaser Three-one out," the voice said, fading to nothingness in the middle of the final syllable.

"Highball, this is Six," Huber said. Deseau had turned to look at him. "Halt at Michael Foxtrot Four-one-six, Five-one-four. Fox elements will provide security while Rocker elements—"

The artillery.

"—carry out their fire mission. Break. Rocker One-six, I want to be moving again as soon as possible. Copy? Six over."

"*Roger, Highball Six,*" Lieutenant Basingstoke replied crisply. He had more time in grade as well as more time in the Regiment than Huber. Huber suspected that Basingstoke thought he should've been task force commander in Huber's place, which was just another piece of evidence as to why a redleg lieutenant didn't have sufficient judgment to command a mobile force. "*You don't want us to reload the gun vehicles before proceeding, then? Rocker One-six over.*"

"Negative!" Huber responded. He bit off the words, "You bloody fool!" but he suspected his tone implied them, which was just fine with him. "Rocker, I don't want to be halted in enemy-controlled territory an instant longer than we have to be, especially after we've been shooting artillery so they know *exactly* where we are. Six out."

Learoyd pulled *Fencing Master* into the halt location the AI had chosen for them. Huber looked up, frowning. The patches of sky overhead weren't sufficient for the Automatic Air Defense System to burst incoming shells a safe distance away. So long as the task force kept moving they were probably all right, but now, halted—

Well, Central knew the score; and anyway, the Regiment wasn't a democracy. *Ours not to reason why…*

The hogs swung into position, their turrets rotating and launch tubes rising while the vehicles were still in motion. The ammunition haulers pulled off to either side of the guns. The F-2 combat cars tried to keep outside the scattered trucks, but this wasn't a defensive position in any sense of the term. The Lord save Highball's souls if any Solace forces were close enough to take advantage of the situation.

"Lieutenant?" said Padova, leaning close to shout over the idling fans. "I didn't think we were going to hear anything from Central on this run. That we were on our own?"

Huber shrugged. His shoulders ached from the weight of his armor, but that was nothing new. "The operation was pretty spur of the moment, Rita," he said. "I guess they're flying it by the seat of their pants, just like we are."

The howitzers fired, rippling with a half-second between discharges so that the shockwaves from the shells didn't interfere with other rounds in the salvo. The nearest gun was within ten meters of *Fencing Master*. Huber's helmet damped the blasts so they didn't break his eardrums, but the pressure of 200-mm shells tearing skyward squeezed his whole body like loads of sand.

The hogs weighed forty tonnes apiece, and the steel skirts of their plenum chambers stabilized them better than conventional trails and recoil spades could do. Despite that the big vehicles jounced so hard when they fired that puffs of dirt and leaf litter spurted out of their fan intakes.

The rounds didn't reach terminal velocity for seven seconds, but the *crack!* of each going supersonic stabbed through the deeper, world-filling snarl of the rocket motors. Overhead, branches whipped and shredded leaves swirled in roaring eddies.

Huber'd wondered how the guns would fire through dense foliage, but that obviously wasn't a problem. The shells could course correct if they had to, but the disparity between the massive projectiles and the leaves made Huber grimace at the foolishness of his concern.

The first howitzer launched a second round immediately after Gun Six fired its first; the third followed three seconds later. As the launch tube sank back to its travel position, the hog's driver began spinning up his fans: they'd been shut down while the gun was firing lest the blades whip into their housings and wreck the nacelle.

"*Highball Six!*" Lieutenant Basingstoke said, his voice crackling with the effort of Huber's commo helmet to make it audible over the thunderous conclusion of the fire mission. "*Rocker elements are ready to move. Rock—*"

Gun Six fired its third and final round. The shriek of the shells arching southward seemed like silence after the cacophony of the preceding seconds.

"*—er One-six over.*"

"All Highball units," Huber said. The whole operation had taken less time than switching drivers; a minute at the outside. "Resume march order. Six out."

He grinned wryly. While he didn't suppose Lieutenant Basingstoke was going to become a bosom buddy, at least he knew his job.

And because he was thinking that, Huber said, "Rocker One-six, this is Highball Six. It's a pleasure to serve with real professionals, Lieutenant. Please convey my congratulations to your troopers. Six over."

Foghorn slid out of sight among the trees. Learoyd brought *Fencing Master* up, following thirty meters behind the lead car. That was a greater interval than they'd maintain when the task force had reached a constant speed.

"*Highball Six, this is Rocker One-six,*" Basingstoke said. "*I've passed on your congratulations to my gunners.*" After a pause he added, "*I'm glad we were able to perform to the standard the infantry and your combat car crews have demonstrated in order to get us this far. Rocker One-six out.*"

Huber looked up at branches whipping past against a dark sky. He grinned faintly. "Thank you, Rocker One-six," he said. "Six out."

He wondered how much farther Task Force Huber was going to get. *Who knows? Maybe all the way.*

And then what? Huber added to himself; but that was a problem for another day.

Huber awakened from a doze. He'd been hunched into the back corner of the fighting compartment, held upright by ammo boxes and a carton of rations. Fields of dark green soybeans rolled to either horizon beyond the iridium walls, punctuated by stretches of native vegetation.

According to the briefing cubes, Solace was several times as populous as all the Outer States put together. Those people were heavily concentrated in the center of the country around Bezant and Port Plattner, however, with the remainder of the country given over to the collective farms which produced food for the entire planet.

Huber frowned as he thought about the rations. He'd swallowed a tube of something a little after dawn as they negotiated the foothills of the Solace Highlands, but he'd had nothing since. He didn't feel hungry but supposed he ought to eat something.

It was an effort to get anything down because he was so fatigued by the constant vibration. Besides, the poppers made food taste like it'd been scraped from the bottom of a latrine. That wasn't much of a change from what ration tubes ordinarily tasted like, of course.

He jolted alert, suddenly aware of why he'd awakened. Padova'd been on duty with the C&C display while he rested. She was trained but she didn't have the sixth sense for what wasn't *right* that'd come with a year or two of combat operations.

"I've got the watch," Huber said. He took the controller from Padova's hand as he spoke, lurching upright. She jumped aside, startled and maybe a little snappish at the lack of ceremony. The reaction passed before it got to her tongue, which was just as well.

As Huber adjusted the display to make explicit what instinct already told him, he said, "Highball, we're going to have to adjust course to the left by thirty degrees. There's a monorail line eighteen klicks ahead, and if we continue as planned we'll be spotted by a train headed southward. We'll—"

He stopped because he'd caught the fine overtone to the sensor data, the descant he'd ignored for the moment while he focused on the electronic signature of a six-car train heading south at 120 kph. Task Force Huber could avoid observation from a train at ground level, but—

"Bloody Hell!" Huber snarled, interrupting himself. "This is going to take a moment, troopers. There's aircars scouting for the train and they'll spot us sure!"

"Six, this is Two-six," Lieutenant Messeman said on the command channel. *"I suggest it's a troop train and the aircars are escorts. Over."*

"Roger," said Huber, because it couldn't be anything else once Messeman had stated the obvious. He shook his head angrily. He must still be waking up. He couldn't afford to miss cues; he couldn't, and the troopers who were his responsibility couldn't afford him missing them either.

"Roger," Huber repeated, but with a note of decision. There was nothing wrong with his tactical appreciation once he got his mind in gear. "Highball, we can't avoid them so we'll engage and keep moving. Fox will attack on a company front—"

That was a bit of an overstatement, given that the Fox elements under Huber's command were two understrength platoons, but it'd do.

"—from point Echo Michael Four-two, Six-one. X-Ray elements continue in march order. Fox elements form to the right on Three-six in line abreast with five, I repeat five, meter intervals. Execute! Six out."

Padova looked at him wonderingly. It was too bad Learoyd wasn't on the right gun, but the newbie was going to have to get her feet wet some time. This was probably as safe a place to do it as any.

"Crew," Huber said, switching his helmet to intercom. *Foghorn* was moving up on their right with the other cars of F-3 slanted farther back as they drove through the soybeans to their stations. Lieutenant Messeman's platoon would take longer to join from the middle and rear of the column, but it'd be in line by the time it needed to be. "Frenchie, set our guns to take out the scouts when we're sure of getting them both."

The aircars were keeping station to either side of the track, five hundred meters up and a kilometer ahead of the train. They were looking for trouble on the line rather than scouting more generally, but even so from their altitude they were bound to notice the Slammers' vehicles.

Deseau keyed the command into the pad on his tribarrel's receiver. Instead of executing immediately he said, "*You don't think it'll warn them, El-Tee?*"

"It's a train," Huber snapped. "They're not going to turn around, they won't even be able to slow down."

Deseau grimaced and pushed EXECUTE. *Fencing Master*'s tribarrels slewed to the right and elevated under the control of the gunnery computer.

"The C&C box'll divide our fire so that the whole train's covered," Huber continued, deliberately speaking to his whole crew over the intercom rather than embarrassing Padova by singling her out for the explanation. "We'll shoot it up on the fly, not because that'll damage the enemy but—"

Fencing Master's tribarrels fired, six-round bursts from the paired wing guns and about ten from Deseau's as it destroyed an aircar by itself. Padova jumped, instinct telling her that the gun'd gone off by accident. She blushed and scowled when she realized what had happened.

Above the horizon to the north, a cottony puff bloomed and threw out glittering sparks. The flash of the explosion had been lost in the distance, even to Huber who'd been looking for it.

"—because if we don't, we'll have whatever military force is aboard that train chasing us," Huber continued, giving no sign that he'd noticed Padova's mistake. "We're going to have enough to do worrying about what's in front without somebody catching us from behind."

The gunnery computer returned the tribarrels to their previous alignment. Huber and Deseau touched their grips, swiveling their weapons slightly to make sure that a circuitry glitch hadn't locked them; Padova quickly copied the veterans. *Yeah, she'll do.*

A column of black smoke twisted skyward near where the white puff had appeared in the sky. The second Solace scout hadn't blown up in the air, but its wreckage had ignited the brush when it hit the ground.

"*Six, this is Two-six,*" Messeman said. "*I'll take my Two-zero car out of central control to cut the rail in front of the train. All right? Over.*"

"Roger, Two-six," Huber said. He thought Messeman was being overcautious, but that still left seven combat cars to deal with a six-car train.

Sunlight gleamed on the elevated rail and the line of pylons supporting it across the dark green fields. The train itself wasn't in sight yet, but at their closing speed it wouldn't be long. Huber settled behind his gun, staring into the holographic sight picture.

Fencing Master came over a rise too slight to notice on a contour map but all the difference in the world when you were using line-of-sight weapons. The train, a jointed tube of plastic and light metal, shimmered into view, slung beneath the elevated track.

"Open fire," Huber said calmly. His thumbs squeezed the butterfly trigger.

Padova's bolts were high—meters high, well above even the rail—but Huber and Deseau were both dead on the final car from their first rounds. Huber traversed his gun clockwise from the back of the target forward. Frenchie simply let the train's own forward motion carry it through his three-second burst so that his bolts crossed with his lieutenant's in the middle of the target. By that time Padova corrected her aim by sawing her muzzles downward.

The car fell apart, metal frame and thermoplastic paneling alike blazing at the touch of fifty separate hits, each a torch of plasma. The Solace mercenaries on the train carried grenades and ammunition, but those sparkling secondary explosions did little to increase the destruction which the powerguns had caused directly.

The second car back had something more impressive in it, perhaps a pallet of anti-armor missiles. When it detonated, the shockwave destroyed the whole front half of the train in a red flash so vivid that even daylight blanched. The low pressure that followed the initial wave front sucked topsoil into a dense black mushroom through which the rear cars cascaded as blazing debris.

"Cease fire!" Huber ordered. "Don't waste ammo, troopers, we've worked ourselves out of a job."

He took a deep breath; his nose filters released now that the air was fit to breathe again. Plasma bolts burned oxygen to ozone, and the matrix holding the copper atoms in alignment broke down into unpleasant compounds when the energy was released. Huber's faceshield had blocked the direct intensity of the bolts to save his retinas, but enough cyan light had reflected into the corners of his eyes that shimmers of purple and orange filtered his vision.

"Reform in march order," Huber concluded hoarsely. "Six out."

"*They didn't have a chance,*" Padova said. She sounded as though she was on the verge of collapse. "*They couldn't shoot back, they were helpless!*"

"*It's better when they don't shoot back,*" Learoyd said from the front compartment. He'd buttoned up before they went into action; now the hatch opened and the driver's seat rose on its hydraulic jack, lifting his head back into the open. "*They might've got lucky, even at this range.*"

"*Some a' them caught us with our pants down when we landed here,*" Frenchie Deseau said harshly. "*We weren't so fucking helpless! Ain't that so, El-Tee?*"

Huber flipped up his faceshield and rubbed his eyes, remembering unwillingly the ratfuck when a Solace commando ambushed F-3 disembarking from the starship that had just brought them to Plattner's World. *A buzzbomb trailing gray exhaust smoke as it curved for Arne Huber's head…*

And afterward, the windrow of bodies scythed down by a touch of Huber's thumb to the close-in defense system.

"No," he said in a husky whisper. "We weren't helpless. We're Hammer's Slammers."

Task Force Huber continued to slice its way north, moving at an even hundred kph across the treeless fields.

"Highball Six, this is Flasher Six," the voice said faintly. The signal wobbled and was so attenuated that Huber could barely make out the words. *"Do you copy, over?"*

Ionization track transmissions could carry video under the proper circumstances, but communications between moving vehicles were another matter. Huber would've said it was impossible without a precise location for the recipient, but apparently that wasn't quite true.

"Flasher Six, this is Highball Six," he said, shutting his mind to the present circumstances though his eyes remained open. Deseau and Learoyd glanced over when he replied to the transmission, then returned to their guns with the extra alertness of men who know something unseen is likely to affect them. "Go ahead, over."

Huber had no idea who Flasher Six was nor what he commanded. The AI could probably tell him, but right now Huber had too little brain to clutter it up with needless detail.

Fencing Master's sending unit had the reference signal from the original transmission to go on, so Huber could reasonably expect his reply to get through. It must have done so, because a moment later the much clearer voice responded, *"Highball, you're in position to anchor a Solace artillery regiment. I need you to adjust your course to follow the Masterton River, a few degrees east of the original plot. I'm downloading the course data—"*

A pause. An icon blinked in the lower left corner of Huber's faceshield, then became solid green when the AI determined that the transmission was complete and intelligible.

"—now. Central delegated control to me because they haven't been able to get through to you directly. Flasher over."

Task Force Huber was winding through slopes too steep and rocky to be easily cultivated. Shrubs and twisted trees with small leaves were the only vegetation they'd seen for ten kilometers. That was why they'd been routed this way, of course: the chance of somebody accurately reporting their location and course to Solace Command was very slight.

Huber was behind schedule, and the notion of further delay irritated him more than it might've done if he hadn't been so tired. He glared at the transmitted course he'd projected onto a terrain overlay and said, "Flasher, what is it that you want us to do? We're to attack an artillery *regiment?* Highball over."

"Negative, Highball, negative!" Flasher Six snapped. *"These are the Firelords! There's an eight-gun battery of calliopes with each battalion and they'd cut you to pieces. Your revised course will take you through a town with a guardpost that'll alert Solace Command. That'll give the Firelords enough warning to block the head of the valley with their calliopes and take you under fire with their rockets. We'll handle it from there. Over."*

Huber called up the Firelords from *Fencing Master*'s data bank; his frown grew deeper. They were one of several regiments fielded from the Hackabe Cluster. Their truck-mounted bombardment rockets were relatively unsophisticated and short ranged but they could put down a huge volume of fire in a short time.

"Flasher," Huber said, switching his faceshield back to the course display, "the Firelords'll be able to saturate our defenses if they try hard enough. I'll have to put all my tribarrels on air defense, and even then it's going to be close. Are you sure about this? Over."

"*Roger, Highball!*" Flasher said in a tone of obvious irritation. "*Your infantry component will have to handle local security. Are you able to comply, over?*"

"Roger, Flasher," Huber said. It wasn't the first time he'd gotten orders he didn't like. It wouldn't be the last, either—if he survived this one. "Highball Six out."

He paused a moment to collect his mind. The AI was laying out courses and plotting fields of fire; doing its job, as happy as a machine could be. And Arne Huber was a soldier, so he'd do his job also. If it didn't make him happy, sometimes, he and all the other troopers in the Regiment had decided—if only by default—that it made them happier than other lines of work.

"*Trouble, El-Tee?*" Deseau asked without looking up from his sight picture. He'd been covering the left front while Huber was getting their orders.

"Hey, we're alive, Frenchie," Huber said. "That's something, right?"

He looked at the new plot on the C&C display, took a deep breath, and said over the briefing channel, "Highball, this is Six. There's been a change of plan. We're to proceed up the valley of the Masterton River, through a place called Millhouse Crossing. There's a Militia guardpost there."

In briefing mode, the unit commanders could respond directly and lower-ranking personnel could caret Huber's display for permission to speak. Nobody said anything for the moment.

He continued, "We'll shoot up the post on the move, but be aware that they may shoot back. We'll continue another fifteen klicks to where the road drops down into the plains around Hundred Hectare Lake. We'll halt short of there because an artillery regiment is set up beside the lake, the Firelords. We're to keep their attention while a friendly unit takes care of them. Any questions? Over."

"*If they're so fucking friendly,*" Deseau said over *Fencing Master*'s intercom, "*then let them draw fire and we'll shoot up the redlegs. How about that?*"

There was a pause as the rest of the task force stared at the transmitted map; at least the unit commanders would also check out the Firelords. The first response was from Lieutenant Basingstoke, saying, "*Highball Six, this is Rocker One-six. The Firelords can launch nearly fifteen hundred fifteen-centimeter rockets within five seconds. You can't—the task force cannot, I believe—defend against a barrage like that. Over.*"

Huber sighed, though he supposed it was just as well that somebody'd raised the point directly. "One-six," he said, "I agree with your calculations, but we have our orders. We're going to do our best and hope that the Firelords don't think it's worth emptying their racks all in one go. Over."

Somebody swore softly. It could've been any of the platoon leaders. Blood and Martyrs, it could've been Huber himself muttering the words that were dancing through his mind.

"All right, troopers," Huber said to the fraught silence. "You've got your orders. We've all got our orders. Car Three-six leads from here till we're through this. Highball Six out."

Padova obediently increased speed by five kph, pulling around *Foghorn* as Sergeant Nagano's driver swung to the left in obedience to the directions from the C&C box. As soon as they were into the broader part of the valley, they'd form with the combat cars in line abreast by platoons at the front and rear of the task force. The X-Ray vehicles would crowd as tightly together between the cars as movement safety would allow.

Bombardment rockets had a wide footprint but they weren't individually accurate, so reducing the target made the tribarrels' task of defense easier. Not easy, but an old soldier was one who'd learned to take every advantage there was.

Padova took them up a swale cutting into the ridge to the right. Deseau looked at the landscape. By crossing the ridge, they'd enter a better-watered valley where the data bank said the locals grew crops on terraces.

"Ever want to be a farmer, Bert?" Deseau asked.

"No, Frenchie," Learoyd said.

Deseau shrugged. *"Yeah, me neither,"* he said. *"Besides, I like shooting people."*

He laughed, but Huber wasn't sure he was joking.

Fencing Master nosed through the spike-leafed trees straggling along the crest. They were similar to giants Huber'd seen in the lowland forests, but here the tallest were only ten meters high and their leaves had a grayish cast.

Limestone scraped beneath *Fencing Master*'s skirts as they started down the eastern slope. The landscape immediately became greener, and after less than a minute they'd snorted out of wasteland into a peanut field.

A man—no, a woman—was cultivating the far end of the field with a capacitor-powered tractor. The farmer saw *Fencing Master* and stood up on her seat. As *Foghorn* slid out of the scrub with the rest of the column following, she leaped into the field and began crawling away while the tractor continued its original course. The peanut bushes wobbled, marking her course. Deseau laughed.

"It's like a different planet," Padova said, taking them down the path to the next terrace, a meter lower. *Fencing Master* was wider than the farm machinery, so they jolted as their skirts plowed the retaining wall and upper terrace into a broader ramp. The valley opened into more fields interspersed with the roofs of houses and sheds. *"All green and pretty."*

An aircar heading south a kilometer away suddenly turned in the air and started back the way it'd come. Learoyd and Deseau fired. Half the vehicle including the rear fan disintegrated. The forward portion spun into the ground and erupted in flames.

"Just wait a bit, Rita," Frenchie said with a chuckle.

The Solace Militia used civilian vehicles with no markings that'd show at a quick glimpse through a gunsight. That aircar might've been a farm couple coming home with all their children, but Huber would've fired also if he hadn't been concentrating on other business. He had to cover the sensor readouts as well as the position of his task force.

Killing civilians—maybe civilians—wasn't a part of the work that Huber much cared for, but you'd go crazy if you let yourself worry about the things you couldn't change. Go crazy or shoot yourself.

In the interests of command, *Fencing Master* should've been farther back in the column with *Foghorn* or *Fancy Pants* leading… but Huber was making the choice, and he knew that afterward the CO had less to explain to the survivors if he'd been leading from the front. He had less to explain to himself, too, if he was one of those survivors.

Padova increased speed, crossing the fields at forty kph and using the extra inertia to help break down the retaining walls before accelerating again. Huber frowned, but the rest of the column kept station. Since *Fencing Master* was widening the ramps, the following vehicles didn't have to slow as much to negotiate the terraces.

The valley's lower levels were planted in rice, a green much brighter than the leaves of the peanut bushes. The paddies were flooded; showers of spray, muck, and young plants erupted as the Slammers drove through. Upper fields began to drain as the column's passage opened the dikes.

Occasionally someone stepped out of a wood-framed dwelling or glanced up in a field to see what the noise was. Some continued to stare as the column howled by, perhaps thinking they were mercenaries under contract to the Solace government.

Twice an aircar appeared in the far distance. A tribarrel in air defense mode ripped each out of the sky.

The Masterton River here was twenty meters wide, too narrow to rate as a river back on Friesland. Even so, it carried more tumbling water than Huber'd have wanted to take his combat cars over without being sure of a ford.

No need to cross, of course. There was plenty of room on the broad bottom terrace to form on a platoon front. *Foghorn* came up on the right of *Fencing Master,* with Gabinus' Three-eight and *Fancy Pants* falling in alongside.

Funnel-mouthed fish weirs lined both banks. The small boys tipping them up to check the catch turned to watch the passing armored vehicles. *Fencing Master* still set the pace. Padova continued to accelerate now that they were no longer descending the slope.

The town, Millhouse Crossing, was two rows of buildings which began as a straggle of shacks with board walls and roofs of corrugated plastic. Further on the houses were masonry and two or three stories high. The road was barely wide enough for the recovery vehicle, and even the combat cars would have to go through one at a time.

A black-and-yellow Solace flag flew over the cupola of a building in the center of town. All the F-3 vehicles fired as soon as the guardpost came in view, shattering the stuccoed limestone in dazzles of cyan and white.

Chickens were running in nervous circles in the street. A cart and small tractor stood forlorn beside a roofed marketplace on the inland side. The cart was half-loaded, but its owner and every other human in Millhouse Crossing was trying to hide.

"Highball, form on Three-six in line ahead," Huber said. "We'll go back to platoon front on the—"

As *Fencing Master* drew ahead again, Deseau decided he had a fair shot at the facade of the guardpost—and took it. He was more right than not, placing most of his ten-round burst in the ground floor of the government building, though a pair of 2-cm bolts blew in the arched entryway of the private house next door.

"—other side of town. Six out."

Huber swiveled his gun so that it covered building fronts a hundred meters ahead on his side. Padova brushed a pair of shacks that'd been built closer to the road than most of the row, knocking them to scrap. A sheet of plywood flipped outward and slapped down over a screened intake on *Fencing Master*'s port side; it clung there, partially blocking the duct, till Padova deliberately swerved through another shack and swept the debris off. A brief snowstorm of chicken feathers sprayed from beneath the skirts.

They howled past a house painted pale green. In the corner of his eye Huber saw a white face staring from the interior. The spectator was no threat, and besides Huber's attention was focused on the magnified image of buildings well in the distance. A sniper directly alongside would be for *Foghorn*'s gunners to deal with.

Learoyd's gun hammered, the bolts' intense cyan reflecting from the soft pastels of the building fronts. His burst fanned the interior of the government building which Deseau's gun had already set alight. As *Fencing Master* passed, orange flame *whuffed!* from the window openings, a gas stove adding its note to the ongoing destruction.

Fencing Master hit the cart in the roadway, flinging its contents into the air, and bunted the tractor through the lightly framed market stalls. Huber flinched reflexively as cans of meat bounced off the armor beside him. Civilians scrambled out of the wreckage running in circles much as the chickens had moments before.

The rest of the way was clear. Padova kept *Fencing Master* on the raised roadbed through the village, then dropped into the left-hand paddy at a slant to let the rest of the platoon fall in beside them. High-pressure air squirting from beneath the plenum chambers excavated furrows twice the width of the vehicles themselves, gouging out the young rice.

The crop could be replanted; the damaged buildings could be repaired. In a few years, people in Millhouse Crossing would no longer talk about the day Hammer's Slammers roared through. Nothing really matters but life itself, and death.

The village was twelve kilometers from the mouth of the valley. According to the terrain display, the Masterton River dropped twenty meters in the next five hundred, boiling over a series of cataracts that closed it to navigation, and from there meandered another eight klicks to Hundred Hectare Lake.

In the geologic past the lake had been of twice its present area. When the water drained, the original shoreline remained as a limestone escarpment on the south and western margins. Though never more than a few meters high, it was sufficient to cover an artillery regiment against powerguns firing from the Masterton Valley.

Under other circumstances, Huber might've considered taking his combat cars in a balls-to-the-wall charge across the farmland south of the lake. The Firelords' calliopes, emplaced on the escarpment and manned by professionals, made that notion suicide.

Another option—the one Huber would've picked—was to have halted well beyond the twenty-kilometer range of the Firelords' bombardment rockets and let Battery Alpha clear the problem. Again the calliopes were the difficulty. Saturating the Firelords' air defenses would require much of the ammunition the battery was carrying, and there wouldn't be any resupply until after—and if—the Regiment captured Port Plattner.

Which left the third option, Flasher Six dealing with the Firelords in his own good time and fashion, while Task Force Huber took whatever was thrown at them. Maybe next time his troopers'd be dishing it out while somebody else drew fire....

The sensor display gave Huber the warning: not movement but a radio signal from the hills overlooking the broad pass to the north. A Solace lookout was signaling back to headquarters near the lakeside.

"Highball!" Huber called. He didn't aim his own gun; he had other duties. "Tar—"

Deseau must've expected an outpost and set his AI to caret RF sources. Most civilians would be using land lines, but a mercenary unit would generally depend on its own communications system. While Huber was still speaking, Frenchie acted. A three-round ranging burst hiss/CRACKed from his tribarrel, vivid even in sunlight.

"—get at vector zero-seven degrees, radio trans—"

Nobody was good enough to hit a target ten kilometers away with his first shot. Deseau adjusted his aim, dialed up the magnification on his holographic sights, and engaged the gun's stabilizer. Learoyd leaned over his own gun, importing the target information from Deseau's weapon instead of duplicating the effort.

"—mitter. Fire at—"

Deseau and Learoyd fired together. Their tribarrels spat streams in near parallel, merging optically as they snapped through the sunlight ahead of the task force.

"—will!"

The distant slope winked—cyan from the impacting plasma, red and gushing gray steam where brush burned explosively. There was a burp of orange and the radio signal cut off.

"Got 'em!" Deseau shouted as he and Learoyd took their thumbs from their triggers. He wasn't on intercom, but Huber could easily hear his excited voice. "Got the bastards!"

Fancy Pants and Three-eight ripped ropes of blue-green hellfire toward the pass. A stretch of hillside where the vegetation was dry began to burn with some enthusiasm. Another gun, this one from F-2 aiming past the X-Ray vehicles, joined in.

"Cease fire!" Huber ordered. "Six to Highball, cease fire! Save your gunbarrels, troopers, because we're going to need them bad. Out!"

"*Here it comes,*" Deseau said, reading the flicker of saffron from beyond the mouth of the valley. "*For what we are about to receive, the Lord make us thankful.*"

The sensor suite analyzed the sound some ten seconds after Frenchie had correctly identified the exhaust flashes reflected from clouds of dust: rocket motors igniting, sixty of them rippling in groups of six every second. A Firelord battery had just launched half the rockets on its six trucks.

"Fox elements," Huber said, "put all your guns, I repeat *all* your guns in air defense mode. Have your backup weapons ready to deal with ground threats."

He pressed his hands against his armored chest to keep from balling them into fists till they cramped.

"Troopers," he went on, "this is going to be hard but we're going to do it. Hold station on Three-six, watch for problems on the ground, and let our gunnery computers do their job. They can handle it if anything can. Six out. Break."

The armored vehicles bucked through the muck of the paddies, throwing up curtains of spray to the rear and sides. The mid-afternoon sun struck it into rainbows, dazzlingly beautiful over the bright green rice plants.

"Padova," Huber continued, "keep picking up the pace as long as the rest of Highball can stay with us. Don't let 'em string out, but the Firelords may not have us under direct observation. I'd like to be somewhere other than where they calculate. Out."

"*Roger*," the driver said. She sounded focused but not concerned. Huber couldn't tell without checking whether *Fencing Master*'s speed increased, but he figured he'd delegated the decision to the person best able to make it.

Deseau set the tribarrels on air defense; the guns lifted their triple muzzles toward the northern sky like hounds casting for a distant scent. He took his 2-cm weapon out of the clip that held it to his gun's pintle; Learoyd held his sub-machine gun in his right hand as he snapped the loading tube out of the receiver, then in again to make sure it had locked home. Huber grinned tightly and drew his own 2-cm weapon from its muzzle-down nest between ammo boxes at the rear of the compartment.

All the tribarrels in the task force opened fire, their barrel clusters rotating as they slashed the northern sky. The Command and Control box coordinated the cars' individual AIs so that all the incoming missiles were hit without duplication. Red flashes and soot-black smoke filled the air beyond the mouth of the valley. A rocket, gutted but not destroyed, spun in a vertical helix and plunged back the way it had come.

The guns fell silent; then Deseau's weapon stuttered another four-round burst. A final rocket exploded, much closer than the smoky graveyard of its fellows. The tribarrel originally tasked with that target must have jammed before it finished the job, so Frenchie's gun was covering.

"*Hold for a jolt!*" Padova called, her voice rising.

The sky ahead flashed yellow-gray again, silhouetting the hills. For a moment Huber, focused on the C&C display, thought the driver also meant the next inbound salvo.

Fencing Master's bow lifted, spilling pressure. The combat car hurtled onward on inertia, its skirts skimming but not slamming straight into the cross dike which had just appeared at the end of the paddy.

Fencing Master came down like a dropped plate. The Lord's *Blood!* but they hit. Padova'd executed the maneuver perfectly, but there was no way you could sail thirty tonnes of iridium into watery muck and the passengers have a good time. Huber had the coaming in his left hand and his tribarrel's gunshield in his right; otherwise he'd have hurtled out of the compartment.

"Padova, slow down!" Huber bellowed, though the driver had already cut back on the car's speed by bringing the fan nacelles closer to vertical. "Highball, watch for the fucking dike here! Six out!"

He glanced to the right to see how the other cars of the platoon had handled the obstruction. Three-eight's driver had negotiated it flawlessly and was still parallel to *Fencing Master*. Sergeant Tranter must've seen the dike coming and warned his driver, because *Fancy Pants* had slowed to climb it in rulebook fashion and was now lurching down the other side.

Foghorn had tried to plow straight through. The dike was only a hand's breadth above the water and some forty centimeters down to the floor of the paddy. It was a meter thick, though, and over the width of a combat car's skirts even mud weighed several tonnes. The crew in the fighting compartment were all down, though the left wing gunner was trying to lift himself with a hand on the coaming. The car wallowed; the driver'd lost control when the shock curtains deployed automatically to save his life.

All the tribarrels fired again, those mounted on *Foghorn* along with the rest; the impact hadn't affected the gunnery computer. That was a good thing, because this time the Firelords had launched 240 rounds, a battalion half-emptying its racks.

Plasma bolts stabbed home. Flame and dirty smoke spread across the sky in a solid mass, replacing the dispersing rags of the previous salvo.

"Sir, I didn't see the wall!" Padova said. *"Via, sir, I'm sorry!"*

"Roger that," Huber said. F-3 had gotten straightened out and was cautiously accelerating across the second paddy. Nagano and both his wing gunners were on their feet again, though *Foghorn*'s guns pecked the sky in short bursts regardless of what the crew was doing. The X-Ray element had reached the dike and was crossing in good order, in part because of the holes the combat cars had torn. "Drive on."

The crackling roar of the first salvo's destruction rolled over Task Force Huber as the second flashed and spurted a little nearer. The tribarrels continued to fire, switching from target to fresh target as the rockets curved downward. The math was easy—two hundred and forty incoming projectiles, twenty-four guns to sweep them out of the sky—

Or not.

The left wing gun spun and stopped. It was properly Huber's weapon, but Deseau was at it before Huber could react. Without even a pause to check the gun's diagnostics, Deseau snatched open the feed trough and used his knifeblade to lever out the disk that'd kinked and jammed. Grinning at Huber, he charged the gun and stepped back as it resumed blasting cyan bolts through barrels already white hot.

Huber tensed, waiting for the third salvo; possibly more than a thousand rockets, launched against combat cars whose guns were dangerously hot from dealing with the previous hundreds of projectiles. Instead, cyan light flickered behind the hills. Moments later, rolling orange fireballs mushroomed in response.

"*Highball, this is Flasher Six,*" the unfamiliar voice called. The tone of crowing triumph was evident despite the compressed and tenuous transmission. "*Thanks for your help, troopers. We've got it from now. Flasher out.*"

"*The hell he says!*" Deseau snarled, turning a furious face toward Huber. "*El-Tee, are you going to let them tankers have all the fun? We're not, are we?*"

Another volley of 20-cm bolts speared into the plains from higher ground somewhere to the northeast. Again whole truckloads of bombardment rockets exploded, the fuel and warheads going off in split seconds. Flasher Six commanded at least a company of tanks; their main guns were raking the Firelords, probably from beyond the distance an unaided human eye could see.

Tribarrels didn't have that range… but the combat cars weren't nearly that far away, either. Huber checked the terrain display and made an instant decision. *Like Frenchie says, why should the tankers have all the fun?*

"Highball, this is Six," he said. He might get in trouble for this in the after-action debriefing, but that would be a long time coming—if he survived. "X-Ray elements will halt inside the valley at point Delta Michael Four-one, Three-seven. India elements will dismount to provide security. Fox elements will take hull-down positions in the valley mouth—"

The C&C display obligingly detailed firing positions west of the river for each of the eight combat cars.

"—and engage the enemy. Hit the calliopes first, troopers, and any vehicles that aren't running—but my guess is that with the panzers shooting them up they're going to have forgotten about us till we give 'em reason to remember. Six out."

Padova tilted her fans for greater forward thrust. Lieutenant Messeman's cars were passing through the X-Ray element, slewing from side to side in the wakes of the big vehicles. The terraces narrowed on the steeper slopes above the cataracts; the C&C box had set their course along the road in line ahead now that air defense was no longer the primary concern.

Huber hadn't taken the guns out of air defense mode, though, because there was still a chance that the Firelords would try to carry their enemies with them to Hell. A slim chance. They were all mercenaries; their war was a business, not a holy crusade.

Sensor suites gave the task force few details of what to expect in the plains below. At this distance electronic and sonic signatures couldn't pinpoint targets, and the cars didn't have a line of sight. Obviously Flasher had the enemy under direct observation, but the link between the tank unit and Highball was too marginal for complex data transmission.

There shouldn't be a big problem. The artillerymen were so busy getting out of the frying pan that they weren't going to worry about the fire.

Because of the angle, F-2's cars were in position before *Fencing Master* tore through the stunted nut trees on the upper slope. Messeman's gunners opened fire while Deseau screamed angry curses at Padova. She ignored him, swinging them with necessary caution around a spur of rock into the position the AI had chosen. Here they'd be sheltered from possible snipers higher up the hill.

The plains beyond were full of targets. After a volley into their rocket-laden trucks had put the Firelords off-balance, Flasher concentrated on the calliopes in firing positions on the lip of the escarpment. The multi-barreled 3-cm powerguns could be dangerous even to tanks at long range. Main gun bolts had blown all of the calliopes to shimmering vapor before the combat cars nosed over the rise, but there were enough other things to shoot at.

Huber swung his tribarrel onto a ten-wheeled truck trying to flee through a field of sorghum. He squeezed and watched his plasma snap in cyan brilliance across the bed loaded with bombardment rockets in five forward-slanting racks. Before the third bolt hit, the vehicle erupted into rolling orange fury, searing a black circle from the crops.

The Firelords had set up between the ridge and the lakeside, shielded from the task force. When the tanks began to rake them from the flank and rear, some of the hundreds of vehicles—not just rocket trucks but also the command, service, and transportation vehicles that an artillery regiment requires—tried to escape west along the lake's margin. Others—the truck Huber hit was one—had climbed out of the bowl and spread out across the fields.

Another volley of 20-cm bolts lashed the milling chaos, setting off further secondary explosions. The billowing flames and blast-flung debris curtained the survivors to some degree from the tanks fifty, eighty—maybe over a hundred kilometers distant, but the combat cars had good visibility.

Huber ripped a tank truck. It turned out to be a water purification vehicle, not a fuel tanker, but it gushed steam and began to burn anyway.

Three white flares burst over the center of the encampment. A man jumped onto the TOC, a cluster of sandbagged trailers, waving a towel—beige, but Huber understood—over his head. All around him was blazing wreckage, but apart from a few hits by 2-cm bolts the TOC had been spared. The Slammers had concentrated on targets that'd give the greatest value in terms of secondary explosions, and there was no lack of those in an artillery regiment.

"*Enemy commander!*" said a hoarse voice. Huber's AI noted that the fellow was broadcasting on several frequencies, desperately hoping that one would get through to the gunners shooting his troops like ducks in a barrel. "*The Firelords surrender on standard terms. I repeat, we surrender on terms. Cease fire! Cease fire!*"

"Highball, cease fire!" Huber repeated, and as he did so another volley of tank bolts lanced into the lakeside with fresh mushroomings of flame. Flasher couldn't pick up the radio signal—a truckload of exploding rockets had knocked down the transmitter masts—and the white flares could be easily overlooked in the general fiery destruction.

"Flasher Six!" Huber shouted, the AI switching his transmission to the ionization track system. "Cease fire! All Flasher units, cease fire! They're surrendering!"

Explosions continued to rumble in the plains below, but the ice-pick sharpness of plasma bolts no longer added to it. Even before they got Huber's warning, the Flasher gunners would've noticed that Highball had stopped firing. A blast had knocked the officer with the towel to his knees, but he kept his hand high and waving.

"Firelords, this is Slammers command," Huber said, responding on the highest of the frequencies the Firelords had used. He *wasn't* in command, of course, Flasher Six was, but the tanker couldn't communicate with the poor bastards down below. "We accept your parole. Hold in place until my superiors can make arrangements for your exchange. Ah, that may be several days. We will not, I repeat not, be halting at this location. Slammers over."

"Roger, Slammers," the enemy commander said, relief and weariness both evident in his voice. "We've got enough to occupy us here for longer than a few fucking days. Can you spare us medical personnel? Over."

"Negative, Firelords," Huber said. "I hope your next contract works out better for you. Slammers out."

He lifted off his commo helmet and closed his eyes, letting reaction wash over him. He was exhausted, not from physical exertion—though there'd been plenty of that, jolting around in the fighting compartment during the run—but from the adrenaline blazing in him as shells rained down and he could do nothing but watch and pray his equipment worked.

He settled the helmet back in place and said, "Booster," to activate the C&C box, "plot our course north from this location."

On the plains below, fuel and munitions continued to erupt. It didn't make Huber feel much better to realize that the destruction would've been just as bad if those rockets had landed on Task Force Huber instead of going off in their racks.

It was an hour short of full darkness, but stars showed around the eastern horizon; stars, and perhaps one or more of the planet's seven small moons. Sunset silhouetted the three grain elevators a kilometer to the west where monorail lines merged at a railhead. Timers had turned on the mercury vapor lights attached to the service catwalks as the task force arrived, but there was no sign of life in the huge structures or the houses at their base.

"Suppose we oughta do a little reconnaissance by fire, El-Tee?" Deseau said hopefully. He patted his tribarrel's receiver.

Padova and Learoyd slept on the ground beside *Fencing Master*. They hadn't strung the tarp, just spread it over the stubble as a ground cloth. The car's idling drive fans whispered a trooper's lullaby.

"Do I think you should use up another set of barrels just because you like to see things burn, Frenchie?" Huber said, smiling faintly. "No, I don't. We'll have plenty to shoot at for real in a few hours, don't worry."

A tribarrel across the perimeter snarled a short burst. Huber jerked his head around, following the line of fire to a flash in the distant sky.

"*Highball, Fox Two-six,*" Lieutenant Messeman reported. "*Air defense splashed an aircar, that's all. Out.*"

Probably civilians who hadn't gotten the word that a Slammers task force had driven into the heart of their country. Huber'd lost count of the number of aircars they'd shot down on this run; thirty-odd, he thought, but poppers always washed the past out of his mind. He needed the stimulant a lot more than he needed to remember what was over and done with, that was for sure.

The tracked excavator whined thunderously as it dug in the second of the six hogs. The note of its cutting head dopplered up and down, its speed depending on the depth of the cut and the number of rocks in the soil.

The task force was carrying minimal supplies, so the excavator didn't have plasticizer to add to the earth it spewed in an arc forward of the cut. The berm would still stop small arms and shell fragments. If Battery Alpha needed more than that, the Colonel had lost his gamble and the troopers of Task Force Huber were probably dead meat.

Lieutenant Basingstoke, half a dozen of his people, and three techs from the recovery vehicle, stood beside the hog whose starboard fans had cut out twice during the run. Sergeant Tranter had joined them. He wasn't in Maintenance anymore, but neither was he a man to ignore a problem he could help with just because it'd stopped being his job.

Huber looked westward. Lights were on in the spaceport seven klicks away, backlighting the smooth hillcrest between it and Task Force Huber.

He could imagine the panic at Port Plattner, military and civilians reacting to the unexpected threat in as many ways as there were officials involved. They'd be trying to black out the facilities, not that it would make much difference to the Slammers' optics, but they hadn't yet succeeded. The port was designed to be illuminated for round-the-clock ship landings. Nobody'd planned for what to do when a hostile armored regiment drove a thousand kilometers to attack from all sides.

The sky continued to darken. Huber always felt particularly lonely at night; in daytime he could pretend almost any landscape was a part of Nieuw Friesland that he just hadn't seen before, but the stars were inescapably alien.

Grinning wryly at himself, he said, "Frenchie, hold the fort till I'm back. I'm going to talk to the redlegs."

Another thought struck him and he said, "Fox Two-six, this is Six. Join me and Rocker One-six. Out."

He lifted himself from the fighting compartment as Messeman responded with a laconic, "*Roger.*"

The cutting head hummed to idle as the excavator backed up the ramp from the gun position it'd just dug. Waddling like a bulldog, it followed the sergeant from the engineer section as he walked backward to guide it to the next pit. A hog drove into the just-completed gun position and shut down its fans. The hull was below the original surface level, and the howitzer's barrel slanted up at twenty degrees to clear the berm.

Huber nodded to the munitions trucks loaded with 200-mm rockets. He said to Lieutenant Basingstoke, "I hope the engineers have time to dig those in too, Lieutenant. After watching what happened to the Firelords when their ammo started going off."

"If we begin firing at maximum rate…" Basingstoke said. He was a tall, hollow-cheeked man. His pale blond hair made him look older than he was, but Huber suspected he'd never really been young. "We'll expend all the ammunition we've carried in less than ten minutes. No doubt that will reduce the risk."

He smiled like a skull. Huber smiled back when he realized that the artillery officer had made a joke.

Lieutenant Messeman trotted over, looking back toward his cars and speaking into his commo helmet on the F-2 frequency. He turned and glared at Huber, not really angry but the sort of little man who generally sounded as though he was.

"Any word on when we'll be moving?" he demanded. "We *are* moving, aren't we? We're not going to have to nursemaid the artillery while the rest of the Regiment attacks?"

Basingstoke stiffened. Before he could speak—and they were all tired, but Blood and Martyrs, didn't Messeman have any sense at all?—Huber snapped, "We're going to leave the two combat cars which I determine to be sufficient for air defense, Lieutenant. That's one from each platoon. Personally, I expect to be thankful for all the artillery support we can get when we attack."

Messeman grimaced but shrugged. "Yeah, I'll leave Two-four. The patch we put on the plenum chamber after the breakout's starting to crack. They can use the time to weld it properly."

"Seven kilometers," Basingstoke said, glancing to the west. The crest showed up more sharply against the port lighting as the sky darkened. "That's closer to the target than I care to be, but—"

He gave the other officers another skull smile.

"—I've been glad to have the combat cars' company for as long as possible, and I realize that means following you to your attack positions."

Tranter crawled out of an access hatch in the hog's plenum chamber. He was a big, red-haired man who moved so gracefully that you generally forgot that his right leg was a biomechanical replacement for the one severed when a tank fell off a jack.

"Got it, Lieutenant!" he called cheerfully to Basingstoke. "They pinched a cable when they replaced your Starboard Three, so when the nacelles're canted hard right you get a short. The wrenches'll have it rerouted in ten minutes."

"Three-eight'll be staying here with the hogs, Sergeant," Huber said, looking over his shoulder. The combat cars faced outward around the artillery vehicles. The circuit was too open for defense against serious ground attack but admirably suited to stop incoming shells and possible Solace infiltrators. If the Waldheim Dragoons and the scattering of Militiamen and other mercenaries in Port Plattner mounted an attack before the Regiment was ready to strike, the cars' sensor suites would give Huber sufficient warning to change his dispositions.

"Roger," Tranter said, nodding. "Ah, El-Tee? Can I swap out Chisum on Three-eight for Stoddard on my car? Stoddard pukes every time he takes a popper, so he's pretty washed out after this run."

"Right, the cars here'll be in air defense mode unless a lot of wheels fall off," Huber said, frowning to hear that Stoddard couldn't take stimulants. That didn't handicap a trooper quite as badly as blindness would, but it wasn't something a platoon leader wanted to hear about a useful man. "Want me to…?"

"I'll tell him," Tranter said, throwing Huber a brilliant smile again as he strode off to inform Chisum and Gabinus, Three-eight's commander. Tranter wore a slip-over shoe on his right foot to raise it to the height of the boot on his left, giving his leg movements an unbalanced look.

The excavator started on a fifth gun pit. Messeman watched a hog slide into the one just completed with the delicacy required by tight quarters. He said, "Ah, Six? Will we be getting a view of the target before we go in?"

"What I've been told," Huber said, "is that they'll launch a commo and observation constellation just before we drop the hammer. They're estimating that the new satellites will survive two minutes, certainly no more than five. That's why they're saving it till everything's ready."

Messeman sighed. "Sure, makes sense," he said. "I like to tell my people what we're getting into, that's all."

"Tell them there's nobody on the planet as good as they are, Lieutenant," Huber said. His glance took in Lieutenant Basingstoke as well. "We proved that getting here. Tell them one more push and we'll be able to stand down."

Messeman and Basingstoke nodded agreement; Huber gave them a thumbs-up and headed back to *Fencing Master*.

It was true, as far as it went: one push and a stand-down.

If they survived.

And until the next time.

Automatic weapons had been firing from the port area at intervals ever since sunset three hours ago. Occasional tracers ricocheted high enough to be seen over the hills. Less often, a tribarrel flickered across the cloud bases like distant cyan lightning. That'd be another task force splashing an aircar or something equally insignificant… except for the poor bastards on the receiving end.

The alert signal at the upper left corner of Huber's faceshield was the first message he'd gotten from Central since the fire mission before they'd reached the Solace Highlands. He let out his breath in a gasp.

There might not have been a Central anymore. Base Alpha might have fallen and the Solace forces begun mopping up the Slammers task force by task force, bringing to bear as much weight as they needed to crush each hard nut. Huber'd kept his fear below the surface of his mind, but it'd been there nonetheless.

"All units, prepare to receive orders and target information," said a voice as emotionless as the surf on a rocky shore. *"Don't get ahead of your start times, and once you commit don't, I repeat do not, stop shooting until you're told to. Regiment One out."*

The data dump started at once, progressing for thirty seconds instead of concluding instantaneously. Satellite reconnaissance was updating the information at the same time those satellites transmitted it to the Regiment's scattered elements. Port

Plattner, an oval five kilometers by three, expanded on the Command and Control display. There'd been six warehouse complexes spaced about the perimeter when the satellites shut down thirty-six hours before; now there was a seventh beside the huge starship on northwest edge, twelve large temporary buildings with more under construction.

"Regiment One? That's Major Steuben," Deseau muttered, unusually worried for him. *"Is he in fucking charge now?"*

"Shut up, Frenchie," Huber snapped as he scrolled through the download. He was more irritated than he'd have been if a newbie like Padova had made the comment. Deseau should've known they didn't have enough data to guess what was going on. Steuben might be in command of Base Alpha because his White Mice were defending it, but that didn't mean the Colonel and Major Pritchard were casualties.

It didn't mean they *weren't* casualties, either.

"Right!" Huber muttered when he had the situation clear. At least it was clear enough that he knew staring at it longer wasn't going to change anything in a good way. "Red and Blue elements—"

F-2 and F-3 respectively, each with a squad of infantry in support.

"—will proceed to designated positions on the reverse slope—"

The download from Central set out the east side of the terminal building as the general objective for Highball's action elements, but Central hadn't known what strength Huber would have available for the attack. Huber's C&C box had broken the assignment into individual targets. Losing two cars and six infantry was probably better than Operations had calculated, though under normal circumstances twenty percent was a horrendous casualty rate.

"—and hold there till two-two-three-seven hours, when—"

Battery Alpha opened fire, loosing thunder and the long crackling lightning of sustainer motors as the missiles streaked west so low that they barely cleared the ridgeline. The hogs rocked from the backblasts, slamming their skirts against the hard clay substrate.

"—we'll cross the crest and attack our objectives at forty kph. White element under Sergeant Marano—"

The remaining two combat cars and eleven infantry—some of whom were walking wounded only if they didn't have to walk very far.

"—remains here to provide security for the X-Ray element. Any questions? Over."

"Let's do it, El-Tee," Sergeant Nagano said. He raised his gauntleted left hand from *Foghorn*, the thumb up.

"Roger that," Huber said, after a ten-second pause to be sure that nobody had anything substantive to add. "Move out, troopers. Keep it slow till we're in position, and nobody crosses the start line till it's time. Six out."

Fencing Master started forward, barely ambling. The other cars—particularly Messeman's trio from the east arc of the circle—had farther to go to get into position. Padova wasn't letting eagerness make her screw up.

The bone-shaking roar of the rocket howitzers paused on a long snarl as the last of the six rounds in the ready magazines streaked westward. Another battery took up the bombardment as Basingstoke's hogs cycled missiles from their storage magazines in the rear hull into their turrets to resume firing.

The hogs were launching firecracker rounds, anti-personnel cargo shells designed to dump thousands of bomblets each. Powerguns from the port's air defenses stabbed the sky for several seconds, bursting all the incoming rounds before they could open over the target. Then one got through.

Huber knew what it was like on the ground—and what it would've been like for Task Force Huber if the Firelords had gotten lucky with their less-sophisticated equivalents. When the bomblets swept over the defenses as a sea of white fire, shrapnel would kill the crews and disable gun mechanisms. Then the next round—and the next twenty rounds—would get through.

The cars aligned themselves to the right of *Fencing Master* at twenty-meter intervals. The eighteen infantrymen were twenty meters behind, their skimmers bobbling in the wake of the cars. They looked hopelessly vulnerable to Huber, but he knew from conversations that most infantrymen regarded combat cars as big targets, and tanks as bigger targets yet. They'd come in handy for clearing the terminal building, if they got that far.

Padova raised her speed to ten kph but didn't accelerate further. Huber frowned with instinctive impatience, then understood. "Highball," he said, "we're timing—"

Padova was timing.

"—our approach so we'll reach our attack positions at exactly the time to go over the crest. That way we'll already have forward inertia instead of lifting from a halt. Six out, break."

His frown deepened as he continued, "Trooper Padova, using initiative is fine, but don't play games or you'll be playing them in another unit. Tell me what you're planning the next time, all right?"

"*Sorry, sir,*" the driver said, sounding like she meant it. "*I wasn't… sorry, it won't happen again.*"

The cars and skimmers passed to the south of the grain elevators and their clustered dwellings. Deseau looked back over his shoulder, his hand resting lightly on the butt of his 2-cm weapon. If a sniper or Solace artillery observer appeared among the buildings now, the forward tribarrel wouldn't bear on it.

Huber smiled wryly. Frenchie was an optimistic man, in his way.

A line of posts supported plastic netting and a top strand of barbed wire, fencing to keep pastured cattle from straying into the railhead. All six cars hit it within an eyeblink of one another, smashing the fence down with no more trouble than they took with the spiky bushes which dotted the cropped grassland on the other side. Huber had been ready to duck if the wire flew toward him, but instead it curled around the next post to the left.

Learoyd was singing, mostly under his breath so it didn't trip the intercom. Occasional phrases buzzed in Huber's ears: "*… and best… lost sinners was slain.…*"

Fencing Master accelerated smoothly despite the increasing slope. The fans were biting deeper, but their note didn't change because Padova matched her blade incidence flawlessly against the increased power she was dialing in. The cars were nearing the crest. On the other side, sparkling explosions backlit stubble and the thicket of brush which grew from exposed rocks where mowers couldn't reach.

A salvo from Battery Alpha shrieked overhead, so deafeningly close that *Fencing Master* shimmied. Huber's exposed skin prickled and he heard an abrasive snarl against his helmet. He didn't know whether he was feeling debris from the exhaust or grit swept up from the ground by the shells' passage. Deseau shouted in angry surprise, though there was no real harm done.

It would've been a bad time to cross the ridge ahead of orders, though. A really bad time.

"Highball…" Huber said, judging the time by *Fencing Master*'s speed, not the clock he could call onto his faceshield if he wanted to.

"Execute!"

Battery Alpha's salvo of cargo shells opened just on the other side of the ridge. This close, the red flashes of the charges that expelled the contents were startlingly visible. The bomblets scattered on separate ballistic courses toward the terminal, detonating like so many thousand grenades just as the combat cars came over the rise. From where Huber watched, three kilometers away, the sea of glittering white radiance was beautiful.

His helmet gave him targets, first a calliope dug into the ground at the edge of the meters-thick concrete pad which supported starships as they landed and lifted off. Huber put a burst into it, his plasma glancing from the iridium gunbarrels but vaporizing the steel frame and trunnion. The gun was silent, its barrels already cooled to red heat: bomblets had killed its crew or driven it to cover.

Powerguns slashed the port's flat concrete expanse from all directions, tribarrels and the tanks' 20-cm main guns. Buildings, vehicles, and stacks of cargo on the immense concrete pad were burning.

There were over twenty starships on the pad. They weren't deliberate targets, but bolts splashed them with cyan highlights.

As Huber switched his aim to a wheeled vehicle racing away from the terminal, a last salvo struck the temporary buildings being erected next to the starship in the northwest. Nothing happened for a moment because instead of bomblets the rounds carried fuel-air warheads.

The delayed blast spilled air from *Fencing Master*'s plenum chamber and slammed the car down hard. Huber shouted, instinctively afraid that he'd been flung out of the fighting compartment. He bashed his chest into the grips of his tribarrel. The clamshell armor saved his ribs, but he'd have bruises in the morning.

Padova got them under weigh again, straightening their course; the blast had slewed the car a quarter-turn clockwise while shock curtains deployed around the driver. A column of kinked black smoke rose from where the shells had landed.

The pad wasn't cratered: the explosive had spread in a thin smooth sheet before it went off, and concrete has great compression strength. The structures which had covered more than a thousand square meters of the pad were gone except for twisted fragments which had fallen back after the blast blew everything skyward. The starship, thick-hulled and weighing over 150,000 tonnes, appeared undamaged. The valves had been wrenched off the two open cargo hatches, however.

Huber found the truck he'd been aiming at; the shockwave had shoved it into the loading dock which extended from the back of the terminal building. He gave it a three-round burst from reflex, watching it burst into flames as his AI found him something more useful to shoot at.

Deseau and Learoyd were firing at gun positions on the roof of the terminal, though nothing moved there except the haze of smoke from the anti-personnel bomblets which had gone off seconds before. Instead of a nearby target, Huber's helmet targeted a line of vehicles on the northern edge of the pad. At least a company of the Waldheim Dragoons were using blast deflectors as breastworks against the Slammers attacking from that side. Tribarrels on the Waldheim APCs and 10-cm powerguns on their tanks stabbed the distant hills.

The walls now raised from the pad were meant to deflect a giant starship's full takeoff thrust skyward so it wouldn't knock down everything within a kilometer. The structures were sufficient to stop even a 20-cm bolt, but the cars approaching from southeast had a clear shot at the sheltering vehicles.

Huber set the target and brought up his sight's magnification. He was using light amplification rather than thermal viewing; the many fires dotting the port's flat expanse provided more than enough illumination. When his pipper centered on a tank's turret ring, he thumbed the trigger and let the stabilizer hold his bolts on target. The tank's own ammunition blew it up in a cyan flash.

Huber shifted to the next target over, an APC rocking in the shockwave of the tank's destruction. Before he could fire, a 20-cm bolt hit the lightly armored vehicle and sprayed molten blobs of it a hundred meters away.

Fencing Master continued to advance. The ten-story terminal building blocked Huber's line of sight to the Dragoons; his faceshield careted windows instead. He squeezed, slewing the tribarrel to help the car's forward motion draw his burst across the seventh floor from left to right. The rooms were dark till the bolts hit, but gulps of orange flame followed each cyan flash as plasma ignited the furnishings.

An equipment park on the southwest side of the pad had taken a pasting from incendiaries. Hundreds of vehicles were alight. Every so often one erupted with greater enthusiasm like a bubble rising in a caldera to scatter blazing rock high in the air. Eight combat cars skirted the park to the south, moving fast. Their tribarrels raked the back side of the terminal building.

At the beginning of the war, Solace had started building concrete-roofed dugouts at intervals around the perimeter of Port Plattner. The work had stopped when Solace Command realized that the Outer States were barely capable of defense, and even those completed—three of them in the sector Central had assigned to Huber's troops—appeared to be unmanned.

Deseau and Learoyd had burned the firing slit of the southernmost to twice its original size. Now as *Fencing Master* swept around the squat structure, Learoyd depressed his tribarrel and fired a long burst down the entrance ramp at the back. The steel door gushed red sparks and ruptured inward, but there was no secondary explosion.

White flares popped from the roof of the terminal building. More flares followed from a dozen points across Port Plattner, including the northern perimeter where the Waldheim Dragoons had been fighting. "*UC forces, we surrender!*" a woman's voice cried. "*Terminal control surrenders, by the Lord's mercy we surrender!*"

She must have been using the port's starship communications system because her high-output transmission blanketed all frequencies. Every floor of the terminal building was ablaze, but those were merely administrative offices. The actual control room was in a sub-basement, armored against the chance of a starship crash.

Fencing Master turned left, away from the base of the terminal. Padova dropped the car twice onto the sodded lawn to scrub off inertia that wanted to carry them into the burning building. The other Highball cars were braking in roostertails of red sparks as their skirts skidded on concrete. The terminal was a tower of flame, lashing the ground with pulses of heat.

"*Sir, what should I do!*" Padova said. They were moving slowly south along the face of the building, crushing ornamental shrubs under their skirts. *Foghorn* and *Fancy Pants* followed, while Lieutenant Messeman's cars had halted on the other side of a wing-shaped entrance marquee which extended twenty meters from the front entrance.

"*All Slammers units,*" a familiar voice growled. "*This is Regiment Six, troopers. Cease fire unless you're fired on. Under no circumstances fire on the starships that'll start land-ing shortly. Hammer out.*"

Deseau tracked a man running across the pad to the left. He didn't shoot, but he was touching the trigger. Huber hooked a thumb to back him off, then said, "High-ball, we'll laager a hundred meters back the way we came. Infantry in the center of the circle."

He looked at the plot the C&C box suggested, approved it, and concluded, "Six out."

That was far enough from the terminal building that they wouldn't broil, though Huber wanted to keep Highball reasonably close to its objective until somebody got around to ordering them to move. The Lord knew when that'd be, given what the Colonel and his staff had on their plate right now.

The eight vehicles crossing the pad from the west slowed as they approached the terminal. Huber's eyes narrowed: one was a command car, a high-sided box built on the chassis of a combat car to hold far more communications and display options than could be fitted into a C&C box. Mostly they were staff vehicles, though Huber knew a couple of line company commanders preferred them to combat cars.

The shooting had probably stopped, though it was hard to say because munitions continued to explode. That wouldn't end for days, not with the number of fires burning across the huge port. You could get killed just as dead when a truck blew up as you could by somebody aiming at you....

That reminded Huber of casualties. He checked the readout on his faceshield and saw to his pleasant surprise that all the personnel were green—infantry included—except for a cross-hatched icon on *Foghorn*. "Three-one, what's your casualty?" he said.

"Six, the right gun blew back and burned Quincy both arms," Sergeant Nagano replied. *"We got him sedated and covered in SpraySeal. He'll be all right, I guess, but he won't be much good in the field for a few months. Over."*

"Highball Six," broke in another voice before Huber could reply, *"this is Regiment Six. We're joining your laager but leaving you in local control. Out."*

Huber felt a momentary jolt, but that was ingrained reflex; his conscious mind was far too exhausted to be concerned. "Roger, Six," he said. "Break. Highball, spread the laager to accommodate eight more cars. The command group's joining us. Highball Six out."

The eight vehicles with Colonel Hammer, five of them from K Company, idled toward Highball. The cars of Huber's original command reformed as the eastern half of a circle instead of the complete circuit. Instead of steering *Fencing Master* straight to its new location and rotating the bow out, Padova drove the car sideways. She was bragging, but Huber was too wrung out to call her down for it.

"Guess they didn't have a walkover like we did," Deseau said as he gave the newcomers a professional once-over. Three of the combat cars had holes in their plenum chambers; one was shot up badly enough that its skirts dragged. It probably couldn't have kept up with the rest of the unit if they hadn't been crossing such a smooth, hard surface. *"Nobody even shot at us that I saw."*

"They shot at us, Frenchie," Learoyd said. He tapped the bulkhead beside him with the knife he was using to scrape his ejection port.

Huber leaned forward to look past the trooper. Three projectiles, each separated from the next by a hand's breadth, had dimpled the iridium inward. The third was deep enough that the armor had started to crack.

"From the bunker when we got close," Learoyd explained; he sounded apologetic. *"I guess I shouldn't've quit shooting when something blew up inside."*

The impacts must've been audible in the next county, but Huber hadn't been aware of them, nor Deseau either it seemed. Aloud Huber said, "No harm done, Learoyd. Nobody'd guess their compartmentalization was that good, and it's not like there wasn't anything else needing attention."

The laager was complete with two meters between adjacent cars: tight, but giving them room to maneuver fast if something unexpected happened. The right wing gunner of the car next to *Fencing Master* raised his faceshield and shouted over the idling fans, "How's your leg, Lieutenant?"

"Sir!" Huber said. He'd expected Colonel Hammer to be in the command car. "Sir, my leg's fine, I guess, but I haven't been using it much except to stand on."

Huber's left leg ached like a wall was leaning on it, but the rest of his body wasn't much better. His skin itched and the slickness where his clamshell rubbed over his hipbones was either popped blisters or blood. In the morning, that might matter; right now, Arne Huber was alive and that was good enough.

Huber's AI pulsed a warning on his faceshield. The task force was still under combat conditions, and a pair of aircars were approaching from the northeast a thousand meters up. The cars' tribarrels weren't on air defense, and the AI thought maybe they ought to be.

"They got running lights on, El-Tee," Deseau said, swinging his gun onto the aircars manually. *"They're not trying to sneak up on us, but maybe they're just too smart to try what wouldn't work."*

"Put that gun on safe, trooper!" Colonel Hammer roared. Then he snapped his faceshield down and continued, *"All Slammers units, do not shoot. Under no circumstances harm the incoming aircars. They're bringing Solace representatives to treat with us! Six out."*

The aircars hovered a kilometer from the perimeter of Port Plattner. Hammer continued an animated conversation with someone on a push that didn't include Highball Six. After nearly a minute's discussion, the aircars mushed toward the laager together. The command car's rear door opened; Major Pritchard stepped out of the vehicle.

Colonel Hammer nodded approval and swung his legs over the coaming of his fighting compartment to stand on the plenum chamber. He looked at Huber, grinned, and said, "Come along with me, Lieutenant. We're going to take the surrender of the Republic of Solace.

The two squads of infantry tilted their skimmers on end and stacked them in groups of three between the combat cars of Highball section. Sergeant Tranter swung down a cooler from *Fancy Pants* since the infantry's supports were back with the hogs.

The troopers looked more concerned with the Colonel and his operations officer in the center of the circle than they were with the crackling destruction that covered most of the near distance. They'd seen destruction more often than they'd been this close to the Colonel, after all.

The aircars hovered for a moment, then landed a hundred meters out from the laager. Hammer grimaced and snapped to Pritchard, "Get 'em in here, Major. Do they think we're going to walk over to them?"

Huber wasn't sure he *could* walk that far. His left leg had been numb till he dropped from the plenum chamber to the ground. That shock had seemed to drive a hot steel rod straight up from his heel to the hip joint. His knee didn't want to bend, and every time he moved the rod burned hotter.

Pritchard spoke into his commo helmet. He must have had a link to the aircars through his command vehicle, because after a moment they lifted and crawled toward the laager in ground effect. He smiled tightly to Hammer and Huber, saying, "The gentleman from Nonesuch was concerned that the terminal might fall in this direction. I assured him that the shell of a ferroconcrete building will remain standing after it's burned itself out."

His grin grew even harder. "I've got a lot of experience with that, of course. We all have."

"Right," said Hammer. "That's why they hire us." He glanced at Huber and added, "You've met Mister Lindeyar already, haven't you, Lieutenant?"

"Him?" said Huber, shocked out of his torpor. He wasn't sure he'd heard right; or if he had, that his brain hadn't taken a shock during the battle that was making him remember things that'd never happened. "There was a Lindeyar at Benjamin, but what's that got to do with Solace?"

A starship was dropping slowly. It was still at high altitude but the effort of supporting its mass in a controlled descent made it pulsingly noticeable. Hammer'd mentioned ships landing, so Huber supposed it part of the plan. Somebody's plan, and no concern for a line lieutenant.

"Sigmund Lindeyar is the Nonesuch representative for all of Plattner's World, not just to the United Cities," Major Pritchard said, sounding detached. "Quite an important man back home, I gather."

Hammer spat on the dirt at his feet. "Yeah," he said, releasing the catches on the right side of his clamshell. "And if you don't believe us, just ask Lindeyar himself."

The aircars landed again, this time a few meters short of the bows of the combat cars. The slick-finished limousines reflected the surging firelight like pools of oil; by contrast, *Foghorn* and *Fancy Pants* were hulking gray boulders, scarred by the ages.

The starship continued to drop, balanced on the repulsion of two self-generated electromagnetic fields. Violet corona discharges danced across the heavens, crackling and roaring. Huber glanced at it, then frowned as he looked higher in the sky. A second starship was descending, and he thought a third waited above the second.

"El-Tee, there's a couple more aircars coming up from the south," Deseau said over *Fencing Master*'s intercom. *"I don't guess there's a problem—they're responding with Regimental IFF—but I figured I'd mention it."*

Huber nodded to Deseau. Learoyd had the receiver cover of the left wing tribarrel raised to adjust the feed mechanism. The crew of a CO's vehicle caught a lot of extra work, which bothered Huber. Neither Deseau nor Learoyd seemed to notice, let alone care.

And it wasn't like either one of them wanted to be platoon leader.

A group of military and civilian personnel were getting out of one of the aircars. Among them was an attractive—

Via! The attractive young woman was Daphne Priamedes, and the senior officer whom she'd bent to help to exit was her father, Colonel Apollonio Priamedes. Huber'd never expected to see either one of them again.

Lindeyar had arrived in the other vehicle, alone except for three bodyguards. Huber looked at him and smiled wryly. *How many people have I killed in the last two days? And not one of them anybody I knew, let alone disliked.*

"Colonel?" Huber said aloud. "There's two more aircars coming from the south. I guess you've already got that under control, but—"

"But you thought you'd make sure I had the information," Hammer said with an approving nod. "Right, I do."

He gestured to the southern sky. "That's the UC delegation," he said. "They're our principals on this contract so they need to be here."

The first starship settled onto the far end of the pad, close by the ship that had brought the Waldheim Dragoons. The new vessel was about the size of the one that had held an entire brigade of armored cavalry. Its sizzling discharge ceased, but the concrete continued to vibrate at a dense bass note.

Lindeyar straightened the fall of his jacket and strode into the laager past the combat cars. His bodyguards waited beyond the circle.

The civilians who'd arrived in the other vehicle huddled for a moment. The old man wearing a fur stole and cap of office directed a question at Colonel Priamedes with a peevish expression.

Priamedes snapped a reply and walked after Lindeyar, his daughter at his side. Daphne kept her face blank, but Huber could see from the way she held herself that she was ready to grab her father if his body failed him. Exchanging looks of indignation, the four civilians followed.

The two aircars coming from the south landed with a brusque lack of finesse; one even bounced. Huber leaned back slightly to get a better look between two vehicles of Lieutenant Messeman's platoon. He'd been right about what he thought he'd seen: the four civilians getting out of the aircars were members of the UC Senate whom he'd seen before when he was assigned to duties in Benjamin, but White Mice were driving and guarding them. Their battledress was as ragged as Huber's own, and one trooper's plastron had been seared down to the ceramic core.

The man in the fur cap glared at Hammer. "You sir!" he said. "I'm President Rihorta. Colonel Priamedes tells me you're the chief of these hirelings. May I ask why it's necessary to hold these discussions in such a, such a—"

At a loss for words, he waved a hand toward the chaos beyond. His sleeves were fur-trimmed also. As if on cue, a fuel tank in the vehicle park exploded, sending a bubble of orange fire skyward.

"—a place?"

"Well, Mr. President…" Hammer said, putting a hand under his breastplate to take some of its chafing weight off his shoulders. "If I needed a better reason than that I felt like it, I'd say because it'll convince you that you don't have any choice. I could burn all of Bezant down around your ears even easier than I took the spaceport that your survival depends on."

"Bezant is a civilian center, not a proper target of military operations," Colonel Priamedes said in a tight voice.

"Is it?" Hammer snapped at the Solace officer. "I could say the same about Benjamin, couldn't I?"

He waved his hand curtly. "But we're not here to discuss, gentlemen," he went on. "We already did all the discussing we needed to with those—"

He pointed to the bullet-gouged hull of the combat car he'd arrived in.

"—and with the hogs. We're here to dictate the end of the war on such terms as seem good to our principals."

The UC senators walked between the combat cars with as much hesitation as the Solace delegation had shown. One of them was coughing. The air reeked of smoke and ozone, so familiar to Huber that he hadn't thought about it till he watched the civilians' grimaces and shallow breaths.

A woman of thirty wearing battledress of an unfamiliar pattern entered the laager with the UC civilians. She nodded to Hammer, then stood at parade rest and watched the by play with eyes that were never still.

"Masters and mistresses," Hammer said. His tone was even, but Huber noticed he gripped his breastplate fiercely enough to mottle his knuckles. "You politicians probably know each other—"

The delegations exchanged wary glances, even faint nods. They had more in common with one another than they did with the soldiers and war material surrounding them.

"—and you know Mister Lindeyar—"

The Nonesuch official looked around the gathering, his face without expression.

"—but you may not know Mistress Dozier, who's the Bonding Authority representative with responsibilities for the contracts here on Plattner's World."

The woman in battledress said, "Good day. I'm here solely as an observer, of course. My organization has no interest in the negotiations between principals except to see that all parties adhere to the contracts which we oversee."

The second starship was in its final approach. Hammer raised his hand in bar. President Rihorta started speaking anyway, but the overwhelming *CRACKLE CRACKLE CRACKLE* penetrated even his self-absorption after a moment.

When the sound and dazzling corona died away, Sigmund Lindeyar said, "Rather than draw these proceedings out unnecessarily, I'm going to take charge now. Nonesuch has been subsidizing the mercenaries which the Outer States have hired for this conflict. In fact some eighty percent of the charges have come from our coffers—"

"What!" said President Rihorta. "But you've been insisting we raise port duties to upgrade the facilities!"

"You traitorous scum," Colonel Priamedes said in a quiet voice, stepping toward Lindeyar. Daphne tried to stop him. Huber placed himself in front of the Solace officer and held till weakness and Daphne's efforts forced Priamedes back.

His knees started to buckle. Huber caught him and shifted around to his right side, continuing to support Priamedes while Daphne held her father's other arm.

"I'm scarcely a traitor, Colonel," Lindeyar said with a chuckle. He fluffed the lapel of his jacket. "I've been quite successful in advancing the interests of my nation… which is Nonesuch, you will recall."

The UC delegates were whispering among themselves. Lindeyar fixed them with his cold eyes and said, "Now as for you gentlemen—"

The word was a sneer.

"—the first thing you need to know is that my government has withdrawn its financial support. I've already informed the Bonding Authority—"

Mistress Dozier nodded agreement.

"—that as of this moment, Nonesuch will no longer pay the wages of the mercenaries employed on Plattner's World. Therefore unless the UC and its local partners are capable of paying those charges by themselves, the war is over and all the mercenaries will go home immediately. Can you pay, gentlemen?"

The four UC senators gaped at Lindeyar. Minister Graciano said, "Good Lord, man, of course we can't. But why would we want to? We've won. This is what we've been hoping for all along!"

"Mister Lindeyar," Major Pritchard said, "there was discussion about transferring the contract of Hammer's Regiment to Nonesuch directly."

Lindeyar met the unspoken question with a wintry smile. "Was there?" he said. "Perhaps there was. In the event, however, my government has decided to depend on its national forces for defense of its new concession here on Plattner's World."

The third starship landed near the two which had arrived minutes before. Huber couldn't see the ships from where he stood, but while everyone waited for the roar to quiet he shifted the upper right quadrant of his faceshield to the view from an H Company tank on the north side of Port Plattner.

Hatches on the first ship began to open as soon as the third touched down. The crew had been waiting till that moment. As close as the vessels were to one another, there might have been danger if the first-landed had begun disembarking previously.

The first personnel out were ship's crewmen, adjusting the ramps with hydraulic jacks. Starship personnel were used to the agonizing disorientation of interstellar travel. They had the same splitting headaches, the same blurred vision, and the same nausea as those who traveled less often, but they'd learned to work through the pain.

The noise died away. As Huber cut his remote to return to Lindeyar's response, he saw huge tanks on caterpillar treads starting to roll out of the starship.

"That's right, you've won, gentlemen," Lindeyar said with dripping disdain. "Go home and tell your people about your victory. Celebrate!"

He swung his blond, handsome head about the circle like a wolf surveying the henhouse he's just entered. "As for you, Mister President and *your* fellows, our terms are simple: Port Plattner is now an extraterritorial division of the Polity of Nonesuch. Port controls and fees are no longer your concern. If you choose to argue the matter, then we'll take over the administration of all Solace."

He pointed his left arm to the north, fingers outstretched, though he didn't turn his head away from the Solace delegation. "There's a division of the Nonesuch National Guard on the ground already. We can bring more troops in if we have to, but given the condition of your forces that obviously won't be necessary. And if you're thinking of mercenaries—I'm afraid you've overextended your off-planet credit already. Now that you no longer hold Port Plattner, Solace is bankrupt. The money you've placed with the Bonding Authority will just cover repatriation of the units already contracted to you, and the Authority won't approve any further hires."

All eyes turned to Mistress Dozier. She shrugged and said without emphasis, "The Authority isn't in the business of making moral judgments. We're employed—"

Her face hardened.

"—by all parties, let me remind you, to enforce contracts, nothing more. Mister Lindeyar has correctly stated the situation insofar as the Bonding Authority is concerned."

Colonel Priamedes' head lolled on Huber's shoulder. "Papa?" Daphne whispered urgently.

Huber touched the colonel's throat with an index and middle finger; his pulse was strong. Priamedes hadn't recovered from the knocks he'd taken at Northern Star Farms, and the present events were simply more than his system could handle without shutting down.

Huber's leg didn't hurt anymore; the adrenaline surging through him was the best medicine for pain. He didn't know how long he could keep this up, but for the time being he could do his job—whatever that job turned out to be. He eyed Sigmund Lindeyar without expression.

"I don't have to explain this to Colonel Hammer," Lindeyar said, "but for the rest of you I'll point out that any mercenary unit which works without a paid contract becomes an outlaw in the eyes of the Bonding Authority. Civilization can't survive with bands of mad dogs roving from planet to planet without rules."

Hammer began to laugh so hard that his loose breastplate flapped back and forth. He said, "Oh, what a principled gentleman you are, Master Lindeyar!" and then bent over again in another spasm of mirth.

"On behalf of the Colonel," Major Pritchard said as the delegates of both sides stared at Hammer in disbelief, "I can assure you that Hammer's Regiment is scrupulously careful to operate within the constraints of the Bonding Authority. We aren't vigilantes who imagine that it's our duty to impose justice...."

Pritchard swept the politicians with a gaze as contemptuous as that of Lindeyar a few moments earlier. He went on, "And if we were, we'd be hard put to find an employer who could meet our standards, wouldn't we?"

Lindeyar seemed more disconcerted by Hammer's laughter than he might have been by anger. He looked at the bodyguards standing by the aircar he'd arrived in: all three had their hands in plain sight. When he followed their gaze back, he saw Deseau's tribarrel aimed at them. Frenchie grinned down and pointed his right index finger at Lindeyar's face like a pistol.

In a careful voice, Lindeyar said, "Of course, Colonel Hammer, your troops' performance on Plattner's World won't go unnoticed, particularly the brilliant stroke by which you captured the port here. I'm sure you'll have no difficulty finding employment in the near future."

Hammer straightened. The laughter was gone; he gave Lindeyar a look of cold appraisal.

"I worry about a lot of things, Mr. Lindeyar," he said. "It's my job to worry; I'm in charge. But I've never had to worry about somebody hiring us. My Slammers are the best there is, and the whole universe knew it before we came here to Plattner's World."

Lindeyar nodded, licking his lips. "Yes, of course," he said. He cleared his throat before going on, "Since there's no need to conclude the formalities at this moment, I'll be off to other matters which require my attention. President Rihorta, I'll be in touch with you regarding the wording of your government's concession of Port Plattner."

He backed away from the circle, smiling fitfully each time his eyes met those of one of the Slammers. His hip bumped *Foghorn*'s skirt; he turned with a shocked expression, then walked at an increasing pace to his aircar.

Colonel Priamedes was able to support his own weight again. Huber released him and stepped aside, though Daphne kept hold of her father's other arm.

"I guess you people have things you'd better be about as well," Hammer said, surveying the delegations. All the civilians seemed to be on the verge of collapse; Priamedes, whose difficulties were merely physical, had gotten his color back and now stood straight. "Go on and do them."

He focused on Minister Graciano. "You and I'll talk regarding financial arrangements tomorrow. Mistress Dozier, you'll be present?"

"Yes, of course," the Bonding Authority representative said.

Lindeyar's aircar lifted and curved toward the ships disgorging a Nonesuch armored division. Huber'd left his 2-cm weapon in *Fencing Master*, so all he had was the pistol on his equipment belt. He'd never been much good with a pistol; but if he fired in the direction of the aircar, Frenchie would swat it out of the air in blazing fragments.

That'd be a violation of the contract, of course. The Colonel would have him executed immediately as the only way to prevent the Regiment from being outlawed and disbanded.

We're not in the business of dispensing justice....

The delegations started moving away toward their own vehicles. Daphne Priamedes said, "It's over for us, now—Solace and the Outer States as well now that Nonesuch has the port. 'Woe to the conquered.' That's how it's always been."

Arne Huber thought about Sergeant Jellicoe, about *Flame Farter*'s two crewmen and all the other troopers he'd lost here on Plattner's World. He watched the aircar landing among the disembarking Nonesuch soldiers and said aloud, "Yeah, I suppose. But it's not just to the conquered, sometimes."

Arne Huber stood on the berm against which *Fencing Master* nestled bow-on, surveying the landscape. It'd been a field of spring wheat before the engineers gouged Firebase One out of it two days ago and moved a third of the Regiment's combat elements into it.

Huber hadn't been a farmer; he'd seen no magic in the original flat expanse of green shoots stretching to the hills ten kilometers away. He was willing to grant that it'd been more attractive than this scraped yellow wasteland, though.

Deseau crawled carefully out of the plenum chamber. He was a small man, but battle and the hard run had left him stiff. You could hurt yourself on sharp, rusty metal when your muscles don't work the way you expect them to. He stepped away from the access port before he dusted his trousers with his hands; Padova followed him out. He grinned at Huber and said, "Funny to be on Plattner's World and not be skating in mud, ain't it, El-Tee?"

A dirigible slinging three pallets of howitzer ammunition was crawling upwind to the cargo pad. The big airships didn't overfly the firebase: they dropped their loads outside the berm, from where trucks with troopers driving hauled the material the short remainder of the way.

"Hadn't really thought about it, Frenchie," Huber said. His eyes were on the dirigible, but he wasn't really thinking about that either. "I can't say I like the dust here in the highlands a lot better."

"Hey, Learoyd?" Deseau called to the trooper in the fighting compartment. "Slide into the front, will you, and run up Port Two?"

Learoyd didn't work in the plenum chamber unless he had to. He was too big for the hatches even when he was fit, and now his right arm was in a surface cast to keep him from rubbing off the medication that the Medicomp had applied when things settled down enough for the support equipment and personnel to arrive from Base Alpha. A fresh set of barrels for the 2-cm automatics had arrived, so Learoyd was working on the tribarrels while the other crewmen realigned the nacelle that'd taken a knock from the dense rootball of a tree *Fencing Master* had driven over.

"I'll do it," said Padova, mounting the bow with a hop and a grab for the first handhold on the hull proper. Rita'd settled in during the run and the three days of quiet following Port Plattner; now she was a member of *Fencing Master*'s crew, not just a skilled driver.

"Any word about when we might be moving out, El-Tee?" Deseau asked, shielding his eyes with his hand as he looked up at Huber. "I mean, we're off the clock, right? Paying for our own time."

A dotted line of dirigibles stretched to the southern horizon: Huber could see at least a dozen airships at once. There'd been a solid stream of airships transferring supplies and material from the UC ever since the Regiment pulled twenty kilometers back and set up three firebases equidistant from Port Plattner. They'd leave in a single giant transport from Port Plattner rather than in dribs and drabs from makeshift starports in the UC, so Huber supposed it made sense. Not that anybody cared what he thought.

"So far as anybody's told me, Frenchie," he said, "we're going to stay here till we've all grown long white beards. I don't expect that's what'll happen, but your guess is as good as mine."

Padova switched on the portside fans and ran them up together. Huber cocked his head, listening with a critical ear for any imbalance in the harmonics. So far as he could tell, the nacelles were tuned as sweetly as if they'd just been blueprinted in the factory.

"El-Tee?" called Learoyd. He pointed to *Fencing Master*'s port wing gun, slewing incrementally under the control of gunnery computer. "There's something coming."

Huber looked south again, noticing this time that two enclosed aircars were approaching fast below the dirigibles. His eyes narrowed: the cars' IFF must have been responding correctly or else the tribarrels on air defense would've shot them out of the sky a minute ago, but the drivers were taking a chance anyway. Even with the war over…

"Hey, what d'ye have?" Deseau said. He couldn't see what was happening from ground level, but he'd noticed Learoyd's and Huber's interest. Instead of immediately jumping onto the plenum chamber to see for himself, he first latched the access port closed so that *Fencing Master* would be able to maneuver again.

The aircars came over the berm twenty meters up, braking to a hover with a slickness that showed the drivers were expert. They set down in front of the TOC, between two of Battery Alpha's dug-in howitzers; dust skittered, dancing away to the west.

Huber jumped from the berm to the plenum chamber, his boots clanging. He climbed into the fighting compartment just as Deseau did; both men reflexively checked their tribarrels. Learoyd locked down the third barrel on his gun and slipped the adjustment wrench into its pouch on his belt.

"What d'ye think, El-Tee?" Deseau asked. "Did that bastard Lindeyar have second thoughts about terminating our contract?"

"None of them are Lindeyar," Learoyd said. "They're the other politicians' cars."

Fencing Master's tribarrels couldn't bear on the aircars because they were straight behind them, and anyway you didn't point a gun across a firebase unless you wanted to lose your rank. Frenchie was holding his 2-cm weapon in the crook of his arm, and Learoyd unclipped his sub-machine gun from the bracket on the inside of the armor.

The limousines' doors opened. Huber recognized Minister Graciano and his three colleagues, and the woman in battledress getting out of the front was Mistress Dozier. From the other aircar came President Rihorta and another member of the Solace delegation. The man accompanying those two was a stranger.

Aloud Huber said, "I don't know who the tall guy is. He's off-planet, that's for sure. I've never seen a hat like that—"

It was more of a turban; the stranger donned and adjusted it carefully before proceeding with the others toward the ramp down to the TOC.

"—on Plattner's World before."

"That's the Colonel waiting in the entrance for 'em," Deseau said. "I swear it is!"

"What do we do now, El-Tee?" Learoyd said. He knew the situation'd changed. He wasn't worried, just looking for direction from somebody smarter than he was.

"We wait for orders, trooper," Huber said. He pursed his lips, then added, "And while we're waiting, I think we've got room here to stow another case of tribarrel ammo. Let's see if the quartermaster can help us out."

Huber's mind registered motion—a streak of light across the purple-black sky. He opened his mouth to shout a warning over the squadron net, then realized it was a shooting star rather than incoming artillery.

Padova stood on the plenum chamber where she could quickly slide down the driver's hatch. She looked into the fighting compartment and shook her head. "How can Frenchie sleep?" she muttered.

"I'm on watch, Rita," Learoyd said. "Why shouldn't he sleep? The El-Tee's awake too."

He blinked. "And you."

"Frenchie's been here a lot of times, Rita," Huber said, using that formation instead of "Frenchie's a veteran," which the driver might find insulting. "As soon as there's a reason, he'll be up and doing his job."

He grinned with a kind of affection he felt only because he and Deseau were part of the same family. "Besides, if the job's killing, Frenchie could do that without waking up."

Padova'd seen the elephant by now, that was for sure; but there was a difference between one hard run punctuated by firefights and the bone-deep awareness that this might be the last chance to sleep for days or longer. Frenchie's *body* understood that sleeping curled up on the floor of the fighting compartment was best present use of his time.

"You think it's going to be fighting again, don't you?" Padova said angrily. "But who? The only people who could hire us is Nonesuch, and who would they need us to fight? They've got a fucking division on the ground, we saw them land it!"

"We're going to fight Nonesuch, Rita," Learoyd said calmly. He withdrew the loading tube from his backup sub-machine gun, wiped it with an oily cloth, and clicked it home in the receiver again. "We're going to take the port back."

"And who the bloody hell is *paying* us to attack Nonesuch!" the driver snarled, balling her fists in frustration. "Are we going outlaw, is that what you mean?"

"I don't know who's paying us," Learoyd said, bending to check the bearing in the pintle supporting his tribarrel. "But there's nobody else to fight here, so we're fighting Nonesuch."

He shrugged. "The El-Tee knows we're getting ready to fight, we all know that. So it has to be Nonesuch."

Huber looked at Learoyd's round, placid face; as calm as a custard, reddened as usual by sun and wind. None of them understood how the Regiment could be going into battle again on Plattner's World. Learoyd was the only one who wasn't bothered by ignorance: he didn't expect to understand things.

"Yeah, Bert's right," Huber said. "Curst if I know how or why, but I can't say I'm sorry. I didn't like Lindeyar when I first met him, and he hasn't improved with time."

Padova hugged herself in frustration. "If we're really going to fight," she said, looking in the direction of the TOC, "why hasn't Central signaled us to stand to?"

"Do you see anybody in the base who isn't at his action station?" Huber said. "An alert might warn other people. Everybody's waiting for it, even Frenchie. Especially Frenchie."

He brought up the F-3 stats again on the C&C display. They were still at four cars. Sergeant Bielsky was bringing a repaired vehicle up from Benjamin, but he wouldn't arrive for thirty hours. The four cars of the present complement had shaken down during the run and attack, even Gabinus' Three-eight—which now had *Flamingo Girl* painted in fluorescent blue on both sides of the fighting compartment. All the guns had been rebarreled, all the fans were running within seventy percent of optimum, and each car had a full crew.

He glanced at Learoyd, his right arm in a stiff bend though the hand was free to grip with. Replacements had flown up from the UC in aircars, but there was no way in hell that Deseau—the car commander—or Huber wanted to go into battle with a trooper they didn't know in place of Learoyd with one arm. There were a couple more wounded crewmen in F-3 for the same reason; it wasn't ideal, but...

Huber chuckled.

"Sir?" Padova said, frowning at what she didn't understand.

"Kind of an old joke," he said. "If everything was ideal, nobody'd be hiring mercenaries, would they?"

He chuckled again; and as he did so, the alert signal pulsed red. Sergeant Deseau was on his feet, reaching for his tribarrel's grips before his eyes could focus.

Colonel Hammer's voice rasped in their commo helmets, *"Troopers, the United Cities and Republic of Solace in combination have hired us to wrest control of Port Plattner from the foreign invaders now holding it. Normally I don't discuss the financial details of the Regiment's contracts, but in this particular case I'll mention that our payment is guaranteed by a consortium of planets which in the past have purchased about half the Thalderol base produced on Plattner's World. They seem to feel it wouldn't be to their benefit if Nonesuch controlled access to the product."*

Deseau whooped and clapped his hands. Padova had already dropped into the driver's compartment. Huber switched the C&C box to display the download that would shortly arrive from Central.

"Your assignments are on the way," Hammer continued. *"Artillery prep will begin in three minutes, and the action elements will begin moving out of the firebases at the same time. Don't get overeager—we want plenty of time for the shells to soften 'em up. For this operation we won't enable the lockout on our guns. I'd rather take the risk of being shot by a friendly than having a software glitch keep me from nailing a hostile because there's a friendly on the other side of him. But remember, the terrain is dead flat and your gun'll shoot any bloody thing that you aim at."*

The hogs of Battery Alpha elevated their launch tubes. They faced outward in a clock pattern centered on the TOC; now their turrets rotated so that the whole battery was aligned to the northwest, the direction of Port Plattner.

"I don't want any of you to think this'll be easy," Hammer continued. *"They've got a hundred and fifty tanks and their other vehicles mount tribarrels too. It doesn't matter how slow and clumsy they are, because they aren't coming to us—we have to go to them. But troopers—we've faced worse. Get out there now and help me show people what happens when you try to cheat the Slammers! Six out."*

The satellites were up again; some satellites, anyhow. The download had full real-time coverage of the port. Approaches, lines of sight, threats and targets—the initial targets being the threats, of course—shimmered onto the holographic display in standard color overlays, as familiar to Huber as the grips of his tribarrel.

Four Nonesuch tanks moved in echelon to join the twelve parked in front of the smoldering terminal building. Each was built around a centerline 25-cm powergun. Though the big weapons could only be adjusted a few degrees in azimuth, their bolts were powerful enough to penetrate even the thick plating of a starship.

A line of dun-colored space-frame tents, sandbagged to the concrete, stood beside the vehicles. More tents—thousands of them—dotted the edges of the pad, most of them serving the infantry riding APCs. The latter, tracked like the tanks, had iridium armor and mounted a tribarrel in a one-man cupola.

Nonesuch fatigue parties worked on the perimeter bunkers without heavy equipment. Soldiers were mixing concrete in hand troughs. Huber wondered whether Lindeyar and his cronies had tried to buy construction mixers from Solace and been refused, or if this was merely a stopgap until dedicated support units arrived aboard later vessels.

Three ships, even such large ones, were barely enough to carry a division; the Nonesuch planners had concentrated wholly on combat personnel and equipment, accepting discomfort and inefficiency in order to frighten their possible opponents into quiescence. So far as the Solace Militia went, that may have been a good plan....

"*Fox, this is Fox Six,*" Captain Gillig said. Her voice had a pleasant alto lilt even when she was giving battle orders. "*Fox Three will trail on the approach, but we'll attack with all platoons in line. There's a tank company in our sector, but the panzers'll deal with it while we hit targets of opportunity. With a division to choose from, there shouldn't be any lack of those.*"

Deseau turned to Huber and said, "*Hey, El-Tee? I couldn't believe that bastard Lindeyar was going to get away with shafting us. Could you?*"

Huber thought for a moment. Given the delays in star travel, this coalition must have taken weeks or even months to put together. Hammer must have started planning it almost as soon as the Regiment arrived on Plattner's World.

"I did believe it, Frenchie," he said. "But that's all right—I'm just a line lieutenant. So long as I do my job, I can leave the rest to the Colonel."

The hogs lit the night with flaring backblasts, beginning to shower 200-mm missiles on the enemy. The roar shook the ground. Moving as smoothly as water swirling down a drain, 1st Squadron's tanks and combat cars slid from the firebase, advancing toward Port Plattner twenty klicks away.

"*Target!*" said a machine voice in Huber's ear as *Fencing Master* led the rest of F-3 out of the angled passage through the berm. His faceshield gave him a vector.

So far as Huber could tell, the careted point on the crest ten kilometers distant was a few meters of brush and low trees, no different from everything for a klick to either side, but you didn't argue when Central told you to shoot. He laid his tribarrel on, careful not to overcorrect as the stabilizer fought with the combat car's motion, and dialed up magnification as the sight picture slewed toward the target. Huber was using a false-color infrared display, so the caret was a black wedge thrusting down from the top of the image.

He actually saw them in the instant his thumbs squeezed: three soldiers wearing drapes that almost erased their thermal signature, pointing a passive observation device toward Firebase One. They'd remained hidden till now, so they must have just attempted to send information back to Port Plattner.

Huber grinned with fierce pride that the *hiss/CRACK!* of his tribarrel's first round preceded the sound of *Fencing Master*'s other two guns by a fraction of a second. He didn't often beat Frenchie and Learoyd to the punch, and neither did anybody else.

The eleven tanks of D Company—two more, deadlined for repairs but able to shoot, remained behind in the firebase for defense—had been first through the berm and were deploying across the wheat in line abreast. Colonel Hammer's combat car and that of the S-3—Huber wondered whether Major Pritchard was in it, as he certainly would choose to be, or if he'd been forced to remain in the TOC to coordinate the attack—followed, taking the right of the tanks along with two five-car platoons of G Company; the remaining platoon and the command cars of Regimental HQ Section remained behind as base defense. Captain Gillig and the sergeant major were next out, followed by F-1, F-2, and finally F-3.

The engineers had sited the firebase on a low rise, so *Fencing Master* in the entrance was slightly above the vehicles already spreading out to the northwest. Central tasked Huber and his crew because they had the best line on the target. Huber'd chafed to wait for everybody else to get under weigh before his cars did, but it'd worked out after all.

There's a lot of chance in life and especially in battle. Arne Huber just happened to be in the right place at the right time to send a burst of plasma bolts snapping straight as a plumb line into what till that instant was three enemy soldiers. His faceshield blocked their cyan core, but dazzle reflecting from the landscape quivered across his retinas.

Huber's first round hit the observation device, probably a high-resolution thermal imager. It contained enough metal to erupt into a blaze of white and green sparks. After that it was hard to say who hit what, because the three tribarrels put ten or a dozen rounds apiece into the target.

Huber switched his gunsight back to its normal seven-point-five-degree field. The freshly lit fire on the ridgeline was only a quiver at this distance. In the magnified image Huber had seen an arm fly from an exploding torso and white-hot fragments blasted from the granite outcrop behind the scouts.

His gunbarrels shimmered, sinking back from yellow heat. The cluster continued to spin, pulling air through the open breeches to cool the bores.

Padova followed the course Captain Gillig's C&C box had programmed. She didn't ask about the shooting. Huber supposed she was scared—as the good Lord knew he was himself—but she'd shaken down just fine. She'd be driving *Fencing Master* until she got a promotion, which at the rate she was going wouldn't be long.

F-3 followed two hundred meters behind the first and second platoons on the left flank, a reserve not only for Fox Company but for the whole squadron. Despite satellite coverage and the Regiment's sensor suites, there was always risk of an attack from some direction other than straight ahead. Huber's cars stayed back to deal with it.

"Good to burn in our guns like that," Deseau said as his cluster stopped rotating. *"A few rounds to make sure the barrels're seated and there's no cracks in the castings."*

Cyan bolts streaked up from the northwest horizon, ending in yellow flashes made ragged by the smoke of the explosions. Despite the decoy missiles of the first salvos, the Nonesuch defenses—over eight hundred tribarrels on the APCs and tanks—were shooting down the firecracker rounds that followed. The Nonesuch command hadn't been caught napping, more's the pity....

The lead combat cars began firing. Flashes and the sparkling detonations of submunitions bloomed on the other side of the high ground separating 1st Squadron from the port. At least one Nonesuch artillery battery was firing on the attackers, a *much* faster response than Huber had expected from planetary forces which probably had no experience of real warfare. The shells didn't get through, but if the Nonesuch tankers were as good as their artillerymen this was going to be a very long night for the Slammers.

A long night, or a short one.

Much brighter cyan flashes lit the night: the tanks of Dog Company punched the ridgeline five klicks away with their main guns. Their thunder echoed across the fields.

Huber checked the C&C display, then said, "Fox Three, there was a Nonesuch infantry company picketed on the reverse slope. They moved into position and the panzers are taking care of them. Three-six out."

One of the eight Nonesuch APCs opened fire before it had reached the crest. The bolts of its tribarrels streaked five hundred meters over the Slammers in a rising slant. When the APC advanced high enough that its gun might have been able to bear on the attackers, the tank which had been waiting for a target fired. A brilliant secondary explosion lifted skyward a divot of soil and wood-chips.

Moments later, a *bum! bum! bum!* directly overhead made Huber twist to look up. Cargo shells from Battery Alpha had opened at low altitude, sending fingers of smoke toward the ridgeline. Their thousands of anti-personnel bomblets hit to carpet the target with lingering white flashes, scouring the hasty positions of Nonesuch infantry who'd dismounted before their APCs tried to engage.

Dirty smoke hung over half a kilometer of the hilltop. Huber could penetrate it with thermal imaging, but there was nothing to see except bare rock and the pulped remnants of the trees and shrubs that had grown there moments before. The enemy troops and their equipment had vanished except for the continuing sizzle of a battery pack shorting through commo gear, forming a hotspot on the image.

"Nothing for us there," Deseau said cheerfully. He patted his tribarrel's receiver. *"Well, we'll have our chance yet tonight, I figure."*

"Fox Three, this is Fox Six," Captain Gillig ordered. *"Move up on the left flank of Fox One, keeping ten meter intervals between vehicles. We'll take firing positions*

below the crest. Six out."

Huber tensed as his faceshield flashed warnings. Chuckling, he relaxed. The squadron had torn through the fence separating the wheatfield from the pasture on the rougher terrain to the north. Wire flew up in springy coils around the vehicles, and the tug jerked the posts out of the ground in front of F-3. The motion was the same quick flicker men would make leaping to cover.

The northern sky quivered as with heat lightning. "*Hoo-boy!*" Deseau said. "*Some a' them firecracker rounds are landing where they ought to. I tell you, with a division of 'em down there, I don't mind a bit a' help from the cannon cockers.*"

"*We get paid the same if we get shot at or if we don't, Frenchie,*" Padova said. Her voice sounded artificially bright, but *Fencing Master* slid as if on rails to where it belonged on the left flank of the Squadron. "*I'd just as soon get easy money.*"

Deseau laughed. Huber glanced at him, then looked away. Frenchie wasn't suicidal: he figured the risks that came with the job were plenty bad enough without doing crazy stuff. But when Frenchie had a chance to kill, the fact he might die didn't concern him.

Fencing Master started up the final rise, tearing through three-meter shrubs with as little difficulty as it'd had with the wheat. Huber glanced back. Plenum chamber pressures compressed and deformed the loose earth of the plowed fields. Each of the vehicles had left a trench the full width of its skirts with a mound of soil and young shoots to either side.

Huber kept most of his attention on the Command and Control display. His cars were in the same condition as when they left the firebase, fully ready for battle if not for a rear-area inspection. The rest of the squadron was in similar shape, though a Golf Company car had lost a pair of fans and lagged behind on the slope. Sometimes bad luck was the only kind of luck there was; but if the car had been in Huber's platoon, tomorrow its sergeant/commander would be proving the problem wasn't because of a maintenance failure.

If the sergeant/commander survived, of course. And if Huber did.

Three shells from the Nonesuch battery burst several klicks back, sending spouts of black earth into the sky. Air defense hadn't bothered with them since they were no more danger to the Slammers than they were to the guns which'd fired them.

"Fox Three, this is Three-six," Huber said, glad to have good news to point out to his troopers a few seconds before they jumped into a tough one. "The hostiles are shooting where we used to be, so they don't have us under direct observation. When we reach our firing positions, we're going to get the first shot. If we can't kick their asses then, Via! we don't belong in this line of work! Six—"

Because of the way the ridge curved, *Fencing Master* pushed through the brush into a clear view of Port Plattner a heartbeat before the rest of the squadron did. Huber already had his tribarrel aimed at a predicted location even before his faceshield gave him real targets.

He squeezed the butterfly trigger as he shouted, "—out!" to his platoon.

A company of ten Nonesuch APCs had left the pad and was driving toward the ridge at the best speed turbine engines could move their caterpillar tracks. Their side armor, though thinner than that of the combat cars, was iridium, but hatches on the roofs of their troop compartments were thrown back so that the infantry in back could use their personal weapons.

Huber depressed his tribarrel and raked the hatches. Nonesuch troops carried powerguns; the blue-green flash of their stored ammunition melted the APC's frame from the inside so that the bow tilted upward. Fuel cells on the underside blew a circle of orange flames around the glowing wreckage.

Tanks and combat cars were firing all along the ridgeline. Though Huber couldn't have seen most of the Slammers' vehicles even if he'd taken the time to look to his side, streams of cyan plasma from their tribarrels and the tanks' stunning, world-searing flashes stabbed downward into easily visible targets.

The tanks were in hull-down positions where the firecracker rounds had scraped and sculpted the ground in erasing the Nonesuch picket. They shot as quickly as their gunners could work the foot-trips of their main guns, aiming at the company of Nonesuch tanks below. A 20-cm bolt hit massive frontal armor, rocking the target back on its treads in blinding coruscance.

To Huber's half-conscious horror, the centerline 25-cm gun shot back despite the Slammer's direct hit. The bolt gouged the hillside at least fifty meters from the nearest target, but the fact the tank fired at all was amazing.

A second bolt from the same Slammers tank struck where the armor glowed pulsingly white from the first. This time the glacis failed. The 25-cm magazine detonated, scooping the hull empty. The thick shell remained as a white-hot monument.

Huber swung his gun onto a company of buttoned-up APCs moving slantwise left to right in two echelons. They were several kilometers away, still on the concrete, when Huber hit the nearest vehicle in the lead row. Its side armor blew inward under the hammer of his 2-cm bolts. As the rest of the line drew ahead, Huber shifted his aim slightly onto the next APC and slashed it open the same way.

Huber steadied on the third APC, but as he did so the four second echelon vehicles opened fire on *Fencing Master* with their cupola tribarrels. One of them walked his burst up the sod, then splashed two bolts on *Fencing Master*'s bow slope and a third into the armor of the fighting compartment.

The combat car rocked at each impact. Huber's helmet deadened the clangs, but the jolts transmitted through the floor of the compartment buckled his knees. Before the Nonesuch gunner could finish the job, Deseau raked the APCs' cupolas, dismounting their tribarrels in rainbow brilliance.

Huber's third target exploded in a mushroom of crimson flame. As he hammered through the cab of the fourth and last, he saw Deseau's and Learoyd's guns crossing his burst to slaughter the soldiers bailing out of the vehicles Frenchie had disarmed.

The infantry weren't much of a threat now even if they got clear, but Huber shifted his own fire onto a car that his troopers hadn't hit yet. Body parts flew up at his lash before a secondary explosion finished the job in a saffron fireball.

Despite the filters over Huber's nostrils, *Fencing Master* stank of ozone and the vile slickness of burned metal. Vaporized iridium had burned the side of his neck, and his seared left sleeve stuck to his elbow. *Blood and Martyrs, that was close!*

Fencing Master jumped again. *We're hit!* but it wasn't incoming: a strip of the automatic defense array at the top of the skirts had gone off, sending a load of small osmium slugs out toward the left front. They met the anti-tank missile homing on the combat car.

The warhead detonated partially in a red flash. Bits of the debris sprayed *Fencing Master*. The concussion staggered Huber and a chunk of the rocket motor whanged the hull, but that was a cheap price. If the round'd hit squarely, the jet from its shaped charge would've gutted *Fencing Master* like a trout.

A 25-cm bolt hit close by, vaporizing a combat car forward of the rear bulkhead. A cloud of glowing iridium shimmered through all the colors of the spectrum, turning the ridgeline as bright as noon in Hell.

"*Shall I back up? Shall I back us up?*" Padova shouted into the intercom. *Fencing Master* lifted, quivering on plenum chamber pressure instead of resting its skirts firmly on the ground.

"Set us down!" Huber shouted, swinging his gun onto the pair of Nonesuch tanks sheltering at the side of a starship like tortoises in the lee of a high cliff. His tribarrel floated on a frictionless magnetic bearing, but inertia made slewing it a deliberate business. "Give us a solid—"

He had his target, not the glacis that could resist a tank's main gun nor the treads which a tribarrel could weld, immobilizing the huge vehicle without affecting its firepower. Huber aimed at the bore of the main gun, the 25-cm tunnel glowing from the bolt with which it had turned a combat car and its crew into fiery gases.

"—platform!"

Fencing Master thudded back to the ground as Huber's thumbs squeezed, but the stabilizer was locked on. His stream of blue-green bolts flared and sparkled against the tank's muzzle, its gun tube, and the mantle which covered the glacis opening.

A 25-cm bolt put such stresses on the bore that the guns' rate of fire was necessarily low, no more than two rounds per minute. Huber'd laid his tribarrel on the first tank nonetheless because that gunner'd proved he had the Slammers' elevation. Even the centerline gun's limited traverse would be sufficient to sweep six or eight vehicles to either side of the one it'd destroyed.

It was a calculated gamble, though, because the other tank was able to fire *now*. When a vivid cyan flash enveloped it, instinct told Huber this was a bolt which might blast *Fencing Master* and its crew to dissociated atoms.

The Nonesuch tank hadn't fired. A pair of 20-cm bolts had hit it simultaneously, lighting the concrete field with a rainbow bubble similar to what the combat car had become a moment before. Huber's faceshield blacked out almost totally. He kept his thumbs on the trigger, burning out his bores as he slashed his own massive target.

His faceshield cleared except for the streams from *Fencing Master*'s three tribarrels and the smudge of reflection where they hammered together into the Nonesuch tank. Then the tank and the world vanished again.

The protective black curtain cleared seconds later as the shockwave reached the ridgeline. The roof of the tank's fighting compartment toppled back toward the chassis which had been cleaned of its contents like a raccoon-licked clamshell. The tank's gunner had chambered another round. 2-cm bolts glancing down the bore from *Fencing Master* had detonated it before the breech was fully locked.

Focused on his gunsight, Huber hadn't heard the freight-train roar of 200-mm rockets passing low overhead, nor the *plop plop plop* of small charges ejecting sub-munitions from the carrier shells. The Nonesuch air defenses had been able to stop most of the incoming while it was simply them against the hogs, but when the Slammers' vehicles appeared on the ridgeline the Nonesuch tribarrels were switched to direct fire. There was nothing to stop salvos from the batteries surrounding Port Plattner.

Each shell's twelve sub-munitions went off between twenty and forty meters above the ground, a yellow flash and a rag of smoke as the explosive charge forged a plate of uranium into a white-hot spike and drove it downward toward the Nonesuch vehicle its sensors had chosen. The hogs were firing anti-tank shells, not firecracker rounds that barely scratched the paint of armored vehicles.

The self-forging fragments shattered the Nonesuch defenses already bruised by powerguns firing from the high ground surrounding the port. They punched through roof plating, relatively thin even on the tanks. Inside, the friction-heated uranium turned into balls of flame enveloping everything in the penetrated compartment. Hundreds of Nonesuch vehicles vanished into simultaneous blow-torch flames: fuel, flesh and munitions, all pulverized, all burning at the temperature of a star's surface.

Two more salvos popped in the air and raged on the ground. The thunderclaps of detonations died away, though some of the burning vehicles screamed as they lit the night with jets of fire.

Huber's gun had jammed, but nobody in 1st Squadron was shooting anymore. There were cyan flickers on the pad's northern perimeter, but that might have been guns continuing to fire as they melted into the vehicles on which they were mounted.

"Cease fire!" Colonel Hammer rasped. *"All Slammers units, cease fire! Nonesuch representatives on the starships have offered their surrender. Cease fire, troopers, it's over!"*

Huber took his hands from the grips of his weapon. The barrel cluster continued to spin, a white blur that made the air throb as it threw off heat. Huber had a multitool in his belt pouch, but when he reached for it to clear the jam he realized that his fingers didn't want to close properly.

Deseau's tribarrel had jammed also. He held his backup 2-cm weapon, but he wasn't shooting into the thousands of helpless human targets sprawling and staggering on the concrete below. The hell-strewn carnage was enough even for Frenchie.

Learoyd took off his commo helmet to rub his bald scalp with his left hand. The skin of his chin and throat below the faceshield's protection was black where iridium vaporized from his gun bores had redeposited itself. He looked older than Huber had ever seen him before.

"Fox Three-six to Fox Three," Huber said in a voice that caught at every syllable. "Good work, troopers. Nobody ever commanded a better unit than I did tonight."

He swallowed and added the words that almost hadn't gotten past his swollen throat. "Three-six out."

Then, because his head throbbed and any constriction was an agony he couldn't bear for the moment, Huber took off his helmet. He regretted the decision immediately with the first breath he took of the unfiltered atmosphere.

He turned and vomited over the side of the fighting compartment. No matter how often he encountered it, the smell of burned human flesh always turned Arne Huber's stomach.

"Hey El-Tee!" said Deseau, standing with Padova on the plenum chamber to brace the replacement plate while Learoyd applied the cold weld. "That black-haired piece you met the first time the wogs threw in the towel? She's coming to see you."

"He's not an el-tee anymore, Frenchie," Learoyd said, laying his bead along the seam as evenly as the fully-mechanized factory operation which put *Fencing Master* together to begin with. "He's a captain now."

Huber looked over his shoulder in the direction of Frenchie's gaze. He wasn't sure how Daphne Priamedes would take to being called a "black-haired piece," but it was accurate given Deseau's frame of reference. The other part, though…

Huber got up from the empty ten-liter coolant drum he was using as a seat while he worked at the Command and Control box. He wiped his hands on his utility blouse—newly issued three days before and still clean enough—and said quietly, "I met her in Benjamin, Frenchie, back when I was in Operations."

"Captain Huber?" Daphne called from the ground. "I hope you don't mind my coming to offer you lunch. The orderly said that you have an office but that you usually worked in your combat car."

Huber shut down the display. "Glad to see you, Daphne," he said as he swung himself, left leg first, over the side of the fighting compartment. "I could use a break, but I don't know about lunch. Maybe…"

He paused as he slid to the ground, careful to take the shock on his right boot. He'd been going to say, "…the canteen," but the facilities here at Base Beta consisted of a plastic prefab with extruded furniture and dispensers for a basic range of products. Bezant was only twelve klicks away, so there was no need for the Regiment itself to provide off-duty troops with anything impressive.

Daphne flashed a smile of cool triumph. "I thought you might say that," she said, "so I've brought a cooler in the car. I thought we'd fly to a grove where we could find some quiet."

Huber looked down at his uniform. He hadn't been doing much manual labor—well, *much*—but he'd have wanted to change before an interview with Hammer; or with Joachim Steuben, now that he thought about it.

Daphne repeated the cool smile. "Come along, Arne," she said. "The trees won't care any more than I do. I left my aircar by the TOC."

She crooked her elbow for him to take and started off. Base Beta was an expansion of Firebase One, no prettier than it'd been before Engineer Section trebled its area to hold all three squadrons. As he passed *Fancy Pants*, Huber saw Tranter looking out of an access port and said, "Hold the fort for an hour, Sarge. If anybody really needs me, I've got my commo helmet."

"Roger that, sir," Tranter said cheerfully. He was holding a multitool and a pair of pliers, doing technician's work and pleased at the chance.

"Hey El-Tee?" Deseau shouted from *Fencing Master*, loudly enough that half the camp could hear him. "If there's any left that you don't need, remember me'n Learoyd."

Daphne appeared not to notice the comment, unless the faint smile was her response.

Huber cleared his throat, taking stock of the situation. Daphne was wearing a pants suit, simply cut and of sturdy—but probably expensive—material. It would've been proper garb if Huber'd decided to put on his dress uniform and take her to one of the top restaurants in Bezant, but it wasn't out of place in a firebase either.

Well, he'd never doubted that she was smart.

A starship lifted, its corona shiveringly bright even in broad daylight. The rumble of shoving such a mass skyward trembled through Huber's bootsoles, though the airborne sound was distance-muted and slow to arrive.

Huber nodded toward the rising vessel and said, "This time they're repatriating the other mercenary units before they terminate our contract. It'll probably take a while to find so much shipping."

"Yes, but the amount of trade Port Plattner carried before the war is simplifying the problem," Daphne said. They'd reached her car, parked on the concertina-wired pad under the guns of an A Company combat car. The Colonel and the staff he'd brought with him on the run north were sharing space in the trailers with the squadron commanders. That must've been tight, though Huber had his own problems. Tents beside the buried trailers provided overflow for activities that nobody would care about if the shooting started again.

"As for continuing to pay your hire until all the other forces are off-planet…" Daphne continued in a wry, possibly amused, tone. "That was a condition Colonel Hammer set on agreeing to allow us to employ the Slammers. Though I think that after seeing the mistake Nonesuch made, we would have decided to find the money whether or not it was a contract term."

The sergeant in charge of the White Mice at the aircar pad spoke to one of her troopers, who swung open the bar wrapped in razor ribbon. Huber noticed the sergeant's arm was in a surface cast, then recognized her as the commander of the resupply aircars. He nodded and said, "I'm glad you came through all right, Sergeant."

"Same to you, Captain," she said, surprised and obviously pleased at his notice. "And congratulations on your promotion."

They stepped into the fenced area. Daphne's limousine was as much of a contrast to the battered utility vehicles as she herself was to the several contract drivers resting in what shade they could find.

"I haven't congratulated you on your promotion, Arne," she said. She opened the door, then bent to touch the switch which slid the hardtop in three sections down into the seatback. "I'm very glad things worked out for you."

Does she know what she's saying? Huber wondered; but maybe she did. Various things Daphne'd said showed that she was far enough up in the government of Solace that she could probably learn anything she wanted to.

"Yeah," he said, getting into the front passenger seat. "The Colonel offered me an infantry company before we headed north, but I wouldn't have known what I was doing. I'm glad I waited."

Waited for a 25-cm bolt to turn Captain Gillig, a good officer and a first-rate bridge player, into a cloud of dissociated atoms. A bolt that could just as easily have hit fifty meters south and done the same thing to Lieutenant Arne Huber and his crew. There were religious people—some of them troopers—who believed everything happened by plan, and maybe they were right. Huber himself, though, couldn't imagine a plan that balanced details so minute and decided that tonight a particular lieutenant would be promoted instead of being ionized....

Daphne ran her fans up to speed, then adjusted blade angle to lift the car off the ground in a jackrabbit start. Huber remembered that on pavement she'd been more sedate; she was outrunning the cloud of dust her fans raised from the scraped, sun-burned, clay.

"To be honest," she said, her attention apparently focused on her instruments and the eastern horizon, "I thought you might already have looked me up now that the war's over."

Huber didn't speak for a moment. He *had* thought about it. He'd decided that she wouldn't be interested; that she wouldn't have time; and that anyway, he flat didn't have the energy to get involved in anything more than a business transaction which cost about three Frisian thalers at the going rate of exchange.

Aloud he said, "Daphne, I just got promoted to command of Fox Company. I'm trying to integrate new personnel and equipment as well as repair what we can."

What remained of Captain Gillig's *Fantom Lady* would stand, probably forever, on the crest where it'd been hit. The eight fan nacelles hadn't been damaged, so Maintenance had stripped them off the hulk.

Relatives of the crew would be told their loved ones were buried on Plattner's World. That was mostly true, except for the atoms that other 1st Squadron troopers had inhaled.

Huber laughed. "No rest for the wicked, you know."

Daphne looked at him with unexpected sharpness. "Don't say that," she said. "You're not wicked. You saved our planet. Saved us from ourselves, if you want to know the truth!"

Did you have friends working in the terminal building when I shot it up, honey? Did you have a cousin paying his vehicle taxes when we blasted the police post at Millhouse Crossing? Other people did!

"Ma'am," said Huber, speaking very slowly and distinctly because this mattered to him. "I appreciate what you're saying, but don't kid yourself. If there's such a thing as wicked, then some of what I do qualifies. Some of what I've done on Plattner's World."

"I don't think you appreciate how true that is of other people too, Arne," Daphne said. She looked at him steadily, then put a hand on his thigh and squeezed before returning her attention to the horizon and steering yoke.

Well, that answered a question which, despite Deseau's certainty, had remained open in Huber's mind. Frenchie didn't have much to do with women like Daphne Priamedes.

He grinned. Neither did Arne Huber, if it came to that.

"The alliance of nations on Plattner's World which hired your Regiment," Daphne said, switching subjects with the grace of a mirror trick, "will continue to operate the port as a common facility rather than a part of Solace. We'll be raising the price of Moss and of Thalderol base to pay for port renovations."

She looked at Huber and grinned coldly.

"Which will be extensive, as you might imagine."

"Yeah," Huber said, "I can."

Just clearing wrecked equipment would be a bitch of a job: the melted hull of a two-hundred-tonne tank wasn't going to move easily, and thousands of plasma bolts had not only scarred the surface but also shattered the concrete deep into the pad's interior. The terminal building was gone, and the guidance pods which humped at regular intervals across the pad were scarred by shrapnel from the firecracker rounds if they hadn't been blasted by stray powergun bolts.

"Your backers are agreeing to the price rise?" Huber said. "The planets who funded us the second time, I mean."

"Their rates will go up ten percent," Daphne said primly. "They're quite comfortable with that. The rate to Nonesuch will go up thirty percent."

She looked at Huber and added, "I suppose you're surprised that we don't refuse to sell Thalderol base to Nonesuch regardless of the price?"

"No ma'am," Huber said, fighting to control his grin. What a question to ask a mercenary soldier! "I'm not surprised. I'd say it was a good plan to keep Nonesuch from getting so desperate that they'd try a rematch despite all."

Daphne smiled wryly. "Yes," she said, "I suppose it is at that, though I don't believe anyone was thinking in those terms when we came to the decision. We just wanted to set the rate at the maximum we thought they'd pay. We need the money rather badly, you see."

They both laughed; the tension of moments before was gone and nothing was hiding in the background so far as Huber could tell. Well, no conflict, anyway.

The aircar was five hundred meters above the ground, mushing along at about eighty kph. They'd flown beyond the wheatfields; below was pasture in which large roan cattle wandered in loose herds. Brush and small trees grew in swales, green against the rusty color of the grass at this season. Fencelines occasionally glinted from one horizon to the other, but there were kilometers between tracts.

Huber took off his commo helmet and set it in the compartment behind him.

He probably wasn't going to be back in the hour he'd told Tranter, and that was all right too.

"A nice day," he said, stretching in his seat before he put an arm over Daphne's shoulders.

"Yes," she said, setting the aircar's autopilot as she leaned toward Huber. "A nice day for normal things instead of with guns and destruction."

They kissed, wriggling closer in their bucket seats.

In his mind, Port Plattner blazed with plasma bolts and the rich, red light of burning tents. *But for me,* Huber thought as he raised his hand to her breast, *guns and destruction* are *what's normal.*

CALLIOPE

THE DARKNESS

"Hi, Lieutenant," someone said as he walked into Ruthven's room. "Good to see you up and around. I gotta do a few tests with you back in the bed, though."

On the electronic window, a brisk wind was scudding snow over drifts and damaged armored vehicles. Ruthven turned from it; a jab of pain blasted the world into white, buzzing fragments. It centered on his left hip, but for a few heartbeats it involved every nerve in his body.

"Your leg's still catching you?" said Drayer. He was the senior medic on this ward. "Well, it'll do that for a while, sir. But they did a great job putting you back together. It's just pain, you know? There's nothing wrong really."

Pain like this isn't nothing, thought Ruthven. If he hadn't been nauseous he might've tried to put Drayer's head through the wall; but he had no strength, and anyway, there was no room for anger just now in the blurred gray confines of his mind.

He eased his weight back onto his left leg; it reacted normally, though the muscles trembled slightly. The agony of a few moments past was gone as thoroughly as if it'd happened when he was an infant, twenty-odd years earlier.

"Anyway, come lie down," Drayer said. "This won't take but a…"

He noticed the window image for the first time. "Blood and Martyrs, sir!" he said. What d'ye want to look at that for? You can set these panels to show you anyplace, you know? I got the beaches on Sooner's World up on all my walls. Let me tell you, walking to my quarters across that muck is plenty view of it for me!"

Ruthven glanced back at the window, catching himself in mid-motion; his hip ignored him, the way a hip ought to do. The snow was dirty, and what appeared to be patches of mud were probably lubricating oil. The Slammers' hospital here on Pontefract shared a compound with the repair yard, a choice that probably reflected somebody's sense of humor.

"That's all right," Ruthven said, walking to the bed; monitoring devices were embedded in the frame. "I chose it deliberately."

He grinned faintly as he settled onto the mattress. The juxtaposition of wrecked personnel and wrecked equipment reflected *his* sense of humor too, it seemed.

Drayer knelt to fit his recorder into the footboard. "Well, if that's what you want," he said. "Me, I was hoping we'd be leaving as soon as the Colonel got transport lined up. The government found the money for another three months, though."

Drayer looked up; a sharp-featured little man, efficient and willing to grab a bedpan when the ward was short-handed. But by the Lord and Martyrs, his talent for saying exactly the wrong thing amounted to sheer genius.

"Had you heard that, sir?" Drayer said, obviously hopeful that he'd given an officer the inside dope on something. "Though I swear, I don't see where they found it. You wouldn't think this pit could raise the money to hire the Regiment for nine months."

"They're probably mortgaging the amber concession for the next twenty years," Ruthven said. He braced himself to move again.

The fat of beasts in Pontefract's ancient seas had fossilized into translucent masses which fluoresced in a thousand beautiful pastels. Ruthven didn't know why it was called amber.

"Twenty years?" Drayer sneered. "The Royalists won't last twenty days after we ship out!"

"It'll still be worth some banker's gamble at enough of a discount," Ruthven said. "And the Five Worlds may run out of money to supply the Lord's Army, after all."

He lifted his legs onto the mattress, waiting for the pain; it didn't come. It wouldn't come, he supposed, until he stopped thinking about it every time he moved... and then it'd grin at him as it sank its fangs in.

"Well, I don't know squat about bankers, that's the truth," Drayer said with a chuckle. "I just know I won't be sorry to leave this pit. Though..."

He bent to remove the recorder.

"...I guess they're all pits, right, sir? If they was paradise, they wouldn't need the Slammers, would they?"

"I suppose some contract worlds are better than others," Ruthven said, looking at the repair yard. Base Hammer here in the lowlands seemed to get more snow than Platoon E/1 had in the hills. He'd been in the hospital for three weeks, though; the weather might've changed in that length of time. "I've only been with the Regiment two years, so I'm not the one to say."

Drayer's brow furrowed as he concentrated on the bed's holographic readout. He looked up beaming and said, "Say, Lieutenant, you're so close to a hundred percent it don't signify. You oughta be up and dancing, not just looking out the window!"

"I'll put learning to dance on my list," Ruthven said, managing a smile with effort. "Right now I think I'll get some more sleep, though."

"Sure, you do that, sir," said Drayer, never quick at taking a hint. "Doc Parvati'll be in this afternoon to certify you, I'll bet. Tonight or tomorrow, just as sure as Pontefract's a pit."

He slid his recorder into its belt sheath and looked around the room once more.

"Well, I got three more to check, Lieutenant, so I'll be pushing on. None of them doing as well as you, I'll tell you. Anything more I can…"

The medic's eyes lighted on the gold-bordered file folder leaning against the water pitcher on Ruthven's side-table. The recruiter'd been by this morning, before Drayer came on duty.

"Blood and Martyrs, sir!" he said. "I saw Mahone in the lobby but I didn't know she'd come to see you. So you're transferring back to the Frisian Defense Forces, is that it?"

"Not exactly 'back,'" Ruthven said. He gave up the pretense of closing his eyes. "I joined the Slammers straight out of the Academy."

Sometimes he thought about ordering Drayer to get his butt out of the room, but Ruthven'd had enough conflict when he was in the field. Right now he just wanted to sleep, and he wouldn't do that if he let himself get worked up.

"Well, I be curst!" the medic said. "You're one lucky dog, sir. Here I'm going on about wanting to leave this place and you're on your way back to good booze and women you don't got to pay! Congratulations!"

"Thank you, Technician," Ruthven said. "But now I need sleep more than liquor or women or anything else. All right?"

"You bet, sir!" Drayer said as he hustled out the door at last. "Say, wait till I tell Nichols in Supply about this!"

Ruthven closed his eyes again. Instead of going to sleep, though, his mind drifted back to the hills last month when E/1 arrived at Fire Support Base Courage.

"El-Tee?" said Sergeant Hassel, E/1's platoon sergeant but doubling as leader of First Squad from lack of non-coms. *"We got something up here you maybe want to take a look at before we go belting on int' the firebase, over."*

"Platoon, hold in place," Ruthven ordered from the command car, shrinking the map layout on his display to expand the visual feed from Hassel some 500 meters ahead. The platoon went to ground, troopers rolling off their skimmers and scanning the windblown scrub through their weapons' sights.

Melisant, driving the high-sided command car today, nosed them against the bank to the right of the road and unlocked the tribarrel on the roof of the rear compartment. She used the gunnery screen at her station instead of climbing out of her hatch and taking the gun's spade grips in her hands. The screen provided better all-round visibility as well as being safer for the gunner, but many of the ex-farmers in the Regiment felt acutely uncomfortable if they had to hunch down in a box when somebody might start shooting at them.

Ruthven expanded the image by four, then thirty-two times, letting the computer boost brightness and contrast. The command car's electronics gave him clearer vision than Hassel's own, though the sergeant can't have been in any doubt about what he was seeing. It was a pretty standard offering by the Lord's Army, after all.

"Right," Ruthven said aloud. "Unit, there's three Royalists crucified upside down by the road. We'll go uphill of them. Nobody comes within a hundred meters of the bodies in case they're boobytrapped, got it? Six out."

As he spoke, his finger traced a virtual course on the display; the electronics transmitted the image to the visors of his troopers. They were veterans and didn't need their hands held…but it was the platoon leader's job, and Ruthven took his job seriously.

The Lord knew there were enough ways to get handed your head even if you stayed as careful as a diamond cutter. The Lord *knew*.

Instead of answering verbally, the squad leaders' icons on Ruthven's display flashed green. Seven troopers of Sergeant Rennie's Third Squad—the other two escorted the gun jeep covering the rear—were already on the high ground, guiding their skimmers through trees which'd wrapped their limbs about their boles at the onset of winter. The thin soil kept the trees apart, and the undergrowth was already gray and brittle; Heavy Weapons' jeeps, two with tribarrels and the third with a mortar, wouldn't have a problem either. The command car, though…

Well, it didn't matter that a command car's high center of gravity and poor power-to-weight ratio made it a bad choice for breaking trail in wooded hills. This wasn't a choice, it was a military necessity unless Ruthven wanted to take the chance that the bodies weren't bait. His two years' experience in the field wasn't much for the Slammers, but it'd been plenty to teach him to avoid unnecessary risks.

The victims had been tied to the crosses with their own intestines, but that was just the usual fun and games for the Lord's Army. Ruthven grinned. If he'd had a better opinion of the Royalists, he might've been able to convince himself the Regiment was Doing Good on Pontefract. Fortunately, Colonel Hammer didn't require his platoon leaders to maintain feelings of moral superiority over their enemies.

His eyes on the dots of his troopers slanting across the terrain display, Ruthven keyed his microphone and said, "Courage Command, this is Echo One-six. Come in Courage Command, over."

The combat car's display showed that the transmitter in Lieutenant-Colonel Carrera's headquarters was one of half a dozen in Firebase Courage which were live, but nobody replied. Ruthven grimaced. He wasn't comfortable communicating with the Royalists to begin with, since any message which the Royalists could hear, the Lord's Army could overhear. It added insult to injury that the fools weren't responding.

The car bucked as the forward skirts dug into an outcrop with a *skreel!* of steel on stone. Ruthven expected they'd have to back and fill, but Melisant kicked her nacelles out and lifted them over the obstacle. She was driving primarily because her skimmer…now strapped to the side of the car in hopes of being able to repair it at the Royalist base…was wonky, but she was probably as good at the job as anybody in the platoon.

"Courage Command, this is Echo One-six," Ruthven repeated, keeping his voice calm but wondering if showing his irritation would help get the Royalists' attention. "Respond ASAP to arrange linkup, if you please. Over."

The car shifted back to level from its strongly nose-up attitude, though it continued to rock side to side. Ruthven had a real-time panorama at the top of his display, but he didn't bother checking it. His responsibility was the whole platoon, not the problems of weaving the car through woodland.

"*Echo One-six, my colonel say, 'Who are you?'*" replied a voice from the firebase. "*We must know who you are, over!*"

Ruthven sighed. It could've been worse. Of course, it might still get worse.

"Unit, hold in place till I sort this," he said aloud. Rennie's squad, now in the lead, must be nearly in sight of the firebase by now. "Break. Courage Command, this is Echo One-six. We're the unit sent to reinforce you. Please confirm that your troops are expecting us and won't open fire."

He hesitated three long heartbeats while deciding whether to say what was going through his mind, then said it: "Courage, we're the Slammers. If we're shot at, we'll shoot back. With everything we've got. Over."

Third Squad *was* in sight of the Royalists: the feed from Rennie's skimmer showed the firebase as a scar of felled trees on the hill 700 meters from him. Ruthven frowned; he was looking down into the firebase. The ridge by which E/1 had approached was a good fifty meters higher than the knoll where the Royalists had sited their guns.

"*You must not shoot!*" squealed a new voice from the Royalist firebase; a senior officer had apparently taken over from the radioman. "*We will not shoot! You must come in and help us at once!*"

Ruthven grinned faintly. "Courage, I'll give you three minutes to make sure all your bunkers get the word," he said. "We don't want any mistakes. Echo One-six out."

"*Hey El-Tee?*" said Sergeant Wegelin on the command push; he was crewing the tribarrel at the end of the column. "*What d'ye mean, come in shooting with everything we got? We're not exactly a tank company, you know, over.*"

"They don't know that, Wegs," Ruthven said, smiling more broadly as he examined the real-time visuals. "And anyway, I don't think we'd need panzers to put paid to this lot, over."

Fire Support Base Courage housed four 120-mm howitzers with an infantry battalion for protection. Treetrunks had been bulldozed into a wall around the camp, but they wouldn't stop light cannon shells as effectively as an earthen berm. The Slammers' powerguns would turn the wood into a huge bonfire.

"*Why in hell did they set up with this ridge above them, d'ye suppose?*" asked Hassel. Though the platoon sergeant had his own line of sight to the firebase, the display indicated he was using Wegelin's higher vantage point. "*We could put the guns out of action with four shots, over.*"

"*Because I never met nobody wearing a uniform here who knows how to pour piss outa a boot, Top,*" said Wegelin. "*Over.*"

"The ridge's too narrow for a battalion and the guns," said Ruthven. He was using text crawls to monitor the panicked orders flying across the firebase, but he didn't see any reason to wait in respectful silence for the Royalists to get their act in order. "They should've left a detachment…"

"*Echo One-six, you must come in now,*" Lieutenant-Colonel Carrera said sharply.

"Quickly, before the Dogs take advantage! Quick! Quick!"

"Break," said Ruthven, closing his conversation with his squad leaders. "Rennie, take your squad in. Wegelin, stay on overwatch. I'll follow Rennie, then Sellars, Wegelin, and you bring up the rear, Hassel. Six Out."

Again green blips signaled Received and Understood. Sergeant Rennie knelt on his skimmer to lead the way down and up the wooded saddle to the firebase. His troopers were lying flat with their control sticks folded down. That wasn't a good way to drive, but it made them very difficult targets in case somebody in the garrison hadn't gotten the word after all.

Rennie wasn't the brightest squad leader in the Regiment, but he was reflexively brave and never hesitated to take a personal risk to spare his troopers. They'd have followed him to Hell.

Melisant was sending power to the fans before Ruthven'd finished giving his orders, but the command car lifted awkwardly and only slowly started to wallow forward. The grace with which the troopers flitted around him made Ruthven feel like a hog surrounded by flies, but the skimmers'd run out of juice in a matter of hours without the car's fusion bottle to recharge them. He knew he was doing his proper job here inside the vehicle, though he didn't *feel* like he was.

The gun jeep that'd been reinforcing the lead squad didn't follow Rennie's troopers. The driver/assistant gunner waved as the combat car swept past; the jeep was hunkered down in a notch on the reverse slope that gave it a line of fire to the four howitzers and most of the interior of the firebase.

Sergeant Wegelin'd probably ordered the crew to keep under cover till he came up with the other gun and mortar. That wasn't precisely disobeying Ruthven's instructions, but it came bloody close; and Wegelin was probably right in his caution, so the El-Tee would keep his mouth shut. That was a lot of what a junior lieutenant did when he had good non-coms....

The infantry moved toward the firebase through the stumps and brush in a skirmish line, but Melisant swung the car onto the road as soon as she reached the swale connecting the knolls. The track'd been cut with a bulldozer rather than properly graded, but the car's air cushion smoothed the ride nicely. The deep ruts from wheeled vehicles were frozen now and had snow on their southern edges.

Royalists cheered from the top of the wall. The soldiers were male but there were scores of women and children in the compound as well, some of them waving garments.

Ruthven grimaced, thinking of what'd happen if the Lord's Army overran the place. His job was to prevent that, but if the rebels were in the strength Intelligence thought they were...well, one platoon, even a bloody good platoon like E/1, wasn't going to be able to do the job without help that the Royalists might not be able to provide.

The firebase entrance was a simple gap in the wall, but bulldozers had scraped a pile of trunks and dirt as a screen ten meters in front of it. Semi-trailers bringing in supplies would have a hard time with the angle, but Melisant should be able to guide the combat car through without trouble.

There were three strands of barbed wire in front of the wall. That gave negligible protection against assault, but maybe it'd hearten the defenders: placebo effects were real in more areas than medicine.

Ruthven grinned. It wasn't much of a joke, but in a situation like this you took any chance for a laugh that you got.

Rennie parked his skimmer beside the entrance and hopped up the front of the wall like a baboon with a 2-cm gun; he stood facing inward. His troopers split to either side, four of them joining him on the main wall while the other two mounted the screen and looked back to cover the rest of the column.

"Melisant, ease off a bit," Ruthven said over the intercom as he opened the roof hatch. "We don't want to spook our allies, over."

"*You mean they'll mess their pants, El-Tee?*" Melisant said. "*Yeah, we don't want that. Out.*"

The fan note didn't change, but the driver let gravity slow the heavy vehicle as they started up the slope toward the entrance. Ruthven thumbed the lift button and a hydraulic jack raised his seat until his head and shoulders were above the hatch coaming. This way the Royalists could see *him* instead of watching forty tonnes of steel and iridium growl toward them impassively.

Ruthven tried to keep his face impassive as he eyed the barrier. It was a tangle of protruding roots and branches, no harder to climb than a ladder. Defenders firing over the top from the other side would have very little advantage over an attacking force. The common soldiers carried locally made automatic rifles, but the three blockhouses spaced around the wall mounted pulsed lasers; each weapon had its own fusion bottle.

The Lord's Army wasn't any better equipped, but the Prophet Isaiah certainly did a better job of building enthusiasm in his followers than King Jorge II did. Rumor had it that Jorge and his three mistresses had left Pontefract for a safer planet several months ago… and this time rumor was dead right. Ruthven'd heard that from a buddy on Colonel Hammer's staff.

The command car eased through the S-bend at the base entrance. Melisant was squaring the corners, apparently to impress the locals. Ruthven looked down at them, trying to keep a friendly smile. They were impressed, all right, waving and cheering so loudly that sometimes he could hear them over the car's howling fans.

Good Lord they're young! he thought. It really was a war of children. Most of the Royalist soldiers were teenagers and so undernourished they looked barely pubescent, while the Lord's Army recruited ten year olds at gunpoint from outlying villages.

It'd go on for as long as King Jorge managed to pay the Slammers and the Five Worlds Consortium shipped arms to the Prophet. A whole generation was dying in childhood.

History was a required subject at the Academy; Ruthven had done well in it. The realities of field service had provided color for those textual accounts of revolts, rebellions, and popular movements, however. That color was blood red.

He'd expected a vehicular circuit inside the wall, but the interior of the compound was sprinkled randomly with shanties and lean-tos except for the road from the gate to a clearing in the center. The four howitzers were emplaced evenly around the open area, each in a low sandbagged ring which again must've been built for its morale value.

"*You want us up between the guns, El-Tee?*" Melisant asked. "*Looks like they dump the resupply there and the troops hoof it back to their billets, right? Over.*"

"Roger that," Ruthven said. "Break, Unit, we'll form in the central clearing while I figure out what to do next. Six out."

Blood and Martyrs! This's looking more and more like a ratfuck. Ruthven hadn't been thrilled by the assignment from the start, but until E/1 got to Firebase Courage he hadn't have guessed how bad things really were.

He'd expected the Royalist troops to be ill-trained and poorly equipped…because all Royalist field units were: the defense budget never percolated far from the gaudily dressed officers in the capital, Zaragoza. He *hadn't* expected Fire Support Base Courage to be so ineptly constructed, though. It was a wonder that the Lord's Army hadn't rolled over the position long before.

The Headquarters complex was four aluminum trailers which'd been buried in the ground to the right of the gate. A tower in the middle of them carried satellite and short-wave antennas, making the identification obvious and coincidentally providing an aiming point to the Prophet's gunners. The Lord's Army had only small arms, but painting a big bull's-eye on your Tactical Operations Center still isn't a good plan.

An officer in a green dress uniform with gold crossbelts was coming up the steps from one of the trailers, steadying his bicorn hat. The three aides accompanying him were less gorgeously dressed; that, rather than the rank tabs on his epaulets, identified Lieutenant-Colonel Carrera.

Ruthven dropped into the compartment again. As soon as Melisant brought the car to a halt, he swung the rear hatch down into a ramp and stepped out to meet the Royalist officers.

Carrera stopped where he was and braced to attention. A rabbity aide with frayed cuffs scurried to Ruthven and said, "Sir, you are the commander? My colonel asks, what is your rank?"

Ruthven frowned. Instead of answering, he walked over to Carrera and said, "Colonel? I'm Lieutenant Henry Ruthven, in command of Platoon E/1 of Hammer's Regiment. We've been sent to you as reinforcements."

"A lieutenant?" the Royalist officer said in amazement. "One platoon only? And where are the rest of your tanks? This one thing…"

He flicked his swagger stick toward the command car.

"…this is not enough, surely! We must have more tanks!"

What Major Pritchard, the Slammers Operations Officer, had actually said when he assigned Ruthven was, "to put some backbone into the garrison." It wouldn't have been polite or politic either one to have repeated the phrasing, but now Ruthven half-wished he had.

"We're infantry, Colonel," Ruthven said calmly, because it was his job…his duty…to be calm and polite. "We don't have any tanks at all, but I think you'll find we can handle things here. We've got sensors to give plenty of warning of enemy intentions. We've got our own powerguns, and we have direct communications to a battery of the Regiment's hogs."

"Oh, this is not right," Carrera said, turning and walking back toward his trailer. "My cousin promised me, *promised* me, tanks and there is only this tank."

"Sir?" said Ruthven. Sellars was bringing her squad in; the jeeps of Heavy Weapons followed closely. "Colonel! We need to make arrangements for the siting of my troops."

"Take care of him, Mendes," Carrera called over his shoulder. "I have been betrayed. It is out of my hands, now."

Carrera's aides had started to leave with him. A pudgy man in his forties, a captain if Ruthven had the collar insignia right, stopped and turned with a stricken look. The Royalists didn't wear name tags, but he was presumably Mendes.

"Right, Captain," Ruthven said with a breezy assertiveness that he figured was the best option. "I think under the circumstances we'll be best served by retaining my troops as a concentrated reserve here in the center of the firebase. We're highly mobile, you see. We'll place sensors around the perimeter to give us warning of attack as early as troops there could do."

That was true, but the real reason Ruthven'd decided to keep E/1 concentrated was so that his troopers could support one another. Self-preservation was starting to look like the primary goal for this operation. The Slammers'd been hired to fight and they *would* fight, but Hank Ruthven knew the Colonel hadn't given him troopers in order to get them killed for nothing.

All elements of E/1 were now within the compound. Hassel'd put the troopers with 2-cm shoulder weapons on the wall aiming northeast, toward the ridge they'd just come from. Both the tribarrels covered the high ground also.

The ten troopers with sub-machine guns faced in, keeping an eye on Ruthven and the babbling crowd of Royalists. They weren't threatening; just watchful. With their mirrored faceshields down they looked like Death's Little Helpers, though, and they could become that in an eyeblink if anybody gave them reason.

"We'll need the use of your digging equipment," Ruthven continued. "The bulldozer and whatever else you have; a backhoe, perhaps?"

"We have nothing," Mendes said.

Ruthven's face hardened; he gestured with his left hand toward the dug-in trailers. His right, resting on the receiver of his slung sub-machine gun, slipped down to the grip.

"They went back!" Mendes said. "They came, yes, but they went back! We have nothing here, only the guns; and no tractors to move them!"

Bloody hell, that was true! Ruthven'd assumed he wasn't getting signatures from heavy equipment during E/1's approach simply because nothing was running at the moment, but the shanties scattered within the compound would make it impossible for even a jeep to move through them.

"Right," said Ruthven. "Then I'll need a labor party from your men, Captain. We have a few power augers, but there's a great deal of work to do before nightfall. For all our sakes. However the first requirement is to garrison that knob."

He gestured toward the high ground. When Mendes didn't turn his head, Ruthven put his hand on the Royalist's shoulder and rotated him gently, then pointed again.

"It's not safe to give the enemy that vantage point," Ruthven said. To any real soldier, that'd be as obvious as saying, "Water is wet," but real soldiers were bloody thin on the ground on Pontefract.

And it seemed they all wore Slammers uniforms.

"Oh, we can't do that!" Mendes said. "That is too far away!"

"Together we can," Ruthven said. "I'll put a squad there, and you'll supply a platoon. We'll rotate the troops every day. Dug in and with fire support from here, they'll be an anvil that we can smash the rebels if they try anything."

"Oh," said Mendes. "Oh. Oh."

He wasn't agreeing…or disagreeing, so far as Ruthven could tell. He sounded like a man gasping for breath.

"Right!" Ruthven said cheerfully, clapping the Royalist on the shoulder. "Now, let's get to your ops room and set up the assignments, shall we?"

He'd put Rennie's squad on the ridge the first night, though he might also take Sellars' up for the afternoon to get the position cleared. He could only hope that the Royalists would work well under Slammers' direction; that happened often enough on this sort of planet.

"Top?" Ruthven said to Hassel over the command push as he walked Mendes toward the trailers. He'd cut the whole platoon in on the discussion through the intercom, though he was blocking incoming messages unless they were red-tagged. "Take charge here while I get things sorted with our allies."

He paused. Because Mendes could theoretically hear him…in fact the Royalist officer appeared to be in shock…Ruthven chose the next words carefully: "And Top? I know what you're thinking because I'm thinking the same thing. But this is going to work if there's *any* way in hell I can make it work. Six out."

"Good morning, Hank," a professionally cheerful voice said. "Oh! Were you napping? I didn't mean to wake you up."

"Just thinking, Lisa," Ruthven said, opening his eyes and smiling at Lisa Mahone, the Frisian recruiting officer. Apologetically he added, "I, ah… I haven't gotten around to the papers, yet."

He thought he saw Mahone's eyes harden, but she sat down on the side of his bed and patted his right leg in a display of apparent affection. She said, "Well, I've used the time to your advantage, Hank. I told you I *hoped* I'd be able to get Personnel to grant you a two-step promotion? They've agreed to it! I'm authorized to change the recruitment agreement right now."

She leaned forward to take the folder from the side table, her hip brushing Ruthven's thigh. "How does that sound, *Captain* Ruthven?"

"It's hard to express, Lisa," Ruthven said, forcing a smile to make the words sound positive. He slitted his eyes so that they'd appear closed. In truth he *didn't* know what he thought about the business; it seemed to be happening to somebody else. Maybe it was drugs still in his system, though Drayer'd sworn that they'd tapered his dosage down to zero thirty-six hours ago.

Ruthven watched silently as Mahone amended the recruitment agreement in a firm, clear hand. She was an attractive woman with dark, shoulder-length hair and a perfect complexion. Her pants suit was severely tailored, but the shirt beneath her pale green jacket was frilled and had a deep neckline.

The gold-bordered folder not only acted as a hard backing for Mahone's stylus, it recorded the handwritten changes and transmitted them to the hospital's data bank. There they became part of the regimental files, to be downloaded or transmitted by any authorized personnel.

Mahone wasn't as young as Ruthven'd thought when she approached him three days earlier, though. Perhaps the drugs really had worn off.

"I have to admit that I didn't have to do much convincing," she said in the same bright voice as she appeared to read the document in front of her. "My superiors were just as impressed by your record as I am. Very few graduates in the top ten percent of their class join mercenary units straight out of the Academy."

"I wanted to be a soldier," Ruthven said. This time his wry smile was real, but it was directed at his naive former self. "I thought I ought to learn what being a soldier was really about. I wanted to see the elephant, if you know the term."

"Seeing the elephant," had been used by soldiers as a euphemism for battle from a very long time back. It might even be as old as "buying the farm," a euphemism for death.

"And you certainly did," Mahone said. "Your combat experience is a big plus."

She met his eyes with every appearance of candor and said, "The Frisian Defense Forces haven't fought a serious war since the Melpomene Emergency fifteen years ago. You knew that: that's why you enlisted in Hammer's Regiment when you wanted to see action. I know it too, and most importantly, the General Staff in Burcana knows it. The Defense Forces are willing to pay very well for the experience that our troops haven't gotten directly."

Mahone smiled like a porcelain doll, smooth and perfect, and held the folder out to Ruthven. "You bought that experience dearly, Captain," she said. "Now's the time to cash in on your investment."

Ruthven winced. It was a tiny movement, but Mahone caught it.

"Hank?" she said, lowering the folder while keeping it still within reach. She stroked Ruthven's thigh again and said, "Is it your leg?"

"Yeah," Ruthven lied. "Look, Lisa…can you come back later? I want to, ah, stand up and walk around a bit, if that's all right. By myself."

"Of course, Hank," Mahone said, smiling sympathetically. "I'll leave these here and come by this evening. If you like you can just sign them and I'll pick them up without bothering you if you're asleep."

Mahone set the folder upright on the table, between the pitcher and waterglass. Straightening she glanced, apparently by coincidence, at the electronic window.

"Thank the Lord you don't have to go back to *that*, right?" she said. She smiled and swept gracefully out of the room.

Ruthven continued to lie on the bed for nearly a minute after the latch clicked. Then he got up slowly and walked to the window. He'd been thinking of Sergeant Rennie. That, not his leg, had made him wince.

They'd met on Atchafalaya. It'd been Ruthven's first day in the field, and it was Trooper Rennie then....

"Here you go, Chief," said the driver of the jeep that'd brought Ruthven from E Company headquarters. "Last stop this run."

It was raining and well after local midnight. This sector was under blackout conditions; water running down the inside of Ruthven's faceshield blurred his light-enhanced vision and dripped on the tip of his nose. It was cold, colder than he'd dreamed it got on Atchafalaya, and he was more alone than he'd ever before felt in his life.

"Sir, you gotta get out," the driver said more forcefully. "I need t' get back to Captain Dolgosh."

Besides the jeep's idling fans, the only sound in the forest was rain dripping into the puddles beneath the trees. Air-plants hung in sheets from high branches, twisting and shimmering in the downpour. Ruthven couldn't see anything human in the landscape.

"Where do I...?" he said.

Two figures came out of the blurred darkness. "Hold here, Adkins," one of them said. "I'll be going back with you. It won't be long."

"If you say so, El-Tee," the driver said. In bright contrast to his resigned agreement he added, "Hey, it's captain now, right? That was sure good news, sir. Nobody deserved it more!"

"Lieutenant Ruthven?" the newcomer continued brusquely, ignoring the congratulations. He was built like a fireplug and his voice rasped. "I'm Lyauty, you're taking E/1 over from me. I thought I'd stick around long enough to introduce you to your squad leaders."

"Ah, thank you very much, Captain," Ruthven said. He'd heard the man he was replacing'd been promoted to the command of Company K. That'd worried him because it meant Lyauty must be a good officer. *How am I going to measure up?*

The trooper who'd accompanied Lyauty was looking in the direction they'd come from, watching their backtrail. He had his right hand on the grip of his 2-cm weapon; the stubby iridium barrel was cradled in the crook of his left elbow. He hadn't spoken.

"This your gear?" Lyauty said, reaching into the back of the jeep before Ruthven could forestall him. *I thought the trooper would carry the duffle bag.* "Via, Lieutenant! Is this *all* yours? We're in forward positions here!"

"I, ah," Ruthven said. "Well, clean uniforms, mostly. And, ah, some food items. And the assigned equipment, of course."

The driver snickered. "He's got his own auger, sir," he said.

"Right," said Lyauty in sudden harshness. "And you let him bring it. Well, Adkins, for that you can haul his bag over to the car. I've got Sellars on commo watch. The two of you sort it out. Leave him a proper field kit and I'll take the rest back to Regiment with me to store."

"Sorry, sir," the driver muttered. "I shoulda said something."

"Come along, Ruthven," Lyauty said. "Sorry about the trail, but you'll get used to it. Say, this is Trooper Rennie. I've got him assigned as my runner. You can make your own choice, of course, but I'd recommend you spend a few days getting the feel of the platoon before you start making changes."

The trooper leading them into the forest turned his head; in greeting, Ruthven supposed, but the fellow didn't raise his faceshield. He was as featureless as a billiard ball.

Ruthven turned his head toward Lyauty behind him. "A power auger is assigned equipment, sir," he said in an undertone.

"Right," said the captain. "We've got three of them in the platoon. A bloody useful piece of kit, but not as useful as extra rations and ammo if things go wrong. The brass at Regiment can afford to count on resupply because it's not their ass swinging in the breeze if the truck doesn't make it forward. Here in the field we pretty much go by our own priorities."

The trail zigzagged steeply upward; Rennie in the lead was using his left hand to pull himself over the worst spots, holding his 2-cm weapon like a huge pistol. Ruthven's sub-machine gun was strapped firmly across his chest, leaving both hands free. Even so he stumbled repeatedly and once clanged flat on the wet rock.

"It's not much farther, Lieutenant," Lyauty said. "Another hundred meters up is all."

"I thought…" Ruthven said. He slipped and caught himself on all fours. As he started to get up, the toe of his left boot skidded back and slammed him down again. The sub-machine gun pounded against his body armor.

"I thought your headquarters would be the command vehicle," he said in a rush, trying to ignore the pain of his bruised ribs.

"We couldn't get the car to the top of this cone," Lyauty said. "I've been leaving it below with three troopers, rotating them every night when the rations come up."

"The jeeps couldn't climb above that last switchback," said Trooper Rennie. "We had to hump the tribarrels from there, and that's hell's own job."

There was a tearing hiss above. Ruthven jerked his head up. The foliage was sparse on this steep slope, so he was able to catch a glimpse of a green ball streaking across the sky from the west.

"Is that a rocket?" said Ruthven. Then, "That was a rocket!"

"It wasn't aimed at us, Lieutenant," Lyauty said wearily. "Anyway, our bunkers're on the reverse slope, though we've got fighting positions forward too if we need them."

"I just thought…" Ruthven said. "I thought we, ah… I thought that incoming artillery was destroyed in the air."

"They can't hit anything with bombardment rockets," Lyauty said. "Anyway, they can't hit us. To use the tribarrel in the command car for air defense, we'd have to shift it into a clearing. That'd make *it* a target."

"We're infantry, Lieutenant," Rennie said over his shoulder. "If you want to call attention to yourself, you ought to've put in for tanks."

Ruthven opened his mouth to dress the trooper down for insolence. He closed it again, having decided it was Lyauty's job properly since he hadn't formally handed over command of the platoon.

"We can hit hard when we need to, Lieutenant," Lyauty said. "But until then, yeah…keeping a low profile is a good plan."

"Who you got with you, Rennie?" a voice called from the darkness above them.

Ruthven looked up. He couldn't see anybody, just an outcrop over which a gnarled tree managed to grow. His torso beneath the clamshell body armor was sweating profusely, but his hands were numb from gripping wet rocks and branches.

"Six's come up, Hassel," Rennie said. "And we got the new El-Tee along."

"Sir?" said a man kneeling beside the outcrop. "Come on up but keep low. If you stand here, the Wops get your head in silhouette. I'm Hassel, First Squad."

"It's Hassel's bunker, properly," Lyauty said. "I asked the other squad leaders to come here tonight so I can introduce you."

Another man stepped into the night; this time Ruthven saw his arm sweep back the curtain of light-diffusing fabric hanging over a hole in the side of the hillside. "This the new El-Tee?" he said.

"Right, Wegs," said Lyauty. "His name's Ruthven. Lieutenant, Sergeant Wegelin's your Heavy Weapons squad leader. Come on, let's get under cover."

"Yessir, two tribarrels and two mortars instead of three of each," said Wegelin as he held the curtain for Hassel, then Ruthven after a directive jab from Lyauty's knuckles. "And if you think that's bad, then we only got three working jeeps. It don't matter here since we offloaded the guns, but we'll be screwed good if they expect us to displace on our own."

Ruthven hit his head—his helmet, but it still staggered him—on the transom, then missed the two steps down. He'd have fallen on his face if the tall man waiting—he had to hunch to clear the ceiling—hadn't caught him.

"Have you heard something about us displacing, Wegs?" the man said, stepping back when he was sure Ruthven had his feet. "Because I haven't. Talk about getting the shaft! E/1 sure has this time."

"Troops, this is Lieutenant Ruthven who's taking over from me," Lyauty said. "Lieutenant, that's van Ronk, your platoon sergeant, Axbird who's got Second Squad…"

"How-do, Lieutenant," said a short woman who at first seemed plump. When she lifted her rain cape to pour a cup of cacao from the pot bubbling on a ledge cut into the side of the bunker, Ruthven realized she was wearing at least three bandoliers laden with equipment and ammunition.

"And that's Purchas there on watch," Lyauty said, nodding to the man in the southeast corner. "He's Third Squad."

Purchas was on an ammo box, using a holographic display which rested on a similar box against the bunker wall. He didn't turn around.

"We pipe the sensors through optical fibers," Lyauty explained, gesturing to the skein of filaments entering the bunker by a hole in the roof. Rain dripped through also, pooling on the floor of gritty mud. "Below the ridgeline there's a microwave cone aimed back at the command car. We need the car for the link to Central, but other than that we're on our own here."

Everybody'd raised their faceshields; Ruthven raised his too, though the bunker's only illumination was that scatter from the sensor display. *My eyes'll adapt. Won't they?*

"If you're wondering, there isn't a separate command bunker," Lyauty said. "You can change that if you want, but I feel like moving to a different squad each night keeps me in the loop better."

Everybody was looking at Ruthven. Well, everybody but Purchas. They expected him to say something.

Ruthven's lips were sticking together. "I…" he said. "Ah, I see."

"Well, I'll leave you to it, then," Lyauty said. "This is as good a platoon as there is in the Slammers, Ruthven. You're a lucky man."

He turned toward the curtained entrance. "Ah, excuse me, sir," Ruthven said. *How do I address the man? Oh Lord, oh Lord!* "Ah, my sleeping bag is with my other gear. Ah, in the jeep."

"No sweat, Lieutenant," said Trooper Rennie, pointing to the bag roughly folded on a wall niche. The outside was of resistant fabric; beneath were layers of micro-insulation and a soft lining. This cover was torn, and from what Ruthven could see, the lining was as muddy as the floor. "There's an extra in each of the squad bunkers. You and me won't both be sleeping at the same time."

Lyauty cleared his throat. "Well," he said, "keep your heads down, troopers. I'll be thinking about you, believe me."

He muttered something else as he stepped back into the rain. Ruthven thought he heard, "I've got half a mind…" but it might not have been that.

The bunker was cold and it stank. Sweat and rain water were cooling between Ruthven's skin and his body armor, and he was sure he'd chafed blisters over his hipbones. Another rocket screamed through the sky; this time it hit close enough to shake dirt from the bunker ceiling.

Ruthven looked at his new subordinates. Their expressions were watchful, hostile, and in the case of Purchas completely dismissive.

He wished he were back on Nieuw Friesland. He wished he were anyplace else but here.

Lieutenant Henry Ruthven wished he were dead.

There was a knock on a door down the corridor. "El-Tee, is that you?" somebody called. Ruthven, his face blanking, stepped quickly around the bed to get to the door.

Muffled words answered unintelligibly. "Sorry," said the familiar voice. "I'm looking for Lieutenant Ruthven and…"

"Axbird, is that you?" Ruthven said, stepping into the corridor. "Via, Sergeant, I thought you'd already shipped out! Come on in…I've got a bottle of something you'll like."

"Don't mind if I do, El-Tee," Axbird said. "Tell the truth, there isn't a hell of a lot I don't like, so long as it comes out of a bottle. Or a can…I'm democratic that way."

E/1's former platoon sergeant had gained weight…a lot of weight…since her injury, though that hadn't been but…well, it'd been four months. Longer than Ruthven would've guessed without thinking about it. But still, a lot of weight.

The skin of her face was as smooth as burnished metal. Her eyes had the milky look of a molting snake's, and she had an egg-shaped device clipped above each ear.

Ruthven backed into his room and rotated the chair for Axbird, primarily to call it to her attention. A buzzbomb had hit the side of the command car while she was inside with her faceshield raised. The jet from the warhead's shaped charge had missed her…had missed everything, in fact; patched, the car was still in service with E/1…but it'd vaporized iridium from the opposite bulkhead. That glowing cloud had bathed her face.

Axbird entered with the careful deliberation of a robot. She wasn't using a cane, but she held her hands out at waist height as though preparing to catch herself. When she reached the chair, she put one hand on the back and tapped the device above her right ear. "How do you like them, El-Tee?" she said with a plastic smile. "I always wanted to have black eyes. Didn't say they shouldn't be lidar transceivers, though. That's what you get for not specifying, hey?"

"You're getting around very well, Axbird," Ruthven lied. He squatted to rummage in the cabinet under his side table. There was only one glass, and the brandy was too good to pour into the plastic tumbler by the water pitcher.

"I'm still getting used to them," Axbird said. "Dialing 'em in, you know? They say I'll get so I can tell the numbers, but right now I'm counting doorways."

"There's a linen closet in the middle of the corridor," Ruthven said apologetically. He offered her the glass, wondering if she could see his expression. Probably not; probably never again.

Axbird drank the brandy without lowering the glass from her lips. "Via, I needed that," she muttered, wiping her mouth with the back of her hand. She forced another grin and said, "How are you doing, sir? I heard you guys really got it in the neck."

"It was bad enough," Ruthven agreed carefully. He'd hesitated a moment, but he took the glass and refilled it for her. "Thank the Lord for Fire Central."

"You can't trust wogs," Axbird said. Her voice rose. "We might as well kill 'em all. Every fucking one of 'em!"

"There's better local forces and worse ones, Sergeant," Ruthven said with deliberate formality. "I'd say the Royalists here were pretty middling. They'd do well enough if they got any support from their own government."

"Yeah, I suppose," Axbird said. She was trembling; she held the glass in both hands to keep from spilling. "You trust your buddies and screw the rest, every one of 'em."

A rebel sapper had gotten close enough to nail the command car with a buzzbomb because the Royalists holding that section of the perimeter had all been asleep. The car's Automatic Defense System hadn't been live within the compound; it wouldn't have been safe with so many friendlies running around.

"Sorry, El-Tee," Axbird said. She seemed to have gotten control of herself again. "Yeah, remember on Diderot where our so-called allies were trying to earn the bounties the Chartists were offering on a Slammer's head?"

"Umm, that was before my time, Axbird," Ruthven said, sitting on his bed. He held the brandy bottle but he didn't think a drink would help him right now. "I joined on Atchafalaya, remember."

"Oh, right," said Axbird. She drank, guiding the glass to her lips with both hands. "Right, Diderot was back when I was a trooper."

For a moment she was silent, her cloudy eyes staring into space. Ruthven wondered if he should say something…and wondered what he *could* say…but Axbird resumed: "They got a great spot lined up for me, El-Tee. The Colonel did, I mean: a condo right on the beach on San Carlos. It's on Mainland because, well…until I get these dialed in better, you know."

Her right hand gestured toward the lidar earpiece, then quickly closed again on her empty glass.

"And for maintenance at first, I don't want to be out on my own island," she continued in a tone of birdlike perkiness. "But I can be. I can buy my own bloody island, El-Tee, I'm on full pay for the rest of my life! That'll run to a lotta brandy, don't you know?"

"Here, I'll fill that," Ruthven said, leaning forward with the bottle. He took the glass in his own hand before he started to pour. "Are you from San Carlos originally, then?"

"Naw," Axbird said. "I'm from Camside, sir. Haven't been back since I enlisted, though, twelve years."

She stared off into space. Her eyes moved normally; Ruthven wondered how much sight remained to them. Probably no more than being able to tell light from dark, though that'd be some help when she was on her own.

"I thought of going back, you know?" she said. "My pension'd make me a big deal on Camside, leastways unless things've changed a bloody great lot since I shipped out. But I thought, who do I know there? There's nobody, nobody ever who'd understand what it means to be a Slammer. What do I care about them?"

Axbird drank convulsively, dribbling brandy from the corners of her mouth. She started to lower the glass and instead dropped it. It bounced once, then shattered.

"Oh Lord, sir!" she said, her voice rising into a wail. She lurched to her feet. Tears were streaming from beneath the lids of her ruined eyes. "What do *I* care about wogs, on Camside or any bloody place?"

She was wearing hospital slippers. Ruthven got up quickly and gripped her shoulder to keep her from stepping in the glass she probably couldn't see. Axbird threw her arms around him.

"Oh, Lord, El-Tee!" she said. "There's nobody who'll understand! There'll never be anybody!"

Ruthven held the sobbing woman. His eyes were closed. He was remembering E/1's second and last night in Fire Support Base Courage. *Nobody'll ever understand.*

"El-Tee!" said Rennie in a hoarse whisper. "Sir, wake up. The bastards're bugging out!"

Ruthven jerked upright. He'd been sleeping in the rear compartment of the command car while Rennie sat at the console with the sensor readouts and commo gear. The squad leaders each took a two-hour watch, debriefing Ruthven when they were relieved or if anything significant appeared.

As it'd done, apparently.

Melisant'd been sleeping on top of the cab; her boots clunked against armor as she slid down behind the controls. The tone of Rennie's voice through the open hatch had snapped her awake, so she was heading for her action station like the good trooper she was.

Rennie had the sensor display filling most of the holographic screen; commo was a narrow sidebar, unimportant for the time being. People…hundreds of people…were clustered at the firebase entrance. They were leaving on foot, heading eastward along the road. From the south, west, and north other groups of people were approaching.

Those coming toward the base were rebels of the Lord's Army, armed to the teeth. Judging from the lack of metal for the magnetic sensors to pick up, the Royalists had left their weapons behind.

"Them wogs're just walking outa the base!" Rennie said. "They musta been talking to the rebs, don't you guess?"

"More to the point, they're walking out on us," Ruthven muttered. "Rouse the platoon…but quiet, don't let the locals know we've tumbled to what's going on."

He uncaged and pressed the panic button that automatically copied all platoon communications to Base Hammer, through the satellite net if it was up or by bouncing off cosmic ray tracks if it wasn't. It was faster than making a separate transmission to Regiment, and there was *bloody* little time. The rebels'd be climbing over the wall in a few minutes, and when that happened it'd all be over for E/1.

Ruthven raised the platform to put his head and shoulders through the roof hatch. Using his helmet's thermal imaging, he could see that the howitzer crews were gone too. The guns hadn't been disabled: explosions or the roar of thermite grenades would've warned the Slammers. In all likelihood, the Lord's Army had offered the Royalists their lives, in exchange for all their arms and for the Slammers who'd been sent as reinforcements.

It was at best an open question as to whether the rebels intended to honor their bargain. They'd left the road clear for half a klick from the firebase entrance, but the figures concealed in the brush there to either side looked to Ruthven like a kill zone placed far enough out that the victims couldn't run back to safety.

On the other hand, the Royalists hadn't exactly delivered Platoon E/1 into the Prophet's hands either.

"Unit, listen up," Ruthven said. The troopers in the firebase were gathered close enough that his helmet intercom reached them unaided, but the command car's powerful transceivers were relaying the signal to Sergeant Sellars' squad on the knoll to the northeast. "We can't hold this place, it's too big, but we can break out and join Second Squad. All together in a tight perimeter we can hold till help comes."

Via, what was the closest friendly unit? Maybe G Troop's combat cars, based with a regimental howitzer battery at Firebase Groening? But that was forty klicks away, and it wouldn't be safe for them to come direct by the road.

"I'm taking the car out by the entrance," he continued aloud. "We can't get over the wall or through it. Wegelin, your jeeps follow me."

Maybe a tank could push a hole in the tangle of treetrunks, but a command car couldn't and overloaded jeeps *certainly* couldn't. Nor did they have enough excess power to climb the irregular surface.

"The rest of you lift over the wall in the zero to forty-five-degree quadrant," Ruthven said. That'd spread the troopers enough that they wouldn't get in each other's way while awkwardly jumping the trees. "The skimmers can do it if you're careful. I'll call a fire mission on the rebs coming from the north. When it lands, that's our signal to roll. Any questions?"

"*El-Tee, I was a redleg on Andersholz before I joined the Regiment,*" said Wegelin. "*I can fire them one-twenties. The wogs keep'em loaded but powered down, you see.*"

Ruthven tried to make sense of what Wegelin had just said. He hadn't known the Heavy Weapons sergeant had been an artilleryman, but he didn't see what difference it made now. They could startle the rebs and cause casualties by firing the Royalist guns in their faces as they climbed the wall, but it sure wouldn't drive them away.

"*What I mean, sir,*" Wegelin continued, "*is a charger of five HE rounds'll give us a hole any bloody place you want to go through the wall. Not at the gate where they'll be expecting us, I mean, over.*"

"Can you manage that in two minutes, over?" Ruthven said as he dropped into the van's interior. Rennie'd vacated the console and was on his way out of the compartment, returning to his squad.

Ruthven checked the display. Rennie'd prepped fire missions on each of the four rebel concentrations; three moved as the company-sized groups advanced on the firebase.

"*We're on our way, out,*" the sergeant responded. As he spoke, icons on Ruthven's display showed the jeeps sprinting to the northernmost howitzer; the sound of their fans burred faintly through the open hatches. The big gun wasn't far from where Wegelin's squad was to begin with, but he obviously wanted them all to be able to jump into the jeeps as soon as they'd set up the burst.

"Unit," Ruthven said. He placed his right index finger on the terrain map image of the firebase wall, exporting the image to all his troopers. "Adjust the previous order. The car and jeeps will be leaving the firebase *here*. I don't know what the shells are going to do…"

One possibility was that they'd blast the existing tangle into something worse, so that the skimmers couldn't get over or through either one. It was still the best choice on offer.

"…and if you want to follow me through what I hope'll be a gap, that's fine. But *don't* get in the way, troopers, this car's a pig. We're going to be a full honk, and we won't be able to dodge. Questions, over?"

Nobody spoke, but three green icons blipped onto the top of the display. *Via, they're pros, they're the best platoon in the bloody regiment, they really are….*

"*Six, we got the tube ready!*" Sergeant Wegelin said as his icon lit also. "*Five rounds, HE, and I've programmed her to traverse right three mils at each round. We're ready, over!*"

The Royalist howitzers had their own power supplies to adjust elevation and traverse; they could even crawl across terrain by themselves, though very slowly. The northern weapon was now live, a bright image on Ruthven's display and a whine through the hatch as its pumps pressurized the hydraulic system.

"Fire Central, this is Echo One-six," Ruthven said, calling the Regiment's artillery controller but distributing the exchange to his troopers on an output-only channel. "Request Fire Order One…"

Targeting the rebels approaching from the northeast. They were coming uphill by now. That plus the stumps and broken rocks of the roughly cleared terrain had slowed them.

"…HE, repeat HE only, we're too close for firecracker rounds, time of impact fifty-five, repeat five-five seconds from…"

His index finger tapped a marker into the transmission.

"… *now*, over."

"*Roger, Echo One-six,*" replied a voice barely identifiable as female through the tight compression. She was so calm she sounded bored. Then, "*On the way, out.*"

"Echo One-Four-six," Ruthven said. *I probably sound bored too.* "This is Six. Take the wall down in three-five, I repeat three-five, seconds. Break. Unit, wait for our hogs, don't get hasty. Then its time to kick ass, troopers, out!"

The command car's fans were howling. The vehicle slid forward; forty tonnes accelerates slowly, so Melisant was getting an early start. *They'll hear us, but screw'em. They'll hear more than our fans real soon.*

Ruthven started to close the back ramp but Melisant had already taken care of that.

He went up through the roof hatch and took the tribarrel's grips in his hands.

There were a lot of reasons to stay down in the body. Communications with E/1 and Central were better inside; he could operate the gun just as well from the console and had a better display than his visor gave him; and the vehicle's armor, though light, might save him from shrapnel or a bullet that'd otherwise rob the platoon of its commander. There wasn't a trooper in E/1 who'd think their El-Tee was a coward if he stayed in the compartment.

But Ruthven himself'd worry that he was a coward in the dark silences before dawn, especially if he survived and some of his troopers didn't. And somebody was going to die. That was as sure as sunrise, even if E/1 got luckier than any veteran expected.

The long-barreled 120-mm howitzer belched a bottle-shaped yellow flash toward the perimeter wall; companion flares spewed out and back from both sides through the muzzle brake's baffles. The tube recoiled and the blast slapped Ruthven. The commo helmet's active sound cancellation saved his hearing, but the shockwave pushed him against the hatch ring. Even at this distance, unburned powder grains speckled his throat and bare hands.

The wall erupted, leaking the shellburst's red flash through the treetrunks it blew apart. Royalist shanties flattened, flung outward in a cone spreading from the howitzer. A huge dust cloud rose from the shock-pummeled compound.

The command car hit the ground, plowing a track through the hard soil. The steel skirt rang, scattering sparks when it hit embedded stones as the vehicle bucked and pitched.

Either the shockwave had startled Melisant into chopping her throttles, or she'd realized it'd be a disaster to get in front of the howitzer while it was still firing. The Regiment used rocket howitzers rather than tube artillery. She probably hadn't expected the muzzle blast of a long-range gun to be so punishing.

Ruthven hadn't expected it either. Being told something by an Academy lecturer wasn't the same as being hit by what felt like a hundred-kilo sandbag in the field.

The howitzer returned to battery and slammed again, then *again*, *again*, and *again*. The interval between shots was less than two seconds. The last shell screamed toward the northwest horizon as the gun fell over on its side. Rapid fire at zero elevation had lifted the recoil spades at the end of the gun's trail.

Between the third round and the fourth, the salvo from the hogs at Firebase Groening burst outside the encampment as a white glare which silhouetted the flying treetrunks. Central'd fused the shells to go off just above the surface instead of burying themselves before exploding.

Fragments of casing screeched across the hillside in an interlocking web more deadly than any spider's. A large chunk…maybe the baseplate of a Royalist shell… howled through Firebase Courage in a flat red streak. It didn't miss the command car by much, but it missed….

"Go!" Ruthven shouted. "Go! Go! Go!"

The car was accelerating again. After Melisant'd gotten them stopped the first time, she'd gimbaled the nacelles vertical and kept the fans at maximum output. They'd been hovering at ten centimeters on a pillow of air, not exactly flying—the vehicle remained in ground effect—but shuddering to every shockwave.

The elevation, though slight, gave the car a gravity boost when Melisant shoved the steering yoke forward. They gathered speed quickly despite ticks and bounces from debris scattered across the interior of the firebase. Flames spurted beneath the plenum chamber when they crossed the former perimeter; the 120-mm shells had started small fires in the wood, and the drive fans whipped them into hungry enthusiasm.

There were some larger chunks for them to kick aside, but the trees no longer formed an interlocked mass that could resist a forty-tonne battering ram. Showers of sparks and blazing torches flew ahead of the skirts. Then the car was through and heading down the slope into what remained of a company of the Lord's Army.

Ruthven snapped a short burst at what looked in his visor's thermal image like a rebel kneeling only twenty meters away. The car skidded enough to throw his bolts wide, but before he could correct he realized that he was shooting at a legless, headless torso impaled on a sapling.

Cyan bolts snapped through the night, igniting the brush. Nobody could aim accurately from a skimmer at speed, but in the corner of his eye Ruthven saw a secondary explosion. A trooper'd gotten lucky, hitting a rebel's buzzbomb and detonating the warhead.

Red tracers and muzzle flashes danced in the darkness also, but most of the rebels firing were in the companies to the south and east. The party on which the hogs had unloaded were largely silent, dead or stunned by the 20-cm shells. One rebel opened up from a gully to E/1's left front, but at least a dozen powerguns replied to the chattering rifle. Either somebody hit the reb, or he decided that huddling out of sight was a better idea than martyrdom for the Prophet after all; at any rate, the shooting stopped.

The command car reached the ground slope rising toward Second Squad. The brush and canes hadn't been cleared here; they averaged maybe two meters high, and there were occasional much taller trees.

Melisant kept moving, but she had to slow to twenty kph. They'd drawn well ahead of the jeeps and skimmers on the downhill run, but now the smaller vehicles were able to slip between clumps which the car had to fight through.

For a wonder, Sergeant Sellars was keeping her Royalists from shooting down at Ruthven's force. Maybe Second Squad was holding the locals at gunpoint to enforce fire discipline… and then again, maybe that detached platoon'd bugged out when the shooting started. Either way, Ruthven was going to put Sellars in for both a medal and a promotion when this was over.

If I'm around to make the recommendation. If she's around to get it.

Badly aimed rifle fire had been zipping overhead since the beginning of the breakout, but now a machine gun on a fixed mount cut branches nearby. Ruthven rotated his tribarrel to the right. Bullets whanged off the car's high side. The machine gunner was part of the unit that'd been waiting down the road for the Royalist garrison. He was bloody good to hit a moving target at 600 meters, even with the advantage of a tripod.

Ruthven fired a short burst. His tribarrel was stabilized, but the lurching car threw him around violently even though the weapon held its point of aim. His bolts vanished into the night, leaving only faintly glowing tracks on their way toward interplanetary vacuum.

Ruthven took a deep breath, letting the car bump into a small depression. When they started up the other side, into a belt of canes trailing hair-fine filaments, he fired. This time his shots merged with the muzzle flashes of the rebel machine gun. Plasma licked a white flare of burning steel.

Got you, you bastard! Ruthven thought. Three rebels with buzzbombs rose out of the swale ten meters ahead of the car.

Ruthven swung the tribarrel back toward the new targets. The rebels to left and right fired: glowing gas spurted from the back of the launching tubes, and the bulbous missiles streaked toward the vehicle behind quick red sparks.

The car's Automatic Defense System banged twice, blasting tungsten pellets from the strips just above the skirts. They shredded the buzzbombs in the air, killing one of the rebels who happened to be in the way of the remainder of the charge.

Ruthven shot before his gun was on target, hoping his blue-green bolts chewing the landscape would startle the rebels. The remaining rebel fired. Because the car's bow was canted upward, the third buzzbomb approached from too low to trip the ADS. The warhead burst against the skirts, punching a white-hot spear through the plenum chamber and up into the driver's compartment.

Several lift fans shut off; pressurized air from the remaining nacelles roared through the hole blown in the steel. The car grounded, rocked forward in a near somersault, and slammed to rest on its skirts.

The first impact smashed Ruthven's thighs against the hatch coaming; pain was a sun-white blur filling his mind. When the car's bow lifted, it tossed him onto the bales of rations and personal gear in the roof rack. Ruthven was only vaguely aware of the final shock hurling him off the crippled vehicle.

He opened his eyes. He was on his back with the landscape shimmering in and out of focus. He must've been unconscious, but he didn't know how long. The car was downslope from him. One of its fans continued to scream, but the others were silent. Black smoke boiled out of the driver's compartment.

He tried to stand up but his legs didn't move. *Have they been blown off? They couldn't be, I'd have bled out.* He'd lost his helmet, so the visor no longer protected his eyes from the sky-searing bolts of plasma being fired from the knoll above him. The afterimages of each track wobbled from orange to purple and back across his retinas.

Ruthven rolled over, still dazed. Pain yawned in a gaping cavern centered on his right leg. He must've screamed but he couldn't hear the sound. When the jolt from the injured leg sucked inward and vanished, his throat felt raw.

"It's the El-Tee!" somebody cried. "Cover me, I'm going to get him."

Another buzzbomb detonated with a hollow *Whoomp!* on the right side of the command car. Momentarily, a pearly bubble swelled bigger than the vehicle itself. The jet penetrated the thin armor, crossed the compartment, and sprayed out the left side.

Ruthven started crawling, pushing himself with his left foot and dragging his right as though the leg were tied to his hip with a rope. He couldn't feel it now except as a dull throbbing *somewhere*.

He wasn't trying to get to safety: he knew his safest course would be to lie silently in a dip, hoping to go unobserved or pass for dead. He wasn't thinking clearly, but his troopers were on the knoll so that's where he was going.

A rebel ran out from behind the command car shouting, "Protect me, Lord!"

Ruthven glanced back. His sub-machine gun was in the vehicle, but he wore a pistol. He scrabbled for it but his equipment belt was twisted; he couldn't find the holster.

The rebel thrust his automatic rifle out in both hands; the butt wasn't anywhere near his shoulder. "Die, unbeliever!" he screamed. A 2-cm powergun bolt decapitated him. The rifle fired as he spasmed backward.

One bullet struck Ruthven in the small of the back. It didn't penetrate his ceramic body armor, but the impact was like a sledgehammer. Bits of bullet jacket sprayed Ruthven's right arm and cheek.

He pushed himself upward again, moaning deep in his throat. He thought he might be talking to himself. A skimmer snarled through the high grass and circled to a halt alongside, the bow facing uphill. Nozzles pressurized by the single fan sprayed grit across Ruthven's bare face.

"El-Tee, grab on!" Rennie shouted, leaning from the flat platform to seize Ruthven's belt. "Grab!"

Ruthven turned on his side and reached out. He got a tie-down in his left hand and the shoulder clamp of the sergeant's armor in his right. Rennie was already slamming power to the lift fan, trying to throw his weight out to the right to balance the drag of Ruthven's body.

The skimmer wasn't meant to carry two, but it slowly accelerated despite the excess burden. Ruthven bounced through brush, sometimes hitting a rock. His left boot acted as a skid, but often enough his hip or the length of his leg scraped as the skimmer ambled uphill. A burst of sub-machine gun fire, a nervous flickering against the brighter, saturated flashes of 2-cm weapons, crackled close overhead, but Ruthven couldn't see what the shooter was aiming at.

The skimmer jolted over a shrub whose roots had held the windswept soil in a lump higher than the ground to either side. Ruthven flew free and rolled. Every time his right leg hit the ground, a flash of pain cut out that fraction of the night.

A tribarrel chugged from behind, raking the slope up which they'd come. Ruthven was within the new perimeter. Half a dozen Royalists huddled nearby with terrified expressions, but E/1 itself had enough firepower to halt the rebels. They'd already been hammered, and now more shells screamed down like a regiment of flaming banshees.

Firebase Groening was northeast of Firebase Courage, so the hogs were overfiring E/1's present perimeter to reach the rebels. Somebody…Sergeant Hassel?…must be calling in concentrations, relaying the messages through the command car. The vehicle was out of action, but its radios were still working.

Rennie spun the skimmer to a halt. "Made it!" he shouted. "We bloody well made it!"

Ruthven found his holster and managed to lift the flap. Beside him, Rennie hunched to remove his 2-cm weapon from the rail where he'd clamped it to free both hands for the rescue.

A buzzbomb skimmed the top of the knoll, missing the tribarrel at which it'd been aimed and striking Sergeant Rennie in the middle of the back. There was a white flash.

The shells from Firebase Groening landed like an earthquake on the rebels who'd overrun the Royalist camp and were now starting uphill toward E/1. In the light of the huge explosions, Ruthven saw Rennie's head fly high in the air. The sergeant had lost his helmet, and his expression was as innocent as a child's.

"Good afternoon, Lieutenant Ruthven," Doctor Parvati said as he stepped into the room without knocking. "You are up? And packing already, I see. It is good that you should be optimistic, but let us take things one step at a time, shall we? Lie down on your bed, please, so that I can check you."

Ruthven wondered if Parvati'd put a slight emphasis on the phrase "one step." Probably not, and even if he had it'd been meant as a harmless joke. *I have to watch myself. I'm pretty near the edge, and if I start overreacting, well….*

"Look, Doc," he said, straightening but not moving away from the barracks bag he was filling from the locker he'd kept under the bed. "You saw the reading that Drayer took this noon, right? I'm kinda in a hurry."

"I have gone over the noon readings, yes," Parvati said calmly. He was a small, slight man with only a chaplet of hair remaining, though by his face he was in his early youth. "Now I would like to take more readings."

When Ruthven still hesitated, Parvati added, "I do not tell you how to do your job, Lieutenant. Please grant me the same courtesy."

"Right," said Ruthven after a further moment. He pushed the locker to the side and paused. The garments were new, sent over from Quartermaster's Stores. The gear on the command car's rack had burned when they shot at rebs trying to get to the tribarrel. The utilities Ruthven worn during the firefight had been cut off him as soon as he arrived here.

He sat on the bed and carefully swung his legs up. He'd been afraid of another blinding jolt, but he felt nothing worse than a twinge in his back. Funny how it was his left hip rather than the smashed right femur where the pain hit him now. He'd scraped some on the left side, but he'd have said that was nothing to mention.

"So," said Parvati, reading the diagnostic results with his hands crossed behind his back. The holographic display was merely a distortion in the air from where Ruthven lay looking at the doctor. "So."

"I was talking to Sergeant Axbird this afternoon," Ruthven said to keep from fidgeting. "She was my platoon sergeant, you know. I was wondering how she was coming along?"

Parvati looked at Ruthven through the display. After a moment he said, "Mistress Axbird's physical recovery has gone as far as it can. How she does now depends on her own abilities and the degree to which she learns to use her new prosthetics. If you are her friend, you will encourage her to show more initiative in that regard."

"Ah," Ruthven said. "I see. *I'm* cleared for duty, though, Doctor. Right?"

He wondered if he ought to stand up again. Parvati always used the bed's own display instead of downloading the information into a clipboard.

"Are you still feeling pain in your hip, Lieutenant?" the doctor asked, apparently oblivious of Ruthven's question.

"No," Ruthven lied. "Well, not really. You know, I get a little, you know, tickle from time to time. I guess that'll go away pretty quick, right?"

It struck Ruthven that the diagnostic display would include blood pressure, heart rate, and all the other physical indicators of stress. He jumped up quickly. Pain exploded from his hip; he staggered forward. His mouth was open to gasp, but his paralyzed diaphragm couldn't force the air out of his lungs.

"Lieutenant?" Parvati said, stepping forward.

"I'm all right!" said Ruthven. Sweat beaded his forehead. "I just tripped on the locker! Bloody thing!"

"I see," said Parvati in a neutral tone. "Well, Lieutenant, your recovery seems to be proceeding most satisfactorily. I'd like you to remain here for a few days, however, so that some of my colleagues can check you over."

"You mean Psych, don't you?" Ruthven said. His hands clenched and unclenched. "Look, Doc, I don't need that and I *sure* don't want it. Just sign me out, got it?"

"Lieutenant Ruthven, you were seriously injured," the doctor said calmly. "I would be derelict in my duties if I didn't consider the possibility that the damage I was able to see had not caused additional damage beyond my purview. I wish to refer you to specialists in psychological trauma, yes."

"Do you?" Ruthven said. His voice was rising, but he couldn't help it. "Well, you let *me* worry about that, all right? You're a nice guy, Doc, but you said it: my psychology is none of your business! Now, you clear me back to my unit, or I'll take it over your head. You can explain to Colonel Hammer why you're dicking around a platoon leader whose troops need him in the field!"

"I see," said the doctor without any inflection. "I do not have the authority to hold you against your will, Lieutenant, but for your own sake I wish you would reconsider."

"You said that," Ruthven said. He bent and picked up his barracks bag. "Now, you do your job and let me get back to mine."

Parvati made a slight bow. "As you wish," he said. He touched the controller in his hand; the hologram vanished like cobwebs in a storm. "I will have an orderly come to take your bag."

"Don't worry about that," Ruthven said harshly. "I can get it over to the transient barracks myself. They'll find me a bunk there if there isn't a way to get to E/1 still tonight. I just want to be out of this place ASAP."

He didn't know where the platoon was or who was commanding in his absence. Hassel, he hoped; it'd be awkward if Central'd brought in another officer already. He wondered how many replacements they'd gotten after the ratfuck at Firebase Courage.

"As you wish," Parvati repeated, opening the door and stepping back for Ruthven to lead. "Ah? By the water pitcher, Lieutenant? The file is yours, I believe?"

Ruthven didn't look over his shoulder. "No, not mine," he said. "I was thinking about, you know, transferring out, but I couldn't leave my platoon. E/1 really needs me, you know."

He walked into the corridor, as tight as a compressed spring. Even before Axbird had come to see him, he'd been thinking of night and darkness and the faceless horror of living among people who didn't know what it was like. Who'd *never* know what it was like.

The troopers of Platoon E/1 did need Henry Ruthven, he was sure.

But not as much as I need them, in the night and the unending darkness.

JIM

The Hammer series exists because Jim Baen first bought individual stories, then the books themselves. These three volumes of The Complete Hammer's Slammers *are therefore the right place to print my obituary to my friend Jim.*

Jim Baen called me on the afternoon of June 11, 2006. He generally phoned on weekends, and we'd usually talk a couple more times in the course of a week; but this was the last time.

In the course of the conversation he said, "You've got to write my obituary, you know." I laughed (I'll get to that) and said, "Sure, if I'm around—but remember, I'm the one who rides the motorcycle."

So I'm writing this. Part of it's adapted from the profile I did in 2000 for the program book of the Chicago Worldcon at which Jim was Editor Guest of Honor. They cut my original title, which Jim loved: The God of Baendom. I guess they thought it was undignified and whimsical.

The title *was* undignified and whimsical. So was Jim.

James Patrick Baen was born October 22, 1943, on the Pennsylvania-New York border, a long way by road or in culture from New York City. He was introduced to SF early through the magazines in a step-uncle's attic, including the November, 1957, issue of *Astounding* with "The Gentle Earth" by Christopher Anvil.

The two books Jim most remembered as being formative influences were *Fire-Hunter* by Jim Kjelgaard and *Against the Fall of Night* by Arthur C. Clarke. The theme of both short novels is that a youth from a decaying culture escapes the trap of accepted wisdom and saves his people despite themselves. This is a fair description of Jim's life in SF: he was always his own man, always a maverick, and very often brilliantly successful because he didn't listen to what other people thought.

For example, the traditional model of electronic publishing required that the works be encrypted. Jim thought that just made it hard for people to read books, the worst mistake a publisher could make. His e-texts were DRM-free and in a variety of common formats.

While e-publishing has been a costly waste of effort for others, Baen Books quickly began earning more from electronic sales than it did from book sales in Canada

($6,000/month). By the time of Jim's death, the figure had risen to ten times that.

Jim didn't forget his friends. In later years he arranged for the expansion of *Fire-Hunter* so that he could republish it (as *The Hunter Returns*, originally the title of the Charles R. Knight painting Jim put on the cover).

Though Clarke didn't need help to keep his books in print the way Kjelgaard did, Jim didn't forget him either. Jim called me for help a week before his stroke, because Amazon.com had asked him to list the ten SF novels that everyone needed to read to understand the field. *Against the Fall of Night* was one of the titles that we settled on.

Jim's father died at age fifty; he and his stepfather didn't warm to one another. Jim left home at seventeen and lived on the streets for several months, losing weight that he couldn't at the time afford. He enlisted in the army as the only available alternative to starving to death.

Jim spent his military career in Bavaria where he worked for the Army Security Agency as a Morse Code Intercept Operator, monitoring transmissions from a Soviet callsign that was probably an armored corps. One night he determined that "his" Soviet formation was moving swiftly toward the border. This turned out to be an unannounced training exercise—but if World War III had broken out in 1960, Jim would've been the person who announced it.

Jim entered CUNY on the GI Bill and became a Hippie. Among other jobs he managed a Greenwich Village coffee house, sometimes acting as barker as well: "Come in and see tomorrow's stars today!" None of the entertainers became tomorrow's stars, but that experience of unabashed huckstering is part of the reason that Jim himself did.

Jim's first job in publishing was as an assistant in the Complaints Department of Ace Books. He was good at it—so good that management tried to promote him to running the department. He turned the offer down, however, because he really wanted to be an SF editor.

In 1973 Jim was hired at *Galaxy* and *If* magazines when Judy-Lynn Benjamin left. He became assistant to Ejler Jakobson, who with Bernie Williams taught Jim the elements of slash-and-burn editing.

Unfortunately, this was a necessary skill for an editor in Jim's position. The publisher wasn't in a hurry to pay authors, so established writers who could sell elsewhere preferred to do so. *Galaxy* and *If* published a lot of first stories and not a few rejects by major names. Material like that had to be edited for intelligibility and the printer's deadline, not nuances of prose style.

Apart from basic technique Jim had very little to learn from his senior, who shortly thereafter left to pursue other opportunities. Jim's first act as editor was to recall stories that his predecessor had rejected over Jim's recommendation. When in later years I thanked him for retrieving the first two Hammer stories, Jim responded, "Oh, David—Jake rejected *much* better stories than yours!" (Among them was Ursula K. LeGuin's Nebula winner, "The Day Before the Revolution".)

Ace Books, in many ways the standard bearer of SF paperback publishing in the

Fifties, had fallen on hard times in the Seventies. Charter Communications bought the company and installed Tom Doherty as publisher. Tom hired Jim to run the SF line. The first thing the new team did was to pay Ace's back (and in some cases, *way* back) royalties. By the time the famous SFWA (Science Fiction Writers of America) audit of Ace Books was complete, the money had already been paid to the authors; a matter of some embarrassment to the SFWA officers who were aware of the facts.

Ace regained its position as an SF line where readers could depend on getting a good story. (To Homer, that was the essence of art; not all writers and editors of more recent times would have agreed.) As well as pleasing readers, the Ace SF line made money for the company; unfortunately (due to decisions from far above the level of publisher) SF came to be the only part of the company that *did* make money. Tom left Ace in 1980, founded Tor Books, and hired Jim to set up the Tor SF line.

Which Jim did, following the same pattern that had revived Ace: a focus on story and a mix of established authors with first-timers whom Jim thought just might have what it took. It worked again.

In fact it worked so well that when Simon & Schuster went through a series of upheavals in its Pocket Books line in 1983, management decided to hire Jim as their new SF editor. Jim thought about the offer, then made a counter-offer: with the backing of two friends, he would form a separate company which would provide S&S with an SF line to distribute. S&S agreed and Baen Books was born.

Jim used the same formulas with his new line as he had at Ace and Tor, and again he succeeded. If that were easy, then past decades wouldn't be littered with the detritus of so many other people's attempts to do the same thing.

Even more than had been the case at Ace and Tor, Jim was his own art director at Baen Books—and he really directed, rather than viewing his job as one of coddling artists. Baen Books gained a distinct look. Like the book contents, the covers weren't to everyone's taste—but they worked.

Jim had the advantage over *some* editors in that he knew what a story is. He had the advantage over *most* editors in being able to spot talent before somebody else had published it. (Lois Bujold, Eric Flint, John Ringo, and Dave Weber were all Baen discoveries whom Jim promoted to stardom.)

Furthermore, he never stopped developing new writers. The week before his stroke, Jim bought a first novel from a writer whom Baen Books had been grooming through short stories over the past year.

The most important thing of all which Jim brought to his company was a personal vision. Baen Books didn't try to be for everybody, but it *was* always true to itself. In that as in so many other ways, the company mirrored Jim himself.

When Jim called me on June 11, he told me he was dying. *I* thought he was simply having a bad interaction among prescription drugs. Though the stroke that killed him occurred the next day in hospital, Jim was right and I was wrong—again.

After that opening, Jim said, "I'm just going to say it: we've known each other all these years and you seem to like me. Why?"

That's a hell of a thing to be hit with out of the blue. Jim had always known that he was socially awkward and that he not infrequently rubbed people the wrong way, but it wasn't something we discussed. (And it's obviously not a subject on which I could be of much help.)

If I'd been a different person, I'd have started out by listing the things he did right: for example, that I'd never met a more loving father than Jim was to his two daughters. Being me, I instead answered the question a number of us ask ourselves: "How can you like a person who's behaved the way you know I have?" I said that his flaws were childish ones, tantrums and sulking; not, *never* in my experience, studied cruelty. He agreed with that.

And then I thought further and said that when I was sure my career was tanking—

"*You* thought that? When was that?"

In the mid Nineties, I explained, when Military SF was going down the tubes with the downsizing of the military. But when I was at my lowest point, which was very low, I thought, "I can write two books a year. And Jim will pay me $20K apiece for them—"

"I'd have paid a lot more than that!"

And I explained that this wasn't about reality: this was me in the irrational depths of real depression. And even when I was most depressed and most irrational, I knew in my heart that Jim Baen would pay me enough to keep me alive, because he was that sort of person. He'd done that for Keith Laumer whom he disliked, because Laumer had been an author Jim looked for when he was starting to read SF.

I *could not* get so crazy and depressed that I didn't trust Jim Baen to stand by me if I needed him. I don't know a better statement than that to sum up what was important about Jim, as a man and as a friend.